THE PORTABLE

Rabelais

The Viking Portable Library

Each Portable Library volume is made up of representative works of a favorite modern or classic author, or is a comprehensive anthology on a special subject. The format is designed for compactness and for pleasurable reading. The books average about 700 pages in length. Each is intended to fill a need not hitherto met by any single book. Each is edited by an authority distinguished in his field, who adds a thoroughgoing introductory essay and other helpful material. Most "Portables" are available both in durable cloth and in stiff paper covers.

THE PORTABLE

Rabelais

SELECTED, TRANSLATED, & EDITED BY

SAMUEL PUTNAM

The Viking Press

THE PORTABLE RABELAIS

PUBLISHED BY THE VIKING PRESS IN JULY 1946

PUBLISHED ON THE SAME DAY IN THE DOMINION OF CANADA
BY THE MACMILLAN COMPANY OF CANADA LIMITED

TWENTIETH PRINTING MARCH 1971

SBN 670-58733-8 (HARDBOUND)
SBN 670-01021-9 (PAPERBOUND)

LIBRARY OF CONGRESS CATALOG CARD NUMBER: 46-6714

SET IN CALEDONIA, ELECTRA, DEEPDENE, AND CIVILITÉ TYPES
AND PRINTED IN U. S. A. BY THE COLONIAL PRESS INC.

FOR MY SON

Hilary Whitehall Putnam

THIS EDITION OF A GREAT EDUCATOR

> "Somme, que je voy un abyssme de science:
> car, doresnavant que tu deviens homme et te
> fais grand, il te fauldra yssir de ceste tran-
> quillité et repos d'estude et apprendre la che-
> valerie et les armes. . . ."
>
> BOOK II, CHAPTER viii

Contents

II. Gargantua in Paris

III. The Old Education and the New

IV. The Cake-Peddlers' War

V. The Abbey of Thélème

BOOK SECOND: PANTAGRUEL, KING OF THE DIPSODES, RESTORED TO THE LIFE

I. The Childhood and Youth of Pantagruel

THE THIRD BOOK OF THE HEROIC DEEDS AND SAYINGS OF THE WORTHY PANTAGRUEL

THE FOURTH BOOK OF THE HEROIC DEEDS AND SAYINGS OF THE WORTHY PANTAGRUEL

Introduction

Following the dog's example, you will have to be wise in sniffing, smelling, and estimating these fine and meaty books; swiftness in the chase and boldness in the attack are what is called for; after which, by careful reading and frequent meditation, you should break the bone and suck the substantific marrow—that is to say, the meaning of the Pythagorean symbols which I employ—in the certain hope that you will be rendered prudent and valorous by such a reading; for in the course of it you will find things of quite a different taste and a doctrine more abstruse which shall reveal to you most high sacraments and horrific mysteries in what concerns our religion, as well as the state and our political and economic life.

PROLOGUE TO BOOK FIRST

I

FRANÇOIS RABELAIS is almost universally admitted to be one of the world's great writers, one whose place is in the company of Aristophanes, Cervantes, and the Shakespeare who gave us a Falstaff; he ranks with Dante, Camões, and the author of *Don Quixote* as (in Chateaubriand's phrase) the creator of a literature. Just as the old French literature ends with the *Cent Nouvelles Nouvelles,* marking the expiration of the late-medieval impulse, so does the new begin with Rabelais and the

1

Renaissance, with that demon of thirst, Pantagruel, and the horrific deeds of the great Gargantua. This alone, apart from his girth and stature as an artist, would confer upon Maître François a very considerable literary-historical importance, in view of the heavy debt which other literatures owe to the French. Rabelais' significance, however, is a good deal larger than that: embodying the very breath and spirit and boundless *thirst* of the Renaissance era—a thirst for new and ever widening horizons, for human freedom and the good life for all— he was the first great and truly popular writer of modern times.

Too big for his contemporaries to grasp in all his elusive many-sidedness, he was commonly regarded by them as an erudite buffoon; and this reputation, unfortunately, has clung to him down the centuries. The men of his own vital and ventripotent age may perhaps be forgiven: they were too close up for perspective; and this possibly may apply to a Montaigne who, in the half-century following Rabelais' death, found the latter's writings to be, merely, *"dignes qu'on s'y amuse,"* although it is more likely that the ecclesiastical censorship had something to do with the formulation of this opinion.[1] In the seventeenth century Molière and La Fontaine were to become the Maître's disciples, and on the eve of the French Revolution a Jean-Jacques Rousseau and others were to draw inspiration from his Abbey of Thélème; yet Voltaire could still allude to him as a "drunken philosopher who wrote only when he was

---

[1] Montaigne's modern translator, E. J. Trenchman, in a note to the two-volume Oxford University Press edition of 1927, has this to say (Vol. I, p. 399): "It seems odd that Montaigne should class Rabelais among books 'simply amusing,' and one can hardly believe that he did not see the deep meaning underlying the work. In his day there might have been danger in discussing its more serious import. Hence we may believe that the above words are a blind."

intoxicated," and could describe the *Gargantua and Pantagruel* as "an extravagant and unintelligible book . . . prodigal of erudition, ordures, and boredom"—a judgment which reminds one of certain present day criticisms of James Joyce!

Voltaire's verdict was the prevalent one at the beginning of the nineteenth century. It was Balzac, the realist, on the one hand, and, on the other hand, the French romanticists who initiated the modern discovery of the authentic Rabelais beneath the seeming mountain of "ordure" and Gargantuan jest; scenting the presence of a "substantific marrow," they started gnawing at the "Pythagorean" bone, and Chateaubriand, Victor Hugo, Flaubert, Barbey d'Aurévilly, Sainte-Beuve, Taine, Michelet, and Guizot, among others, now paid tribute to the writer who not only had "created French letters" [2] but who, in Etienne Pasquier's words, was in a very real sense "the father of our idiom." The praise is not always unqualified, by any means, and is frequently more than a little dubious or muddled in character. Thus Hugo, seeing Rabelais as one who "enthrones a dynasty of bellies" (Grandgousier, Gargantua, Pantagruel), proceeds to dub him "the Aeschylus of grub" and, with this for a theme, goes off into a romantic rhapsody; while Taine for his part descries in the Rabelaisian chronicle an "epic brain" behind the "bizarre language," the "insane imagination," and "an enormous amount of filth," which leads him to conclude that the author on the whole is "too excessive and too eccentric," and that his audience, accordingly, must be one limited to "drunkards and scholars."

The realists did better by Rabelais than did the romantics. Typical of the latter's effusions is Barbey

---

[2] Chateaubriand: "Rabelais has created French letters. Montaigne, La Fontaine, Molière are his descendants."

d'Aurévilly's: "My adorable old Rabelais! . . . A mastodon radiantly emerged from chaos into the blue of a nascent world." With this, contrast Balzac: "The greatest mind in modern humanity, the man who sums up Pythagoras, Hippocrates, Aristotle, and Dante." On the side of form it is Flaubert who speaks of Rabelais' "nervous, clear, substantial, muscularly protruding, bister-colored phrase," and who names as favorite bedside authors Montaigne, Rabelais, Regnier, La Bruyère, and Le Sage.

The historians, likewise, have their pertinent word. "I shall be heard not without astonishment," says Guizot, "when I name Rabelais as one of those who have thought and spoken most clearly on the subject of education, prior to Locke and Rousseau." And Michelet stresses the invaluable historical contribution which the writer who penned (or, more likely, dictated) the "Remarks of the Drunkards" chapter and similar passages has made in preserving for us the conversation of sixteenth-century France: ". . . greater than Aristophanes and Voltaire . . . superior even to Cervantes. Aristophanes and Rabelais . . . the two gigantic phenomena of literature . . . the two gigantic representatives of Antiquity and the Middle Ages."

In brief, Rabelais was slowly but surely coming into his own at last, after three centuries of neglect, misrepresentation, and contemptuous treatment on the part of recognized critics, during which time his influence had none the less remained a living and informing one, shaping the speech, the literature, and the ideas of his countrymen. True, the old legend of the "jolly winebibber of Chinon," the "drunken monk," the "drunken philosopher," the big-bellied glutton, etc., lingered on—myths of this kind die hard always—and there were still those who were able to discern in the founder of Pantagruelism no more than a "clowning Homer" (*Homère bouffon*) or Homeric clown. But with it all there was an ever growing perception of Rabelais' true and impressive stature as a man of the modern world; as a writer whose thinking, under the masks of humor, satire, and allegory, pointed new paths for his fellow men; and as an artist whom we today, in this age of Freud, Joyce, Proust, the subconscious and the dream, are only beginning to appreciate at his proper worth.

II

As FOR the reader who is acquainted with Rabelais only through the medium of an English translation, he in the past has been in a peculiar position, which has led to his forming a picture of the author that is often almost wholly false, or in any event, nearly always, a distorted one. The result is that Rabelais remains practically unknown, save as a name, to the English-speaking world, or else is known for what he was not: a bibulous, gormandizing "philosopher" shaking his sides in laughter[3] at the follies of humankind and the essential vanity of life. And if this is the picture that has come to be, the blame must be ascribed, without any malice or denigration, to—Sir Thomas Urquhart of Cromarty!

For Rabelais' seventeenth-century translator, the sixteenth-century Nash, and the eighteenth-century Sterne are the Maître's outstanding disciples in English (the question of a Rabelais influence in Joyce is a debatable one). That Sir Thomas was a creative genius in his own right, no one, probably, would deny. He deserves a place in any history of our literature, and especially in

---

[3] Compare Pope's lines addressed to Swift, at the beginning of the *Dunciad:*

Whether thou choose Cervantes' serious air,
Or laugh and shake in Rabelais' easy chair.

any account of our prose. If this place is not commonly accorded him, it is doubtless for the reason that he is looked upon as a translator rather than as a creator, whereas the truth of the matter is that he is too much the creator to be able to subordinate himself in a manner that is entirely satisfactory always to the task of carrying over the thought and expression of another. There is in him much, very much, of Rabelais' own lust for life and language, of the Rabelaisian atmosphere and effect; yet when all is said, the resulting product is Urquhart rather than Rabelais, an Urquhart who, taking off from the *Gargantua and Pantagruel*, ends by giving us a *new* masterpiece for our shelves, a masterpiece of seventeenth-century English prose.[4]

Seventeenth-century prose—there comes the rub; for there is no denying that many persons today find the Urquhart version, even with modern editing, extremely difficult when not unintelligible reading; and so, Rabelais continues to be for them almost as much of a closed book as he is in the original. Frequently, and most regrettably, they turn away from him in distaste or despair, convinced that this great mind of which Balzac speaks, a mind that has so much to say to the men of the present, holds nothing for them.

To this the Urquhart enthusiast, who is likely to be a bit of a fanatic in his devotion to Sir Thomas, may retort that Rabelais is not for the *polloi*, and that the one who cannot decipher him in the Squire of Cromarty's rendering was not intended to make his acquaintance; but such a point of view is unacceptable to those familiar with the real Rabelais, the author of popular best-sellers which were relished alike by the learned and the un-

---

[4] One of Rabelais' modern translators, Mr. W. F. Smith, has remarked how often he is struck by the seeming inevitability of Sir Thomas' renderings. One cannot but agree with this.

learned of his time. While there are in the *Gargantua and Pantagruel* certain passages—not too many of them —that, as Professor Abel Lefranc has observed, were no doubt over the head of the average reader in sixteenth-century France, the bulk of the work was not. That work, on the contrary, is distinctly popular in genesis and inspiration and in its prevailing tone and was never intended to become the object of a cult on the part of a select few.

If Rabelais today appears to be obscure, so obscure as to make it difficult to conceive of him as ever having been a writer for the masses, this is principally due to the highly topical character of his pages. Incidents and allusions which are dark to us were, we must remember, perfectly clear to those for whom he wrote and called for no more mental effort on their part than the morning newspaper, the daily cartoon or comic strip requires of us. An inordinately hot, dry summer of which everyone was talking set him off on his literary career with the first book of the *Pantagruel* (what we know as Book Second); and a quarrel between two country gentlemen, one of whom was his father, over fishing rights in a stream provided the plot for his *Gargantua* with its inimitable episode of the Picrocholine war. And so it goes: one might run through his romance, as the modern scholar has done, clothing allusions that otherwise are mere sound and fury with the warm and palpitating flesh of life and giving to the drolleries an added and even more mirthful zest.

But this is something that is displeasing to the one who would make of Rabelais an esoteric cult, and he will have none of it. He is humorously stern toward those who look in the writings of the Maître for anything beyond humor—humor and the upturned tankard. To him, such as these are "whey-faced dry-as-dusts who

never trolled a catch or drained a bumper." Believing
with La Bruyère that "whatever one may say, he
(Rabelais) will always be inexplicable," this type of
critic or reader rejects and resents any attempt on the
part of scholars to paint in the philosophical, literary,
and social-political-economic background of the Rabelaisian opus, preferring to keep for himself the conception that his own imagination has formed, out of his
Urquhart or out of the void, even though it has no correspondence in reality.

To the present translator such an attitude seems a
deliberate and somewhat sophomoric self-stultification. It
is true enough that some of Rabelais' early commentators,
such as M. Eloi Johanneau of the French Variorum edition, are at times almost as funny as their author at his
best; but fanciful "interpretations" of this sort which
would find a historical equivalent for every character and
incident have nothing to do with the painstaking investi-
gations of the modern student who ever since the middle
of the last century has been doing his best to lay bare the
mind of Rabelais, the homely real-life sources of his art,
his method of composition, the "influences to be found
in his work," and his outlook upon the world as given
expression in his writings. Surely, these are things that
we do want to know; and surely, too, if properly
handled, they need not detract in the least from our enjoyment of the one whom Professor Lefranc has termed
"the pride and hope of the Renaissance," but rather
should add to the intellectual and aesthetic pleasure that
we derive from him.

Of all the writers of the Renaissance, Rabelais, remarks
Lefranc, was "the one most desirous of linking his work
with all the social, political, religious, scientific, and even
colonial preoccupations of his age." Are we, then, to
brush all this aside and listen only to Rabelais the

Laugher, "because to laugh is natural to man"? The fact of the matter is: those who would forbid us to look for that substantial core of meaning that the author himself urges us to seek, have a philosophy of their own of which they would make Rabelais the exponent, but which, as it happens, was not his; for their amiable skepticism— there's-nothing-to-be-done-about-it-and-what's-the - use - anyhow-so-laugh-or-smile-and-drain-another - bumper — is wholly alien to Maître François of the dusty feet, whose life, as Michelet has put it, was "a restless, wandering, fugitive one," and who, from his early convent days to the eve of his death, was almost constantly embroiled in an ideological fray of one sort or another.

The ordinary English language reader, meanwhile, dependent upon Urquhart and his expounders, gets exceedingly little of this background which is so indispensable to the understanding and full enjoyment of Rabelais. Sir Thomas himself was unfamiliar with many of the allusions in his author which have only been cleared up by late-nineteeth- and twentieth-century scholars, particularly the Lefranc group and the members of the Société des Etudes Rabelaisiennes. As a consequence, in order to cover up his ignorance of the real-life context or his uncertainty as to the meaning involved, Urquhart very often improvises, expands, and embroiders upon the text, dumping into it upon occasion all the synonyms for a French word that he has found in his Cotgrave.[5] And this it is that gives him at times that very modern air!

---

[5] Randle Cotgrave: A Dictionary of the French and English Tongues, London, Islip, 1611. There is no point here in going into the actual mistranslations, which are rather numerous, of Urquhart and his continuator, Peter Motteux, translator of Books IV and V. This subject has been dealt with by the present writer in an appendix to his American translation of Rabelais: All the Extant Works of François Rabelais, an American Translation, with a Critical

It was Rabelais' big-bellied, ribald side that especially appealed to his translator's temperament and genius, and this Urquhart does indeed convey; when in doubt, he usually leans to the ventripotent or the smutty. A case in point is the list of Gargantua's games, in Book First, Chapter XXII. Reading Urquhart, one gets the impression of an underlying erotic significance which often is not there in the original. *"A la soulle,"* for example, becomes "at the soilie smutchie," which sounds vaguely suggestive; but in reality, this is simply a variety of ball game. The same is true of the list as a whole, the great majority of these diversions being ordinary pastimes such as hopscotch, blindman's-buff, hide-and-seek, and the like, favorites with children since time immemorial—Rabelais' and "kiddies'" games!

In view of all this, it is not hard to see how a false or grossly distorted conception of Rabelais should have come to be created in the minds of those who read him only in English and without benefit of the research specialist's labors. Nor is it surprising that Anatole France's work on the subject, published in the late twenties, should have met with a lukewarm reception in this country, the reviewers objecting to it on the ground that it was too intellectualized. "I cannot see the man for the mind," one of them complains; and he adds that "the jolly winebibber of Chinon" is missing. In this version the endeavor of the editor-translator will be to let the man and his mind speak for themselves through as faithful as possible a presentation of Rabelais' writings, based upon a critical study of the various texts as revised by

Text, Variant Readings, Variorum Notes, and Drawings Attributed to Rabelais, New York, Covici-Friede, 1929. Motteux is greatly inferior to Urquhart and, a rabid Protestant, at times lets his religious bias interfere, as when, on at least one occasion, he deliberately omits an important passage unfavorable to the Calvinists.

the author and with such, and only so much, commentary as may be needed to render the text comprehensible to the present-day reader.

And what of Urquhart, then? The writer recalls a remark of Ernest Hemingway's over a café table years ago, apropos of the Goodspeed Bible. "Why!" exclaimed Hemingway, "they'd take away one of the few real pieces of literature that we have!" There are those who will feel that way about Sir Thomas. But let them not be alarmed. Why not keep our Urquhart—and our Rabelais, too?

III

IF ONE is to understand François Rabelais and get the most that is to be had from his writings, one must have an understanding, an appreciation of the age in which he lived, an age whose spirit and teeming life is superbly embodied for us in his *Gargantua and Pantagruel* as in no other work of literature. It might seem that it was unnecessary to dwell on the character and significance of the Renaissance, inasmuch as this is something that "every schoolboy" is supposed to know. We are all familiar, or should be, with the great world-changing events that began to occur about the middle of the fifteenth century: the fall of Constantinople, which threw open the treasures of Byzantine art and culture to the western world; the introduction of gunpowder and cannon in the west (see Grandgousier's lament upon this subject), which brought to a lingering end the Age of Chivalry and the Bayards; the discovery of America, with all its tremendous, far-reaching consequences; the discovery, by Copernicus and others, of a new heaven as well as a new earth; the revival of classical learning (which had really begun in the fourteenth century, with the finding of Cicero's *Familiar Letters* at Verona in

1345); the invention of printing, which was vastly to aid in the diffusion of knowledge, and which was to render possible the mass-consumption of such literary productions as the Gargantuan Chronicle (the *Grandes Cronicques*) and Rabelais' own masterpiece; and finally, the revolt against the papacy—a national as well as a religious revolt—and the Protestant Reformation.

A mere list of these events is breath-taking, if one pauses to consider what each of them in itself signified and the effect of the whole. Is it any wonder if this was an age that was looked upon as a veritable "rebirth" of mankind, coming after the darkness of a "Gothic night"? The only age with which we may properly compare it is our own: that portentous crossroads at which we stand today, with the discovery of the atom bomb and the unfolding potentialities of atomic energy. If we do not at once grasp the comparison, it is for the reason that the miracles of four hundred years ago have long since become the commonplaces of the present.

It was a time of seemingly infinite possibilities, when it appeared that anything might happen, for good or ill; for the men of the sixteenth century trembled at gunpowder as we do at the explosive power of the atom. It was a day of limitless horizons, but horizons that were all too cramped, still, for the insatiable inquiring spirits of the Renaissance which were ever seeking to push them back. This, in Professor Lefranc's words, was "the period of the great awakening," when "every one, in spite of imminent hardships and impending struggles, felt joyous and alert. A boundless curiosity laid hold of minds. This was the moment when it seemed that one could hear, throughout France one might say, that formidable and symbolic cry that Gargantua gave upon coming into the light of this world: 'A drink! A drink! A drink!'" Here we have the true, the right Rabelaisian thirst and the

wine that was craved by the Renaissance humanists.[6]
Rabelais, Erasmus, Reuchlin, Budé, Sir Thomas More—
they were drunk with something more than the tavern
vintage, though they would not have disdained the
latter; for, being humanists who believed in the dignity,
the rights and pleasures of the human body—and none
believed in them more firmly than did Dr. François
Rabelais, the physician of the new era—they were opposed to anything that savored of medieval asceticism.
There is no contradiction here, but rather the relation
of part to whole.

It is against the background of this vital, creative
epoch, which attained a peak of intensity about the year
1530, that Rabelais' work must be set. For he is nothing
if not the man of the Renaissance, whose writings reflect
every deep-going concern of his age. Beginning under
the influence of Budé and the "love of Greek," he is,
first of all, the humanist *par excellence*, and as such is
far more complete, rounded, and typical a figure than
any of the other great ones of his time. The map of a
swiftly expanding world is mirrored in the fantastic voyages of his Pantagruel; and it is believed possible that
he may have met and talked with Jacques Cartier. In
any event, he was undoubtedly influenced by the geographers, cosmographers, mapmakers, and travelers of the

---

[6] Rabelais had employed the symbol of thirst prior to his *Gargantua and Pantagruel*. The title-page of his edition of the *Aphorisms*
of Hippocrates bears the couplet:

Hic medicae fons est exundantissimus artis.

Hinc, mage ni sapiat pigra lacuna, bibe.

"Here is the overflowing fount of healing lore. Hence, drink, unless
the stagnant water of a ditch tastes better to you." And the object
of Pantagruel's quest, Bacbuc, or the Holy Bottle, has reference to
the proverb, "*In vino veritas*." There is the further fact that Pantagruel is by tradition the inspirer of thirst, and the author, who is
led to take up the tale as the result of a throat-parching summer,
is simply following out the medieval mythos.

day—Grynaeus, André Thevet, Ramusio, and others—
and his Book Fourth clearly points to the search for a
northwest passage to the Indies. Astronomy, representing
a consciousness of the new heavens, similarly attracts
him, as is to be seen in the stress upon this science in
the education that is given to the young Gargantua.
Science in general fascinates him, especially humanistic medicine, zoology, botany, and pharmacology; and
his first literary labors consisted in editing the medical
texts of Hippocrates, Galen, and the Italian Manardi.

It is not only the sciences but the arts as well that
occupy Maître François' attention; and here the influence
of the Italian renascence is highly visible; for the French
Renaissance may be said to have begun on that August
day in 1494 (Rabelais was probably about six months
old at the time) when the armies of Charles VIII set out
to cross the Alps. Architecture, warfare, equitation, fencing as they appear in his descriptions—see the Abbey of
Thélème, the Picrocholine episode, and the account of
Gargantua's schooling—all are after the new models
from the southern peninsula. And Rabelais' knowledge
in each of these provinces is very exact, so exact that a
modern architect has been able to reconstruct his
Thélème, a military expert has approved his strategy,
and a nautical authority has been found to be wrong in
criticizing his use of seafaring terms! In all of which we
may behold the humanist, in love at once with learning
and with life.

"For humanism," says John Addington Symonds,
"which was the vital element in the Revival of Learning,
consists mainly of a just perception of the dignity of man
as a rational, volitional and sentient being, born upon
this earth with a right to use and enjoy it. Humanism
. . . involved a vivid recognition of the goodliness of

man and nature, displayed in the great monuments of human power, recovered from the past."

It was this humanist creed that led Rabelais to abandon one phase of the Renaissance, represented by the Protestant Reformation, for the reason that, having at first vigorously espoused the Protestant cause as is shown by certain passages in his work, he soon discovered that "the demoniacal Calvins, those impostors of Geneva"— those "predestinators," as he elsewhere calls them—were fundamentally opposed to the ideal of the full, free life for all, for which humanism stood. True, he seems to have retained his devotion to "the good apostle, St. Paul," and his fondness for "a good evangelic preacher," but that was about as far as it went. Though he was hounded through life by the theologians of the Sorbonne and though his Catholic orthodoxy is decidedly open to question, he could not go along with the reformationists; for Calvinism, with its denial of the moral freedom of the individual, was repugnant to his sense of life.

If François Rabelais was a man of the Renaissance, it must not be forgotten that he was, by that very fact, a man *out of* the Middle Ages; and this is true not only of Rabelais but of the sixteenth-century humanists in general.[7] It is especially on the literary and philosophic sides that this medieval influence is to be discerned. He was steeped in the old *chansons de geste* and, like Petrarch, may have turned his hand to revising one or two of them. The medieval farce *Patelin* gives him a literary method, that of the *fatrasie*, or cock-and-bull chain (compare the *coq-à-l'âne* of Marot), which he

---

[7] On the relation of the Renaissance to the much misunderstood Middle Ages, the reader may be referred to the introduction to the present writer's biography of Rabelais: *François Rabelais, Man of the Renaissance*, New York, Jonathan Cape and Harrison Smith, 1929; London, Jonathan Cape, 1930.

employs so admirably and which could hardly have
been without its effect upon a James Joyce. He was likewise deeply imbued with the philosophy of the later
Middle Ages; and notwithstanding all the uproarious
fun that he has with the Schoolmen, there was in him
much of the scholastic; as someone has remarked, the
"sel franciscain" was to be with him to the end. He was
familiar, also, with the medieval preachers and their
sermons—has not Anatole France discovered a clerical
tang to his humor?—and as we shall see, he even imi-
tates their pulpit obscenities.

Like his fellow humanists, Rabelais stands on the
threshold between two worlds, the old world and the
new; but it is to the future that he points, always, rather
than to a past which he is unable to shake off in its entirety. This should become evident as we glance at the
all too few facts that we have concerning his vagrant,
storm-tossed life.

IV

"Would that it were possible to do a life of Rabelais!"
the historian Michelet once exclaimed; and this, indeed,
has been a task of which even the boldest and best informed have been wary until a comparatively recent
date. The undertaking remains a perilous one, for there
are still wide gaps in Maître François' career as it is
known to us; there are periods when he drops from sight
completely so far as the record goes, for years at a time.
The modern Rabelais specialist has done and is doing
much to fill these gaps, and it is his labors that have rendered possible such an account as that by M. Jean
Plattard (*François Rabelais*, Paris, 1932). But with it
all, our knowledge is scant enough; and the danger is
that, in the absence of documentation, a biographer will

be tempted to fall back upon legend, tradition, or conjecture by way of filling in the blanks.

The author's name, even, has been tampered with, some seeking for it a fantastic derivation from the Hebrew (*rab*, master, and *lez*, a jester), while others maliciously would derive it from the Latin words, *rabie laesus* (bitten with rabies, or madness); the truth of the matter being, more likely, that it is related to the French *érable* and means simply a maple grove.

We do not so much as know for a certainty when Rabelais was born, the dates that have been given for his birth ranging from 1483 to 1500. Most authorities are now agreed that the correct date is some time around 1495; and basing himself upon what he regards as internal evidence in the text, Lefranc would fix it as the night of February 3 or the morning of February 4, 1494. The place of birth was not Chinon, as has been stated in the past, but the little farm owned by the Rabelais family at nearby La Devinière, and the infant François was doubtless baptized in the Benedictine abbey church of Saint-Pierre de Seuilly.

Another legend that must go: Rabelais' father was neither a tavernkeeper nor an apothecary, but a member of the legal profession (*licencié ès lois*), the family being of the well-to-do middle class, with not inconsiderable property-holdings. Rabelais' mother was a Dusoul, and the Gallet, Delopiteau, and Pavin families were related to his own. He had two brothers, Jamet and Antoine, and a sister, Françoise; and if he himself did not later share in the division of the family estate, this was in all probability due to the fact that, having entered a religious order, he was, as the saying went, "legally dead" (*civilement mort*).

If there is a doubt as to the place where the young François received his education—whether with the

Benedictines of Seuilly or as a novice with the Franciscans of La Baumette—there is no doubt as to the monastic and scholastic character of that training, which, in
its medieval texts and routine and even in the matter of
children's games, must have resembled in many ways
the upbringing of Gargantua before Ponocrates took him
in hand. We know that Rabelais eventually became a
member of the Gray Friars, or Franciscan Order, entering the monastery of Puy-Saint-Martin at Fontenay-le-
Comte, in Bas-Poitou, and that he was ordained a priest.
It was here that he became impregnated with the teachings of Duns Scotus and other Schoolmen; and he has
given us in his work more than one reminiscence of convent life in the form of jibes, snatches of song, etc., not
to speak of his inimitable and altogether delectable Friar
John. As for his "trailing his monk's robe over the
hedges," that is, giving himself over to drinking and
debauchery while residing within convent walls, it may
merely be repeated that there is absolutely no foundation for this report. He did get into serious trouble while
in the monastery, that is true. It was not, however, over
wine or women, but over Greek books—a far blacker
sin in the eyes of the anti-humanist heresy-hunters of
the Sorbonne. For François and his young companion,
Pierre Amy, had become converts to the new learning,
devotees of "bonnes lettres," and would appear to have
collected a small classical library, which was taken from
them by their ecclesiastical superiors. In the meantime,
they had struck up a three-cornered correspondence with
the leading humanist of the realm, Guillaume Budé, and,
powerful influence having been brought to bear in their
behalf, their books were restored to them.

This, certainly, does not sound like the escapade of
a "drunken monk"; it sounds a good deal more like
Rabelais' own Friar Claude of the Hauts-Barrois, who, in

Friar John's words, did "nothing but study any more."
The upshot of the affair was that both Rabelais and his
friend Amy were granted permission to leave the Franciscan for the more enlightened and liberal Benedictine
Order, François receiving a papal authorization for the
change.

Meanwhile, events of large significance were occurring
in the world outside. It was on December 10, 1521, that
Martin Luther burned the papal bull, *Exurge Domine,* at
Wittenberg, and three years later the break between the
humanists and the theologians began, with the publication of the *Commentaries* of Erasmus on the Greek
text of St. Luke. This was the greater storm that was
brewing, of which the little tempest in the monastery had
been no more than a back-eddying gust.

From his early years Rabelais would seem to have
been a lover of good company, good conversation, and
the pleasant things of life, and the companions of his
choice were the learned and the wise, the friends of the
humanities and the masters of the art of graceful living.
If the reports that we have are true, he was an excellent
talker and, by reason of his erudition and brilliant conversation, was greatly sought after as a guest. This it
was that made him welcome in the households of the
great and powerful who were at the same time patrons
of the new learning. All his life long he was to have such
friends, and they were to stand him in good stead; they
probably saved him more than once from going to the
stake. That he valued them, there is no doubt; but this
does not mean that he was either a sycophant or a snob.
The patron was a necessary institution in those parlous
times for one who chose to speak his mind so freely and
to jest at things held sacred by men with the power of
life and death in their hands. It was the combination of
his personal charm and the functioning of a sort of hu-

manist freemasonry that was to provide a constant shelter against the wrath of the Sorbonnists who were forever on his trail.

Already in his monastery days we find him in such a setting, as he walks and talks in the garden of André Tiraqueau, a learned jurist of the epoch and the author of a well-known work on the marriage laws (*De Legibus Connubialibus*). Tiraqueau was the leader of a Hellenist coterie at Fontenay-le-Comte, and the two young friars from the neighboring convent would attend the gatherings of this exclusively masculine group, where the chief topic of conversation was the "woman question," the famous *"querelle des femmes,"* a violent controversy which had been raging since some time back in the fifteenth century and which was to continue through a number of decades of the sixteenth, reaching a climax in the 1530's, just as Rabelais came to writing maturity. It was, perhaps, in Tiraqueau's garden that the creator of Dr. Rondibilis first became interested in the theme which he was to develop in so hilarious a fashion in the second book of his *Pantagruel* (Book Third). The nature of this controversy and Maître François' position in it will be considered in more detail later. Here, it may merely be stated that he *appears* from the start as an anti-feminist, by espousing the side of Tiraqueau against the spokesmen for the feminine sex.

All this shows that Rabelais at an early period of his career was becoming immersed in the vigorous intellectual life of his century, and such preoccupations and friendships as these were to have an influence upon his work and were to be reflected there in numerous allusions, anecdotes, and episodes. Tiraqueau's legal cast of mind, for one thing, probably had its effect upon Rabelais' thinking; for despite his satirical, bitter, and forthright attacks upon the profession—see his Judge Bridlegoose in Book Third, the case of Lords Kissarse and Suckpoop in Book Second, his Shysteroos (*Chicquanous*) in Book Fourth, etc.—Rabelais has much of the lawyer in his mental make-up (his father had been one before him, remember, and it seems likely that he had studied law at some time or other). He is as deeply versed in medieval jurisprudence as in medieval philosophy, and each of these disciplines holds a kind of fascination for him.

It is to this period, while he was sojourning with another of his patrons, Geoffroy d'Estissac, Bishop of Maillezais, Abbot of Saint-Pierre-de-Maillezais, and Prior of Ligugé, that we owe Rabelais' first literary work that has come down to us, a production in verse entitled *Epistle to Bouchet*. Bouchet was a prolific and very bad poet who also had been staying at the priory, and during his temporary absence he and François exchanged letters in rhyme, a fashionable pastime in those days. As for Rabelais' verse, it is quite as bad as that of his correspondent; for although his contemporaries occasionally referred to him as "poet," he seldom rises above doggerel and never above the mediocre. He can be looked upon as a poet only in the broadest, etymologic sense, as a *maker* or creator.

While residing at Fontenay-le-Comte, in the monastery or at the priory of Ligugé, Maître François must have roamed the countryside, exploring its every nook and cranny, absorbing its rich, succulent speech and popular lore, and meeting its well-known characters, such as Friar John; for his pages are crammed with allusions to this region and his idiom is that of Poitou rather than the "language of Touraine," as Balzac assumed when he sat down to produce his *tour de force*, the *Contes Drolatiques*.

Rabelais all this time was growing older, and his

position in life was still a very unsettled one. Assuming that he was born in 1494 or 1495, he was around thirty years of age when he penned his *Epistle to Bouchet* (probably in 1526). If there appears to be a certain retardation in his career, this is to be explained by his long residence in a monastery. And then, in September 1526, he disappears so far as any record of him is concerned and is not heard of again until September 1530, exactly four years later. It is altogether likely that these were his student *Wanderjahre*, in the course of which he made a tour of the universities of France, following an itinerary much the same as that of Pantagruel as described in Book Second, Chapter v, and ending like Pantagruel's on the Parisian Left Bank. This, at any rate, is the view of Lefranc. Somewhere en route he may have enrolled as a law student for a time. And it was while thus traversing his native land that he picked up much of the lore and wisdom which he was to pour into his romance, and formed a number of friendships which were to play a part in his later life.

In Paris, it would seem that he resided at the Hôtel-Saint-Denis, town house of the Benedictine Order, on the present site of Numbers 54-56-58 of the Rue Saint-André-des-Arts, at the corner of this street and the Rue des Grands-Augustins, to the left as one goes down to the Seine. Did he, too, visit the famous "Fodder Street" and take part in or witness the disputations there? (See, in Book Second, Panurge's debate with the "great English scholar.") One thing is certain: he became thoroughly familiar with student jargon and student types, with that Babel of tongues to be found in the quarter of the schools, and with the psychology of the Parisian populace (see his Limousin student, Panurge's linguistic exercises, etc.).

On September 17, 1530, following the biographic

hiatus that has been noted, we find Maître François putting down a gold crown and enrolling as a medical student at the University of Montpellier. The next year, we hear of his taking part in a university farce, of which he may have been the author, on the "Man Who Married a Dumb Wife" theme. Having begun as a priest and a friar and having probably tried the law and given it up, Rabelais has now found his calling, that of physician, and is henceforth to be known as "Master François Rabelais, Doctor of Medicine," even though he does not actually attain his doctorate until seven years later. This does not mean that he left the Church; the Holy See was to grant him a dispensation to practice his profession while wearing the priestly garb, provided he did not make use of scalpel or cautery, which were forbidden to the clergy, and provided, also, that he did not practice it for gain. He was to continue within the fold and was to die a country curate; but it was medicine that was to become the centering activity of his life, his literary work being regarded by him as a kind of therapeutic for his patients—the therapeutic of laughter.

Rabelais' mind, in short, was essentially the product of three disciplines: theology, law, and medicine; with the influence of classical antiquity running through it all. It is not possible to understand him otherwise.

It may have been a medical student's need of money— "lack of money, there's no affliction like it"—that led to Rabelais' becoming a writer of popular romances. In the late spring or early summer (May-June) of 1532, he appears at Lyon, which was then the center of the printing industry and the second literary capital of France, being the home of a brilliant humanist group. Whatever the reason, he now turns editor, reviser, and translator of medical and, perhaps, other texts as well, including the old romance *Pierre de Provence*. In other words, he becomes a kind of superior literary hack and is soon to be editing and writing introductions for Galen, Hippocrates, and the *Medical Letters* of Manardi, the physician of Ferrara.

For in Lyon at this time, to quote from an old poet, a "million black teeth" (*un grand million de dents noires*) were "working in and out of fair time," the allusion being to the new invention of movable type and the custom of bringing out new books at the four seasonal fairs for which the city was famous (foreshadowing the habits of the present-day publisher). At the autumn fair, held in August, 1532, the season's bestseller was a volume bearing the title, *The Great and Inestimable Chronicles of the Great and Enormous Giant Gargantua*, etc. (the *Grandes Cronicques*). This work in the past has been attributed to Rabelais, but it is now known that, while he may have had a hand in its revision, he was not the author of it. It is the work referred to in the Prologue to Book Second: "The printers have sold more copies of that work in two months than they have Bibles in nine years." Its success was to inspire Maître François to go back and Rabelaisianize the Gargantua myth in a work of his own published two years later; but meanwhile, the first book of his *Pantagruel* (Book Second) was already completed; it was printed in October and put on sale at the November fair.

As has been said, it was the great summer drought of 1532 that gave Rabelais the idea for his *Pantagruel*. That summer was the hottest and the driest within the memory of anyone living. As is usual in such cases, and as we gather from the chroniclers of the time, the weather must have been a chief topic, if not the sole topic, of conversation; and the proverbial name of Pantagruel, the "little devil" of thirst out of the late-medieval mystery plays, who went about casting salt down people's throats, must have been on the lips of many whose parched gullets were almost literally "spitting cotton." If Rabelais was looking for a theme, he with his fertile, gigantesque imagination needed to look no farther; and so it was that his "Pantagruel, King of the Dipsodes" (that is, the Thirsty Ones), was born. The work was signed with the anagram, "Alcofribas Nasier."

It was just as his *Pantagruel* was being put on sale that Dr. François obtained, on November 1, 1532, the post of physician to the Hôtel-Dieu, or city hospital, of Lyon, at a stipend of forty French pounds a year. He appears to have filled the position to the satisfaction of all, and it is said that as a result of his ministrations the death-rate fell two or three per cent. Toward the end of this year he decided, for one reason or another, to re-visit "my own cow country," La Devinière.

About the time that he returned to La Devinière, a row over river rights was going on there, between Gaucher de Sainte-Marthe, Seigneur de Chapeau (on the Loire, near Saumur), on the one hand, and his neighbors headed by Antoine Rabelais, François' father, on the other hand. It was a typical back-country feud and must have struck the newly fledged writer of romances as very funny, indeed, seeing that he has made such sport of it in his Picrocholine episode. That best-seller, the *Grandes Cronicques,* was still fresh in mind; and so, the idea occurred to him of taking this rustic incident and combining it with the Gargantua legend of the late Middle Ages of which the author of the *Chronicle* had made use. Such is the *"trame réelle,"* the real-life basis of Book First, that "perfect picture of rural manners," as Professor Lefranc has termed it. Even Friar John has been identified as being, in all probability, the procurator of the Abbey of Seuilly, the "monk of Seuilly" to whom reference is made. Once again, out of the simple every-

day life about him, Rabelais had shaped an important
segment of his romance, one which may well stand by
itself and which long since has taken its place among
world classics as a masterpiece of humor and rollicking
satire.

The *Gargantua* did not see the light of print until the
fall of 1534, some two years after the publication of the
first book of the *Pantagruel;* and to keep the pot boiling,
Maître François became a compiler of almanacs—
almanacs of a humorous, distinctly Rabelaisian variety.
The *Pantagrueline Prognostication* and the *Almanac for
the Year 1533* were, accordingly, his next works to
appear.

On October 23, 1533, Rabelais for the first time ran
afoul of the theologians of the Sorbonne, when his
Pantagruel was suppressed by them as being sacrilegious
and obscene. This may have had something to do with
his departure for Rome early in 1534, in the suite of
Jean du Bellay, Bishop of Paris and later Cardinal. Du
Bellay was another humanist patron, one who may have
been a friend of the Maître's youth. The author of the
Gargantua and Pantagruel was to make a number of
journeys to Italy in the course of his life, and that he employed his time to good advantage on this first occasion
is indicated by the fact that, upon his return he brought
out an edition of Marliani's *Topographia Antiquae
Romae,* dedicated to his patron.

When the *Gargantua* was published in the fall of 1534,
it met with the same fate as its predecessor at the hands
of the Sorbonne. For the "Affair of the Placards" had
occurred—anti-Catholic and atheistic placards which
had blossomed over the realm on the night of October
17-18, one of them even being affixed to the King's bed-
chamber—and a violent reaction against the Protestants
and reformers in general had set in. With fagots flaming

all around him, Rabelais again drops from sight for the first months of 1535, and his *Almanac* for that year is marked by a more serious tone. By spring the persecution had died down and the fugitives began returning. Maître François was back in Lyon when Jean du Bellay passed through the city on his way to Rome to be made a cardinal, and once more he was called upon to accompany the prelate as his physician. While in Rome this time, he filed a petition for apostasy, for having laid aside his monk's robe without permission; and on January 17, 1536, Pope Paul III granted him an absolution, along with permission to enter the Benedictine monastery of his choice and to continue the practice of medicine under the conditions that have been mentioned. Rabelais' appeal to the Pope, written in Latin, and three of his letters from Italy have come down to us.

In June, 1536, the war between Francis I and the Emperor Charles V began. This war was reflected ten years later, as Paris itself was being threatened by the imperial armies, in the ardent patriotism of the Prologue to Book Third. In August of the same year (1536) Rabelais became a canon of Saint-Maur, which made him a secular priest. He was now free of his monk's robe at last, though in somewhat irregular fashion, apparently through the conniving of his ecclesiastical superiors. There was some complaint as to this, the matter was taken up with Rome, and there was a second appeal to the Pope; but what the pontiff's answer was, is not known.

In the summer of 1537 Dr. François is directing anatomical demonstrations at Lyon, and he returns to Montpellier to lecture there. Etienne Dolet and others have testified to Rabelais' skill as a physician. Marvelous cures, widely talked about, were attributed to him. As an instructor in medicine he attracted much attention by the practice of dissection on cadavers, by his botanical and pharmacological erudition, and by lecturing, humanist that he was, directly from the Greek text of his authors. Modern medical men have credited him with a number of discoveries: the uterine origin of hysteria in woman (see his famous Dr. Rondibilis passage, Book Third), though this is open to question and the theory itself has since been discredited; the value of laughter as an emotional release; new methods in the treatment of syphilis; etc.

If ever a man's life was marked by ups-and-downs, it was his. One moment we find him taking to his heels— "doing a duck" (*faire la cane*), to employ his own expression—in order to keep from being burned alive; and not long afterward, we encounter him in the entourage of royalty at a meeting of two of the most powerful monarchs of the age. The explanation lies in his relations to the French throne on the one hand and to the Church on the other. The brilliant Renaissance court of Francis I, where the new influence coming out of Italy (including the influence of Boccaccio) prevailed, was naturally fond of this bold and sprightly satirist and appreciated his writings as much as churchmen like du Bellay and d'Estissac, who were at the same time humanists, did his conversation. For this reason, if for no other, the King was inclined to stand between Maître François and the wrath of the Sorbonnists. But there were other reasons. Due in part to the influence of his sister, Marguerite, and in part to his need of the Lutheran princes in his struggle with Charles, Francis was inclined to look with favor, or at least with tolerance, on the reformers within the Church. This attitude, however, was subject to sudden and violent change where the royal power and prerogatives were involved, as shown by the Affair of the

Placards; and in any case, there was a limit to which the kingly protection might serve when theologians were thundering at one who was all too patently tainted with heresy.

Rabelais was to experience one of these sudden and dramatic turns of fortune in connection with the historic meeting of Charles and Francis at Aigues-Mortes, on July 14, 1538. His standing at court was shown by the fact that he was present in the French monarch's train; but the outcome of this glittering event, which had been arranged by Pope Paul III as a means of bringing about a reconciliation between warring factions within the Church, was anything but favorable to the cause for which Rabelais and his friends stood. The Aigues-Mortes meeting was followed by another swing of the court from reform to orthodoxy and an attempt to wipe out heresy from the realm. As a result, Rabelais was compelled to tone down his writings from then on and to put a curb on his exuberance. The effect is to be seen in Books Third and Fourth and in the revision of the first two books for the 1542 and 1552 editions, where the author is frequently to be discovered substituting "sophist" for "theologian" and making similar discreet changes.

Another period of biographic darkness follows, from August, 1538, to July, 1540. Possibly it was during these years that Rabelais became the father of a bastard son, by the name of Théodule, who according to the record died in infancy and whose funeral was attended by princes of the Church. That is all we know about the incident. "Rabelais' bastard"—the phrase must continue to tantalize us.

In 1540, the Maître was in Turin, in the service of Guillaume du Bellay, Sieur de Langey and brother of the cardinal. Langey was noted as a wise and humane administrator, and it is to him that Rabelais owes the ideas on the treatment of conquered peoples which he sets forth in his work. In 1541, the author completed the definitive revision of Books I and II, and these books were reprinted the year following. It was at this juncture, just as he was beginning to feel that perhaps he had succeeded in appeasing the censors, that he was horrified to learn of an unauthorized and unexpurgated edition brought out by his old-time friend, Etienne Dolet, who thenceforth was to become a bitter enemy in Rabelais' eyes. The consequence was that the *Gargantua* and the *Pantagruel* were once more censured by Parliament, on complaint of the theological faculty of the Sorbonne, and its author was openly accused of impiety and heresy by the King's Arabic reader, Guillaume Postel.

Following a period of more than two years, from July, 1543, to September, 1545, during which he appeared once again to have "ducked" from his persecutors, Rabelais on September 19 of the latter year was granted, for the first time, a royal privilege for the printing of his works, and the following year Book Third was published under his own name, "M. François Rabelais, Doctor of Medicine." This would indicate that he was in favor at court once more. Possibly, it is the lack of royal protection that accounts for his prolonged literary silence, from 1534 to 1546.

Whatever the explanation, this section of Rabelais' continuing romance was worth waiting for. Book Third is his great book, his book of ripened wisdom. Erudite and humanist in character, with a heavy Platonist influence, it is still, in spite of its erudition, one of the lightest and airiest portions of his work as a whole and is at the same time, like all his writings, exceedingly topical. The subject that is uppermost in the conversations at court, the "woman question," becomes its central theme, for the sake of which the course of the narrative is changed. The gigantesque element, it is to be noted, disappears almost entirely, and Pantagruel is now the wise man of philosophy, expounding the way of life which Rabelais calls "Pantagruelism." The character of Panurge, by contrast—and this shows that the author is drawing ever closer to life—steadily degenerates, and the story tends to become something like a *roman de moeurs.*

Despite the concessions that had been made to the theologians, and notwithstanding its royal privilege, Book Third was banned some time prior to April 25, 1546. Things were beginning to go against Maître François; old friends were deserting, and the stake was always there; and so it is that we find him going into voluntary exile in the provincial city of Metz, where he is said to have resided in a house in the Jewish quarter, and where he was probably employed as a municipal physician. While here, he occupied himself with the composition of Book Fourth.

In 1547, Henry II, friend and patron of du Bellay, ascended the throne and Rabelais went to Rome to join the cardinal—his fourth visit to Italy, his third stay in the Eternal City. A partial edition of Book Fourth, consisting of eleven chapters and a prologue, appeared in 1548. For some reason, the text breaks off in the middle of a phrase. Rabelais' *Almanac for the Year 1548* was also published at this time.

In its final form, Book Fourth saw the light in 1552. This is the book into which the author has distilled the passion for discovery and the geographic curiosity of his age and in so doing has reflected the royal policy of colonial and maritime expansion. With its "Papimaniacs" and its bitter attacks on the Decretals, it also mirrors Henry II's quarrel with the See of Rome, and Rabelais is to be seen taking what is in reality a Gallican or national-Catholic position. It is less erudite than the preceding books, lacking the wealth of classical allusions to be found in them, but it is, perhaps, the nearest of all to the life of the times in its subject matter and in the rich flavor of its popular speech.

While Rabelais was still in Rome, an heir was born to Henry II and Catherine de' Medici, on February 3, 1549, and in honor of this event Cardinal du Bellay decided to stage a celebration in the form of an elaborate sham battle. Maître François has left us a vivid description of this in the account of the affair which he penned for the Cardinal de Guise, under the title of *Sciomachia,* a piece of writing which shows him to have been an excellent reporter.

In August 1550, after another disappearance of nearly a year, Rabelais was made the object of a vitriolic attack by Gabriel de Puy-Herbaut (Puits-Herbaut), a monk of Fontevraut known as the "mad Putherb" (from the Latin form of his name, Putherbus). In his attack, Puy-Herbaut was supported by the court poet, Charles de Sainte-Marthe, son of Gaucher de Sainte-Marthe, the ancient enemy of Antoine Rabelais, François' father. Thus did the old country feud which had inspired the *Gargantua* come back to the author of that work in his declining years. Rabelais was so discouraged with it all that, as he tells us, he came near resolving "not to write another iota."

Early the following year, through the influence of du Bellay, the monk who had shed his robe and the writer who so often had assailed the theologians was installed as curate of Saint-Martin-de-Meudon; for his ambition all his life long seems to have been the humble one of obtaining a comfortable living in the Church.

In April 1552, a reconciliation was effected between

the King of France and the Holy See as represented by Pope Julius III, and Rabelais' Gallican views, expressed in Book Fourth, were no longer popular at court. That book, as a matter of fact, had already been suppressed, on March 1, 1552, one of the magistrates who stopped the sale being Rabelais' old friend and first patron, André Tiraqueau. In October of this year a rumor spread in Lyon that Maître François was in prison.

There is no evidence that Rabelais ever actually fulfilled his curate's functions, either at Meudon or at Saint-Christophe-de-Jambet, in the Sarthe, another benefice which had been bestowed upon him, although a pleasant legend long persisted as to his teaching little children the plain song in his old age. Ill health caused him to resign both livings on January 9, 1553. It was about this time that he was given the honorary court post of *maître des requêtes*. He died not long afterward, "at Paris, in a house in the Rue des Jardins," if tradition be true, and he is said to have been "buried in St. Paul's Cemetery . . . at the foot of a tree which is still standing today" (this from an old record). The date of his death like that of his birth is uncertain. The one commonly accepted is April 9, 1553.

It was not until nine years after its author's death that the *Isle Sonante,* or first version of Book Fifth, was given to the world. This book represents a working over of Rabelais' posthumous notes and papers; and while critical opinion is tending to swing back to a belief in its *essential* authenticity (for example, Lefranc), it would appear to be Rabelais' work only in spots, and in any event, is creatively decidedly inferior to the other books.

v

Such was the troubled but ever full and varied life of
François Rabelais. Such was the outward man; what of
his mind and his outlook on the world?

The first thing that impresses one is what M. Lazare
Sainéan has called his "encyclopedic brain"; he has been
termed "a living encyclopedia," "the Pliny of his day,"
etc. His culture, it may be repeated, was fourfold: ecclesiastic (scholastic), juridical, medical, and humanistic. His intellect was a profoundly inquiring one; he was
ever the *"amateur de peregrinité,"* the lover of the
curious and the strange; yet with it all he remains per-
sistently close to life, the tumultuously stirring life of that
great age in which he lived, the life of the people about
him, as well as the life of the mind. To speak the simple
truth, his interests are as broad as life itself, and he, if
any man, might say that nothing human was alien to
him.

As a writer, he molded and shaped the language that
his countrymen were to speak, drawing upon the wealth
of popular idiom while enriching his native tongue with
needed borrowings from the Greek and Latin.[5] As a
literary creator, he is of epic proportions. His masterpiece may have been, as Anatole France remarks, a
chance one, but it is a masterpiece for all of that, one
of the treasures of world literature. Rabelais' place as a
humorist is beside Aristophanes, as one of the greatest
that we have known. But he was so much more than a
humorist! As we have seen, however exaggerated and
gigantesque the form that his imagination assumes, he
is basically realist in inspiration. A medical man of today,

---

[5] Many of these neologisms "stuck"; others did not.

Dr. Isidor Coriat, has spoken of "the dream-like character of Rabelais' thinking"; and the fact of the matter is that, in the structure which he rears upon his realistic base, he does at times appear to adumbrate in rather a startling manner the twentieth-century Freudians, Joyceans, and even the Surrealists (see his "Anatomy of Lentkeeper," Book Fourth).

At this point, the question of "influences" may be raised, seeing that there is scarcely such a thing as literary parthenogenesis. An inspection of his work shows clearly that his three principal masters were Lucian, Villon, and his heretical-minded contemporary, Jean Le Maire de Belges. From Sir Thomas More he borrowed the name and idea of Utopia; and Clement Marot, the humanist jurisconsults, and such Italian Renaissance writters as Pulci, Folengo, and Boiardo, as well as Plutarch, Pliny the Elder, and other authors of classical antiquity also contributed to his pages. Like a Shakespeare or a Picasso, like the great artist always, he took his material where he found it and never failed to make it his own.

But, someone may ask, what of the "obscenity" in Rabelais, his "coarseness" and "pornography," of which we have heard so much? The answer here is, simply, that he was speaking the language of his day, following the fashion and the *mores* of an age. Read his contemporaries, read those old pulpit exhorters, the *"prêcheurs libres"*: Olivier Maillard, Jean Bourgeois, Jean Raulin, and others. Does not Calvin employ the untranslatable epithet *"merdailles"* in addressing his congregation? And much has been heard of Luther and his reported *Tischreden*. As the Abbé Galliani has observed, "the obscenity of Rabelais is naïve; it is like a poor man's backside." It is one of the popular elements in his work, one of the things that he gets from the people, and is as healthy as the smell of a barnyard on a bright spring morning.[9]

On the side of content, there can be no doubt that, underlying the humor, the satire, the riotous imagination, there is a very definite philosophy of life, a philosophy that represents an admixture of Zeno and Epicurus, with a metaphysic provided by the followers of the Hermes Trismegistus. It is hard to believe with Professor Lefranc that the *Gargantua and Pantagruel* contains a "secret doctrine" of an atheistic kind. This, it seems to the present writer, is to fall into the humorlessness and fact-twisting of the older commentators. Rabelais was looked upon as an atheist by some of his enemies while he lived, but this proves little. Certainly, he was far from being an orthodox Catholic, even though for reasons of his own he chose to remain within the Church, and it is doubtful if "theist" or "deist" would quite cover the case. He was the nearest of all, it would seem, to being a pantheist; and it is likely that his religion is to be summed up in a phrase which he takes from Rossali, one of the glossarists on the *Hermes:* "the deathless circle of God"—or, in Pascal's famous *pensée:* "an infinite sphere, the center of which is everywhere, the circumference nowhere."

To his philosophy Rabelais gives the name of "Pantagruelism," which has been defined as "a moral doctrine

---

[9] An American physician, Dr. Douglass W. Montgomery, writing in the *Medical Record*, is of the opinion that Rabelais' "grossness" is due to his profession and hospital experiences; it is a doctor's naturalistic attitude. Rabelais, he adds, is not gross but "contemporaneously objective." Compare William Carlos Williams' view: ". . . the truth about Rabelais, now common property. He was not at all the fat-headed *débauché* we used to think him, gross, guffawing vulgarly, but a priest 'sensitized' to all such grossness . . . the old master, the old Catholic and the old priest." At bottom, Rabelais' attitude toward sex, into which there enters a large element of horse-play, will be found to be essentially a *healthy* one, the expression of a superabundant physical vitality—there are no "complexes" here.

that implies a constant elevation and breadth of soul," or, in the Maître's own words: "a certain cheerfulness of disposition preserved in spite of fortuitous circumstances." Pantagruel, as Lefranc points out, is "a model of moral equilibrium and tranquil wisdom." This "cheerful stoicism" does not, however, constitute the sum of Rabelais' world-view. His work is the deepest, most far-reaching expression that we have of that consuming thirst for the abundant life that was characteristic of the men of the Renaissance. This is brought out superlatively well in his Abbey of Thélème, which, as M. Plattard says, is a reflection of its creator's basic naturalistic philosophy and sense of life. Thélème is far from being, as Florio saw it, "the epicure's and glutton's home," and its rule, *"Fay ce que vouldras,"* has been grossly misinterpreted by some, as justifying a reign of unbridled instinct and desire. If one looks closely, one will perceive that what Rabelais is saying here is that unspoiled human nature is essentially, potentially good; "man can be beautiful" and can make a good life for himself. In other words, he is asserting a faith in human progress and perfectibility that is the heart of the humanist-Renaissance creed, the ideal of the free life, a dream that sees man, liberated from all mysticism and asceticism, walking upright in the sun and finding it a joyous experience.

It is toward this ideal, this dream, that Rabelais the educator shapes his thought. We have heard Guizot speaking of him in the same breath with Locke and Rousseau; and Sainte-Beuve, in one of his *Causeries,* devotes a paper to Maître François' educational method. While there are in it certain survivals of scholasticism, the program laid down is on the whole remarkable for its modernity, particularly for its stress on object-teaching, physical education, the natural sciences, and on "industry and the processes of trade." It is true that education as conceived by Rabelais in the case of the kingly Gargantua is still largely aristocratic in character, an affair of the gentleman and the scholar (*clerc*)—for like Castiglione, he is concerned with depicting the perfect prince of the new Renaissance type—but it is none the less democratic in its broad tendencies; for he himself, despite a certain obvious respect for birth and breeding (which has in it something of the modern eugenic attitude), a respect for place and power and a fondness for the refinements and softer things of life, is, when all is said, a man of the people who speaks the people's language. This is apparent from the influence he exerted at the time of the French Revolution.[10]

In almost all his attitudes, if indeed not all, Rabelais is unmistakably progressive. Like Erasmus, Budé, and Sir Thomas More, he is opposed in principle to war, but he makes something very like the modern distinction between wars of aggression and wars for defense. In the first chapter of his Book Third, he outlines a new mode of treatment for the conquered, one that combines the ideal of justice with political realism. In his passage on Sir Gaster (Sir Belly) in Book Fourth, he displays a profound awareness of the basic economic forces in society and the relation of those forces to the arts of man. And in the course of Panurge's dissertation on borrowers and lenders, in Book Third, he paints for us a glowing picture of a new and interdependent world and a society based upon a free interchange between human beings such as many of us today have come to conceive.

On one question alone he would appear, upon a

---

[10] See the work by Pierre Louis Ginguené: *De l'Autorité de Rabelais dans la Révolution Présente et de la Constitution Civile du Clergé*, published, significantly, in the year 1791. Some scholars (e.g., M. Georges Lote: *La Vie et L'Oeuvre de François Rabelais*, Paris, 1938) would deny this influence; they see, rather, a diminution of interest in the Maître in the eighteenth century.

superficial inspection, to take a reactionary position, representing a throwback to the Middle Ages, and that is with respect to women. Regarded during his lifetime as a violent anti-feminist, he was attacked by the defenders of the sex, and "Pantagruelist" came to be synonymous with woman-hater. Yet in his Abbey of Thélème, embodying his vision of an ideal society, woman has an honored place beside man; and even in the rowdy Book Third, if we look behind all the fun that is poked at cuckolds and the institution of marriage, we shall see that what Rabelais in reality is satirizing, and rather subtly, too, is masculine jealousy and the domination and seclusion of woman by the male; and we shall further perceive that he has very definite ideas as to what constitutes a self-respecting marriage, based upon a true companionship between the contracting parties. For all of its harangues against women, his Book Third, it may be noted, is dedicated to the greatest feminist of the day, Marguerite of Navarre. Perhaps we may solve the seeming contradiction if we remember that at the time Rabelais wrote a strenuous effort was being made to revive the old medieval ideal of *"courtoisie,"* and it was this false and enslaving brand of chivalry that Maître François was assailing, just as Cervantes was to do, a little later, in *Don Quixote.*

If Rabelais has given us the fullest and most vital expression of his age that is to be found in literature, it is for the reason that he was not merely the man of his age but the man of tomorrow as well. Life with him was a matter of ever receding horizons. That is what makes him seem so close to us—so close and so contemporary.

VI

In the selection of the passages contained in this volume, the primary purpose has been to present a coherent picture of Rabelais the writer and Rabelais the thinker—in other words, a picture of the author's mind as revealed in his creative work. All the best known portions of the *Gargantua and Pantagruel*, those commonly regarded as being most characteristically "Rabelaisian," will be found here, along with others which are ordinarily overlooked but which are important for the light they have to throw on Maître François' intellectual attitudes and development. The posthumous Fifth Book is not represented. Not only is its authenticity still open to question; its creative inferiority to the other books is apparent to anyone. It is the *Gargantua* and the three books of the *Pantagruel*, published during his lifetime and revised by him, by which Rabelais must be judged.

In connection with the text, the critical edition of the works of Rabelais by Professor Abel Lefranc and his colleagues, long in course of publication by Champion, Paris, has in general been followed as a basis, especially in the matter of sentence division and punctuation; and it goes without saying that this edition has likewise been of inestimable service in clearing up points of language and obscure allusions. With regard to language, M. Lazare Sainéan's notes in the Lefranc edition and his monumental work, *La Langue de Rabelais*, Paris, 1922, have served as a court of final appeal. Special indebtedness must also be acknowledged to M. Jean Plattard on the humanist-educational, M. Henri Clouzot on the historical-biographical, and M. Paul Dorveaux on the medical side. M. Plattard's illuminating volume, *François Rabelais* (Paris, 1932), has already been mentioned. M. Clouzot was, years ago, one of the first modern editors to attempt a biographical "*Notice.*"

As for the translation itself, there has been no attempt at an unduly modernized version; but rather, an effort has been made to preserve a judicious balance between the old and the new in language, by avoiding on the one hand unnecessary archaisms employed merely for the sake of effect, and on the other hand, contemporary English or American expressions that would be out of place and would jar upon the reader. It is, as may be imagined, not an easy balance to maintain. One thing that should be borne in mind is that Rabelais' sixteenth-century readers encountered a somewhat similar incongruity, or seeming incongruity, in the Maître's pages, with the thundering oaths and coarse, ribald, thoroughly colloquial and contemporaneous speech of Panurge, Friar John, and others standing in sharp contrast to the wealth of classical erudition which was constantly being displayed. This, after all, *is* Rabelais, and he is not to be made over. In any event, there would seem to be no point in undertaking to rewrite Urquhart.

A word may perhaps be said here as to Rabelais' rhythm. The impression that most of us have of that rhythm is derived from Urquhart; and Sir Thomas, due either to uncertainty or to sheer creative vitality, often runs riot with his author. The "big-bellied" quality of Rabelais' prose lies in the mouth-filling word or phrase rather than in the roll of the sentence; his sentence structure, as a matter of fact, as shown by such a reconstitution of his text as that which the Lefranc editors give us, is prevailingly short, simple, and direct.

Closely associated with the question of translation is that of notes. What is one to do where there are so many allusions that call for an explanation? Write the notes into the text? That seems hardly fair to the author, since it not only puts into his mouth things that he did not say and possibly never would have said, but also spoils the rhythm of the original. There appeared to be nothing for it but to hold the notes down to a minimum and place them at the end of each chapter, where they may be made use of or not by the reader as he may choose. Only occasionally, when it seemed natural and did not destroy the rhythm, has the translation of a Latin phrase been embodied in the text.

Acknowledgment is due Crown Publishers, holders of the copyright, for their very kind permission to make use of such portions of his original full-length version as the translator might see fit. The Introduction contains a good deal of material from the translator's book, *François Rabelais, Man of the Renaissance*, published by Jonathan Cape and Harrison Smith, in 1929.

Mr. Albert Mordell, author of *The Erotic Motive in Literature*, is to be thanked for valuable suggestions regarding the text and the Introduction and for assistance with Rabelais' Hebraisms.

The translator further would express his deep sense of gratitude to Mr. Pascal Covici, who, some twenty years ago, persuaded him to attempt the formidable task of doing Rabelais into English and who made it possible for him to complete his Renaissance studies in France. The encouragement received from the late Hugo P. Thieme of the Romance languages department of the University of Michigan is likewise gratefully remembered.

Above all, he is profoundly grateful to his wife, Riva Putnam, for her unfailing inspiration and assistance.

SAMUEL PUTNAM

Book First

Book First

BOOK FIRST

The Most Horrific Life

OF THE

GREAT GARGANTUA

FATHER OF PANTAGRUEL

Composed in Days of Old by M. Alcofribas

Abstractor of Quintessence

BOOK FULL OF PANTAGRUELISM

Of the five books into which Rabelais' masterpiece is divided, the Gargantua, or Book First, is in reality the second in point of time. There is internal evidence to this effect, as may readily be perceived by any reader. Thus, in ending Book Second, the author says: "Here I shall bring to a close this first book." And in Book First, Chapter 1, we find: "I send you back to the great Pantagrueline Chronicle"—that is, to Book Second. The fact that, in the title of Book First, Gargantua is referred to as the "father of Pantagruel" is also significant; and his genealogy, it will be noted, is given in Book Second, as it would not have been, presumably, had the Gargantua already been published.

We now know how all this happened: how the work

by another hand, entitled the Great and Inestimable Chronicles of the Great and Enormous Giant, Gargantua, *had been placed on sale at the Lyon fair in August, 1532, just as Rabelais, inspired by the great drought of that summer, was putting the finishing touches to his* Pantagruel; *how Maître François, toward the close of the year, went back to visit "my own cow country, to see if any of my folks are still alive," and how there, in the vicinity of La Devinière, he found himself in the midst of a country row over fishing rights in the Loire; and finally, how he proceeded to combine this episode with the old Gargantua myth, giving to the whole his own inimitable verve.*

This book falls roughly into five parts: the first, Chapters i-xv, *deals with the birth and early upbringing of Gargantua; the second, Chapters* xvi-xx, *deals with his Parisian adventures; the third, Chapters* xxi-xxiv, *might bear the title,* The Old Education and the New; *the fourth, Chapters* xxv-lii, *is an account of the Cake-Peddlers' War and introduces one of Rabelais' most delightful characters, Friar John Hackem (Urquhart's "Freer Jhon of the funnels and gobbets"); the fifth, Chapters* liii-lviii, *has to do with the building of the Abbey of Thélème. These divisions and their titles do not appear in Rabelais' text but have been supplied by the present editor.*

The title-page announces that this book is

ON SALE AT LYON, AT FRANÇOIS JUSTE'S
OPPOSITE OUR LADY OF COMFORT

M. D. XLII.

In addition to the Prologue, there is an initial "Aux Lecteurs" in verse.

To the Readers

My friends, who are about to read this book,
Please rid yourselves of every predilection;
You'll find no scandal, if you do not look,
For it contains no evil or infection.
True, you'll discover, upon close inspection,
It teaches little, except how to laugh:
The best of arguments; the rest is chaff,
Viewing the grief that threatens your brief span;
For smiles, not tears, make the better autograph,
Because to laugh is natural to man.

Author's Prologue

MOST illustrious Drinkers and you, most precious
Syphilitics, for it is to you, not to others, that my writings
are dedicated:

Alcibiades, in the dialogue of Plato entitled the *Symposium*, praising his preceptor, Socrates, who was, without question, the prince of philosophers, says, among
other things, that his master was like the Sileni. Sileni, in
the old days, were little boxes, such as may now be seen
in apothecaries' shops, painted over with merry and
frivolous figures, such as harpies, satyrs, bridled goslings,
horned hares, saddled ducks, flying goats, and harnessed
deer, with other pictures of the same sort, designed to
give pleasure and to excite folks to laughter; for such a
fellow was Silenus, master of the good Bacchus. But

inside these boxes were kept fine drugs, like balm, ambergris, amomum, musk, and civet, as well as medicinal stones and other precious things. And so, Alcibiades said that Socrates was like a Silenus, for the reason that, viewing him from the outside and judging him by his external appearance, you would not have given an onionpeel for him, so ugly was he of body and so ridiculous of mien, with a hooked nose, the stare of a bull, and the face of a fool, simple in manners, a rustic in clothing, poor in fortune, unfortunate in women, unfit for all public duties, always laughing, always drinking his share with anybody and everybody, always making light of himself, always dissimulating his own divine wisdom. But opening this box, you would have found in it a celestial and priceless drug, a more than human understanding, marvelous virtues, an invincible courage, a sobriety without its like, an unfaltering contentment, a perfect assurance, and an incredible contempt for all those things for which human beings lie awake, run about, labor, sail the seas, and fight.

Now what, in your opinion, is the drift of this prelude, this feeler? It is simply that you, my good disciples, and certain other foolish loafers, reading the hilarious titles of some of our books, *Gargantua, Pantagruel, Pint-Flogger, The Dignity of Codpieces, Peas and Bacon cum commento*, etc., may all too readily assume that there is to be found inside nothing but mockeries, pranks, and hilarious concoctions, seeing that the sign hung out in front, that is to say, the title, is, without further inquiry, commonly received with jest and derision. But such levity is not becoming in judging the works of men, for you yourselves say that the robe does not make the monk; and many a one goes clad in monastic garb who, on the inside, is anything but a monk, while many another wears a Spanish cape who, so far as his courage is concerned, shows no allegiance to Spain. That is why it is imperative to open the book and to weigh carefully what is to be found there. You then will realize that the drug contained in it is a good deal more valuable than might have been presumed from the box—that is to say, that the matters there treated are not so foolish as the title on the outside would indicate.

And even supposing that you do find matter there that is sufficiently entertaining and that corresponds well enough with the title, you are never under the necessity of pausing over it, as you would stop and listen to the Siren's song, but you rather should interpret in a higher sense that which you may, perhaps, believe to have been uttered out of pure light-heartedness.

Didn't you ever do any bottle-opening? Son of a bitch! Then, try to recall the countenance you had upon such occasion. Or have you never seen a dog falling upon a marrow-bone? He is, as Plato says, *lib. ii. de Rep.*, the most philosophic beast in the world. If you have observed him, you must have noted with what devotion he watches that bone, with what care he guards it, with what fervor he holds on to it, with what prudence he bites into it, with what affection he breaks it, and with what diligence he sucks it. What leads him to do this? What is the hope behind his effort? What does he expect to gain? Nothing more than a little marrow. It is true that this little is more delicious than large quantities of any other kind of meat, for the reason that marrow is a form of nourishment which nature has worked out to perfection, as Galen tells us, *iii, Facu. natural.*, and *xi., De usu partium.*

Following the dog's example, you will have to be wise in sniffing, smelling, and estimating these fine and meaty books; swiftness in the chase and boldness in the attack are what is called for; after which, by careful reading and frequent meditation, you should break the bone and suck the substantific marrow—that is to say, the meaning of the Pythagorean symbols which I employ—in the certain hope that you will be rendered prudent and valorous by such a reading; for in the course of it you will find things of quite a different taste and a doctrine more abstruse that shall reveal to you most high sacraments and horrific mysteries in what concerns our religion, as well as the state and our political and economic life.

Do you believe, upon your word, that Homer, when he was writing the *Iliad* and *Odyssey*, ever thought of the allegories which Plutarch, Heraclides, Ponticus, Eustathius, and Phornutus have plugged into those works, and which Politian has pilfered from these others? If you think so, you do not come within either hand or foot of my opinion, which is that all those things were as little dreamed of by Homer as the sacraments of the Gospel were by Ovid, in the latter's *Metamorphoses*, though a certain silly monk, a sponger if there ever was one, will take it upon himself to prove the latter case, whenever he happens to meet any folks as foolish as himself and (as the proverb has it) a lid worthy of such a kettle.

If you refuse to believe any such thing, why should you not do the same for these new and merry *Chronicles,* since, in dictating them, I thought no more of all this than did you, who were, it may be, engaged in drinking, like myself? For in the composition of this masterly work I did not waste nor spend any more time than that allotted to my bodily refection, by which I would have you understand: eating and drinking. Such, indeed, is the proper time to write of these high matters and profound sciences, as Homer, paragon of all philologists, well knew, and Ennius, father of the Latin poets, as Horace bears witness, even though one lout has said that Horace's verses smell more of wine than they do of oil.

A certain beggarly rascal has said the same thing of my books; but a turd for him! The odor of wine, oh, how much more dainty, pleasing, irresistible, celestial and delicious it is than that of oil! And I shall feel that I have won as much glory, when it is said of me that I have spent more on wine than on oil, as Demosthenes felt was his, when it was said of him that he had spent more on oil than on wine. For me, there is only honor and glory in being looked upon as a good fellow and a good companion; and in this name, I am welcome in any good company of Pantagruelists. Demosthenes was reproached by one ill-natured chap with the charge that his orations smelled like the apron of a foul and filthy oil-merchant.

However, you are to interpret all that I do and say in the very best part, holding in reverence the cheese-shaped brain that feeds you these fine puff-balls; and to the best of your ability, always keep me good company.

And now, my dears, hop to it, and gaily read the rest, wholly at your bodies' ease and to the profit of your loins. But listen, ass-wallopers—may a chancre lame you!—remember to drink a like health to me, and I will pledge you on the spot.

I. The Birth and Early Upbringing of Gargantua

(CHAPTERS I-XV)

The Gargantua myth is an old one, the tale forming part of the collection known as the Bibliothèque Bleue. *The earliest allusion to the name is to be found in a record of the bishopric of Limoges, of the latter half of the fifteenth century. In the early 1530's, the legend appears to have taken on new life, and there are a number of references to it in the farces of the period. From one of these, the* Farce du Goutteux *(Farce of the Gouty One) Rabelais may have borrowed at once his vinous coloring and his idea of literary therapeutics—a gouty patient being healed by procuring a copy of the book. There is also a work by François Girault, entitled* The Great and Marvelous Life of the Right Powerful and Redoubtable King Gargantua, *and purportedly "translated from the Greek and Latin into French," which contains a number of incidents, such as the carrying away of the Parisian bells, that are suggestive of Rabelais' creation.*

By the time Maître François came to deal with him, Gargantua had taken on certain definite characteristics: his gigantic stature, his gigantic strength, his gigantic appetite. An authority on French folklore, M. Paul Sébillot, has summed the matter up as follows:

"The conclusion seems to be that there has existed in

the past a vast legendary cycle, the giant heroes of which were in the habit of residing in or passing through a certain place, being noted for their strength, their enormous size, their appetites, and their huge strides. To these general attributes have been added fragmentary traits borrowed either from the legendary Hercules, or from eastern giants, or even from the saints. Each of these personages originally possessed an individual existence and a name. Later, at a period difficult to determine with precision, they for the most part lost their individualities and were absorbed by a single Gargantua, just as the Roman Hercules had ended by taking on the attributes of all congenerous heroes. This hypothesis, as I see it, is confirmed by the existence in many countries of giants possessing the same functions and qualities as Gargantua, even though their legends may have been to a greater degree effaced, while certain of them have lost their very names."

One thinks of our American Paul Bunyan and other figures. And is not the Superman of the contemporary comic strip a derivative of these?

The Genealogy and Antiquity of Gargantua

I SEND you back to the *Great Pantagrueline Chronicle,* if you would form an idea of the genealogy of Gargantua and of the antiquity from which he has come down to us. From it you will learn in full how the Giants were born into this world, and how from them, in direct line, sprang Gargantua, father of Pantagruel; and so, do not be put out with me if for the present I pass on, although the subject is such a one that the oftener it is recalled, the more pleasing it is to your Lordships, for which you have the authority of Plato in his *Philebo* and his *Gorgias,* as

well as of Flaccus, who says that there are certain subjects such as these very ones, no doubt, that are the more
delectable the more often they are discussed.

Would to God that every one were as certain of his
genealogy from Noah's ark down to the present day! It is
my opinion that a number are today emperors, kings,
dukes, princes, and popes of the earth who are descended
from certain porters and pardon-peddlers, just as, on the
other hand, a number are almshouse beggars, needy and
miserable, who are of the blood and lineage of great
kings and emperors, as a result of the marvelous passing
of realms and empires:

From the Assyrians to the Medes;
From the Medes to the Persians;
From the Persians to the Macedonians;
From the Macedonians to the Romans;
From the Romans to the Greeks;
From the Greeks to the French.

And in order to give you an idea of who it is that is
speaking to you, I will say that I believe that I am
descended from some rich king or prince of former times,
for you never saw a chap who had a greater longing to be
a king, and a wealthy one, than I, so that I might be able
to dispense good cheer, not have to work, not have to
worry about anything at all, but be able to enrich my
friends and all others who are good and wise. But in this,
I comfort myself that in the other world I shall be greater
than at present I should dare to hope. And with a like or
a better thought, comfort your own misfortune, and drink
hearty, if it can be done.

But to come back to our sheep, I was telling you that,
by a sovereign gift of the heavens, the antiquity and
genealogy of Gargantua had been preserved for us more
nearly whole than any other, except that of the Messiah,
of which I say nothing, for it is none of my business, and

moreover, the devils, that is to say, the slanderers and hypocrites, would oppose me in this. The document was found by one Jean Audeau in a meadow which he had near the Gualeau Arch, below the farm known as L'Olive, on the road to Narsay. In making ditches in this meadow, the diggers, with their mattocks, came upon a great bronze tomb, immeasurably long, the end of which they never found, as it was too deeply buried in the sluices of the Vienne. Opening this tomb in a certain place, marked above with a goblet, around which had been written, in Etruscan characters, HIC BIBITUR, they found nine flagons, arranged in the same order as that in which ninepins are set up in Gascony, the middle one of which covered a great, thick, fat, fuddled, pretty little moldy booklet, more, but not better, smelling than the rose. In this, the said genealogy was found, written out at length, in chancellery letters, not on paper, not on parchment, not on wax, but on a piece of elm-bark, so worn with age that it was barely possible to recognize three of the characters in a row.

I (although unworthy) was summoned; and by great dint of spectacles, practicing the art by which one may read invisible letters, as Aristotle teaches, I translated this booklet, as you may see in your pantagruelizing, that is to say, drinking your fill, as you read of the horrific deeds of Pantagruel.

At the end of the book was a little treatise entitled the "Antidoted Baubles." The rats and cockroaches, or (if I must be exact) other malign beasts, had gnawed away the beginning; the rest I have appended below, out of reverence for antiquity.

There follows a verse composition in fourteen stanzas, 112 lines, of which no one yet has ever been able to make sense. This was a literary genre known in Rabelais' time as the "enigme." It is possible that the "enigma" in question here has its roots deep in the events of the Reformation era; but to the modern reader it means what it did to the Maître's contemporaries—precisely nothing.

How Gargantua Was Carried Eleven Months in His Mother's Belly

GRANDGOUSIER was a jolly good fellow in his day, liking to drink hearty as well as any man in the world at that time, and he was very fond of salty food. For this reason, he ordinarily had on hand a good supply of Mayence and Bayonne hams, a lot of smoked beef-tongues, an abundance of chitterlings in season and salt-beef with mustard, a store of fish-eggs, salted, pressed, and dried, and plenty of sausages—not those of Bologna (for he was afraid of the Lombard poison) but those from Bigorre, from Longaulnay, from La Brenne and from Rouergue.

When he was of manly age, he was married to Gargamelle, daughter of the King of the Butterflies, a pretty wench with a good mug on her. And these two often played the beast-with-two-backs, rubbing their bacons together hilariously, and doing it so often that she became pregnant with a fine son and carried him up to the eleventh month.

For women may carry their big bellies as long, and even longer, especially when it is some masterpiece of a personage that is to be born, and one who is to do great deeds in his time. Thus, Homer tells us that the child with which Neptune impregnated the Nymph was born after a year had rolled by; that was the twelfth month. Since (as A. Gellius says, *lib. iii*) this long time was befitting to the majesty of Neptune, in order that the child might be formed to perfection. For similar reason, Jupiter caused the night which he spent in bed with Alcemene to last forty-eight hours, for in a less time, he would not have been able to forge Hercules, who rid the world of monsters and tyrants.

Those gentlemen, the ancient Pantagruelists, have confirmed what I say, and have declared not only possible, but also legitimate, the child born of a woman eleven months after the death of her husband:

Hippocrates, *lib. De alimento;*

Pliny, *lib. vii, cap. v;*

Plautus, in his *Cistellaria;*

Marcus Varro, in the satire entitled *The Testament,* adducing the authority of Aristotle to prove his point;

Censorinus, *lib, De die natali;*

Aristotle, *lib. vii, cap. iii et iiii, De nat. animalium;*

Gellius, *lib. iii, cap. xvi;*

Servius, in explaining this line of Vergil's *Eclogues:* *Matri longa decem,* etc.,

and a thousand other fools, whose number has been increased by the lawyers, *ff. De suis, et legit., 1. Intestato, ſ fi,* and *Autent., De restitut. et ea que parit in xi mense.* What is more, they have scribbled their bacon-filching law: Gallus, *ff. De lib. et posthu., et septimo ff. De stat. homil.,* and certain others which for the present I do not dare to mention, by means of which laws, widow-ladies may openly play at press-rump, whenever they get a bid, and with all their stakes, two months after the death of their husbands.

I beg you, my good and lusty lubbers, if you find any of the sort who are worth unbuttoning a fellow's breeches for, mount 'em and bring 'em to me. For if they become pregnant in the third month, their offspring will become the heir of the deceased; and so, once you know they are gone, push boldly on, and let the good ship go free, seeing that the paunch is full!—like Julia, daughter of the Emperor Octavianus, who never abandoned herself to her drummer-boys except when she knew that she was pregnant, just as a ship never takes on a pilot until she is calked and loaded. And if anyone blames them for having their holes patched while they are pregnant, in view of the fact that beasts never permit a male upon their bellies in such a case, they will reply that those are beasts, but they are women, well instructed in the fine and jolly little privileges of superfetation which reminds one of Populia's reply, as reported by Macrobius, *lib. ii, Saturnal:* If the devil doesn't want them to become pregnant, he ought to twist off the spigot and plug up the bunghole.

In the foregoing passage, Rabelais is probably satirizing the pedants, and in particular, the pedantic jurisconsults of his time. He here alludes to Hippocrates' treatise On Nourishment; *to Book* VII, *Chapter v, of Pliny the Elder's* Natural History; *to Plautus' play, the* Cistellaria; *to the work entitled* On the Natal Day, *by the third-century grammarian, Censorinus; to a satire by Varro; and to several passages in the* Digests *or* Pandects *of Justinian that have to do with the subject of births. For effect, he retains the legal form and phraseology.*

How Gargamelle, Being Pregnant with Gargantua, Ate a Great Abundance of Tripe

THE occasion and the manner of Gargamelle's giving birth was this, and if you don't believe it, I hope your bottom drops out. Hers dropped out one afternoon, the third day of February, from having eaten too many *gaudebillaux*. *Gaudebillaux* are the fat tripe of *coiraux*. *Coiraux* are beef fattened in the stall and in the *guimaulx* meadows. *Guimaulx* meadows are those that bear grass two times a year. Of these fat oxen, they had killed three-hundred-sixty-seven-thousand-fourteen, to be salted down Shrove Tuesday, so that, in the spring, they might have a lot of beef in season, as a spicy and commemorative offering to their palates at the beginning of their meals, to enable them to enter into their wine in better fashion.

The tripe were plentiful, you understand, and they were so dainty that everyone licked his fingers. But the great mischief was this, that it was not possible to keep them long, for they would have stunk, which would have been indecent; and so, they decided to gulp them down, without losing a mouthful. For this purpose, they invited in all the citizens of Cinais, Seuilly, La Roche-Clermault and Vaugaudry, without leaving out Coudray-Montpensier, Gué de Vede, and other neighbors, all good drinkers, good companions, and up-and-coming ninepin-players.

Grandgousier, big-hearted fellow that he was, took a very great pleasure in all this and ordered them to spare no expense. But he kept warning his wife all the time, that she should eat the least of any, in view of the fact that she was approaching her term, and this mess of tripe was not a highly commendable dish.

"A person would, like as not, eat dung," he said, "who eats the sack that holds it."

Notwithstanding these remonstrances, she proceeded to eat sixteen hogsheads, two barrels, and six jugs full of them. O the fine fecal matter that must have puffed up inside her!

After dinner, they all went pell-mell to the Willow-

Grove; and there, upon the thick grass, they danced to the sound of joyous flutes and melodious bagpipes, so gaily that it was a heavenly pleasure just to see them having so merry a time.

The Remarks of the Drunkards

THEN they started talking about having a little after-dinner snack on the spot; and at once, the flagons began to go, the hams to trot, the goblets to fly, and the big bowls to jingle.

"Draw one!"

"Set 'em up!"

"Keep 'em coming!"

"Mix me one!"

"Slip me mine without a chaser—that's the way, my friend."

"Throw this one down you like a man!"

"Produce the claret, and fill her up till she weeps."

"To hell with thirst!"

"I was burning up, but this ought to do the trick."

"'Pon my word, old girl, I don't seem to be able to get into form."

"What's the matter, dearie—catch a cold?"

"You said it."

"Saint Quenet's belly! Let's talk about drinking."

"I only drink by the clock, like the Pope's mule."

"I only drink out of my breviary, like a good guardian father."

"Which came first, thirst or drinking?"

"Thirst, for who would have drunk if he wasn't thirsty in the good old days?"

"Drink, for *privatio presupponit habitum.* I'm a scholar. *Foecundi calices quem non fecere disertum?*"

"We poor innocents drink all too much without being thirsty."

"Not I. Sinner that I am, I never drink without thirst, if not present, at least future—to head it off, you understand. I drink for the thirst to come. I drink everlastingly. With me, it's an eternity of drinking and a drinking of eternity."

"Let's sing something; drink up, and let's intone a motet!"

"Where's my intoner?"

"What's the matter here! It looks as if I only drank by proxy."

"Which is it you do, wet your gullet to dry it or dry it to wet it?"

"I don't know anything about the theory of the thing, but I manage to get along in practice."

"Drink up!"

"I drink, I wet my whistle, I sprinkle my throat, and all out of fear of dying."

"Keep on drinking, and you'll never die."

"If I don't drink, I'm dry, and that means I'm dead already. My soul flies away to some frog-pond. For the soul never inhabits a dry spot."

"O you wine-servers, creators of new forms, make of me, a non-drinker, a drinker!"

"A perennial inundation for these dry and withered old bowels of mine!"

"It's no use drinking, unless you feel it as it goes down."

"This one's bound for my veins; my kidneys aren't going to get any of it."

"I don't mind if I wash the tripe of the calf I dressed this morning."

"My stomach's well ballasted."

"If the paper with the list of my debts could drink

the way I do, my creditors would have plenty of wine when they came around to collect."

"That hand of yours is spoiling your nose."

"Oh, how many others are going in before this one comes out!"

"If you drink your glass shallow like that, you'll burst your belly-band."

"This is what you call bird-sniping with flagons for decoys."

"What's the difference between a bottle and a flagon?"

"A lot of difference. You close a bottle with a stopper and a flagon (if it's a female one you mean) with a vice."

"That's telling him!"

"Our fathers drank well and emptied their pots."

"Ha! yes, their chamber-pots—drink up!"

"Haven't you anything to send to the river? This one's going to wash the tripe."

"I don't drink any more than a sponge."

"I drink like a Templar."

"And I *tanquam sponsus*. Like a bridegroom."

"*Sicut terra sine aqua* for me."

"What's a synonym for ham?"

"It's a warrant for drinks; it's a wine-chute. With a chute you let wine down into the cellar; with ham, you lower it into your stomach."

"Hey, there, give me a drink, give me a drink there! *Respice personam; pone pro duos; bus non est in usu.* (That means: have respect for present company and pour for two. If I say '*pro duos*' instead of '*pro duobus*,' that's because *bus*— 'I've *had* a drink'—is not in use.")

"If I went up as this goes down, I'd have been high in the air long ago."

"That's the way Jacques Coeur got rich."

"There's profit in a drunkard's itch."

"That's the way Bacchus conquered India."

"And philosophy Melind."

"A little rain lays a big wind, and long drinking routs thunder."

"If my urine tasted like this, should you like to sample it?"

"I hold mine back when I'm drinking."

"Fill them up, boy! I hereby enter an appearance, in due course."

"Drink, Bill! There's another jug still."

"I appeal from thirst; it's a cruel and unusual punishment. Boy, take up my appeal in proper form."

"Pass me what's left on the plate over there."

"I used to drink all there was; now I leave nothing."

"Let's not be in a hurry; let's get all that's coming to us."

"Here is some tripe that you can bet your money on—you'll be wanting more of it—it's from the dun steer with the black stripe."

"For God's sake, let's curry him down to a fare-you-well."

"Drink up, or I will——"

"No, no!"

"Well, then, drink up, please."

"Sparrows don't eat unless you spank their tails; I won't drink if you're not polite to me."

"*Lagona edatera!* Here's to you! There's not a rabbit-hole in my body where this wine is not ferreting out thirst."

"It's whipping mine up very nicely."

"It's going to drive mine away altogether."

"Let us proclaim to the sound of flagons and bottles that no one who has lost his thirst shall come looking for it here; as a result of prolonged enemas of drinking, we've got rid of it—out of doors."

"God Almighty made the planets, and we make the plates clean (*platz netz*)."

"It is God's own word I speak: *Sitio*. I've got a thirst."

"I'm a father-confessor, and I'm telling you that the stone called ἄσβεστος (asbestos) is not more inextinguishable than my paternal craving for a drink."

"Appetite comes with eating, says Hangest of Mans; thirst leaves with drinking."

"What's a good remedy for thirst?"

"It's the opposite to the one for dog-bite; always run after the dog, and he will never bite you; always drink before you're thirsty, and thirst will never catch up with you."

"Hey, there, wake up! Ah, that's the time I caught you napping. O eternal Sandman of the wine cups, preserve us from slumber. Argus had a hundred eyes to see with, but a wine-server needs a hundred hands, like Briareus, so he won't get tired pouring."

"Wet her down; there'll be plenty of time to dry her out afterwards!"

"A little of the white! Pour, pour like the devil! Pour there and fill her up; my tongue's hanging out."

"Drink, *Landsmann!*"

"Here's to you, mate! Down the hatch!"

"Ha! That one went down easy enough."

"*O lacrima Christi!* Tears of Christ!"

"It's from La Devinière; it's Burgundy grape!"

"What good white wine!"

" 'Pon my soul, it's like velvet!"

"Ha, ha! but it's good stuff, all wool and a yard wide."

"Brace up, old man!"

"We're not going to lose this trick, for I've just raised—my elbow."

"*Ex hoc in hoc.* From glass to mouth. You all saw me;

there's no sleight-of-hand about it. When it comes to this sort of thing, I'm past master (*maistre passé*)."

"Ahem! Ahem! And I'm Parson Matthew (*Prebstre Macé*)."

"What a life for us drinkers! But think of the thirsty ones!"

"Here, boy, be a good lad, please, and fill her up."

"Crown her 'till she's cardinal-red on top."

"*Natura abhorret vacuum.* Nature abhors a vacuum."

"Do you think a fly would find any leavings here?"

"Breton fashion, bottoms up!"

"Fall to! Don't leave a drop!"

"Gulp it down; it's medicine!"

The company of drinkers portrayed above is a mixed one, a number of the individuals being readily recognizable. There is the man of law, who speaks of producing the claret, of entering an appearance with the wine-server, of taking an appeal from thirst, etc. Representatives of the clergy, possibly monks from a neighboring monastery, are present, including the good father superior who only satisfies his "paternal thirst" out of his breviary. There are at least a couple of women, one of whom has caught a cold, who distract the men from their favorite topic, which is drinking. And it is probably a Swiss soldier or lansquenet who exclaims, "Drink, Landsmann!" (Lans, tringue). A Basque expression like "Lagona edatera" (meaning drinking companion) is also to be noted.

The conversation of those in their cups is not infrequently a disjointed affair, but there is a considerable continuity in the present instance, more than at first may be apparent, with one remark leading to another through an association of thoughts, words, or sounds. There are occasional snatches of song, as in the lines beginning "That's the way Jacques Coeur got rich"—*Jacques Coeur being a fifteenth-century forerunner of the modern big bankers (there is an allusion to him in Verse 285 of Villon's* Testament*). Similarly,* "Drink, Bill! There's another jug still" (Hume, Guillot! Encores y en a il un pot) *and* "Ah! that's the time I caught you napping" (Je vous y prens, je vous resveille) *may be tags of old songs now lost. One of the interlocutors quotes the well-known line of Horace (Epistles,* i, v, 19), Foecundi calices, *etc.:* "Brimming bowls—whom have they not made eloquent?"

There is a jibe at the legal profession in the humorous pomposity, "Privatio presupponit habitum (*Privation presupposes habit*)," *and a play on the* "substantial forms" *of the scholastics in* "Make of me, a non-drinker, a drinker." *In observing that* "the soul never inhabits a dry spot," *the speaker is drawing upon the pseudo-Saint-Augustine (*"Anima certe quia spiritus est, in sicco habitare non potest—*The soul, assuredly, being spirit, cannot dwell in an arid place"). Some of the Biblical allusions are none too reverent in tone, as when use is made of Christ's word on the cross:* "Sitio—*I am athirst*" (John, xix, 28), *or, in a couple of instances, of passages from the* Psalms: "tanquam sponsus—*like a bridegroom*" (Psalms, xviii, 6); *and* "sicut terra sine aqua—*like a land without water*" (Psalms, cxlii, 6). *Even the reference to the famous Neapolitan wine,* lacrima Christi, *is faintly sacrilegious, being reminiscent of the famous remark of the Master of Arts of Cologne:* "Utinam Christus vellet etiam flere in patria nostra—*Would that Christ would weep a little in our country, also!*"

Puns, it will be noticed, play an important part in this dialogue: planets and platz netz, *or clean plates;*

past master (maistre passé) *and Parson Matthew* (prebstre Macé)—*the "parson" in question being a character who appears in a number of works of the period, but who has not been identified by scholars; the play on* sommelier, *wine-server, and* sommeil, *sleep; etc.*

How Gargantua Was Born in a Very Strange Fashion

WHILE they were carrying on this bibulous small talk, Gargamelle commenced to feel bad down below; and then, Grandgousier rose from the grass and began to comfort her, very decently, thinking that she was about to give birth, and telling her that she should sit there on the lawn, under the willows, and that she would soon be growing a pair of new hoofs, like a horse put out to grass, adding that she ought to pluck up fresh courage, to be ready for the arrival of her new little darling. He also told her that while the pain might be a trifle annoying, it would not last very long, and the joy she would then feel would take away all the discomfort, so that she would not even be able to remember it.

"I will prove it," he went on. "Our Savior says, in the Gospel, *John, xvi:* 'A woman when she is in travail hath sorrow, because her hour is come: but as soon as she is delivered of the child, she remembereth no more the anguish.'"

"Ha!" she exclaimed, "that's well said, and I would much rather listen to such sayings from the Gospel, since I get more profit from them, than to the Life of St. Margaret or some hypocritical tale like that."

"Only have the courage of a sheep," he told her, "get rid of this one, and we'll soon make another."

"Ha!" she replied, "it's easy enough for you to talk,

you men! Well, then, in God's name, I'll do my best, since you insist. But I wish to God you had cut it off."

"Cut what off?" said Grandgousier.

"Oh," she said, "you're a man. You understand well enough."

"My member?" said he. "Goats' blood! All right, if you want me to, have them bring a knife."

"Oh, no," she cried, "God forbid! I pray God to forgive me; I didn't mean it, and I hope you won't pay the least bit of attention to what I said. But I've a lot to do today, unless God helps me, and all on account of that member of yours, God love it!"

"Courage, courage," said he. "Don't you worry about that: just leave all that to the four front-oxen. I'm going to go take a little nip of something or other. If anything happens, I'll be close by. Just put your hands to your mouth and call, and I'll be right with you."

A short while afterward, she commenced to breathe hard and to moan and cry. Immediately, a lot of midwives came running up from all sides. Feeling her down below, they found some filthy membranes that smelled very bad, and they thought that this was the child; but it was only her bottom dropping out, due to the relaxing of the right intestine, the one you call the rump-gut, all as a result of the tripe she had eaten, as we have set forth above.

Then a dirty old hag who happened to be among those present and who had a reputation for being a great doctor, coming from Brisepaille near Saint-Genou and being around sixty years old, proceeded to concoct a horrible astringent for her, as a result of which all Gargamelle's membranes were so obstructed and constricted that you would have had hard work prying them open with your teeth, which is quite a horrible thing to think about.

Just as the devil, at St. Martin's mass, when he was writing down the cackle of the two sporting lasses, had to make use of a good set of teeth to stretch his parchment.

On account of this inconvenience, the cotyledons of the matrix were relaxed, and the infant, leaping up, entered the hollow vein and climbed over the diaphragm to her shoulders (where the said vein divides into two parts) and there he took the left hand path and came out by the left ear.

This infant did not, as soon as he was born, begin to cry "Mie, mie" like other children; but in a loud voice, he bawled "Give me a drink! a drink! a drink!" as though he were inviting all the world to have a drink with him, and so lustily that he was heard throughout the land of Beuxes and Vivarais ("Booze" and "Bibbers").

I doubt whether you will quite believe my account of this strange nativity. If you don't believe it, I don't care; but a good fellow, a man of good sense, ought always to believe what anybody tells him and whatever he sees in print.

"Does not Solomon say, *Proverbs, xiv, Innocens credit omni verbo?* And St. Paul, *First Corinthians, xiii, Caritas omnia credit?* Why will you not believe this? For the reason, you say, that it does not seem at all likely. I tell you that, for this very reason alone, you ought to believe it, in perfect faith, since the Sorbonnists say that faith lies in believing things that possess no appearance of likelihood."

Is it against law, against faith, against reason, against Holy Writ? For my part, I find nothing in the Bible that is opposed to all this. If God had wanted to have it that way, should you say he couldn't have done it? Ah, for heaven's sake, don't get all balled up over foolish thoughts like that, for I am telling you that with God nothing is impossible. And if he willed it so, all women after this would give birth through the ear.

Bacchus, wasn't he engendered from Jupiter's thigh?

Rentrock, wasn't he born from his mother's heel?

Scrunchfly from his nurse's slipper?

Minerva, wasn't she born from Jupiter's brain, by way of his ear?

Adonis from the bark of a myrrh tree?

Castor and Pollux from the shell of an egg laid and hatched by Leda?

But you would be still more astonished and dumbfounded, if I were at once to lay before you that whole chapter of Pliny in which he speaks of strange births and those contrary to nature. For I was never so self-assured a liar as he. Read the seventh book of his *Natural History, cap. iii,* and don't come pestering my head any more with your silly objections.

There are two passages in the preceding section which Rabelais discreetly omitted from the revised edition of 1542. One consists of the two paragraphs containing the allusion to the Gospel of John *and the* Life of St. Margaret. *The other is the paragraph quoting the book of* Proverbs *and* First Corinthians.

There are a number of folklore references: the devil in church writing down the chatter of the Gauloises, or sporting lasses; the allusions to such folk characters as Rocquetaillade, or Rentrock, and Crocquemouche, or Scrunchfly; etc. (The name Roquetaillade persists in several regions of France.) "Leave all that to the four front-oxen" similarly represents a popular saying and perhaps a legend.

The pun on Beuxes and Vivarais (in Rabelais' text,

*spelled Beusse and Bibaroys) is dependent upon pro-
nunciation, a Gascon pronunciation in the latter case,
marked by a confusion of the v and b sounds, which
leads to a play on the Latin* bibere, *while Beuxes or
Beusse connotes the participle* bu(s) *from the French*
boire, *to drink.*

*The mode of Gargantua's birth is Rabelais' own addi-
tion to the Gargantua myth.*

How Gargantua Was Named, and How He Sucked Wine

THAT good fellow, Grandgousier, while drinking and
having a jolly time with the others, heard the horrible
cry his son had given upon coming into the light of
this world, when the child brayed out, demanding "A
drink! a drink! a drink!"; and he remarked, "QUE GRAND
TU AS (*supple le gosier*). What a big and nimble throat
you have!" Upon hearing this, those present declared
that, really, the child ought to have the name of GAR-
GANTUA, since this had been the first word his father had
spoken after his birth—in imitation of the example of
the ancient Hebrews. Grandgousier very kindly conde-
scended, and the child's mother was very well satisfied.
And to appease the newborn, they gave him a good stiff
drink, and he was carried to the font and there baptized, as is the custom with good Christians.

And they set aside seventeen-thousand-nine-hundred-
thirteen cows of Pontille and Bréhémont for his ordinary
milk diet; for it was not possible to find sufficient nourishment in the whole country, in view of the great quantity of milk required to sustain him. But how many
Scotistical doctors there were who asserted that his
mother might have nursed him easily enough, and that

it would have been possible to draw from her breasts fourteen-hundred-two great barrels and nine pails of milk every time. All of which is not very likely. And indeed, this proposition has been declared mammilarily scandalous and offensive to pious ears and one that smells of heresy a long way off.

This state of affairs lasted until he was a year and ten months old, at which time, on the advice of the doctors, they began lugging him about. They made for him a fine ox-cart, the invention of Jean Denyau, in which they trundled him merrily here and there. And it was a sight to see, for he had a good mug on him and nearly eighteen chins. He cried very little but dirtied his pants at all hours, for he was marvellously phlegmatic in the buttocks, as much by natural constitution as from the disposition he had accidentally acquired through having imbibed too much of the Septembral juice.

But he never drank a drop without good reason. For if he happened to be put out, irritated, angry, or merely out of sorts, if he stamped his foot, if he wept, if he cried, they would bring him something to drink, and this at once would put him in a good humor, and he would become as coy and happy as you pleased. One of his maids has told me, swearing to it upon her word, that he was so accustomed to this treatment that at the very sound of pints and flagons, he would fall into an ecstasy, as though he were tasting the joys of paradise. And so, seeing that he had so divine a disposition, to amuse him every morning they would ring glasses with a knife in front of him, or flagons with their stoppers, or pints with their lids, at which sound, he would become very gay and leap for joy, and would rock himself back and forth in his cradle, dandling his head, monochordizing with his fingers, and barytoning with his behind.

It will be observed that the setting continues to be Rabelais' own La Devinière country. The name, Jean Denyau (or Deniau) is a case in point. It was the name of a number of tenants of the Abbey of Seuilly. Professor Lefranc believes the Jean Denyau in question may have been a wheelwright of the neighborhood.

A "Scotistical" doctor is a disciple of Duns Scotus. There are several other word-coinages in this section.

How They Dressed Gargantua

WHEN he had reached this age, his father ordered that they should dress him up in his own livery, which was blue and white. And so they fell to and made it, cutting and sewing it after the fashion that was then current. From the ancient records in the Chamber of Accounts at Montsoreau, I find that he was clad in the following fashion:

For his shirt, they took nine hundred ells of Châtellerault cloth, with nine hundred for the gussets, made in the form of squares, which were placed under his armpits. And they were not pleated, for the pleating of shirts was not invented until after the shirt-makers, having broken off the points of their needles, had begun doing business with the hind-end.

For his doublet, they took eight-hundred-thirteen ells of white satin and for his laces fifteen-hundred-nine-and-a-half dog-skins. It was about this time that the fashionable began attaching their breeches to their doublets, instead of attaching their doublets to their breeches, for that is a thing against nature, as Occam has demonstrated at length, in his treatise on the *Exponibles* of M. Highbreeches.

For Gargantua's breeches, they took eleven-hundred-five-and-a-third ells of white broadcloth. They were cut in the form of striped columns, scalloped in the rear, in order not to overheat his loins. The pleats inside were puffed out, as much as necessary, with blue damask. And it is to be noted that he had very fine legs, well proportioned to the rest of his stature.

For his codpiece, they took sixteen and a quarter ells of the same cloth. It was in the form of a buttress, securely and jovially fastened with a pair of pretty gold buckles, which held two enameled crotchets, in each of which was enchased a huge emerald as big as an orange. For (as Orpheus says, *lib. De lapidibus,* and Pliny, *lib. ult.*) this stone has an erective virtue and one very comforting to the natural member. The bulge of the codpiece was nearly six feet long, scalloped like the breeches, with the blue damask floating down in front. Viewing the fine gold-thread embroidery and the curious gold knots, adorned with fine diamonds, fine rubies, fine turquoises, fine emeralds, and Persian pearls, you would have compared the effect to that of a handsome cornucopia, such as may be seen in ancient monuments, and such as Rhea gave the two nymphs, Adrastea and Ida, Jupiter's nurses. It was always gallant, succulent, dripping, always verdant, always flourishing, always fructifying, full of temperament, full of flowers, fruits, and all delights. I call upon God to be my witness, if it wasn't a sight worth seeing. But I will tell you more about it in the book which I have written *On the Dignity of Codpieces.* I will tell you one thing, right here, however, and that is that it was very long and very ample, and that it was well furnished and well victualed inside, being in no way like those hypocritical codpieces that a lot of lily-boys wear, which are only filled with wind, to the great detriment of the feminine sex.

For his shoes, they took four-hundred-six ells of bright-blue velvet; and they were very prettily shaped, with parallel and cross-lines combining in uniform cylinders. For the soles, they employed eleven hundred brown cowhides, shaped like a codfish's tail.

For his jacket, they took eighteen hundred ells of dyed-in-the-grain blue velvet, embroidered around the edges with pretty vine-branches and in the middle with silver needlework pints, with a maze of gold links and a great many pearls, all this denoting that he was to be a great pint-licker in his time.

His girdle was made of three hundred ells and a half of silk serge, half white and half blue (if I am not greatly mistaken).

His sword did not come from Valencia nor his dagger from Saragossa, for his father hated all those drunken half-Moorish hidalgos like the very devil; but instead, he had a fine wooden sword and a dagger of cured leather, with as much nice gilt paint on it as anyone could have wished.

His purse was made of an elephant's penis, which had been given him by Herr Pracontal, procurator of Libya.

For his cloak, they took nine-thousand-five-hundred-ninety-nine-and-one-third ells of blue damask, as before, the whole being diagonally threaded in gold, which, when you saw it at the right distance, appeared to be of that nameless shade sometimes seen on the necks of turtle-doves; and a marvelously pleasing sight it was.

For his bonnet, they took three-hundred-two-and-a-quarter ells of white velvet. It was large and round in shape and of a size to fit his head. For his father said that those Moorish bonnets, made like a pastry-crust, would sooner or later bring bad luck to the cropped heads that wore them.

For his plume, they took a great handsome blue pelican feather, from the land of the savage Hircanians, and this hung down very prettily over his right ear.

For his emblem, he had, in the form of a gold plate weighing more than forty-five pounds, a suitable enameled device, portraying a human body with two heads, one turned toward the other, and with four arms, four feet, and two behinds; for Plato, *In Symposio,* tells us that human nature was like this in its mysterious beginnings; and around this device was inscribed, in Ionic letters: AGAPE OY ZETEI TA HEAUTES—"Love seeketh not its own."

To hang about his neck, he had a gold chain weighing one-hundred-sixty-six-thousand-seven-hundred-eight-and-two-thirds pounds, made up in the form of huge berries, between which were inlaid great green jaspers, engraved and carved in the form of dragons, all surrounded with rays and sparks, such as King Nekhepso once wore. It came down as far as his navel, and all his life long he felt the good effects of it, a circumstance which the old Greek physicians would very well have understood.

For his gloves, they took sixteen hobgoblins' skins, with three werewolf-hides to embroider them. They were made of this material by prescription of the Cabalists of Saint-Louand.

As for his rings (which his father wished him to wear in order to revive the ancient sign of nobility) he had on the index finger of his left hand a carbuncle as big as an ostrich's egg, enchased with seraph-gold, very cunningly. On the medical finger of the same hand he had a ring made of four metals welded together, in the most wonderful fashion you ever saw, in such a way that the steel did not rub the gold nor the silver the copper. All this was made by Captain Chappuis and Alcofribas, his worthy assistant. On the medical finger of the right hand he had a ring made in spiral form, in which had been enchased a perfect balas-ruby, a pointed diamond, and a Pison emerald, all of inestimable price. For Hans Carvel, high lapidary to the King of Melinde, estimated them at a value of sixty-nine-million-eight-hundred-ninety-four-thousand-eighteen big woolly sheep (or Agnus Dei gold-pieces), and the estimate of the Fuggers of Augsburg was quite as high.

A number of the allusions in this passage may call for an explanation for the modern reader. William of Occam (who died in 1347), an English Franciscan, was a Schoolman known as "the Invincible Doctor." He was an opponent of Duns Scotus and leader of the nominalist school. The Exponibles, or Exponibilia, figured in the treatises on logic of the era, as a part of the Parva Logicalia that followed the Syllogism. Once again, Rabelais is having fun with the scholastics.

The "De lapidibus" is a treatise on the natural or magic properties of precious stones, written in Greek (περὶ λίθων) in the time of Constantine and attributed to Orpheus. Pliny has a long passage on emeralds in the thirty-seventh and last book of his Natural History, but does not allude to the peculiarity mentioned by Rabelais. As a matter of fact, Maître François is attributing to this stone a property directly opposite to the one assigned it in the old medical works.

Gargantua's emblem is reminiscent of the hermaph-roditic figure described by Plato in the Symposium (189 E). The Greek quotation from St. Paul is, of course, from First Corinthians, xiii, 5.

As for the personages mentioned, aside from Nek-hepso, Pharaoh of Egypt (681-674 B.C.), who was known as an astrologer and magician, they are for the most part *either fictitious (possibly with veiled allusions), as in the case of "M. Highbreeches" (M. Haultechaussade) and Alcofribas (Rabelais' own pseudonym), or of doubtful or unestablished identity—Pracontal, Captain Chappuis, Hans Carvel, etc.* ——*The Fuggers were bankers of Augsburg whose wealth was proverbial in the sixteenth century, as that of the Rothschilds was later to be. The "Cabalists of Saint-Louand" is probably a sarcastic reference to the monks and prior of that place, which is a village on the right bank of the Vienne, a little below Chinon. The "drunken half-Moorish hidalgos" have been seen as the hard drinking and quarrelsome Spanish adventurers who overran the Continent during the wars of the sixteenth century.*

"Seraph-gold" is pure gold, like the Egyptian and Persian coins bearing this name. A Pison emerald is one from the region of the Pison River, which flowed through the Garden of Eden. "Big woolly sheep" (moutons à la grande laine") were large gold pieces with an Agnus Dei inscription on one side. The "medical finger" —the digitus medicus *of Pliny (xxx, 12)—is the fourth or ring finger, so called, it is said, because the ancients used that finger to stir their medical potions.*

Rabelais then devotes a couple of chapters to a learned humanist disquisition, on "The Colors and Livery of Gargantua" and "What Is Signified by the Colors Blue and White," that makes rather dull reading today, after which he goes on with the story of Gargantua's upbringing.

Gargantua's Adolescence

GARGANTUA, from the age of three to five years, was brought up and instructed in all proper discipline, by order of his father; and this period he spent like the little children of the country, namely: in drinking, eating, and sleeping; in eating, sleeping, and drinking; in sleeping, drinking, and eating.

He wallowed in the mud, smudged his nose, dirtied his face, ran his shoes over at the heels, frequently caught flies with his mouth, and liked to chase the butterflies of his father's realm. He pissed over his shoes, shit in his shirt, wiped his nose on his sleeve, dropped snot in his soup, and paddled around everywhere. He drank out of his slipper and ordinarily scratched his belly with a basket. He sharpened his teeth on a top, washed his hands in his porridge, and combed his hair with a goblet. He would set his butt on the ground between two chairs and cover his head with a wet sack. He drank when he ate his soup, ate his cake without bread, bit when he laughed and laughed when he bit, often spit in the basin, farted from fatness, pissed against the sun, and hid himself in the water from fear of the rain. He struck when the iron was cold, moped around, was as sweet as sugar when he wanted to be, flayed the fox, said the monkey's paternoster, went back to his sheep, turned the sows out to hay, beat the dog in front of the lion, put the cart in front of the oxen, scratched himself where he didn't itch, tried to pump everybody, reached for too much and got little, ate his white bread first, put horseshoes on the geese, tickled himself to make himself laugh, was always running to the kitchen, offered sheaves of hay to the gods, had them sing the *Magnificat* at matins and found it quite all right, ate cabbage and passed white beets, knew flies when he saw 'em in milk and pulled their legs off, scratched paper and smeared parchment, drew on the goat's leather, reckoned without his host, beat the bush without getting the birdie, believed that clouds were brass canopies and kidneys were lanterns, took two miller's fees for one sack of grain, played the ass to get the bran, made a hammer out of his thumb, took the cranes at the first leap, wanted the hauberks made link by link, always looked a gift horse in the mouth, jumped from the cock to the ass, put one ripe one between two green ones, made a ditch of the earth taken from the ditch, guarded the moon from the wolves, if the clouds fell hoped to catch larks, made a virtue of necessity, made soup of such bread, cared as little for the shorn as for the shaven, and, every morning, flayed the fox. His father's pups ate from his plate, and he ate from the plate with them. He bit their ears, they scratched his nose; he blew up their bungholes, and they licked his chops.

And do you know what, my lads? I hope you drink so much you tumble over arse-backwards, if this little lecher wasn't always feeling his nurses, upside down, backside frontwards. Giddy-up, old girl! For he had already commenced to give his codpiece a little exercise; and each day, his nurses would adorn it with pretty bouquets, pretty ribbons, pretty flowers, and pretty tassels; and they would pass their time in making it come up between their hands, like a suppository; then they would burst out laughing, when it began to prick up its little ears, as though this were the best joke in the world.

One of them would call it my little spout, another my peg, another my coral-branch, another my stopper, my plug, my centerbit, my ramrod, my gimlet, my trinket, my rough-and-ready-stiff-and-steady, my prop, my little red sausage, my little booby-prize.

"It belongs to me," said one.

"It's mine," said another.

"What about me," said another, "am I to have none of it? Faith, I'll cut it off, then!"

"Ha, cut it off!" said another. "That would hurt him. Madame, are you in the habit of cutting little children's things off? He'd be Monsieur-without-a-Tail, then."

And to amuse him like the little children of the country, they made him a lovely whirligig, from the wings of a windmill of Mirebalais.

The foregoing passage is a take-off on popular proverbs, proverbial expressions, and platitudes. Thus, a proverb like "He is a fool who covers himself with a wet sack" throws a light on Gargantua's action. To "spit in the basin" or "flay the fox" is to vomit. To "piss against the sun" is to offer offense to a friend or protector. The "monkey's paternoster" refers to the sound that monkeys make with their lips. To "turn the sows out to hay" (a futile thing) is to change the subject of a conversation without rhyme or reason. To "beat the dog in front of the lion" is to berate an unimportant or less important individual in front of a person of consequence, one's remarks being in reality directed at the latter. Offering sheaves of hay, instead of wheat or corn, to the gods is another foolish procedure. To "draw on the goat's leather" is to tipple, and to "jump from the cock to the ass" is to leap from one subject to another (this gave rise to a literary form, the "coq-à-l'âne"). There are also certain literary reminiscences: to "come back to one's sheep" being an allusion to the medieval farce, Patelin, while Gargantua's mistaking the clouds for "brass canopies" recalls Villon (Testament, 689), and his "taking the cranes at the first leap" suggests the Roman de la Rose, where the phrase, "prendre au ciel la grue," (to take the crane in the heavens) is synonymous with an impossible undertaking.

Gargantua's Hobby-Horses

THEN, in order that all his life he might be a good rider, they built for him a fine large wooden horse, which he made prance, leap, vault, buck, and dance all at once, causing it to walk, trot, pace, gallop, and amble, now like a Scotch nag, now like a broken-pacer, now like a camel, now like a wild ass; and he would change the color of his steed's hair (as the monks do their dalmatics, according to the feast-day) to bay-brown, to chestnut, to dappled gray, to mouse-color, to deer-color, to roan, to cow-color, to sickle-striped, to mottled, to piebald, to white.

He himself, out of a huge logging truck, made a hunting horse, another one out of the beam of a winepress for everyday use, and a mule with a saddle-cloth for his room, out of a great oak. In addition to these, he had ten or a dozen for relay purposes, and seven for the post; and he put them all to bed alongside him at night.

One day, Lord Breadinbag came to call upon Gargantua's father, in high state and with a great train, and on the very same day, the Duke of Freemeal and Count Wetwhistle also came to pay a visit. Faith, if the house wasn't a little small for so many folks, and especially the stables. And so it was, the maître-d'hôtel and the steward of the said Lord Breadinbag, in order to find out if there were any other stables vacant about the place, went to the young lad, Gargantua, to inquire of the latter privately, where the stables with the big chargers were, reflecting that children are more than likely to reveal everything they know.

Then, Gargantua led them up the great steps of the castle, passing through the second hall into a large gallery, through which they entered a massive tower. As they mounted the tower, by another flight of steps, the steward observed to the maître-d'hôtel:

"This youngster is playing a trick on us, for the stables are never at the top of the house."

"That's where you're all wrong," said the maître-d'hôtel, "for I know plenty of places, at Lyon, at Baumette, at Chinon and elsewhere, where the stables are at the very top of the house; and it may be, too, there's a road in behind, leading up here. But I'll ask him and find out."

Then he said to Gargantua:

"My little dear, where are you taking us?"

"To the stable," replied Gargantua, "where my chargers are. We're almost there. Just climb these stairs."

Then, passing through another large hall, he led them to his bedroom and, opening the door:

"There," he said, "are the stables you were asking about. There is my jennet, there is my gelding, my Lavedan, my broken-pacer."

And then, presenting them with a full-grown handspike, he added:

"I am going to make you a present of this Frieslander; I got him from Frankfort, but he's yours now; he's a good little plug and will stand a lot of working out. With a tercel, half a dozen spaniels and a brace of grayhounds, you're king of the partridges and rabbits for all this winter."

"By Jove!" they said, "that's one on us. The monk's with us right now."

"No, he isn't," said Gargantua. "He hasn't been here for three days."

You may decide for yourselves which it was that the pair of them were the more inclined to do, to hide their heads in shame or to burst out laughing. As they wer*

descending the stairs in great confusion Gargantua inquired: "Should you like a halter?"

"What do you mean?" said they.

"Here are five turds," he said, "to make a muzzle for
you."

"For today, at least," remarked the maître-d'hôtel,
"though we may be roasted, we shan't burn, for this lad
certainly has rubbed the old pig's fat into us, if you
want my opinion. Little sweetheart, you have hay on
your horns all right. I can see you're going to be pope
(*pape*) some day."

"That's what I intend to be," said Gargantua, "and
then you shall be a butterfly (*papillon*), and this nice
little popinjay (*papegai*) shall be a hypocrite (*pape-
lard*), ready-made."

"Well, well," said the steward.

"But," demanded Gargantua, "do you know how many
stitches there are in my mother's shimmy?"

"Sixteen," said the steward.

"It's not the gospel truth you speak," said Gargantua,
"for she has *cent* (a hundred) in front and scent behind,
and you were all wrong in your count."

"When?" said the steward.

"When they made a spout of your nose," said Gargantua, "to drain a barrel of dung, and a funnel of your
throat to put it into another tub, because the bottom had
dropped out of the first one."

"Good God!" cried the maître-d'hôtel, "but we've
come upon a talker. Mr. Chatterbox, I'm sure God will
keep you from spoiling, because you're so fresh in the
mouth."

As they descended the steps in great haste, they
dropped the big handspike, with which Gargantua had
loaded them down, under the archway of the stair.

"What the devil kind of horsemen are you!" exclaimed

Gargantua. "Your bobtail goes back on you in a pinch. Supposing you had to go from here to Cahusac, which should you prefer, to ride a goose or lead a sow in leash?"

"I'd prefer to have a drink," said the steward.

Saying this, they entered the lower hall, where the whole troop was, and in telling the story of what had just happened, they set the whole crowd to laughing like a swarm of flies.

"Stables at the very top of the house": "the houses of Chinon, built at the foot of the hill where the chateau stands, still have cellars or stables hollowed out of the side of the embankment; access to them is by a flight of steps, and the 'stable' may thus be higher than the house" (Lefranc edition). ——A Lavedan steed is one from the old viscounty of Lavedan in Gascony; these horses were noted for their speed. ——"The monk's with us": to "give the monk" to someone is equivalent to our "give the bird." ——To "rub the pig's fat into" (larder) someone is to get the better of him in repartee. —— "You have hay on your horns": allusion to the custom of putting hay on the horns of cattle that were for sale at a fair.

How Grandgousier Learned of Gargantua's Marvelous Mind through the Latter's Invention of a Rump-Wiper

About the end of the fifth year, Grandgousier, returning from the conquest of the Canarians, paid his son Gargantua a visit. He was as happy as a father could be at seeing such a child of his; and hugging and kissing him, he proceeded to ask him little childish questions of various sorts. And he also had his share of drinks with the boy and the nurses, questioning the latter very carefully, among other things, as to whether they had kept their charge neat and clean. To this, Gargantua replied that he himself had given orders on this point, and that in all the country there was not any cleaner a lad than he.

"How is that?" inquired Grandgousier.

"I," replied Gargantua, "after long and careful experiment, have discovered a means of wiping my rump that is the most lordly, the most excellent, and the most expedient ever seen."

"What is that?" Grandgousier wanted to know.

"I'll tell you about it, straight off," said Gargantua. "I wiped myself once with a lady's velvet mask, and I found it did very nicely, for the softness of the silk gave my bottom very great pleasure. Another time, I tried a hat of hers, and it was the same. Another time, I tried a neckerchief, and another time some bright satin earpieces, but the gilt on them, like a lot of dingleberries, took all the skin off my behind—may St. Anthony's fire burn out the rumpgut of the goldsmith that made them and the lady that wore them!

"I cured myself of this by wiping with a page's bonnet, prettily decked out with a Swiss feather. Then, doing my business behind a bush, I found a March-cat, and I wiped myself with him, but his claws exulcerated my entire perineum. I cured myself of this, the next day, by wiping on my mother's gloves, well perfumed, if not with benzoin, with smell of loin.

"Then, I wiped myself with sage, with fennel, with anet, with sweet marjoram, with roses, with gourd-leaves, with cabbages, with beets, with a vine-branch, with marshmallows, with mullein (which is arse-red), with lettuce, and with spinach-leaves—all of them did my leg a lot of good—with mercury, with parsley, with nettles, with comfrey—but from this I got the bloody flux of Lombardy, which I cured by wiping myself with my codpiece.

"Then, I wiped myself on the sheets, on the bed-clothes, on the curtains, on a cushion, on a rug, on a green carpet, on a duster, on a napkin, on a handkerchief, and on a dressing gown. And I found more pleasure in all of them than mangy curs do when you scratch 'em."

"Well," said Grandgousier, "but what rump-wiper did you find the best?"

"I was coming to that," said Gargantua. "You shall know the *tu autem* right away. I wiped myself with hay, with straw, with oakum, with floss, with wool, with paper —but

> "He always leaves bait on his balls
>   Who his dirty arse with paper mauls."

"What!" exclaimed Grandgousier, "my little jacka-napes, have you been at the wine-jug, that you're making rhymes already?"

"Yea, verily, Your Majesty," replied Gargantua, "I'm quite a rhymer, I am; I often rhyme till I get rummy. Listen to what our privy has to say to the folks that come there to do their business:

> Squirthard,
> Farthard,
> Turd in us;
> Your lard
> Bombard,
> Discard
> On us.
> Clutter us,
> Splutter us,
> Guttur us,

But with St. Anthony's fire be charred,

> If a muss
> You leave with us,
> You ornery cuss.

Wipe your arse, or you are barred.

"Do you want to hear more?"

"Yes, indeed," replied Grandgousier.

"All right, then," said Gargantua, "here goes:

A ROUNDELAY

In dunging t'other day, I felt
The debt I to my arse did owe:
The odor was not orchard-blow:
It was the worst that I had smelt.
  Oh, if fate had but kindly dealt,
And sent a little one I know,
    While I was dunging.
  Down on my knees I'd not have knelt,
But, quite naïvely, would have stopped her flow,
While with her fingers, back below,
She kept me clean where turds did melt,
    While I was dunging.

"Now, tell me I'm not a poet. But *mer Dé*—Mother of God, or *merde* to you! I didn't make 'em up, at all. Hearing this old grandmother that you see here recite 'em, I stuffed 'em into the bag of my memory."

"But," said Grandgousier, "let's go back to what we were talking about."

"What," said Gargantua, "dunging?"

"No," said Grandgousier, "wiping the rump."

"Look," said Gargantua, "will you bet me a half-keg of Breton wine that I don't make a monkey out of you over this?"

"That I will, right enough," said Grandgousier.

"Well, then," said Gargantua, "there's no need to wipe

your rump unless it's dirty; it can't be dirty, unless you've been dunging; so therefore, you have to dung before you wipe your rump."

"My, my," said Grandgousier, "what good sense you have, my little lad! One of these fine days, by God, I'm going to have you made a Doctor of Jovial Science, for you're a good deal wiser than your years. And now, please, go on with your rump-wiping discourse; and by my beard, in place of a half-keg, you shall have sixty barrels, and it's real Breton wine I mean, the kind that grows, not in Brittany, but in the good land of Verron."

"I wiped myself afterward," Gargantua went on, "with a kerchief, with a pillow, with a slipper, with a purse, with a basket—but, oh, what an unpleasant rump-wiper that was—and finally with a hat—and make a note of this, that some hats are shorn, others shaggy, others velvety, others of taffeta, and still others of satin. The best of all are the shaggy ones, for the reason that they make a very neat abstersion of the fecal matter.

"Then, I wiped myself with a hen, with a rooster, with a pullet, with a calf's skin, with a hare, with a pigeon, with a cormorant, with a lawyer's bag, with a chin-band, with a hood, with a decoy-bird. But in conclusion, I will state and maintain that there is no rump-wiper like a good downy goose, providing that you hold its head between your legs. And you may believe me, on my word of honor, that you will feel in your bunghole a miraculous pleasure, from the softness of the down as well as from the moderate heat of the goose, which is readily communicated to the rump-gut and other intestines, until it reaches the region of the heart and brain. And do not think that the beatitude of the heroes and demigods in the Elysian Fields comes from their asphodel or their ambrosia or their nectar, as these old women tell us. In

my humble opinion, it comes from the fact that they
wipe their arses with the neck of a goose. And such, also,
is the opinion of Master John of Scotland.

*The above passage is one of the most famous in Rabe-
lais, and one of the broadest in its popular brand of
humor. This chapter is one of five that Mr. W. F. Smith,
in his translation, saw fit to leave in the original French—
he tells us that his "pen recoiled" from doing them into
English.*

*"Conquest of the Canarians": allusion to the inhabi-
tants of the Canary Islands, or to Canaria, the land of
medieval tradition. ——"St. Anthony's fire": this has
been identified by a modern medical authority as
ergotism, due to intoxication with the ergot of cereals;
it is accompanied by symptoms of erysipelas and gan-
grene. ——"Well perfumed, if not with benzoin, with
smell of loin": this is a pun on* benjoin(t) *(benzoin, or
"well joined") and* maujoin(t) *("badly joined," that is, a
"crack," in the erotic sense). ——"You shall know the
tu autem": that is to say, the end of the matter; from the
words at the close of the breviary:* Tu autem, Domine,
miserere nobis *(But thou, O Lord, have mercy on us).
——"I often rhyme till I get rummy":* en rimant souvent
m'enrime; *a play on* s'enrhumer, *to catch a cold.* ——
"Doctor of Jovial Science": docteur en gaie science,
allusion to the titles of bachelor and doctor en gay saber
given to laureates of the Jeux Floraux, *or Floral Games,
of Toulouse. ——"In the good land of Verron": a fertile
tract at the junction of the Loire and Vienne rivers. ——
"Master John of Scotland": Duns Scotus. The entire
chapter is something of a satire on the sophistries of the
Schoolmen.*

How Gargantua Was Instructed by a Sophist in Latin Letters

WHEN he had heard these remarks, the good Grand-gousier was ravished with admiration, as he considered the rare good sense and marvelous understanding of his son Gargantua. And he said to the nurses:

"Philip, King of Macedonia, discovered the good sense of his son Alexander through the latter's clever manner of handling a horse. For this horse I am telling you about was so terribly wild that no one dared mount him, seeing he had thrown all his would-be riders, breaking one's neck, another's legs, another's head, and another's jaw-bones. Observing all this in the Hippodrome (which was the place where they walked their steeds and put them through their paces), Alexander perceived that the animal's wildness was merely due to the fact that he was frightened by his own shadow. And so, mounting him, he proceeded to run the horse against the sun, in such a manner that the shadow fell behind; and by this means, he tamed him to his will. From this, the father learned what a superb mind the son possessed, and as a consequence, had the lad well taught by Aristotle, who at that time was esteemed above all the philosophers of Greece.

"And I want to tell you that from this one conversation which I have just had with my son Gargantua, in your presence, I know there is something uncanny about his understanding, so sharp, subtle, profound, and well balanced do I perceive him to be. He will attain the highest degree of wisdom, if he is well instructed. For this reason, I'd like to turn him over to some learned man and have him educated according to his capacity; and I don't want to spare any expense."

Accordingly, they had him instructed by a great doctor, a sophist, Master Tubal Holofernes by name, who taught him his alphabet so well that he could say it backwards and by heart; and at this, he spent five years and three months. Then, they read him *Donatus, Facetus, Theodolus,* and *Alanus in parabolis;* and at this, he was thirteen years, six months, and two weeks.

But note that, in the meanwhile, he had been taught to write in Gothic letters, and he copied out all of his books by hand, for the art of printing was not yet in use. And he carried around with him, ordinarily, a big writing-desk, weighing more than seven-hundred-thousand pounds, the pen-rack of which was as big as the great pillars of Ainay, while the inkhorn that hung down from it by huge iron chains had the capacity of a ton of merchandise.

Then, they read him *De modis significandi,* with the commentaries of Windjammer, Stoopandfetchit, Toomany, Gualehaul, John Calf, Badpenny, Pussybumper, and a lot of others; and he was at this more than eighteen years and eleven months. And he knew them all so well that, at school contests, he could say them by heart, backwards. And he would prove to his mother, on his fingers, that *de modis significandi non erat scientia.*

Whereupon, they read him the *Compost,* or Church Calendar, on which he spent sixteen years and two months, when his preceptor died——

> And he died in the year fourteen-twenty,
> Of the syphilis, which he had a-plenty.

After this, he had another old codger named Master Jobie Bridle, who read him Ugutio, Everard's *Graecismus,* the *Doctrinal,* the *Parts,* the *Quid est,* the *Supple-*

mentum, the *Mamotrectus,* the *De moribus in mensa servandis,* Seneca's *De quatuor virtutibus cardinalibus,* Passavantus *Cum commento,* the *Dormi secure* for holy days, and certain other works of similar grist, by the reading of which he became as wise as any that we ourselves have ever baked in an oven.

Rabelais is here satirizing the education that was given the young by the clergy, in his day: the texts, the educational methods (e.g., reading to the pupil, oral repetition, etc.), and the inordinate length of time that was spent upon such mind-dulling exercises. Indeed, the entire picture of Gargantua's upbringing may be regarded as constituting such a satire. The title of this chapter originally read: "How Gargantua Was Instructed by a Theologian," etc. The word "sophist" was later substituted for "theologian," both in the title and in the body of the chapter.

Of the texts referred to, the Donatus *was a Latin grammar in use in the schools in the Middle Ages; the* Facetus, Theodulus, *and* Alanus in parabolis *formed part of a collection known as the "eight moral authors," which was in school use down to the middle of the sixteenth century. The* De modis significandi, *variously attributed to Thomas Aquinas, Duns Scotus, and others, was a treatise on speculative grammar and enjoyed a great vogue in the Middle Ages; Erasmus alludes to it as a work that made dunces of the youth of his day; Rabelais' German translator, Gottlob Regis, terms it a "barbarisches Buch." Ugutio, Bishop of Pisa, author of a Latin vocabulary for school use, already discredited in the sixteenth century, is depicted by Erasmus as one of the champions of barbarism. The* Graecismus *was the thirteenth-century lexicon of Latin words drawn from the*

Greek, compiled by Everard of Béthune. The Doctrinal, *another thirteenth-century work, was the* Doctrinale puerorum *of Alexandre de Villedieu, a grammatical treatise in leonine verse. The* Parts *was a work entitled* De octo partibus orationis. *The* Quid est *was probably a school question-and-answer book. The* Supplementum, *or Supplement, may refer to any one of a number of works bearing that title. The* Mamotrectus *was a text for the religious instruction of the young; it was ridiculed by Erasmus. The* De moribus, *etc., was a manual of table etiquette. The* "Seneca" *is a work by Martin of Braga, sixth-century Bishop of Mondonedo.* Passavantus *was Iacobo Passavanti, a Florentine monk of the fourteenth century, author of the* Specchio della Vera Penitenza *(Mirror of True Penitence), greatly admired by Tuscans for the purity of its style; it was accompanied by a commentary. The* Dormi secure *was a collection of ready-made sermons for preachers, so that they might be able to "sleep in peace."*

Most of these were works which, having enjoyed a wide popularity in their day, were being discredited by the New Learning. Not all the humanists, however, would have agreed with Rabelais in every instance; many would not have been so sweeping in their condemnation.

The names Tubal (Tubalain) and Holofernes are from the Old Testament and the Apocrypha; see Genesis, iv, 22, and the book of Judith. The names Windjammer, Stoopandfetchit, etc., are fictitious, but Gualehaul is one of the principal characters in the romance of Lancelot and is also a knight in a fifteenth-century mystery play.

The anecdote of Alexander and his horse is from Plutarch's Life of Alexander. The verse couplet quoted is from an epitaph composed by Clement Marot.

How Gargantua Was Placed under Other Pedagogues

AT LAST Gargantua's father perceived that although his son studied very hard and spent all his time at it, he was getting nothing out of it. What was worse, the lad was becoming a fool, a ninny, a dreamer, and a dunce. When the old man complained of this to Don Philippe des Marais, Viceroy of Banterpope, he was told that it would be better for his son to learn nothing at all than to spend his time reading such books under such teachers, for the scholarship of the latter was but stupidity and their wisdom but puffery, and such pedagogues merely bastardized good and noble minds and utterly corrupted the flower of youth.

"If you don't believe it," he said, "you have but to take any one of these young chaps of today who have studied but a couple of years. In case he doesn't display better judgment, better ability in conversation, and a better vocabulary than your son, as well as better manners and worldly poise, then I'm nothing, hereafter, but a bacon-slicer of La Brenne."

This pleased Grandgousier very much, and he gave orders that the test should be made.

Accordingly, that evening at supper, the said Des Marais brought in a young page of his of Ville-Gongis, a lad named Eudemon, so sleek of hair, so well dressed, so well brushed, so frank in his bearing that he rather resembled a little angel than a human being. Then Des Marais said to Grandgousier:

"Do you see this young fellow? He's not yet twelve. And now, if you like, let's see what a difference there is between the learning of those silly old fogies, your mateologians, and that of the young folks of the present generation."

Grandgousier liked the idea, and commanded the page to hold forth.

Then Eudemon, begging permission to do so of the said Viceroy, his master, with hat in hand, an open face, a rosy mouth, self-assured eyes, and a gaze fixed upon Gargantua in youthful modesty, stood squarely on his feet and began eulogizing and magnifying, first of all Gargantua's virtues and good manners, secondly his learning, thirdly his nobility, and fourthly his physical charms. And for his fifth point, he gently exhorted the lad to revere and obey his father, who had been at such pains to have him well taught. In conclusion, he begged Gargantua to take him as the least of his servants; since at the moment, he asked no other gift of the heavens than that Gargantua might be so gracious as to employ him in some pleasant and acceptable service.

All this was uttered with gestures so appropriate, a pronunciation so distinct, in a voice so eloquent, with language so ornate, and in such good Latin, that the speaker resembled a Gracchus, a Cicero, or an Aemilius of times past rather than a youth of the current century.

But all Gargantua did was to start bawling like a cow. He hid his face in his hat, and it was as impossible to get a word out of him as it is to draw a fart from a dead donkey.

At this, his father was so irate that he wanted to kill Master Jobie. But Des Marais kept him from this, by talking to him, soothingly, until the old man's anger had died down a little. Then, the latter commanded that Master Jobie be paid his wages, that they let him drink his fill like a good sophist, and send him forthwith to all the devils in hell.

"For once, at least," he said, "he won't cost his host much, if he dies as drunk as an Englishman."

When Master Jobie had left the house, Grandgousier consulted with the Viceroy as to what tutor they should procure for Gargantua, and it was decided between them that Ponocrates, Eudemon's teacher, should have the post, and that the three of them together should go to Paris to find out what the youth of France were then engaged in studying.

Rabelais is here contrasting the new education and the old through their youthful products. Eudemon, it will be noted, speaks in Latin, the language of the learned, and follows the scholastic mode of presenting and sustaining a thesis. In his delivery he observes the rules laid down in a work published about 1500, entitled L'art et science de bien parler.

The identity of Des Marais remains uncertain. ——La Brenne is a region in the Department of l'Indre; in "bacon-slicer of La Brenne," Rabelais is perhaps aiming at an unpopular cleric. ——Ville-Gongis is in the arrondissement of Chateauroux, l'Indre. ——"Mateologians" is a coinage from the New Testament *Greek and means "vain speakers." As only the learned knew Greek, Maître François did not deem it necessary to elide this term. ——"Drink his fill like a good sophist" originally read "like a theologian."*

⊛

II. Gargantua in Paris

(CHAPTERS XVI-XX)

Paris does not play the part in the Gargantua *that it does in the* Pantagruel *(Book Second). Indeed, one rather gets the impression that this interlude has been introduced chiefly for the sake of the Notre-Dame bells episode and that amusing character, Janotus de Bragmardo. The Parisian descriptions in Book First are much less vivid than those of the author's own Chinon country—less vivid, also, than those in Book Second. This, in all probability, is to be explained by the fact that the first book of the* Pantagruel *was written immediately following or shortly after Rabelais' visit to the capital, as a climax to his tour of the universities of France; whereas the* Gargantua *came, in good part, as a result of his La Devinière visit.*

For lovers of Paris, with a knowledge of French, who may care to run down the subject, a study of the topography of Maître François' sojourn in that city will be found in the Revue des Etudes Rabelaisiennes *for 1908. Rabelais mentions only the University, Notre-Dame, the Hôtel de Nesle, the Jeu de Paume de Braque, the Porte Saint-Victor, Montmartre, and some half-dozen localities in the environs of the metropolis.*

His description, however, of the atmosphere of Paris and the character of its inhabitants remains startlingly exact to this day: the cosmopolitanism and babel of tongues, the curiosity of Parisians and their love of the new, their "overbearing" tendency, their "proud-talking," etc. It was in this age that Ariosto, speaking of Paris, wrote (Orlando Furioso, xvi, 35): *"There is not a land in Christendom that does not have citizens there."*

How Gargantua Was Sent to Paris, the Enormous Mare That Carried Him, and How She Routed the Ox-Flies of La Beauce

ABOUT this same time Fayolles, fourth king of Numidia, sent to Grandgousier from the land of Africa a mare that was the largest and most enormous ever seen, as well as the most monstrous (for you know very well that Africa always has something new to offer). She was as big as six elephants and had feet that were cloven into fingers, like Julius Caesar's nag, while her ears were as long and drooping as those of the nanny-goats of Languedoc, and she had a little horn in her rump. In addition, she had a burnt-chestnut hide, with dappled-gray spots forming a kind of trellis-work; but above all, she had a horrible tail, for it was more or less as big as the pillar of Saint-Mars near Langeais, and quite as square, being tufted and laced like corn-tassels.

If you wonder at this, you might well wonder more at the tails of the Scythian rams, which weighed more than thirty pounds, and of those Syrian sheep, which (if Thenaud is telling the truth) had to have a cart hitched on behind to carry their tails, because they were so long and heavy—you get no tail like that, you back-country whoremasters, you! And this mare was brought by sea, in three caracks and a brig, to the port of Olonne in the Talmondais.

When Grandgousier saw her, he exclaimed:

"Just the thing to carry my son to Paris! Now, by God, everything is going to be all right. He'll be a great scholar in time to come. If it weren't for Messieurs the beasts, we'd all be living like scholars. I mean——"

The next day, after they had had a little drink, of course, Gargantua, his tutor Ponocrates, and their servants took the road, and with them Eudemon, the young page. And since the weather was fair and mild, his father had him wear a pair of fawn-colored boots—Babin would have called them brodequins.

They went along in high spirits, keeping good cheer always, until they were above Orléans, in which place there was a large forest, eighty-eight miles long and forty-three miles wide, or thereabouts. This forest was horribly fertile in ox-flies and hornets, so that it was a veritable slaughter for the poor mares, the asses, and the horses. But Gargantua's mare very decently avenged all the outrages here perpetrated upon her kind by a trick of which none had any suspicion; for as soon as they had entered this forest and the hornets had begun their assault, she unsheathed her tail and flourished it about so effectively that she not only scattered them all, but knocked down the whole wood at the same time: crissways, crosswise, here and there, on this side and that, length and breadth, above and below, she felled it as a mower does grass; so that, when she was through, there was neither wood nor hornets, but the entire region had been reduced to open country.

At this, Gargantua was highly gratified, without taking any further credit to himself, and remarked to the others: "Very nice, this" (*beau ce*); and so the country, after that, was called *La Beauce*. But all the lunch they got was a lot of gaping, in memory of which, to this day, the gentry of Beauce are in the habit of making a breakfast of yawns, and find it very satisfactory, since they hock and spit all the better for it afterwards.

They finally reached Paris, where Gargantua rested for two or three days, dispensing good cheer with his followers, while they made inquiries as to what learned gentry there were in the city at that time, and investigated the kind of wine drunk there.

The Fayolles mentioned at the beginning of this chapter, according to a modern authority (M. Henri Clouzot), is "very probably François de Fayolles, second son of Jean de Fayolles, Captain of Coulonges-les-Royaux and relative of d'Estissac"; d'Estissac was Rabelais' friend and patron. ——The monk, Jehan Thenaud, was the author of an overseas travel narrative (cf. Herodotus, iii, 113). ——There was a family of shoemakers by the name of Babin at Chinon. ——"Scythian rams": Scythia, for the cartographers of Rabelais' time, was the present Siberia; Clouzot thinks the allusion here is to Tibet, which was renowned for its sheep and goats. ——"Port of Olonne in the Talmondais": today, Sables-d'Olonne (Vendée), a port of Bas-Poitou, near Fontenay and Maillezais, and an important harbor from the sixteenth to the eighteenth century; the Talmondais is a part of La Vendée. La Beauce, according to Professor Lefranc, is "a region rich in grain, but without trees, including a part of Orléanais, Blésois, Chartrain, and Dunois (departments of Loiret, Loire-et-Cher, Eure-et-Loire)"; the name Beauce goes back to pre-Roman times. ——"Africa always has something new to offer": a saying of the ancients; see Pliny, Natural History, viii, 16; Flaubert is said to have been haunted by this phrase, which he found to be "full of ostriches, giraffes, hippopotamuses, Negroes, and gold dust"; and Erasmus, in his Adages (III, vii, 10), *makes use of it under the Latin form:* "Semper Africa novi aliquid apportat." ———*The story of Caesar's nag is likewise from Pliny* (Natural History, viii, 42). ———*"The pillar of Saint-Mars near Langeais": an ancient monument, believed to have served, originally, to indicate territorial boundaries; it overlooks the Loire, about one kilometer from the town of Saint-Mars, in the district of Chinon.* ———*The carack was a large Genoese boat of the era (Italian:* caracca). ———*Fawn-colored boots were commonly worn by amorous swains at the end of the fifteenth century.* ———*The incident of the felling of the trees by Gargantua's mare occurs in the* Grandes Cronicques, *the work that inspired Rabelais to treat the Gargantua myth.* ———*The habit of breakfasting on yawns was proverbially attributed to the inhabitants of La Beauce.*

How Gargantua Paid His Respects to the Parisians, and How He Took the Great Bells from the Church of Notre-Dame

A FEW days afterward, when they were sufficiently rested, Gargantua went into the town and was a cause of great wonderment to all who saw him. For the people of Paris are so stupid, such ninnies, and so foolish by nature that a juggler, a pardon-peddler, or relic-seller, a mule with bells, or a fiddler in the middle of a public square will gather a bigger crowd than a good evangelic preacher ever could. So annoying were they in following Gargantua about that the latter was compelled to seek a rest on the towers of Notre-Dame Church. Gazing down from this retreat and seeing so many people all about him, he remarked, in a voice that was loud and clear:

"I suppose these rascals expect me to pay my own welcome and *proficiat,* do they? That's fair enough. I'm going to give them wine, but it will be a vintage *par rys*—of a kind to make you laugh."

With this, he smilingly unbuttoned his handsome codpiece; and drawing out his *mentula,* he drenched them all with such a bitter deluge of urine that he thereby drowned two-hundred-sixty-thousand-four-hundred-eighteen, not counting the women and little children. A certain number escaped this doughty pisser by lightness of foot; and these, when they had reached a point above the University, sweating, coughing, spitting, and out of breath, all began cursing and swearing, some in wrath while others were laughing fit to burst:

"By the wounds of God! I deny God! God's blood! Did you see that! *La merde*— Mother of God to you! *Po cab de bious*— God's head! *Das dich Gots leyden schend*— may God's passion confound you! *Pote de Christo*— Christ's power, or Our Lady's muff! St. Quenet's belly! God's holy name! By St. Fiacre of Brie! St. Ninian! I make a vow to St. Theobald! Crucified Christ! Holy Sunday! May the devil take me! Word of a gentleman! By St. Chitterling! By St. Godegran, who was martyrized with *pommes cuites!* By St. Foutin, the fornicating apostle! By St. Vitus! Carymary, carymara! By St. Mamie, but we are done for from laughing (*par rys*)."

And so, the city was named Paris from then on. Up to that time it had been called Leucetia (Lutetia), as Strabo tells us, *lib. iii,* that is to say, *White* in Greek, on account of the white rumps of the ladies there.

At the imposition of this new name, all those present began swearing, each one by the saints of his parish; for the Parisians, who are made up and pieced together of all nations, are by nature both good swearers (*jureurs*) and good jurists, and a trifle over-bearing with it all, for which reason, in the opinion of Joaninus de Barranco, *Libro de copiositate reverentiarum,* they are called *Parrhesians* in Greek, that is to say proud-talkers.

At this point, Gargantua's gaze fell upon the great bells which are in the towers, and he started ringing them very melodiously. As he did so, the thought occurred to him that they would make good jingle-bells for his mare's neck, as he was planning to send her back to his father loaded down with *fromage de Brie* and fresh herrings. And so, he proceeded to carry them home with him.

There came, then, a ham-begging commander of St. Anthony to make his swinish plea. This fellow, although he could be heard far enough away to cause the bacon to tremble in the salting-vat, thought he would be able to make away with them on the sly; but he was compelled to be honest and leave them behind, not because they were too hot, but because they were a little too heavy to carry. It is not the commander of Bourg I mean, for he's too good a friend of mine.

At this, all the town was moved to the point of sedition, for you are doubtless aware that they are so ready at this sort of thing that foreign nations are inclined to wonder at the patience of the King of France; for their monarchs do not, in all justice, restrain them, in view of the inconveniences that would ensue from day to day. Would to God I knew the workshop in which such schisms and conspiracies are forged so that I might lay the evidence before the confraternities of my parish! You may know that the place where the people, all excited and stirred up, came together was Nesle, where there formerly stood, but stands no longer, the oracle of Lutetia. There, the case was discussed, and the inconvenience shown of having the bells carried off.

After they had argued the *pro et contra,* it was concluded, by aid of the syllogism known as *Baralipton,* that they should dispatch the oldest and most efficient of the Faculty to interview Gargantua, and to remonstrate with him on the terrible inconvenience attending the loss of the bells. And notwithstanding the objections of certain of the University, who asserted that this mission was one that called for an orator rather than a sophist, they selected for the business one Master Janotus de Bragmardo.

This is one of the most famous episodes in the whole of the Gargantua and Pantagruel—*possibly, all in all, the best known—and has repeatedly inspired the Rabelais illustrator. It is, at the same time, one of the most irreverent, and in an effort to avert the wrath of the theologians of the Sorbonne, the author in revision toned it down very considerably in places. One of his major elisions has here been restored: the passage containing the oaths that the Parisians swore, beginning with "By the wounds of God!" and ending with "By St. Vitus!" (A passage, incidentally, that Urquhart does not give.)* ——*"The place where they came together was Nesle" (the* hôtel *royale de Nesle): in place of "Nesle," the earlier editions have "the Sorbonne."* ——*Where the present version reads: "wonder at the patience of the Kings of France," a bold phrase occurs in the edition of 1535: "at the patience, or (better) the stupidity," etc.* ——*In place of the rather meaningless pleasantry, "so that I might lay them before the confraternities of my parish," the 1535 edition reads: "just to see if I would not make some fine slabs of dung out of them."*

It is passages such as these that appear to provide

some ground for the belief, held by Professor Lefranc and others, that Rabelais was deliberately engaged in covert atheistic propaganda.

Of the saints mentioned, several are fictitious: St. Quenet; St. Chitterling, an "ithyphallic saint," according to M. Lazare Sainéan; St. Foutin, an erotic deformation of St. Photin; and St. Mamie, an allusion to the virgin and martyr, Mamyca, and to the proverb, "to pay one's devotions to St. Mamie," which was equivalent to "go see one's mistress."

This polyglot passage reflects that admixture of races at Paris of which Ariosto speaks. Among those present are Germans, Italians, men from Provence, the Scotchman who swears by St. Ninian, and others. There are a number of puns: as mer Dé, Mother of God or merde; Pote de Christo (pote in Italian meaning sometimes power and sometimes the female pudenda); St. Foutin, a play on the verb foutre; etc. The pommes cuites of St. Godegran were possibly a specialty of a wine-shop, the Grand Godet in the Place de Grève, that is mentioned by Villon (Testament, 1039). Carymary, carymara is roughly equivalent to hocus pocus.

The "point above the University" to which the victims of the Gargantuan flood retired was Mount Saint-Geneviève, highest point of the "University Quarter."

A proficiat is a tribute paid to a bishop by way of welcome. It is not Strabo, but the Emperor Julian in his Misopogon who gives Paris the name of Leuketia, from the Greek leukos, white; Strabo's name for Paris is Loukotokia. ——"Joaninus de Barranco": both the author and the work attributed to him are probably fictitious. ——"Ham-begging commander of St. Anthony": members of the Order of St. Anthony had the reputation of being able to cure sick hogs placed under the protection of their patron. As a reward, at hog-killing time, they were *presented with bacon or ham.* ——*"Nothing is too hot or heavy" (for someone to carry off) was a popular saying.* ——*"Commander of Bourg": Antoine de Saxe, commander of Saint-Antoine-de-Bourg-en-Bresse, author of a number of volumes of verse.* ——*"An orator, rather than a sophist": that is, a member of the Faculty of Arts, rather than a theologian.* ——*Attempts to identify Master Janotus de Bragmardo have been in vain.*

Like Gargantua's mare, the episode of the bells is not Rabelais' invention, but occurs in the Grandes Cronicques.

How Janotus de Bragmardo Was Sent to Recover the Big Bells from Gargantua

MASTER JANOTUS, shorn like Julius Caesar, having put on his antique *liripipium,* and having well antidoted his stomach with oven-cakes and holy water from the cellar, betook himself to Gargantua's lodgings, driving in front of him three red-muzzled calves of ushers, and dragging after him five or six artless masters of arts, all of them as dirty as could be.

As they came in, Ponocrates met them. He was frightened at first, when he saw them disguised like that, and thought they were some silly masqueraders. And so, he asked one of the aforesaid artless masters of the outfit what was the meaning of this mummery. Then he learned that they had come to demand that the bells be restored to them.

As soon as he heard this, Ponocrates ran to tell the news to Gargantua, so that the latter might be ready with an answer, and might make up his mind on the spot as to what was to be done. Gargantua, thus warned, called to one side Ponocrates his tutor, Philotomus his maître-d'hôtel, Gymnastes his squire, and Eudemon, and at once proceeded to confer with them as to what he should do and say.

All were of the opinion that they ought to lead their visitors to the butler's pantry and there give them a good stiff drink. And in order that this old codger might not be all puffed up at having got the bells back, it was decided that while he was drinking, they should send for the town marshal, the rector of the Faculty, and the vicar of the church, to whom, before the sophist had stated his business, the bells should be turned over. After which, they would listen to the fellow's fine speech. This was done, and when the personages mentioned had arrived, the sophist was ushered into the room and began his speech as follows, coughing as he did so.

A liripipium *was a doctor's gown with a tail.* ——*In place of* "a good stiff drink," *the earlier editions have* "a theologian's drink," *and in place of* "the sophist was ushered," *etc., they have* "the theologian."

The Harangue of Master Janotus de Bragmardo, Delivered before Gargantua, for the Purpose of Recovering the Bells

"Ahem! ahem! ahem! *Mna dies.* G'day, Sir, g'day to you, *et vobis,* Gentlemen. It would be only decent for you to give us back our bells for we have great need of them. Hem! haw! ah-ah-sh! We've refused good money for them before now, from the folks of Londres in—Cahors, and we've done the same with those of Bordeaux in Brie, who wanted to buy them on account of the substantific quality of their elementary complexion, which is

intronificated in the terrestreity of their quiddative nature, in extranizing the haloes around the sun and moon
and the whirlwinds upon our vineyards—not ours, really,
you understand, but those round about us. For if we
lose our wine, we lose everything, both rent and law.

"If you return them at my request, I will earn six span
of sausages and a good pair of breeches, which will do
my legs a lot of good, if they keep their promise to me.
Ho! By God, *Domine*, a pair of breeches is not to be
sneezed at. *Et vir sapiens non abhorrebit eam.* And a
wise man will not spurn them. Ha, ha! You don't get a
pair of breeches by wishing for 'em. I know that's true
so far as I'm concerned. Just think, *Domine*, it's eighteen
days now that I've been matagrabolizing this fine speech.
*Reddite quae sunt Caesaris Caesari, et quae sunt Dei
Deo.* Render unto Caesar—*Ibi jacet lepus.* There lies the
rub.

"'Pon my word, *Domine*, if you'd like to have a bite
of supper with me some time, *in camera*—I swear to
Christ!—*charitatis, nos faciemus bonum cherubin*—
we'll keep good cherubim—I mean good cheer. *Ego
occidi unum porcum, et ego habet bon vino.* I've just
killed a pig and I've got a little jug. But you can't make
bad Latin out of good wine.

"Moreover, *de parte Dei, date nobis bellas nostras.* In
God's name, give us back our bells. Hold on a minute,
and I'll present you, on behalf of the Faculty, with a
copy of the *Sermones de Utino*—*utinam*, provided that
—you return our bells. *Vultis etiam pardonos?* Should
you gentlemen like some pardons also? *Per diem*—
I mean, *per Deum*—*vos habebitis et nihil payabitis.*
You shall have them and pay nothing.

"O Sir, *Domine*, *belligivaminor nobis!* Give us our
bells. As a matter of fact, *est bonum urbis.* They're the
property of the city. They're for everybody's use. If your

mare likes 'em, so does our Faculty, *quae comparata est insipientibus, et similis facta est eis.* Which is likened unto the senseless ones and has been made like unto them. *Psalmo nescio quo.* Some Psalm or other, I don't know which, although I've got it down, right enough, in my notebook, *et est unum bonum Achilles,* that is to say, an incontrovertible argument. Hem! hem! ahem! ah-ash!

"Look here, I'll prove to you that you ought to give them to me. *Ego sic argumentor.* This is my argument: *Omnis bella bellabilis in bellerio bellando, bellans bellativo bellare facit bellabiter bellantes.* Every bellable bell belling in the belfry, belling bellatively, makes the bellers bell bellfully. *Parisius habet bellas.* There are bells in Paris. *Ergo gluc.* There you are, and it proves nothing.

"Ha! ha! ha! that was some speech! It's in *tertio prime,* the third mode of the first syllogistic figure, in *Darii* or somewhere else. 'Pon my soul, I've seen the time when I was a devil of an arguer, but I'm no good at it any more; all I think about now is good wine, a good bed, my back to the fire, my belly to the table, and a good deep bowl.

"Hey, *Domine,* I beg you, *in nomine Patris et Filii et Spiritus Sancti, Amen,* to give us back our bells, and may God keep you from harm and Our Lady from health— I mean, Our Lady of Health—*qui vivit et regnat per omnia secula seculorum, Amen.* Hem! haw! ah-ash! ash-shaw!

"*Verum enim vero, quando quidem, dubio procul, edepol, quoniam, ita certe, meus Deus fidus.* For verily, yea, verily, whereas, beyond a doubt, in the name of Pollux, thus, certainly, so be it, God of the faithful. A city without bells is like a blind man without a cane, like an ass without a crupper, and a cow without jingles; and until you give 'em back to us, we shall not cease to

cry after you like a blind man who has lost his cane, to
bray like an ass without a crupper, and to bellow like a
cow whose jingles have been taken from her.

"A certain Latinizer, living near the City Hospital,
once said, alleging the authority of one Tamponus—my
mistake: I mean Pontanus, the secular poet—that he
wished all bells were made of feathers and the clapper
of a fox's tail, because they gave him the chronic—er,
colic—in the tripes of his brain when he was composing
his carminiform verses. But bing, bang, bing, this way,
that way, tother way, he was declared a heretic—we
turn 'em out just like that, like wax-figures. And so saith
the deponent. *Valete et plaudite. Calepinus recensui.* I,
Calepino, have made this recension.

*This speech by Master Janotus, with its execrable and
macaronic Latin, its pompous word-coinages, and the
like, is a hilarious satire on Rabelais' bitter and life-long
enemies, the scholastic theologians of the Sorbonne: their
ignorance; their grandiloquence; their indolence and
self-indulgence.* ——"Mna dies": *jumbled pronunciation
of* bona dies. ——*Londres is a tiny hamlet of Quercy,
canton of Seiches, arrondissement of Marmande (Lot-
et-Garonne); Bordeaux is a village of the Parisian sub-
urbs, canton of Claye, arrondissement of Meaux en Brie.*
——"Ibi jacet lepus": *literally, "there lies the hare,"
the* "lepus" *being the crucial point of an argument, the
problem or difficulty involved.* ——*The* "camera charitatis" *was the reception room for guests in monasteries.*
——"Sermones de Utino": *allusion to the sermons of a
Dominican preacher, Léonard Matthei (Leonardus Udi-
nus), published at Lyon, in 1501; the* "Utino" *is for the
sake of the play on* utinam. ——*Pontanus was an Italian
scholar and bad poet;* "carminiform verses" *are* "verse-*

like verses" (from the Latin carmen). ——*The Calepinus referred to is Ambrosio Calepino, monk of Bergamo, author of a well-known Latin dictionary;* recensui *was the word commonly employed by one who had completed the copying or collation of a manuscript—in this case, a Latin expert!*

How the Sophist Carried His Cloth Away, and How He Brought Suit against the Other Masters

THE sophist had no sooner finished than Ponocrates and Eudemon burst out laughing, so heartily that they thought they were going to render up their souls to God, just as Crassus did when he saw a big-balled ass eating thistles; and there was Philemon, who, when he saw an ass eating the figs that had been prepared for his own dinner, laughed until he died. Master Janotus began laughing with them, and even went them one better; and they all laughed until the tears came into their eyes, through the vehement concussion of the substance of the brain, which caused the lachrymal humidities to be squeezed out and to run down along the optic nerves. As a result, they were a good example of Democritus heraclitizing, and of Heraclitus democratizing.

When they had quite finished laughing, Gargantua held a conference with his followers as to what was to be done. Ponocrates was of the opinion that they ought to give this fine orator another drink. And in view of the fact that he had provided them with more good sport, and had made them laugh more than the comedian Crackbrain ever could have done, he thought they ought to give the fellow the ten span of sausages mentioned in his jolly speech, along with a pair of trousers, three hundred big chumps of cordwood, twenty-five barrels of wine, a bed with a three-layer mattress of goose-feathers, and a very deep and capacious bowl, for these were the things the sophister had stated were necessary to his old age.

Everything was done as planned, the only thing being that Gargantua doubted if they would be able to find, right away, breeches suitable to the old fellow's legs; he was doubtful, also, as to what cut would be most becoming to the orator—the martingale, which has a draw-bridge effect in the seat, to permit doing one's business more easily; the sailor-style, which affords more comfort for the kidneys; the Swiss, which is warmer on the belly; or the codfish-tail, which is cooler on the loins. He accordingly had them take along seven ells of black cloth, with three of white for the lining. The wood was borne by workmen, the masters of arts carried the sausages and bowls, while Master Janot himself insisted upon carrying the cloth. One of the other masters, Jousse Bandouille by name, remonstrated with him, telling him it was not respectable nor decent for one of his rank to do so and that he ought to turn it over to one of the others.

"Ha!" exclaimed Janotus, "you big blockhead, your conclusions are not at all *in modo et figura*. Don't you see, this is what the *Suppositions* and the *Parva Logicalia* are good for? *Pannus pro quo supponit?*"

"*Confuse*," replied Bandouille, "*et distributive*. Confusedly and distributively."

"You numskull," said Janotus, "I didn't ask you, *qua modo supponit*, in what manner it corresponds, but *pro quo*, to what. The answer, blockhead, is: *pro tibiis meis*, to my shanks. And for that reason, I propose to carry it myself. *Egomet, sicut suppositum portat adpositum*, as the supposition carries the apposition."

And so, he proceeded to sneak it away, as Patelin did *his* cloth.

But the best of all was when the old duffer, at a plenary session held in the church of the Mathurins, put up a vainglorious plea for the breeches and sausages which his colleagues had promised him but which they now peremptorily refused him on the ground that he had already got some from Gargantua, according to the information they had received. He remonstrated with them, telling them that these had been gratis, and had been given out of Gargantua's liberality, so that they were in no wise absolved from their promises. Notwithstanding this, they told him that he should be content with reason, and that he was not going to get any further handout.

"Reason!" exclaimed Janotus. "We never use it here. Miserable traitors, you're a lot of good-for-nothings; you're the scum of the earth, I'm well aware of that. Never limp in front of the lame; I'm one of you when it comes to wrong-doing. God's spleen! I'll tell the King of the disgraceful carryings-on here, and I'm a scurvy rascal if he doesn't have you all burned alive as buggers, traitors, heretics, and seducers, enemies of God and of virtue!"

Following these words, they drew up an indictment against him, and he, in turn, summoned them to appear. In short, the case went to court and is there yet. The Sorbonnists, thereupon, made a vow not to take a bath, while Master Janotus and his adherents vowed not to wipe their noses, until there was a definite decision in the matter. For which reason, they are, to this day, both dirty and snotty, for the court has not had time as yet to examine carefully all the documents in the case. The decision will be handed down at the next Greek Calends, that is to say, never; for, as you know, the procedure of these magistrates is beyond the power of nature and contrary to their own statutes. The statutes of Paris keep chirping that God alone can make things infinite. Nature can make nothing immortal, since she puts an end and a period to all the things that she produces; for *omnia orta cadunt,* etc., all things that rise have a fall. But these windjamming loafers surely make the cases pending before them both infinite and immortal; and by so doing, they have occasioned and verified the saying of Chilon, the Lacedaemonian, carved up at Delphi, to the effect that misery is the companion of lawsuits and that folks who go to law are wretched, for the reason that they will die before they ever get the rights for which they are suing.

In this chapter, as in preceding ones, the earlier editions have "theologian" for "sophist" and "the Sorbonnists" for "the masters" (the reading "Sorbonnists" has been restored in the final paragraph). ——"As Crassus did": according to Pliny (Natural History, vii, 19), *Crassus was one of those men who never laughed; this appears to have been the only time; Erasmus has the anecdote* (Adages, I, x, 71). *——"As Philemon did": the anecdote is related by Lucian* (Macrobii, 25) *and Valerius Maximus (ix, 12). ——"Democritus heraclitizing . . . Heraclitus democratizing": Democritus being the laughing, Heraclitus the weeping, philosopher. ——"The comedian, Crackbrain": Songecreux, the sobriquet of the famous comic actor, Jehan de l'Espine, known as "du Pontalais." ——"Ten span of sausages": it was six in Master Janotus' speech. ——"The Suppositions": the* Suppositiones *were a section of the* Parva Logicalia, *which formed a part of the scholastic course of instruction. ——"Confuse et distributive": reference to the*

Suppositio confusa et distributiva *of the* Parva Logicalia.
——*"The church of the Mathurins": the Sorbonne held sessions here down to the time of the Revolution; earlier editions have "at the Sorbonne."* ——*"All things that rise have a fall": Sallust,* De Bello Jugurthino, ii, 3. ——*"Carved up at Delphi": Pliny,* Natural History, **VII,** 32.

III. The Old Education and the New

(CHAPTERS XXI-XXIV)

Rabelais the educator—and this is one of the most important aspects of Rabelais the writer—is nowhere more in evidence than in his Gargantua, *or what is commonly known as his first book. The idea of describing the educational methods, old and new, good and bad, to which his gigantesque young hero was subjected, is original with him; there is nothing of this in the* Grandes Cronicques. *Already, in his* Pantagruel, *in the famous letter of Gargantua to his son (Book Second, Chapter* VIII, *Maître François had outlined the typical scheme of education for the* clerc, *or scholar, as advocated by Erasmus and other humanists—one that envisaged an encyclopedic erudition, the object being to make of the pupil an "abysm of knowledge." In this, he was not original; it was when, in turning to the* Gargantua *myth, he found himself once more confronted with the question, that he was led to deepen his ideas on the subject, and it is here that he makes his distinctive contributions.*

After giving us a picture of the old monastic type of schooling as personified by Master Tubal Holofernes, a picture that he greatly exaggerates for the sake of effect, the author goes on to depict a system of pedagogy which, while humanistic in character, represents, basically, his own best thought in this domain, his own permeating life-view. This new education, of which Ponoc-

117

ates is the exemplar, looks to the normal and harmonious development of all man's energies and capacities; its purpose is to stimulate activity and to make of work and study one of life's supreme pleasures. The gap between the two systems is an enormous one, and in his romance Rabelais leaps it by having recourse to a magic potion, which does away with the necessity of a lengthy description of the slow process of transformation in the individual.

Rabelais' contribution is distinctly on the side of pedagogic method. Education for him is rooted in the concrete realities of daily living, the "lessons of things." It is not a matter of the intellect alone, but of physical and moral culture as well—the classic ideal of mens sana in corpore sano, with Rabelais the physician laying a particular stress on hygiene. Sainte-Beuve, in a paper on Rabelais in his Causeries du Lundi, has excellently summed up the character of this new pedagogy, which, he says, "lies in the combination of play and study, in learning things by making use of them, in putting books and the things of life side by side, theory and practice, body and mind, gymnastics and music, as with the Greeks, without, however, modelling ourselves on the past, but having regard continually to the present and future." In addition to all this, as a modern French educator and Rabelais authority, M. Jean Plattard, has pointed out, there is inherent in this system a "confidence in the natural goodness of man, an act of faith in the progress of humanity."

The Studies of Gargantua under His Sophist Teachers

THE first few days having thus passed, and the bells having been put back in their place, the citizens of Paris, by way of showing their gratitude for this honorable action, offered to keep and support Gargantua's mare, which suited him very well; and so, he sent the animal to live in the Forest of Bière, or Fontainebleau. I believe, she is not there any more.

This matter having been attended to, Gargantua wanted with all his heart to study according to Ponocrates' directions; but the latter, to begin with, ordered him to go on in the manner to which he was accustomed, so that he, Ponocrates, might be able to find out by what means over so long a period of time the lad's former teachers had succeeded in rendering their pupil so stupid, so silly, and so utterly ignorant.

Gargantua then spent his time in some such fashion as this. He ordinarily awoke between eight and nine o'clock, whether it was day or not; for such were the orders of his former tutors, who would quote the saying of David: "*Vanum est vobis ante lucem surgere.*" It is vain for you to rise up early!" Then he would skip, bound, and wallow in the straw-mattress of his bed for some time, in order the better to revive his animal spirits.

He dressed according to the season, but he liked to wear a great long robe of thick wool, lined with fox-fur. Afterwards, he would comb his hair with Almain's comb, which was his four fingers and a thumb; for his teachers had told him that to comb, wash, or clean one's self in any other manner was time lost in this world.

Then he did his business, urinated, puked up his

guts, belched, farted, yawned, spat, coughed, hiccuped, sneezed, and blew his nose like an arch-deacon; following which, he had a bite of breakfast, to overcome the dew and the bad air. His breakfast consisted of fine tripe fried, fine rashers, fine hams, a fine mess of grilled kid, and a plentiful supply of convent soup.

Ponocrates remonstrated with him, telling him he ought not to eat immediately upon getting out of bed, without first having taken a little exercise. But Gargantua replied:

"What! Don't I get enough exercise? I wallow around six or seven times in bed before rising. Isn't that enough? Pope Alexander did the same, on the advice of his Jewish physician, and he lived until he died, in spite of the croakers. My first teachers got me into the habit, by telling me that breakfast was good for the memory; and so, the first thing they did was take a drink. I find it's a very good habit, and I eat all the better for it at dinnertime.

"And Master Tubal, who was head of his class in Paris, told me that there was not so much in running fast as there was in getting an early start; accordingly, for the welfare of humanity, we shouldn't drink, drink, drink, like ducks, but rather, we ought to do our drinking in the morning. *Unde versus:*

> "To get up in the morning is a bitter pill;
> To drink in the morning is better still."

After he had had a good hearty breakfast, Gargantua would go to church, and they would bring him, in a large basket, a huge breviary, wrapped up like a slipper, and a heavy one it was, too—heavy with grime as well as with clasps and parchment—weighing a little more or less than eleven-hundred-six pounds; and then, he would hear twenty-six or thirty masses. Meanwhile, his official chaplain would come in, all tucked up in an overcoat, like a peewit, and with his breath well antidoted with much syrup-of-the-vine. With him, Gargantua would mumble over all his *kyrie-eleisons,* and would pick them so clean that not a morsel would fall to the ground.

As he left the church, they would bring him, upon an ox-cart, a lot of St. Claude rosaries, each one of them as big as a hat-block; and promenading through the cloisters, the galleries, or the garden, he would say more of them than sixteen hermits could.

Then he would study for a miserly half-hour, or thereabouts, with his eyes fixed on his book. But (as the comic poet says) his soul was in the kitchen.

Then, having urinated a good jugful, he would sit down at table. And since he was naturally phlegmatic, he would begin his meal with a few dozen hams, smoked beef-tongues, caviar, sausages, and such like precursors of wine. While he was thus engaged, four of his servants, one after another, would continually cast heaping shovelfuls of mustard into his mouth. Then he would drink a horrific quantity of white wine, to relieve his kidneys; after which, he would eat, according to the season, whatever meats suited his appetite; and he only stopped eating when he felt his belly pulling down.

As for drinking, there was neither end nor canon to that, for he would remark that the limits and the bounds of drinking were when the corks in one's shoes swelled up more than half a foot high.

Jacques Almain, doctor of the University of Paris and author of a treatise on logic, is said to have been renowned for his slovenliness. ——Pope Alexander vi *had a physician, Bonnet de Lates, who was a converted*

Provençal Jew. ——*St. Claude was famous for its rosaries.* ——*"His soul was in the kitchen":* Terence, Eunuchus, iv, 8: "Jamdudum animus est in patinis."

Gargantua's Games

THEN, distractedly gnawing over a slice of Graces, he would wash his hands in fresh wine, pick his teeth with a piece of pork, and chat gayly with his companions. After which, when the green cover had been spread out, they would bring in many cards, dice, and plenty of tables. And then Gargantua would play.

Rabelais here gives a list of 217 games. These fall into four general groups: card games; table games, such as chess and the like; games of skill; and miscellaneous diversions, including simple amusements, "fool-killer" games, etc. Many of these pastimes have been identified by scholars; others remain unknown or doubtful. Some of them, but not too many, are erotic or "obscene" in character, or have to do with excretory processes. On the whole, however, these are, simply, the adult and juvenile amusements of an age.

After he had had a good time playing, and had strained, passed, and winnowed his time, it was no more than right that he should have a little drink and that meant eleven sixteen-gallon bumpers per man. And as soon as he had had a bite of supper, he would stretch out on a nice bench, or in a nice wide bed, and sleep for two or three hours, without thinking or speaking any evil.

When he awoke, he would wiggle his ears a little. In the meanwhile, they had brought in some fresh wine, and he would drink more heartily than ever. Ponocrates would remonstrate with him, to the effect that it was bad to drink like that, immediately after sleeping.

"It is the life the Fathers lived," Gargantua would answer him. "I naturally sleep salty, and a little nap is as good to me as a rasher of ham."

Then he would commence to study a bit, and out would come the beads. In order to get them over with in better form, he would mount an old she-mule that had served nine kings. And in this fashion, mumbling with his mouth and dangling his head, he would go to see some rabbit ferreted out.

Upon his return, he would take himself off to the kitchen to see what kind of roast there was on the spit.

He would then have, I am telling you, upon my word! a very good supper; he liked to invite a few of the neighbors, and together they would swill down plenty and tell stories, old and new. Among others, Gargantua had for domestic retainers the Lords of Fou, of Gourville, of Grignault, and of Marigny.

After supper, the pretty wooden Gospels would come in, that is to say, a supply of game-boards; and they would play flush, "One, Two, Three" or "Chip in All Your Stakes," to make short work of it. Or it might be, they would go see some of the lasses in the neighborhood, with a few little suppers, collations, and postcollations thrown in. Then he would sleep, without taking his halter off, until eight o'clock the next morning.

The names Fou, Gourville, Grignault, and Marigny are those of well-known families; Rabelais may have had certain individuals in mind. ——"Wooden Gospels":

game-boards were so called for the reason that they opened like books or Gospels. ——"Collations and post-collations": an allusion to monastery feastings.

How Gargantua Was Instructed by Ponocrates in Such a Manner That He Did Not Waste an Hour of the Day

As PONOCRATES grew familiar with Gargantua's vicious manner of life, he began to plan a different course of instruction for the lad; but at first he let the latter go his own way, remembering that nature does not endure sudden changes without great violence.

To make a better beginning of his task, he consulted a learned physician of the day, one Master Theodore, as to whether or not it would be possible to bring Gargantua back into the right path. Master Theodore proceeded, in canonical fashion, to purge the youth with Anticyrian hellebore, and by means of this medication, succeeded in cleansing him of all his abnormal and perverse mental habits. By this means, also, Ponocrates made Gargantua forget all that he had learned under his former teachers, as Timotheus did with his disciples who had been taught by other musicians. In order to get better results, Ponocrates introduced his pupil to such learned men as were at hand; and by force of their example the boy's mind expanded and he conceived a desire to study in a different manner than the one to which he had been accustomed; he began to want to make the most of his talents. Ponocrates soon had him so trained that he did not lose a single hour of the day, but, most commendably, spent all his time in learning and the acquirement of knowledge.

In accordance with this new regime, Gargantua awoke about four o'clock in the morning. While his attendants were rubbing him down, another would read him certain passages from the Holy Scriptures, in a loud, clear tone of voice, with a suitable enunciation. This task was assigned to a young page, a native of Basché, Anagnostes by name. According to the drift of the passage that was read to him, Gargantua would, frequently, fall into a revery and adore, pray, and supplicate the good God, whose majesty and marvelous judgments the Bible reading had made plain.

Then he would go into a closet to attend to the natural excretory functions of his body. There his teacher would repeat what had been read to him, explaining the more obscure and difficult points.

Returning, they would consider the state of the heavens, to see if it was such as their observations of the night before had led them to expect, making note also of what signs the sun, as well as the moon, was entering that day.

This done, Gargantua was dressed, combed, curled, trigged out, and perfumed, during which time they would repeat to him the lessons of the day before. He himself would say them by heart, making certain practical and human applications, and this exercise would sometimes be prolonged for two or three hours, although ordinarily it ended when Gargantua was fully dressed. And then, for three solid hours, they would read to him.

When this was over, they would go out, still talking about what they had just read, and find some sport at Bracque or in the meadows, playing ball, tennis or three-cornered toss-ball, briskly exercising their bodies as they, before, had exercised their souls.

Their sport was quite free and easy, for they would quit whenever they pleased and they ordinarily stopped when they were sweating all over or when they were exhausted. Then they would be very thoroughly rubbed and dried, would change their shirts, and would stroll leisurely back to see if dinner was ready. While they were waiting, they would recite, clearly and eloquently, such sentences as they had remembered from the morning's reading. In the meanwhile, Monsignor Appetite would put in an appearance, and they would all sit down, in orderly fashion, at the table.

At the beginning of the meal, they would read to Gargantua some pleasing tale of ancient prowess, and this would last until he had had his wine. Then (if he liked) they would continue the reading, or else they would fall to chatting merrily, speaking first of the virtues, properties, nature, and efficacy of everything that was on the table: of the bread, the wine, the water, the salt, the meats, the fish, the fruits, the roots and herbs, and the manner in which all these were served. By so doing, they became familiar, in a short time, with all the passages relating to these topics to be found in Pliny, Athenaeus, Dioscorides, Julius Pollux, Galen, Porphyry, Oppian, Polybius, Heliodorus, Aristotle, Aelian, and others. In the course of such conversations, to make sure of their points, they would often have the books in question brought to the table. As for Gargantua, he remembered so well everything that was said that there was not a physician anywhere who knew one-half as much as he did.

After this, they would speak of the lessons that had been read that morning and, finishing the meal with a little quince marmalade, Gargantua would pick his teeth with a piece of mastic, wash his hands and eyes in good fresh water, and return thanks to God in a few melodious canticles, in praise of the divine munificence and benignity. At this point they would bring in cards, not for playing, but that they might learn a thousand new and fine points, all of which had something to do with arithmetic. As a result, Gargantua became very fond of the science of numbers, and every day, after dinner and after supper, he would pass the time in this manner as pleasantly as he formerly had in playing cards or dice. Indeed, he became so skilled in the theory and practice of the subject that the Englishman, Tunstal, who had written a comprehensive treatise on it, confessed that, by comparison with Gargantua, he understood it no better than he did High German.

The same was true of other mathematical sciences, such as geometry, astronomy, and music. For as they waited for their meal to digest, they would construct any number of amusing instruments and geometric figures, and they would also put the astronomic rules into practice. Afterwards, they would have the best time in the world, singing quartettes or quintettes, or anything that pleased them. As for musical instruments, Gargantua learned to play the lute, the spinet, the harp, the German flute with nine holes, the viol, and the trombone.

When an hour had been thus spent and the process of digestion was finished, Gargantua would get rid of his natural excrements, and then would return to his chief studies for three hours or more, repeating the reading of the morning, going on with the book on which he was engaged, practicing penmanship and drawing, and learning to form the old Gothic and the Roman characters.

Then they would leave the house, accompanied by a young gentleman of Touraine, named Squire Gymnastes, who would proceed to teach them the art of horsemanship. Changing his clothes, Gargantua would mount a courser, a charger, a jennet or Berber, a light, fleet-footed steed, and would put the animal through a hundred paces, making him leap in the air, take the ditch, vault the hurdle, or turn short about in a circle, sometimes to the right, sometimes to the left. He never broke a lance, for it is the greatest stupidity in the world to have to confess: "I have broken ten lances in a tournament or in a battle." A carpenter could do as well as that. The glorious and the praiseworthy thing is, with one lance, to have broken the heads of ten enemies.

And so, with his steel-pointed weapon held stiff and firm, he would pierce a coat-of-mail, fell a tree, snare a ring, or pick up a warrior's saddle, a hauberk or a gauntlet. All this he did, armed from head to foot. As for flourishes and all the little tricks in handling a horse, no one was better at this than he. The high-jumper of Ferrara was but a monkey in comparison. Gargantua was particularly clever at leaping quickly from one horse to another without a fall (these horses were known as desultories); and he was equally good at mounting from either side, lance in hand, without a stirrup; he was able, finally, to guide his steed as he wished without a bridle; for such accomplishments as these are called for in military life.

Other days, he would practice with the battle-ax, which he handled so well, so smoothly, and with so much assurance, performing all the customary feats with it, including the great sweeping side-cut, that he was looked upon as a knight-at-arms, on the field and in all trials of strength. Then he would brandish the pike and twirl the two-handed sword, the bastard-sword used by archers, the Spanish rapier, the dagger, and the poniard—all of this, armed or unarmed, equipped with his buckler, with only his cloak, or with a small round shield.

He would hunt the stag, the roebuck, the bear, the doe, the wild boar, the hare, the partridge, the pheasant, and the bustard. He would play with the big ball and make it bound in the air, with his foot or with his fist. He would wrestle, run and jump—not three steps and a jump, not the hop-step-and-jump, not the German jump —"For," as Gymnastes remarked, "all those are useless and of no account in war"—but with one leap, he would bound over a ditch, leap a hedge, or run six paces straight up the side of a wall, and in this manner seize hold of a window as high up as a lance.

He was fond of swimming in deep water, on his belly, on his back, on his side, with his whole body, or with his feet alone; or with one hand in the air, holding up a book, he would cross the River Seine without wetting the volume, in the meanwhile dragging along his cloak by his teeth, in the manner of Julius Caesar. Then, with one hand, he would hoist himself into a boat. From the boat, he would dive back into the water, head first, going to the very bottom, down among the rocks, into all the pits and caverns. Then he would turn the boat, steer it and propel it, now rapidly, now slowly, now upstream, now down. He would hold it steady in the middle of a dam. He would guide it with one hand and, in the other, flourish a big oar. He would spread the sail, climb the masts among the rigging, run along the yards, adjust the compass, set the ropes against the wind, and hold the steering wheel firm.

Coming out of the water, he would take a good stiff run up the mountain and come down the other side with the same impetuosity. He would climb trees like a cat, leaping from one to another like a squirrel, and would fell huge limbs like another Milo.

With two steel-pointed poniards and a pair of stone-punchers that had been previously tried out, he would run up the side of a house like a rat and come down in such fashion that he would not be a bit the worse for his fall. He would practice throwing the dart, the bar, a stone, the javelin, the partisan, and the halberd; he would stretch the bow taut and, with sheer strength, would bend the big crossbow. He would sight the arquebus, mount the cannon, and shoot at paper pigeons and other targets, aiming sometimes up, sometimes down, sometimes from the front, sometimes from the side, and sometimes from behind, like the Parthians.

They would stretch a cable for his benefit, from some high tower to the ground. He would climb this, hand over hand, and then come down it, so firmly and with so good an aim that you could not have done as well on a meadow. They would make him a huge perch between two trees, and from this he would hang by his hands and dart back and forth along it, his feet touching nothing all the while, so fast that one could hardly have kept up with him by running at top-speed.

To exercise his chest and lungs, he would yell like all the devils in hell. I heard him once, calling Eudemon, all the way from the Porte Saint-Victor to Montmartre. Stentor never had such a voice at the Battle of Troy.

To develop his muscles, they made him a pair of heavy salmon-shaped lead pieces, each weighing 870,000 pounds, to which he gave the name of *halteres,* or dumbbells. He would lift one of these in each hand, raise the two of them above his head, and hold them there, without moving, for three quarters of an hour and more, which is an inimitable feat of strength.

He played barriers with the best of them and, when it came to the test, was so sturdy on his feet that he could dare the gamest of them to budge him from his place, like Milo of old, in imitation of whom he held a pomegranate in his hand as a prize for the one who could oust him.

Having spent his time in this manner, and having been rubbed down, cleaned, and refreshed with a change of clothes, he would return home in very leisurely fashion; and as they passed meadows or other green places, he

and his companions would stop to notice the trees and
the plants, comparing them with what had been written
about them in such old authors as Theophrastus, Dioscorides, Marinus, Pliny, Nicander, Macer, and Galen.
And they would carry handfuls home, where a young
page named Rhizotome would take charge of the specimens, along with the mattocks, picks, hoes, spades,
pruning-knives, and other implements necessary to good
botanizing.

Having reached home, while supper was being prepared, they would repeat a few of the passages that had
been read; then they would sit down at table. It is to be
noted, here, that Gargantua's dinner was a sober and a
frugal one, since he ate only enough at that time to
muzzle the barkings of his stomach; but his supper was
copious and large, for at this meal he took as much as
he needed to sustain and nourish him, which is the diet
prescribed by any good and reliable system of hygiene,
although a lot of wrangling, addlepated, blockhead
physicians such as are turned out by the sophists will
advise the contrary.

During this meal, the reading begun at dinner was
continued as long as they thought proper; the rest of
the time being spent in pleasant, literate, and instructive
conversation. After grace had been said, they would
begin singing and playing on musical instruments, or
would amuse themselves with such light pastimes as are
to be found in cards, dice, and gaming-boxes. On certain
evenings, they would continue having a good time and
enjoying themselves until bedtime came. On other
occasions, they would go to call on learned men, or
those who had traveled in foreign lands.

As the night wore on, before retiring, they would re-
pair to the most open place in the house, in order to gaze
on the face of the heavens, and there they would make

note of the comets, if any, and of the figuration, situation, aspect, oppositions, and conjunctions of the stars.

After which, with his teacher, in the manner of the Pythagoreans, Gargantua would repeat briefly all that he had read, seen, learned, done, and heard in the course of the entire day. Praying God their creator, adoring Him, reaffirming their faith in Him, glorifying Him for His immense goodness, and rendering Him thanks for all time past, they would commend themselves to His divine clemency for all time to come. This done, they would seek their repose.

This chapter and the following one contain the heart of Rabelais' educational doctrine. It is a wholly serious passage, with not a frivolous word or allusion; the author's ordinarily irresistible impulse to humor for once is held in restraint. These pages appear to have been written at a time when he was close to the Protestant reform movement, before the break between the humanists and the Calvinists had occurred; it does not sound in the least like an under-cover atheist speaking here. The emphasis on physical culture and on bodily hygiene (the doctor speaking) cannot fail to be noted.

"Anticyrian hellebore": so called from the Greek island of Anticyra; it was believed by the ancients to be a remedy against insanity and other cerebral maladies; it is mentioned by Horace (Ars Poetica, 309), Pliny (xxv, 25), Aulus Gellius (xvii, 15), and Dioscorides (iv, 145, 146); see the Adages of Erasmus (i, viii, 52 and 53).
——The anecdote of Timotheus is related by Quintilian; but according to the latter's account (Institutiones, ii, 3), the music master employed the hellebore to induce his pupils to pay a higher fee! ——There is no humorous intent in having Gargantua read to in the water-closet;

Pope Gregory I *held that Psalms might be sung anywhere, even in the privy.* ——"*Some sport at Bracque*":
allusion to the tennis court of that name. ——"*The
Englishman, Tunstal*": *Cuthbert Tunstal (1479-1559),
Bishop of Durham, first secretary to Henry* VIII, *author
of a treatise on arithmetic.* ——"*The high-jumper of
Ferrara*": *this may be a reminiscence of Rabelais' sojourn
in Italy.* ——"*These horses were known as desultories*":
"*desultorii equi,*" *that is, horses belonging to a desultor,
a leaper, vaulter, circus-rider; they are mentioned by
Livy* (XXIII, *xxix,* 5), *Suetonius* (*Caesar,* 39), *and Cicero
(Pro Murena,* 27). ——"*Another Milo*": *the story is told
by Pausanias* (VI, *xiv,* 5-8); *Milo, in attempting to split
a fallen tree trunk that lay in his path, had his hands
caught and was devoured by wolves.* ——"*Halteres, or
dumb-bells*": *these are mentioned by the poet Martial*
(XIV, 49; VII, *lxvii,* 6). ——*Macer was the author of a
Latin poem on plants, printed for the first time at Naples
in 1477.*

*It will be noted that elements of the old pedagogy
remain, such as the stress on repetition and memory
exercises, the practice of reading to the pupil, etc. But
the new far outbalances the old.*

How Gargantua Employed His Time in Rainy Weather

IF IT happened that the day was rainy and intemperate,
all the time before dinner was employed as usual, except
that it was necessary to light a clean, pleasant fire to correct the inclemency of the weather. But after dinner, in
place of outdoor exercises, they would stay in the house
and, as a means of apotherapy, would make sport of
baling hay, splitting and sawing wood, and threshing

sheaves in the barn. Then they would study the arts of painting and sculpture, or would revive the ancient game of knuckle-bones, or dice, as Leonicus has described it, and as our good friend Lascaris plays it. And as they played, they would recall those passages from ancient authors in which there is some mention of or metaphor applicable to this game.

They likewise would go to see how metals were drawn or artillery was cast; or else they would go visit the lapi-daries, the goldsmiths, the carvers of precious stones, the alchemists, the money-coiners, the upholsterers, the weavers, the velvet-workers, the watch makers, the looking-glass-makers, the printers, the organ-makers, the dyers, and workmen of other sorts. And everywhere they went, they would set up the wine, and would think and learn a lot about industry and the processes of the various trades.

At other times, they would attend public readings, state occasions, oratorical and declamation contests, or would go to listen to the pleadings of learned jurists or to the sermons of evangelic preachers.

They would also go to the halls and other places set aside for fencing, and there they would try their hands at all weapons, against the masters themselves, and would make it plain to the latter that they knew quite as much, and even more, about the art than did those whose trade it was.

In place of botanizing, they would visit the shops of the druggists, the herbalists, and the apothecaries, and would observe carefully the fruits, roots, leaves, gums, seeds, and foreign ointments, as well as the manner in which these were adulterated.

They would go see the jugglers, mountebanks, and quack-medicine vendors, observing their gestures, their tricks, their antics, and their persuasive chatter, especially those of Chauny in Picardy, for these latter are by nature great talkers and great windbags, when it comes to spinning a yarn about green monkeys and that sort of thing.

Returning for supper, they would eat more soberly than they did other days, and would consume food that was more desiccative and extenuating, in order that the intemperate humidity of the air, communicated to the body by an unavoidable propinquity, might be corrected by this means, and in order that they might not be any the worse from lack of that exercise to which they were accustomed.

This was Gargantua's program, and he kept it up from day to day, profiting by it, I would have you know, as much as any young fellow of his age could have done who was endowed with native good sense and who enjoyed the advantage of such continuous exercise. Although it seemed hard at first, it became, as he went on, so light, so pleasant, so altogether delightful, that it was more like a king's sport than a student's curriculum.

In order to relieve the intense mental strain, Ponocrates, once a month, would pick some clear, fine day, and they would leave the city early in the morning and go to Gentilly, or to Boulogne, or to Montrouge, or to Pont-de-Charenton, or to Vanves, or to Saint-Cloud. There they would spend the entire day in having the best time they could contrive, laughing, joking, drinking their fill, playing, singing, dancing, gamboling in some fine meadow, hunting sparrows' nests, catching quails, or fishing for frogs and crayfish.

But while this day was spent without books and formal readings, it was not spent without profit, for in the pleasant meadow, they would recite by heart certain charming verses of Vergil's *Georgics,* of Hesiod, or of Politian's *Rusticus,* and would compose a few amusing

Latin epigrams, and then would turn these into rondeaux
and ballads in the French language.

As they had their lunch, they would separate the water
from the wine—as Cato teaches, *De re rust.*, and as
Pliny also does—by means of an ivy goblet. They would
wash the wine in a basin full of water; then they would
draw it off with a funnel. They would pass the water
from one glass to another, and would construct a number
of little automatic devices, that is to say, such as worked
by themselves.

*"Apotherapy": a regime adapted to restoring or
nourishing the strength of the body; Rabelais borrows
the term from Galen. ——Nicolaus Leonicus Thomaeus
was an Italian humanist, author of a dialogue on the
game of dice,* Sannutus, sive de ludo talario, *published
at Lyon in 1532. ——The Greek scholar, Janus Lascaris, was librarian to François I. ——"Politian's Rusticus": a Latin poem composed by the fifteenth-century
Italian scholar, Angelo Poliziano, in imitation of Hesiod's*
Days *and Vergil's* Georgics.

IV. The Cake-Peddlers' War

(CHAPTERS XXV-XLI)

The episode that follows, which is the narrative core of the Gargantua, *or* Book First, *is now known to be based upon events, persons, and places in real life. This discovery is due to the researches of modern scholars, particularly those of Professor Abel Lefranc, and is supported not only by overwhelming internal evidence in the text, but by certain external documents as well. There would, in short, appear to be no doubt that the Cake-Peddlers' War represents the literary use which Rabelais made of a country quarrel between the squire of Lerné, Gaucher de Sainte-Marthe, and a faction headed by Maître François' lawyer father, Antoine Rabelais, the big man of the neighboring village of Seuilly. As Professor Lefranc puts it, this is "a peasants' dispute, followed by a brawl. . . . No detail, no remark, is invented: it is life itself. . . . Places are cited with a scrupulous precision. No element of fantasy intervenes up until the opening of hostilities. Rabelais has related for us a true adventure which undoubtedly took place at the moment of his arrival in the Chinon country, in the month of September. Everything leads us to believe that he had a first-hand acquaintance with the events he is describing. . . . Once again we have proof that Rabelais invents nothing out of whole cloth, but a precise fact or circumstance will be found underlying his most fanciful conceptions, and often the greater part of the accompanying details as well. At every instant we are able to verify this law of his mind, and I am sure that the more one scrutinizes his work, the better one will be able to see how this explanation accounts for his method of composition."*

Gaucher de Sainte-Marthe, the Picrochole of the story, belonged to an old and illustrious family; he was the owner of a number of estates, a royal councillor, and physician-in-ordinary to the King; he was also physician to the Abbess of Fontevrault and to the Constable Charles de Bourbon, and his son, Charles de Sainte-Marthe, became a distinguished court poet. He appears to have been a headstrong individual, capable of causing an entire community to rise up against him, which is the thing that happened, when, for his own pleasure and profit as a fisherman, he built a double row of stakes across the river Loire, thus seriously interfering with navigation. Nor is it strange that the litigating opposition should have been headed by Rabelais' father, who was a man of the law and the bigwig of the rival village.

The Picrocholine episode, however, is of broader interest in that it reveals to a large extent Rabelais' views on the subject of war. That he made a distinction between just and unjust wars, between defensive wars and wars of aggression, is clear; and it is equally clear, from this and other portions of his work, that he hated war as an institution. He also had his own ideas on the treatment of a conquered enemy, ideas that in his time were humane and progressive.

The Cake-Peddlers' War also introduces one of Rabelais' most delightful character creations: Friar John Hackem—not, alas! "Friar John of the funnels and gobbets," as Urquhart and other translators have it; for the monk's name in French, "Frère Jean des Entom-

meures," is connected with *entamure, a slice or gash, and
has reference to his battling disposition, not to his drinking capacity. It is practically certain that Friar John in
real life (he has a number of possible literary forbears)
was a monk of Seuilly and a dignitary of the abbey there.
This lovable character affords the author an opportunity
of depicting the slothful, ignorant, and anything but
ascetic life that was led by many of the monastics of his
day; and as he goes on, Rabelais makes it plain that if he
admires Friar John, it is on account of the latter's activity, because this is one monk who is not idle, but who
works and accomplishes something.*

How There Arose between the Cake-Peddlers of Lerné and Gargantua's Countrymen the Great Quarrel from Which Huge Wars Were to Spring

AT THAT time, which was the vintage season, at the beginning of autumn, the shepherds of the country were
engaged in guarding their vines, to prevent the starlings
from eating the grapes. And it was at this very time that
the cake-peddlers of Lerné happened to be passing along
the highway, with ten or a dozen loads of cakes, on their
way to the city. The shepherds thereupon courteously
requested the bakers' men to sell them a few cakes at
the market price.

And note right here that grapes and freshly-baked
cakes make a most heavenly breakfast, especially when
the grapes in question are black Burgundies, fig-grapes,
muscâdines, sour grapes or diarrhetic ones—these last,
for the benefit of those who are constipated in the belly,
for they make you squirt the length of a good long pole;

and frequently, when those who have eaten them think they are going to pass wind, they pass something else, and hence it is that such persons are known as "vintage-thinkers."

The cake-peddlers were by no means inclined to grant the shepherds' request, but (what was worse) proceeded to insult the latter terribly, calling them "scum of the earth, toothless bastards, red-headed rogues, chippy-chasers, filthy wretches of the kind that dung in the bed, big lubbers, sneaky curs, lazy hounds, pretty boys, pot-bellies, windjammers, good-for-nothings, clodhoppers, bad customers, greedy beggars, blowhards, mamma's darlings, monkey-faces, loafers, bums, big boobs, scoundrels, simpletons, silly jokers, dudes, teeth-chattering tramps, dirty cowherds, and dung-dripping shepherds," with other like defamatory epithets, adding that it was not for the likes of them to be eating these fine cakes, but that they ought to be satisfied with coarse, lumpy bread and big round loaves.

To these insults one of the shepherds named Forgier, a personable young lad with an excellent reputation, calmly replied as follows:

"Since when have you fellows begun to sprout horns that you're becoming so arrogant? I must say, you used to be glad enough to supply us, but now you refuse. That's not very neighborly; we don't do that to you when you come here to buy our good wheat to make your cakes. We would have been willing to let you have our grapes at the market price; but now, *mer Dé* and *merde,* you're going to be sorry for what you've done; you'll be hearing from us one of these days; we'll do the same thing to you, and then you'll remember."

Whereupon Marquet, major domo of the cake-merchants' confraternity, took him up:

" 'Pon my word, but you're certainly cocky this morning; you must have eaten too much millet last night. But come here, come here, I'll give you some of *my* cakes."

And so Forgier, thinking nothing of it, came up, drawing a ten-penny piece from his girdle, in the belief that Marquet was going to produce some cakes; but the latter, instead, lashed him with his whip across the legs, with so much force that you could see the welts. Marquet then started to run away, but Forgier yelled "Murder!" with all his might and, at the same time, hurled after his adversary a big club that he carried under his arm. The missile struck Marquet on the head, at the coronal suture, on the right side, under the crotaphite or temporal artery, causing him to tumble from his mare more dead than alive.

In the meantime, some farmers who were shelling nuts near by, came running up with their long poles and began beating the bakers' men as though they were threshing green rye. The other shepherds and their women folk, hearing Forgier's cries, came running also, with their slings and arm-shooters, and pursued the enemy with such a shower of stones that it was more like a hailstorm than anything else. They finally overtook the fugitives and proceeded to help themselves to four or five dozen cakes, being careful, however, to pay the customary price and giving the bakers, in addition, a hundred nuts and three basketfuls of white grapes. Then the bakers' men assisted Marquet, who was badly wounded, to mount again, and they all returned to Lerné, without keeping on to Parilly, cursing roundly and muttering dire threats against the cowherds, the shepherds, and the farmers of Seuilly and Cinais.

When the cake-peddlers were gone the shepherds and their lasses made merry with a fine lot of grapes and cakes. They had a gay time together to the pleasant music of the bagpipe, making great fun of those braggarts who had got the worst of it from having crossed themselves with the wrong hand that morning. And with the juice of large white and black grapes they massaged Forgier's legs so effectively that he was cured in no time at all.

Here we have the typical "incident" that starts a war. The places mentioned are all in the Chinon region. ——"On their way to the city": that is, to Chinon. ——Parilly is a hamlet in the neighborhood of Chinon (Indre-et-Loire). ——Cinais is a canton in the arrondissement of Chinon, to the northeast of La Devinière. ——The individuals, also, are close to life. There were inhabitants by the name of Forgier in the parishes of Cinais and Seuilly; one of them was a tenant of the Abbey of Seuilly from 1549-1556. Marquet has been identified as Michel Marquet, king's secretary in 1489 and receiver-general of Touraine, father of Marie Marquet, who was married in 1508 to Gaucher de Sainte-Marthe. ——"Arm-shooters": these "brassiers" were probably a kind of sling carried on the arm.

How the Inhabitants of Lerné, under the Command of Picrochole, Their King, Suddenly Assaulted Gargantua's Shepherds

WHEN the bakers' men had returned to Lerné, they at once, without stopping to eat or drink, betook themselves to the Capitol, and there, in the presence of their king, Picrochole, the third of that name, set forth their complaint, displaying their broken baskets, their bonnets in tatters, and their ripped cloaks, and telling how their cakes had been taken away from them; they also told how Marquet had been dangerously wounded, adding that all this had been done by Grandgousier's shepherds and tenant farmers, near the great highway on the other side of Seuilly.

Picrochole, beside himself, flew into a furious rage and, without pausing to think of the what or how, had them at once cry ban and arrière-ban throughout the country, commanding that each and every one, on pain of the noose, should assemble armed in the Great Square in front of the Castle, at the hour of noon.

In order the better to assure his enterprise, he had them beat the drum all around the town. He himself, while they were preparing his dinner, went to watch his artillery being mounted and his colors run up, and to see to it that his men had plenty of munitions, as well as armor and rations.

As he ate his dinner he distributed the commissions. In accordance with his orders Lord Raggedyass was put in charge of the advance-guard, which consisted of sixteen-thousand-fourteen arquebusiers and thirty-five-thousand-eleven volunteer infantrymen.

The Grand-Squire Braghard was placed in charge of the artillery, which included nine-hundred-fourteen big bronze pieces, in the form of cannons, double-cannons, basilisks, serpentines, culverins, siege-guns, falcons, or small cannon, light artillery, small culverins, and others.

The rear-guard was commanded by the Duke of Scratchpenny, while in the line of battle were the king and princes of the realm.

Thus summarily accoutred, they dispatched, before setting out, three hundred light-horse under the command of Captain Windbag, to reconnoiter the country and to see if there were any ambuscades round about. But after a diligent search the skirmishers found the

whole land silent and peaceful, without any assemblage
of any sort.

In the meanwhile, Picrochole had commanded them
to forward-march, each under his own standard. And
so, without any military order, their ranks in confusion,
they took the field, despoiling and laying waste everything that came in their way, sparing neither poor nor
rich, neither sacred place nor profane. They drove off
oxen, cows, bulls, calves, heifers, lambs, sheep, nanny-
goats and billy-goats, hens, capons, pullets, goslings,
ganders, geese, hogs, sows, and pigs. They knocked
down the nuts, picked the vines clean, carried off the
hedges, and shook all the fruit from the trees.

It was, in short, an indescribable havoc that they
wrought. They did not find a single person who offered
any resistance, but all, rather, threw themselves on the
enemy's mercy, begging to be treated humanely, in
view of the fact that they had always been good and
amiable neighbors, and that they never had committed
any outrage that would justify such mistreatment, adding that God would speedily punish their oppressors.
The only answer that Picrochole's men made to these
remonstrances was that they would teach them how to
eat cakes.

   *The name Picrochole literally means one who has a
choleric disposition (Greek: pikros, bitter, and cholos,
wrath); this accords with what is known of the temperament of Gaucher de Sainte-Marthe. ——"To the Capitol": to the seignorial château of Lerné.*

How a Monk of Seuilly Saved the Abbey Close from Being Sacked by the Enemy

THEY went on in this rowdy fashion, plundering and thieving, until they arrived at Seuilly, where they robbed both men and women and took whatever they could lay their hands on. Nothing was either too hot or too heavy for them. Although there were cases of the plague in most of the houses, they went in everywhere and carried off everything that was there. And not a single one of them caught the pestilence, which is quite a marvelous thing, for the curates, vicars, preachers, physicians, surgeons, and apothecaries who went to visit, treat, cure, preach, and administer to the sick all died of infection, while these devilish pillagers and murderers all escaped. How does that come, Gentlemen? Think it over, I beg of you.

When the town had been plundered in this manner they went on to the abbey, creating a horrible uproar; but they found it well locked and barred, whereupon the principal section of the army proceeded toward the Gué de Vède, with the exception of seven companies of foot-soldiers and two hundred lancers, who stayed and broke down the walls of the close, in order to lay waste the vineyard.

The poor devils of monks did not know which of their saints to call upon, but kept ringing the bell all the time, *ad Capitulum capitulantes:* "To the chapter meeting all those who have a voice there." It was decided that they should form a solemn procession, with appropriate chants and litanies, *contra hostium insidias,* against the wiles of the enemy, and with responses *pro pace,* or prayers for peace.

In the abbey, there happened to be at this time a

cloistered monk by the name of Friar John Hackem, young, gallant, spruce, good-natured, quite handy, bold, adventurous, level-headed, tall, lean, with a good chin and plenty of nose, a fine dispatcher of prayers and masses, an expert blinker of vigils—in short, a true monk, if ever there was one since this monking world of ours first monked a monkery. For the rest, he was a scholar to the teeth, in the matter of his breviary.

This friar, hearing the noise which the enemy was making in the close, went out to see what was doing and, perceiving that the vineyard on which a whole year's drinking depended was being ravished, he came back to the church where his brother monks were huddled, as frightened as a crew of bell-founders when they have broken their mold and spoiled the bell. He was just in time to hear them chanting: *Ini, nim, pe, ne, ne, ne, ne, ne, ne, tum, ne, num, num, ini, i, mi, i, mi, co, o, ne, no, o, o, ne, no, ne, no, no, rum, ne, num, num.*" ("*Impetum inimicorum ne timueritis*— Ye shall not fear the assault of the enemy," was what they were trying to sing.)

"That's a fine song and dance!" he exclaimed. "In the name of God, why don't you sing:

Farewell, baskets, the vintage is in?

I hope I go to the devil, if they're not in our close, hacking down so many grapes and vines that, by God, there won't be any pickings there for four years to come. St. James' belly! what are we going to drink in the meanwhile, we poor devils? O Lord God, *da mihi potum!* Give me something to drink!"

Then the prior of the cloister spoke up: "What's this drunkard doing here? Arrest him! To think of his disturbing divine service like this!"

"But," remonstrated the monk, "what about the wine service? Let's see that it is not disturbed; for you your-

self, Sir Prior, like to drink of the best there is, like any
decent fellow; for an honest man never hates good wine:
that's a monastic apothegm. But these responses you're
singing here are out of season, by God!

"Tell me, why is it our prayers are so short in time
of vintage and harvest and so long in Advent and all
through the winter? The late Friar Macé Pelosse of
blessed memory, a true supporter, damme, of our religion, once told me, as I recall, the reason was that in the
former season we press and make the wine, while in
winter we drink it.

"Listen, Gentlemen, all of you who like your wine,
follow me; for by Christ, may St. Anthony burn me up,
if those who haven't taken care of the vines are going
to drink the juice! God's belly! think of the Church's
property! Ha! no, no! The devil! St. Thomas, the Englishman, would have died for that; and if I die, shan't I
be a saint like him? But I'm not going to die; that's the
medicine I'm going to give them."

Saying this, he dropped his big robe and seized a staff
of the cross, made of the heart of a sorbapple-tree, long
as a lance, round, with a good grip, and decorated after
a fashion with fleurs-de-lis, almost all of which had been
rubbed off. Then he sallied forth, in a handsome cassock,
using his cowl for a scarf; and with the staff of the cross,
he proceeded to lay about him briskly on the heads of
the enemy, who, without any ranks, banner, trumpet or
drum, were engaged in despoiling the vineyard—for
the standard-bearers and color-bearers had laid their
standards and their colors against the wall, the drum-
mers had caved in one side of their drums in order to fill
their instruments with grapes; the trumpets were full of
vine-branches, and all was in confusion. Friar John came
down upon them so stiffly, without even shouting a
warning, that he bowled them over like pigs, slashing

this way and that, as in the old-fashioned mode of fencing.

He beat in some of their heads, broke the arms and legs of others, unjointed the neck-vertebrae of still others, dislocated the loins of others still, bashed in their noses, gouged out their eyes, split their jaw-bones, sunk their teeth in their chops, crushed their shoulder-blades, mangled their shins, unhinged their hips, and hewed to pieces the bones of their forearms and shanks. If any of them tried to hide in the thicket he broke their back-bones and tore them in two like dogs. If any tried to save themselves by flight, he stove their heads into bits, by way of the lambdoid suture. If any climbed a tree, thinking they would be safe there, he impaled them through the guts on his stick.

If any of his old acquaintances called to him: "Hey, there! Friar John, my friend, I surrender!" he would answer: "You're jolly well right, you do; but just the same, I'm going to send your soul to all the devils in hell!"

And then, he would give them a few quick knockout blows.

If, on the other hand, any were rash enough to stand up to him, he would display the strength of his muscles by running them through the chest, piercing the medias-tinum and the heart. Giving it to others under their shortribs, he would turn their stomachs upside down, so that they died at once. He would give a good wallop in the navel to others and make their guts pop out, while some he ran through the testicles, piercing their rump-guts.

You may take my word for it, it was the most horrible spectacle that was ever seen.

Some called on St. Barbara, others on St. George,

others on St. Touchmenot, others on Our Lady of Cunault, Our Lady of Loretto, Our Lady of Glad Tidings, Our Lady of Lenou, Our Lady of Rivière. Some made vows to St. James, some to the Holy Shroud of Chanbery (but it was burned up, three months afterward, so thoroughly that not a stitch of it was saved), others to the relic of Cadouin, to St. John of Angely, to St. Eutropius of Saintes, to St. Mexme of Chinon, to St. Martin of Candes, to St. Cloud of Cinais, to the relics of Javarzay, and to a myriad other good little saints.

Some died without speaking, others spoke without dying; some died while they spoke, others spoke while they died. Others cried out, in a loud voice: "Confession! Confession! *Confiteor, Miserere, In manus!*"

So great was the outcry of the wounded that the Prior of the Abbey, with all his monks, came sallying forth. When they saw the poor devils lying among the vines and wounded to the point of death, they began confessing some of them. While the priests were thus busied, the little monklings ran up to the place where Friar John was, inquiring what he wanted them to do to help him. He told them to slit the throats of those on the ground. And so, laying their capes on the nearest arbor, they began finishing off the ones he already had done in. Should you like to know with what implements? With those small-bladed knives with which the little children of our country are in the habit of opening walnuts.

Then Friar John with his staff of the cross went over to the breach which the enemy had made. Some of the monklings carried the colors and standards into their rooms to make garters out of them. But when those of the enemy who had been confessed wanted to escape through the breach, the Friar belabored them with blows, saying:

"These fellows have confessed and repented and have won pardons, and so, they're going to heaven, straight as a sickle, or as the road to Faye."

Thus, by Friar John's prowess, that whole section of the army which had entered the close was routed, to the number of thirteen-thousand-six-hundred-twenty-two, without counting the women and children, that's always understood. Maugis, the hermit, did not conduct himself so valiantly with his pilgrim's staff against the Saracens—the Maugis whose exploits are related along with the deeds of the four sons of Aymon—as did this monk, that day he met the enemy with a staff of the cross.

"Gué de Vède": a hamlet of a few houses east of La Devinière, so named from the ford (gué) at that point. ——Friar John, it will be noted, is "lean" (maigre); he does not have the figure commonly associated with a gormandizing monk. ——"A fine dispatcher of prayers and masses . . . blinker of vigils": capable of getting them over in a hurry, or in the blink of an eye. ——"The late Friar Macé Pelosse": this individual has not been identified; he may be the "Parson Matthew" (Prebstre Macé) mentioned in the "Remarks of the Drunkards" passage. ——"St. Thomas, the Englishman": St. Thomas à Becket, Archbishop of Canterbury. ——"The road to Faye": this road, in the Chinon region, was rocky and winding, due to the elevated situation of the town; there is also a play on Faye and foye (foi), faith, that is to say, the path of the faith, or the road to heaven. ——"The four sons of Aymon": allusion to a romance of chivalry, the Histoire des Quatre Fils Aymon, printed about 1480.

How Picrochole Assaulted La Roche-Clermault, and Grandgousier's Regrets and Difficulties in Undertaking a War

WHILE the monk was skirmishing, in the manner we have described, against those who had entered the close, Picrochole, in great haste, was passing the Gué de Vède with his followers and was assailing La Roche-Clermault, at which place he met with no resistance whatsoever. Since it was already dark, he decided to put himself and his men up in that town for the night, and to seek there a little relief from the bad humor that was gnawing him.

In the morning, he assaulted the outer bastions and the castle and proceeded to fortify them thoroughly, stocking them with the requisite munitions, with the idea of making a stand there, in case he should be attacked, since the position was a strong one, both naturally, owing to its situation, and artificially.

Let us leave them there now and return to our friend, Gargantua, who is at Paris, wholly intent upon his literary studies and athletic exercises, and to that good old man, Grandgousier, his father, who, after supper, is warming his balls at a great clear fire and, while waiting for the chestnuts to roast, is writing on the hearth with the burnt end of a stick that is used to poke the fire, relating, as he does so, charming tales of days gone by, for the benefit of his wife and family.

At this moment, one of the shepherds who was guarding his vineyards, a fellow called Pillot, came to Grandgousier and told the latter the whole story of the outrages and pillagings which Picrochole, king of Lerné, was committing in his, Grandgousier's, territory and dominions, and how Picrochole had plundered, sacked, and laid waste the whole country, with the exception of the Close of Seuilly which Friar John Hackem had saved for his sovereign's sake; and how, finally, at that very moment, Picrochole was in La Roche-Clermault, and was there engaged in fortifying himself and his men with all speed.

"Alas! alas!" exclaimed Grandgousier. "What is this, my good folks?" Am I dreaming, or is this the truth they're telling me? So Picrochole, my old, old friend, bound to me by race and treaty, would attack me, would he? Who has put him up to this? Who is behind it? Who has advised him to do it? Oh! Oh! Oh! Oh! My God! My Savior! Help me, inspire me, counsel me what to do! I protest, I swear to Thee—even as I implore Thine assistance!—that I have never done anything to displease Picrochole, nor done any harm to his people, nor have I, at any time, pillaged his lands; but quite the contrary, I have aided him with men, money, influence, and advice on every occasion when I knew how to be of service to him. And to think that he now should commit such an outrage against me—why, it can only be the Evil One that makes him do it. O Thou good God! Thou knowest my courage, for from Thee nothing is hidden. If it is simply that he has suddenly gone mad, and that Thou hast sent me to restore him to his senses, do Thou, then, give me both the strength and the wisdom to bring him once more under the yoke of Thy holy will, through proper discipline.

"Oh! Oh! Oh! my good folks, my friends and faithful servants, must I embarrass you by calling upon you to aid me in this matter? Alas! my old age now desires only repose, and all my life long I have sought nothing so much as peace; but I perceive that I must once more weight down my tired and feeble old shoulders with a warrior's harness and take the lance and mace in my trembling hand, in order to rescue my poor subjects and assure their safety. That is only reasonable, after all, since by their labor I am supported and by their sweat I am nourished, I, my children, and my family.

"Nevertheless, I shall not undertake a war until I have tried out all the arts and means of peace: on that, I am resolved."

And then, he summoned his council and laid the matter before them, just as it stood. It was decided that some prudent man should be sent to Picrochole, to find out why the latter had thus suddenly broken the peace, and why he had invaded territories to which he could lay not the slightest claim. In addition, a messenger was to be dispatched to Gargantua and his companions, so that they might be able to help maintain peace and defend their country in its hour of need. Grandgousier approved all these decisions and commanded that they be put into effect. He accordingly, that very hour, sent his Basque lackey to find Gargantua, as speedily as possible; and the old man sat down and wrote his son as follows:

The Tenor of the Letter Which Grandgousier Wrote to Gargantua

THE intensity of your studies makes it advisable that, for some time to come, I should not disturb that philosophical leisure of yours; and I should not be doing so now, if the confidence I had reposed in my old friends and former confederates had not played me false and, thus, imperiled the security of my old age. But since it appears to be my fatal destiny to be put out by those in whom I have trusted most, it becomes necessary for me to sum-

mon you back to help defend the people and the inheritance that by natural right have been intrusted to you.

For just as arms on the outside are weak, if there is
not good counsel inside the house, so study and good
training are futile, if, at the opportune moment, they are
not put into execution and effect by Virtue.

My plan is not to provoke, but to appease; not to attack, but to defend; not to make conquests, but to guard
my faithful subjects and hereditary dominions, which
dominions Picrochole, without just cause or occasion, has
hostilely entered. From day to day, he goes on with his
mad enterprise, committing excesses that are intolerable
to any free-born man.

I have taken it upon myself as a duty to moderate his
tyrannic wrath, offering him all that I thought might
reasonably content him. I have sent to him a number of
times, to find out in what, by whom, or in what manner
he felt that he had been insulted, but I have received
from him no response beyond a wilful defiance, along
with the statement that the only right he claimed in my
lands was his own advantage. By this, I know that the
eternal God has abandoned him to the direction of his
own free will and his senses, which are always worth-
less when not constantly guided by Divine Grace. And
so, I cannot help feeling that, under an ill sign, he has
been sent to me that I might put him in his place and
bring him back to reason.

Therefore, my well-loved son, as soon as you have read
this letter return as quickly as you can, not so much to
aid me (a debt you owe by nature) as to succor your
own people, who are, by reason, yours to safeguard and
protect. The whole thing shall be done with as little
spilling of blood as may be; and if it is possible, by more
expedient means, through the precautions and the ruses

of war, we shall save every soul of them and send them all back happy to their firesides.

My very dear son, may the peace of Christ, our Redeemer, be with you. My greetings to Ponocrates, Gymnastes, and Eudemon.

The twentieth of September,

Your father,

GRANDGOUSIER.

How Ulrich Gallet Was Sent to Picrochole

THE letter having been dictated and signed, Grandgousier commanded that Ulrich Gallet, his Master of Requests, a man wise and discreet whose virtue and good sense he had tested under a number of contentious circumstances, should go to Picrochole, to lay before the latter the sense of the council.

That very hour the worthy Gallet set out. Having crossed the ford, he inquired of the miller concerning Picrochole's activities; whereupon he learned that the soldiers had left the miller neither cock nor hen, and that they were fortified in La Roche-Clermault. The miller advised him not to go any further, from fear of the sentries, for they were in a very bad humor, he said. Gallet could easily believe this; and so, for that night, he slept at the miller's house.

The next morning he betook himself with his trumpet to the gate of the castle, and there requested the guards to permit him to speak with the king, inasmuch as he had something to say which it was to His Majesty's advantage to hear.

When these words had been repeated to the king, the latter refused to allow his men to open the gate to the

messenger, but going up on the ramparts, he called down
to the ambassador:

"Well, what's new? What have you to say?"

Then the ambassador spoke as follows:

*There was at Chinon a Jean Gallet, king's counsel and
relative and colleague of Rabelais' father.*

Gallet's Speech to Picrochole

No MORE just cause of grief can arise among human
beings than when, from a quarter from which they might
rightfully have hoped for grace and benevolence, they
receive only hurt and harm. And it is not without good
cause (even though it may be without good reason) that
many persons under such circumstances find an in-
dignity of this sort less tolerable than the loss of their
lives; and in cases where by force or other means they
have not been able to correct such a state of affairs, they
even have ended by depriving themselves of the light of
life.

Hence, it is not in the least strange if King Grandgousier, my master, upon learning of your mad and
hostile invasion, has been greatly displeased and finds
it all very hard to understand. The wonder would be if
he had not been moved by the incomparable excesses
which you and your followers have committed in his
land and among his subjects; for you have not failed, in
any instance, to set an example of utter inhumanity. No
human being can know how all this pains him, on account of the heart-felt affection with which he always
has cherished his subjects. It is beyond human compre-
hension to understand how grieved he is and the more

so that all these sorrows should have been caused him,
and all these wrongs done him, by you and yours, who,
as far back as the mind of man can remember, have been
bound by the ties of friendship, you and your fathers, to
him and to his ancestors. This bond, up to the present,
has been looked upon as sacred, having been inviol-
ably maintained, guarded, and watched over—so well
guarded that not only his own people, but even foreign
nations, such as the Poitevins, Bretons, the inhabitants
of Le Maine, and those who dwell beyond the Canary
Islands and Isabella have been of the opinion, in the
past, that it would be as easy to demolish the firmament
and to rear the abysses above the clouds as it would be
to sunder your alliance; and they have so feared that
alliance, in the enterprises they have undertaken, that
they have never dared provoke, irritate, or damage one
of you, from fear of the other.

But there is more to be said. This sacred friendship
of yours has so echoed to heaven that there are very few
today, inhabiting the Continent or the islands of the
ocean, who have not, ambitiously, aspired to be received
into that pact, upon your own conditions, respecting
your confederation as highly as they do their own lands
and dominions. As a result, as far back as can be remembered, there has not been any prince or league so
mad or so proud as to dare invade, I will not say your
own territories, but even those of your allies. And if,
acting upon ill-considered advice, any of them have
formed any new plans of encroachment, the very name
of your alliance, repeated in their hearing, has been
sufficient, at once, to dissuade them from their designs.

What madness is it, then, that now leads you, thus
summarily breaking off this alliance and trampling all
the bonds of friendship under foot, contrary to all lawful rights—what is it leads you, in this hostile manner,

to invade these territories of your former ally, without having been in any manner endamaged, irritated, or provoked by him? Where is good faith? Where is law? Where is reason? Where is your humanity? Where is your fear of God? Do you think that such an outrage as this can remain hidden from the eternal mind of a Sovereign God, who is the just retributor of all our enterprises? If you think so, you are wrong, for all things come before His judgment.

Is it your own fatal destiny or the influence of the stars which impels you, in this manner, to abandon your ease and repose? Thus do all things have a period and a close; and when they have reached a certain superlative point they fall in ruins, for they cannot long remain at such a point. Such is the end of those who have not learned, by reason and temperance, to moderate their own good fortune and prosperity.

But if it has been predestined that your happiness and repose should now come to an end, must it be through your inconveniencing my king, by whom you were set up? If your house must fall in ruins, must it be on the fireside of the one who erected it? The thing is so beyond the bounds of all reason, so abhorrent to common sense that it hardly can be conceived by human understanding; and those in foreign lands will find it incredible, until the outcome of the event makes it plain to them that there is nothing any longer holy or sacred to those who once have freed themselves from God and reason, in order to follow their own perverse inclinations.

If any wrong had been done by us to your subjects or your dominions, if we had shown any favor to your enemies, if in all things we had not aided you, if your good name or your honor had been injured by us, or, to state it better, if the spirit of the devil, tempting you to evil, had, by means of fallacious appearances and deceit-

ful visions, put it into your head that we had done things
not worthy of our ancient friendship toward you—then
you ought first to have made inquiries as to the truth of
these things, after which you should have admonished
us, and we would have seen to it that you had the utmost
satisfaction.

But O eternal God! what is the object of this undertaking of yours? Would you, like a perfidious tyrant, thus
pillage and lay waste my master's realm? Have you
found him so ignorant and so stupid that he would not,
or so destitute of men, money, and counsellors in the
art of war that he could not, resist your unjust assault?
Leave here at once; and by tomorrow see to it that you
shall have retired for good into your own territory, without causing any trouble or disturbance along the way.
Moreover, pay a thousand bezants in gold for the damage you have done in this land. Half of it shall be paid
tomorrow; the rest you may pay at the next Ides of May,
leaving with us, in the meanwhile, for hostages, the
Dukes of Windmill, Dragass, and Riffraff, together with
Prince Scratchemhard and Viscount Lousy.

*In the light of mid-twentieth-century events, this pas-
sage has rather a weirdly contemporary sound—do we
not have here the ruthless, power-mad aggressor and his
acts of atrocity, the confederation or league to halt aggression and preserve the peace, the principle of liberty
or death in the face of aggression, and, finally, the rep-
arations to be inflicted upon the aggressor? That Rabelais was opposed in principle to wars of conquest and
that he believed in the virtue of a defensive alliance of
nations by way of preventing them, would seem to be
fairly obvious; for this is another serious-minded passage.
If the author at the end gives play to his humor, in the*

*names bestowed upon Picrochole's hostages, this, as
M. Lazare Sainéan points out, is to indicate the un-
savory character of that sovereign's advisers.*

*"Foreign nations such as the Poitevins, Bretons, the
inhabitants of Le Maine": an allusion to the victory of
Charles VIII, at Saint-Aubin-de-Cormier, in 1488, and
the annexation of Brittany to France.* ——*"Isabella":
the first city built by Europeans in America, founded
by Columbus in Hispaniola, or Haiti, in 1493.* ——*"A
thousand bezants": the bezant was a Byzantine coin, of
gold or silver, widely used in France in the twelfth and
thirteenth centuries; it varied in value between the English sovereign and half-sovereign.*

Picrochole's only response to Grandgousier's message,
as delivered by Ulrich Gallet, was: "Come and take
them," this being the reply of Leonidas to Xerxes, when
the latter called upon him to lay down his arms. He also
kept muttering something about some cakes. When this
was reported to Grandgousier, that monarch, in a further
effort to avert hostilities, ordered an investigation to be
made to ascertain precisely what had happened between the bakers' men and his own people. Upon learning that four or five dozen cakes had been taken by his
subjects, he commanded that five cartloads be given in
restitution and that a wagon-load of cakes be presented
to the injured Marquet, along with a sum of money "to
pay the barbers who had dressed his wounds" and a perpetual freehold in a certain farm. Gallet was then dispatched to carry out these orders; but Picrochole, on the
advice of Captain Braghard, merely seized the cakes and
the money, the oxen and the carts, and sent the envoys
back with a warning not to come again.

How Certain of Picrochole's Officers by Their Hasty Advice Put Him in Extreme Peril

AFTER the cakes had been taken, there appeared before Picrochole the Duke of Riffraff, Count Bullybluster, and Captain Smeartail. They said to him:

"Sire, today we are going to make you the happiest, most chivalrous prince that ever was, since the death of Alexander of Macedon."

"Put on your hats, gentlemen, put on your hats," said Picrochole.

"Many thanks," said they. "Sire, we have only come to do our duty. This, then, is what we have to suggest: that you should leave here, in the garrison, a captain with a small company to guard the place—for it impresses us as being quite strong enough, both by natural situation and by reason of the fortifications which you have erected—and then, that you should divide your army in two, as you could do, very cleverly. One part will then go to fall upon Grandgousier and his followers. He's sure to be easily routed at the very first skirmish. There you will get piles of money, for the old miser has it and to spare. Old miser, we said, for the reason that a true prince never has a sou. To hoard up money is a miserly trick.

"The other part of your army, in the meanwhile, will march on Aunis, Saintonge, Angoumois, and Gascony, as well as Périgord, Médoc, and Landes. Without resistance, you will take towns, castles, and fortresses. At Bayonne, Saint-Jean-de-Luz, and Fuenterrabia, you will seize all the ships and coast down toward Galicia and Portugal, plundering all the maritime places as far down as Lisbon, where you will find waiting for you all the reinforcements that a conqueror needs. Holy Christ! Spain will surrender right enough, for they're nothing but a lot of clodhoppers. You will pass through the Seville Strait, and there you will erect two columns, more magnificent than those of Hercules, to the perpetual memory of your name. And that strait shall be called the Picrocholine Sea. Having passed through the Picrocholine Sea, what do you think? Barbarossa will be your slave——"

"I'll show him mercy," said Picrochole.

"That is all very well," said they, "providing he's willing to be baptized. And then, you will take the realms of Tunis, Bizerta, Algiers, Bône, Cyrene, and all Barbary, in short. Passing on, you will take possession of the Majorca and Minorca Islands, Sardinia, Corsica, and the other islands of the Balearic Sea and the Gulf of Genoa. Coasting along to your left, you will overcome the whole of Provence and the seacoast of Gaul, Genoa, Florence, Lucca, and then—good-by, Rome! That poor Monsignor, the Pope, will die of fright.

"'Pon my word," said Picrochole, "I'm not going to kiss his slipper."

"Next you take Italy, then Naples, Calabria, Apulia, and Sicily, sacking them all, and Malta along with them. All I hope is, those jolly Knights that used to be at Rhodes try to resist you. I'd just like to see the color of their urine!"

"I shouldn't mind going to Loretto," said Picrochole.

"No, no," said they, "that'll be on the way back. From there, you will take Candia, Cyprus, Rhodes, and the Cyclades, and fall on Morea. St. Ninian! It's ours already! God help Jerusalem! for the Sultan can't stand up to you for a minute."

"I," said Picrochole, "will rebuild Solomon's Temple."

"Not yet," said they, "wait a minute. Never be so sudden about your plans. Do you know what Octavianus Augustus says? *Festina lente.* Hasten slowly. First, you want to take Asia Minor, Caria, Lycia, Pamphylia, Cilicia, Lydia, Phrygia, Mysia, Bithynia, Carrasia, Adalia, Samagaria, Kastamuni, Luga, Sebasta, and everything to the Euphrates."

"Shall we see Babylon and Mount Sinai?" inquired Picrochole.

"There's no need of that at this time," said they. "Isn't it enough trouble to have crossed the Hircanian Sea and to have straddled the two Armenias and the three Arabias?"

"Good Lord!" cried Picrochole, "we're out of our senses! We're done for!"

"What's the matter?" said they.

"What are we going to drink in those deserts? For Julian Augustus and his whole army died there of thirst, if what they say is true."

"We've taken care of everything," said they. "By way of the Syrian Sea, you will have nine-thousand-fourteen great ships, loaded down with the best wine in the world. They will have come in at Jaffa. There they will have found twenty-two-hundred-thousand camels and sixteen hundred elephants, which you will have taken in a hunt near Sidjilmassa, when you first entered Libya. In addition, you shall have the whole caravan of Mecca. Won't that be enough to keep you in wine?"

"Well," said he, "but it won't be fresh."

"Gods and little fishes!" said they. "A bold conqueror like you, who pretends and aspires to the empire of the universe, can't always have things just so! You ought to thank God that you and your men have come through, safe and sound, as far as the Tigris River."

"But," said Picrochole, "that part of our army that is routing that old toper, Grandgousier—what are they doing all this time?"

"They've not been asleep," was the reply. "We're going to meet up with them very soon. They've taken Brittany for you, Normandy, Flanders, Hainaut, Brabant, Artois, Holland, and Zeeland. They have crossed the Rhine, over the bellies of the Swiss and the Lansquenets, and one wing has conquered Luxembourg, Lorraine, Champagne, and Savoy, all the way to Lyon. There they found your troops returning from the naval conquest of the Mediterranean Sea, and they have reassembled in Bohemia, after having sacked Swabia, Würtemburg, Bavaria, Austria, Moravia, and Styria. Then they have swooped down on Lübeck, Norway, Sweden, Denmark, Gothland, Greenland, and the Hanseatics, all the way to the Arctic Sea. This done, they have conquered the Orkney Islands and subjugated Scotland, England, and Ireland. Sailing from there, by way of the Sandy Sea and Sarmatia, they have conquered Prussia, Poland, Lithuania, Russia, Wallachia, Transylvania and Hungary, Bulgaria, Turkey—and there they are at Constantinople!"

"Let's go join 'em right away," said Picrochole, "for I want to be emperor of the Trebizond, too. Aren't we going to kill off all those Turkish and Mohammedan dogs?"

"What the devil else should we do?" said they. "And you will give their lands and goods to those who have served you faithfully."

"That's only reasonable," said Picrochole. "That's only justice. I hereby make you a present of Carmania, Syria, and the whole of Palestine."

"Ha! Sire," said they, "that's very decent of you. Many thanks. May God prosper you always."

Now there happened to be, among those present, a certain old gentleman who had had considerable experience in enterprises of various sorts, a true old warhorse by the name of Echephron. Hearing these remarks, he spoke up and said:

"I'm very much afraid that all this is like the farce of the jug of milk and the shoemaker who dreamed that he was rich. Then the jug broke, and he woke up—without any dinner. What do you expect to get by all these great conquests? What will be the outcome of all your toil and trouble?"

"It will be," said Picrochole, "that we shall be able to come back, sit down, and take it easy."

To this, Echephron replied:

"And in case you never come back? For it's a long and dangerous journey you're embarking on. Wouldn't it be better to take it a little easy right now, without running into all these dangers?"

"Oh!" put in Bullybluster, "here's a nice one for you, by God! I suppose we ought to hide in the chimney-corner and spend all the rest of our lives with the women-folk, stringing pearls or spinning, like Sardanapalus.

> Who neither adventures
> Horse nor mule,
> Says Solomon——"

"Who adventures too much,"

said Echephron,

> "Loses horse and mule,
> Marcoul replied."

"Enough!" exclaimed Picrochole, "let us proceed. I fear nothing except those devilish legions of Grand-gousier's. What if, while we're in Mesopotamia, they should fall upon our tail? What would we do then?"

"That's all right," said Smeartail. "A little order which you'll send to the Muscovites will bring you, in a minute, four-hundred-fifty-thousand picked soldiers. Oh, if you would only make me your lieutenant, I'd kill a comb for a drygoods-merchant! I'd bite 'em, I'd fall on 'em, I'd strike 'em, I'd catch 'em, I'd kill 'em, I'd do for 'em."

"Hurry up! Hurry up!" said Picrochole, "let's be going. And let him that loves me follow me!"

Rabelais in the above passage drew inspiration from the conversation of Pyrhhus and Cineas in Plutarch's Life of Pyrrhus, *and from the dialogue of Lucian entitled* Navigium seu Vota. *This chapter might almost be a satire on the visions of modern would-be world conquerors and their advisers—even to the "Picrocholine Sea," or "mare nostrum"!*

"Those jolly Knights that used to be at Rhodes": the Knights of St. John of Jerusalem, who were driven out of the Island of Rhodes by Solyman II, in 1522; the Emperor Charles V set them up in the Island of Malta, in 1530. ——"Samagaria . . . Luga": these two places are unknown. ——"The two Armenias and the three Arabias": Great and Little Armenia; Arabia Deserta, Arabia Felix, and Arabia Petraea. ——"The Sandy Sea": probably the Baltic. ——The verses quoted are from the Dialogues of Salomon and Marcoul, *a highly popular work in the Middle Ages; in these dialogues the wisdom of Solomon is set over against the jocular reflections of a man of the people who is an incarnation of good common sense.*

Upon receiving Grandgousier's letter, Gargantua at once set out from Paris. On the advice of an old friend and ally, the Lord of Vauguyon, Gymnastes was sent

*ahead to reconnoiter the enemy. Having fallen in with
a detachment under command of one Captain Bumper,
the young squire discomfited Picrochole's men by performing a number of acrobatic feats upon his horse,
thereby convincing them that he was a devil out of hell.
He ended by slaying Captain Bumper and massacring
his followers, after which he returned to make his report
to Gargantua.*

How Gargantua Demolished the Castle of Gué de Vède, and How They Crossed the Ford

WHEN Gymnastes returned, he informed Gargantua and
his followers of the state in which he had found the
enemy, and of the trick which he, all alone, had played
on the whole mob of them, adding that the foe was but
a lot of rascals, pillagers, and brigands, ignorant of all
military discipline, and that the best thing to do was
boldly to proceed against them at once, as it would be
a very easy matter to knock them all in the heads like
beasts.

Then it was, Gargantua mounted his big mare and
set out, accompanied by the persons we have mentioned above. And finding in his path a great tall tree
(one commonly known as St. Martin's Tree for the
reason that it had grown from a pilgrim's staff which
St. Martin formerly had planted there) he remarked:

"The very thing I needed. This tree will make me a
staff and a lance, at the same time."

With no effort whatever he wrenched it from the earth
and, removing the branches, trimmed it down to suit his
purpose.

In the meanwhile, his mare was making water to

relieve her belly; and she made so much that she created a deluge for seven leagues around, and all the urine flowed down to the Gué de Vède, until the ford became so swollen with the current that the enemy's entire band was drowned in most horrible fashion, with the exception of a few who had taken the road toward the hills, at the left.

Gargantua, having come to the Wood of Vède, was advised by Eudemon that a remnant of the enemy had taken refuge inside the castle. To make sure of this, Gargantua cried out, at the top of his voice:

"Are you there, or aren't you? If you are there, out with you; if you're not there, that's all I have to say."

A certain dastardly cannoneer who was stationed at the machicolation at that moment fired a cannon-ball at Gargantua, dealing the latter a furious blow on the right temple; but Gargantua never noticed it, any more than if he had been hit by a plum.

"What's that?" he asked. "Are you throwing grape-seed at us? That's a vintage that is going to cost you dear."

For he really thought that the cannon-ball was a grape-seed.

Those who were inside the castle, and who had been busy with their plunderings, hearing the noise, now came running to the towers and fortifications; and from there, they fired more than nine-thousand-twenty-five rounds with the small cannons and arquebuses, aiming them all straight at Gargantua's head. The fusillade came so thick and fast that Gargantua exclaimed:

"Ponocrates, my friend, these flies will blind me yet; reach me one of those willow-boughs to chase them away."

For he thought the lead balls and artillery-stones were ox-flies.

Ponocrates then informed him that these "flies" were nothing other than rounds of artillery that were being fired from the castle. Thereupon, Gargantua proceeded to shake his big tree against the castle, and with great blows, he laid low towers and fortifications and brought the whole structure tumbling to the ground. By this means, all those inside were crushed and broken to bits.

Leaving this place, they came to the mill-bridge, and there found the whole ford filled with dead bodies, piled so high they had choked the mill-race. These were the bodies of the ones who had perished in the urinal flood from Gargantua's mare. As they stood there, deliberating how they were going to cross over, in view of the obstructing cadavers, Gymnastes remarked:

"If the devils have crossed I surely can!"

"The devils," remarked Eudemon, "have crossed in order to carry off the souls of the damned."

"St. Ninian!" exclaimed Ponocrates. "Then, as a necessary consequence, he *will* cross."

"That I will," said Gymnastes, "or else stay right here where I am!"

And spur to his horse, he passed over clean, without his nag's being the least bit frightened by the dead bodies. For Gymnastes had trained his steed, according to the teaching of Aelian, not to fear either souls or dead bodies. He had done this, not by slaying people, as Diomedes slew the Thracians, and as Ulysses placed the bodies of his enemies under his horses' feet (so Homer tells us), but by putting a dummy in the hay of his horse's stall and making the animal walk over this when he fed him his oats.

The three others followed without any mishap, except for Eudemon, whose mount sank its right foot up to the knee in the paunch of a big fat rascal who was lying drowned, on his backside. The horse was unable to get his foot out, and remained impaled there, until Gargantua, with the end of his stick, pushed the rest of the fellow's guts into the water, the horse, in the meanwhile, lifting its foot out. And (a marvelous thing in veterinary science) the animal, from having touched the bowels of that big lout, was cured of a splint which it had in that foot.

"Artillery-stones": stones hurled by certain machines of war. ——*"According to the teaching of Aelian":* Aelian (De Natura Animalium, xvi, 25, *and* De Equorum apud Persos Disciplina) *quotes Homer as to the methods of Diomedes and Ulysses, contrasting the custom of the Persians, who placed straw mannikins under their horses' hoofs.*

How Gargantua, in Combing His Hair, Combed Out Cannon-Balls

HAVING left the banks of the Vède behind them, it was not long until they arrived at Grandgousier's castle, where the old man was waiting for them with great impatience. Upon their arrival, they were met with open arms. You never in your life saw folks any happier than they were. The *Supplementum Supplementi Chronicorum* states that Gargamelle thereupon died of joy. So far as I am concerned, I know nothing about this, and care still less, about her or any other female.

It is the truth that I am telling you now: Gargantua, having brushed up his clothes a bit, had started to smooth back his hair with his comb (which was a hundred reeds in size, furnished with large, whole elephant-teeth), when, at each stroke, there fell out more than seven bales of cannon-balls, which had lodged there at the demolition of the Wood of Vède. Perceiving this, Grandgousier, his father, thought they were lice, and said to him:

"Well, well, my good lad, so you've brought us some of those sparrow-hawks of Montaigu, have you? It was not my intention to put you in school there."

At this, Ponocrates spoke up:

"My Lord, don't think for a minute that I've had him in college of lice called Montaigu. I'd rather enroll him among the beggars of Saint Innocent's, when I think of the enormous cruelty and vile treatment which I know is to be found in that institution; for convicts among the Moors and Tartars, murderers in criminal prison—even, I might say, the very dogs in your house—are better off than are the poor devils in that college. And if I were king of Paris, may the devil take me, if I wouldn't set fire to it and burn up principal and regents who permit such inhumanity to be practiced in front of their very eyes."

Then, picking up one of the balls, he added:

"These are cannon-shot which your son, Gargantua, just missed receiving, from the hands of your traitorous enemies, as he went through the Wood of Vède. But they were suitably punished; all perished in the ruins of the castle, as the Philistines did through the genius of Samson, and as those did who were crushed by the Tower of Siloam, according to what we read in *Luke. xiii.* It is my opinion that we ought to follow them up now while the time is ripe. For Opportunity has all her hair on the front of her head. Once she has passed, you cannot recall her. She is bald at the back of her head and she never, never returns."

"But," said Grandgousier, "we shan't do that just now; for I have made up my mind to give you this evening a banquet of welcome."

As he said this, the servants set about preparing the supper. As extra fare, they roasted sixteen oxen, three heifers, thirty-two calves, sixty-three milk-kids, ninety-five sheep, three hundred young suckling pigs, with fine must-sauce, two-hundred-twenty partridges, seven hundred woodcocks, four hundred capons from the country of Loudun and of Cornouailles, six thousand hens and as many pigeons, six hundred fattened pullets, fourteen hundred young hare, three-hundred-three bustards, and one-thousand-seven-hundred young capons. As for game, that was not so readily to be had, with the exception of eleven wild boars, sent by the Abbot of Turpenay, and eighteen fallow-deer, a gift of Lord Grandmont, together with one-hundred-forty pheasants which Lord Essards sent, along with a few dozen woodpigeons, river-fowl, teals, bitterns, curlews, plovers, francolins, brants, red-shanks, young lapwings, sheldrakes, spoonbills, spotted herons, young herons, water-hens, white herons, storks, lesser bustards, orange-colored flamingoes (that is *phoenicopteres*), beach-swallows, turkey-hens, as well as a quantity of couscous and a plentiful supply of soup.

In short, there was an abundance of food of all sorts, very worthily prepared by Lickgravy, Shakepot, and Squeezejuice, Grandgousier's cooks, while Johnny, Mickey, and Bumperclean saw to it that the drinks kept coming.

"Supplementum Supplementi Chronicorum": *the Supplement to the Supplement of the Chronicles, a work that existed only in Rabelais' imagination.* ——"I know

nothing about this and care still less": this has been seen
as one of the evidences of Maître François' anti-feminist
attitude. ——"*The beggars of Saint Innocent's"*: the
Cemetery of the Innocents in Paris, situated near Les
Halles and one of the oldest in the city, was noted for
its mendicants. ——"*From the country of Loudun and
of Cornouailles"*: Loudun, famed for its capons, is in the
Chinon region; Cornouailles is in lower Brittany. ——
"*The Abbot of Turpenay"*: the Abbey of Turpenay, of
the Order of St. Benedict, was in the district of Chinon.

How Gargantua Ate Six Pilgrims in a Salad

IT IS proper that we relate here what happened to the six
pilgrims who came from Saint-Sébastien, near Nantes
and who, from fear of the enemy, had taken refuge that
night in the garden, hiding themselves under the pea-
stalks, among the cabbages and lettuce.

Gargantua, feeling a trifle dry, inquired if they could
not get him a little lettuce to make a salad. And I am
telling you that they had the finest and the biggest
lettuce in the country, for the plants were as large as
plum or walnut trees. Gargantua decided that he would
go look for himself, which he did, bringing away with
him, in his hand, as much as he thought he wanted. At
the same time, he carried off the six pilgrims, who were
so terrified that they did not dare either to speak or to
cough.

As he first washed the leaves off at the fountain, the
pilgrims said to one another, in a low voice:

"What are we going to do? We'll drown here, among
all this lettuce. Shall we speak up? But if we do, he'll kill
us as spies."

As they were deliberating in this manner, Gargantua

put them, along with the lettuce, into one of the household plates, which was as big as the wine-vat of Cîteaux,
and with a dash of oil, vinegar, and salt he thereupon
gobbled them up, as a little appetizer. He already had
had five of them in his mouth, while the sixth was in his
plate, hidden under a lettuce-leaf, with the exception of
his staff, which stuck out above. Noticing this, Grandgousier remarked to Gargantua:

"I think that's a snail's horn there; don't eat it."

"Why not?" demanded Gargantua. "They're good to
eat, all this month."

In drawing out the staff, he drew up the pilgrim with
it, and gulped him down right heartily. Then he took a
horrifying swig of black Burgundy-grape, while waiting
for supper to be served.

The pilgrims who had been thus devoured rescued
themselves as best they could from the mill of his teeth.
They thought they had been cast into some underground
dungeon. And then, when Gargantua took that mighty
swig, they thought, for sure, that they were going to
drown in his mouth, as the winy torrent almost carried
them down into the gulf of his stomach. Leaping about
by the aid of their staffs, like Saint-Michel pilgrims, they
took refuge against the wall formed by his teeth. But
unfortunately, one of them, as he explored the country
with his staff, to see if they were safe, happened to strike
roughly against the cavity of a hollow tooth, hitting the
jawbone-nerve. This caused Gargantua great pain, and
he commenced to bawl with rage at the suffering he was
forced to endure. In order to relieve his pain, he had
them bring his toothpicks; and making for the hard-
walnut tree, he straightway routed out your pilgrim
gentlemen.

He snatched one of them up by the legs, another by

the shoulders, another by the knapsack, another by the poke, and another by the scarf. As for the poor haircloth beggar who had struck the nerve with his staff, Gargantua seized him by the codpiece. This proved to be a lucky thing for the pilgrim, for in so seizing him, Gargantua pierced an inguinal bubo which had been making a martyr of the poor devil ever since he and his companions had passed Ancenis. The pilgrims, thus routed out, scampered away across the vineyard, and Gargantua's pain was eased.

At that very moment, he was called in by Eudemon to supper, for all was in readiness.

"But first," said he, "I'm going to get rid of my pain through my kidneys!"

Then he made water so copiously that the urine cut off the pilgrims' path, and they were forced to ferry the big canal that arose in front of them. Attempting to cross in the shelter of a thicket, they all, with the exception of Fournillier, fell straight into a net that had been spread to trap wolves. They contrived to escape from this, through the efforts of Fournillier, who broke through the snares and ropes. When they were loose, they lodged for the rest of that night in a shanty near Coudray. There, the rest of them were greatly comforted in their misfortunes by the kind words of one of their number named Tiredfoot, who insisted that this adventure of theirs had been predicted by David, in Psalm. . . .

"*Cum exurgerent homines in nos: Fortes vivos deglutissent nos*. When men rose up against us: They had swallowed us up alive."

"When we were eaten in a salad with a grain of salt."

"*Cum irasceretur furor eorum in nos: Forsitan aqua absorbuisset nos*. When their wrath was kindled against us: Then the waters had overwhelmed us."

"When he took that ungodly swig."

"*Torrentem pertransavit anima nostra.* The stream had gone over our soul."

"When we crossed the big canal."

"*Forsitan pertransisset anima nostra aquam intolerabilem.* Then the proud waters had gone over our soul."

"The water of his urine which cut off our path."

"*Benedictus Dominus, qui non dedit nos in captionem dentibus eorum. Anima nostra, sicut passer, erepta est de lacqueo venantium.* Blessed be the Lord who hath not given us a prey to their teeth. Our soul is escaped as a bird out of the snare of the fowlers."

"When we fell into the trap——"

"*Lacqueus contritus est.* The snare is broken."

"By Fournillier."

"*Et nos liberati sumus. Adjutorium nostrum,*" etc.

"And we are escaped. Our help," etc.

How the Monk Was Feasted by Gargantua, and the Fine Talk They Had at Supper

WHEN Gargantua sat down to table, Grandgousier, after the first few mouthfuls had been disposed of, began to relate the origin and the causes of the war which had broken out between himself and Picrochole. He told how Friar John Hackem had triumphantly defended the abbey-close, and went on to praise the latter's prowess above that of Camillus, Scipio, Pompey, Caesar, and Themistocles. At this, Gargantua requested that they send for the monk immediately, in order that they might consult with him as to what was the best thing to do. The others agreed, and the steward was dispatched. He soon came back, bringing with him, in jovial style, the friar and his staff of the cross, mounted upon Grandgousier's mule. As the monk came in, a thousand warm greetings, a thousand embraces, a thousand good-day's were exchanged.

"Hey, there, Friar John, my friend!"

"Friar John, my fine cousin!"

"Devil take me, if it isn't Friar John!"

"Welcome, my friend, welcome!"

"Let me hug you!"

"Come over here and let me break your back—that's how glad I am to see you!"

And maybe you think Friar John didn't have a good time out of it all! For there never was a politer or a more agreeable chap than he.

"Here, here," said Gargantua, "draw up a stool alongside me, down at this end."

"That suits me," said the monk, "if it does you. Boy, a little moisture! Pour laddie, pour; I need it to tone up my liver. Let it come; I want to sprinkle my throat!"

"*Deposita cappa*," said Gargantua. "Let's take off that cowl!"

"No, by God, young fellow," said the monk. "There's a chapter in *Statutis Ordinis*—in the Statutes of our Order—that is against that."

"A turd," said Gargantua, "a turd for your chapter. That cowl's breaking your back; take it off."

"No, my friend, let it be; for by God, I drink all the better for it. It makes me feel good all over. If I take it off, these young gents, the pages, will be making garters out of it, as happened to me once at Coulaine. Without it, I wouldn't have any appetite at all, but just let me sit down at a table in this robe, and by God, I'll drink to you and your nag, both of you, and that right hearty. God save us all. I've had supper already, but I shan't eat any the less for that, for I've a well-paved stomach and one as hollow as St. Benedict's boot, always gaping open like a lawyer's bag. 'Of all fishes save the tench, take the wing of a partridge or the rump of a nun.' Wouldn't it be a funny death to die with an erection? Our prior's very fond of the white of a capon."

"In that," said Gymnastes, "he's not a bit like the foxes, for of all the capons, hens, and pullets that they take, they never eat the white meat."

"Why not?" said the monk.

"Because," replied Gymnastes, "there are no cooks to cook it; and if it's not properly cooked, it remains red and not white. The redness of meats is an indication that they are not well done, except in the case of oysters and crayfish, which are heated to a cardinal-red in cooking."

"Corpus Christi!" exclaimed the monk, "as Monsieur Bayard would say. Then the infirmarian of our abbey has a head that's not been well cooked, for his eyes are as red as an alder-tree-bowl. This leveret's rump is good for the gout. Apropos of the trowel, why is it that a young lady's thighs are always nice and cool?"

"That problem," said Gargantua, "is not in Aristotle, nor Alexander of Aphrodisias, nor in Plutarch."

"There are," said the monk, "three reasons why such a place is always naturally cool. *Primo*, because water trickles down it all the time; *secundo*, because it is a shady place, dark and obscure, where the sun never shines; and thirdly, because it is constantly fanned by all the breezes that blow through the northwind-hole, as well as by the shirt and, very frequently, by the old codpiece, as well. Here's to you! Boy, a little drink! Clink, clink, clink! My, but God is good, to give us wine like this! I swear to God that if I had lived in the time of Jesus Christ, I would have seen to it that the Jews didn't take Him in the garden of Olivet. And also may the devil run away with me, if I wouldn't have strung the hams of those gents, the apostles, who after they had had a nice supper like that, were so cowardly as to desert their good master in a pinch! I hate, worse than poison, a fellow who runs away, when he ought to stay and juggle knives. Ha! if I could only be king of France for eighty or a hundred years! I'd make cropped curs out of all those turntails of Pavia. Plague take 'em! Why didn't they die there, on the spot, instead of leaving their good prince in such a pickle? Isn't it better and more honorable to die fighting like a brave man than to live by fleeing like a coward? We're not going to have many goslings to eat this year. Hey! my friend, pass the pig. The Devil! there's no more must-sauce. *Germanavit radix Jesse.* 'And there shall come forth a rod out of the stem of Jesse.' Upon my life, I'm dying of thirst. This wine's not the worst in the world. What kind of wine do you drink at Paris? Damme if I didn't keep open house there once, for more than six months at a stretch, to all comers. You don't happen to know Friar Claude of the Hauts-Barrois do you? Oh, what a fine fellow he is! But I don't know what bug he's got now. He does nothing but study, from fear of the mumps. Our late abbot used to say that it is a monstrous thing to see a learned monk. By God, sir, my friend, *magis magnos clericos non sunt magis magnos sapientes.* What I mean is: The greatest clerics are not the greatest scholars. You never saw so many hares as there are this year, but I haven't been able to get hold of either a goshawk or a tercelet anywhere. Monsieur de la Bellonnière had promised me a lanner, but he wrote to me not long ago that it had become asthmatic. The partridges will be biting our ears off this season, but I don't enjoy bird-stalking any more, since I catch cold so easily. If I don't run around and work myself up into a lather, I don't feel easy. It's true, in jumping the hedges and the bushes, my frock sometimes leaves a little wool behind it. But I've just got hold of a nice greyhound. Damme, if a hare gets away from *him*. A flunky was taking him home to Monsieur de Maule-vrier, when I swiped him. Do you think I did wrong?"

"No, Friar John," said Gymnastes, "no, by all the devils in hell, no."

"Well," said the monk, "here's to those same devils, as long as there's any of 'em left. In God's name, what would that lame old duck have done with a hound like that? Holy Christ, he'd like it better if you made him a present of a good pair of oxen."

"How does it come," inquired Ponocrates, "that you curse so much, Friar John?"

"That," said the monk, "is merely to adorn my language a little. That's just a little color that I picked up from my studies in Ciceronian rhetoric."

"As happened to me once at Coulaine": Coulaine is the name of a château in the canton of Chinon. ——*"As Monsieur Bayard would say": the famous Chevalier Bayard, whose oath is said to have been: "Feste Dieu Bayard!"*——*"Apropos of the trowel": the beginning of a popular saying: "Apropos of the trowel, God keep you from harm, Mason."* ——*"Those turntails of Pavia": the battle of Pavia in which the French suffered a humiliating defeat and François I was captured by the Emperor Charles V.* ——*"And there shall come forth a rod out of the stem of Jesse": Isaiah, xi, 1.* ——*"Friar Claude of the Hauts-Barrois": the meaning of "Hauts-Barrois" is in doubt.* ——*"Monsieur de la Bellonnière: Bellonnière is the name of a château.* ——*"Monsieur de Maulevrier": Urquhart renders this as "My Lord Hunt-little," but it appears to be the name of a real person, probably Michel de Ballan, Seigneur de Maulevrier.*

Why It Is Monks Are Shunned by Everybody, and Why It Is That Some Have Longer Noses Than Others

"On my word as a Christian," said Eudemon, "I am amazed when I stop to think what a decent sort of chap this monk is, for he's the life of the party. Why is it, then, I wonder, that monks—joy-killers, as they call them— are always chased out when good fellows get together, just as bees chase the drones from their hives? *Ignavum fucos pecus,* says Maro, *a praesepibus arcent.* The lazy horde of drones they drive from the hives."

To this, Gargantua replied:

"There is nothing truer than that the robe and cowl draw down upon themselves all sorts of hard feelings, insults, and curses, on the part of everybody, just as the wind known as Caecias draws the clouds. The chief reason is that monks feed on the excrement of the world, that is to say, on human sins, and, like excrement-eaters, they are always being driven back to their privies, that is, to their convents and abbeys, which are isolated from polite intercourse as are the privies of a house. But if you can understand why it is that a pet monkey in a household is always teased and tormented, then you ought to be able to understand why it is that monks are shunned by everybody, both old and young. The monkey does not watch the house, like a dog; he does not haul a cart like the ox; he produces neither milk like the cow nor wool like the sheep; he does not carry burdens like the horse. All he does is bedung and defile everything, which is the reason why he receives only mockery and blows from everybody.

"Similarly, a monk—I mean the lazy ones—does not labor, like the peasant; he does not guard the country like the soldier; he does not cure the sick like the doctor; he does not preach to nor teach the world like a good evangelic doctor and pedagogue; he does not bring in commodities and public necessities like the merchant. And that is the reason why they are all jeered at and abhorred."

"But," said Grandgousier, "don't they pray God for us?"

"They do nothing of the kind," said Gargantua. "All they do is keep the whole neighborhood awake by jangling their bells."

"Well," said the monk, "a mass, a matins, or a vespers well rung is half sung."

"They mumble over a lot of legends and psalms, which they don't in the least understand; and they say a great many paternosters, interlarded with long Ave Marias, without thinking or caring about what they are saying. And all that I call a mockery of God, not prayer. God help 'em, if they ever pray for us; all they pray for is from fear of losing their round-loaves and their thick soups. All true Christians, of all walks of life, in all places and at all times, have prayed to God, and the Spirit prays and intercedes for them, and God gives them grace. That's the sort our good Friar John is; and that is why everybody likes to have him around. He's not a bigot, he isn't ragged, he's decent, jolly, sensible, an all-around good fellow. He labors, he works, he defends the oppressed, he comforts the afflicted, he comes to the aid of those who are in trouble, he guards the abbey vineyard."

"I do," said the monk, "a good deal more than that; for while dispatching, in the choir, our matins and anniversary masses, I manufacture, at the same time, cords for crossbows, I polish bolts and arrows, and I make nets and traps for catching rabbits. I'm never idle. But come on, drink up! Drink up there! Bring on the fruit of the vine. These are chestnuts from the Wood of Estroc, with nice new wine; they will make a compounder of farts of you. What's the matter? you don't seem to be in form yet. I drink at all fords, by God, like a circuit-rider's horse."

At this point, Gymnastes said to the monk:

"Friar John, knock off that snot-ball that's dangling from the end of your nose."

"Ha ha!" laughed the friar, "am I in danger of drowning, that I'm in water up to the nose? No, no. *Quare? Quia*——

> A lot goes out, but none goes in,
> When there's plenty of wine down in the bin.

My friend, if you had winter boots made out of hide like that, you wouldn't have to be afraid to fish for oysters, for they'd never take water."

"Why is it," inquired Gargantua, "that Friar John has such a fine nose?"

"For the reason," replied Grandgousier, "that God has willed it so, who shapes us in such and such a form, to such and such an end, as a potter does his clay."

"Because," said Ponocrates, "he happened to be the first at the nose-fair. He took the largest and the handsomest there was."

"Whoa, there, giddap!" cried the monk. "According to the true monastic philosophy, it is because my nurse had soft teats, and in sucking her, my nose sank in, as it would in so much butter, and then rose and puffed out, like dough in the kneading-trough. The hard teats of nurses are responsible for pug-nosed children. But speed it up, speed it up! *Ad formam nasi cognoscitur ad te levavi.* By his nose ye shall know him. Unto thee I lift up—I think you know what it is comes up. No, thanks, I don't

go in for sweets. Boy, a little drink! And a little toasted
bread along with it, if you please! It's good for dunking."

*Rabelais gives us here his basic criticism of the
monastic system. The thing to which he primarily
objects, it is clear, is not the licentiousness of the monks;
for he himself, as will be seen shortly from his Abbey of
Thélème, was not a believer in the ascetic life. It is,
rather, the slothfulness of the monastery inmates that
offends him, the social uselessness, as he sees it, of their
occupations—he displays in this passage a keen sense of
the social value of labor. Over against this he sets the
industriousness of Friar John, the social utility and
human helpfulness of the latter's efforts. In the paren-
thetical expression, "I mean the lazy ones (j'entends de
ces ocieux moynes)," he makes it plain, however, that he
is not condemning all monks. Friar John is merely putting
into practice the precept of St. Jerome, addressed to
those in convents: "Be at some work, so that the Devil
will always find you occupied . . . weave rush baskets
. . . and nets for catching fish."*

*This is, none the less, one of the passages in the
Gargantua with a distinct Protestant ring.*

*"Says Maro": Vergil (Publius Vergilius Maro),
Georgics, iv, 168. ——"The wind known as Caecias":
from the Attic Nights of Aulus Gellius (Noctes Atticae,
ii, 22): "There is also a wind by the name of Caecias,
which, Aristotle tells us, blows in such a fashion that it
does not drive the clouds away, but draws them to it."
——"A pet monkey in a household": Rabelais is here
developing a motive from Plutarch's treatise on How to
Distinguish a Friend from a Flatterer. ——"Chestnuts
from the Wood of Estroc": a region in the Vendée that,
in the sixteenth century, was renowned for its chestnuts.*

——"*Like a circuit-rider's horse*": "comme un cheval de promoteur"; *the* promoteur *was an officer exercising ecclesiastic jurisdiction who travelled about the country.* ——"Quare? Quia——": "*Why? Because——.*" ——"*Ad formam nasi cognoscitur*": M. Jean Plattard comments: "*Friar John makes use of this to suggest that 'you can tell by the shape of the nose.'*" ——"*Ad te levavi*": "*Unto thee I lift up mine eyes*," Psalms, cxxiii,7.

When they had done feasting, a conference was held and it was decided that, around midnight, they would all go out to reconnoiter the enemy; meanwhile, they would have a little nap. Being restless, Gargantua was lulled to sleep by the psalm-singing of Friar John; and the latter, who was used to arising in the middle of the night for matins, had them up again in good time. The monk insisted upon taking some more refreshment, and then they armed and equipped themselves. Over his protests, for he wanted only his trusty staff of the cross, Friar John was rigged out in armor from head to foot and mounted upon "a good courser of the realm, a doughty broadsword at his side."

How the Monk Encouraged His Companions, and How He Hanged Himself to a Tree

IN THIS fashion, the noble champions set out upon their adventure, with the object of finding out what course they would have to pursue, and what they would have to guard against, when the great and terrible day of battle came. And as they went, the monk encouraged them, saying:

"Don't be the least bit afraid, my lads; I will guide you safely. God and St. Benedict be with us! If I only had as much strength as I have nerve, crucified Christ! I'd pluck 'em like ducks. I'm not afraid of anything except their artillery. I used to know a prayer, which the sub-sacristan of our abbey taught me, that guaranteed one's person against all gun and cannon-fire. But it wouldn't do me any good, because I have no faith in it. Anyway, my staff of the cross will work wonders. By God, whichever one of you does a duck, damme, if I don't make a monk out of him, in my stead, and harness him with my own cowl, for it's a good remedy against cowardice. Did you ever hear the story about Monsieur de Meurles' greyhound, that wasn't worth a rap on the field? His master put a cowl around his neck, and Jesus Christ, there wasn't a hare or a fox anywhere that could get away from him; and what was more, he covered all the bitches in the country which, before that time, had been out of commission, *et de frigidis et maleficiatis,* 'of them that are cold and impotent'—through evil spells!"

Angrily uttering these words Friar John, as he passed under a walnut tree, in riding toward the Willow Grove, caught the vizor of his helmet in the crotch of a large branch. Notwithstanding this, he stoutly spurred his horse, and the animal, being very high-mettled, suddenly sprang forward, while the monk, who was endeavoring to unloosen his vizor from the crotch, let go the bridle and clung with his hands to the branch, as his steed darted out from under him.

In this fashion, Friar John was left hanging to the walnut tree, crying help, murder, and treason, all the while. Eudemon, who was the first to discover the monk's plight, called out to Gargantua:

"Sire, come and see Absalom hanged."

Coming up, Gargantua gazed at the monk's countenance and the way in which he was hanging.

"You are wrong," he said, "in comparing him to

Absalom, for Absalom was hanged by his hair; but this Friar, who is shorn, is hanging by his ears."

"Help me!" said the monk, "in the devil's name, help me! Is this any time for talk? You're like the decretalist preachers, who say that whoever sees his neighbor in danger of death ought first, under pain of three-pronged excommunication, to admonish the other to confess and to put himself in a state of grace—all this before giving him any help. And so, after this, when I see them in the river and about to drown, in place of running up to lend them a hand, I intend giving them a good long sermon *de contemptu mundi et fuga saeculi,* on contempt of the world and flight from worldly things, and when they're stiff and dead, that will be time enough to go fish them out."

"Stay right where you are, old dear," said Gymnastes. "I'm coming to get you, for you're a nice little *monachus:*

> *Monachus in claustro*
> *Non valet ova duo;*
> *Sed, quando est extra,*
> *Bene valet triginta.*

"A monk in the cloister is not worth two eggs; but when he is out, he's worth all of thirty. I've seen more than five hundred hanged, but I've never seen any hanged with better grace, and if I could do as well, I'd be willing to hang like that all the rest of my life."

"Are you done preaching yet?" said the monk. "Help me, for God's sake, since you won't for the Other's. By the robe that I wear, you'll repent of this *tempore et loco praelibatis,* at the appointed time and place."

Then Gymnastes dismounted from his horse, climbed the walnut tree and, lifting the monk up by the gussets with one hand, unfastened his vizor from the tree-crotch with the other hand, and let him fall to the ground, coming down after him, himself. As soon as the friar was down, he jerked off all his harness and sent one piece hurtling after another, across the field. Then, resuming his staff of the cross, he remounted his horse, which Eudemon had caught, and they all continued merrily on their way, taking the Willow Grove road.

Rabelais then goes on to narrate in detail the engagements of the Picrocholine War, enlivened by a number of incidents: the capture of Friar John by the enemy; the outwitting of his guards by the monk and his escape; the capture of Picrochole's grand squire, Braghard, by the friar and the latter's rescue of the pilgrims who had fled from Gargantua's chops only to fall into the hands of the marauders; the release of the pilgrims by Grandgousier, who sends them home with the advice that they stay there; the humane treatment accorded Braghard by Grandgousier, who loads him down with presents and permits him to return to his king; the quarrel among Picrochole's advisers and the slaying of Braghard; Gargantua's assault on La Roche-Clermault and the routing of Picrochole's army, and finally, Picrochole's flight.

How Picrochole, Fleeing, Was Overtaken by Ill Fortune, and What Gargantua Did after the Battle

PICROCHOLE (thus driven to despair) fled toward L'Ile-Bouchard, but along the Rivière road his horse stumbled and fell to the ground, at which Picrochole was so angry that he slew the beast with his own sword. Then, finding no one who would provide him with another mount, he was about to take an ass belonging to the mill nearby, when the millers leaped upon him and beat him soundly, taking away all his clothes and giving him nothing but an old gunny-sack to wear. Clad in this, the poor devil, wroth as could be, went his way.

Crossing the water at Port-Huault and there relating his misfortunes, he was informed by an old witch that his kingdom would be restored to him at the coming of the Cockcranes. After that, no one knows what became of him. I have often heard that he is, at present, a poor day-laborer at Lyon, as bad-tempered as ever, and always babbling pathetically, to all strangers, about the coming of the Cockcranes, being sure that, according to the old hag's prophecy, he will be restored to his kingdom when they come.

At the conclusion of their return march, Gargantua first took a census of his followers and found that very few of them had perished in battle—none, in fact, except a few foot-soldiers of Captain Tolmerus' company, while Ponocrates had received an arquebus-bullet through his doublet. Then Gargantua made all his men take some refreshment, giving orders to the paymasters to provide the wherewithal for this meal. He further commanded his troops not to commit any outrages in the town, seeing that it now belonged to him. After the meal, they were all to line up in the square in front of the castle, and there to receive six-months' pay, which order was carried out. He then summoned to the same square all that remained of Picrochole's men; and to these, in the presence of all his princes and captains, Gargantua spoke as follows:

The scene of the Picrocholine War continues to the end to be the Chinon country; L'Ile-Bouchard, Rivière, Port-Huault are all in this region. ——"The coming of the Cockcranes": the sense of this expression (venue des cocquecigrues) *is "never."* ——*"Captain Tolmerus": the name in Greek means bold, daring.*

The Speech Which Gargantua Delivered to the Vanquished

OUR fathers, grandfathers, and ancestors from time immemorial have been of the opinion, inspired by their own natural inclinations, that, as a worthy commemoration of their battles, triumphs and victories, it is better to erect trophies and monuments in the hearts of the vanquished, through the benevolence shown the latter by the victors, than to rear imposing pieces of architecture in conquered countries. For they had a higher respect for the living memory which human beings might hold of them, as a result of their generosity, than they did for the mute inscriptions to be found on arches, columns, and pyramids, which are subject at once to atmospheric calamities and to the workings of universal spite.

You ought to remember well enough the clemency which they showed the Bretons at the Battle of Saint-Aubin-du-Cormier, as well as at the demolition of Parthenay. You have heard, and, hearing, you ought to admire, the good treatment they gave the barbarians of Spaniola, who had pillaged, depopulated, and ravaged the maritime coast of Olonne and the Talmondais.

All the heavens were filled with the praise and congratulations which you yourselves and your fathers showered upon them, when Alpharbal, King of Canaria, not satisfied with his good fortune, rashly invaded the land of Aunis, practicing piracy throughout the Armorica Islands and neighboring regions. He was vanquished and captured in an open naval engagement by my father

--may God watch over and protect him. What then? Where other kings and emperors, even those that call themselves Catholic, would have treated him miserably, subjected him to a harsh imprisonment, and held him for an unreasonable ransom, my father dealt with him courteously and amiably, put him up in the palace and, exhibiting an incredible degree of mildness, sent him back home under a body-guard, laden down with gifts and overwhelmed with all the gracious offices of friendship.

What was the outcome? Alpharbal, returning to his own land, assembled all the princes and dignitaries of his realm, related to them the humane treatment which he had received at our hands, and begged them to see to it that the world should have an example of their own gracious honorableness, as it had had of our honorable graciousness. It was, accordingly, decreed by unanimous consent that all their lands, dominions, and their realm should be offered to us, to be disposed of as we might see fit.

Alpharbal himself at once returned, with nine-thousand-thirty-eight great merchant-vessels, bringing with him not only the treasures of his house and royal line, but that of nearly all the country as well; for as he was about to set sail, to take advantage of an east-northeast wind, all his subjects came thronging down and proceeded to cast into the boats gold, silver, rings, jewels, spices, drugs, and aromatic odors; parrots, pelicans, long-tailed monkeys, civets, genets, and porcupines. There was not a single decent mother's son of them that did not, then and there, throw in the most precious thing he happened to possess.

When Alpharbal arrived, he wanted to kiss my father's feet, but this was not permitted, as being unworthy of him. Instead, he and my father embraced each other as friends. He presented his gifts, but they were not accepted, for the reason that they were excessive. Alpharbal then offered to become my father's voluntary serf and vassal, he and his posterity. This offer, likewise was not accepted, as not being just. By a decree of state, Alpharbal yielded his lands and his realm, offering the signed deeds and conveyances, sealed and ratified by all the proper parties. This was absolutely refused, and the contracts cast into the fire.

The upshot of the matter was that my father was overcome with sympathy, and began to weep copiously, as he thought of the frank goodwill and the simplicity of the Canarians. And so, with exquisitively chosen words and sentences beautifully framed, he endeavored to make light of the good turn he had done them, stating that all he had done was not worth a fig and that if he had shown them any decency it was no more than he had been bound to do. But Alpharbal only thought the more of it.

What was the result of it all? Whereas for Alpharbal's ransom, if we had wanted to be as hard as possible in the matter, we might, tyrannically, have exacted two million crowns, retaining his eldest sons as hostages, they, as it was, made themselves our perpetual tributaries and obliged themselves to pay us each year two millions in refined twenty-four-carat gold. They paid us that sum the first year; the second year, they voluntarily paid two-million-three-hundred-thousand crowns; the third year, two-million-six-hundred-thousand; the fourth year, three millions—constantly, and of their own free will, increasing the amount until we were obliged to forbid them to bring us any more.

All this is characteristic of gratitude; since time, which gnaws away and diminishes all other things, augments and increases the sense of benefits received, for the reason that a good turn freely rendered a reasonable man grows continually and becomes ennobled in his thought and memory. Not wishing, therefore, to be lacking in that mildness which I should inherit from my forbears, I hereby absolve and acquit you all. You are, every man of you, as free and untrammeled as you were before.

Moreover, upon leaving the gates, you shall be given three-months' pay to enable you to return to your households and your families; and you shall be conducted there in safety by six hundred men-at-arms and eight thousand foot-soldiers under the command of my squire, Alexander, to make sure that the peasants do not molest you. May God be with you!

I regret, with all my heart, that Picrochole is not here; for I would have given him to understand that it was without any will of my own, without any hope of adding either to my own material welfare or to my fame, that this war was declared. But since he is among the missing, and no one knows where he is nor how he vanished, I hereby decree that his realm shall go, in its entirety, to his son, who, seeing that he is still too young (for he is not yet five), shall be governed and instructed by the elder princes and learned men of the realm. And since a kingdom so desolated by war may readily be brought to ruin, if some restraint is not imposed on the covetousness and the avarice of its administrators, I hereby order that Ponocrates shall be the superintendent of all these regents, being herewith invested with all requisite authority, and that he shall remain with the young heir until he is sure that the latter is capable of ruling and reigning by himself.

I am aware, however, that a too spineless and relaxed complacency, displayed in the pardoning of malefactors, does not but encourage the delinquents to commit mischief the more thoughtlessly the next time, on account of the confidence they have that they will once more be

pardoned. I also recall the fact that Moses, the mildest
man on earth in his day, sternly punished the mutinous
and seditious among the people of Israel. I remember
that Julius Caesar—so mild a commander as to lead
Cicero to say of him that there was nothing more
sovereign about his fortune than the fact that he could,
and nothing better about his virtue than the fact that he
always would, pardon and save every one—I remember
that this same Caesar, nevertheless, in certain instances
rigorously punished the instigators of rebellion.

In accordance, therefore, with such examples as these,
I would have you leave with me before you go: first, that
fine specimen of a Marquet who was the primary cause
of this war through his overweening presumptiousness;
secondly, his companions, the other cake-peddlers, who
neglected to restrain his hot-headedness upon the spot;
and finally, all the counselors, captains, officers, and
domestics of Picrochole who may have incited, advised,
or spurred him on, through flattery, thus to forsake his
own dominions and to come disturbing us.

*This speech, like a number of other passages in Ra-
belais, is a sample of humanistic eloquence, patterned
after Ciceronian models. At the same time, there can be
no doubt that it gives expression to the author's own
ideas on the subject of the treatment of conquered
peoples whose rulers have been guilty of aggression—
ideas that are startlingly modern in character, particularly
with regard to the distinction that is made between the
guilty and the innocent and the stress upon the necessity
of punishing the former.*

*"Atmospheric calamities and . . . the workings of
universal spite": Rabelais is here developing a thought
from Pliny the Younger's Panegyric of Trajan; compare*

Horace, Odes, III, xxx: "Exegi monumentum aere perennius." ——*"Battle of Saint-Aubin-du-Cormier":* in this battle, on July 28, 1488, the French army won a victory over the Bretons, and the commander of the Breton forces, Louis, Duke of Orléans, later Louis XII of France, was made a prisoner. ——*"The demolition of Parthenay":* on March 28, 1487, the commander of this garrison surrendered it to Charles VIII, after securing a pardon and permission to retire. ——*"The barbarians of Spaniola":* Spaniola was the name given by Columbus to the island of Haiti; the invasion, of course, is purely mythical. ——*"Olonne and the Talmondais":* Olonne is the present day Sables d'Olonne, on the west coast of France; the Talmondais is the region around Talmont, in the Vendée. ——*"Alpharbal, King of Canaria":* Rabelais has previously alluded to this imaginary defeat of the "Canarians" by Grandgousier. ——*"The Armorica Islands":* the islands now known as the Noirmoutiers, off the French west coast. ——*"So mild a commander as to lead Cicero to say of him,"* Cicero, Pro Ligario, 12.

Following *Gargantua's* address, they buried the dead and dressed the wounded, and held a magnificent state banquet in honor of those warriors who had distinguished themselves. Gargantua then proceeded to reward Ponocrates, Gymnastes, Eudemon, and his other aides with grants of money, castles, and land. It was when he came to Friar John that a question arose as to the nature of the reward to be conferred upon the monk; and this leads to one of Rabelais' most profoundly significant passages, the chapters on the Abbey of Thélème, in which he sets forth his ideas of a free society, even though it may be a society that exists only in the land of Utopia and his own imagination.

V. The Abbey of Thélème

(CHAPTERS LII-LVII)

Rabelais' vision of the Abbey of Thélème is, as M. Jean Plattard has observed, essentially a monk's dream.

"Above all," the French scholar continues, "it is the dream of a monk, who, disgusted with the monastic spirit and suffering from too rigid a discipline, imagines that the first condition of happiness would lie in the suppression of all rule and all restraint. . . . It is probable that, before Rabelais' time, many a monk had dreamed just such a dream as this. Undoubtedly, it would not be impossible to discover, in their (the monks') writings, something in the way of a precedent fantasy, embodying this conception of a 'convent', founded in opposition to all the principles of ordinary convents. Two writers whom Rabelais knew well, Jean Le Maire de Belges, in his Temple de Venus, and Coquillart, in his Droits nouveaux, De Presumptionibus, had conceived monasteries where everything—ceremonies, prayers, customs—bore some relation to the cult of Venus or of love.

"But the Abbey of Thélème is a fantasy that stems from Rabelais' own temperament, and from his intellectual preoccupations about the year 1533. Thélème is open to all . . . that is to say, to the whole phalanx of humanists, who were awaiting a reform in the Church, and who joined their efforts to those of the future reformationists, down to the day when the French ref-

196

ormation became, definitely, Calvinism. Thélème was to be, primarily, an asylum for all of those who were struggling against the powers of Gothic darkness, against 'hypocrites', and against the Sorbonne. Rabelais does not appear to suspect that there are, in the camp of the humanists, united under the same banner, from the necessity of resisting a common enemy, certain minds of tendencies widely diverse from his own; nor did he know that those whom he later was to brand with the name of 'predistinators' would not think of stooping to lead the epicurean life that enchanted his own imagination."

M. Plattard then goes on to point out that the principles underlying the foundation of Thélème are, essentially, those of Rabelais' basic naturalistic philosophy, his sense of life.

"The ascetic regime," he says, "which was part of the very spirit of the institution of monasticism, is as contrary to Rabelais' temperament as it was to the mind of Erasmus. The latter, in the Praise of Folly, had ridiculed the Judaic practices of the monks. . . . Thus, for Erasmus, the monastic rule is an absurd one, for the reason that it has nothing in common with the law of charity, which is of the very essence of Christianity. As for Rabelais, he condemns it in the name of nature's law. Monastic asceticism is contrary to his very sense of life."

The older commentators went far afield in their efforts to find the sources of, or precedents for, this Rabelaisian "abbey"; but the best source of all is that which is constituted by Rabelais' own mind and intellectual interests.

As to the question of the location of Thélème, Professor Lefranc thinks that it may, tentatively, be situated near "the point of confluence of the Indre and the Loire, upon the banks of the latter stream, to the east of Huismes"; and he adds: "It is plausible to assume that Pantagruel resides at Thélème during Book Third."

How Gargantua Had the Abbey of Thélème Built for the Monk

THERE remained the monk to provide for. Gargantua wanted to make him Abbot of Seuilly, but the friar refused. He wanted to give him the Abbey of Bourgueil or that of Saint-Florent, whichever might suit him best, or both, if he had a fancy for them. But the monk gave a peremptory reply to the effect that he would not take upon himself any office involving the government of others.

"For how," he demanded, "could I govern others, who cannot even govern myself? If you are of the opinion that I have done you, or may be able to do you in the future, any worthy service, give me leave to found an abbey according to my own plan."

This request pleased Gargantua, and the latter offered his whole province of Thélème, lying along the River Loire, at a distance of two leagues from the great Forest of Port-Huault. The monk then asked that he be permitted to found a convent that should be exactly the opposite of all other institutions of the sort.

"In the first place, then," said Gargantua, "you don't want to build any walls around it; for all the other abbeys have plenty of those."

"Right you are," said the monk, "for where there is a wall (*mur*) in front and behind there is bound to be a lot of *murmur*—ing, jealousy and plotting on the inside."

Moreover, in view of the fact that in certain convents in this world there is a custom, if any woman (by which, I mean any modest or respectable one) enters the place, to clean up thoroughly after her wherever she has been —in view of this fact, a regulation was drawn up to the effect that if any monk or nun should happen to enter this new convent, all the places they had set foot in were to be thoroughly scoured and scrubbed. And since, in other convents, everything is run, ruled, and fixed by hours, it was decreed that in this one there should not be any clock or dial of any sort, but that whatever work there was should be done whenever occasion offered. For, as Gargantua remarked, the greatest loss of time he knew was to watch the hands of the clock. What good came of it? It was the greatest foolishness in the world to regulate one's conduct by the tinkling of a time-piece, instead of by intelligence and good common sense.

Another feature: Since in those days women were not put into convents unless they were blind in one eye, lame, hunchbacked, ugly, misshapen, crazy, silly, deformed, and generally of no account, and since men did not enter a monastery unless they were snotty-nosed, underbred, dunces, and trouble-makers at home—

"Speaking of that," said the monk, "of what use is a woman who is neither good nor good to look at?"

"Put her in a convent," said Gargantua.

"Yes," said the monk, "and set her to making shirts."

And so, it was decided that in this convent they would receive only the pretty ones, the ones with good figures and sunny dispositions, and only the handsome, well set-up, good-natured men.

Item: Since in the convents of women, men never entered, except under-handedly and by stealth, it was provided that, in this one, there should be no women unless there were men also, and no men unless there were also women.

Item: Inasmuch as many men, as well as women, once received into a convent were forced and compelled, after a year of probation, to remain there all the rest of their natural lives—in view of this, it was provided that, here, both men and women should be absolutely free to pick up and leave whenever they happened to feel like it.

Item: Whereas, ordinarily, the religious take three vows, namely, those of chastity, poverty and obedience, it was provided that, in this abbey, one might honorably marry, that each one should be rich, and that all should live in utter freedom.

With regard to the lawful age for entering, the women should be received from the age of ten to fifteen years, the men from the age of twelve to eighteen.

The name, Thélème, is derived from the Greek thelema, meaning will or desire. It indicates the spirit of the place, whose motto is: "Fay ce que vouldras. Do as thou wouldst." This "abbey" may be an imaginary one, but Rabelais is at pains to locate it with relative precision. "It is situated," says M. Henri Clouzot, "in the islet of thickly grown meadows, hemmed in between the Indre, the old Cher, and the Loire, where the fine cows of Bréhémont graze" (these, it may be recalled, were the cows that provided the infant Gargantua with his "ordinary milk diet"). ——"The Abbey of Bourgueil or that of Saint-Florent": the Benedictine Abbey of Saint-Pierre de Bourgueil, founded in the tenth century, was one of the richest in Anjou; Saint-Hilaire-Saint-Florent was in the canton and district of Saumur (Maine-et-Loire) and was one of the oldest and richest in the west of France.

How the Abbey of the Thelemites Was Built and Endowed

FOR the building and furnishing of the abbey, Gargantua made a ready-money levy of two-million-seven-hundred-thousand-eight-hundred-thirty-one of the coins known as "big wooly sheep"; and for each year, until everything should be in perfect shape, he turned over, out of the toll-receipts of the Dive River, one-million-six-hundred-sixty-nine-thousand "sunny crowns" and the same number of "seven-chick pieces." For the foundation and support of the abbey, he made a perpetual grant of two-million-three-hundred-sixty-nine-thousand-five-hundred-fourteen "rose nobles," in the form of ground-rent, free and exempt of all encumbrances, and payable every year at the abbey gate, all of this being duly witnessed in the form of letters of conveyance.

As for the building itself, it was in the form of a hexagon, so constructed that at every corner there was a great round tower sixty paces in diameter, all these being of the same size and appearance. The River Loire flowed along the north elevation. Upon the bank of this river stood one of the towers, named Arctic, while, proceeding toward the east, there was another, named Calaer, following it another, named Anatole, then another, named Mesembrine, another after it, named Hesperia, and finally, one named Cryere. Between every two towers, there was a distance of three-hundred-twelve paces. To the building proper, there were six stories in all, counting the underground cellars as one. The second story was vaulted, in the form of a basket-handle. The rest were stuccoed with plaster of Paris, in the manner of lamp-bottoms, the roof being covered over with a fine slate, while the ridge-coping was lead, adorned with little mannikins and animal-figures, well grouped and gilded. The eaves-troughs, which jutted out from the walls, between the mullioned windows, were painted with diagonal gold-and-blue figures, all the way down to the ground, where they ended in huge rain-spouts, all of which led under the house to the river.

This building was a hundred times more magnificent than the one at Bonivet, at Chambord, or at Chantilly; for in it there were nine-thousand-three-hundred-thirty-two rooms, each equipped with a dressing-room, a study, a wardrobe, and a chapel, and each opening into a large hall. Between the towers, in the center of the main building, was a winding-stair, the steps of which were partly of porphyry, partly of Numidian stone, and partly of serpentine marble, each step being twenty-two feet long and three fingers thick, with an even dozen between each pair of landings. On each landing were two fine antique arches, admitting the daylight, while through these arches, one entered a loggia of the width of the stair, the stair itself running all the way to the roof and ending in a pavilion. From this stair one could enter, from either side, a large hall, and from this hall the rooms.

From the tower known as Arctic to the one called Cryere, there were fine large libraries, in Greek, Latin, Hebrew, French, Tuscan, and Spanish, separated from each other according to the different languages. In the middle of the building was another and marvelous stairway, the entrance to which was from outside the house, by way of an arch thirty-six feet wide. This stair was so symmetrical and capacious that six men-at-arms, their lances at rest, could ride up abreast, all the way to the roof. From the tower Anatole to Mesembrine, there were large and splendid galleries, all containing paintings representative of deeds of ancient prowess, along with historical and geographical scenes. In the center of this elevation was still another gateway and stair, like the one on the river-side. Over this gate, there was inscribed, in large old-fashioned letters, the following poem:

The architecture of the Abbey of Thélème as described by Rabelais has been found to be precise. Taking the indications given, a modern French architectural authority, M. Charles Lenormant, has actually drawn up the plan and elevation of the structure, as has his colleague, M. Arthur Heulhard. This, remarks M. Plattard, is "a Renaissance château of the type considered most magnificent about 1533; it preserves the general character of a feudal castle, with certain additional and luxurious features. . . . All the details might have been found in other edifices of the age. In his journeyings across France, Rabelais had become familiar with the subject."

Of the coins mentioned in the first paragraph, the moutons à la grande laine, *or "big wooly sheep," were gold pieces bearing an Agnus Dei inscription and worth about sixteen francs each (the sum represented is approximately 43,216,296 francs); the "sunny crowns"* (escuz au soleil) *bore the figure of the sun and were worth from thirty-six to forty-five sous; the "seven-chick pieces"* (a l'estoille pousinnière) *are Rabelais' own invention, so named from the seven-starred constellation of the Pleiades, supposed to resemble a flock of chickens; the* nobles à la rose, *or "rose nobles," struck off by Edward* II *and bearing the roses of York and Lancaster,*

*had a value equivalent to twenty-five francs; the present
value of the sum here stated, then, would be 59,237,850
francs.*

*The names of the abbey towers are taken from the
Greek, Calaer meaning "fine air," Anatole "eastern,"
Mesembrine "southern," Hesperia "of the evening" or
"western," and Cryere "frozen" or "icy," this last tower
being situated between the north and west and thus
exposed to the northwest wind.*

*Bonivet, Chambord, and Chantilly were famous
châteaux of the era. ——"Serpentine marble": green
marble with red and white spots.*

*It is to be noted that Rabelais has no space reserved
for the English or German tongues; they were not considered literary languages in his day.*

Inscription Over the Great Portal of Thélème

You hypocrites and two-faced, please stay out:
Grinning old apes, potbellied snivelbeaks,
Stiffnecks and blockheads, worse than Goths, no doubt
Magogs and Ostrogoths we read about;
You hairshirt whiners and you slippered sneaks;
You fur-lined beggars and you nervy freaks;
You bloated dunces, trouble-makers all;
Go somewhere else to open up your stall.

> Your cursed ways
> Would fill my peaceful days
> With nasty strife;
> With your lying life,
> You'd spoil my roundelays—
> With your cursed ways.

Stay out, you lawyers, with your endless guts,
You clerks and barristers, you public pests,
You Scribes and Pharisees, with your "if's" and "but's,"
You hoary judges (Lord, how each one struts!):
You feed, like dogs, on squabbles and bequests;
You'll find your salary in the hangman's nests;
Go there and bray, for here there is no guile
That you can take to court, to start a trial.

No trials or jangles
Or legal wrangles:
We're here to be amused.
If your jaws must be used,
You've bags full of tangles,
Trials and jangles.

Stay out, you usurers and misers all,
Gluttons for gold, and how you hoard the stuff!
Greedy windjammers, with a world of gall,
Hunchbacked, snubnosed, your money-jars full, you bawl
For more and more; you never have enough;
Your stomachs never turn, for they are tough,
As you heap your piles, each miser-faced poltroon:
I hope Old Death effaces you, right soon!

That inhuman mug
Makes us shrug:
Take it to another shop,
And please don't stop,
But elsewhere lug
That inhuman mug!

Stay out of here, at morning, noon and night,
Jealous old curs, dotards that whine and moan,

All trouble-makers, full of stubborn spite,
Phantom avengers of a Husband's plight,
Whether Greek or Latin, worst wolves ever known;
You syphilitics, mangy to the bone,
Go take your wolfish sores, and let them feed at ease—
Those cakey crusts, signs of a foul disease.

> Honor, praise, delight
> Rule here, day and night;
> We're gay, and we agree,
> We're healthy, bodily;
> And so, we have a right
> To honor, praise, delight.

But welcome here, and very welcome be,
And doubly welcome, all noble gentlemen.
This is the place where taxes all are free,
And incomes plenty, to live merrily,
However fast you come—I shan't "say when":
Then, be my cronies in this charming den;
Be spruce and jolly, gay and always mellow,
Each one of us a very pleasant fellow.

> Companions clean,
> Refined, serene,
> Free from avarice;
> For civilized bliss,
> See, the tools are keen,
> Companions clean.

And enter here, all you who preach and teach
The living Gospel, though the heathen raves:
You'll find a refuge here beyond their reach,
Against the hostile error you impeach,
Which through the world spreads poison, and depraves;

Come in, for here we found a faith that saves;
By voice and letter, let's confound the herd
Of enemies of God's own Holy Word.

> The word of grace
> We'll not efface
> From this holy place;
> Let each embrace,
> And himself enlace
> With the word of grace.

Enter, also, ladies of high degree!
Feel free to enter and be happy here,
Each face with beauty flowering heavenly,
With upright carriage, pleasing modesty:
This is the house where honor's held most dear,
Gift of a noble lord whom we revere,
Our patron, who's established it for you,
And given us his gold, to see it through.

> Gold given by gift
> Gives golden shrift—
> To the giver a gift,
> And very fine thrift,
> A wise man's shift,
> Is gold given by gift.

The foregoing inscription is a species of composition of which various examples are afforded by the medieval mystery plays and farces; it is the genre known as the cri, *a proclamation or invitation issued to a number of persons enumerated by the poet. The form was one suited to the rhetorical taste of the age; it fell into discredit about the middle of the sixteenth century, but was*

*still in vogue at the time that Rabelais wrote. Pro-
sodically, the piece is an imitative tour de force, and not
a highly successful one. It is, however, more or less
typical of the author's verse efforts.*

*Rabelais here lists those whom he would exclude from
his ideal society: the bigots and hypocrites, for whom he
finds any number of synonyms, ecclesiastic penitents,
beggars, and the like; the legal tribe; misers and usurers;
jealous husbands and others of their kind; syphilitics;
etc. Those whom he would admit are the well bred and
refined, the healthy, the clean-living, preachers of "the
living Gospel," and members of the feminine sex who
are comely and modest.*

*"Goths . . . Magogs and Ostrogoths": a play on the
Gog and Magog of Ezekiel and the Apocalypse; these
names spread to popular romances during the Middle
Ages and became identified with the Goths and Ostrogoths.*

*While Rabelais is following a highly artificial literary
form, he none the less makes use of the vigorous language of the people.*

What Kind of Dwelling the Thelemites Had

In the middle of the lower court was a magnificent fountain of beautiful alabaster, above which were the three
Graces with cornucopias, casting out water through their
breasts, mouths, ears, eyes, and the other openings of
their bodies.

The interior of the portion of the dwelling that
opened upon this court rested upon great pillars of
chalcedony and of porphyry, fashioned with the finest of
antique workmanship. Above were splendid galleries,
long and wide, adorned with paintings, with the horns of

deer, unicorns, rhinoceroses, and hippopotamuses, as well as with elephants' teeth and other objects interesting to look upon.

The ladies' quarters extended from the tower Arctic to the Mesembrine gate. The men occupied the rest of the house. In front of the ladies' quarters, in order that the occupants might have something to amuse them, there had been set up, between the first two outside towers, the lists, the hippodrome, the theatre, and the swimming-pools, with wonderful triple-stage baths, well provided with all necessary equipment and plentifully supplied with water of myrrh.

Next the river was a fine pleasure-garden, in the center of which was a handsome labyrinth. Between the towers were the tennis courts and the ball-grounds. On the side by the tower Cryere was the orchard, full of all sorts of fruit-trees, all of them set out in the form of quincunxes. Beyond was the large park, filled with every sort of savage beast. Between the third pair of towers were the targets for arquebus, archery, and crossbow practice. The servants' quarters were outside the tower Hesperia and consisted of one floor only, and beyond these quarters were the stables. In front of the latter stood the falcon-house, looked after by falconers most expert in their art. It was furnished annually by the Candians, the Venetians, and the Sarmatians, with all kinds of out-of-the-ordinary birds: eagles, gerfalcons, goshawks, sakers, lanners, falcons, sparrow-hawks, merlins, and others, all so well trained and domesticated that, when these birds set out from the castle for a little sport in the fields, they would take everything that came in their way. The hunting-kennels were a little farther off, down toward the park.

All the halls, rooms and closets were tapestried in various manners, according to the season of the year. The whole floor was covered with green cloth. The bedding was of embroidered work. In each dressing-room was a crystal mirror, with chasings of fine gold, the edges being trimmed with pearls; and this mirror was of such a size that—it is the truth I am telling you—it was possible to see the whole figure in it at once. As one came out of the halls into the ladies' quarters, he at once encountered the perfumers and the hair-dressers, through whose hands the gentlemen passed when they came to visit the ladies. These functionaries each morning supplied the women's chambers with rose, orange, and "angel" water; and in each room a precious incense-dish was vaporous with all sorts of aromatic drugs.

"Ball-grounds": the game was played with a large in-flated ball (ballon), *resembling our football.* ——*"Angel water": water of myrrh, so called on account of the high esteem in which it was held.*

How the Monks and Nuns of Thélème Were Clad

THE LADIES, when the abbey was first founded, dressed themselves according to their own fancy and good judgment. Later they of their own free will introduced a reform. In accordance with this revised rule, they went clad as follows:

They wore scarlet or kermes-colored stockings, and these extended above their knees for a distance of three inches, to be precise, the borders being of certain fine embroideries and pinkings. Their garters were of the same color as their bracelets, and clasped the leg above and below the knee. Their shoes, pumps, and slippers were of brilliant-colored velvet, red or violet, shaped in the form of a lobster's barbel.

Above the chemise, they wore a fine bodice, of a certain silk-camlet material, and a taffeta petticoat, white, red, tan, gray, etc. Over this went a skirt of silver taffeta, made with embroideries of fine gold or elaborate needlework, or, as the wearer's fancy might dictate, and depending upon the weather, of satin, of damask, or of velvet, being orange, tan, green, ash-gray, blue, bright yellow, brilliant red, or white in color, and being made of cloth-of-gold, silver tissue, thread-work, or embroidery, according to the feast-days. Their gowns, which were in keeping with the season, were of gold tissue or silver crisping, and were made of red satin, covered with gold needle-work, or of white, blue, black, or tan taffeta, silk serge, silk-camlet, velvet, silver-cloth, silver-tissue, or of velvet or satin with gold facings of varying design.

In summer, on certain days, in place of gowns they wore cloaks of the above-mentioned materials, or sleeveless jackets, cut in the Moorish fashion and made of violet-colored velvet, with crispings of gold over silver needlework, or with gold knots, set off at the seams with little Indian pearls. And they always had a fine plume, matching the color of their sleeves and well trimmed with golden spangles.

In winter, they wore taffeta gowns of the colors mentioned, trimmed with the fur of lynxes, black-spotted weasels, Calabrian or Siberian sables, and other precious skins. Their chaplets, rings, gold-chains, and goldwork-necklaces contained fine stones: carbuncles, rubies, balas rubies, diamonds, sapphires, emeralds, turquoises, garnets, agates, beryls, and pearls great and small.

Their head-dress, likewise, depended upon the weather. In winter, it was after the French fashion; in spring, after the Spanish style; in summer, after the

Tuscan. That is, excepting feast-days and Sundays, when they wore the French coiffure, for the reason that it is more respectable and better in keeping with matronly modesty.

The men dressed after a fashion of their own. Their stockings were of broadcloth or of serge, and were scarlet, kermes-hued, white, or black in color. Their hose were of velvet and of the same colors, or very nearly the same, being embroidered and cut to suit the fancy. Their doublets were of cloth-of-gold, silver-cloth, velvet, satin, damask, or taffeta, of the same shades, all being cut, embroidered, and fitted in a most excellent fashion. Their girdles were of the same-colored silk, the buckles being of well enameled gold. Their jackets and vests were of cloth-of-gold, gold-tissue, silver-cloth, or velvet. Their robes were as precious as the ladies' gowns, the girdles being of silk, of the same color as the doublet. Each one carried a fine sword at his side, with a gilded handle, the scabbard being of velvet, of the same shade as the stockings, while the tip was of gold or goldsmith-work, with a dagger to match. Their bonnets were of black velvet, trimmed with a great many berry-like ornaments and gold buttons, and the white plume was most prettily divided by golden spangles, from the ends of which dangled handsome rubies, emeralds, etc.

Such a sympathy existed between the men and the women that each day they were similarly dressed; and in order that they might not fail on this point, there were certain gentlemen whose duty it was to inform the men each morning what livery the ladies proposed to wear that day, for everything depended upon the will of the fair ones. In connection with all these handsome garments and rich adornments, you are not to think that either sex lost any time whatsoever, for the masters of the wardrobe had the clothing all laid out each morning, and the ladies of the chamber were so well trained that in no time at all their mistresses were dressed and their toilets completed from head to foot.

In order to provide the more conveniently for these habiliments, there was, near the wood of Thélème, a large group of houses extending for half a league, houses that were well lighted and well equipped, in which dwelt the goldsmiths, lapidaries, embroiderers, tailors, gold-thread-workers, velvet-makers, tapestry-makers, and upholsterers; and there each one labored at his trade and the whole product went for the monks and nuns of the abbey. These workmen were supplied with material by my Lord Nausicletus, who every year sent them seven ships from the Pearl and Cannibal Islands, laden with gold-nuggets, raw silk, pearls, and precious stones. And if certain pearls showed signs of aging and of losing their native luster, the workmen by their art would renew these, by feeding them to handsome cocks, in the same manner in which one gives a purge to falcons.

Rabelais is here describing the costume worn by the wealthy and fashionable of his period, and once again he is very exact. He is familiar with all the complexities of the feminine toilet and accurately distinguishes one garment from another. He has a typically Renaissance taste for luxurious materials that makes one think of a seventeenth-century Rembrandt.

"My Lord Nausicletus": this is the name given by Homer, in the Odyssey, *to the Pheacians; it means, renowned for his ships, or for his exploits upon the sea.*

——*"The Pearl and Cannibal Islands": in the nomenclature of Rabelais' time, these were the southern Antilles.*

———*"By feeding them to handsome cocks": this mode of restoring pearls is described by Averroes, twelfth-century Arabic philosopher and physician.*

How the Thelemites Were Governed in Their Mode of Living

THEIR whole life was spent, not in accordance with laws, statutes, or rules, but according to their own will and free judgment. They rose from bed when they felt like it and drank, ate, worked, and slept when the desire came to them. No one woke them, no one forced them to drink or eat or do any other thing. For this was the system that Gargantua had established. In the rule of their order there was but this one clause:

DO WHAT THOU WOULDST

for the reason that those who are free born and well born, well brought up, and used to decent society possess, by nature, a certain instinct and spur, which always impels them to virtuous deeds and restrains them from vice, an instinct which is the thing called honor. These same ones, when, through vile subjection and constraint, they are repressed and held down, proceed to employ that same noble inclination to virtue in throwing off and breaking the yoke of servitude, for we always want to come to forbidden things; and we always desire that which is denied us.

In the enjoyment of their liberty, the Thelemites entered into a laudable emulation in doing, all of them, anything which they thought would be pleasing to one of their number. If anyone, male or female, remarked: "Let us drink," they all drank. If anyone said: "Let us play," they all played. If anyone suggested: "Let us go find some sport in the fields," they all went there. If it was hawking or hunting, the ladies went mounted upon pretty and easy-paced nags or proud-stepping palfreys, each of them bearing upon her daintily gloved wrist a sparrow-hawk, a lanneret, or a merlin. The men carried the other birds.

They were all so nobly educated that there was not, in their whole number, a single one, man or woman, who was not able to read, write, sing, play musical instruments, and speak five or six languages, composing in these languages both poetry and prose.

In short, there never were seen knights so bold, so gallant, so clever on horse and on foot, more vigorous, or more adept at handling all kinds of weapons than were they. There never were seen ladies so well groomed, so pretty, less boring, or more skilled at hand and needlework and in every respectable feminine activity. For this reason, when the time came that any member of this abbey, either at the request of his relatives or from some other cause, wished to leave, he always took with him one of the ladies, the one who had taken him for her devoted follower, and the two of them were then married. And if they had lived at Thélème in devotion and friendship, they found even more of both after their marriage, and remained as ardent lovers at the end of their days, as they had been on the first day of their honeymoon.

I must not forget to describe for you an enigma that was found, as they were digging the foundations of the abbey, one written on a bronze tablet. That enigma was as follows:

"The life that the Thelemites led," remarks Plattard, "is that of the great lettered lords of Italy and France

*in the time of François I. . . . Liberal culture holds,
naturally, a large place in this humanist dream.
. . . Their (the Thelemites') leisurely and polished life
recalls that of certain Italian courts, of which Castiglione
has drawn us a picture in his* Il Cortegiano. *. . . It is
interesting to note that, for Rabelais, the basis of the
moral life for the élite gathered at Thélème is honor, the
principle of that moral aristocracy which rules in the
romances of chivalry, and which was to find expression
in the seventeenth century in the concept of* l'honnête
homme.' " *In the era of the French Revolution, Rabelais'
vision of Thélème was to influence Rousseau and
Utopian-socialist thought.*

The Gargantua, or Book First, closes with an "Enigma
in the Form of a Prophecy," written in verse. Like the
"antidoted Baubles" at the beginning of the book, this
composition undoubtedly has veiled reference to events
of the Reformation period. Only a small part of the
"enigma," however, was written by Rabelais—the first
two and last ten of the fifty-five lines of which it is composed. The rest is by his friend, the court poet, Mellin de
Saint-Gellais, commonly known as "Merlin." Maître
François must have had Saint-Gellais' permission to
make use of the piece in this fashion. As M. Plattard
concludes: "It is not here that the reader is to look for
that recondite enlightenment promised him in the Prologue. The 'substantific marrow' is to be found, rather, in
those chapters in which Rabelais openly lays bare his
ideas on education, war, monks, superstitions, and the
ideal of the free life."

END OF THE GARGANTUA, OR BOOK FIRST

Book Second

〜〜〜〜〜〜〜〜〜 ＊ 〜〜〜〜〜〜〜〜〜

BOOK SECOND

PANTAGRUEL

King of the Dipsodes

RESTORED TO THE LIFE

WITH

HIS DEEDS AND

DREADFUL FEATS OF PROWESS

Composed by the Late M. Alcofribas

Abstractor of Quintessence

*In this book we have Rabelais' first published work of
a literary character. As we now know, it must have appeared in the autumn of 1532, or about two years before
the Gargantua. It was probably put on sale at the Lyon
fair which began on November 3rd of that year. The
oldest known edition bears the imprint of Claude Nourry,
called "the Prince," and the definitive edition of 1542
that of François Juste, both printers being located "opposite Our Lady of Comfort."*

*The Pantagruel is the work that Chateaubriand had in
mind when he observed that Rabelais "created French
letters." Professor Lefranc refers to it as a "masterpiece
of living reality, profound satire, and inimitable verve,"*

219

and adds that it has "remained without a second in our literature."

Both the Gargantua *and the* Pantagruel, *as we have seen, have a real-life basis, the former having been inspired by a back-country quarrel, while the latter took shape in the author's mind as the result of the great drought of 1532.* Pantagruel, *or* Panthagruel, *is a "little devil" who makes an appearance or is mentioned in passing in a number of medieval mystery plays, and particularly in a composition of the later fifteenth century, by one Simon Greban, entitled the* Mystery of the Acts of the Apostles *(Mystère des Actes des Apôtres). As evolved in these dramas, the character is that of a demon who leaps down people's gullets, producing a violent sore throat and rendering speech impossible, or who casts salt into their mouths or otherwise produces a consuming thirst; until, eventually, the name comes to be practically synonymous with thirst itself. Accordingly, in Rabelais' romance, Pantagruel is the "King of the Dipsodes," or Thirsty Ones. Etymologically, like Grandgousier, Gargantua, and Gargamelle, the name has reference to the throat, in the sense of suffocation. (Compare the burlesque derivation which Maître François gives at the beginning of his narrative.)*

It is interesting to note that, aside from the mystery plays referred to, there is no popular folklore literature embodying the Pantagrueline legend, of which Rabelais is, one may say, the creator; for taking the hints in the old mysteries he has worked them up into literature. Subsequent to Rabelais, there is, naturally, a host of bookish allusions.

There is a heavy influence of Lucian in this book, affecting at once the author's ideas and his choice of a setting. A French translation of Lucian's Dialogues, *by Geoffroy Tory, had appeared in 1529; and there is no doubt that Rabelais was influenced not only by this rendering, and by the translator's preface in which he defends the use of the vernacular, but by Tory's original work, the* Champ Fleury, *as well, especially when he comes to satirize pedantic tendencies to deform the French tongue through "Latinizings" in the manner of the Limousin student.*

Another prominent influence is that of Sir Thomas More, from whom Rabelais borrows the idea and name of Utopia.

There are also evocations of the old French romances of chivalry and their heroes; of the fifteenth-century farce, Patelin; *of Villon, Jean Le Maire de Belges, and the Italian burlesque epic-writers, Pulci, Folengo, and Boiardo.*

Book Second possesses the least unity of any of the five books of Rabelais' romance. It may be divided into three distinct parts, the first treating of the childhood and youth of Pantagruel (Chapter I-VI), the second dealing with the visit of the young Pantagruel to Paris and his friendship with Panurge (Chapters VII-XXII), and the third covering the expedition to Utopia (Chapters XXIII-XXXIV). The third part, it would seem, was worked out by the author before the second, at about the same time as the opening chapters of the book. We have, therefore, in the opening and closing pages of this book, Rabelais' first serious literary efforts.

The second part is the most remarkable from the point of view of literature. It contains pages which the other books, while undoubtedly better composed, have not surpassed. For one thing, we may note in this part the absence of the gigantesque motive, of the abnormal element; while Gargantua's letter to Pantagruel has been characterized as "the most ardent hymn ever composed to the glory of the Renaissance" (Lefranc). On the other hand, in the opening pages of this book, those in which, it might seem, Rabelais had set out more or less deliberately, in imitation of the Grandes Cronicques, to write a best-seller, something that would catch and hold the public eye—in these pages will be found a more popular style, a more directly popular appeal; whereas the closing part of the book has been conceived in a tone of bold satire.

This book, as has been hinted, displays weaknesses of composition, but in boldness of ideas Rabelais has, it may be, gone farther here than anywhere else in the course of his work.

It is to be noted that the author's native Chinon plays but a very small part in this book, Paris constituting the principal scene. It seems clear that Rabelais must have visited Paris before 1532, and it is possible that he had paid two visits to the capital before that date.

Book Second is highly topical in character. In addition to the memorable heat and drought of 1532, a number of events of the time are to be discerned in these pages, including the pardon and jubilee decreed to France by Pope Clement VII; the panic over the Turks, in May, 1532; the arrest of a number of usurers by royal order the same year; the plague of 1532; etc.

In connection with Book Second, Lefranc makes much of what he is pleased to term Rabelais' "atheism," as exhibited in the author's travesties of sacred things—for example, of the genealogy of Christ (compare the genealogy of Pantagruel). Calvin describes the Pantagruel as "obscene" and speaks of "that devil named Pantagruel and all his ordures and villainies"; and Robert Estienne, in the preface to his Gospel of St. Matthew, reproaches the ecclesiastic authorities for not *burning Rabelais and "his cursed and blasphemous works," the* Gargantua *and the* Pantagruel.

The book is preceded by a "Decastich of Master Hugues Salel." Salel was a poet of the time (1504-1543) who enjoyed a great reputation as a translator of portions of the Iliad; *his works were published at Paris, in 1540. In a couple of the earlier editions the decastich is followed by the words: "Long live all good Pantagruelists!"*

Author's Prologue

MOST illustrious and most chivalrous champions, gentlemen and others, you who are so heartily devoted to all the
gracious little forms of courtesy, you have already seen,
read, and are familiar with the *Great and Inestimable
Chronicles of the Enormous Giant Gargantua,* and, like
true believers, have right gallantly given them credence;
and more than once you have passed the time with the
ladies—God bless 'em—and the young ladies, when
you were out of any other conversation, by telling them
fine long stories from those chronicles, for all of which
you deserve great praise, and your name ought to go
down in history.

And if you take my advice, each one of you will leave
his task, cease worrying about his trade, forget all about
his own business, and give his whole attention to these
stories, so that his mind may not be distracted or en-
cumbered in any manner, until he has learned them all
by heart, in order that if, by any chance, all the
printeries should go out of business or all books should
be destroyed, in time to come each one of you would still
be able faithfully to teach these tales to his children and
to pass them on down, from hand to hand, to his heirs
and assignees forever, like a religious Cabala. For there
is in them, it may be, more meat than a lot of big pock-
marked windbags may think, who understand a good
deal less about such little pastimes as these than Raclet
does about the *Institutes.*

I have known a good many high and mighty lords

who, when they were hunting big game or flying falcons for ducks, if it happened that the animal did not fall into the trap or the falcon showed signs of giving up the chase and they saw that the prey was gaining by force of wing, were very much annoyed, as you can well enough understand; but their refuge and their consolation (and a good precaution against catching cold, as well) was to repeat the Inestimable Deeds of that same Gargantua. There are certain others (and this is no laughing matter) who, when they were suffering intensely from toothache, after having spent all they had on doctors without getting any relief, have been able to find no more effective remedy than that of placing those same *Chronicles* between two very hot cloths and applying them to the sore spot, sinapizing them with a little powdered dung.

But what shall I say of those poor syphilitics and gouty ones? Oh! how many times have we seen them, when they were well anointed and thoroughly greased, their faces glistening like the doorknob of a meat-larder, their teeth jumping like the keys of an organ-board or spinet that is being played upon, and their gullets foaming like a wild boar which the hounds have cornered in the nets! And what did they do then? All the consolation they had was to listen to the reading of a few pages of that same book; and we have seen some who will give themselves to a hundred big barrelfuls of old devils, if they didn't feel an obvious relief from the reading of that book while they were being thus held in limbo—neither more nor less than do women who are in a family way, when someone reads to them the *Life of St. Margaret*.

And do you think that is nothing at all? Find me a book in any language, in any science or branch of learning whatsoever, that has such virtues, properties, and prerogatives, and I will buy you a half-pint of tripe. No, gentlemen, no: I tell you, it is without a peer, incomparable, and utterly unprecedented; and I will stick to it through hell-fire. As for those who would uphold any other opinion, look upon them as slanderers, predestinators, impostors, and seducers.

It is true enough that one may find in a few good, high-grade books certain occult properties, among which books I would include *Pintlicker, Orlando Furioso, Robert the Devil, Fierabras, Fearless William, Huon of Bordeaux, Mandeville,* and *Matabrune,* but they are not to be compared to the one of which we are speaking. Everyone must have learned, by infallible experience, of the great profit and utility to be derived from that same *Gargantuan Chronicle,* seeing that the printers have sold more copies of this work in two months than they have Bibles in nine years.

Being desirous, then—I, your humble servant—of adding to your pleasure, I hereby make you a present of another book of the same stamp—if, indeed, it is not a little more commendable and worthy of confidence than was the other one; for do not believe (unless you wish to go wrong) that I am speaking as the Jews do of the Law. I was not born under any such star as that, and I would never think of treacherously assuring you of a thing that was not true. I speak here as a jolly old papal buzzard— what am I saying? I mean a fuzzard—of the martyred lovers and a guzzard of amours. *Quod vidimus testamur.* We bear witness to that which we have seen. By which I mean, the horrifying deeds of prowess of Pantagruel, in whose service I have been ever since I was a page down to the present time. It is by his leave that I have come to visit my own cow-country, to find out if any of my folks are still alive.

But to put an end to this Prologue, may I jolly well give myself to a hundred thousand basketfuls of devils, body and soul, tripe and bowels, in case there is a single lying word in this whole story. Likewise, may St. Anthony's fire burn you up, may the epilepsy whirl you around, may the lightning strike you, may an ulcer eat you, may the bloody flux take you, and may the fine fire of the old rickrack—as fine as a hair from an old cow's back—covered with quicksilver ('pon my soul)—run straight up your old bunghole; and, like Sodom and Gomorrha, may you fall into a gulf of fire and brimstone, in case you do not believe absolutely everything that I am about to tell you in this present *Chronicle*.

The work referred to throughout this Prologue is not Rabelais' own Gargantua, but the Grandes Cronicques. ——"Like true believers": The early editions have: "believed them just as you would the text of the Bible or of the Holy Gospel." ——"Than Raclet does about the Institutes": allusion to Raimbert Raclet, professor of law at Dôle, and to the Institutes of Justinian. —— "Sinapizing them with a little powdered dung": in "sinapizing" (compare the English sinapism), Rabelais is adding a word to the French language, from the Latin sinapizare, Greek sinapizein, meaning to poultice with mustard; the "powdered dung" (pouldre d'oribus), literally, "powder of gold," has reference to the color of excrement, the term being a popular one for a remedy without effect. ——"Like the doorknob of a meat-larder": the knob glistens from the imprint of greasy hands. ——"Predestinators": aimed at Calvin and his followers. ——"Pintlicker," etc.: the Pintlicker is an imaginary work, although it is possible that this (Fesse-pinte) is the name of a folklore character mentioned in some popular work of the period; of the other works, the Orlando Furioso is Ariosto's famous masterpiece; Robert le Diable, Fierabras, Guillaume sans Peur, and

Huon de Bordeaux *all belonged to the popular literature,
or* Bibliothèque Bleue; *the* Fierabras *was the first
romance of chivalry to find its way into print (Geneva,
1478);* "Fearless William," *hero of an old* chanson de
geste, *was the most intrepid of the four sons of Aymon
(a tale mentioned in Book First);* Huon, *or* Hugon, *Duke
of Bordeaux, was a famous paladin under Charlemagne
(all these are mythical personages); the* Mandeville
(Montevielle) *is* The Travels of Sir John Mandeville;
no work entitled Matabrune *is known to scholars.* ———
"A jolly old papal buzzard," *etc.: an untranslatable play
on words, revolving about the term* protonotaire, *or
(apostolic) prothonotary (of the See of Rome); Rabelais'*
onocrotale *is literally a pelican, while "fuzzard" and
"guzzard" are for his "crotenotaire" (allusion to excrement) and "crocquenotaire"; the apostolic prothonotaries
were known for their amours.* ———"The old rickrack"
(ricquracque): *the reference is to the effects of debauchery; or, according to Cotgrave, to erysipelas.)*

፭፭፭፭፭፭፭፭፭፭ * ፭፭፭፭፭፭፭፭፭

I. The Childhood and Youth of Pantagruel

(CHAPTERS I-VI)

The Origin and Antiquity of the Great Pantagruel

IT MAY not be a useless nor an idle proceeding, in view of the fact that we have plenty of leisure on our hands, to refresh your minds regarding the primary source and origin of our friend, Pantagruel. For I notice that all good historians do this in their Chronicles, not only the Arabians, the Barbarians, and the Latins, but also the Greeks and Gentiles, who were endless drinkers. It is fitting, here, that you should make a note of the fact that, at the beginning of the world—I am speaking from a long way off, for it is more than forty times forty nights, calculating according to the method of the ancient Druids—at the beginning of the world, shortly after Abel had been killed by his brother Cain, the earth, imbued with the blood of the righteous, was one year so very fertile in all the fruits that are produced from its flanks, and especially in medlars, that that year has been known from time immemorial as the year of the great medlars, since three of them made a bushelful.

That was the year the Calends were discovered by the Greek almanacs. The month of March fell in Lent, and the middle of August was in May. In the month of October, as I recall, or perhaps it was September (if I am not mistaken, for I wish to guard carefully against that), there came the week so renowned in History, that is known as the Week of the Three Thursdays. There were three of them that week, on account of irregular leap years, as a result of which, the sun stumbled a little to the left, like a bandy-legged person, the moon varied from its course more than five fathoms, and there was clearly to be perceived a movement of trepidation in that part of the firmament known as *Aplanes,* or the heaven of fixed stars. This movement was so intense that the middle star of the Pleiades, leaving its companions, declined toward the equinoctial, while the star called the Ear of Corn left the Virgin to retire toward Libra, which things are very appalling and very hard matters for astrologists to bite into. And incidentally they would have to have rather long teeth to be able to reach so far.

You may very well imagine that people were glad enough to eat those medlars I was telling you of, for they were very good to look at and delicious to the taste, as well. But like Noah, that holy man (to whom we are all under such obligations for his having planted the vine, from which we get that nectar-like, delicious, precious, celestial, joyous, and deific liquor called wine) —just as Noah was deceived in drinking the wine, being unaware of its great and powerful virtues, so the men and women of that day took great pleasure in eating this fine large fruit. But many varied accidents came to them as a result of it, for all of them experienced a most horrible swelling of their bodies, though not all in the same place.

For some swelled up in the belly, and their bellies became hunchbacked, like a huge wine-vat, of whom it is written: *Ventrem omnipotentem,* or Belly Almighty.

These were all good folks and jolly good fellows, and of their race was born Saint Potbelly and Shrove-Tuesday.

Others swelled up in the shoulders and became so hunchbacked in that portion of their anatomy that they were called Montifers, that is to say mountain-bearers, specimens of whom you can still see everywhere, of various sexes and in various walks of life; and from this race sprang Aesop, whose splendid deeds and sayings you have in writing.

The swelling of others took place in the length of that number which is known as Nature's Workman, as a result of which they came to be possessed of marvelously long, big, fat, thick, and juicy ones, crested after the antique fashion. Their members were so long that they employed them as girdles, wrapping them five or six times around their bodies. And if it happened that the member was in form, with the wind to its poop, you would have said, upon seeing these chaps, that they must be soldiers with lances at rest ready to joust with the dummy. Their race is lost, as the women tell us; for these latter are continually lamenting the fact that

> There are no more of those big ones, etc.,—

you know the rest of the song.

Others grew so enormously in the region of their testicles that three of those organs were enough to fill a hogshead. From them have come the big balls of Lorraine, which will never stay in a codpiece, but are always falling down to the bottom of their owners' breeches.

Others grew in their legs, and to see them, you would have said that they were cranes or flamingos, or else, people walking on stilts; and the little schoolroom rowdies are in the habit of calling them by the name of *Jambus*, in grammar class.

Others grew so in their noses that this member came

to resemble the beak of a still, being all diapered and spangled with pimples, swarming with purple-colored tufts, and enameled, studded, and embroidered with gueules. You have seen noses like that on Canon Bigbelly and on Dr. Woodenfoot, the physician of Angers. There were very few of this race that cared much about a dose of barley-water, but all were connoisseurs of the Septembral juice. Naso, the Big Nose, and Ovid sprang from them, and all those of whom it is written: *Ne reminiscaris.*

Others grew in their ears. Some had such big ones that they could use one of them for their doublet, breeches, and jacket, and with the other cover themselves, as they would with a Spanish cape; and it is said that this race still exists in Bourbonnais, for which reason they are commonly known as "the long ears of Bourbonnais."

Others grew in the length of their bodies, and from these come the giants, and through them, Pantagruel.

Rabelais then proceeds to give a long and fanciful genealogy for his hero. This genealogy embraces four distinct classes of names: those drawn from the Bible and Biblical mythology; those drawn from Greek and Roman mythology; those drawn from the medieval romances of chivalry; and, lastly, invented, purely fictitious names. Voltaire believed that this was "a highly scandalous parody of the most respectable genealogies."

I understand well enough how, in reading this passage, a reasonable doubt may well arise in your minds. You may ask how it is possible that things should be so, in view of the fact that, at the time of the flood,

everybody perished except Noah and seven persons who
were with him in the ark, in which number the Hurtaly
above mentioned is not included. The point is, undoubtedly, well taken, and quite obvious; but my answer
shall satisfy you, or else my brain is badly calked. Seeing
that I was not there at the time, and so am not in a
position to give you an eye-witness's account, I will cite
for you the authority of the Masorites, those well-hung
lads and fine Jewish bagpipers, who assert that, in
reality, the said Hurtaly was not in Noah's ark at all. He
had not been able to get in, for he was too big; instead,
he sat a-straddle of it, one leg this way and one leg that
way, like little children on their wooden hobbyhorses,
or like the big bull's-horn-blower of Berne who was
killed at the battle of Marignano, and who had for a
mount a huge rock-throwing cannon which is a beast
with a jolly nice ambling gait, I may tell you, and one
with which no one could find any fault. In this manner, I
swear to God, Hurtaly saved that ark from shipwreck,
for he would give it a shove with his legs and turn it
whichever way he chose with his foot, as one does the
helm of a ship. Those that were inside sent him up
plenty of victuals through the chimney, being grateful
for the good turn he was doing them, and sometimes
they would converse together as Icaromenippus did with
Jupiter, according to Lucian's report.

Do you think you have all this through your noodles?
Drink up then, a good stiff drink without a chaser, for
if you don't believe it, neither do I, said she.

*"Not only the Arabians, the Barbarians, and the
Latins"; three of the earlier editions have a variant read-
ing here: "Not only the Greeks, the Arabians, and the
Ethnics, but also the authors of the Holy Scripture, like*

Monsignor St. Luke and St. Matthew." ——"*There are no more of those big ones*": this was a real song, the words of which have been found. ——"*By the name of Jambus*": a play on the French jambe, a leg, and iambus, a metrical foot. ——"*Naso, the Big Nose, and Ovid*": this, of course is one and the same person, Publius Ovidius Naso. ——"*Ne reminiscaris*": from the litany, "Ne reminiscaris delicta nostra, *Remember not our sins,*" a play on the Latin ne and the French nez, or nose. —— "*The Hurtaly above mentioned*": in his genealogy of Pantagruel, Rabelais lists "Hurtaly, *who was a fine eater of soups and reigned at the time of the deluge*"; Hurtaly was an antediluvian Biblical giant. ——"*The bull's-horn-blower of Berne*": the sonneur de corne de taureau in Swiss companies was the one who gave the signal for the battle; the feat mentioned here is a historic one; reference is to the defeat of the Swiss by François I, at Marignano, on September 13-14, 1515. ——"*As Icaromenippus did with Jupiter*": in Lucian's Icaromenippus, *the philosopher merely views the trap-doors through which prayers ascend to Jove.* ——"*Neither do I, said she*": possibly the tag of a popular song or saying.

The Nativity of the Most Redoubtable Pantagruel

GARGANTUA, at the age of five-hundred-twenty-four years, begot his son Pantagruel, with his wife, whose name was Badebec, daughter of the King of the Amaurots in Utopia. She died in childbirth, for the child was so marvelously big and heavy that he was unable to come to light without suffocating his mother.

But in order to understand fully the cause and reason of that name which was given him in baptism, you should note that there was, that year, so great a drought throughout all the land of Africa that thirty-six months, three weeks, four days, and a little more than thirteen hours passed without any rain, and with the sun so intense that all the earth was dried up. It was not more scorched in the time of Elijah than it was then, for there was not a single tree on the earth that had either leaf or flower. The grass was without any green, the river-beds were empty, and the fountains were dry; the poor fish, tired of their own element, wandered over the earth, crying horribly; the birds fell from the air for lack of dew; and the wolves, foxes, deer, wild boars, fallow-deer, hares, rabbits, weasels, martins, badgers, and other beasts were to be found dead in the fields, their jaws dropping open.

As for human beings, that was a great pity. You might have seen them with their tongues hanging out, like rabbits which have been running for six hours; some cast themselves into wells, while others crawled into the bellies of cows to find a little shade. These latter were the ones whom Homer calls *Alibantes*. The whole country was at anchor. It was a pitiable thing to see the effort which human beings expended in protecting themselves against that horrible thirst. It was all they could do to save the holy water in the churches from being used up; but an order went out from the council of Messieurs the Cardinals and the Holy Father that no one was to take more than a single lick at it. And so, whenever anyone entered a church, you might have seen a score of poor thirsty devils running up behind the one who distributed the water, their chops open, in the hope of catching some little drop, like the Wicked Rich Man, for they did not want any to go to waste. Oh, how happy that year was the one who had a nice, cool, well-furnished cellar!

The philosopher, in raising the question why sea water is salty, relates that at the time when Phoebus turned over the driving of his lucific chariot to his son, Phaeton, the said Phaeton, poorly trained in the art and being unable to follow the ecliptic line between the two tropics of the sun's course, wandered from his path and came so near the earth that he dried up all the countries lying underneath, burning up a great part of the heavens, that part which the philosophers call the *Via lactea*, or *Milky Way*, and which winebibbers have named *St. James' Way*, although the smartest among the poets tell us that it is the place where Juno's milk fell when she was suckling Hercules. And so the earth was so scorched that it fell into an enormous sweat, sweating out all the sea, which for that reason is salty, because all sweat is salty. You will agree that this is true, if you care to taste your own, or, if you like, that of syphilitics when they are being given a sweat bath: it is all one to me.

An almost exactly parallel case occurred during this year that I have been telling you about, for one Friday, when everybody was engaged in devotions and they were having a fine procession, with many litanies and beautiful chants, begging Almighty God that he would deign to look upon them with an eye of mercy in their discomfort—while this was taking place, there were clearly seen going up from the earth great drops of water, as when someone is sweating copiously. And the poor people began to rejoice, as if it had been something that was to do them good, for as certain of them remarked, there was not a single drop of moisture in the air from which they might hope for rain, and so the earth was supplying the lack. Other learned ones declared that this was the rain of the antipodes, of which Seneca tells us in the fourth book *Quaestionum natu-*

ralium, in speaking of the origin and sources of the Nile; but these latter were mistaken; for when the procession was over and everybody began trying to catch a little of this dew, so that they might be able to drink a good cupful, they found that it was nothing but brine, worse-tasting and saltier than sea-water.

And since it was this very day that Pantagruel was born, his father named him as he did; for *Panta* in Greek is equivalent to all, and *Gruel* in the Hagarene language means thirsty, the inference being that at the hour of the child's birth, the world was all athirst. Moreover, his father, in a mood of prophecy, foresaw that his son would one day be the Ruler of the Thirsty Ones, as was shown him at that very hour by a most obvious sign. For as the mother, Badebec, was giving birth, and as the mid-wives were waiting to receive the child, there came out first from the mother's belly sixty-eight mule drivers, each one leading by the halter a mule loaded with salt; after these came nine dromedaries loaded with hams and smoked beef-tongues, seven camels loaded with eels, and, finally, twenty-four cartloads of leeks, garlic, onions, and shallots, all of which greatly frightened the said mid-wives. But some among them spoke up and said:

"That's a goodly store; and it's a lucky thing, for we drink only in miserly fashion (*lachement*) these days, not in good old *Landsman* fashion. It is a good sign, for those are the goads of wine."

And while they were cackling away like this, with small talk among themselves, lo and behold, Pantagruel came out, all covered with fur like a bear, which led one of the old women present to remark, in a tone of prophecy:

"He's born with hair; that means he will do marvelous things, and if he lives, he'll live to a certain age."

*This passage gives a humorous and fabulously exag-
gerated account of the great drought of 1532. ——The
name Badebec is still common in French patois, with the
general sense of a stolid, silent, gaping-mouthed, or foolish individual, gaping-mouthed being the proper signifi-
cation. ——The Utopia referred to is that of Sir Thomas
More. ——"Whom Homer calls Alibantes": it is Plutarch, not Homer, who calls them this; see the former's
Table Talk, Book VIII, Question x, 3; the name means
the desiccated ones. ——"The Wicked Rich Man":
allusion to Lazarus and the rich man in hell, Luke, XVI,
19-25. ——"The philosopher, in raising the question
why sea water is salty": Empedocles, in Plutarch,* On
the Opinions of the Philosophers, II, 6. ——*"The ecliptic
line between the two tropics": the ecliptic is the line
followed by the sun in its course; and "the tropics are
the two lines which, in the Ptolemaic system, bound the
declinations of the sun; one of them passes through the
sign of Cancer, the other through Capricorn" (Plattard).*
——*"St. James' Way": popular and legendary name of
the Milky Way in France and other Catholic countries,
supposed to point the route for pilgrims to Santiago de
Compostella. ——"The fourth book* Quaestionum natu-
ralium": the reference is doubtful; in the third book of
his* Quaestiones Naturales *Seneca quotes an opinion of
Theophrastus which might apply to the explanation
given by Rabelais.*

*One of the earlier editions (Poitiers, 1533) contains a
couple of passages that have not been included here for
the reason that their authenticity is doubtful.*

The Mourning Which Gargantua Observed upon the Death of His Wife Badebec

WHEN Pantagruel was born, who do you think was astonished and perplexed? It was Gargantua, his father. For seeing, on the one hand, his wife Badebec dead and, on the other hand, his son Pantagruel born, so handsome and so big, he did not know what to say or what to do. The doubt that troubled his mind lay in deciding whether he ought to weep from sorrow for his wife or laugh for joy over his son. On the one hand and on the other, he found good logical arguments, enough to suffocate him, and he drew them all up, very nicely, *in modo et figura*, in true syllogistic fashion; but he was not able to resolve the question; and so for this reason he remained entangled like a mouse caught in pitch or like a kite snared in a trap.

"Shall I weep," he said. "Yes, and why? My good wife is dead, who was the most this and the most that of any woman that ever was. I'll never see her again; I'll never get another one like her; that is an inestimable loss to me. Oh my God! What have I done to Thee that Thou shouldst punish me thus? Why didst Thou not send death to me before Thou didst to her? For to live without her is for me but to languish! Ha! Badebec, my darling, my sweetie, my little twat (it was all of four and a half acres big, plus two fields each large enough to plant a dozen bushels of grain each), my honey lump, my cod-piece, my old shoe, my slipper, I'll never see you again. Ha! Poor Pantagruel, you've lost your good mother, your gentle nurse, your well beloved lady. Ha! False Death, art so malevolent, art so outrageous towards me that thou wouldst take from me her to whom immortality belonged as of right!"

In saying this, he began to weep like a cow; but all of a sudden he started laughing like a calf, as he remembered Pantagruel:

"Ho! my little son," he said, "my cod, my little hoofy, what a darling you are, and how grateful I am to God for having given me so fine a son, so gay, so smiling, so pretty! Ho, ho, ho, ho! how content I am! Let's drink up, ho! Away with all melancholy. Bring on the best there is, rinse the glasses, lay the cloth, chase those dogs away there, stir up the fire, light the candles, close that door, bring on that soup-bread, give those poor beggars what they want and send them on their way, and take my cloak, for I'm going to strip to my doublet, that I may be the better able to show these old ladies a good time."

As he said this, he heard the Litany and the *Mememto's* of the priests, who were putting his wife into the ground. He thereupon broke off his cheerful remarks and was suddenly ravished once more but in a different manner:

"Lord God, must I become sad again? That annoys me. I am no longer young, I'm getting along in years, the weather is dangerous, and I may catch some kind of fever. That's what drives me crazy. On the word of a gentleman, it would be better to weep less and drink more. My wife is dead; well! by God (*da jurandi*, pardon me for swearing), I shan't be able to resurrect her by my tears. She's well off; she's in paradise at least, if there's nothing better than that. She's praying God for us; she's quite happy where she is; she doesn't have to worry any more over our miseries and calamities. That's our own lookout. But God help the survivors; I ought to be thinking about finding me another one!

"But here's what you can do," he said to the *sages-femmes,* "wise women"—"Where are they? Good folks, I can't see you— Go to her burial, and I will stay here in the meanwhile and rock my son; for I'm not feeling very well, and I'm afraid I'm in danger of falling sick. Take a stout drink before you go; you'll find it's good stuff, and you may believe me upon my word of honor."

Obeying his orders, they went to the funeral and burial, while the poor Gargantua remained at home. In the meanwhile the latter composed an epitaph to be engraved on his wife's tombstone which ran as follows:

SHE DIED OF CHILD, AND THAT'S NO RIDDLE

THE NOBLE BADEBEC, FOR THIS

IS THE TRUTH; HER FACE WAS LIKE A FIDDLE,

A SPANISH BODY, HER BELLY SWISS.

THEN PRAY TO GOD TO GIVE HER BLISS,

AND PARDON HER—SHE SINNED, NO DOUBT.

HERE LIES ONE NOT TOO REMISS,

WHO DIED THE DAY THAT SHE PASSED OUT.

This passage, like the slighting allusion to Garga-melle's death in the Gargantua, *is commonly cited as one of the evidences of Rabelais' anti-feminism. The doubting and derogatory manner in which he speaks of heaven is viewed as a manifestation of his atheism.*

Pantagruel's Infancy

I FIND, in the ancient historiographers and poets, that a number of persons have been born into this world in very strange ways, which it would take too long to relate here: read the seventh book of Pliny, if you have the leisure. But you never heard of a case so marvelous as that of Pantagruel; for it is hard to believe how he grew in body and in strength in so short a time. Hercules who killed two serpents in his cradle was as nothing compared to him, for those serpents were very small and fragile ones. But Pantagruel while he was still an infant-in-arms did some very amazing things.

I shall not take time here to tell you how, at every meal, he sucked the milk of four-thousand-six-hundred cows, nor how, in order to provide him with a saucepan in which to boil his milk they kept all the saucepan-makers busy at Saumur in Anjou, at Villedieu in Normandy and at Framont in Lorraine, or how they served him his broth in a great stone trough, which is still to be seen at Bourges, near the Palace. But his teeth were already so big and strong that he bit a big slice out of that trough, as may be seen very plainly even now.

One day, towards morning, when they wanted to make him suck one of his cows (for he never had any other nurses, as History tells us), he succeeded in getting one of his arms out of the wrappings with which they had bound him in his cradle, and seizing that cow for you underneath one ham, he bit off two of her teats and half of her belly, along with her liver and her kidneys, and he would have eaten the whole cow, if it had not been that she bellowed horribly, as if the wolves had been at her legs. Hearing her cry, everybody came running up and took the said cow away from Pantagruel; but in spite of all they could do, her ham remained in his hands. He gulped it down very nicely, as you might a sausage, and when they wanted to take away the bone, he swallowed that too, as quickly as a cormorant would a little fish; and afterwards he began to babble: "Good,

good, good," for he could not as yet speak very plainly, giving them to understand by this that he found it very good, and that all he wanted was a little more of the same.

After this incident, those who had charge of him took care to fasten him in with big cables like those which are manufactured at Tain, for the transporting of salt to Lyon, or like those of the big ship Françoise, which is in the Port of Grace in Normandy. On one occasion, when a big bear that his father was raising escaped and came running up to lick his face (for his nurses had not washed his chops very well), he broke those cables, as easily as Samson among the Philistines broke his; and, by your leave, he took my Mister Bear and tore him to pieces like a hen, and made a good warm mouthful out of him for one meal. At this Gargantua, fearing that the child might hurt himself, had four large iron chains made to bind him, and he also had them manufacture a number of buttresses, to which his cradle was firmly attached. Of these chains, you have one at La Rochelle, which is raised at night between the two great towers of the harbor; the second is at Lyon, the third at Angers, while the fourth was carried away by some of the devils to use in tying up Lucifer, who happened to break loose about that time, owing to a colic that gave him extraordinary torment, the result of his having eaten the fricasseed soul of a sergeant for breakfast. And so, you may very well believe what Nicolas de Lyra has to say concerning that passage of the *Psalter* where it is written: *Et Og regem Basan*, "and Og, the King of Bashan," to the effect that this Og, while still very small, was so strong and robust that they had to fasten him in his cradle with chains of iron. As a result of all this, Pantagruel remained calm and quiet for he could not so easily break those chains, seeing that he did not have room enough in the cradle to give free play to his arms.

But here is what happened one day when they were having a great feast, his father, Gargantua, being engaged in giving a sumptuous banquet to all the princes of his Court. I can readily believe that the courtiers were so taken up with the dinner-service that they gave small thought to poor little Pantagruel, who thus remained *a reculorum,* as the schoolboys say, or off in one corner. But what do you think the latter did?

What did he do, my good folks? Listen:

First, he tried to break the chains of his cradle with his arms, but he was not able to do so, for the chains were too strong. Then, he stamped with his feet until he had kicked the bottom out of the cradle, which was made of a great beam sixty-three inches square; and as soon as he had got his feet out, he wriggled the rest of his body through, as best he could, until his feet were touching the ground. Whereupon, with great strength, he lifted his cradle on his back, so that it was bound to him there like a tortoise climbing a wall, and to see him, you would have thought that this was a big five-hundred-ton carack standing on end.

In this fashion, he entered the hall where the banquet was going on, in so bold a manner that he gave everyone present a good fright; but since his arms were bound inside, he was not able to reach out for anything to eat. Accordingly, with a great effort he bent over to take up a few mouthfuls with his tongue. Perceiving this, his father understood quite well that they had left the lad without feeding him; and on the advice of the princes and lords present, he commanded that they should undo the chains. Gargantua's physicians also stated that if they kept the boy in a cradle like that, he would be subject all his life to the gravel. When they had unchained him, they made him sit down, and he then ate quite heartily; but first, Pantagruel broke his cradle into more than five-hundred-thousand bits, with one blow of his fist, striking it squarely in the middle, and swearing all the while that he would never go back to it any more.

The preceding chapter is especially close to life. For instance, Saumur in the department of Maine-et-Loire and Villedieu-les-Poëles in the canton of Avranche (Manches) were noted for their poëliers, or makers of braziers, while Framont (Rabelais has Bramont) in Alsace was known from the thirteenth to the nineteenth century for its iron mines and forges and for the manufacture of utensils. The stone trough of Bourges in the thirteenth century stood in front of the municipal palace of Jean de Berry, today the prefecture of Cher; it was a stone vat known as "the giant's dish," which served once a year to hold the wine that was distributed to the poor. The "Grande Françoise," named after François 1, was a triumph of naval construction of the age, including among other things a tennis court, a smithy, a windmill, and a chapel; but when an attempt was made to launch it in 1533 it turned over on its side and sank. There were great harbor chains, of the sort mentioned, at Rochelle, Lyon, and Angers.

Nicolas de Lyra was an Italian Franciscan of the fourteenth century, author of a famous commentary on the Bible. ——"Og, the King of Bashan": see Psalms, cxxxvi, 20, and Deuteronomy, iii, 11; De Lyra in his commentary says nothing about the chains.

Deeds of the Noble Pantagruel in His Youth

THUS Pantagruel grew from day to day and derived much profit from it all, as anyone could see; and at this his father, from natural affection, rejoiced. They had a crossbow made for him while he was still a little shaver, so that he could amuse himself with the birdies; and that crossbow at present is known as the Great Crossbow of Chantelle. Then they sent him to school to acquire learning and to spend his youth.

In accordance with this plan he came to Poitiers to study and profited much from his stay there. While he was in this city he noticed that the students had certain periods of leisure, but did not know what to do to pass the time; and he was sorry for them. And so one day he took from a great rock-quarry named Passelourdin a huge stone, more than forty yards square and about ten-and-a-half feet in thickness, and placed this stone, with no effort at all, upon four pillars in the middle of a field, so that the students, when they did not know what else to do, might find a pastime in climbing it and feasting on the top, with many flagons, hams, and pastries, carving their names upon it with a knife. This rock, at present, is called the Upraised Stone. In memory of this feat, no one to this day is permitted to matriculate in the University of Poitiers until he has drunk from the Caballine fountain of Croutelle, passed by Passelourdin, and climbed the Stone in question.

Afterward, in reading the stirring Chronicles of his ancestors, he discovered that Geoffrey of Lusignan, known as "Big-Toothed Geoffrey," the grandfather of the cousin-in-law of the eldest sister of the aunt of the son-in-law of the uncle of the daughter-in-law of his step-

mother, had been buried at Maillezais; and so, he took
campos or leave of absence for a day, in order to visit
the place like the dutiful chap that he was. Leaving
Poitiers with some of his companions, he went by way of
Ligugé, stopping off to visit the noble Ardillon who was
abbot there, then by way of Lusignan, Sanxay, Celles,
Coulonges, and Fontenay-le-Comte, pausing in the last-
named place to greet the learned Tiraqueau; and from
there he and his comrades proceeded to Maillezais,
where he visited the sepulchre of that same Geoffrey
with the big tooth. He was a little afraid, at first, when
he saw his ancestor's portrait, for it is the picture of a
man in a great fury, half drawing his curved sword from
its scabbard. Pantagruel inquired the cause of this,
whereupon the canons of the place informed him, there
was no explanation, save that

Pictoribus atque poetis, etc.,

that is to say, that painters and poets possess the liberty
of painting anything they choose in any manner that
pleases them. But Pantagruel was not satisfied with
their reply, and said:

"He is not painted that way without good reason,
and I have no doubt that at his death someone did him
a wrong, for which he is demanding vengeance of his
relatives. I am going to look into this a little further
and do whatever I see fit."

He did not after this return to Poitiers, for the reason
that he wished to visit the other universities of France.
And so, going on to La Rochelle, he set sail for Bordeaux,
in which place he did not find a great deal of sport—
nothing, indeed, except a few longshoremen playing
cards on the beach. From there, he came on to Toulouse,
where he learned to dance very well and how to juggle
the two-handed sword, as is the custom among the stu-

dents of that university; but he did not stay there very long, when he perceived that they were in the habit of burning their regents alive, like red herrings. Speaking of this, he remarked:

"I hope to God I never die like that, for I am naturally quite thirsty enough, without being heated any more."

Then he came on to Montpellier, where he found very good wines of Mirevaux and some jolly company; and there he thought he would start studying medicine. But he decided that the calling was far too tiresome and melancholy a one, and that physicians always smelled of enemas, like old devils. Accordingly, he resolved to study law; but seeing that there were but three lousy wretches and one bald-headed legist in the place, he took his departure; and, along the way, did the distance between the Pont du Gard and the amphitheatre of Nîmes in less than three hours, which seems an accomplishment more nearly divine than human. He then came to Avignon, and he had not been there three days before he fell in love, for the women there are very fond of the game of press-rump, seeing that the town is in papal territory.

Upon perceiving this, his tutor, named Epistemon, brought him to Valence in Dauphiny; but he soon perceived that there was not much sport here, either, and that the ruffians of the city were in the habit of beating the students, whom they despised. One fine Sunday when everybody was engaged in public dancing, a certain student wished to take part in the dance, but the ruffians I have mentioned would not permit him to do so. When he saw this, Pantagruel chased all the rowdies as far as the banks of the Rhone, and he would have seen to it that they were all drowned if they had not hidden themselves in the earth like moles a good half-league under the Rhone. The hole may be seen there yet.

After this he departed, and with three steps and a jump came to Angers, where he found himself very well taken care of, and he would have stayed there some little while if it had not been that the plague drove him away. From there he came to Bourges where he studied for quite a long time, and to considerable advantage, in the college of law. He would remark, upon occasion, that law books impressed him as being a handsome golden robe of state, and an enormously precious one, but one, nevertheless, embroidered with dung.

"For," he would say, "there are no books in the world so fine, so ornate, so elegant as are the texts of the *Pandects;* but their embroidery, that is to say, the *Gloss of Accursius,* is so befouled, so infamous, and so infectious that there is nothing in it but ordure and vileness."

Leaving Bourges, he went to Orléans, and there encountered a number of roistering students who proceeded to stage a great celebration in honor of his coming. In a short time he had learned from them how to play tennis so well that he was master of the game; for the students of that place make a fine sport of it. Sometimes they would take him to the Islands to amuse himself at the game of push-on; but so far as racking his brains with study was concerned, he was very careful not to do anything of the sort, from fear of hurting his eyesight. For as a certain one of the regents would sometimes remark in his lectures, there is nothing so harmful to the sight as a malady of the eyes.

One day when one of the students of his acquaintance, who did not have any more learning than he could carry, but who, as compensation, knew how to dance and play tennis very well, was made a licentiate in law,

Pantagruel drew up a coat-of-arms and a device for the graduates of the university, the motto reading as follows:

> A tennis ball in your belly-band,
> And a racquet in your hand,
> A law-book in your doctor's hood,
> Scrape your feet, and scrape 'em good,
> And you're a doctor, understand.

This passage is of particular interest from the biographic point of view, as providing possibly a more or less true-to-life account of Rabelais' own student Wanderjahre. There is to be perceived, for one thing, a certain wavering between law and medicine, with a decided leaning to the latter. The author also makes plain his attitude toward the legal profession, makes it clear that his quarrel is with the glossarists like Accursius (most famous of the medieval commentators) and not with the Pandects themselves. There are reminiscences, in this chapter, of friends and scenes of his youth, of such personages as the jurist, André Tiraqueau, and Antoine Ardillon, Augustinian Abbot of Fontaine-le-Comte, near Ligugé, and of the priory of Maillezais, where Maître François' patron, Geoffroy d'Estissac, kept open house to the humanists.

The Upraised Stone (Pierre Levée) is a partly crumbling dolmen along the road from Saint-Saturnin to Vandouzil, in the region of Poitiers, the table formed by this rock being still intact in the eighteenth century. The fountain of Croutelle was south of Poitiers; Rabelais terms it "Caballine" in allusion to the Hippocrene Spring which the steed Pegasus caused to gush forth on Parnassus, with a blow of his hoof. A warrior's head believed to be that of Geoffroy de Lusignan ("Big-Toothed Geoffrey"), who burned the Abbey of Maillezais in 1223 and was compelled by the Pope to rebuild it, was uncovered by excavations in the choir of the church in 1834. The cavern into which Pantagruel drives the Valence rowdies was one under the church of Saint-Pierre, in the faubourg *of the city. The only purely fanciful allusion (apparently) is to the crossbow of Chantelle.*

The burning of regents at Toulouse has reference to the burning alive, in June 1532, of Jean de Caturce of Limoux, who held the chair of law at the university. The plague of Angers is the one that broke out in August, 1518, and lasted into 1519, compelling François i *to leave Anjou.*

The quotation from Horace is from the Ars *Poetica, 9-10.* ——*"Seeing that the town is in papal territory": under the government of the Holy See, manners in Avignon were notoriously lax.* ——*The name Epistemon signifies "one who knows."* ——*"The game of push-on":* pouss'avant *was a variety of ball-game, but it has here an erotic sense.* ——*"Scrape your feet": this was the "respectable" slow dance* (basse dance au talon) *in which the feet did not leave the floor.*

How Pantagruel Met a Native of Limousin Who Mangled the French Language

ONE day or other, I cannot tell you just when it was, Pantagruel with his companions was taking a little after-supper stroll, in the vicinity of the gate by which one leaves for Paris. There he met a student, as jaunty as could be, coming along the same road; and after they had exchanged greetings, Pantagruel inquired of the stranger:

"Where do you come from, my friend, at this time of day?"

The student replied:

"From the alme, inclyte, and celebrate Academy that is vocitated Lutetia."

"What's he saying?" Pantagruel put the question to one of his followers.

"He comes from Paris," was the reply.

"So," said Pantagruel, "you come from Paris, do you? And what kind of sport do you young gentlemen students find down Paris way?"

The other replied:

"We transfretate the Sequan at the dilucule and crepuscule; we deambulate through the compites and quadrivies of the urbe; we despumate the Latial verbocination and, like verisimile armorabonds, captate the benevolence of the omnijugal, omniform, and omnigenous feminine sex. On certain diecules we invisit the lupanars, and in a venereic ecstasy we inculcate our vereters into the penetissim recesses of the pudends of those amicabillissim meretricules. Then we cauponisate, in the meritory taverns known as the Pine Apple, the Castle, the Madeleine, and the Mule, some fine vervecine spatules, perforaminated with petrosil; and if, by fort fortune, there should be a rarity or penury of pecune in our marsupies, and the latter should be exhausted of ferruginous metal, we, for the scot, demit our codices and oppignerates vestes, prestolating the arrival of tabellaries from the patriotic lares and penates."

At which, Pantagruel exclaimed:

"What the devil kind of language is this? By God! but I'm beginning to think you're some kind of heretic."

"Signor, no," said the student, "for libentissimally, as soon as there illucesces any minutule slice of day, I demigrate into one of those so well architected minsters, and there, irrorating myself with fine lustral water,

I mumble a cut of some missic precation of our sacri-
ficules; and submurmurillating my horarian precules, I
elue and absterge my anime of its nocturnal inquina-
ments. I revere the Olympicoles, I venere latrially the
supernal Astripotent, I dilige and redame my proxims, I
observe the decalogic prescripts and, according to the
facultatule of my vires, do not discede from them by an
unguicular late. It is quite veriform that, inasmuch as
Mammon does not supergurgitate a drop in my loculs,
I am somewhat rare and lent at supererogating the
eleemosyns to those egenes hostially queritating their
stipe."

"Oh, a turd, a turd," said Pantagruel, "what's the fool
trying to say? I think he's making up some diabolical
language as he goes along, and that he's trying to be-
witch us all, like a magician."

One of his companions then spoke up.

"My lord, this chap, undoubtedly, is trying to ape
the language of the Parisians, but all he does is to flay
the Latin, while he thinks he's Pindarizing. He probably
imagines that his French is simply grand, just because
he disdains the common manner of speaking."

"Is that true?" Pantagruel demanded; and the student
replied:

"Signor, Messire, my genie is not nate apt at doing
what that flagitiose nebulon speaks of, namely, excoriating the cuticule of our Gallic vernacule; but viceversally,
I gnave opere and by veles and rames enite to locuple-
tate it with a Latinicome redundancy."

"By God!" cried Pantagruel, "I'll teach you how to
speak. But first, tell me, where are you from?"

"The primeve origin," replied the student, "of my aves
and ataves was indigene to the Lemovick regions, where
requiesces the corpor of the hagiotate St. Martial."

"I understand well enough, now," said Pantagruel. "You are a Limousin, for all your blather, and you're just trying to imitate the Parisians. Come here, till I give you a combing down!"

Then, he took the student by the throat, saying to him: "You flay the Latin; but, so help me St. John, I'll make you flay the fox, for I'm going to flay you alive!"

At this, the poor Limousin began to cry:

"Hey, squire! Ho, St. Martial! Help! awk, awk! Let me go, for God's sake! Keep your hands off me!"

"Now," remarked Pantagruel, "you're talking something like."

And so, he left him there; for the poor Limousin had dunged all over his breeches, which were cut in the back in the codfish-tail-fashion, and not with a full bottom.

"St. Alpantin!" exclaimed Pantagruel, "what a skunk! To the devil with this turnip-eater; he stinks too much!"

And so, he let him go.

But the student remorsefully remembered the adventure all his life, and was always so thirsty that he would sometimes remark that Pantagruel was holding him by the throat. And after a few years, he died the death of Roland, thus fulfilling divine vengeance and demonstrating what the philosopher and Aulus Gellius have to say, that it is better to speak the customary language and, as Octavianus Augustus once observed, to avoid exotic words, as the masters of ships avoid rocks at sea.

For the benefit of those readers who desire it, a "translation" of the Limousin student's jargon is given.

To Pantagruel's first question the student replies: "From the cherishing, illustrious, and celebrated Academy that is called Lutetia (Paris)."

*Being interpreted, the passage beginning "We trans-
fretate the Sequan" reads as follows:*

We cross the Seine at dawn and twilight; we walk
through the squares and street-corners of the city; we spout
(literally, foam or froth) Latin and, like true lovers, capture
the benevolent feminine sex of all shapes, kinds, and degrees
of servitude (omnijugal). On certain days, we visit the
houses of prostitution, and in a venereal ecstasy, we insert
our penes into the deepest recesses of the pudenda of those
most amiable whores. Then we eat, in the (pay-) taverns
known as the Pine Apple, the Castle, the Madeleine, and the
Mule, some fine shoulders of mutton interlarded with parsley; and if, by ill fortune, there should be a scarcity of
money in our pocket-books, then we put our books and
clothes in hock, while we wait for money (messengers) from
home.

The passage beginning "Signor, no" reads:

My lord, no, for most willingly, as soon as the faintest
glow of day appears, I go into one of those well built
churches, and there, sprinkling myself with holy water, I
mumble some of the prayers of our services; and as I murmur my prayers at the proper hour, I wash and cleanse my
soul of its nocturnal stains. I revere the gods (literally: the
dwellers on Olympus), I worshipfully venerate the Almighty
(literally: the Sovereign of the Stars), I cherish my neighbor and return his love, I observe the commandments (prescriptions) of the Decalogue and, according to the (faculty
of) strength that is in me, do not depart from them by a
nail's breadth. It is quite true that, inasmuch as Mammon
does not drop any money into my purse, I am somewhat
slow about indulging in any supererogatory charity to the
poor, who beg their pennies from door to door.

The passage beginning "Signor, Messire":

My genius is not naturally (literally: by birth; Latin,
aptus natus) apt at doing what that insulting wretch speaks
of, namely, excoriating the cuticle of our Gallic vernacular;
but vice versa, I lend all the help I can and do all in my

power (literally: force myself by means of sails and oars) to enrich it with a Latin-like redundancy.

The passage beginning "the primitive origin of my aves":

The primitive (primeval) origin of my fathers and grandfathers was in the Limousin regions, where rests the body of the most holy St. Martial.

The significance of Rabelais' Limousin student is perhaps best brought out by quoting M. Jean Plattard:

At the time Rabelais wrote there was in the world of students a "pig-Latin" (*écorche-latin*) jargon, the principle of which was to substitute for French words Latin words turned into French. Geoffroy Tory, in his *Champ Fleury* (1529), protests against the argot of these Latin-skimmers. The phrase that he cites, as a specimen of this jargon, is . . . almost the first sentence of the Limousin student. Rabelais, in this episode, has, therefore, merely sought to ridicule the jargon of the schools, not intending, by any means, to criticize the Latinizing writers; since, following their example, he himself has skimmed the Latin and abused neologisms drawn from that language, particularly in his 'harangues'. . . . But a distinction was made, at that time, between terms drawn from the Latin, which had no equivalents in the language, and the pig-Latin jargon, which undertook to substitute pedantic vocables for usual terms.

"The gate by which one leaves for Paris": the north gate of the enceinte at Orléans; the gate no longer exists, but a section of the street that led to it has been preserved. ——"The meritory taverns": i.e., the pay-taverns; these were actual fifteenth-century students' hostelries. ——"I'll make you flay the fox": i.e., vomit. ——"St. Alpatin": a facetious saint of the old mystery plays and romances of chivalry. ——"Turnip-eater": an epithet applied to the natives of Limousin. ——"Died the death of Roland": a death due to thirst, according to *popular tradition.* ———*"The philosopher and Aulus Gellius"*: Favorinus, *in Book* VII, *Chapter* x, *of the* Attic Nights (Noctes Atticae). ———*"As Octavianus Augustus once observed"*: Rabelais, *quoting from memory, makes free with a passage in Aulus Gellius (passage cited).*

II. Pantagruel Visits Paris and Meets Panurge

(CHAPTERS VII-XXII)

How Pantagruel Came to Paris

AFTER Pantagruel had studied most diligently at Orléans, he considered visiting the great University of Paris. But before setting out, he was told that there was an enormous bell at St. Aignan's, in Orléans, which had been buried in the earth for more than two-hundred-fourteen years, for the reason that it was so big and heavy that no mechanism of any sort could so much as lift it out of the ground, although they had applied all the methods described in Vitruvius' *De architectura,* Alberti's *De Re edificatoria,* Euclides, Theon, Archimedes, and Heron's *De ingeniis,* with no effect whatsoever.

Being quite disposed to listen to the humble request of the citizens and inhabitants of the city, he decided to carry the bell to its destined loft. He went at once to the place where it was, and lifted it from the ground with his little finger, as easily as you would have lifted the bell around a sparrow-hawk's neck. But before carrying it to the belfry, Pantagruel thought he would serenade the city by ringing it through the streets, with one hand. This amused everybody very much, but a

great misfortune resulted from it; for as he was ringing
the bell, in this manner all the fine wine of Orléans
turned and spoiled. But nobody knew anything about
this until the night following, when all felt so thirsty
from having drunk this spoiled wine that the only
thing they could do was to spit Maltese cotton, and remark: "We've got the old Pantagruel; our throats are
salty."

When he had accomplished this feat, Pantagruel came
on to Paris with his followers, and upon his arrival in
that city the entire populace turned out to see him;
for, as you are well enough aware, the people of Paris
are by nature silly, in sharps and flats. They surveyed
Pantagruel with astonishment, and not without considerable apprehension, being alarmed lest he should carry
off the Palace into some country *a remotis,* as his father
had carried away the bells of Notre-Dame, to hang them
around his mare's neck.

After he had lived there for some space of time,
ardently pursuing his studies in all of the seven liberal
arts, Pantagruel was heard to observe that it was a good
city to live in but not to die in, seeing that the beggars
of St. Innocent were in the habit of warming their rumps
on the bones of the dead.

*Of the writers mentioned above, Marcus Vitruvius
Pollio, Roman engineer and writer on architecture, was
well known to Renaissance humanists; the first edition
of Leone-Battista Alberti's treatise was published at
Florence in 1485, and tended to diffuse a taste for
classic architecture among the learned of the age; Theon
of Smyrna (second century,* A.D.*) wrote commentaries
on the Platonic mathematicians, and there was another
Theon (fourth century) who wrote on mathematics and*

left a treatise on Ptolomaeus; Heron of Alexandria was a third-century engineer and mathematician, author of a number of works dealing with mechanics, although the De ingeniis *is imaginary on Rabelais' part; Euclides and Archimedes need no identification.* ——"*Spit Maltese cotton*": cf. *Villon's* Testament, *729; also, our American phrase, "spit cotton."* ——"*In sharps and flats*": *in every way.*

Rabelais then goes on to tell how Pantagruel discovered the library of St. Victor, in the ancient abbey of that name, which in the sixteenth century was outside the walls of the city of Paris. This library was "a most magnificent one, especially rich in books of a certain kind." The phrase "of a certain kind" is a cautious statement; for St. Victor's was commonly regarded by the humanists as the most formidable theological arsenal of the age. The author thereupon proceeds to list more than a hundred humorous mock-titles of works which this library was supposed to contain. A few of the titles are real or but slightly modified, but the majority are pure invention, and practically every one would require a fairly extended gloss to render it wholly intelligible. Accordingly, while the passage is a famous one (Voltaire, among others, was delighted with it) it has had to be omitted here. It is a thoroughly enjoyable aside, but so far as the thread of the Pantagrueline narrative or the major course of Rabelais' thought is concerned, it will not be missed.

The Letter Which Pantagruel at Paris Received from His Father Gargantua

PANTAGRUEL studied very hard, you may be sure of that, and profited greatly from it; for he had a two-fold understanding, while his memory was as capacious as a dozen casks and flagons of olive oil. And while he was residing there, he received one day a letter from his father, which read as follows:

My very dear Son:

Among all the gifts, graces, and prerogatives with which that sovereign plastician, Almighty God, has endowed and adorned human nature in its beginnings, it seems to me the peculiarly excellent one is that by means of which, in the mortal state, one may acquire a species of immortality, and in the course of a transitory life be able to perpetuate his name and his seed. This is done through that line that issues from us in legitimate marriage. By this means, there is restored to us in a manner that which was taken away through the sin of our first parents, of whom it was said that, inasmuch as they had not been obedient to the commandment of God the Creator, they should die, and that, through their death, the magnificent plastic creation which man had been should be reduced to nothingness. By this means of seminal propagation, there remains for the children that which was lost to the parents, and for the grandchildren that which, otherwise, would have perished with the children; and so, successively, down to the hour of the last judgment when Jesus Christ shall have rendered to God the Father His specific realm, beyond all danger and contamination of sin; for then shall cease all begettings and corruptions, and the elements shall forego their incessant transmutations, in view of the fact that the peace that is so desired shall then have been consummated and perfected, and all things shall have been brought to their period and their close.

It is not, therefore, without just and equitable cause that I render thanks to God, my Saviour, for having given me the power to behold my hoary old age flowering again in your youth: for when, by the pleasure of Him who rules and moderates all things, my soul shall leave this human habitation, I shall not feel that I am wholly dying in thus passing from one place to another, so long as, in you and through you, my visible image remains in this world, living, seeing, and moving among men of honor and my own good friends, as I was wont to do. My own conduct has been, thanks to the aid of divine grace—not, I confess, without sin, for we are all sinners, and must be continually beseeching God to efface our sins—but at least, without reproach.

For this reason, since my bodily image remains in you, if the manners of my soul should not likewise shine there, then you would not be held to have been the guardian and the treasury of that immortality which should adhere to our name; and the pleasure I should take in beholding you would accordingly be small, when I perceived that the lesser part of me, which is the body, remained, while the better part, which is the soul, through which our name is still blessed among men, had become degenerate and bastardized. I say this, not out of any doubt of your virtue, of which you have already given me proof, but to encourage you, rather, to profit still further, and to go on from good to better. And I am now writing you, not so much to exhort you to live in this virtuous manner, as to urge you to rejoice at the fact that you are so living and have so lived, that you may take fresh courage for the future. In order to perfect and consummate that future, it would be well for you to recall frequently the fact that I have spared no expense on you, but have aided you as though I had no other treasure in this world than the joy, once in my life, of seeing you absolutely perfect in virtue, decency, and wisdom, as well as in all generous and worthy accomplishments, with the assurance of leaving you after my death as a mirror depicting the person of me, your father—if not altogether as excellent and as well formed an image as I might wish you to be, still all that I might wish, certainly, in your desires.

But while my late father of blessed memory, Grandgousier, devoted all his attention to seeing that I should profit from and be perfected in political wisdom, and while my studious labors were equal to his desires and perhaps even surpassed them, nevertheless, as you can readily understand, the times were not so propitious to letters as they are at present and I never had an abundance of such tutors as you have. The times then were dark, reflecting the unfortunate calamities brought about by the Goths who had destroyed all fine literature; but through divine goodness, in my own lifetime light and dignity have been restored to the art of letters, and I now see such an improvement that at the present time I should find great difficulty in being received into the first class of little rowdies—I who, in the prime of my manhood, and not wrongly so, was looked upon as the most learned man of the century. I do not say this in any spirit of vain boasting, even though I might permissibly do so—you have authority for it in Marcus Tullius, in his book on *Old Age,* as well as in that maxim of Plutarch's that is to be found in his book entitled *How One May Praise One's Self Without Reproach*—but I make the statement, rather, to give you the desire of climbing higher still.

Now all the branches of science have been reëstablished and languages have been restored: Greek, without which it is a crime for anyone to call himself a scholar, Hebrew, Chaldaic, and Latin; while printed books in current use are very elegant and correct. The latter were invented during my lifetime, through divine inspiration, just as, on the other hand, artillery was invented through the suggestion of the devil. The world is now full of scholarly men, learned teachers, and most ample libraries; indeed, I do not think that in the time of Plato, of Cicero, or of Papinian, there ever were so many advantages for study as one may find today. No one, longer, has any business going out in public or being seen in company, unless he has been well polished in the workshop of Minerva. I see brigands, hangmen, freebooters, and grooms nowadays who are more learned than were the doctors and preachers of my time. What's this I'm saying? Why, even the women and the girls have aspired to the credit of sharing this heavenly manna of fine learning. Things have come to such a pass that, old as I am, I have felt it necessary to take up the study of Greek, which I had not contemned, like Cato, but which I never had had the time to learn in my youth. And I take a great deal of pleasure now in reading the *Morals* of Plutarch, the beautiful *Dialogues* of Plato, the *Monuments* of Pausanias, and the *Antiquities* of Athenaeus, as I wait for the hour when it shall please God, my Creator, to send for me and to command me to depart this earth.

For this reason, my son, I would admonish you to employ your youth in getting all the profit you can from your studies and from virtue. You are at Paris and you have your tutor, Epistemon; the latter by word-of-mouth instruction, the former by praiseworthy examples, should be able to provide you with an education.

It is my intention and desire that you should learn all languages perfectly: first, the Greek as Quintilian advises; secondly, the Latin; and finally, the Hebrew, for the sake of the Holy Scriptures, along with the Chaldaic and the Arabic, for the same purpose. And I would have you form your style after the Greek, in imitation of Plato, as well as on the Latin, after Cicero. Let there be no bit of history with which you are not perfectly familiar. In this you will find the various works which have been written on cosmography to be of great help.

As for the liberal arts, geometry, arithmetic, and music, I gave you some taste for these while you were still a little shaver of five or six; keep them up; and as for astronomy, endeavor to master all its laws; do not bother about divinatory astrology and the art of Lully, for they are mere abuses and vanities.

As for civil law, I would have you know by heart the best texts and compare them with philosophy.

As for a knowledge of the facts of nature, I would have you apply yourself to this study with such curiosity that there should be no sea, river, or stream of which you do not know the fish; you should likewise be familiar with all the birds of the air, all the trees, shrubs, and thickets of the forest, all the grasses of the earth, all the metals hidden in the bellies of the abysses, and the precious stones of all the East and South: let nothing be unknown to you.

Then, very carefully, go back to the books of the Greek, Arabic, and Latin physicians, not disdaining the Talmudists and the Cabalists, and by means of frequent dissections, see to it that you acquire a perfect knowledge of that other world which is man. And at certain hours of the day, form the habit of spending some time with the Holy Scriptures. First in Greek, the New Testament and the Epistles of the Apostles; and then, in Hebrew, the Old Testament.

In short, let me see you an abysm of science, for when you shall have become a full-grown man, you will have to forsake your quiet life and leisurely studies, to master the art of knighthood and of arms, in order to be able to defend my household and to succor my friends in all their undertakings against the assaults of evildoers.

In conclusion, I would have you make a test, to see how much profit you have drawn from your studies; and I do not believe you can do this in any better fashion than by sustaining theses in all branches of science, in public and against each and every comer, and by keeping the company of the learned, of whom there are as many at Paris as there are anywhere else.

But since, according to the wise Solomon, wisdom does not enter the malevolent soul, and since science without conscience is but the ruin of the soul, it behooves you to serve, love, and fear God and to let all your thoughts and hopes rest in Him, being joined to Him through a faith formed of charity, in such a manner that you can never be sundered from Him by means of sin. Look upon the scandals of the world with suspicion. Do not set your heart upon vain things, for this life is transient but the word of God endures eternally. Be of service to all your neighbors and love them as yourself. Respect your teachers, shun the company of those whom you would not want to be like, and do not receive in vain the graces which God has bestowed upon you. And when you feel that you have acquired all the knowledge that is to be had where you now are, come back to me,

so that I may see you and give you my blessing before
I die.

My son, may the peace and grace of Our Lord be with
you! Amen.

From Utopia, this seventeenth day of the month of
March.

Your Father,

GARGANTUA.

When he had received and read this letter, Pantagruel
took fresh courage, and was inflamed to profit more than
ever from his studies; to such a degree that, seeing him
so study and profit, you would have said that his mind
among his books was like a fire among brushwood, so
violent was he and so indefatigable.

*This is that "ardent hymn . . . to the glory of the
Renaissance" of which Professor Lefranc has spoken.
"This letter," observes M. Plattard, "constitutes one of
the gravest chapters in the Pantagruel. Rabelais is here
celebrating the restoration, that is to say, the renaissance,
of learning (bonnes lettres) and is outlining the program
of encyclopedic instruction which he looks upon as
suited to every person called upon to occupy an elevated
position in society. This program conforms to the intellectual ideal of the humanists of the time. Its elements
may be found in various contemporary writings . . .
but one would be wrong in taking these writings as the
sources from which Rabelais has directly borrowed his
ideas in this chapter; those ideas were common at the
time to all the humanists." Gargantua's letter has also
inspired one of the most eloquent passages in Guizot
(Annales d'Education). It is to be noted that the course*

of humanistic studies here outlined is designed to fit the young Pantagruel, not for a cloistered, but for an active life. The stress on activity once more.

"That sovereign plastician": plasmateur *is one of* Rabelais' *neologisms, one that did not stick in the language; a few lines farther on (*"magnificent plastic creation"*) he employs* plasmature. ——"Calamities brought about by the Goths": *among the humanists the term tended to become synonymous with barbarians, and was applied in particular to the benighted ones of the Middle Ages.* ——"Marcus Tullius . . . on old age": *see the* De Senectute, 9 *and* 10. ——"That maxim of Plutarch's": Peri tou heauton epainein anepiphthonos (De se ipsum citra invidiam laudando), xx; *Plutarch's point of view is that old men of reputation and virtue should be permitted, and even encouraged, to boast of themselves in order to excite the emulation of youth.* ——"In the time of . . . Papinian": *the Roman jurisconsult Aemilius Papinianus (d. 212 A.D.) flourished during the reign of Septimus Severus.* ——"The art of Lully": *allusion to the alchemist and philosopher of the latter half of the thirteenth century, Raymond Lully, the* "doctor illuminatus."

How Pantagruel Came Upon Panurge Whom He Loved All His Life

ONE day, as he was walking outside the city in the direction of St. Anthony's Abbey, conversing and philosophizing with his followers and other students, Pantagruel came upon a tall, handsome chap who was physically very well set up, but who had been grievously wounded in several parts of his body, and who was in so bad a condition generally that he looked as though he had been attacked by dogs; to tell the truth, he greatly resembled an apple-picker from the Perche country.

The moment he caught sight of him, at a distance, Pantagruel remarked to the others:

"Do you see that fellow coming there, down the Charenton-Bridge Road? Take my word for it, he may be down on his luck now, but he comes of good and well-to-do stock, I can tell that by looking at his face; it is escapades such as those with a little curiosity are always getting into that have made a beggar out of him."

And so, when the stranger had come up to them, Pantagruel said to him:

"My friend, stop a moment, please, and answer a few questions. You will not be sorry for it for I should like very much to be of some assistance to you; I can see that you are in trouble and I am very sorry for you. But first tell me, friend: who are you, where do you come from, where are you going, what is your business, and what is your name?"

The fellow answered him in the Germanic language:

Juncker, Gott geb euch glueck unnd hail. Zuvor, lieber Juncker, ich las euch wissen das da ir mich von fragt, ist ein arm unnd erbarmglich ding, unnd wer vil darvon zu sagen, welches euch verdruslich zu boeren, unnd mir zu erzelen wer, vievol die Poeten unnd Orators vorzeiten haben gesagt in irem Spuerchen unnd Sentenzen, das die Gedechtnus des Ellends unnd Armuot vorlangs erlitten ist ain grosser Lust.

To this, Pantagruel replied:

"My friend, I do not understand a word of that gibberish; and so, if you wish us to understand you, speak some other language."

Then, the fellow replied:

Al barildim gotfano dech min brin alabo dordin falbroth ringuam albaras. Nin porth zadikim almucathin

*milko prin al elmim enthoth dal hebin ensouim; kuthim
al dumalkatim nim broth dechoth porth min michais im
endoth, pruch dal maisoulum hol moth dansrilim lupal-
das im voldemoth. Nin bur diavosth mnarbotim dal
gousch palfrapin duch im scoth pruch galeth dal Chinon
min foulchrich al conin butathen doth dal prim.*

"Do you understand any of that?" inquired Pantagruel of the others.

"It is my opinion," said Epistemon, "that that is the
language of the antipodes, and the devil himself could
not make head nor tail of it."

Then Pantagruel turning to the stranger said:

"Old man, I do not know whether the walls understand you or not, but none of us does, that is one sure
thing."

Then the fellow said:

*Signor mio, voi videte per exemplo che la cornamusa
non suona mai, s'ela non a il ventre pieno; cosi io pari-
mente non vi saprei contare le mie fortune, se prima il
tribulato ventre non a la solita refectione, al quale è
adviso che le mani et li denti abbui perso il loro ordine
naturale et del tuto annichillati.*

"I understand just about as much of that," said Epistemon, "as I did of the other." Then Panurge went on:

*Lard, ghest tholb be sua virtiuss be intelligence ass yi
body schal biss be naturall relvtht, tholb suld of me pety
have, for nature hass ulss egualy maide; bot fortune sum
exaltit hess, an oyis deprevit. Non ye less viois mou
virtius de previt and virtiuss men discrivis, for, anen
ye lad end, iss non gud.*

"Less than ever," said Pantagruel. Then Panurge said:

*Jona andie, guassa goussyetan behar da erremedio, be-
harde, versela ysser lan da. Anbates, otoyyes nausu, eyn
essassu gourr ay proposian or dine den. Non yssena bayta
fascheria egabe, genherassy badia sadassu noura assia.*

*Aran hondovan gualde eydassu nay dassuna. Estou
oussyc eguinan soury hin, er darstura eguy harm, Genicoa plasar vadu.*

"Are you, then, God, or *Genicoa* in the Basque
tongue?" inquired Eudemon.

Then Carpalim spoke up: "St. Ninian, but you're a
Scotchman, or else I didn't hear you right."

To which Panurge replied:

*Prug frest strinst sorgdmand strochdt drhds pag
brledand Gravot Chavigny Pomardiere rusth pkallhdracg
Deviniere pres Nays, Bcuille kalmuch monach drupp
delmeupplistrincq dlrnd dodelb up drent loch minc
stzrinquald de vins ders cordelis hur jocstzampenards.*

"Are you talking Christian, my friend," said Epistemon, "or Patelinese?"

"No, it's Lanternese."

Panurge's reply was:

*Herre, ie en spreke anders gheen taele dan kersten
taele; my dunct nochtans, al en seg ie v niet een wordt,
myuen noot v claert ghenonch wat ie beglere; gheest
my unyt bermherticheyt yet waer un ie ghevoet mach
zunch.*

"Quite as plain as the rest," said Pantagruel.

Panurge continued:

*Seignor, de tanto hablar yo soy cansado. Por que
supplico a Vostra Reverentia que mire a los preceptos
evangeliquos, para que ellos movani Vostra Reverentia a lo qu'es de consciencia, y, sy ellos non bastarent
para mover Vostra Reverentia a piedad, supplico que
mire a la piedad natural, la qual yo creo que le movra,
como es de razon, y con esto non digo mas.*

"Yea, my friend," said Pantagruel, "I have no doubt
whatsoever that you can speak a number of languages
very well, but tell us what you want in some tongue that
we can understand."

Panurge then said:

Myn Herre, endog jeg med inghen tunge talede, lygeson boeen, ocg uskvvlig creatner! myne kleebon, och myne legoms magerhed uudviser allygue klalig huvad tyng meg meest behoff girereb, som aer sandeligh mad och drycke: hwarfor forbarme teg omsyder offvermeg, och bef ael at gyffuc meg nogeth, aff huylket jeg kand styre myne groeendes maghe, lygeruss son mand Cerbero en soppe forsetthr. Soa shal tue loeffve lenge och lyska-light.

"I think," said Eusthenes, "that must be the way the Goths used to talk, and that, God forgive me, that's the way we'd all be talking, if we spoke through our hindends."

The fellow went on:

Adoni, scolom lecha. Im ischar harob hal habdeca, bemeherab thithen li kikar lehem, chancathub: "Laab al Adonai chonen ral."

"This time," said Epistemon, "I understand well enough, for that is the Hebraic tongue, most grammatically spoken."

Panurge continued:

Despota ti nyn panagathe, doiti sy mi uc artodotis? Horas gar limo analiscomenon eme atlhios. Ce en to mctaxy eme uc eleis udamos, zetis de par emu ha u chre, ce homos philologi pamdes homologusi tote logus te ce rhemeta peritta hyrparchin, opote pragma asto pasi delon esti. Entha gar anancei monon logi isin, hina pragmata, (hon peri amphibetumen), me prosphoros epiphenete.

"Why!" exclaimed Carpalim, Pantagruel's lackey, "that's Greek! I understand every word he said. And how's that? Have you lived in Greece?"

The answer was:

Agonou dont oussoys vou denaguez algarou, nou den

farou zamist vous mariston ulbrou, fousquez vou brol,
tam bredaguez moupreton den goul houst, daguez
daguez nou croupys fost bardounnoflist nou grou. Agou
paston tol nalprissys hourtou los ecbatonous prou dhou-
quys brol panygou den bascrou noudous caguons goul-
fren goul oust troppassou.

"It seems to me, I understand that," said Pantagruel,
"for it is the language of my own country, Utopia, or
something that sounds a whole lot like it." He was about
to say more, when Panurge interrupted him:

Jam toties vos per sacra perque deos deasque omnis
obtestatus sum ut, si qua vos pietas movet, egestatem
meam solaremini, nec hilum proficio clamans et ejulans.
Sinite, quaeso, sinite, viri impii
  Quo me fata vocant
abire, nec ultra vanis vestris interpellationibus obtundatis,
memores veteris illius adagi quo venter famelicus auri-
culis carere dicitur.

"That is all right, my friend," said Pantagruel, "but
don't you know how to speak French?"

"Very well indeed, my lord," the fellow replied.
"Thank God. It's my native and mother tongue, for I was
born and reared in the garden of France, that is, in
Touraine."

"Then," said Pantagruel, "tell us what your name is
and where you come from; for upon my word, I have
taken such a fancy to you, that if it suits you, you need
never stir from my side, and you and I will make just
such another pair of friends as Aeneas and Achates
were."

"My lord," was the reply, "my true and proper baptis-
mal name is Panurge; and just at present I come from
Turkey, where I was taken prisoner on the ill-fated
expedition to Mytilene. I should be very glad to tell you
all my adventures, for they are more marvelous than

those of Ulysses; but since you have invited me to stay with you, an invitation which I very willingly accept, with the promise never to leave you, even though you go through hell—since I'm staying on, we'll have plenty of time later for all that. Just now I feel a very urgent impulse to eat. My teeth are on edge, my belly is empty, my throat is dry, and my appetite is barking. Everything is all set. If you want to put me to work it will be a sight for sore eyes to watch me eat. For God's sake, tell them to speed it up."

Pantagruel then gave orders that they should take him home and bring him plenty of victuals. This was done and Panurge ate heartily that night and went to bed with the chickens, sleeping until dinner-time next day, when he made the distance between his bed and the table in three hops and a jump.

With this episode, one of the most famous characters in the whole of Rabelais makes his appearance: the roguish, blustering, tail-turning Panurge, who as the Falstaffian fidus Achates of Pantagruel is to run through the rest of the romance, and who, like his master, is to become the central figure of a fair-sized literature. Panurge is an incarnation of cunning, the name being from the Greek: panourgos, "apt at everything, a knave"; it is an epithet applied to the fox by classic authors. Numerous vain attempts have been made at a real-life identification of this character, with some commentators discovering an embodiment of Maître François himself. As he sketched in his Panurge, Rabelais probably had in mind Villon's Repues franches, Pierre Faifeu, and the Franc-Archer de Bagnolet. Lefranc sees a not unlikely origin of the name and type in a late-medieval mystery

*play. The bookish aspect, however, is not to be over-
stressed; for the author may have known a flesh-and-
blood Panurge in the student quarter of Paris.*

*In this passage Panurge speaks a baker's dozen of real
languages or dialects and three imaginary tongues. The
real ones include German, Italian, Scotch, Basque,
Dutch, Spanish, Danish, Hebrew, classical Greek, and
Latin.*

*A translation of the first passage, "in the Germanic
language," reads:*

Young gentleman, may God give you happiness and
prosperity. In the first place, my dear young gentleman, I
would have you know that what you ask of me pains me
deeply and would make a long story, a tiresome one for
you to listen to and for me to tell, even though the old poets
and orators, in their sententious maxims, do say that the
memory of the hardships and sufferings one has endured is
a great joy.

*The passage beginning "Al barildim gotfano," etc.,
was made up by Rabelais out of whole cloth. This, says
M. Sainéan, is "a factitious language, in which one dis-
cerns certain proper names . . . certain technical terms
. . . and certain common nouns . . . along with an
erotic expression: foulthrich al conin." Further on, the
author gives us two more specimens of such jargon.*

*The Italian passage, "Signor mio," etc., reads in
English:*

My lord, you can see, for example, that the bagpipe
never plays unless it has a full belly. It's the same way with
me. I cannot tell you my troubles, if this beastly belly of
mine does not have its customary refreshment. It thinks that
my hands and teeth have forgotten how to work, or that I
have none any more.

*The fragment beginning "Lard, ghest tholb," accord-
ing to M. Sainéan, "is from the Scotch and was un-*

doubtedly supplied Rabelais by a student of that nation at Paris. Scotch was completely unknown in the sixteenth century, and later editions of the Pantagruel replace it with English; but the original linguistic character of the fragment is brought out in the remark that immediately follows in the first edition: 'St. Ninian, but you're a Scotchman.'" A translation follows:

My lord, if you are as powerful in intelligence as you are naturally big of body, you ought to take pity on me, for nature has made us equals; but fortune has exalted some and debased others. None the less, virtue is frequently disdained and virtuous men are held in contempt, for before the last end, none is good.

As for the Basque fragment, "Jona andie," etc., no two commentators give the same rendering. The general sense (according to Lefranc) is:

Monsignor (great lord), for all ills there must be a remedy; to do what is right, that is the hard thing. I have begged you so! Let us get some sort of system into this thing; I shall not mind in the least, if you give me a bite to eat. After that, ask me whatever you please. And it would not be a bad thing on your part, if you were to stand treat, God willing.

The passage beginning "Prug frest strinst," etc., is another forged dialect, possibly based upon a cryptogram: a few proper names are recognizable.

The passage beginning "Herre, ie en spreke," etc., is in Dutch, probably the work, M. Sainéan thinks, of a Dutch student at Paris. Its sense is:

My lord, I do not speak any language that is not Christian; but it seems to me that, without my uttering a single word, my tatters ought to tell you what I want. Be charitable enough to give me a little refreshment.

The Spanish fragment, "Seignor de tanto hablar," etc., means:

My lord, I am tired of so much talking. And so, I beseech Your Reverence to consider the gospel teachings, that you may be led to do what your conscience directs; and if they should not be sufficient to move Your Reverence to pity, I beg that you will have recourse to that natural sympathy which, I am sure, cannot fail to sway you; and so, I shall say no more about it.

The passage, "Myn Herre," etc., is archaic Danish. According to a Danish authority (M. A. Rothe, of Copenhagen), the meaning is:

Sir, even in the event that, like children and brute beasts, I did not speak any language, my clothing and the emaciation of my body still ought to indicate clearly enough what I stand in need of, which is, as a matter of fact, something to eat and something to drink. Have pity on me, then, and order them to give me something that will enable me to master my barking stomach, just as one would set a bowl of soup in front of Cerberus. If you do so, you will live long and prosper.

The Hebrew passage, "Adoni, scolom lecha," etc., is, according to Sainéan, "certainly the work of a rabbi consulted by our author. The accomplishments of Rabelais in Hebrew are scarcely worth the mentioning. His enthusiasm for the sacred tongue, manifested in Gargantua's letter to Pantagruel, is an indication of the aspirations of the age rather than the expression of reality." The passage in English (based upon De Sacy's transliteration) would read:

Sir, peace be with you. If you wish to do good to your servant, give me at once a crumb of bread, as it is written: He lends to the Lord who has pity on the poor man.

The classical Greek fragment, "Despota ti nyn," etc., is transliterated in accordance with the modern oriental pronunciation, as Reuchlin, Lascaris, and Budé had recommended, contrary to Erasmus, who was respon-

sible for the adoption of the pronunciation at present employed in the schools. Those familiar with classic Greek will find no difficulty in transliterating it back. In English it reads:

Excellent master, why do you not give me some bread? You see me miserably perishing of hunger, and yet, you are without pity for me, but insist upon asking me questions out of season. But all lovers of literature agree that speech and words are superfluous, when the facts speak for themselves. Words are only necessary when the facts under discussion are not evident.

The passage "Agonou dont oussoys," etc., is in yet another imaginary tongue. Panurge's final linguistic effort, "Jam toties," etc., is, of course, in Latin. For those who need it, an English translation is appended:

Already, many times, by all that is sacred, by the gods and goddesses, I have begged you, if any pity is capable of moving you, to relieve my distress, but without profiting any from my supplications and my prayers. Let me, then, I beg you, let me go where fate calls me, impious men, and do not weary me any longer with your vain questions, but rather remember the old adage: A hungry belly has no ears.

"St. Anthony's Abbey": St. Anthony of the Fields (Saint-Antoine des Champs), on the present site of the Hôpital de Saint-Antoine, at Paris. ——"An apple-picker from the Perche country": a cider-growing region, included in the present departments of the Orne, the Sarthe, the Eure-et-Loir, and the Loir-et-Cher. —— "Down the Charenton-Bridge Road": the present Rue de Charenton from the Place de la Bastille to Charenton. "The meeting of Pantagruel and Panurge may, then, be located at the intersection of the present Rue du Faubourg Saint-Antoine and the Rue de Charenton" (Clouzot). ——"The language of the antipodes": i.e., of the natives of the New World, recently discovered by

Columbus. ——*"Are you talking Christian . . . or Patelinese?"* alluding to the jargon in the old farce, Patelin. *"No, it's Lanternese": language of the imaginary "Lanternese country" to which reference is made in Book Third and later.* ——*The name Eusthenes, that of one of Pantagruel's followers, is from the Greek and means "powerful, robust."* ——*"Venter famelicus auriculis carere dicitur (a hungry belly has no ears)": see the Adages of Erasmus,* II, 8, 84.

In connection with the linguistic passages in the preceding episode, no attempt has been made to modernize them, as some editors and translators (including Urquhart) have done; the text of the Lefranc edition has been followed.

How Pantagruel Equitably Settled a Dispute That Was Marvelously Obscure and Hard to Decide, So Justly That His Judgment Was Said to Be Highly Admirable

PANTAGRUEL, remembering well his father's letter of advice, desired one day to try out his learning. And so, in all the public squares of the city, he tacked up Theses, to the number of nine-thousand-seven-hundred-sixty-four, in every branch of knowledge, dealing with those points that were the most doubtful in all the sciences.

First in the Rue du Fouarre he held forth against all the regents, liberal-arts students, and orators and set them all on their behinds. Then at the Sorbonne he held forth against the theologians, for a period of six weeks, from four o'clock in the morning until six at night, with the exception of a two-hour interval which he took off for lunch and refreshment. This disputation was attended by a majority of the lords of the Court, masters of requests, presiding magistrates, counselors, members of the Chamber of Accounts, secretaries, advocates, and others, as well as by the sheriffs of the city, along with the physicians and the authorities on canonical law. And it is to be noted that the majority of these were of the sort who were inclined to take the bit in their teeth; but notwithstanding their *ergo's* and their sophisms, Pantagruel talked them all down and showed them that they were nothing but a lot of petticoated calves.

At this, everybody began to go around making a to-do about his wonderful learning, even to the women-folks, including the laundresses, marriage-brokers, baker-women, cutlery-merchants' wives, and others, who, as he went down the street, would cry out: "That's him." In all of which he took as much pleasure as did Demosthenes, prince of Greek orators, when an old hag, squatting on her rump, pointed him out with her finger, saying: "There he goes."

Now at this very time there was a case pending in the courts between two great lords, one of whom was Monsieur Kissarse, the plaintiff, or party of the first part, while the other was Monsieur Suckpoop, the defendant, or party of the second part. The dispute between these two was so knotty a one, and one so hard to decide at law, that the Court of Parliament could make no more out of it than if it had been High Dutch. Then, by the King's command, they called together the four most learned and the fattest of all the members of the French parliament, together with the Grand Council and all the principal regents of the universities, not only of France, but also of England and Italy, such as Jason, Philippus Decius, Petrus de Petronibus, and a lot of other old rabbis. These met together for forty-six weeks without being able to bite into the knot, or to understand the case in such a fashion as to make at all clear the right of the matter, at which they were so put out that they most vilely bedunged themselves from shame.

But one among them, named Du Douhet, the most learned, the cleverest, and the wisest of them all, rose up one day, when he saw that their brains were all philogrobolized, and said to them:

"Gentlemen, we have been here a long time now without accomplishing anything, except to squander time, and without being able to find either brim or bottom to this matter; the more we study it, the less we understand it, which is a great shame for us and a burden on our consciences; and it is my opinion that we shall never get out of this business without disgrace, seeing that all we do in our deliberations is to daydream. But here is what I have to suggest: I am sure you must have heard of that great person named Master Pantagruel, who has been found to be far more learned than the average run of the present age in the great disputations that he has publicly held against all comers. It is my opinion that we ought to call him in and confer with him on this matter, for no man will ever be able to get to the bottom of it, unless it is he."

To this all the councilors and doctors readily assented. They at once sent someone to hunt up Pantagruel, and to beg him to undertake to sieve and sift the case thoroughly and to make to them whatever report he saw fit, in accordance with the rules of legal science; and they placed in his hands all the files and proceedings, which were enough to weigh down four big-balled jackasses. Pantagruel thereupon said to them:

"Gentlemen, are the two lords who are parties to this case still alive?"

The answer was in the affirmative.

"Then what the devil," said he, "is the use of all this

mess of papers and briefs which you are handing me? Isn't it better to hear what they have to say from their own mouths than to read through all this monkey-business, which is nothing but a lot of lies, made up of the diabolic Cautions of Cepola and subversions of the law? For I am sure that you, and all those through whose hands this case has passed, have so bungled it with your pro's and con's that, even though the dispute was a plain and easy one to judge in the first place, you have, by this time, rendered it thoroughly obscure with your stupid and unreasonable reasons, and with the foolish opinions of Accursius, Baldus, Bartolus, Castro, Imola, Hippolytus, Panormitano, Bertachino, Alexander, Curtius, and those other pompous old blockheads who never understood even the simplest law of the *Pandects,* and who never were anything but big booby-calves, ignorant of everything that is necessary to an understanding of jurisprudence. For it is quite certain that they had no knowledge of either the Greek or the Latin language, but only of the Gothic and barbaric tongue. And yet, our laws were first taken from the Greeks, for which you have the word of Ulpian, *l. posteriori De orig. juris,* and all the laws are full of Greek words and maxims; while in the second place, those laws have been turned into a Latin that is the most elegant and ornate to be found anywhere, and I would not even except Sallust, Varro, Cicero, Seneca, T. Livius, nor Quintillian. How then could those old dotards have ever been able to understand the text of the laws, who never saw a good Latin book, as is quite obvious from their style, which is that of a chimney-sweep, a cook, or a scullion, rather than of a jurisconsult?

"Moreover, seeing that our laws have been transplanted from the soil of moral and natural philosophy, how could those fools ever hope to understand them, who, by God! know less about philosophy than does my mule? With regard to literature and the humanities and a knowledge of ancient history, they are less burdened with anything of that sort than a toad is with feathers, despite the fact that the codes are full of such allusions, without a knowledge of which they cannot be understood, as I shall some day set forth more clearly in a written dissertation. For the present, if you care to have me take cognizance of this case, I would first ask you to burn all these papers; and secondly, I would ask you to summon before me the two gentlemen in person; and when I have heard them I will give you my opinion, without any prevarication or dissimulation whatsoever."

To this course some of those present were opposed, for you know that in all gatherings there are more fools than there are wise men, and the majority always dominates the better part, as Titus Livius says, in speaking of the Carthaginians. But the Du Douhet mentioned above manfully upheld the other side, insisting that Pantagruel had spoken the truth, and that all those records, bills, plaintiffs' answers, demurrers, answers to demurrers, and other such deviltries were but subversions of the law, designed to drag out a case, adding that they might all go to the devil if they did not adopt some other course, one in accord with the gospel rule and the principles of philosophic equity. The end of the matter was that all the papers were burned and the two gentlemen personally summoned.

Whereupon, Pantagruel said to them:

"Are you the parties to this dispute?"

"Yes sir," said they.

"Which of you is the plaintiff?"

"I am," said Lord Kissarse.

"Well, my friend, go ahead and lay your case before me, point by point; and be sure you tell the truth; for,

so help me God! if I ca⁺ch you in a single lying word,
I'll wring your head from your shoulders and show you
that, in a court of justice, in the presence of a judge,
nothing is to be spoken but the truth. See to it, then,
that you do not add anything nor leave anything out in
the statement of your case. Proceed."

*According to M. Plattard, in this "case" between the
two lords Rabelais is taking up "a traditional theme of
popular satire, invective against the long-drawn-out
complications of legal procedure, which the royal power
was constantly endeavoring to simplify; he goes on to
hold the glossarists and interpreters of the law responsible for the protraction of trials, thus formulating, in
French and in a work of the imagination, criticisms
which up to that time had been expressed only in Latin
and in technical treatises for the use of scholars. He
thus echoes the protest of Humanism and of the jurists
of the Renaissance against the traditions of medieval
jurisprudence." Others would disagree with this, holding that the episode is too broad, too far-fetched, to
admit of a truly satirical intention on the part of the
author.*

*Rabelais here lists the legal glossarists and commen-
tators that were best known in his day: Jason, or Maïnus
(1485-1519), jurisconsult of Padua, author of commentaries on the* Code *and the* Pandects; *Philippus Decius
(died 1535), professor of law at Pisa and Pavia;
Accursius, who has been previously mentioned; Petrus
Baldus (1323-1400), who taught law at Pavia, Bologna,
and Padua, and whose commentaries were still reprinted in Rabelais' time; Bartolus of Sassoferrato
(1313-1357), professor of law at Bologna and Pisa, surnamed the Torch or Lantern of the Law (Fax Juris or*

Lucerna Juris); *Castro the Neapolitan, professor of law at Florence, Sienna, Bologna, and Padua in the first half of the sixteenth century; Hippolytus, also known as Riminaldus, a fourteenth-century jurisconsult; Panormitano, Nicoló Tedesco (Tedeschi), or Abbas Siculus, Bishop of Palermo (born in 1386), who taught canon law at Sienna, Parma, Bologna, and elsewhere, and who left commentaries on the* Decretals, *etc.; Bertachino of Fermo (1438-1497), a noted legal authority; Alessandro Tartagno ("Alexander"), fifteenth-century jurisconsult, author of commentaries on civil and canonical law; Curtius, pupil of Jason and legal adviser to the Marquis of Montferrat about the year 1470; and Cepola, famous fifteenth-century author of a work on how to evade the law and its punishments—the* Cautelae, *or* "Cautions."

It may be noted that the one legalist who is given favorable mention is the humanist patron, Brian Vallée, Seigneur du Douhet, "a man of letters who had made his home an asylum of the muses" (Clouzot).

"Rue du Fouarre": *Urquhart's "fodder street," where the lecture halls of the Faculty of Arts were situated in the Middle Ages, so called on account of the straw on which the students formerly sat; Dante has an allusion to it* (Paradiso, x, 136-138). ——"Masters of requests": *officers of the royal household.* ——"Along with the physicians": *the members of the medical faculty.* —— "Petrus de Petronibus": *that is to say, Peter Blockhead (in French, Pierre des Lourdauds).* ——"And a lot of other old rabbis": *more literally, rabbinical scholars (rabbinistes).* ——"Their brains were all philogrobolized": *this is Rabelais' own coinage, a combination of Greek and French, applied to those given to sifting things out to such an extent that they become stupefied by their own day-dreaming (Sainéan).* ——"Big boobycalves": *literally, tithing-calves, i.e., the best and fattest of the lot.* ——"l. posteriori De orig. juris": *supplementary book on the origins of the law; Plattard points out that the reference should be to Sextus Pomponius, first-century jurisconsult, instead of Domitius Ulpianus (170?-228 A.D.).* ——"The majority . . . as Titus Livius says": *Livy,* XXI, *4:* "sed ut plerumque fit maior pars meliorem vincit *(but as generally happens, the larger part overcomes the better)."*

"With the exception of the two-hour interval which he took off for lunch and refreshment": following this, the earlier editions have: "Not that he did anything to prevent the Sorbonne theologians from drinking and refreshing themselves in their customary wineshops."

How the Lords Kissarse and Suckpoop Pleaded Their Case before Pantagruel, without Attorneys

THEN Kissarse began, in the following manner:

"Sir, it is true that a good woman of my household was taking eggs to sell at the market."

"Put on your hat, Kissarse," said Pantagruel.

"Many thanks, sir," said Lord Kissarse. "But as I was saying, there passed between the two tropics, on their way to the zenith, six whites and a link, for the reason that the Riphaean Mountains had had that year a great scarcity of booby-catchers, on account of a mutiny of humbugs, instigated among the slangslingers and the Accursian customers, in order to provoke a rebellion of the Swiss, who were assembled to the number of fart-y, to go to a New Year's celebration, on the day when one gives soup to the oxen and the key to the coal-shed to the maids, so that they may give oats to the dogs. All night long, with one hand on the pot, they did

nothing but dispatch bulls on foot and bulls on horse-
back, to hold back the boats; for the tailors, out of the
remnants they had stolen, wanted to make a peashooter
to cover the ocean, which, at that time, was pregnant
with a pot of cabbage, according to the opinion of the
hay-shockers; but the physicians stated that, from its
urine, they could recognize no sign of the foot of bustard, which would show how to eat two-edged swords
with mustard, unless the Gentlemen of the Court gave
a B-flat order to the syphilis not to reap any more harvest
among the silkworms, for the panhandlers had already
made a good beginning at dancing a diapason jig, one
foot in the fire and head in the middle, as good old
Ragot used to say.

"Ha! Gentlemen, God moderates everything according to his pleasure, and against fickle fortune a teamster
broke his whip. That was on the return from Biccocca,
at the time when Master Antitus of Cressbeds took his
bachelor's degree in all branches of nincompoopery,
as the canonical authorities are accustomed to observe:
Beati nincompoopes, quoniam ipsi trippaverunt. Blessed
are the nincompoops, for they shall trip themselves up.

"But what makes Lent so high, by St. Fiacre of Brie,
is nothing else than the fact that

> Pentecost
> Never comes but to my cost;
> But hey, there, giddap,
> A little rain makes a big wind snap.

You are to understand that the sergeant had set the
bull's-eye so high that the clerk was unable, orbicularly,
to lick his fingers, feathered with ganderquills, and
we clearly see that each one is taking himself by the
nose, unless he happens to be gazing, in ocular perspective, toward the chimney, toward the place where
hangs the sign of the wine of the forty girths, which are

necessary for twenty five-year-debtors' pack saddles. At any rate, who would not be willing to let the bird go in front of the cheese cakes before uncovering him, for the memory is often lost when one puts his shoes on backwards? Well, God keep Theobald Mitten from harm."

Then Pantagruel said: "That is very fine, my friend, all very fine; go right ahead, and take your time, but don't get all worked up about it. I understand the case perfectly; proceed."

"Well, Sir," said Kissarse, "that good woman I was telling you of, saying her *gaude's* and her *audi nos'*, could not, in the name of God, cover herself with an upward backhand feint, against the privileges of the University, except by thoroughly and angelically heating herself with a warming pan, covering it with a garden-hedge, and making a flying feint at him, as near as she could to the spot where they sell the old rags which the painters of Flanders use, when they have a mind to put shoes on the grasshoppers, and I am very much astonished at the fact that the world doesn't hatch, in view of the fact that it makes so fine a sitter."

At this point, Lord Suckpoop wanted to interrupt and make a remark, but Pantagruel said to him:

"St. Anthony's belly! Is it your business to speak up without being told? Here I am, sweating away, trying to understand the cause in dispute between you two, and then you'd come balling me up, would you? Keep still, in the devil's name! Keep still! You'll have a chance to say your bellyful, when he's through. Go on," he said to Kissarse, "and take your time."

"Seeing, then," said Kissarse, "that the Pragmatic Sanction made no mention of it, and that the Pope gave each one the privilege of farting at his ease, so long as the wool was not streaked, whatever poverty there might

be in the world, provided that folks did not cross themselves with the sign of the Rabble, the Rainbow, having
been freshly ground down at Milan to let the larks go,
consented that the good woman should squash her
sciatica, through the protest of the little testicled fishes,
which, at that time, were necessary, in order to understand the construction of old boots.

"And so, John Calf, her cousin-german, removed by
one chip from the old block, advised her that she should
not take a chance by splashing around and helping out
with the wash, without first having dipped the paper in
alum, to the tune of scramble, none, play, you're out; for

Non de ponte vadit, qui cum sapientia cadit,

seeing that the Gentlemen of the Accounts could not
agree on the addition of the German flutes, with which
they had built the *Spectacles of the Princes,* newly
printed at Antwerp.

"And there you are, Gentlemen. It's not a very favorable report; and believe my opponent *in sacer verbo
dotis;* for wishing to obey the King's pleasure, I had
armed myself from head to foot with shoe-leather for
my belly, in order to go see how my grape-gatherers
had scalloped their high hats, that they might be able
to play the mannikins better, for the weather was somewhat dangerous for the flux, on account of which a number of militiamen had been turned down at the muster,
notwithstanding the fact that the chimneys were tall
enough, in proportion to the quittor and malanders,
Friend Baudichon.

"And on this account, it was a great year for snail-
shells throughout the Artois country, which was no
small improvement for those gentlemen, the vineyard
basket-carriers, as, without unsheathing, they ate sea-
storks with their belly bands unbuttoned. And I only

wish, for my part, that each one had as fine a voice;
they'd play a much better game of tennis, and as for
those little fine points, which come up in etymologizing
the ladies' high-heeled shoes, they would go down the
Seine much more easily, so that they might always serve
at the Millers' Bridge, as was formerly decreed by the
King of Canaria—the order may still be found in the
registrar's office.

"And so, Sir, I request that your lordship state and
declare what is right in this case, along with costs, damages, and interest."

Then Pantagruel: "My friend, have you nothing more
to say?"

Kissarse replied: "No sir; for I have uttered the whole
tu autem, and have not tampered with a single fact,
upon my honor."

"You, then, Monsieur Suckpoop," said Pantagruel,
"say what you like, and make it brief, without, however,
leaving out anything that may be to the point."

*Rabelais, in this passage and the two immediately
following, is indulging in what was known in his time
as "coq-à-l'âne," or the cock-and-bull chain, with one
word, or even the final syllable of a word, suggesting
another with which a popular locution has associated it.
It would be hopeless to endeavor to make sense of the
whole, for the very good reason that the author's obvious purpose was to keep the passage from making
sense. A comparison of various editions shows that, in
later revisions, frequently, where a passage as originally
written tended to take on a meaning, it has sometimes
been deliberately obscured by the mere interjection of
a nonsensical word or phrase. Maître François here owes
something to the medieval "fatrasie" as exemplified in the*

farce of Patelin; *and one can hardly help thinking of a modern Joyce—although we must remember, always, that where Joyce's intention is serious (the interior monologue), Rabelais is hoaxing. The "Joycean" flavor none the less persists. In any case, like the "Remarks of the Drunkards" chapter, this passage possesses an astonishing linguistic vitality; it is extremely colloquial, going to the very roots of the language. In it will be found proverbs, platitudes, rhyme-tags, snatches from popular songs, and at least a couple of borrowings from the cries of Parisian street vendors.*

"Six whites and a link": pieces of "white" money (blancs) *and the* maille, *an old coin of small value.* —— *"Good old Ragot": famous beggar-chief of the sixteenth century.* ——*"After the return from Biccocca": the battle of Biccocca, April 29, 1522, which cost France the Duchy of Milan; in French,* bicoque *means a shanty or small ramshackle town.* ——*"Scramble, none, play, you're out": this was one of the young Gargantua's games.* ——*"Non* de ponte vadit," *etc.: literally, He does not go from the bridge who falls with wisdom; that is, He does not fall from the bridge who goes with wisdom (walks wisely).* ——*"Spectacles of the Princes": "title of the principal work of the great rhetorician Meschinot, published in 1459 and 1473 . . . . Prudence and Justice were the two lenses, while Strength constituted the mounting and Temperance the riveting" (Plattard).* ——*"In sacer verbo dotis": in sacredotis verbo, on the word of a priest.* ——*"The whole* tu autem": *everything there is to say.*

How Lord Suckpoop Pleaded before Pantagruel

THEN Lord Suckpoop began as follows:

"Sir and Honorable Judges, if the iniquity of men were as easily viewed in categoric judgment as one recognizes flies in milk, the world, four bulls! would not be so eaten up with rats as it is, and many ears would still be upon the earth that have been basely gnawed away by them; for while all that my opponent has said has been the very and whole-cloth truth, so far as the letter and history of the *factum* is concerned, yet, Honorable Judges, cunning, trickery, little hitches are hidden under the rose-jar.

"Should I stand for it if, when I am busy eating my soup like the best of them, without thinking or saying anything out of the way, they come plaguing and pestering my brain, playing a cancan and saying:

> He who drinks as he eats his soup,
> When he is dead, will not see a poop?

"And Holy Virgin! how many great captains have we beheld, on the field of open battle, when they were distributing the thumps of holy bread from the confraternity, in order to dingle-dangle themselves more decently—how many of them have we seen playing the lute, making music with their behinds and taking little hops on the platform. But now that the world has been quite thrown out of pace by the wool and serge of Leicester, one is debauched, the other five, four, and two; and unless the court enters an order to the contrary, it will be as bad a gleaning this year as ever was, or else it will make mugs. If a poor person goes to the hot baths to have his snout brightened with cow-dung or to buy winter boots, and the sergeants, or even the watch, happen to be passing and receive the decoction of a clyster or the fecal matter of a toilet-seat upon their rowdyships, should one, for that reason, trim the heads and fricassee the wooden crowns?

"Sometimes, we think one thing, but God does the other, and when the sun is set, all beasts are in the shade. I do not want to be believed, if I do not prove it smartly, by open and above-board folks. In the year thirty-six, I had bought a German bobtail, tall and short, of good enough wool and dyed-in-the-grain, as the goldsmiths assured me, although the notary had to put in a few *et cetera's*. I am not scholar enough to take the moon in my teeth; but at the butter-jug, where they seal the Vulcanian instruments, the rumor was that salt-beef would enable one to discover the wine without a candle; and even if it was hidden in the bottom of a coalman's sack, barded and caparisoned with chanfrin and leg-harness, requisite for frying the grub well, it is a head of mutton. And it is true what the proverb says, that it is a good thing to see black cows in a burnt wood, when one is playing at making love. I referred the matter to those gentlemen, the scholars, and their conclusion, in *frisesomorum*, was that there is nothing like mowing, in the summertime, in a cellar well furnished with paper and ink, pens and a penknife from Lyon on the Rhone, fiddle diddle dumpling; for as soon as a piece of armor smells of garlic, the rust eats its liver, and then, they do nothing but give a stiff-necked answer and sniff their after-dinner nap; and that is what makes salt so dear.

"Honorable Judges, do not believe that, at the time this good woman I am telling you of was liming the spoonbill for the sergeant's record, in order the better to settle the inheritance, and the black-pudding-haslet was turning its back on the usurers' purses, there was nothing better to do, to protect one's self from cannibals, than to take a bundle of onions, bound with three hundred turnips and a little calf's crow of the best alloy that the alchemists have, and well lute and calcine those slippers, roly-poly, with a fine hayrake-gravy, then hide one's self in some little mole-hole, saving always the bacon-slices.

"And if the dice won't say anything for you except double aces, big-end threes, or speckled aces, throw the lady in a corner of the bed, romp with her, tra la la, and take a good drink, *despicando frogibus,* to all the fine buskin-like boots; that will be for the little molting goslings who play the game of squirrel, as they wait for them to beat the metal and heat the wax for the good-old-ale-drinkers.

"It is quite true that the four bulls in question here had a rather short memory; though in learning the scale, they feared neither cormorant nor Savoy duck, and the good folks of my country had great hopes for them, saying: "Those youngsters will become somebodies in algorism; that shall be a rubric of the law for us." We cannot fail to catch the wolf, building our hedges above the windmill, of which something has been said by the other side. But the old Dickens wanted it and set the Germans on their behinds, which caused all the imps to drink up: *"Herr, trinken, trinken!"* two of my men are in the lurch; for there is no appearance of reason for saying country chicken, at Paris, upon the Petit-Pont; and that, even though they were tufted tomtits or marsh-peewits, unless, it is true, one sacrifices the balls to the ink, fresh from the capitals or lower-case, it's all one to me, so long as the headband doesn't breed worms.

"And even supposing that, when they went to couple the hounds, the monkey-bitches had tooted the prize, before the notary, with his cabalistic art, had drawn up his statement, it does not follow, saving the court's better judgment, that six arpents of whole-cloth meadow would make three vats of fine ink, without blowing in the pan, considering the fact that, at the funeral of King Charles, they had the fleece in open market for two and one, I mean, upon my oath, of wool. And I ordinarily perceive, in all good bagpipes, that when one goes bird-stalking, making three turns with a broom around the chimney and entering his appearance, all he does is strain his guts and blow up his arse, if it happens to be too warm, and, bowl him a ball!

> After they had seen the writs,
> The cows came home, and they were quits.

"And a similar order was entered at Martinmas, in the year seventeen, for the misgovernment of Louze-fougerouse, of which may it please the court to take cognizance. I do not say, as matter of fact, that one may not, in equity and with just title, dispossess those who drink holy water as one does a sickle-sheathed halberd, from which they make suppositories for those who will not give up except for a pretty price.

"*Tunc*, Honorable Judges, *quid juris pro minoribus?* What law is there for minors? For the common interpretation of the Salic Law is to the effect that the first fire-bug who sponges on the cow, who blows his nose in full choir without do-re-me-fa-so-la-si-do-ing the shoemaker's stitches, must, in big-bellied times, sublimate the penury of his member by moss picked when they are catching cold at midnight mass, in order to give the strappado to those white wines of Anjou, that take a scissors-hold, neck-to-neck, Breton fashion.

"Concluding as above, with costs, damages, and interest."

After Lord Suckpoop had finished, Pantagruel said to Lord Kissarse: "My friend, have you no reply to make?"

To which Kissarse answered:

"No, Sir, for I have told only the truth; and for God's sake, give us a decision, for this is costing us a pretty penny, I can assure you of that."

This passage follows the same pattern as the preceding one, of which it is a continuation. There are the same tag-ends of proverbs, popular expressions, and the like; and there are a number of erotic allusions and word-plays, as "dingle-dangle themselves," "entering his appearance," etc.

"Factum": the brief setting forth the facts in the proceeding. ——"The wool and serge of Leicester": reference to the English city, noted for its woolens. —— "Trim the heads and fricassee the wooden crowns": allusion to testons or pieces of money with royal heads on them, while the "trimming" has to do with a process of counterfeiting, and the "crowns" are the well-known coins of that name (not "wooden dishes," as other translators have it). ——"In frisesomorum": "one of the nine modes of the first figure of the syllogism" (Plattard). ——"Despicando frogibus": literally, "despising the frogs" (this is "pig-Latin"; Rabelais writes "despicando grenoillibus").

Pantagruel's Decision in the Dispute between the Two Lords

THEN Pantagruel arose and, assembling all the presiding magistrates, councilors, and doctors there present, said to them:

"Well, Gentlemen, you have heard, *vivae vocis, oraculo*, the case in dispute here; how does it look to you?"

To which they replied:

"We have heard it, that is true, but we have not understood a word of it. To the devil with this case! And so, we beg you, *una voce*, and entreat you to be so kind as to give whatever decision you may see fit, and *ex nunc prout ex tunc*, we will agree to and ratify it with our full consents."

"Well then, gentlemen!" said Pantagruel, "since that is your pleasure, I shall do so; but I do not find this case so difficult. Your paragraph *Caton*, the law *Frater*, the law *Gallus*, the law *Quinque pedum*, the law *Vinum*, the law *Si dominus*, the law *Mater*, the law *Mulier bona*, the law *Si quis*, the law *Pomponius*, the law *Fundi*, the law *Emptor*, the law *Praetor*, the law *Venditor*, and a number of others are a good deal more difficult, in my opinion."

After saying this, he walked up and down the room a couple of times, thinking very deeply, as one could easily tell, for he groaned like a jackass whose belly-band is too tight, as he thought of what he must do in order to be fair to both sides, without showing any favors. Then he came back and sat down, and began to pronounce the following decision:

"Having seen, heard, and well considered the points of difference between the Lords Kissarse and Suckpoop, the Court says to them that, considering the horripilation of the bat, declining stoutly from the summer solstice in order to whisper sweet nothings in the ears of the lollipops, who have been checkmated by a pawn through the unpleasant annoyances of the lucifuges, who are in the Roman climate of a monkey on horseback, bending a crossbow with all his guts—considering this, the plaintiff had just cause to calk the galleon which the good woman inflated, one foot shod and the other bare, reimbursing him, low and stiff in his conscience, with as many bladder-nuts as there is hair on eighteen cows, with an equal number for the embroiderer.

"Likewise, he is declared innocent of the privileged case of small turds, which it was thought he had incurred, since he was no longer able to crap briskly, by the decision of a pair of gloves, perfumed with farts at the nut-grease candle, of the sort they use in his country, the Mirebalais, letting the bowline go with the bronze bullets, with which the stable-valets contestably baked their vegetables, loaded with Bait, with hawk's bells made of Hungary lace, which his brother-in-law memorably carried in a nearby basket, embroidered with gueules, with three chevrons knocked up with dry goods, in the corner kennel from where they shoot the vermiform popinjay with the feather-duster.

"But as for the accusation made against the defendant, that he was a shoe-mender, cheese-eater, and mummy-tarrer, which, in oscillating, has not been found true, as the said defendant has plainly set forth, the court condemns him to three tumblers of curds, seasoned, prelorelitantated, and codpieced, as is the custom of the country, in the case of the said defendant, payable the middle of August, in May; but the said defendant shall be required to furnish hay and oakum to stop the guttural caltrops emburelucocked with gobbets, well sifted with collops.

"And let them be friends as they were before, without costs, for the cause which has been shown."

When this decision had been handed down, the two parties left, each quite content with the court's order, which was an almost unbelievable thing; for it has not happened since the big rain, and will not happen for thirteen jubilees to come, that the two parties to a law suit shall be equally satisfied with a final ruling.

With regard to the councilors and other doctors there present, they remained in an ecstatic fit, for all of three hours, being altogether ravished with admiration at Pantagruel's more than human wisdom, evidenced in the decision which he had given in so difficult and thorny a case as this. And they would have been there yet, if someone had not brought vinegar and rose water to bring them back to their senses and everyday understanding, for which God be praised, far and near!

"Vivae vocis oraculo . . . una voce . . . ex nunc prout ex tunc": *these phrases mean, respectively: "by the living voice of the oracle"; "with one voice"; "from now on as from then on."* ——*"Prelorelitantated . . . emburelucocked": these are coined words; Sainéan thinks that the former* (prelorelitantées) *is probably part of an onomatopoetic refrain.*

Panurge Has a New Way of Building the Walls of Paris

PANTAGRUEL one day, by way of seeking a little recreation from his studies, was strolling toward the Faubourg Saint-Marcel, being desirous of having a look at the Folie-Gobelin. Panurge was with him, having always a flagon under his cloak and a few slices of ham; for without these he never went anywhere, being accustomed to remark that they were his body-guard. He carried no other sword, and when Pantagruel wished to make him a present of one he replied that it would overheat his spleen.

"But how," remonstrated Epistemon, "are you going to defend yourself if you are attacked?"

"With the toe of my shoe," he replied, "providing that upper-thrusts are ruled out."

As they came back, Panurge surveyed the walls of the city of Paris and in derision remarked to Pantagruel:

"What fine walls those are! They would be nice and strong for keeping goslings in a coop! By my beard! but they are absolutely useless to a city like this, for an old cow with one fart could knock down more than a dozen yards of them."

"My friend," said Pantagruel, "do you know what Agesilaus said, when someone asked him why it was the great city of Lacedaemonia was not surrounded with walls? 'Here,' said he, 'are the walls of the city,' pointing to the inhabitants and citizens of the town, who were so well trained in the art of war, so brave, and so well equipped. He meant by that that there are no walls except those of flesh and blood, and that towns and cities can have no fortifications stronger and safer than the virtue of their citizenry. And so it is: this city is so strong in its warlike population that it does not have to worry about any other walls. What is more, supposing they wanted to wall it in, like Strassburg, Orléans, or Ferrara, that would not be possible for the reason that the expense would be too great."

"Well," said Panurge, "but it's a good thing to have a stony face to show when the enemy comes, if it's only to be able to demand: 'Who's down there?' As to the enormous expense that you say would be necessary to wall it in, if the City Fathers would be willing to give me a good jug of wine, I could show them a new way of building walls, very cheap."

"How's that?" said Pantagruel.

"Don't breathe a word about it to anybody," said Panurge, "if I tell you.

"I have noticed that the what-you-may-call-them of the women of this country are cheaper than stone; and it is with them that the walls should be built. They should be arranged in a nice architectural formation, by placing the biggest ones in the front rows and then sloping them down like a donkey's backside, putting in the middle-sized and finally the tiny ones as you go along; then some of them should be sprinkled together, in a few nice little diamond-shaped figures, like the big tower of Bourges, along with plenty of the good stiff broad-and-short-swords that inhabit cloistral codpieces.

"What the devil could knock down a wall like that? There is no metal that is so resistant to blows. And then, when the culverins came to rub up against them, you'd damned soon see the blessed fruit of the old pox distilled in a fine rain. I'm telling you, what the hell! Moreover, the lightning would never strike a wall like that; and why should it, seeing they are all either blest or holy? I can see only one drawback."

"Ho, ho! Ha, ha, ha!" laughed Pantagruel, "and what's that?"

"It is that the flies are awfully fond of that spot and would love to collect there and do their dung; and there you are, the whole thing's spoiled! But here's how you could remedy that. You would have to keep them very well fly-swatted with some nice foxes' tails or a big ass's prick from Provence. And speaking of that, I'm going to tell you, on your way home to supper, a charming little story, which is to be found in *Frater Lubinus, libro De compotationibus mendicantium.*

"In the days when the beasts talked, which was not three days ago, a poor lion, wandering through the forest of Fontainebleau and saying his short prayers, happened to pass under a tree up which a country coal-merchant had climbed to cut down some wood. The merchant, seeing the lion, dropped his hatchet, thereby wounding the beast terribly in one thigh. The lion limped and ran away the best he could through the forest in search of aid, when he happened to meet a carpenter, who very willingly looked at his wound, wiped it as clean as possible, and bandaged it up with moss, telling the lion to be careful to keep the flies away, so they would not do their dung there, while he went to search for the carpenter's herb. And so the lion, his wound having been looked after, was walking through the forest, when he fell in with an old hag who was cutting fagots and gathering wood in that same forest. The hag, seeing the lion coming, was so frightened that she fell down on her back-side while the wind blew her dress, petticoat, and chemise above her shoulders. Be-holding this, the lion, out of pity, came running up to see if she had hurt herself, and looking at her what-you-may-call-it, he exclaimed: 'Oh you poor woman! Who has wounded you like that?' As he said this, he caught sight of a fox, and called to him: 'Brother fox, come here, come here.' When the fox came up, the lion said:

" 'Old fellow, my friend, someone has wounded this good woman here, most viciously, between the legs, and there is an obvious dissolution of continuity. Look how big the wound is, all the way from the rump to the navel; it must measure four, or even five and a half spans. It's a hatchet-wound, and I don't believe it's very old. However, in order to keep the flies from getting at it, swat it well, I beg of you, both inside and out. You have a good long tail. Swat it, my friend, swat it, I beg you, while I go look for some moss to put on it; for we ought

to help one another out in cases like this. And so, swat
it well, my friend, swat it, for this wound must be swatted
very often; otherwise, the lady will not rest easy. And
so, swat it well, old man, swat it well. God has provided
you with plenty of tail; you've a big one and thick
enough; swat it hard, and don't weaken. A good swatter
who, by constantly swatting, swats with his swatter will
never be swatted by flies. Swat, old balls; swat, my little
cutie, and I'll be back in a jiffy.'

"Then he went to look for a supply of moss, and when
he was a long way off, he called back to the fox:

" 'Keep it up, old fellow, swat it well; swat and don't
weaken, and I'll make you official swatter to Don
Pedro of Castille. Swat, that's all; swat; you haven't anything else to do.'

"The poor fox swatted with might and main, this
way and that way, inside and out; but the old hag farted
and pooped and stunk like a hundred devils. The fox
was very uncomfortable, not knowing which way to turn
to avoid the perfume that came from the hag's farts;
and as he turned around, he saw that there was another aperture on her back-side, not so big as the one he
was swatting, from which the wind that was so stinking
and infectious appeared to come.

"The lion finally returned, bringing with him more
than eighteen bales of moss. He proceeded to cram the
moss into the wound, by the aid of a stick that he carried
with him. He had already put in sixteen bales and a half,
when he cried out in astonishment:

" 'What the devil! but this wound is deep. More than
two carloads of moss have already gone in.'

"Whereupon the fox gave him a piece of advice:

" 'Brother lion, my friend, please don't put all the
moss in there; keep a little of it, for there's another little

aperture underneath here that stinks like five hundred devils. I'm poisoned with the smell of it, it's so vile.'

"And so it is, you would have to protect those walls from the flies, and employ hired swatters."

Then Pantagruel spoke:

"How do you know that the shameful members of the women are so cheap as all that? There are many good women in this town, chaste ones and virgins."

"Et ubi prenus?" demanded Panurge. "And where will you find them? I will give you, not my opinion, but the absolute truth. I don't want to boast, but I've stuffed up four-hundred-seventeen of those holes, since I've been in this town, and that's only nine days! This very morning, I found a fellow who, in a knapsack like Aesop's, was carrying around two little girls of the age of two or three at the most, one in front, the other behind. He asked me for alms, but I told him that I had more balls than I had deniers. And afterwards, I said to him:

"'My good man, are those two little girls you have there virgins?'

"'Brother,' he said, 'it's two years now that I've been carrying them like this; and so far as the one in front is concerned, whom I can see all the time, in my opinion she's a virgin, though I wouldn't put my finger in the fire for it; as to the one behind, I know nothing whatever about the matter.'"

"You're good company," declared Pantagruel. "I'd like to have you wear my livery."

And so, they dressed him up very finely and according to the latest fashion, except that Panurge insisted on his codpiece being three feet long and square, not round in shape. It was, accordingly, made that way, and it was certainly a sight to see. And Panurge would frequently remark that the world had yet to learn the

advantage and utility of wearing a long codpiece, but
that they would learn some day, since everything comes
to light in the course of time.

"God keep from harm," he would say, "the fellow
whose long codpiece has saved his life!

"God keep from harm the one whose long codpiece
has been worth to him, in one day, one-hundred-sixty-
thousand-nine crowns!

"God keep from harm the one who by his long
codpiece has saved a whole city from dying of hunger!
By God! I'm going to write a book on *The Advantages
of Long Codpieces,* just as soon as I have a little leisure."

The fact is, he did compose a large volume, and a
very good one, with diagrams, on the subject; but
it has not been printed yet, so far as I know.

*"Toward the Faubourg Saint-Marcel": "the borough
of Saint-Marcel, built around the sanctuary of the
same name—the oldest in Paris, according to the
statement of Gregory of Tours—remained outside the
walls down to the end of the eighteenth century. The
Porte Saint-Marcel, Rue Descartes, at the corner of the
Rue des Fossés Saint-Victor, led to it" (Clouzot). ——
"The Folie-Gobelin": most commentators assume that
this refers to the famous Gobelin manufactory; but Lefranc identifies it as a resort situated in the Faubourg
Saint-Jacques, not far from the Bièvre. ——"Frater
Lubinus, libro . . .": "Friar Wolf's Book on the Drink-
ing-Bouts of Beggars." ——"Carpenter's herb": the mil-
foil or yarrow, reputed to be efficacious in the dressing
of wounds. ——"Her what-you-may-call-it": son comment a nom. ——"Dissolution of continuity": a term
from the scholastic philosophy. ——"Don Pedro of*

Castile": Peter the Cruel, King of Castile about 1350; the association is not clear.

A good part of the central portion of Book Second is taken up with a description of the physical appearance, character, and habits of Panurge; the story which he relates to Pantagruel of how he escaped from the hands of the Turks; the numerous pranks that he played, especially on women; the tale of how he robbed the counters in the churches where pardons were sold; how he married off the old women; the mock suits at law that he instituted; etc. In the midst of all this comes the famous episode of Panurge's debate with *"a great English scholar,"* who by some has been identified as none other than Sir Thomas More, although modern commentators (M. Plattard among them) are inclined to doubt this, as they cannot see the point in Rabelais' holding up to ridicule the author of Utopia, to whom the Maître owes so much.

How a Great English Scholar Wished to Debate with Pantagruel and Was Vanquished by Panurge

IT WAS along about this time that a learned man by the name of Thaumast, having heard of Pantagruel's renown and incomparable erudition, came all the way from England, with the sole intention of seeing Pantagruel and making his acquaintance, in order to satisfy himself that the latter's learning was all that it was reported to be. Having reached Paris, he went directly to Pantagruel's lodging, which was the Hôtel Saint-Denis, where the head of the house at that moment hap-

pened to be walking in the garden with Panurge, philosophizing in the manner of the peripatetics.

As soon as he entered, the visitor began trembling
with fright at seeing so big and portly a specimen. Then,
as the fashion was, he greeted his host very courteously,
saying to him:

"Plato, prince of philosophers, speaks truly when he
tells us that if the image of learning and wisdom were
corporeal and visible to human eyes, it would excite all
the world to admiration, since the very rumor of its
presence, spreading through the air, when received by
the ears of the studious and lovers of wisdom, whom we
call philosophers, no longer leaves these latter any repose but goads and inflames them to run to the place and
behold the person where and in whom learning is said to
have established her temple and set up her oracles. We
have an obvious demonstration of this in the Queen of
Sheba, who came from the uttermost parts of the East
and the Persian Sea, to observe how the wise Solomon
kept his house and to hear his wisdom.

"We have another example in Anacharsis, who came
all the way from Scythia to Athens to see Solon.

"We have another in Pythagoras, who visited the
soothsayers of Memphis.

"Another in Plato, who visited the magicians of
Egypt and Architas of Tarentum.

"Another in Apollonius of Tyana, who went all the
way to Mount Caucasus, passing through the lands of
the Scythians, the Massagetae, and the Indians, navi-
gating the great river Pison, and going as far as the
country of the Brahmans, in order to see Hiarchas, and
who went through Babylonia, Chaldea, Media, Assyria,
Parthia, Syria, Phoenicia, Arabia and Alexandria, all the
way to Ethiopia, to see the Gymnosophists.

"We have a similar case in Titus Livius, to see and

hear whom many students came to Rome from the furthermost parts of France and Spain.

"I should not dare to class myself with those who are so much more perfect than I; but I should like to be looked upon as a student, and as a friend, not only of literature, but of men of letters.

"And so, having heard the report of your inestimable learning, I have left country, relatives, and household and have come here, thinking nothing of the length of the journey, the tiresomeness of a sea-voyage, or the unfamiliarity of countries through which I have passed. I have come solely for the purpose of seeing you and consulting with you respecting certain problems in philosophy, geomancy, and the cabalistic art, problems that to me are very doubtful, and for which I can find no solution that satisfies my mind. If you can solve these problems for me, I shall remain your most humble servant, I and all my heirs, for there is no other gift within my power that I regard as a suitable recompense.

"I will write my questions out, and tomorrow, we will publish them among the learned of the city, so that we may discuss them publicly, in their presence.

"But I wish to explain the manner in which I should like this discussion to be conducted. I do not care to argue pro and con, as do the stupid sophists of this city and elsewhere. Likewise, I do not wish to carry on a discussion in the academic manner, by declamation; neither by means of numbers, as Pythagoras did, and as Pico della Mirandola wanted to do at Rome; but I should like to debate by signs only, without saying a word, for the subjects involved are so difficult that human words would not be sufficient to explain them in a manner to suit me. Therefore, may it please your Magnificence to be present. It will be in the great hall of Navarre, at seven o'clock in the morning."

When he had said this, Pantagruel gave him a most decent answer:

"My lord, of the graces which God has given me, I should not wish to deny anyone a share, in so far as lies within my power; for all good comes from Him, and His pleasure is that it should be multiplied, when one is dealing with the worthy and those fitted to receive the heavenly manna of honorable learning. Since among this number, you occupy the first rank at the present time, as I have very well perceived, I hereby notify you that you will find me ready to comply with any request of yours, according to what little ability is in me; though I ought to be able to learn more from you than you from me. But as you have suggested, we will discuss all doubtful points together, and will search for a solution, even at the bottom of that inexhaustible well where, Heraclitus tells us, the truth lies hidden.

"I am greatly in favor of the mode of debate which you have proposed, that is to say, by signs, without speaking; since by this means, you and I shall be able to understand each other and at the same time, shall be free of those hand-clappings on the part of the booby sophists which are always to be heard when one side is getting the better of an argument.

"Tomorrow, then, I shall not fail to be present at the time and in the place you have mentioned; but I must beg that there be no unseemly contention between us, and that we seek not honor nor the applause of men, but truth alone."

To this, Thaumast replied:

"My lord, may God keep you in His grace, by way of thanking you for the kindness your great Magnificence has shown in being willing to condescend to one of my small worth. Adieu, then, until tomorrow."

"Adieu," said Pantagruel.

Gentlemen, you who read this present narrative, do not think that there were ever two persons more wrought up in their minds than were Thaumast and Pantagruel all that night. Thaumast remarked to the concierge of the Hôtel de Cluny, where he had found a lodging, that, in all his life, he never had been so thirsty as he was that evening.

"I think," he said, "that Pantagruel must have me by the throat. Order some drinks, please, and let's have a little fresh water to gargle my palate."

On the other hand, Pantagruel was keyed to a high pitch, and all night long, did nothing but moon over:

Bede's book, *De numeris et signis;*

Plotinus' book, *De inenarrabilibus;*

Proclus' book, *De magia;*

The works of Artemidorus *Peri onirocriticon;*

Anaxagoras' *Peri semion;*

D'Ynarius' *Peri aphaton;*

The works of Philistion;

Hipponax' *Peri anecphoneton;*

And a lot of others, until Panurge, finally, said to him:

"Stop thinking about all those things and go to bed, for I can see you're so worked up in your mind that you're likely to fall into some kind of ephemeral fever with all this thinking. But first take twenty-five or thirty good stiff drinks; then go to bed and sleep in peace; for in the morning, I will answer Mr. Englishman and argue with him, and if I don't put him *ad metam non loqui,* then you may say what you please to me."

"That is all right," said Pantagruel, "but, Panurge, my friend, he is marvelously learned. How are you going to take care of him?"

"That's easy," said Panurge. "Please don't talk about it any more, but leave it all to me. Is there any man as wise as the devils are?"

"No," said Pantagruel, "indeed, there isn't, without the special gift of divine grace."

"And yet," said Panurge, "I've argued against them many times and have always set them on their behinds. And so far as this wonderful Englishman is concerned, you may rest assured that tomorrow I'm going to make him pass vinegar through his arse-hole, in front of everybody."

Panurge then proceeded to spend the night in drinking with the pages, staking all his breeches-buttons at *Primus, Secundus* and Switches. When the time came, he escorted his master Pantagruel to the appointed place. And you may well believe that there was neither great nor small in Paris who was not among those present, thinking:

"This devil of a Pantagruel, who has argued down all the sly and silly sophists is going to get his now, for this Englishman is another devil from Vauvert. We'll see who gets the best of this."

Everybody was there, and Thaumast was waiting for them when Pantagruel and Panurge reached the hall; and then all the schoolboys, liberal-arts-students, and university electors began clapping their hands, as is their boobyish custom. But Pantagruel cried out in a loud voice, making a noise like a double-barreled cannon:

"Order! hell's fire, order! By God! you bastards, if you ball me up, I'll wring your heads off."

At these words they were all as astonished as a lot of ducks, and would not have dared to cough, even if they had eaten fifteen pounds of feathers. As a matter of fact, at the very sound of that voice, they became so thirsty that their tongues lolled out from their chops for a distance of half a foot. It was as though Pantagruel had salted their throats.

Then Panurge began, saying to the Englishman:

"My lord, have you come here to debate, in a contentious spirit, those propositions which you have submitted, or, rather, to learn and know the truth about these matters?"

To which Thaumast replied:

"My lord, nothing brings me here but the desire to learn and to know the truth about those things concerning which I have been in doubt all my life; I have found neither book nor man who could solve to my satisfaction those doubts that I have set forth. As to contentious discussion, I want none of that; it is too cheap a thing and I leave it to those rascally sophists who, in their disputations, are not looking for the truth but for contradiction and debate."

"Then," said Panurge, "if I, who am the mere disciple of my master, Monsieur Pantagruel, if I am able to satisfy and enlighten you, in every case and on every point, it would be a shame to put my master to the trouble. For this reason, it is more fitting that he should sit as judge at our discussion and give you additional enlightenment, if it should seem to you that my own studious efforts have not been sufficient."

"Indeed," said Thaumast, "that is very well said. Let us begin, then."

It is to be noted, here, that Panurge had placed on the end of his long codpiece a pretty tassel of red, white, green, and blue silk, and that inside it he had stowed away a very nice orange.

The name Thaumast (from the Greek thaumastos) means "admirable, one who occasions wonder and admiration." ——*The Hôtel Saint-Denis, at the corner of the Rue Saint-André-des-Arts and the Rue des Grands-Augustins, to the left as one goes down to the Seine, has been seen as Rabelais' own probable residence during his stay in Paris prior to 1530; for while it originally had been the residence of the abbots of Saint-Denis, since the end of the fifteenth century it had been the town house of the Benedictine order, to which Maître François belonged (Clouzot).* ——*"Plato speaks truly"*: Phaedrus, 250 D, *Remarks on Visual Perception.* ——*"Anacharsis . . . to see Solon"*: Aelianus, Variae Historiae, v, 7. ——*For the other allusions to far-travelers, Pythagoras, Plato, Apollonius of Tyana, and those who came to see Titus Livius, Rabelais is indebted to St. Jerome's epistle prefacing the* Vulgate *(Plattard).* ——*Massagetae: a Scythian people of northern Asia.* ——*"The great river Pison"*: the legendary stream flowing through the Garden of Eden. ——*"To see the Gymnosophists"*: a sect of philosophers said to have been founded in India by Alexander the Great; they went naked, ate no flesh, and devoted themselves to meditation.* ——*"As Pico della Mirandola wanted to do at Rome"*: this Italian philosopher and writer of the latter half of the fifteenth century, in 1486, with the sanction of Pope Innocent* VIII, *offered to maintain 900 theses against all comers, but there is no account of his having wished to dispute by means of numbers.* ——*"In the great hall of Navarre"*: the College of Navarre. ——*"Heraclitus tells us"*: the ancients attributed the saying to Democritus. ——*The works over which Pantagruel pored on the night preceding the debate are: the* Venerable Bede On Numbers and Signs; *Plotinus* On the Unmistakable Things; *Proclus* On Sacrifice and Magic (De Sacrificio et Magia); *Artemidorus* On the Interpretation of Dreams; *Anaxagoras* On Signs *(no work by the Greek philosopher on this subject is known);* D'Ynarius On the Unspeakable Things *(both author and work appear to be Rabelais' invention);* Hipponax On the Things Concerning Which One Should Keep Silent *(the satiric poet of the sixth century* B.C. *is the author of no work bearing this title); Philistion (first century* A.D.*) was the author of mimes, but none of his works have come down to us.* ——*"Primus, Secundus and Switches": two more of Gargantua's games.* ——*"Another devil from Vauvert": allusion to a haunted house, the Hôtel de Vauvert, on the present site of the Observatoire, in Paris; legend attributed the house to Robert le Pieux; it later served as a refuge for vagrants and was finally occupied by the Carthusian monks; the name* Enfer *(hell) remains with the street.* ——*"I leave it to those rascally sophists": a variant reading at this point contains a number of burlesque names hurled at the professors of the Sorbonne.*

How Panurge Got the Better of the English-man, Who Argued with Signs

AND then, everybody being present and listening in dead silence, the Englishman raised his two hands high in the air, one at a time, clenching the extremities of his fingers into the shape known in the Chinon country as the hen's arse; and with one hand he struck the other with his nails four times, then opened his hands and with the palm of one struck the other a resounding slap. Joining them as before, he struck twice, and then four times more, opening them as he did so, then brought them together and stretched them out in front of him, as though he were devoutly praying to God.

Panurge immediately raised his right hand in the air, then placed the thumb of this hand in the nostril of the same side, keeping the four fingers extended and pressed close together in a line parallel to the point of his nose, closing his left eye completely and squinting the right with a deep depression of the eyelid and eyebrow; then he raised his left hand high in the air, keeping the four fingers still tightly pressed together and extended, and with the thumb elevated, holding the hand, thus, in a direct line with the position of the right, with a distance between them of a little over two feet. Having done this, he placed both hands against the earth, then finally brought them up midway, as though sighting straight at the Englishman's nose.

"And if Mercury . . ." said the Englishman.

But Panurge interrupted him:

"Mask, you've spoken!"

Then the Englishman made another sign. He raised his open left hand into the air, then closed the four fingers into his fist and brought the extended thumb to rest on the end of his nose. Afterwards, he suddenly raised his right hand, open, and brought it down, still open, joining the thumb to the place where the little finger of the left hand closed the fist, moving the four fingers of this hand slowly in the air. Then, vice-versa, he did with the right hand what he had done with the left, and with the left what he had done with the right.

Panurge, not in the least taken aback by this, lifted his trismegist codpiece into the air with his left hand, and with his right drew from it a slice of white cow's rib and two pieces of wood of similar shape, one of black ebony, the other of flesh-colored brazilwood; and arranging these neatly between his fingers, he shook them together, making a noise like that which lepers make in Britainy, with their rattles, only a great deal more resounding and melodious, while with his tongue in his cheek he played a merry tune, gazing all the time, steadfastly, at the Englishman.

The theologians, physicians, and surgeons thought

that by such a sign he meant to infer that the Englishman was leprous. The councilors, legists, and decretalists were of the opinion that, by this gesture, Panurge intended to imply that there was some species of human felicity inherent in the leper's condition, as the Savior formerly maintained.

The Englishman was not frightened at this, but raising his two hands in the air, held them in such a position that the three master-fingers closed into his fist; then he passed the thumbs between the index and middle fingers, while the auricular fingers remained stretched out; and in this manner, he presented them to Panurge, then brought them together so that the right thumb touched the left and the left finger touched the right.

At this, Panurge, without saying a word, lifted his hands and made the following sign: with his left hand, he joined the nail of the index finger to the nail of the thumb, making a ring, as it were; then with his right hand, he shut all his fingers into his fist, excepting the index, which he put in and drew out a number of times between the two fingers of the left hand which have been mentioned. Then, with his right hand, he extended the index and middle fingers, spreading them apart from each other as far as he could and moving them toward Thaumast. Following which, he placed the thumb of his left hand under the corner of his left eye, spreading out all the rest of his hand like the wing of a bird or the fin of a fish, moving it very prettily here and there, and doing the same with the right hand at the corner of his right eye.

Thaumast began to turn pale and tremble, then made another sign. With the middle finger of his right hand, he struck the muscle of the palm, under the thumb, then placed the index finger of the right hand into the ring formed by the fingers of the left; but he placed it under, not above, as Panurge had done.

Whereupon, Panurge clapped his hands together and whistled into his palm. Having done this, he once more placed the index finger of his right hand into the ring of the left, drawing it frequently back and forth; then, he stuck out his chin and gazed at Thaumast, intently.

The audience, which knew nothing of the meaning of all these signs, understood well enough that Panurge, without saying a word, was inquiring of Thaumast:

"Well, what have you to say to that?"

The truth is, Thaumast was beginning to ooze great drops of perspiration. He looked like a man who is rapt in exalted contemplation. After thinking for a minute, he placed all the nails of his left hand against those of the right, opening his fingers like semicircles and raising his hands as high as he could in this sign.

At this, Panurge suddenly placed the thumb of his right hand under his jaw-bones and the auricular finger of the same hand into the ring of the left, and with his hands in this position, gnashed his lower teeth against the upper, most melodiously.

Thaumast, with a great effort, rose; but in rising he let a big baker's fart (for the bran came afterwards) and pissed strong vinegar, and stunk like all the devils in hell. The audience began to hold their noses, when they saw that he was beturding himself from anxiety. Then, the Englishman raised his right hand, clenching it in such a manner as to bring the ends of all the fingers together, while the left hand rested squarely upon his breastbone.

At this point, Panurge took his long codpiece with its tassel and stretched it out for a distance of two feet or more. Holding it in the air with his left hand, he took out the orange with his right; then, tossing the orange into the air seven times, he hid it in the fist of his right hand, keeping it elevated all the while; after which, he began to shake out his fine codpiece, calling Thaumast's attention to it.

Thaumast thereupon commenced to puff out his two cheeks like a bagpipe-player, blowing as though he were inflating a pig's bladder.

Then Panurge placed a finger of his left hand in his arse-hole and emitted air with his mouth, making the sound one does when eating oysters in the shell or in sucking soup. When he had done this, he opened his mouth a little and struck it with the palm of his right hand, making a great deep sound that appeared to come from the superficies of his diaphragm, by way of the tracheal artery; and this he did sixteen times.

As for Thaumast, he was now puffing like a goose.

Then Panurge placed the index finger of his right hand in his mouth, squeezing it very tightly with the mouth-muscles. In drawing it out, he made a great sound, of the sort little boys make when they fire beet-balls from an elder-bark-cannon; and he did this nine times.

Whereupon, Thaumast cried:

"Ha! Gentlemen, the great secret!"

And with this, he ran his hand up to the elbow and drew out a dagger which he had there, holding it point downward.

At this, Panurge took his long codpiece and shook it as hard as he could against his thighs, then placed his two hands, joined together in the form of a comb, under his head, sticking out his tongue as far as he could and rolling his eyes around like a dying billy-goat.

"Ha! I understand," said Thaumast, "but what about it?"

As he said this, he placed the handle of his dagger

against his breast and on the point placed the flat of his hand, twirling the end a little with his fingers.

Panurge dropped his head to the left side and placed his middle finger in his right ear, raising the thumb straight up. Then he crossed his arms over his breast, coughed five times and, at the fifth cough, stamped his foot on the ground. After which, he lifted his left arm and, closing all his fingers into his fist, held the thumb against his forehead, striking his breast six times with his right hand.

But Thaumast, as though not satisfied with this, placed the thumb of his left hand on the end of his nose, closing the rest of his hand.

Thereupon, Panurge placed the two master fingers at each side of his mouth, stretching his mouth out as far as possible and displaying all his teeth, while with his two thumbs he pulled down the lids of his eyes, making a face that was quite ugly, or so it seemed to those present.

"The comic effects of this scene," observes M. Plattard, "come at once from the spectacle of a learned man made a fool of by a buffoon and from the misunderstandings arising from this gestural discussion. This theme, which originates in an anecdote related in a gloss of Accursius, had been treated many times before." Rabelais, it would seem, is here borrowing, at least indirectly, from the same Accursius who has been the target of his sarcasms. In the Accursius anecdote, a fool put up by the Romans argues with and discomfits a Greek savant.

"Mask, you've spoken!": allusion to the sixteenth-century masquerades (momons) that were organized at night to take a present to someone; the maskers were supposed to keep silent to avoid being recognized.

——*"His trismegist codpiece"*: literally, *"thrice-great,"*
an epithet applied to Mercury, the Hermes Trismegistus.
——*"Lepers . . . with their rattles"*: *the rattles*
(cliquettes) *were carried by lepers to announce their ap-*
proach. "A *pair of* cliquettes *in decorated wood may be*
seen in the Hôpital Saint-Jean at Bruges" (Clouzot). ——
"Decretalists": *jurists versed in the Decretals, or canon*
law. ——*"As the Savior formerly maintained"*: Luke,
xvi, *19-25, the incident of Lazarus and the rich man in*
hell. ——*"The auricular fingers"*: *the little fingers* (digiti
auriculares). ——*"For the bran came afterwards"*:
word-play on bran *and* bren, *fecal matter, a turd.* ——
"Of the sort little boys make . . .": *the sport of firing*
hemp, carrots, beets, etc., from an elder-bark cannon
still exists in Poitou (where it is known as petouère) *and*
in Lorraine (where it is called peture).

Thaumast Expounds the Virtues and Learning of Panurge

THAUMAST then rose and, removing his bonnet from
his head, thanked Panurge very kindly; after which he
said, in a loud voice so that all present could hear:

"My lords, at this moment, I may well repeat the
Gospel word: *Et ecce plusquam Solomon hic.* And behold, a greater than Solomon is here. You have here in
your midst an incomparable treasure. I refer to Monsieur
Pantagruel, whose renown has brought me all the way
from England, to consult with him concerning certain
insoluble problems in magic, alchemy, the cabala, geomancy, astrology, and philosophy, problems that have
greatly troubled my mind. But now, I am angry with
Fame, who appears to me to have been jealous of him,

seeing that she has reported but the thousandth part of the merit that is in him.

"You have seen how this mere disciple has satisfied me by telling me more than I wanted to know. He has, moreover, laid bare and solved certain other doubtful and immensely important questions. Indeed, I may assure you that he has uncovered the abysmal well of encyclopaedic wisdom, whereas I had not expected to find one man familiar with even the rudiments of all this. I made this discovery while we were debating by means of signs, without saying a word, or even half a word. But in due time I shall set down in writing all that has passed between us and all the problems that we have solved, so that no one may think that all this has been mere buffoonery, and I shall have this statement printed, so that everyone may learn, as I have done.

"From this, you will be able to judge what the master might say to you, if he chose, when his disciple has exhibited such prowess; for *non est discipulus super magistrum*. The disciple is not above his master. In any case, God be praised! And I wish very humbly to thank you all for the honor you have done me upon this occasion. May God reward you eternally!"

Pantagruel in a like manner thanked the audience and, upon leaving, took Thaumast home to dinner with him; and you may believe me when I tell you that they drank with their belly-bands unbuttoned (for in those days it was the custom to fasten-in the belly with buttons, as they fasten collars today). The fact is, they drank to the point of saying "Where do *you* come from?" Holy Virgin! how they did draw on the goat's leather! And the flagons trotted back and forth, as they tooted the old horn.

"Draw one!"

"Set 'em up!"

"Boy, a little wine!"

"Keep it coming, what the devil! keep it coming!"

There was not a mother's son that did not consume twenty-five or thirty barrels. And do you want to know why? It was a case of *Sicut terra sine aqua.* Like unto a land without water. For it was very warm, and what's more, they happened to be thirsty.

With regard to the theses sustained by Thaumast and the significance of the signs employed in the debate, I should be glad to explain them to you in accordance with the statements of the participants; only, I have been told that Thaumast has had a large book on the subject printed at London, in which book he sets forth everything, leaving out nothing. And so, for the present, I shall pass it up.

"And, behold, a greater than Solomon": Matthew, xii, 42; Luke xi, 331. ——"The disciple is not above his master": Matthew, x, 24; Luke, vi, 40; John, xiii, 16. ——"Where do you come from?": to drink until one is unable to recognize one's friends; equivalent to: "Who are you, anyway?" ——"Like unto a land without water": Psalms, cxliii, 6: "My soul thirsteth after thee as a thirsty land." There are snatches of conversation here that Rabelais was later to use in his "Remarks of the Drunkards" chapter.

The author then goes on to narrate how Panurge fell in love with a "haughty Parisian dame," a married lady who rejected his anything but chaste advances; whereupon Panurge played upon her the trick described in the well-known passage that follows.

How Panurge Played a Trick on the Parisian Lady Which She Did Not Like Very Well

Now, as it happened, the next day was Corpus Christi, when all the women came stepping out in their very best clothes. On this particular day, Panurge's lady was dressed in a very handsome satin gown, with a jacket of expensive white velvet. The day before, Panurge had looked all over town until he found a *lykiske orgosa*, or bitch in heat. Roping her with his girdle, he took her to his room and there fed her well all that day and night. The next morning, he killed her and took from her a certain organ, as the Greek geomancers suggest. Chopping this up into as fine pieces as possible, he hid the bits about his person and took them along with him to where the lady was preparing to take part in the procession that is customary on that day.

As he entered, Panurge gave her holy water, addressing her most politely. A little while later, after she had finished her short prayers, he went to take a seat beside her, handing her as he did so a rondeau, couched as follows:

When I paid court to you, my pretty dame,
You were too haughty and quite far from tame;
You told me to pick up my things and pack,
And told me, also, I need not come back,
Although with you I'd squarely played the game.
Supposing that was how you felt, with the same
Politeness I had shown you, you might frame
(Without a pimp) a softer answer: "Jack,
   Let's call it off today."

There's surely no harm done, if I must blame
Your matchless beauty, for kindling into flame
This heart of mine you keep upon the rack:

For I ask nothing but to flop you back
For a somersault, a jolly little game——
　　Let's call it on today.

As she was opening the paper to see what was in it,
Panurge promptly sprinkled his drug over her, on various
parts of her clothing, even to the folds of her sleeves and
of her gown. Then, he remarked to her:

"Lady, poor lovers don't always have an easy time of
it. As for me, I only hope that all the bad nights and all
the bad luck and trouble I have had on account of my
love for you will be deducted from my pains in purga-
tory. You might, at least, pray God to grant me patience
in my affliction."

Panurge had not finished making this little speech
before all the dogs in the church came running up to the
lady, attracted by the odor of the drug with which he
had sprinkled her. Big and small, fat and lean, they all
came up, dangling their members, smelling around her,
and pissing all over her. It was the greatest mischief in
the world. Panurge made a pretence of chasing them
away, then fell back into a side-chapel to see the fun,
for those measly curs were simply urinating all over her
clothes. While a big greyhound was making water on her
head, the others squirted up her sleeves and over her
behind, the little ones pissing on her pumps. The other
women were forced to come to her rescue, but they
had a hard time saving her. Panurge, in the meanwhile,
was laughing his head off, and remarked to one of the
lords of the city:

"I think that lady there must be in heat, or else, some
greyhound has just got done covering her."

When he perceived that all the dogs were snarling
around her, exactly as they do a bitch in heat, Panurge
left and went to look for Pantagruel. Wherever he
found any dogs in the street, he would give them a good

kick, saying: "What's the matter? Aren't you going to the wedding with the rest of your friends? Get along with you, what the devil! get along!"

When he reached home, he said to Pantagruel:

"Master, I beg you, come see how all the dogs in the country are gathered around the prettiest lady in town, doing their best to ball-and-socket her."

Pantagruel was glad enough to come and see the show, which he found quite novel and entertaining. But the real sport came when the procession started. Then, more than six-hundred-thousand-fourteen dogs might have been seen around the lady, causing her a thousand torments. Wherever she went, fresh ones came running up, to follow at her heel and to piss on the ground her dress had touched. Everybody stopped at the sight, and watched the dogs leaping up to her throat and spoiling her finery. The only thing she could do was to go to her own house, and the dogs after her, while all the chambermaids fairly split themselves with laughing.

When she was safely home and had locked the door behind her, all the dogs for a mile and a half around came running up and so thoroughly bepissed the entryway that their urine made a creek on which ducks could have swum. It is this creek which today flows past St. Victor, where, owing to the specific virtue of its dog-piss (as formerly preached by our Master D'Oribus) the Gobelin dye-works have been set up. And may God help us all, a windmill might have ground corn with it, even if not quite so much as is ground by the windmills of Bazacle at Toulouse.

"Lykiske orgosa" (*in the original:* lycisque orgoose): *a number of editions give the French equivalent of the Greek words:* une chienne qui estoit en chaleur; *Lycisca is the name of a bitch in Vergil's Eclogues, III, 18, a source from which Des Periers borrowed the term in his Cymbalum Mundi.* ———*"This stream which today flows past St. Victor": reference to the Bièvre, which traversed the paddock of St. Victor (Clouzot).* ———*"Our Master D'Oribus": Plattard thinks the allusion is, very likely, to one Mathieu Ory, or Orry, a Grand Inquisitor of the Faith, who distinguished himself by his zeal in running down and persecuting heretics* (d'oribus *commonly has a connotation of "golden-colored" excrement).* ——— *"The Gobelin dye-works": home of the famous tapestries, familiar to the tourist visiting Paris.* ———*"The windmills of Bazacle": "a very old mill upon the Garonne, on the western border of Toulouse" (Clouzot).*

III. The Expedition to Utopia

(CHAPTERS XXIII-XXXIV)

In the third and concluding portion of Book Second, the first book of the Pantagruel, *the giant-hero, upon learning that the Dipsodes, or Thirsty Ones, are laying waste the land of Utopia and have laid siege to the capital city of the Amaurotes, leaves Paris with his followers and sets out upon a relief expedition. It is here that the real plot-thread of the main body of Rabelais' romance begins, and this theme—the "navigations of Pantagruel"—will be found running throughout the rest of the work.*

While these last chapters lack the broader interest of many of those in the central portion of the book, they are highly significant as showing Maître François' keen awareness of the age in which he lived, with its tremendous voyages of discovery and its vital and consuming impulse to geographic expansion. The route followed by Pantagruel and the geography involved have been the object of much learned study. Professor Abel Lefranc has published an octavo volume on the subject, with maps (Les Navigations de Pantagruel, *Paris, 1905), and the British scholar, Mr. Arthur Tilley, has made important contributions. The latter has shown that the preface of the* Novus orbis regionum ac insularum veteribus incognitarum *of Grynaeus, printed at Basel, in 1532, contained, in the form of an itinerary of the Spaniards sailing toward the Indies, what was probably Rabelais' source in outlining Pantagruel's journeyings. In Rabelais and the* Novus orbis *the ports of call follow in the same order and the geographical nomenclature is the same. (Mr. Tilley's article, "Rabelais and Geographical Discovery," will be found in the* Modern Language Review, *Vol. II, p. 316 f.) Rabelais' nomenclature as a whole is chiefly of Italian origin, in which connection it is interesting to compare the* Delle Navigazioni e Viaggi *of Giovanni Battista Ramusio (third edition, Venice, 1563).*

Like Sir Thomas More, Rabelais situates the land of Utopia in the Far East, to the north of Cathay, or China, not far from the region designated on the maps as Upper India. He has borrowed from More at least two names, that of the Amaurotes and that of Achoria, while Alymyrodes (name of the inhabitants of a part of Dipsody), on the other hand, appears to be his own invention.

"What, then," inquires Lefranc, "does this crossing of the Atlantic signify, this defeat of the Cannibals, this conquest of the Pearl Islands, and finally, this voyage to the land of the famous Prester John? All this has a meaning: it corresponds to something real, to an idea that profoundly haunted the minds of our author's contemporaries. This was, quite simply, the voyage to the Indies by way of America. . . . He conceived the balance of the story of his young prince as embracing a series of voyages and explorations directed toward the East Indies or the New World, along the Isthmus of Panama—that is to say, toward those regions that excited the most curiosity at the time he began writing. . . ." Later, in accordance with France's changing maritime ambitions, Rabelais was led to alter his plan slightly and to carry his travelers farther to the north (Cartier and the northwest passage), but on the whole he adhered to his original scheme with surprising fidelity. "In one way or another," concludes Lefranc, "Pantag-

ruel was to accomplish the voyage that . . . during the
first part of the sixteenth century remained the objective
of numerous navigators."

How Pantagruel Left Paris, Having Received Word That the Dipsodes Were Invading the Land of the Amaurotes, Together with the Reason That the Leagues Are So Short in France

A SHORT while later, Pantagruel received word that his
father, Gargantua, had been translated by Morgan to
the Land of the Fairies, as Ogier and Arthur formerly
had been, and that the Dipsodes, hearing of this translation, had sallied forth from their domains and had laid
waste a good part of the land of Utopia, being, at the
moment, engaged in besieging the capital city of the
Amaurotes. At this, he set out from Paris, without
saying good-by to any of his friends (for the business was
an urgent one), and so, came directly to Rouen.

On the way, Pantagruel, happening to observe that
the leagues of France were very short, compared to those
of other countries, asked Panurge what the reason for
this was. The latter proceeded to narrate a story which
the monk, Marotus of the Lake, includes in his *Exploits
of the Kings of Canaria.*

"In ancient times," the story ran, "distances in various
countries were not marked by leagues, miles, stadia, or
parasangs. This was not done until King Pharamond
established these divisions, which came about in the
following manner:

"The king had selected, in Paris, a hundred handsome
young bucks, very gallant and capable fellows, and a

hundred pretty lasses of Picardy. He saw to it that they were all well provided for and well groomed for a period of eight days; then he summoned them to him and gave each buck a lass, along with plenty of pocket-money, commanding them to set out for various points and in various directions, and ordering the young fellows, each time they made a stop for the purpose of humping their lasses, to set up a stone; and that was to be a league.

"And so, they set out in high spirits, and seeing that they were all fresh and had had a good rest, they stopped at first to trifle a little at every fence-post. And that is why the leagues of France are so short. But when they had traveled some distance, and were tired as the very devil, and had no more oil left in their lamps, the young blades did not ram it in quite so often, but were very well satisfied (I am referring to the men) with a few measly times a day. And that is why the leagues of Brittany, of Landes, of Germany, and of other more distant countries are so long.

"Other authorities give other explanations, but this strikes me as being the best one."

To this Pantagruel readily agreed.

Departing from Rouen, they came to Honfleur, where Pantagruel, Panurge, Epistemon, Eusthenes, and Carpalim took ship. At this place, as they were waiting for a favorable wind and, in the meanwhile, calking their craft, Pantagruel received from a lady in Paris, whom he had been keeping for some little time, a letter bearing the inscription:

To the best loved by the fair and the least loyal of the brave.

P.N.T.G.R.L.

The name Amaurotes, as has been said, is out of Sir Thomas More; from the Greek amauros, *meaning "dark, obscure."* ——*Morgan was the fay who, after King Arthur's defeat, took him in, cured him of his wounds, and kept him with her.* ——*Ogier the Dane was a legendary paladin of Charlemagne.* ——*"Marotus of the Lake" has not been satisfactorily identified.* ——*The Canarians have been mentioned in Book First.* ——*King Pharamond was a legendary king of the Franks and a Knight of the Round Table.* ——*The length of the league varied in different countries; in France it was, commonly, 4,444½ meters.* ——*"Miles" is a reference to the Roman mile, or a thousand paces. The Greek stadium was equivalent to 606.9 feet. The Persian parasang, familiar to every schoolboy reader of Xenophon, was roughly equivalent to thirty stadia, or three miles.*

With the aid of the ever officious Panurge and Epistemon's knowledge of Hebrew, the lady's mysterious missive was finally deciphered. The author here displays his classical erudition on the subject of invisible inks. The letter was found to contain nothing but a ring set with a false diamond, with an inscription on the inside: "Lama sabachthani," or "Why hast thou forsaken me," the words of Christ on the cross. (This, incidentally, is one of the passages that has been brought forward in support of Rabelais' "atheism.") There is also a play on "dyamant faulx" (false diamond) and "Dy, amant faulx" (tell me, false lover). Epistemon thereupon reminds his master of Aeneas' parting with Dido, of the call of arms and the fact that the ship is "tugging at anchor"; he urges his prince to "cut the knot" and "leave all other thoughts behind him, in coming to the aid of his native city, which was in danger."

Accordingly, when an hour later a northwest wind came up, they took advantage of it and putting out full-sail were soon upon the high seas. Within a few days, after having passed Porto Santo and Madeira, they put in at the Canary Islands. Setting out again from there, they passed Cape Blanco, Senegal, Cape Verde, Gambia, Sagres, Melli, and the Cape of Good Hope, and then put in at the Kingdom of Melinda. Taking advantage of a north wind and setting out from there, they passed Meden, Uti, Udem, Gelasim, the Fairy Islands, and the Kingdom of Achoria, until they at last arrived at the port of Utopia, a little more than three leagues distant from the city of the Amaurotes.

From the geographic point of view, the foregoing passage is a remarkable one, the route followed being precisely that of sixteenth-century navigators who sought the Indies by rounding the Cape of Good Hope. Down through Melinda, all the points mentioned will be found on the map; then, as usual, and for the sake of his narrative, the Maître's imagination intervenes to jumble the real and unreal. "Meden," "Uti," and "Udem" are from the Greek meden, outi, and ouden, meaning "nothing." "Gelasim" is from the Greek gelasimos, meaning "laughable" or "ridiculous," and signifies a land where the inhabitants do nothing but laugh.

We are then given a description of the first encounter of Pantagruel and his followers with the enemy, in which the crafty Panurge, making use of the ship's cables and capstan, traps and burns alive a force of six-hundred-sixty armored knights. By this time the expedition was tired of eating salt meat, and by way of replenishing their supplies with a little fresh venison, a hunt was staged, resulting in a bag of game that was suited to a giant's appetite. After which, they made ready to advance upon the enemy.

How Pantagruel Erected a Monument in Memory of Their Prowess, and Panurge Another in Memory of the Leverets; and How Pantagruel, with His Farts, Begot the Little Men and, with His Poops, the Little Women; and How Panurge Broke a Big Stick over Two Glasses

"BUT before we leave here," said Pantagruel, "in memory of the prowess which you have just exhibited, I desire to erect, upon the spot, a handsome memorial."

Whereupon, singing gay little village songs, they all fell to and set up a large piece of wood, on which they hung a warrior's saddle, a horse's chanfrin, a number of equine ornaments, stirrup-thongs, spurs, a hauberk, a full set of steel armor, a battle-ax, a cavalryman's sword, a gauntlet, a mace, armpit-pads, greaves, a neckpiece, and all the trimmings requisite for a triumphal arch or commemorative monument.

Then, to the eternal memory of the event which had occurred there, Pantagruel composed the following victory-inscription:

'Twas here that four brave fighters bold
Displayed their courage, showed how good sense goes
Farther than armor, as in days of old
Did Fabius and the two Scipios.
They put six-hundred-sixty dirty lice in the throes,
And made the mighty rascals burn like bark;
Thus, kings and dukes, you rooks and pawns, this shows
The worth of genius—more than strength, remark.

For victory,
As all can see,
Is in accord
With the will of the sky,
Where reigns on high
The Almighty Lord.

She comes not to the strong ones nor the great,
But to whom she pleases: this we must believe;
Then, he who longs for riches and high state
Should trust in her, and she will not deceive.

While Pantagruel was engaged in composing the above poem, Panurge stuck up on a big stake the horns, skin, and right front foot of the roebuck, then the ears of the three leverets, the backbone of a rabbit, the jaws of a hare, the wings of two bustards, the feet of four ringdoves, a cruet-stand of vinegar, a salt-horn, the wooden spit they had used, a larding-stick, a filthy kettle all full of holes, a drip-pan in which they had made gravy, an earthen saltcellar, and a goblet of Beauvais. And in imitation of Pantagruel's memorial verses, he composed the following:

'Twas here four drunks, as jolly as you'd wish,
Sat down upon their arses for a feast;
They were bold fellows and all drank like fish,
In honor of old Bacchus, their high priest.
'Twas then that Master Bunny, at the least,
Lost his backbone, as each one there fell to it;
With salt and vinegar, the little beast,
They ran him down; it was a shame to do it.

For the best direction
For protection
Against the heat
Is but to drink
And chink and clink
Your liquor, very neat.

But rabbit-flesh, remember, is very sad
If you have left your vinegar behind;

For vinegar's a rabbit's soul, by gad;
So, you'll do well to keep this point in mind.

Then Pantagruel spoke up:

"Come, my lads: We've spent entirely too much time here, dawdling over our victuals; for it seldom happens that you find a great banqueter performing extraordinary feats of arms. There is no shade like that of army standards, no smoke like that of horses, and no clatter like that of battle-harness."

At this, Epistemon began smiling, and said:

"There is no shade like that of the kitchen, no smoke like that of pastries, and no clatter like that of cups."

To which Panurge added:

"There is no shade like that of curtains, no smoke like that of breasts, and no clatter like that of balls."

Whereupon, rising, Panurge gave a fart, a leap, and a whistle, and cried out gaily, at the top of his voice:

"Long live Pantagruel!"

At this, Pantagruel must needs do the same, but the fart that he let made the earth tremble for nine leagues around, and the foul air he emitted begot more than fifty-three-thousand little men, dwarfs, and misshapen fellows; while with a poop that followed, he begot the same number of little crouching females of a sort you will see in various places, who never grow except like a cow's tail, downward, or else round, like Limousin radishes.

"What!" exclaimed Panurge, "and are your farts as fruitful as all that? By God! but here are some fine little slippers of men for you and some pretty little poops of women; you ought to marry them off together, and they'll beget ox-flies."

This was exactly what Pantagruel did, and he called them Pygmies and sent them to live in an island nearby, where they have greatly multiplied since. But the cranes

are all the time making war on them, though the
Pygmies defend themselves bravely enough, for these
little runts (in Scotland they are called currycomb-
handles) are naturally of a choleric disposition. The
physiological reason is that their heart lies so near their
crap.

Panurge then took two glasses of the same size, that
happened to be there, and filled them with water, as
much as they would hold; following which, he put one
on one stool and the other on another, separating them
by a distance of five feet. Then he took a javelin-staff,
five feet and a half long, and laid it on the two glasses,
in such a manner that the two ends of the staff barely
touched the brims. Having done this, he took a stout
short-lance and said, to Pantagruel and the others:

"Gentlemen, just see how easily we're going to win a
victory over our enemies. For just as I am going to break
this staff on these glasses, without the glasses themselves
being broken or shattered, and what is more, without
spilling a drop of water, just so are we going to break the
heads of those Dipsodes, without a single man's being
wounded, and without the loss of one bit of booty.

"But just so you won't think there is any sleight-of-
hand here, take this short-lance," he said to Eusthenes,
"and hit the staff as hard as you can in the middle."

Eusthenes did so, and the staff was broken into two
clean pieces, while not a drop of water fell from the
glasses.

"I know a lot other tricks," said Panurge; "but come
on; and don't be afraid of anything."

*According to Plattard, Rabelais is here following the
description of ancient memorial monuments as given by*

Alessandro Alessandri, Geniales Dies, i, 22. ——*This is the first French text in which the term* Pygmées *occurs. "Sixteenth-century maps place the Pygmies opposite Japan, to the north of Cathay and the east of Scythia. . . . Without taking Rabelais' geographical data too seriously, this comparison has its value in enabling us to locate the land of Achoria" (Clouzot). "The ancients placed the Pygmies at the far bounds of the world, most often at the sources of the Nile; sometimes in India, the region adjacent to Scythia. . . . The legend that represents the Pygmies, a race of dwarfs, as being in perpetual conflict with the cranes dates from the Homeric epoch" (Plattard). ——"Four brave fighters": Panurge, Carpalim, Eusthenes, and Epistemon, who routed the six-hundred-sixty knights. ——"Dirty lice": morpions, lice of the pubic region, or "crabs." ——"It was a shame to do it": the literal reading is: "ran him down like scorpions."*

The story of Pantagruel's campaign against the Dipsodes and the giants continues; for a prisoner has been taken, and from him it has been learned that Anarch (the "king without a kingdom"), who rules over the "Thirsty Ones," is a great drinker and that giants serve as his body-guard. In many respects, this is the typical gigantesque chronicle of the later Middle Ages and early Renaissance, and is lacking in the homely close-to-life incidents that make the Picrocholine War of Book First such hilarious reading. Yet this chronicle differs from others in the special thirst-inspiring aspects of Rabelais' Pantagruel and the means by which he fights, as is brought out in the episode that follows. (A prisoner had been sent back to King Anarch, to present him with a specially compounded drug.)

How Pantagruel Won a Most Extraordinary Victory over the Dipsodes and the Giants

LET us leave Pantagruel here with his apostles, and speak of King Anarch and his army.

When the prisoner reached camp, he was taken at once to the king; and he told the latter how a great giant named Pantagruel had come to the land, and how this newcomer had defeated and then mercilessly roasted alive all the six-hundred-sixty knights, and how he alone had escaped to bring back the news. Moreover, he told how he had been ordered by this same giant to advise his majesty to invite Pantagruel to dinner, since the latter was planning to attack about dinner-time.

Then, he gave the king the box containing the drug; and no sooner had the king swallowed a spoonful than he at once felt such an overheating of the throat, along with an ulceration of the uvula, that his very tongue began to peel. All the remedies that they offered him were of no avail; the only relief he could find was to drink incessantly, for no sooner did he take a goblet from his mouth than his tongue would begin to burn up. All they could do for him, therefore, was to keep pouring wine into his throat with a funnel.

When they saw what had happened, his captains, pashas, and the members of his body-guard began tasting the drug to see if it would make them equally thirsty; and it had precisely the same effect upon them that it had had upon the king. They all of them began tooting the flagons, and tooting them well, while a rumor ran through the camp that the prisoner was back, that they were to be attacked tomorrow, and that it was for this that the king, his captains, and his bodyguard were making preparations by thus drinking like bellringers. And so it was, every man in the army began swilling, hoisting the flagons, and draining the beakers on his own account. In short, they drank so very, very much that they were soon all snoozing away like pigs, in great disorder, throughout the camp.

And now, to come back to our friend Pantagruel and tell what he is doing all this while.

Setting out from the place where he had erected the memorial, he took the mainmast of their ship in his hand, like a staff, and placed on the top of it two-hundred-thirty-seven puncheons of the white wine of Anjou, the rest being of Rouen. And he fastened to his girdle a barrel brim-full of salt, which he carried as easily as the Lansquenet women do their little baskets. Thus equipped, he set out with his followers.

As they drew near the enemy's camp, Panurge remarked to his master:

"My lord, do you know what you ought to do? You ought to take down a little of that white wine of Anjou from the mast-top and let us all have a drink, right here and now, in true Breton fashion."

To this Pantagruel very readily consented, and they drank so heartily that when they were through there was not a single drop left of the two-hundred-thirty-seven puncheons—with the exception of a leather flask of Tours, which Panurge had filled for himself (he was in the habit of calling this his *vademecum*) and a few paltry lees for vinegar.

After they had drawn on the old goatskin in proper fashion, Panurge gave Pantagruel some devilish combination of drugs to eat, composed of lithontriptic,

nephrocatharticon, and quince-marmalade with cantharides, along with other diuretic spices. After consuming
this, Pantagruel said to Carpalim:

"Go to their town, and slip in like a rat along the
walls, as you know so well how to do, and then suggest
to them that they ought to come out this very minute
and attack the enemy, putting up as stiff a front as they
can. After you have done this climb down, take a lighted
torch, and set fire to all the tents in their camp. Then
yell as loudly as you are able with that lusty voice of
yours, and lose no time in getting out of camp."

"Very well," said Carpalim, "but wouldn't it be a
good thing for me to spike their artillery?"

"No, no," said Pantagruel, "but you may set fire to
their powder."

Mindful of these instructions, Carpalim set out, and
did as Pantagruel had told him to do. As a result all the
fighters in the town at once sallied forth. And when he
had set fire to the tents, Carpalim slipped quietly out
through the enemy's ranks, without the slightest danger
of being perceived, so soundly were they all snoring
away. When he came to their artillery, he touched off
their munitions. But this was dangerous business; the
flash was so quick that it threatened to wrap poor Carpalim, and if it had not been for his miraculous haste he
would have been fricasseed like a pig; but as it was, he
succeeded in making off quicker than a bolt from a
crossbow.

When he was safely out of the trenches he began
yelling so frightfully that it sounded as though all the
devils in hell had been let loose. The enemy awoke at
this, but what do you think? They were as dumbfounded
as at the first matin bell, which in the Luçon country is
known as the scratchballs.

In the meanwhile Pantagruel commenced sowing the salt that he had in his barrel, and since they were all sleeping with their mouths wide open, he filled their gullets full till the poor bastards began coughing like foxes as they cried: "Ha! Pantagruel, you're heating the firebrand inside us."

As for Pantagruel himself, he suddenly felt a great desire to piss, on account of the drug which Panurge had given him; and piss he did, throughout their camp, so copiously and so well that he drowned every last one of them. There was an unusual flood for ten leagues around, and history assures us that if his father's big mare had been there and had pissed a similar amount, there would have been a deluge more enormous than that of Deucalion; for that mare never pissed without making a river bigger than the Rhone and the Danube.

When they beheld this, those who had run out of the camp cried, "Look, they've all been killed; there's their blood." But they were wrong in thinking that Pantagruel's urine was the enemy's blood, for they only saw it by the light of the fire from the burning tents, and perhaps a little moonlight.

The enemy, being now thoroughly awake and observing, on the one hand, the conflagration in their camp and, on the other, the urinal inundation and deluge, did not know what to say or think. Some opined that it was the end of the world and the last judgment, when everything was to be consumed with fire; others, that the sea-gods Neptune, Proteus, Triton, and the others were persecuting them, and that, as a matter of fact, this was salt sea-water.

Ah! who now can relate what Pantagruel did to those three hundred giants! O my muse, my Calliope, my Thalia, inspire me at this moment, refresh my mind, for here is the logical bridge of asses, here is the stumbling-block, here is the difficulty: to describe adequately the horrible battle that now followed.

I would that I had, right now, a bottle of the very best wine that those who are perusing this so veridical history ever drank.

The episode of Pantagruel's urinal flood and the allusion to Gargantua's great mare will remind the reader of Book First; but it is to be remembered that the present book was written before the Gargantua. The reference is, rather, to the Grandes Cronicques and the Chronicques Admirables, in which the incident appears, and which served Rabelais as source-material. We have already come upon snatches of dialogue that he was later to work up into the "Remarks of the Drunkards"; while the episode that is soon to follow, Pantagruel's covering an army with his tongue, corresponds, in a way, to Gargantua's eating the pilgrims in a salad.

The Maître here exhibits his pharmaceutical knowledge (he was noted as a pharmacologist). Lithontriptic is an electuary for dissolving calculi in the bladder and urinary passages. Nephrocatharticon is a kidney-purge. M. Paul Dorveaux, French physician and Rabelais scholar, observes that the diuretic property of cantharides (Spanish fly) had been noted by Hippocrates, Galen, Dioscorides, and others, who recommended that the remedy be employed with discretion.

"After they had drawn on the old goatskin": Urquhart here has a rendering that has become a classic: "after they had whittled and curried the can pretty handsomely." ——"Known as the scratchballs": "a pleasantry referring to one of the instinctive gestures of

the sleeper upon awakening" (Clouzot). ——*"More
enormous than that of Deucalion": for the Greek version of the deluge, see Ovid,* Metamorphoses, i, 318.

There follows an account of "How Pantagruel Routed
the Three Hundred Giants, Clad in Freestone Armor,
and Werewolf, Their Captain."

How Epistemon, Who Had Had His Head Cut Off, Was Cleverly Cured by Panurge; with Some News from the Devils and the Damned

WHEN this gigantic defeat of the enemy had been
achieved, Pantagruel retired to the place where the
flagons were and called Panurge and the others over to
him. They all came up, safe and sound, with the exception of Eusthenes, who had been clawed a little in the
face by one of the giants whose throat he had cut, and
Epistemon, who did not put in an appearance at all, at
which Pantagruel was so grief-stricken that he wanted
to kill himself; but Panurge said:

"Just be patient, my lord, and we'll look for him
among the dead. We'll soon know the truth of the matter."

And so, they started searching for him, and they
found him, stiff and dead, with his head, all bloody, between his arms.

"Ha! old death," exclaimed Eusthenes, "so you've
taken the best man in the world, have you?"

When he heard this, Pantagruel rose, the saddest person you ever saw, and said to Panurge:

"So! old fellow, that sign of yours, with the two

glasses and the javelin-staff, did not work very well, after all, did it?"

But Panurge only replied:

"Don't waste any tears, my lads. He's still warm. I'll cure him for you, and make him as sound as he ever was."

As he said this, he took Epistemon's head and held it against his own codpiece to keep it warm, as well as to keep it out of the draught, while Eusthenes and Carpalim carried the body back to the place where they had had their feast, not from any hope that their comrade would ever be cured, but just so that Pantagruel might be able to view the remains. As they went along, Panurge encouraged them, saying:

"If I don't cure him, I'm willing to lose my own head, which is a fool's bet. So, dry your tears and lend me a hand."

He then thoroughly cleansed the body, neck, and head with a good grade of white wine, after which he sinapized all these parts with powdered extract of dung, which he always carried with him, in one of his pockets. Following which, he anointed them with some kind of ointment or other, and then adjusted them very carefully, vein to vein, nerve to nerve, and vertebra to vertebra, so that Epistemon would not be a stiffneck, for he hated chaps like that worse than poison. When he had done this, he took fifteen or sixteen stitches with the needle, so the head would not fall off again, then rubbed around it a certain salve which he called resuscitative.

Epistemon at once began to breathe, then opened his eyes, then yawned a little, then sneezed, and finally let a good life-sized fart. When he heard this Panurge remarked: "He's cured now, right enough." And he gave him a glass of strong white wine to drink, along with a little sugared toast.

This, then, was the way in which Epistemon was healed, and very cleverly, too, except that he was hoarse for more than three weeks afterward, and had a hacking cough, which he could only get rid of by drinking a lot.

And then Epistemon began telling them how he had seen the devils, had had a heart-to-heart talk with Lucifer and, on the whole, had enjoyed himself very much down there in hell and the Elysian Fields; and he insisted that the devils were not such bad fellows, after all. Speaking of the damned, he expressed regret that Panurge had brought him back to life so soon.

"For I had all kinds of sport, watching them," he said.

"How is that?" inquired Pantagruel.

"They are not so bad off," said Epistemon, "as you might think, though they are in quite different circumstances from what they were in this life.

"For I saw Alexander the Great earning a miserable living by patching old shoes.

"Xerxes was hawking mustard;

"Romulus was a salt-peddler;

"Numa an iron-monger;

"Tarquin a porter;

"Piso a peasant;

"Sulla a ferryman;

"Cyrus a cowherd;

"Themistocles a bottle-vendor;

"Epaminondas a mirror-maker;

"Brutus and Cassius surveyors;

"Demosthenes a vine-dresser;

"Cicero a stoker;

"Fabius a threader of rosary-beads;

"Artaxerxes a rope-maker;

"Aeneas a miller;

"Achilles a scurvy wretch;

"Agamemnon a pot-licker;

"Ulysses a mower;

"Nestor a gold-miner;

"Darius a caretaker of outhouses;

"Ancus Martius a calker;

"Camillus a maker of wooden shoes;

"Marcellus a bean-sheller;

"Drusus a braggart;

"Scipio Africanus, in a pair of wooden clogs, was hawking vinegar-dregs;

"Hasdrubal was a lantern-maker;

"Hannibal a poultry-merchant;

"Priam was selling old rags;

"Lancelot of the Lake was a skinner of dead horses;

"All the Knights of the Round Table were poor day-laborers, plying an oar on the rivers Cocytus, Phlege-thon, Styx, Acheron, and Lethe, whenever the devils wanted a little outing on the water, like the boatmen of Lyon and the gondoliers of Venice. But for each fare, all they get is a punch in the nose, and at night, a little piece of moldy bread.

"Trajan was a frog-fisher;

"Antoninus a lackey;

"Commodus a maker of jade trinkets;

"Pertinax a nut-cracker;

"Lucullus a cook-shop keeper;

"Justinian a maker of cheap toys;

"Hector a gravy-licker, or cook;

"Paris was a poor devil in rags;

"Achilles a hay-bundler;

"Cambyses a mule-driver;

"Artaxerxes a pot-skimmer;

"Nero was a fiddler, and Fierabras, his flunkey, played him a thousand dirty tricks, making his master eat brown bread and drink turned wine, while he himself had the best there was.

"Julius Caesar and Pompey were ship-tarrers;

"Valentine and Orson were rubbers in the hot-baths;

"Gigland and Gauvain were poor swineherds;

"Big-Tooth Geoffrey was a match-seller;

"Jason was a sexton;

"Don Pedro of Castille a pardon-peddling friar;

"Morgan a beer-brewer;

"Huon of Bordeaux was a cooper;

"Pyrrhus was a scullion;

"Antiochus was a chimney-sweep;

"Romulus was a patcher of clogs;

"Octavian a parchment-scraper;

"Nerva a groom;

"Pope Julius a pastry-peddler, but he no longer had his big bogey-man beard;

"John of Paris was a shoe-shiner;

"Arthur of Brittany a hat-cleaner;

"Pierceforest a vineyard-porter;

"Pope Boniface the Eighth was a pot-skimmer;

"Pope Nicholas the Third was a stationer;

"Pope Alexander was rat-catcher;

"Pope Sixtus was a greaser of syphilitic patients———"

"How does that come," Pantagruel interrupted him. "Are there syphilitics down there?"

"Certainly, there are," said Epistemon. "I never saw so many in all my life. Why, there must be more than a hundred-million; for you may take my word for it: those that don't have the old pox in this world are bound to have it in the world to come."

"Holy Christ!" exclaimed Panurge, "then that lets me out; for I've been all the way to the Hole of Gibraltar and the farthest colonies of Hercules, and I've knocked down the ripest there is!"

"Well, Ogier the Dane was an armor-scourer;

"King Tigranes was a roofer;

"Galien the Restorer a mole-catcher;

"The four sons of Aymon were tooth-pullers;

"Pope Calixtus was a barber of women's cracks;

"Pope Urban a bacon-snatcher;

"Melusine was a kitchen-slut;

"Metabrune a laundress;

"Cleopatra an onion-seller;

"Helen a chambermaid-broker;

"Semiramis a lice-killer to beggars;

"Dido was selling mushrooms;

"Penthesilea was a cress-vendor;

"Lucretia the superintendent of a poor-house;

"Hortensia a seamstress;

"Livia a verdigris-grater;

"And so it was, those who had been great lords in this world were gaining a mean and wretched livelihood down there. On the other hand, the philosophers and those who had been beggars in this world were the great lords in those regions.

"For example, I saw Diogenes strutting around in a magnificent purple robe, with a scepter in his hand, and he would drive Alexander the Great into a fury, when the latter had done a bad job patching his shoes, by paying him off with blows of a club.

"I saw Epictetus, all dressed up in the latest French fashion, under a nice arbor, with a lot of young ladies, joking, drinking, dancing, and having a good time, while beside him was a pile of sunny crowns. Above the trellis the following verses had been written up as a motto:

> To leap and dance and sing a song,
> Drink good wine as you run,
> And do nothing all day long
> But count your crowns in the sun.

"When he saw me, he invited me to come and have a drink, as politely as could be, which I was quite willing to do; and we clinked the can most theologically together. While we were thus engaged, Cyrus came up, to beg a denier, in Mercury's name, to buy himself a few onions for his supper.

" 'Nothing doing,' said Epictetus, 'nothing doing. I never give deniers. Here, hold on a minute, you rascal; here's a crown for you; see that you behave yourself.'

"Cyrus was delighted at having fallen into so much pelf; but the other good-for-nothing kings down there, such as Alexander, Darius, and the rest, took it away from him that very night.

"I saw Patelin, Rhadamanthus' cashier, haggling over some little pastries that Pope Julius was hawking. Patelin asked him how much they were a dozen.

" 'Three whites,' said the Pope.

" 'What you mean,' said Patelin, 'is three licks with a cudgel. Hand them over and go get some more.'

"The poor pope went away, crying his eyes out, and told the master-baker for whom he worked that some one had stolen his pastries. Then the baker let him have the old eel-skin, and laid it on so well that the holy father's hide would not have been worth anything even for making bagpipes.

"I saw Master Jean le Maire. He was imitating the pope and making all the poor kings and pontiffs of this world kiss his feet. As they did so, he would put on all sorts of airs and give them his benediction, saying;

" 'Go get some pardons, you rascals, go get some pardons; there's a sale on them today. I hereby absolve you from bread and soup, and dispense you from ever amounting to a damn.'

"And calling Caillette and Triboulet over, he said to them:

"'Gentlemen of the Cardinal College, go ahead and dispatch your bulls: a club across the middle for each one of them.'

"Which was done at once.

"I overheard Master François Villon inquiring of Xerxes:

"'How much mustard do you get for a denier today?'

"'A denier's worth,' said Xerxes.

"'Why plague take you, you old robber!' said Villon. 'A white's only worth a copper denier down here, and here you are, trying to boost the cost of living.'

"And then, Xerxes pissed in his bucket, the way the mustard-sellers do at Paris.

"I saw, also, the Franc-Archer of Bagnollet. He was Inquisitor of Heretics; and coming upon Pierceforest, pissing against a wall on which St. Anthony's fire was painted, he promptly declared him a heretic, and would have had him burned alive, had it not been for Morgan, who, for his *proficiat* and other minor considerations, gave him nine mugs of beer."

At this point, Pantagruel spoke up.

"Your stories are very interesting, but please save them for another time. There is just one thing, however, that I wish you would tell us, right here and now, and that is, how they treat usurers down there."

"When I saw them," said Epistemon, "they were all busy hunting in the gutter for rusty pins and old nails, as you see the beggars doing in this world. But a hundred pounds of that junk is not worth a slice of bread; and besides, business is very bad. And so, the poor bastards sometimes have to go more than three weeks without a bite, or even a crust, to eat. They work day and night, waiting for fair-time to come around; but they're so damnably industrious that they think nothing of all this toil and trouble, provided that, by the end of the year, they succeed in picking up a measly denier or two."

"Well," said Pantagruel, "suppose we have a little drink. Drink up, my lads, drink up; for it is good drinking all this month."

Then they began to bring out their flagons, by the pile, and a fine time they had disposing of the camp munitions. But poor King Anarch was not in a position to enjoy himself to any great extent. Observing this, Panurge spoke up:

"What trade shall we put Monsignor the King to here, so that he'll be an expert at the business, when he has to go down to interview the devils?"

"That is a happy thought," said Pantagruel. "Well, do what you please with him. I make you a present of him."

"Thanks a lot," said Panurge, "I couldn't think of refusing a gift like that, and I'm much obliged to you for it, I am sure."

In this passage in which Rabelais with considerable daring creates an Inferno *of his own, the influence of Lucian becomes highly visible; for it is from Lucian's dialogue, the* Menippos *or Nekyomanteia, that the author has here borrowed his basic idea. Lucian pictures the philosophers, Socrates and Diogenes, as being in hell and taking their revenge on the kings, Xerxes and Alexander. The latter is depicted as patching filthy old shoes in a corner, while Xerxes, Darius, and Polycrates are begging in the street. To this picture of the downfall of the great, become beggars, Lucian opposes the happiness of the philosophers, who continue to philosophize in the enjoyment of complete liberty. "Rabelais has taken his inspiration, though in a very free manner, from this description" (Plattard).*

Of the less familiar personages mentioned: Piso is the name of an old Roman family (from pisum, *a pea); Fabius is the famous Quintus Fabius Maximus, known as "Cunctator," or the Procrastinator, commander against Hannibal, about 210* B.C.; *Ancus Martius was the fourth king of Rome, said to have had salt-works near the sea; Camillus is Marcus Furius Camillus, semi-mythical fourth-century Roman dictator and deliverer of Rome from the Gauls, subject of one of Plutarch's Lives; Marcus Claudius Marcellus, third-century Roman general, was the conqueror of Syracuse; Claudius Nero Drusus, son of Tiberius Nero and Livia, was a first-century general who conducted four campaigns against the Germans, whence his surname, Germanicus; Pertinax is the surname of the second-century Roman emperor, Publius Helvius, who succeeded Commodus, and who was assassinated; Lucius Lucinius Lucullus was the wealthy and luxurious Roman consul of the first half of the first century* B.C. *who defeated Mithridates and Tigranes; Fierabras was a Saracen giant of the romances of chivalry, listed as one of Pantagruel's ancestors; Valentine and Orson were two legendary heroes whose deeds of prowess against the Saracens are related in an old romance, printed at Paris about 1489; Giglan and Gauvain were the heroes of a Breton romance-cycle, printed about 1530 and very popular; we have made the acquaintance of "Big-Tooth Geoffrey," another of Pantagruel's "ancestors"; Godfrey of Bouillon (Billon), Duke of Lower Lorraine, was the leader of the First Crusade, in the eleventh century, and the hero of Tasso's* Jerusalem Delivered; *Don Pedro of Castile, surnamed "the Cruel," was a fourteenth-century king of Leon and Castile; Morgan was the name of a giant-hero of a romance of chivalry that was the source of Pulci's epic, the* Morgante Maggiore, *upon which Rabelais drew; Huon of Bordeaux was a hero of the popular literature, or* Bibliothèque bleue; *Pyrrhus was king of Epirus, fourth to third century,* B.C.; *Antiochus the Great was king of Syria, Babylonia, Media, and part of Asia Minor, third to second century,* B.C., *while Antiochus Epiphanes ruled over Syria, 175-164* B.C.; *Tigranes was the name of several Armenian kings; Galien the Restorer is the hero of a romance* (Galien Rethoré) *printed about 1500, so called because he was "destined to restore chivalry in France"; the romance entitled* The Four Sons of Aymon *has been previously mentioned; no chivalric hero or romance called Metabrune is known to scholars, the allusion being, possibly, to an old* chanson; *Penthesilea was queen of the Amazons in the Trojan War and one of the "neuf preuses," or nine most valiant women of all time, according to popular tradition in the Middle Ages; Hortensia, daughter of the Roman orator, Quintus Hortensius, was famous in antiquity for having successfully pleaded the cause of Roman women threatened with an onerous tax; Livia was the wife of the Emperor Augustus; Caillette was court-fool to Louis* XII, *and Le Feurial, known as Triboulet, was fool to Louis* XII *and Francis* I.

"So that Epistemon would not be a stiffneck": *"stiffneck"* (tortycolly) *is Rabelais' term for hypocrite.* ——— *"Which he called resuscitative"*: *this healing balm will be found in* Don Quixote *and the romances of chivalry.* ———*"Nestor a gold-miner"*: *for the French* harpailleur *Urquhart has* "*a deer-keeper or forester,"* *and LeClercq has* "*forester"; Sainéan, however, linguistic authority on Rabelais, supports the reading given here.* ———*"Jason was a sexton"*: *three editions, including the first, have Baudoin in place of Jason (Baudoin was the younger brother of Godfrey of Bouillon), and there is little doubt*

that Rabelais first wrote Baudoin and for some reason changed it to Jason. ——*"Hole of Gibraltar": the Strait of Gibraltar.* ——*"A pile of sunny crowns": coins bearing the figure of the sun.* ——*"A wall on which St. Anthony's fire was painted": probably the wall of a hospital, "St. Anthony's fire" being erysipelas.* —— *"For his* proficiat": *the* proficiat *was the present made to a bishop by way of welcome.*

We are then told "How Pantagruel Entered the City of the Amaurotes, and How Panurge Married Off King Anarch and Made Him a Green-Sauce Huckster," following which comes a typically Pantagrueline episode.

How Pantagruel with His Tongue Covered an Entire Army, and What the Author Saw in His Mouth

When Pantagruel, with all his followers, entered the land of the Dipsodes, everybody was very glad, and at once surrendered to him. Of their own free will they brought him the keys to all the cities wherever he went, with the exception of the Almyrodes, who were inclined to hold out against him. The latter informed his heralds that they would not surrender except on favorable conditions.

"What!" exclaimed Pantagruel, "do they ask for any better than a hand on the jug and glass in the fist? Come on, let us sack them."

At once, they all fell into ranks, ready for an attack. But on the way as they were proceeding through a large stretch of open country, they were caught in a great downpour of rain. At this, they began to shiver and huddle up against one another. Perceiving this, Pantagruel had their captains tell them that this was nothing at all, that he could see over the clouds, and that it would be nothing more than a light fall of dew; let them keep ranks, and he would see to it that they were sheltered. The men at once dressed ranks. And Pantagruel thrust his long tongue only half way out and covered them as a hen does her chicks.

While all this was taking place, I, who am telling you these very true stories, was hid under a burdock-leaf, no bigger than the bridge of Mantrible; but when I saw them all so well covered, I went to take shelter with them, which I was not able to do; for as the saying is, "There's no cloth left at the end of the yardstick." And so, I climbed up, the best way I could, and traveled a good two leagues over his tongue before entering his mouth. But O ye gods and goddesses! What do you think I saw there? May Jupiter strike me with his three-pointed thunderbolt, if I'm lying! I strolled around there, as one does in St. Sophie's at Constantinople, and I saw rocks as big as the Danish mountains (I suppose they must have been his teeth), and great prairies, and big forests, and huge, strong cities, fully as large as Lyon or Poitiers.

The first person I met was a chap planting cabbages. I inquired of him, in astonishment: "My friend, what are you doing there?"

"I'm planting cabbages," he said.

"But why," I said, "and how?"

"Ha! sir," he said, "we can't all have balls as heavy as a mortar, and we can't all be rich. This is the way I earn my living. I take them and sell them at the market in the city, which is just back there."

"Jesus!" I said. "Is this a new world I'm living in?"

"Nothing of the sort," said he, "it's not new at all; though they do say that outside there's a new land, where they have a sun and a moon and a lot of fine things; but this one is much older."

"Well, my friend," I said, "but what's the name of this city where you take your cabbages?"

"It is called Aspharage," he said, "and they are good Christian folks, and will treat you very nicely."

The short of it was, I made up my mind to go there. On my way, I came upon a fellow trapping pigeons, and I said to him:

"My friend, where do your pigeons come from?"

"They come, sir," he said, "from the other world."

And then I reflected that, when Pantagruel yawned, the pigeons must fly straight down his throat, thinking it a dovecot.

I then entered the city, which I found to be a charming one, strongly fortified and very pleasantly situated. But as I came in, the gate-keepers demanded my health-certificate, at which I was very much astonished; and so, I asked them:

"Gentlemen, is there danger of the plague here?"

"Oh! my lord," they told me, "they're dying all around here, as fast as the cart can travel through the streets."

"Good God!" I said, "and where's all that?"

Then, they informed me that it was in Larynx and Pharynx, which are two great cities, like Rouen and Nantes, rich and very prosperous. And the cause of the plague was a certain stinking and infectious exhalation which had recently issued from the abysses, as a result of which more than two-million-two-hundred-sixty-two-thousand-sixteen persons had died during the last eight days.

I stopped, then, to do a little figuring, and discovered that it must be the stinking breath that came from Pantagruel's stomach, from his having eaten so much garlic-stew, as related above.

Going on from there, I made my way between the rocks, which were his teeth, and even climbed one of them, where I found the prettiest spot in the world, with fine large tennis-courts, handsome promenades, beautiful meadows, many vineyards, and an endless number of Italian summer-houses, scattered through delightful fields. I remained there four months, and never was better off in my life. Then I climbed down the teeth from behind, in the direction of the lips; but on my way, I fell into the hands of brigands, as I was passing through a large forest which is in the neighborhood of the ears. After that, on the slope I came upon a tiny little town (I have forgotten its name), where I had a better time than ever, and earned a little money to live on. Do you want to know how? By sleeping, for they hire people there to sleep by the day, and you can earn five or six sous a day at it; while those that snore loudly enough get as much as seven sous and a half. There I told the senators how I had been robbed, as I was going through the valley, and they assured me that the folks down that way were a villainous lot and natural-born brigands. From this, I learned that, just as we have a country on this side and one on the other side of the mountains, so they have one on this side and that side of the teeth. But it was much more pleasant where I was, and a lot better climate.

I thereupon fell to thinking that it is very true, what they say, that half the world does not know how the other half lives, seeing that no one has as yet written anything about this country, which contains more than twenty-five inhabited realms, not counting the deserts and a great arm of the sea. But I have already composed a large volume, entitled *The History of the Throatians;* for that is the name I have given them, since they dwell in the throat of my master, Pantagruel.

At last, when I was ready to go back, I shinned down his beard, leaped onto his shoulders and, from there, slid to the ground and lay sprawling before him. When he saw me, he said:

"Where do you come from, Alcofribas?"

I replied: "From your throat, sir."

"And since when have you been down there?" said he.

"Ever since you set out against the Almyrodes," I told him.

"That's been more than six months now. And what did you live on? What did you have to drink?"

I replied:

"The same as you, my Lord. I took toll on the daintiest bits that went down your throat."

"Well," he said, "but where did you defecate?"

"In your throat, sir," I said.

"Ha! ha!" said he, "you are a good fellow. Since you have been down there, we, with God's help, have conquered the entire country of the Dipsodes. I hereby make you a present of the castellany of Salmagundi."

"Many thanks, sir," I said. "You are a good deal better to me than I deserve."

In this scene, reminiscent of the pilgrims-in-the-salad episode of Book First, M. Plattard believes that we have, possibly, another borrowing from Lucian; but the Grandes Cronicques (edition of 1533) have the men-of-arms of the city of Reboursin falling into Gargantua's mouth and taking his teeth for rocks. As for Pantagruel's covering the army with his tongue, M. Clouzot calls attention to a similar incident in the Mystère de la Passion.

The name Almyrodes (from the Greek almyros) literally means "the briny ones." ——*The famous bridge of Mantrible plays an important part in the romance of Fierabras.* ——*The mosque of St. Sophia at Constantinople greatly excited the imagination of sixteenth-century travelers and geographers.* ——*"A chap planting cabbages": Plattard thinks this may be from Lucian.* ——*Aspharge, from the Greek, is the "city of the throat."* ——*Salmagundi is, of course, properly a mixed-dish or stew.*

How Pantagruel Fell Ill, and the Manner in Which He Was Cured

A SHORT time afterward, our friend Pantagruel fell ill, being seized with such pains in his stomach that he was unable to eat or drink. And since troubles never come singly, he was afflicted at the same time with a burning of his urine, which caused him more agony than you might think. But his physicians took care of him, and very well, and made him piss away his pain with plenty of lenitive and diuretic drugs. His urine was so extremely hot that it has never cooled off, from that day to this. And as a result, you have in France today in various places where it ran, what are called hot-baths, as, for example:

At Cauterets;
At Limoux;
At Dax;
At Balaruc;
At Neris;
At Bourbon-Lancy and elsewhere.

In Italy:

At Monte Grotto;

At Abano;

At San Pietro of Padua;

At Sant' Elena;

At Casa Nuova;

At San Bartolomeo;

In the County of Bologna;

At Porretta, and a thousand other places.

And I am greatly astonished at a lot of foolish philosophers and physicians, who waste their time arguing about where the heat of these springs comes from, and whether it is due to borax, or to sulphur, or to alum, or to saltpeter in the ore; all they do is to concoct fairy stories, and it would be better for them to go scratch their arses on a thistle than to waste time in discussing something the origin of which they know nothing about. For the answer is easy, and there is no need of looking any farther. The said baths are hot for the reason that they spring from the hot piss of our friend Pantagruel.

And now, in describing for you the manner in which he was cured of his principal ailment, I shall not trouble to tell you how, as a minorative, he took,

Four hundred pounds of scammony colophoniac,

One-hundred-thirty-eight wagon-loads of cassia,

Eleven-thousand-nine-hundred pounds of rhubarb,

Not to mention the other ingredients. I would, merely, inform you that, on the advice of his physicians, it was decided to remove what was causing his stomach-ache; and for this purpose, they fashioned seventeen big copper balls, bigger than the one that is on Vergil's Needle at Rome, constructed in such a manner that they opened in the middle and closed with a spring.

One of his men, carrying a lantern and a lighted torch,

then entered one of these balls, and Pantagruel swallowed him as he would a little pill.

In five other balls were three peasants each, every man with a shovel around his neck.

Into seven other balls went seven porters, each with a basket about his neck: and they were all swallowed like pills.

When they reached the stomach, they touched off the springs and left their cubbyholes, led by the one who carried the lantern. There they groped, for more than a mile and a half around, in a horrible gulf, more stinking and infectious than Mephitis, the Camarina Marshes, or the contaminated Lake of Serbonis of which Strabo writes. And if it had not been that each had properly antidoted his heart, stomach, and wine-jug, commonly known as the noodle, they would have been suffocated and asphyxiated by those abominable vapors. Oh, what a perfume! Oh, what an exhalation, to make a dirty nose-mask for young ladies of fortune!

And so, groping and sniffing around, they finally came to the fecal matter and the corrupt humors, where they found a veritable manure-heap. Then the engineers fell to with their picks, to dig it up, while the others with their shovels filled the baskets. When it had all been cleared away, each went back into his ball. Pantagruel then gagged himself until he puked, and brought them up with no trouble at all, since they were no more in his throat than a fart would be in yours. And they were all very glad to get out of their pills. They reminded me of the Greeks coming out of the Trojan horse. By this means, Pantagruel was cured and was soon convalescing nicely. And you have one of these brass pills, to this day, at Orléans, on the steeple of Holy Cross Church.

This chapter is of special interest by reason of the author's profession. Of the baths mentioned: Cauterets is in the Hautes-Pyrénées; the narrators in the Heptameron were returning from a season at Cauterets when they were halted by a freshet; "Limoux" (in the Aude) probably refers to the mineral springs near that place; Dax is the Aquae Augustae Tarbellicae *of the Romans; Balarucles-Bains is in the canton of Frontignan, arrondissement of Montpellier; Neris is in the canton of Montluçon (Allier), the* Aquae Neri *of the ancients; Bourbon-Lancy is in the canton of Charolles (Saône-et-Loire), the* Aquae Nisinii *of the ancients, a favorite resort of Henri III; Monte Grotto was the most abundant of all the springs in the neighborhood of Abano; Abano, in Venetia near Padua, is the* Aquare Aponenses *of the Romans; "San Pietro of Padua" is today San Pietro Montagnone, four kilometers from Abano; Sant' Elena is the present Sant' Elena Battaglia, four kilometers from Abano and ten kilometers from Padua; Casa Nuova is a spring in the vicinity of Abano; San Bartolomeo is twelve miles from Padua; Porretta is in the province of Bologna.*

"As a minorative": that is, as a mild laxative. —— "Vergil's Needle": allusion to an unidentified obelisk. ——"Mephitis, the Camarina Marshes, or the contaminated Lake of Serbonis": "Mephitis was a goddess worshiped in various places in central Italy and personifying the sulphurous exhalations and vapors coming from a volcanic soil" (Plattard); the Camarina Marshes (now Camarana) are in Sicily (see Vergil, Aeneid, III, 700); the "Lake of Serbonis" (in French, lac de Serbone) is a pleasantry aimed at the Sorbonne. ——"At Orléans, on the steeple of Holy Cross Church": "The spire of the transept of Holy Cross Cathedral at Orléans was adorned with a globe ten feet in circumference, surmounted by a

cross; this enormous 'pill' in gilded copper was destroyed by the Protestants in 1508" (Lefranc).

The Conclusion of the Present Book, and the Author's Excuse

AND now, gentlemen, you have heard the beginning of the horrific history of my lord and master, Pantagruel, and I shall here bring to an end this first book. I have a slight headache, and the stops of my brain feel as though they were a trifle jumbled with this Septembral vintage.

You shall have the rest of the story at the next Frankfort fair. There, you will see how Panurge was married and how his wife made a cuckold of him the very first month of their married life; as well as how Pantagruel discovered the philosophical stone, the manner in which he found it, and the use he made of it; how he crossed the Caspian Mountains, and how he sailed the Atlantic Ocean, and routed the Cannibals, and conquered the Pearl Islands; how he married the daughter of the King of India named Prester John; how he fought the devils, and set fire to five rooms in hell, and plundered the big black room, and cast Proserpina into the fire; how he knocked out four of Lucifer's teeth and one horn off his rump; and how he visited the country of the moon, to find out if the moon was really whole, or if women did have three-quarters of it in their heads; and a thousand other jolly little anecdotes, all very true. It's a fine business, I assure you.

Good night, gentlemen. *Perdonatemi,* and don't be thinking too much about my faults, since you are not in the habit of giving any too much thought to your own.

And if you were to say to me, "Sir, it would not appear to be very wise of you to be spending your time in writing such nonsense and tomfooleries," I should reply that neither is it any the wiser of you to be amusing yourselves by reading such stuff.

But if you read it merely as a pleasant pastime, just as I have written it to pass the time, then you and I are more deserving of pardon than are a lot of Sarabaites, moral lepers, snails, hypocrites, humbugs, whoring monks with their big boots, and other folks like that, who have put on masks to deceive the world. For, giving the public to understand that all they think of is contemplation and devotion, fasting and macerating their sensual nature, and that their only concern is to sustain and nourish the fragile spark of human life that is in them, what they really do is to have a good time, and God knows *what* a time!

Et curios simulant, sed bacchanalia vivunt. They imitate the Curii, but live like bacchanals. You may read it in big and illuminated letters, in their red snouts and pot-bellies, unless they happen to perfume themselves with sulphur.

As to their studies, these are entirely taken up with the reading of Pantagrueline books, not by way of cheerful pastime, but that they may be able to harm someone underhandedly, namely by articling, farticling, and necktwisting, by buttocking, ballocking, and devilsocking, that is, by slandering. In this, they are like those small-town scamps who make a business of digging into and spreading out the dung of little children, in cherry-season, in order to find the stones and sell them to the apothecaries, who make oil of Mahaleb out of them.

I trust that you will flee, abhor, and hate all these as much as I do; and you will be wise in doing so, you may take my word for it. And if you wish to be good Pantagruelists, that is, to live in peace, happiness, and good health, enjoying yourselves always, never put any faith in such folks as that, who look out upon the world through a peephole.

END OF THE CHRONICLES OF PANTAGRUEL, KING OF THE DIPSODES, RESTORED TO THE LIFE, WITH HIS DEEDS AND DREADFUL FEATS OF PROWESS, COMPOSED BY THE LATE M. *Alcofribas*, ABSTRACTOR OF QUINTESSENCE.

This is one of the passages in which Maître François gives vent to his hatred of monastic "hypocrites" and, in particular, of the censors of the Sorbonne, in whom may be seen the correspondents of our Comstocks and Watch-and-Ward societies of today.

The opening sentence has a bearing on the date of composition of the Pantagruel. *"This passage permits us to fix the date of the completion of this book as the month of September, 1532" (Plattard).*

"The philosophical stone": object of the medieval alchemists' quest. ——"Prester John": this personage was variously known as Prestre Jean, Prest Jan, Prestan, Prestegean, etc.; medieval geographers differed widely as to where his realm was situated; Mandeville makes him the sovereign of India; in the New Prologue to Book Fourth, Rabelais refers to him as "King of the Persians." ——"Perdonatemi": Italian for "pardon me." ——"Any too much thought to your own": in the first two editions, Book Second ends at this point. ——"Sarabaites": "name given to certain Egyptian monks who led a disorderly life" (Sainéan); the sense here is "hypocrites." ——"Snails": allusion to the monks' hoods. ——"Big boots": "Bottes were the ecclesiastic footwear par excellence" (Sainéan).

——"*They imitate the Curii*," etc.: *Juvenal*, Satires, ii, 3.
——"*Articling*": *according to one commentator* (*Le Duchat*), *this is* "*to take from the writings of someone certain* articles *to be employed in refuting him as a heretic.*" ——"*Oil of Mahaleb*": *Arabic name of the plum-tree, the* Prunus mahaleb *Linn.* ——"*Through a peephole*": "*through the hole or opening of a hood; these are the monks*" (*Lefranc*).

END OF THE FIRST BOOK OF THE PANTAGRUEL,
OR BOOK SECOND

The Third Book

THE THIRD BOOK

Of the Heroic Deeds and Sayings

OF THE WORTHY

PANTAGRUEL

Composed by M. Fran. Rabelais

Doctor of Medicine

Revised and Corrected by the Author, under the Antique Censorship

The aforesaid author entreats his benevolent readers
to reserve their laughter till the seventy-eighth Book

Book Third has little in common with the two preceding books. Introducing an absolute change of rhythm, it occupies a unique place in the Rabelaisian romance. Whereas the Gargantua and the first book of the Pantagruel are concerned, chiefly, with tales of adventure, in the manner of the old romances of chivalry, Book Third is taken up, for some four-fifths of its space, with the question of whether or not Panurge is to marry. It marks, therefore, a new orientation on the part of its author.

Published after a silence of eleven or twelve years, this book, as Professor Lefranc observes, throws an intense light on the intellectual history both of Rabelais and of his age. It was launched in the midst of a literary battle, one that raged with special violence from about 1542 to about 1550 (the Third Book was published in 1546), and

*it is, in a manner, an episode in this battle. The literary
conflict referred to is the one known as the "Querelle des
femmes," or Woman Question, a controversy that had
been begun as far back as the fifteenth century and had
been carried over into the sixteenth, reaching its peak of
intensity on the eve of the Religious Wars. Dividing
writers and their readers into two sharply defined and
bitterly opposed camps, this controversy had come to
include the entire subject of Feminism.*

*"One may say," continues Lefranc, "that from 1450, or
thereabouts, down to the years that witnessed the beginning of the Reformation, marriage appeared as an
institution badly battered in the breach. The attacks and
satires directed against it are found to be infinitely more
numerous than the panegyrics. It furnished a facile and a
merry theme for a number of semi-popular laments."*

*In order, then, to get at the background of Book
Third, we must associate it with the* Querelle; *and in
doing so, we must take into account certain other works
published on the same theme, pro or con, some of which
directly influenced Rabelais. One of the earliest of these
works is the* Quinze Joyes de Mariage, *or the Fifteen
Joys of Marriage, questionably attributed for long to
Antoine de la Salle, but which may date as far back as
the beginning of the fifteenth century. Another was the*
Arrêts d'Amour, *or Decrees of Love, of Martial de Paris,
known as Martial d'Auvergne.*

*With the sixteenth century, the controversy had taken
on a more serious tone. This was, in no small degree, due
to the revival of classical learning and to the develop-
ments that were taking place in medicine, law, and the
natural sciences. One of the important figures in the
controversy was the juriconsult, Jean Nevizan (died
about 1540), who was the author of a work entitled*
Sylvae nuptialis libri sex. . . . An nubendum sit, vel

U·S AIRWAYS

OLSEN/MARK

US FLIGHT: **755** 30APR

SEAT: **12F**

PARIS – CDG

PHILADELPHIA

API OK   E-TICKET

BISBIV/US

SEQ 175

ZONE 6

US AIRWAYS
DIVIDEND MILES

Dividend Miles Select*

- **Fly for less**
- **Board with Zone 2**

Ask your flight attendant.

*See terms & conditions for complete details at mostmiles.com

non, *six books on the subject: to wed or not to wed,
published at Paris, in 1521, and reprinted at Lyon, in
1526 (it was also reprinted a number of times in the
latter half of the century, and one edition appeared at
Cologne as late as 1656). There would seem to be no
doubt that Rabelais, in the discussions of Book Third,
was inspired by this work.*

Not to be overlooked is Erasmus' Institution of Christian Marriage, *which, dedicated to the Queen of England, appeared in 1526. In this work Erasmus places
marriage above celibacy, stressing the gravity of the
institution. The ideal he urges is that of the male's seeking a cultivated and balanced mind in his mate. It is
probable, thinks Professor Lefranc, that this work had
little influence outside purely literary circles. It may be
noted in passing that the author, in his preceding* Praise
of Folly, *had not been quite so kind to the sex.*

*There is also the work of Rabelais' legal friend André
Tiraqueau, the* De Legibus Connubialibus (On Marriage
Laws), *which appeared in 1513, with revised and en-
larged editions following in 1515, 1524, and 1546 (the
year in which Book Third was published). Tiraqueau's
book did much to stir up the question and to keep it
going. Among the replies it called forth was Bouchard's*
Apology for the Feminine Sex, *the* Tes gynaikeais
phytles, id est Feminei sexus apologia (1522.) *Bouchard
appears to have been another of the writers on whom
Rabelais drew.*

*A feminist treatise that appeared along about this
time adding fuel to the fire, was one* On the Nobility and
Excellence of the Feminine Sex, *the* De Nobilitate et
Praecellentia Feminei Sexus *of Cornelius Agrippa. Commentators agree that the Herr Trippa of Book Third is
Agrippa. The feminists, as well as the anti-feminists,
had their doughty spokesmen.*

"Woman," says Professor Lefranc, "tended to play a larger and larger social rôle; her place was no longer merely at the fireside; her sole mission was no longer to see to the affairs of the household; she was looking forward to an equal footing with man."

All of which, it may be seen, is by way of being a sixteenth-century version of "Woman's Rights."

In the bringing of this question into the foreground, there were a number of factors that acted potently. One was the splendor of the great courts of the time—those of England, France, and Spain—and the political and literary success that women were achieving there. The Queen of Navarre, author of the Heptameron, was not the only outstanding figure. There were a number of others. Among these others, to mention only a few of the better known, were Joan of Aragon, painted by Raphael and celebrated by Niphus in the latter's pioneer work, which some scholars look upon as the beginning of modern aesthetics, the De Pulchro et Amore; Vittoria Colonna, Michelangelo's perduring inamorata; Diane de Poitiers; Anne Boleyn, Henry VIII's beheaded queen, to whom a reference has been seen in this book; Catherine de' Medici; Mary Stuart; Queen Elizabeth; Sir Thomas More's daughters; and any number of others.

As for Rabelais' own attitude on the question, he has been seen as "one of the most notorious, dangerous, and typical enemies of the feminine sex." Much is made of his slighting allusions to women in Books First and Second—apropos of Gargamelle's death, Gargantua's ludicrous mourning for Badebec, etc. There is, it is true, the Abbey of Thélème, where all is to be done "according to the will of the ladies"; and in the first book of the Pantagruel there is a word of praise for those members of the feminine sex who have aspired to the "heavenly manna" of learning. But these, Professor Lefranc thinks,

*were "momentary effusions," and the Gallic scholar goes
on to remark that woman is either absent from the other
portions of the first two books or is there treated with
little sympathy. Thélème, he adds, glorifies women for
the reason that such a glorification is necessary to Rabelais' picture of an anti-monastic society. "In reality,
this former monk was not a lover of women; he obviously
remains faithful to the old* gauloise *tradition . . . with
regard to the weaker sex." And again: "The Franciscan
of Fontenay-le-Comte, friend of Tiraqueau, was ever
alive in him."*

*Professor Lefranc further points out that the two
traditions—the satiric* gauloise *attitude and the idealistic
one—have always existed, side by side, in France. During the decade from 1530 to 1540, an attempt was made
to give the old chivalric ideal of* courtoisie *a new meaning and a new life. The movement grew in strength, and
it is not strange that cries of alarm were soon raised
against it. Among those to sound the alarm was Gratian
(or Gratien) Dupont, Seigneur de Drusac. His* Contro-
verses de sexe masculin et feminin *(Controversies on the
Masculine and the Feminine Sex), a vast poem in three
books containing only a succession of violent invectives
against women, was published at Toulouse, in 1534. (It
may be noted, parenthetically, that the author was reported to have been unhappily married.) This was one of
the works on which Rabelais drew.*

*Another work of the period that may have influenced
Maître François in his treatment of the Woman Ques-
tion in Book Third is a curious one bearing the title:*
Les Angoysses douloureuses qui procèdent d'amours,
contenant tres parties composées par dame Helisenne de
Crenne, laquelle exhorte toutes personnes à ne suyvre
folle amour *(The Pain and Anguish That Come from
Love, in Three Parts, Composed by Dame Helisenne de*

Crenne, Who Exhorts All Persons Not to Be Led Astray by Love's Madness). *Professor Lefranc, after quoting Michelet's "The true Renaissance is the renaissance of the heart," goes on to characterize this product of Dame Helisenne's pen as a book containing "the first cries of the heart and the language of true passion." What was in reality occurring here was a feminine revolt against the tyranny of love that anticipated by a century or so Madame de Lafayette and the* Princesse de Clèves. *Le Motteux and other commentators have believed that Rabelais' Limousin student may, possibly, be a take-off on the author of* Les Angoysses douloureuses.

Yet another document in the feminist-antifeminist warfare which must be mentioned is the Parfaicte Amye (Perfect Woman Friend) *of Antoine Héroët. This book, published at Lyon, in 1542, four years before the appearance of Book Third, ran through many reprints and became a best-seller of the day.*

And in the same year (1542), or thereabouts, a work appeared which would seem to have provided Rabelais with his outline for Book Third. This was the Songe de Pantagruel *of François Hobert, one of the Maître's imitators.*

Not to be forgotten or minimized in connection with the Querelle des femmes *is the personal and literary influence—the philosophic influence, as well—of Marguerite, Queen of Navarre. The author of the* Heptameron *became the center of the neo-Platonic literary movement, which was an integral part of the French Renaissance. It was to this neo-Platonist group, by the way, that Héroët belonged. This coterie, naturally, took the idealistic side in the feminist controversy, and it has been remarked as strange that Rabelais should have dedicated his Third Book to the Queen of Navarre, the ardent champion of her sex. But Marguerite, we are to remem-*

ber, was in a manner Rabelais' patroness, as she was
Marot's. The Queen herself had written a number of
works dealing with the subject of love—La Distinction
du vrai amour; La Mort et Résurrection d'Amour;
Réponse à une chanson faicte par une Dame, etc. See,
also, her epistles in verse to her brother, as well as the
nouvelles contained in the Heptameron. As Lefranc sees
it, the revival of Platonism and the Querelle des femmes
were the two most important phases of the Revival of
Learning for the eight or ten years preceding the advent
of the Pléiade.

In addition to works in French dealing with the
woman question, there were many translations of works
devoted to women and love from the Italian and other
languages, among which may be mentioned Castiglione's
Il Cortegiano.

In short, it was a case in which no writer who was
alive, who had something to say to his age, could stand
aloof or even adopt a neutral position. And Rabelais did
have something to say.

In the words of Lefranc: "No writer . . . between
1540 and 1555 stood aloof from the Querelle des femmes.
How, then, suppose, for a single moment, that the
greatest of them all, the most representative, the one
most desirous of linking his work up with all the social,
political, religious, scientific, and even colonial preoccupations of his age, could have remained outside the
struggle? The hypothesis could not possibly be sustained; a priori, everything contradicts it.

"Rabelais no longer has any attention except for the
redoubtable enigmas centering about the feminine sex
and marriage; he thinks only of making his voice heard
in the general concert. This man, over whom the mysteries of human destiny and human liberty always
exerted so profound and so disturbing an attraction, now

concentrates all his reflective powers upon a partial aspect of this great secret."

As a result of all this, the Rabelaisian word, *Pantagruelist*, came to be synonymous with "woman-hater." Rabelais' position in the Woman Controversy may be said to have been summed up in a work which, coming in 1555, is, really, a résumé of the *Querelle* as a whole. This work was one by François Billon, entitled Le fort inexpugnable de l'honneur du sexe feminin (The Inexpugnable Fortress of Feminine Honor). *The mere space given to Rabelais in this volume is significant, not to speak of the fervor expended upon the creator of Panurge and Pantagruel.*

Nevertheless, to the present translator-editor such conclusions as those set forth above, on the part of Lefranc and others, with regard to Rabelais' attitude on the Woman Question, appear to be somewhat too facile and tinged with more than a little of parti pris. So far as the Maître's contemporaries are concerned, they not only lacked the perspective of distance but were, almost all of them, involved in the wordy fray on one side or the other, the anti-feminists being only too eager to claim the author of the *Pantagruel* as their own. As for a modern Rabelais scholar like Professor Lefranc, he likewise tends to give the impression of being a special pleader, anxious to prove his point and only too ready to brush aside the counter-arguments, while at times, perhaps, over-stressing the evidence favorable to his own side.

François Rabelais is not so simple as all that. He is, indeed, highly complex, both as an individual and as a writer. The very fact that his Book Third is dedicated to the Queen of Navarre, that "abstract spirit, heavenly and rapt," who was the outstanding feminist of her age, *ought to give the over-ardent anti-feminists pause for thought. It ought to stimulate them to carry their analysis a little deeper; in which case they would find that Rabelais is here combatting the old, outmoded, and, in the eyes of many of the Renaissance humanists, essentially false ideal of a lingering medieval chivalry which, stripped of its trappings, was found to be not so chivalrous after all, which actually resulted in the masculine oppression of women, and which was now showing dangerous signs of revival. In other words, he was beginning the task that Cervantes was soon to complete.*

Indeed, if we study closely the remarks of Dr. Rondibilis, together with those of the aged Gargantua in the Trouillogan passage, we shall see that it is not so much feminine fickleness that Rabelais is satirizing as it is masculine jealousy, a jealousy which enslaves the male himself, and that what the author is in reality setting forth is a new and higher, more modern and civilized conception of marriage, based upon mutual trust, respect, and companionship.

To be taken into consideration, also, is the manner in which the anti-feminist theme lends itself to Rabelais' particular brand of humor, his rollicking satire and broad horse-play. So suited is the subject to his peculiar genius as a writer that one has the feeling that he simply cannot resist it. And when to all this is added what well may be, as Lefranc supposes, an individual bent, representing personal tastes, inclinations, and prejudices, we have the always highly complex author—though the adjective "complex" applied to him may come as a surprise to many—who on the one hand could create an Abbey of Thélème and, on the other hand, could sit down and compose Dr. Rondibilis' memorable harangue.

The prominence of the Querelle des femmes *theme, which unquestionably dominates this book, should not cause us to lose sight of the importance of the Prologue as an indication of Rabelais' evolving views on social-political questions. In this case, it is the question of war. Previously we have found him taking, in general, a distinctly anti-militarist, not to say pacifist attitude; but here, in connection with the final struggle between France and the Emperor Charles v, which began in 1542, he is to be heard supporting his monarch and his country's cause, which he regards as a just and holy war, in a tone that has a decided and unpleasant jingoist-imperialist ring—"I am sure that the boundaries of France are going to be superbly extended." Falling back upon the ancients, as usual, he even indulges in a glo-rification of war for its own sake that is hard to recon-cile with the sentiments he has formerly expressed.*

This excess of bellicose ardor is due in part, no doubt, to the heightened patriotism and over-statement that inevitably accompany a war; but in Rabelais' case there were other factors involved. A study of the Maître's writings such as has been made by M. Georges Lote, Lefranc, and others will show that the political and politico-religious ideas there expressed are in general but rather close conformity to the policy of the French throne—to such an extent as to lead to the author's be-ing termed a "royal publicist"; and at this juncture of his career there were special reasons of a personal nature which, in an age when fagots flamed, hardly could have failed to carry weight with one who, like his Pantag-ruel at Toulouse, was "naturally quite thirsty enough, without being heated any more." After years of perse-cution by the ecclesiastic censors of the Sorbonne, and after having had the first two books of his romance sup-pressed, he had at last found a protector in the King himself; and this, it will be noted, is the first book that appears under his own signature and with a royal privilege. Pusillanimity on Rabelais' part? Let us not be too hasty in condemning him. He was, to repeat, essentially a man and writer with something important, something bold, to say to his age; and as he warns us from the start, he meant to say it and, at the same time, avoid the stake if he could. He must be taken as he is: not only a great humanist, but very, very human. And when all is said, he was also very French. Shall we, then, question the sincerity of his patriotism? Especially when we recall that it is in this same book that he gives us (under the guise of Panurge's speech on borrowers and lenders) a picture of a world based on cooperation as opposed to strife, while expressing a view on the treatment of conquered peoples that is startling in its modern humaneness.

Rabelais' quickened interest in the Woman Question seems to have led to certain radical changes in the outline of his romance, in so far as that work may be regarded as having a preconceived plan. It is not until Chapter VII or IX that the author really gets into his theme and into the swing of this book. It is possible, accordingly, that the first chapters were written before he had decided to take up the new theme. Such a change in plan would account for the seeming abandonment of the outline given at the end of Book Second. In order to take his dip into the Querelle des femmes, Rabelais postpones the voyage of Pantagruel and Panurge from Book Third to Book Fourth.

Book Third, "that marvelous Third Book," as Anatole France describes it, "the richest, perhaps the finest, the one that most abounds in comic scenes of any in the Pantagruel," is generally looked upon as the most eru-

dite portion of Rabelais' work. It is the book that contains the most learning, the most quotations and citations. It has been called the book of the humanist, the philologist, the botanist, the physicist. It is such a work as comes from a man's most mature powers, those of a man who has "lived, done, and doubted."

As to "influences," outside those already considered, there are a number of fairly obvious ones to be detected. For example, the Platonist influence is evident, and it is to be noted that Plato is quoted in this book more frequently than anywhere else by Rabelais. Other more or less palpable classic and foreign influences are those of Poggio, Erasmus, Ariosto, Aretino, Lucian, Pliny, Plutarch, etc. Among the numerous Greek and Latin writers from whom the author has borrowed in this book, one might mention Herodotus, Philostratus, Appollonius, Theophrastus, Suetonius, Marcrobius, Lampridius, Spartianus, Trebellius Pollio, Capitolinus, Isidorus, Diogenes Laërtius, Diodorus Siculus, and others.

Among French influences not previously mentioned, one may make out that of Marot, Crétin, Jean Raulin the preacher, Enguerrand, etc. (It is Crétin who appears to have been satirized in the person of Raminagrobis.) As for other and minor influences coming from beyond the French border, there are echoes of the Spanish Guevara and others.

On the other hand, a number of French writers, including Molière and La Fontaine, have drawn rather heavily upon this book, while the English Sterne has made at least one small borrowing.

There is in Book Third much technical and occult lore. In this book, the author displays an intimate familiarity with theology, philosophy, law, medicine, and the natural sciences, while his occult delvings range

from Avicenna and the Hermes Trismegistus to Nostra-
damus and Cornelius Agrippa.

Rabelais also takes occasion here to express himself
on a number of vital issues of the day, such, for in-
stance, as the question of parental consent to marriages,
which provides Pantagruel with a theme for a lengthy
harangue. There is also what has been seen as a satire,
under the form of a eulogy of the Pantagruelion, on the
use of the hempen rope as a punishment for criminals.
The law exempting newlyweds from war proves a fer-
tile theme and Maître François even seizes the oppor-
tunity, in passing, to express a lively opinion on the tech-
nical and comparatively abstruse question of the origin
of language. In short, he is always the humanist, the
man of the Revival of Learning and the Renaissance.

Book Third was published in the year 1546 (in the
autumn of that year, it has been thought). The pub-
lisher was Chrétien Wechel, at the Ecu de Bâle. It is
to be noted that this is the first of the books to appear
under Rabelais' own name. M. Alcofribas, the anagram-
matic "Abstractor of Quintessence," has given way to
François Rabelais, "Doctor of Medicine." In the first
edition, that of 1546 (the text followed here is that of
the definitive edition of 1552), the author takes upon
himself, in addition to "Doctor of Medicine," the title
of "Sacristan of the Hyerean Isles" (the îles d'Hyères.)
As to the formula, "The aforesaid author entreats his
benevolent readers," etc., is merely a parody of one
to be found at the head of certain sixteenth-century
works. In Joachim du Bellay's Deffence et illustra-
tion de la langue françoyse, *for example, we find: "The*
author begs his readers to defer their judgment to the
end of the Book." In the first edition, the words "with

Privilege of the King" are followed by *"for six years."* The first edition bore a Privilege from Francis I, dated 1545. The definitive Michel Fezandat edition of 1552 bears the one from Henry II. It is to be observed, in connection with the former Privilege, that there is a discrepancy in the text as to the length of time for which it is granted. In one place, we read *"ten consecutive years"* and in another *"six consecutive years."*

The decastich *"To the Spirit of the Queen of Navarre"* appears in the first edition, published three years before Marguerite's death. It alludes to the Queen's well-known mystical state of mind during her last days.

As in the case of the other books, the text adopted as a basis has been the last one which, the evidence is, could have had the author's revision during his lifetime, namely, as stated above, the Michel Fezandat small octavo of 1552 (Paris). Variants have been taken from the Editio Princeps (likewise an octavo) of Wechel, Paris, 1546.

Following is the Royal Privilege, prefixed to the first edition of Book Third:

PRIVILEGE ACCORDED BY FRANCIS THE FIRST TO MAÎTRE FRANÇOIS RABELAIS

FRANCIS, by the grace of God, King of France, to the Marshal of Paris, the Bailiff of Rouen, the Seneschals of Lyon, Toulouse, Bordeaux, and Poitou, and to all our officers of justice, or their lieutenants, and to whomsoever it may concern, greetings.

On the part of our dear and loyal friend, Maître François Rabelais, doctor of medicine in our University of Montpellier, it has been set forth that, the said petitioner having heretofore caused to be printed a number of books, notably, two volumes of the *Heroic Deeds and Sayings of Pantag-*

ruel, no less useful than enjoyable, the printers have corrupted and perverted the said books, in a number of places, to the great displeasure and detriment of said author and the prejudice of readers, as a result of which he has refrained from publishing the remainder and sequel of the said *Heroic Deeds and Sayings.* Being, on the other hand, daily besought and importuned by the learned and studious of our realm to cause, for purposes of public utility, the said sequel to be printed, he has implored us to grant him a privilege, in accordance with which no one shall print or place on sale any works of his, except such as he shall cause to be printed by properly authorized publishers, to whom he will turn over his own and true copies, this for the space of ten consecutive years, beginning with the day and date of the printing of the said books.

For these reasons, which have been given due consideration by us, we, desiring that the cause of letters be promoted throughout our realm, for the profit and instruction of our subjects, do hereby grant to the said petitioner privilege, leave, license, and permission to cause to be printed and to place on sale, through such tried and true publishers as may seem good to him, the said subsequent books and portions of the *Heroic Deeds of Pantagruel,* beginning with the third volume, along with power and authority to correct and revise the two first parts heretofore by him composed, and to reprint or cause to be reprinted and placed on sale the said precedent parts, it being by us forbidden and prohibited, to any other printers or others concerned, to print or place on sale the aforementioned books, without the will and consent of the said petitioner, within the term of six consecutive years, beginning with the day and date of the printing of the said books, under pain of sure and heavy punishment, with the confiscation of any books wrongfully so printed, and a summary fine.

To this end, we have granted, and do hereby grant to each one of you whom it may concern, full power, commission, and authority to enforce these presents, and we do hereby order and command all our officers of justice and our subjects to permit, suffer, and allow the said petitioner peaceably to enjoy and make use of this present leave, privilege, and commission, in obedience to this our royal mandate. For such is our pleasure, and so be it.

Given at Paris, the nineteenth day of September, in the

Year of Grace one-thousand-five-hundred-and-forty-five, and in the thirty-first year of our reign.

So signed: *By councilor* DELAUNAY; sealed with a simple end of yellow wax.

Following is the second royal privilege, granted by Henry II.

PRIVILEGE OF THE KING

HENRY, by the grace of God, King of France, to the Marshal of Paris, the Bailiff of Rouen, the Seneschals of Lyon, Toulouse, Bordeaux, Dauphiny, and Poitou, and to all our other officers of justice, or to their lieutenants, and to whomsoever it may concern, greetings.

On the part of our dear and well beloved M. François Rabelais, doctor of medicine, it has been set forth that, the said petitioner having, heretofore, caused to be printed a number of books in Greek, Latin, French, and Tuscan, notably certain volumes of the *Heroic Deeds and Sayings of Pantagruel,* works no less useful than enjoyable, the printers have corrupted, depraved, and perverted the said books in a number of places; that they have, moreover, printed a number of other scandalous books under the name of the said petitioner, to his great displeasure, prejudice, and ignominy, these works having been totally disavowed by him, as false and spurious, and he desiring, in accordance with our own good will and pleasure, to suppress them. All the others are admitted to be his, but perverted beyond recognition, as has been said, and these he desires to revise, correct, and reprint. Likewise to publish and put on sale the sequel to the *Heroic Deeds and Sayings of Pantagruel,* humbly requesting us, in this matter, to concede him from our hand such letters as are necessary and proper. For which reason, we, being generously inclined to the petition and request of the said M. François Rabelais, the deponent, and desiring to treat him well and favorably in this matter, have, for these causes and other worthy considerations, permitted, granted, and accorded, and of our own certain knowledge, full power, and royal authority, do, by these presents, hereby permit, grant, and accord, the power and permission, through such printers as may seem good to him, to print, publish, and put on sale each and all of the said books, and the sequel to *Pantagruel* which has been undertaken and composed by him, both those works which have already been printed, and which shall be, for this purpose, revised and corrected by him, and such other new works as he may plan to publish; also to suppress those that have been falsely attributed to him. And in order that he may be able to bear the expense necessary to the said printing, we have, by these presents, very expressly prohibited and forbidden, and do prohibit and forbid all other bookstores and printers of this our realm, and of our other lands and seigno-ries, to print or cause to be printed, to publish or to place on sale any of the aforesaid books, either old or new, during the time and term of ten consecutive years following, from the day and date of the printing of the said books, without the will and consent of the said deponent, under pain of confiscation of such books as may be found to have been printed to the prejudice of this our present permission, and of a summary fine.

We will and command that you, each and every one whom it may concern, observe, keep, and respect our presents, leave, license, and permission, our prohibitions and restrictions. And if any be found to have violated these, proceed against them, and cause them to be proceeded against, under the aforementioned penalties and otherwise. And see to it that the aforesaid petitioner enjoys full use and makes peaceable employment of the rights herein above conceded, during the said time, at the same time, as has been herein above directed, stopping and putting a stop to all violations and impediments to the contrary. For such is our pleasure. Notwithstanding any decrees, restrictions, mandates, or injunctions contrary hereto. And in order that these presents may be published abroad in many and divers places, We will that, to the *vidimus* of these same presents, done under royal seal, credence be given as to this present original.

Given at St. Germaine-en-Laye, the sixteenth day of August, in the year of Grace one-thousand-five-hundred-and-fifty, and the fourth of our reign.

By the King, the Cardinal of Châtillon being present.

Signed: Du Thier.

François Rabelais

TO THE SPIRIT OF
THE QUEEN OF NAVARRE

O abstract spirit, heavenly and rapt,
Who, frequenting the skies from which you came,
Have left your host and servant, very apt,
Your answering body, always very tame
To your commands, and which you bore with a same
And alien feeling, almost with apathy,
Would you be willing to quit that hostelry,
Your house divine, your home perpetual,
And look below on this third history
Of the joyous deeds of good Pantagruel?

Prologue of the Author

M. FRANÇOIS RABELAIS

FOR THE THIRD BOOK OF THE HEROIC
DEEDS AND SAYINGS OF THE
WORTHY PANTAGRUEL

GOOD folks, most illustrious drinkers, and you, most
precious gouty ones, did you ever see Diogenes, the
Cynic philosopher? If you have seen him, you haven't
lost your eye-sight, or else, I have no intelligence or
logical sense whatsoever. It is a fine thing to behold the

clarity of—wine and gold crowns—I mean the sun. I am willing to stand or fall by the man born blind, of whom so much is made in the most sacred Scriptures, the same who, having permission to ask whatever he wanted, by the command of Him who is all-powerful, and whose word is instantly put into effect, asked nothing except the ability to see.

You—and this is Item No. 1—are no longer young, which means that if you are wise, you will, hereafter, do your philosophizing in wine (and not in vain), rather than metaphysically, and will proceed to join the Bacchic Council, in order that, as you eat your snatches, you may be in a position to give your opinion of the quality, color, odor, excellence, eminence, properties, faculties, virtues, effects, and dignities of the blessed and longed-for wine.

If you have never seen him, as I am readily led to believe, you must at least have heard tell of him. For his name and reputation are quite well enough known everywhere under the heavens. And moreover, you are all of Phrygian extraction, or I am deceived; and if you don't happen to have as many gold crowns as Midas had, you have, at any rate, something or other of his, the possession of which the Persians used to praise in their eavesdroppers, and which the Emperor Antoninus wished he had, in memory of whom the Serpentine of Rohan got its name of Fine Ears.

If you have never heard of him, I should like, at once, to tell you a story about him, as we start in drinking—drink up, then—as I was about to say—listen now—I want to inform you—so that you won't be, like simpleminded rascals, under any false impressions—that he was a rare philosopher and a jolly good fellow, one, you might say, in a thousand. If he had a few imperfections, so have you, so have we all. Nothing, except God, is perfect. And so it was that Alexander the Great (at the very time that he had Aristotle for a teacher in his own house) had so great an esteem for the Cynic that if he had not been Alexander, he would have wanted to be Diogenes the Sinopian.

When Philip, King of Macedon, undertook to besiege and lay low the city of Corinth, the Corinthians, warned by their spies that he was proceeding against them with a large army in martial array, were all greatly frightened, and they had good reason to be. They were very careful to see to it that each citizen had his own duty and task to perform, as they set about their preparations to meet the enemy when he should come and to defend their city. Some removed from the fields to the forests the furniture, cattle, grain, wine, fruit, victuals, and necessary provisions. Others fortified the walls, reared bastions, squared ravelins, dug ditches, cleaned out counter-mines, constructed gabions for defense, arranged platforms, emptied casemates, barred up false passageways, erected cavaliers, repaired counterscarps, greased courtines, ran up turrets, sloped parapets, pierced loopholes, steeled the machicolations, strengthened the Saracen portcullises and cataracts, stationed sentries, and sent out patrols.

Everybody was on the alert; everybody carried the hod. Some scoured corselets, varnished coats of iron, cleaned bards, chanfrins, hauberks, brigandines, casques, visors, lambrequins, battle-axes, helmets, morions, link-harness, warriors' jackets, armlets, tassets, gussets, collars, cuishes, breast-plates, cuirasses, coats-of-mail, big and little bucklers, boots, greaves, foot-armor, and spurs. Others brought up bows, slings, crossbows, balls, catapults, caparisons, grenades, cressets, darts and fire-balls, ballistae, scorpions, and other wartime machines necessary for repelling and destroying the en-emy's battering-rams.

They sharpened bills, pikes, hooks, halberds, crooks, arms, lances, Moorish arrows, iron forks, partisans, crow-bars, axes, darts great and small, javelins, and spears. They filed down scimitars, cutlasses, curved-sabres, cut-ting-arms, swords, small rapiers, pointed-pales, Pistoian and other poniards, dart-sticks, daggers, short-swords, knives, sword-blades, and arrow-heads.

Everybody practiced his big blade; everybody scraped the rust off his broad-sword. There wasn't a woman, no matter how modest or of what age, who did not see to it that her battle-harness was polished up; for you are aware that the women of ancient Corinth were courageous in combat.

Diogenes, seeing them all in such a tumultuous fer-vor, and not having been employed by the officials to do anything, contemplated the countenances of his fel-low citizens for a number of days, without saying a word. Then, as though incited by martial spirit, he girdled up his cloak like a scarf, rolled his sleeves up to the elbows, tucked himself up like an apple-picker, gave his purse, books, and opisthographs to an old friend, and left the city in the direction of the Cranium, which is a hill or promontory of Corinth, a very pretty esplanade.

There he proceeded to roll his terra cotta barrel, which was the only house he had as a protection against the inclemencies of the heavens; and brandishing his arms with great vehemence, he whirled it, twirled it, jumbled it, mumbled it, raked it, quaked it, tumbled it, fisted it, twisted it, cuddled it, fuddled it, rumbled it, fumbled it, eased it, teased it, ramped it, champed it, vamped it, stamped it, jingled it, bungled it, unbungled it, mingled it, scratched it, hatched it, tingled it,

whanged it, banged it, wrangled it, jangled it, strangled
it, swashed it, washed it, nailed it, shackled it, tackled
it, flailed it, festered it, pestered it, retrieved it, battered
it, relieved it, touted it, scouted it, flattered it, cleaved it,
tarred it, coaxed it, sparred it, hoaxed it, spanked it,
banked it, sliced it, joined it, spliced it, charmed it,
armed it, guisarmed it, rigged it, jigged it, and trigged it,
and sent it scooting down the hill into the valley, head-
long from the Cranium. Then, he carried it back from
the valley to the top of the hill, as Sisyphus did his stone,
and it was a wonder he didn't slam-bang the bottom out
of it.

Observing this, one of his friends asked him why it
was he thus tortured body, mind, and barrel. To which
the philosopher replied that, having been given no other
duty to perform for the republic, he thus mauled his
barrel in order that, amid a populace so fervently occupied, he might not seem to be the only laggard and lazy
one.

In like manner, I, while I may be out of the clutter,
am by no means out of the flutter, when I perceive that
I have been given no worthy task, and when I see,
throughout this most noble realm of France, on both
sides of the mountains, everybody busy today, training
and working, some for the fortification and defense of
the fatherland, others with plans to repel the enemy
and take the offensive, the whole being done with fine
strategy and in wonderful order, with obvious profit for
the future; for from now on, I am sure, the boundaries
of France are going to be superbly extended, and the
French are assured of peace; until I scarcely can refrain
from adopting the opinion of our friend, Heraclitus,
when he states that war is the father of all good things;
and I am inclined to think that war in Latin is called
beautiful, not by antiphrasis, as certain patchers of old

Latin junk would have us believe, for the reason that they themselves can see no beauty in it, but, absolutely and simply, for the reason that in war every species of the good and beautiful comes out, while all varieties of ugliness and evil are betrayed. For which reason it was, the wise and pacific King Solomon could not think of any better way to picture for us the unspeakable perfection of Divine Wisdom than by comparing it to the order of an army in camp.

Not having been drafted for the offensive ranks, since they thought me, apparently, too imbecile and too impotent, and, on the other hand, not having been given any defensive employment, even if it was only carrying the hod, hiding away the sod, turning the wheel, or breaking the clod (all of which would have been the same to me), I have felt that it was a more than ordinarily shameful thing to be looked upon as an idle spectator by so valiant, capable, and loyal a people, now, in the full view of all Europe, engaged in acting out this illustrious fable and tragicomedy, without bestirring myself to finish this nothing that is left me, but that is my all.

For very little glory, it seems to me, comes to those who merely use their eyes but who, otherwise, spare their strength, conceal their crowns, hide away their money, and scratch their heads with one finger, like disgusted good-for-nothings that they are, gaping for flies like a parson's calf and pricking up their ears like the asses of Arcady at the musicians' song, indicating, by a silent pantomime, that they give their approval to the prosopopoeia.

Having made this choice and decision, I have thought that it would not be a useless or impertinent business if I were to set in motion my own Diogenic barrel, which is the only thing that remains to me from the shipwreck of the past, at the lighthouse of Bad Luck. And with all this trundling of my barrel, what do you think I ought to do? By the virgin with her skirts tucked up, I don't know yet.

Wait a minute while I take a little suck at this bottle. It is my true, my only Helicon; it is my caballine fountain; it is my one hobby. Here, as I drink, I deliberate, discourse, solve problems, and reach conclusions. After the epilogue, I laugh, I write, I compose, I drink. Ennius wrote while drinking and drank while writing. Aeschylus, if you put any faith in Plutarch, in *Symposiacis*, drank while he composed, and composed while he drank. Homer never wrote on an empty stomach. Cato never wrote except after drinking. I tell you this, so that you may not be able so say that I live without the example of the much praised and better prized. It is good and fresh enough—just entering the second degree, as you might say. And for that, God, the good God of Sabaoth—that is to say, of armies—be eternally praised! And if the rest of you fellows would like to take one big or a couple of small beakers up your sleeves, I haven't anything at all to say against it, provided that you never forget to give God a little bit of praise.

Seeing, then, that this is my lot or my destiny, since it is not permitted to everyone to go to Corinth and live there, I have made up my mind to serve both combatants and non-combatants, so that I may no longer be a useless fellow and a loafer.

As for the mortar-mixers, engineers, and rampart-builders, I will do for them what Neptune and Apollo did in Troy, under Laomedon, what Renaud de Montauban did in his last days. I will wait on the masons, I will put the pot on to boil for the masons, and when the meal is over, with the music of my bagpipe I will tell in rhythmic measures of the dawdling of the dawdlers. That was the way in which Amphion, playing on his lyre, founded, built, and erected the great and celebrated city of Thebes.

As for the warriors, I'd like to tap my barrel once more, and from the draught it contains (with which, from the two preceding volumes, you would have been sufficiently familiar, if those volumes had not been perverted and jumbled through the humbuggery of the printers)—from it, I should like to draw for them a generous third, from the vintage of our postprandial pastimes, and follow it up with a jolly jug of Pantagruelic proverbs. You have my permission to call them Diogenic, if you choose. And inasmuch as I cannot be their comrade, they shall have me for a faithful quartermaster, ready to refresh them, to the best of my ability, upon their return from battle, as well as for a eulogist—and an indefatigable one, I'm telling you—of their deeds of prowess and glorious feats of arms. I shall not fail them, by the *lapathium acutum* of God, unless March fails to come in Lent; but he'll be good and careful not to do that, the old whoremaster!

And yet, I remember having read some place that Ptolemy, son of Lagus, one day, among the other spoils and booty of his conquests, presented to the Egyptians, in full sight of the populace, a Bactrian camel, black all over, and a parti-colored slave, striped in such a manner that one part of his body was black, the other white, the stripes running, not horizontally across the diaphragm, as in the case of the woman sacred to the Indian Venus, who was encountered by the Tyanian philosopher, between the Hydaspes River and the Caspian Mountains, but perpendicularly, which was something not seen before in Egypt. He hoped that, through these novelties, the people's love for him would be increased. But what happened? At sight of the camel, all were frightened and indignant; and at sight of the parti-colored man, some jeered, while others were filled with abhorrence at this view of an infamous monster, that had been created through a mistake of Nature's. In short, the hope he had of pleasing his Egyptian subjects and, by such a means, of increasing the natural affection that they bore him, went trickling through his hands. And he came to understand that beautiful, elegant, and perfect things were more pleasing and delightful to them than ridiculous and monstrous ones. From that day on, he had so great a contempt for the slave, as well as for the camel, that very shortly afterward, either through negligence or from lack of ordinary nourishment, both slave and camel gave up the ghost.

This precedent causes me to vacillate between hope and fear, being apprehensive lest, in place of the pleasure I anticipate, I encounter that which I abhor; in which case, my fortune is chunks of coal, and in place of Venus, I get Spaniel the dog. In place of doing them a service, I may annoy them. In place of amusing them, I may offend them. And my adventure may turn out like Euclion's rooster, so celebrated by Plautus in his *Money-Jug* and by Ausonius in his *Gryphus,* as well as elsewhere—that rooster which, for having uncovered the hoard by scratching, had his slit cropped—I mean, his crop slit.

And if anything like this should happen, should not I play the goat? It has happened before; it may happen again. Hercules forbid that it does! For I recognize in every member of my audience a certain specific and individual quality which our elders termed Pantagruelism, a quality that never permits them to take anything in bad part that they know springs from a good, free, and loyal heart. I see them, every day, willing to accept such payment as this and satisfied with it, even when the currency in question is accompanied by a lack of talent.

Having settled this point, I now return to my barrel. Up and at this wine! Take a good deep swig, my lads! If you don't like it, leave it. I am not one of those pestiferous German swillers, who, by force, outrage, and violence, would compel every *Landsmann* and all their friends to drink, and even to souse and carouse, which is worse. Every good drinker, every good and gouty one, if he is thirsty, let him come to this barrel of mine. If they don't want to drink, they don't have to. If they do want to, and if the wine is to the taste of the lordship of their lordships, then let them drink up, fully, freely, boldly. They need not pay anything, and they need not be sparing. Those are my orders. And don't be afraid that the wine will give out, as it did at the wedding of Cana in Galilee. The more you draw out through the spout, the more I'll pour in through the bunghole. In this way, the barrel will prove inexhaustible. It comes from a live spring and a perpetual vein.

It is like the beverage contained in the cup of Tantalus, figuratively represented amongst the Brahman sages. It is like the mountain of salt in Iberia, rendered so famous by Cato. It is like the golden bough, sacred to the subterranean goddess, so celebrated by Vergil. It is a true cornucopia of merriness and mockery; and if sometimes you seem to be down to the dregs, yet you'll never drink it dry. Good hope lies at the bottom, as it did in Pandora's bottle, and not despair, as in the vat of the Danaïdes.

Note well what I say, and what kind of guests I invite. For in order that none may be under any misapprehension, I will, like Lucilius, who insisted that he only wrote for his fellow citizens of Tarentum and

Cosenza, state here that I have only tapped this barrel for you, good folks, drinkers of the first water and gouty freeholders.

As for the giant Doriphages, the swallowers of early morning mist, they have plenty of passion—I mean to say, occupation—in their rumps and plenty of bags on the hook for venison. Let them graze here, if they like, but these are not their preserves. As for you tasseled big-wigs, you haggling critics, don't speak to me, I beg of you, in the name of the four buttocks that begot you and the lively peg that served as a coupling-pin. And the hypocrites still less, though they all drink a-plenty and are all of them syphilitic, pock-marked, and equipped with an inextinguishable thirst and insatiable appetite. And why? Because they are no good; because they're a bad lot; they are that evil from which we daily pray to God to be delivered. And this, even though they do, sometimes, counterfeit beggars.

Down, you mastiffs! Out of my way! Out of my sun, you pack; to the devil with you! So, you'd come here, buttocking and articling my wine and bepissing my barrel, would you? You behold here the stick that Diogenes, in his will, directed should be laid beside him after his death, so that he would have it to chase away and swat such corpse-eating larvae and hounds of Cerberus as you. And so, down with you, you hypocrites! Back to your sheep, you mastiffs! Out of here, you whiners; what the devil, away with you! Are you still here? I'd give my interest in Papimania to be able to nab you, gr, grr, grrrrr! Will they never go? I hope you're never able to do your business, except from lashes of the stirrup-thong, never able to piss except from the strappado, and never in heat except from blows of a club!

The immediate historical background of this Prologue is worth noting. In September, 1544, following the capture of Saint-Dizier, Charles v had marched on the French capital, which for a period of a couple of weeks was in grave danger of being taken. The treaty of Crépy, on September 18, 1544, put an end to this crisis; but there was great fear of a fresh break with the Emperor, and the entire year of 1545 was devoted to fortifying the realm against attack. This task was intrusted to the Seigneur de Langey, Martin du Bellay, who like his brother the Cardinal was one of Rabelais' patrons. On September 8, 1545, the sudden death of the Duke of Orléans rendered the treaty void and vastly increased the fears of the French; and it was about this time that Maître François must have been writing his Prologue, just before the book went to the printer. The author, it will be observed, speaks of the events he is describing as being "of today." The fortifying of Paris and other cities cost a great deal of money and necessitated heavy additional taxes, which the French and especially the Parisian populace deeply resented. The nation had recently suffered the plague and a rise in the price of wheat, and duties had been levied on nearly all articles of merchandise. Rabelais is here endeavoring to arouse the national conscience in much the same manner as does the propagandist for a modern war-bond campaign. He is fulfilling his function as "royal publicist" by promising his fellow countrymen in return for their sacrifices an era of peace and a France with "superbly extended" boundaries.

Linguistically, the passage is one of the richest in the whole of Rabelais, with its proverbs, rhymes, suggestive sound-tags, onomatopoetic effects, and the like. This is particularly true of those portions describing the warlike preparations of the people and Diogenes' trundling of his barrel.

"*The man born blind*": Matthew, xx, 30-34; Mark, x, 46-52; Luke, xviii, 35-42; John, ix. ——"*As you eat your snatches*": untranslatable word-play on lopiner, *to take a morsel of food,* and opiner, *to give one's opinion.* ——"*Of Phrygian extraction*": *reference to the tradition to be found in old French chronicles to the effect that France had been peopled by Trojan fugitives, led by Francus, Hector's son.* ——"*Serpentine of Rohan*": *this has not been explained.* ——"*Diogenes the Sinopian*": *Sinope in Paphlagonia (Asia Minor) was the philosopher's birthplace.* ——"*Strengthened the . . . cataracts*": *suspended portcullises to be let down on invaders' heads.* ——"*The women of ancient Corinth*": *their combats were those of Venus, Corinth being renowned for its courtesans.* ——"*Opisthographs*": *tablets with writing on both sides.* ——"*In the direction of the Cranium*": *it was here that Diogenes lived in his tub and held his famous conversation with Alexander the Great, when he asked the latter to get out of his sunlight.* ——"*Guisarmed it*": *the* guisarme *was a two-edged battle-ax.* ——"*War in Latin is called beautiful*": *Latin* bellum, *war,* and bellus, *beautiful.* ——"*Order of an army in camp*": Song of Songs, vi, 9. ——"*By the virgin with her skirts tucked up*": *the reference is uncertain; it is possibly to St. Mary the Egyptian before her conversion.* ——"*Plutarch in* Symposiacis": *Plutarch's* Table Talk, *chapter vii; see also Erasmus,* Adages, iv, iii, 59. ——"*It is not permitted to every one to go to Corinth*": *proverbial expression, see Horace,* Epistles, i, xviii, 36. ——"*What Renaud de Montauban did in his last days*": *in the* Four Sons of Aymon, *Renaud out of penitence devotes his last years to serving the masons.* ——"*The humbuggery of the printers*": *Cleuzot observes that "This protestation on Rabelais' part is not to be taken literally; it serves him here rather as an excuse for the boldness of his language, which had brought down upon him the censure of Parliament"; compare the wording of the Royal Privileges.* —— *"Lapathium acutum": an oath based upon a word-play, "lapathium" (pronounced like* la passion*) being the oxy-lapathon, or sorrel (Rumex acutus Linn.) of the Greeks.* ——*"Ptolemy, son of Lagus": Rabelais takes this anec-dote from Lucian by way of the Antiquae Lectiones of Caelius Rhodiginus.* ——*"The Tyanian philosopher": Apollonius of Tyana; see Philostratus, Life of Apollonius of Tyana, iii, 3.* ——*"My fortune is chunks of coal": the expression is from Erasmus, Adages, i, ix, 30.* ——*"In place of Venus . . . Spaniel, the dog": allusion to the lucky throw ("Venus") and the unlucky one ("the dog") in the game of dice.* ——*"Plautus in his Money-Jug": allusion to Plautus' comedy, the Aulularia, iii, 4; a miser buries a jug of gold and a cock that scratches where the treasure lies has its head chopped off.* ——*"Ausonius in his Gryphus": Decius (or Decimus) Magnus Ausonius, fourth-century Latin epigrammatic poet of Bordeaux; Gryphus is the title of the poem supposed to have been discovered by Ausonius amid the dust of a library as Euclion the cock uncovered the miser's gold.* —— *"Should not I play the goat": the verb is* chevroter*, meaning, according to one old commentator, "to be vexed, as she-goats (chèvres) are, which leap about and stamp when one disturbs them"; this is startlingly close to our modern slang phrase, "to be the goat."* ——*"Cana in Galilee": the well-known Gospel episode narrated in the second chapter of John.* ——*"The cup of Tantalus": see Philostratus, Life of Apollonius of Tyana, iii, 25 and 32.* ——*"Rendered so famous by Cato": see the Attic Nights of Aulus Gellius, xi, 22.* ——*"Like the golden*

bough so celebrated by Vergil": Aeneid, vi, 143-4. ——
"Like Lucilius": See Cicero, De Finibus, vii, 1. ——
"Giant Doriphages": the *"doriphages,"* literally, *are*
"devourers of gifts," that is, bribe-takers, allusion being
to the legal profession. ——*"Swallowers of early-morn-
ing mist"*: the judges, who go to court early in the morning. ——*"Plenty of passion . . . in the rump"*: the
word-play, of course, is on passion, *passion,* and au cul
passion, *"passion in the rump,"* which in pronunciation
sounds like occupation, *occupation.* ——*"You tasseled
big-wigs"*: the doctors—and censors—of the Sorbonne.
——*"My interest in Papimania"*: that is, in the land of
fanatical popery; a description of this mythical land is
given in Book Fourth. ——*"I hope you're never able to
do your business,"* etc.: allusion to the effects of flagellation on defecation, urination, and the sexual impulse.

As has been stated, Rabelais began Book Third with
the plan of continuing his account of Pantagruel's
voyage to Utopia and, after half a dozen chapters,
abandoned this theme, or rather, postponed it, in order
to plunge into the Querelle des femmes, with Panurge's
famous *"flea"*—the question as to whether or not he
should marry—as an excuse for this sudden change of
plan. We are told, first, how Pantagruel led a huge
migration of Utopians into the land of the Dipsodes,
or Thirsty Ones, and here the author introduces another
passage in which (as he had done in Book First) he sets
forth his ideas on the just and humane treatment to be
accorded to conquered peoples. Just prior to writing this
book Maître François had been physician-secretary to
Guillaume du Bellay, French governor of the Piedmont,
and had been greatly impressed by this lord's administra-
tion of the province. As Lefranc points out, Rabelais is
here giving us his *"ideal of government and justice"* and

is taking his stand as an opponent of the doctrines of
Machiavelli, siding rather with those "good princes and
great kings" who are "the adornment of their peoples."

How Pantagruel Treated the Dipsodes

PANTAGRUEL's subjects, from the day that they were
born and entered the world, along with their mothers' or
their nurses' milk had sucked in the gentleness and mildness that marked his reign, and on this idea they were
all fed and nourished, so that there would have been
more chance of their surrendering their own lives than
of their proving unfaithful to this first and single yoke
which they owed it to their prince to bear, no matter
where they might be scattered or transplanted.

He wanted this to be true not only of the Utopians and
their children but also of those nations that had been
newly added to his empire; he wanted these latter to
take upon themselves this same fealty and obedience.
Which was what happened, and he was by no means
disappointed in his plans; for if the Utopians in the past
had been loyal and law-abiding citizens, the Dipsodes,
after a few days of association with their new neighbors,
soon outdid the latter, through some natural fervor or
other that is to be found in all human beings at the beginning of all undertakings that are to their liking. Their
only lament, and they called upon all heaven and the
motivating intelligences to bear witness to it, was that
the renown of the good Pantagruel had not sooner been
brought to their attention.

And note here, you drinkers, that the proper method
of treating and holding a newly conquered country, contrary to the opinion which certain tyrannic minds have
entertained, to their own detriment and dishonor, is not

by plundering, forcing, tormenting, ruining, and vexing the people and ruling them with a rod of iron—in short, by consuming and devouring the populace in the manner that led Homer to call an iniquitous king *Demovore,* that is to say, eater-of-the-people. I shall not give you, on this head, any of the old stories; I shall merely recall to your recollections what your fathers—and you yourselves, if you are not too young—have seen.

Like a newborn child, these conquered peoples must be suckled, cradled, and pleased. Like a tree freshly planted, they must be propped, supported, and protected against all ravages, injuries, and calamities. Like one coming out of a long and serious illness and just beginning to convalesce, they must be pampered, spared, and restored in such a fashion that there will come to be for them no other king or prince in the world whom they would less willingly have as an enemy or one whom they would prefer to have as a friend.

Such are the philters, charms, and enchantments of love, by means of which, pacifically, one may retain what has with difficulty been conquered; and the conqueror, be he king, prince, or philosopher, cannot reign more happily than by causing Justice to succeed Courage. His courage is apparent in his victory and conquest; his justice shall be apparent when, with the will and kindly affection of his people, he shall proceed to provide laws, to publish decrees, to establish religions, and to see that each gets his due—just as the noble poet Maro says of Octavianus Augustus:

> He who, as victor, did by force assail,
> By the will of the vanquished made his laws prevail.

This is why Homer, in his *Iliad,* calls the good princes and great kings *kosmetores laon,* that is, the adornments of the people.

This was the idea of Numa Pompilius, second king of the Romans, and a just, politic, and philosophic one, when he ordered that, on the day of the festival of the god Termes, the festival known as the *Terminalia*, nothing should be sacrificed that had died, thereby impressing upon us that all questions pertaining to boundaries, frontiers, and annexations should be settled peacefully, with lasting friendship and good will and without the soiling of hands with blood and pillage. He who takes any other course not only shall lose what he has got but shall have to suffer the scandal and opprobrium that comes with the knowledge that his acquisitions have been wrongly and unjustly achieved, as a result of which what he has acquired shall slip through his hands, since things badly got badly go. And even if he should enjoy the spoils in peace all his life, his gains shall, none the less, perish with his heirs, the shadow on the name of the dead shall be the same, and men shall curse his memory, as that of an unjust conqueror. For as the well-known proverb has it, "Things wrongly acquired, the third generation shall not enjoy."

Note also, you gouty rascals, while we are speaking of this, how Pantagruel made two angels out of one, which is the opposite of the accomplishment of Charlemagne, who made two devils out of one when he transported the Saxons into Flanders and the Flemish into Saxony. For not being able to keep the Saxons, whose territory had been newly added to his empire, in subjection, since they were always rising up in rebellion whenever his attention happened to be distracted in Spain or other distant countries, he decided to transport them into a land that was his own, and one naturally obedient to him, namely Flanders, and to transport the people of Hainaut and the Flemish, who were his natural subjects, into Saxony, inasmuch as he had no doubt of the fealty of the latter, even if they migrated into alien regions. But what happened was that the Saxons obstinately kept up their rebellion, while the Flemish, dwelling in Saxony, imbibed the manners and the contrary habits of the Saxons.

The foregoing passage is a condensation. The title has been supplied by the translator.

"*Certain tyrannic minds*": a likely thrust at Machiavelli, whose work was published in 1532 and, following the marriage of Henry II and Catherine de' Medici, was widely read and discussed in France. ——"*That led Homer to call an iniquitous king Demovore*": this is among the reproaches addressed by Achilles to Agamemnon, Iliad, i, 231; the Greek word is demoboros.—— "*The noble poet Maro*": this is an allusion to Vergil's Georgics, iv, 561-2. ——"*Kosmetores laon*": it has been pointed out that with Homer this is a purely administrative title, meaning marshal or leader of an army. —— "*Things badly got badly go*": Cicero, Philippics, II, xxvii, 65; he quotes the Latin poet Naevius. ——"*As the well-known proverb has it*": the proverb is a Latin one: de male quaesitis vix gaudet tertius haeres. ——"*Charlemagne . . . when he transported the Saxons*": Rabelais probably gets this from some romance of chivalry or some old chronicle, such as that of Sigebert for the year 802.

The Utopians having been settled in the land of the Dipsodes, Panurge is made Castellan of Salmagundi; whereupon, a question arises that provides Maître François with an opportunity to give expression to his view of the ideal world society—perhaps, all in all, the

most profound statement on this subject that we have
from his pen, one that, in any attempt to evaluate his
Weltanschauung, *must be set alongside his Abbey of*
Thélème. *And it may not be without forethought that*
this statement is put into the mouth of the roguish
Panurge, a character who generally serves as comic
relief—the author may have deemed this a safer course.

Panurge Praises Debtors and Borrowers

"But," inquired Pantagruel, "when are you going to get
out of debt?"

"At the Greek Calends," replied Panurge, "when
everybody's happy, and you are your own heir. God keep
me from ever getting out. For that will only be when I
can't find anybody to lend me a denier. He who doesn't
set his yeast at night won't have any dough the next
morning. Are you always in debt to someone? Then,
you're lucky, for there will always be someone to pray
God to give you a good, long, happy life. Since he is
afraid he might lose what you owe him, he will always
speak well of you wherever he goes; and he will always
be getting new creditors for you, hoping that, with them,
you will be able to turn something up, and that he will
be able to fill his own ditch with another's dirt.

"In Gaul, in the old days, when under the rule of the
Druids serfs, varlets, and squires were burned alive at
the funerals and obsequies of their lords and masters,
don't you suppose those rascals had plenty of fear of
their lords' and masters' dying, seeing that they would
then have to die, too? Don't you suppose they constantly
prayed their great god, Mercury, along with Dis, Father
to Gold Crowns, to keep those same lords and masters
in good health for a long time to come? Don't you sup-

pose they were very careful to treat and serve their masters well? For then they could go on living, at least until the time came for them to die. Well, believe me, your creditors will pray God with an even more fervent devotion, from fear that you will die, since they love the sleeve better than the arm, and a denier more than life itself. Look at the money-lenders of Landerousse, who went out and hanged themselves when they saw corn and wine dropping in price and good times coming back again."

Pantagruel making no reply, Panurge went on:

"Holy smoke! when I come to think of it, you've got me up against the wall, when you reprimand me for my debts and creditors; but let me tell you something: that's one time when I look upon myself as most august, reverend, and redoubtable, seeing that contrary to the opinion of all the philosophers, who say that nothing comes from nothing, I, having nothing nor even the beginning of anything, am yet a maker and creator.

"I'm a creator, you say, and of what? Why, look at all those nice, charming little creditors! For creditors are indeed—and I'll stick to it through hell-fire—nice and charming creatures. He who lends nothing is an ugly and an evil one, a creature of hell and the old dickens himself. And what have I made? Debts. Oh, what a rare antique! Debts, I tell you, exceeding in number the syllables resulting from the coupling of all the consonants with all the vowels, as formerly figured out and added up by the noble Xenocrates. If you were to estimate the perfection of debtors by the numerousness of their creditors, you would not be making any great mistake in practical arithmetic.

"Don't you think I feel good, when, every morning, I see around me those same creditors, and all of them so humble, so ready to serve me, and so full of bowings and scrapings? And when I note how, upon my showing a little better face to one than I do to the others, the old bastard thinks he's going to have his settlement first—thinks that he's the first in line, and that my smile means ready money—when I observe all this, it seems to me that I am still playing the part of God, accompanied by all his angels and cherubim, in the passion-play of Saumur. These are my office-seekers, my hangers-on, my bowers, my greeters, my constant petitioners.

"I really think that debts are that mountain of heroic virtues described by Hesiod; and in this science, to which all human beings appear to aspire, I hold my first degree. But few climb up, for the road is too hard, in view of the fact that, today, everybody possesses an ardent passion and a clamorous appetite for making new debts and acquiring new creditors. However, a man doesn't become a debtor merely by wishing to be one; he can't have creditors merely by wanting them. And so, you would like to oust me from this sovereign happiness of mine, would you? You ask me when I am going to get out of debt.

"But there's a lot worse to come. May St. Babolin, the good saint, take me, if all my life I haven't looked upon debts as a connection and a bond between heaven and earth, the one tie that binds the human species—without which, I mean to say, all human beings would perish. It may even be that debts are that great soul of the universe which, according to the Academics, gives life to all things.

"Let that be as it may; but picture in your mind, calmly, some world or other—take, if you think best, the thirtieth of those which the philosopher Metrodorus conceived, or the seventy-eighth of Petronius—a world in which there is neither debtor nor creditor.

"A world without debts! Think of it! The stars will

have no regular course, but all will be in confusion. Jupiter, assuming that he owes nothing to Saturn, will proceed to dispossess the latter from his orbit, and, with his Homeric chain, will hang up all the intelligences, gods, heavens, spirits, genii, heroes, devils, earth, sea, and all the elements. Saturn will ally himself with Mars, and they between them will throw the whole world into an uproar. Mercury, not caring to wait on others, will refuse to be their Camillus, or Errand Boy, as he is called in the Etruscan language, any longer. For he won't owe them anything. Venus will not be venerated, for she will not have let anything. The moon will remain dark and bloody; why should the sun give her any of his light? He is under no obligation to do so. The sun will not shine upon the earth. The stars will not confer their benign influence, for the earth will have ceased lending them nourishment through its vapors and exhalations, by means of which, as Heraclitus asserted, as the Stoics proved, and as Cicero maintained, the stars are fed.

"Among the elements, there will be no coordination, alternation, or transmutation of any kind, for one will not feel obligated to another; one will not have borrowed anything from another. From the earth no water will be produced; water will not be transmuted into air; from the air, no fire will be made; fire will not heat the earth; and the earth will produce nothing but Monsters, Titans, Aloïdae, and Giants. Rains will not rain, light will not shine, wind will not blow, and there will be neither summer nor autumn. Lucifer will break loose and, leaving the depths of hell with his furies, Poenae, and horned devils, will endeavor to dislodge all the gods from the heavens, including the divinities of the major as well as of the minor nations. And this non-lending world will be nothing but a dog-kennel, more contentious and disorderly than the one belonging to the Rector of Paris, and a devil-hatch with more confusion than you will find in the performances at Doué.

"Among human beings, one will no longer greet another. Much good will it do him to yell 'Help! Fire! I'm drowning! Murder!' No one will come to his rescue. Why? He will not have lent anything, and no one will owe him anything. No one will have the slightest interest in his burning, in his shipwreck, in his ruin, or in his death. He hasn't lent them anything, and he's not going to lend them anything in the future. In short, Faith, Hope, and Charity will be banished from the world; for men are born to aid and relieve other men. In place of these virtues will come Defiance, Contempt, Rancor, with all the troop of curses, miseries, and woes.

"You will think that Pandora must have spilled her bottle there. Men will be wolves in the form of men, werewolves and goblins, like Lycaon, Bellerophon, and Nebuchadnezzar; they will be brigands, assassins, poisoners, evil-doers, evil-thinkers, malevolent, hate-bearing, each with his hand against every other man, like Ishmael, like Metabus, like Timon of Athens, the one who, for this reason, was named *misanthropos*. From which it may be seen that it would be an easier thing to rear fish in the air or to pasture deer in the bottom of the ocean than to endure a beggarly world that did not lend anything.

"And if, after the pattern of this snarling and grumpy non-lending world, you go ahead and picture that other smaller world that is man, you will find in the latter a terrible hullabaloo. The head will not want to lend the sight of the eyes to guide the feet and hands, and the feet will not deign to bear the head. The hands will stop working for the latter. The heart will get tired of doing so much work for the other members and will not lend them any more motive force. The lungs will not lend the heart any more breath, and the liver will send the lungs no more blood to keep it going. The bladder will not care to be a creditor to the kidneys, and the urine will be suppressed. The brain, viewing this unnatural order of things, will begin day-dreaming, and will not give any more feeling to the nerves or movement to the muscles.

"To sum it up, in this unhinged world, owing nothing, lending nothing, borrowing nothing, you will behold a more pernicious conspiracy than Aesop ever dreamed of in his fable. There is not the slightest doubt that such an organism would perish; and it would not only perish, but perish very quickly, and that, even though it were Aesculapius himself; and the body would soon go to rot. As for the soul, highly put out about it all, it would go straight to hell, which is precisely the place where my money has gone."

"At the Greek Calends": that is, never. ——*"The money-lenders of Landerousse": allusion not explained.* ——*"As figured out . . . by the noble Xenocrates":* Xenocrates, leader of the Academic school of philosophers, is said to have carried to 100,200,000 the number of syllabic combinations that could be obtained from the Greek alphabet. ——*"Passion-play of Saumur":* allusion to a performance given at Saumur in August, 1534. ——*"Described by Hesiod":* Works and Days, 289. —— *"St. Babolin, the good saint":* this was the first abbot of Saint-Maur, where Rabelais was made a canon. —— *"According to the Academics":* see Plato, Timaeus, 34, B-37 C, cited by St. Augustine, De Civitate Dei, XIII, xvii, 2. ——*"Metrodorus . . . Petronius":* Metrodorus, a disciple of Epicurus who died in the year 277 B.C., maintained that the number of worlds was infinite (Plu-

tarch, On the Opinions of the Philosophers, i, 5); *Petronius, a Pythagorean of the sixth century* B.C., *known only from a passage in Plutarch* (On the Failure of the Oracles, 22 *and* 23), *imagined a universe composed of 186 worlds.* ——*"With his Homeric chain": see the* Iliad, viii, 19 f., *and* xv, 18. ——*"As Cicero maintained":* De Natura Deorum, iii, 14; *see also Plutarch,* On the Opinions of the Philosophers, II, xvii, 2. ——*"Aloïdae, and Giants": the descendants of Aloeus; see the* Odyssey, xi, 307; Iliad, v, 285; *and* Aeneid, vi, 582-4. —— *"Poenae": Personifications of the punishments of the damned.* ——*"The performance at Doué": the "devil-play" of Doué (a small village some twenty kilometers from Saumur) was part of the passion-play at the latter place.* ——*"Like Lycaon, Bellerophon, and Nebuchadnezzar": Lycaon was a king of Arcady, changed into a wolf by Jupiter for having violated the laws of hospitality (Ovid,* Metamorphoses, i); *Bellerophon was the son of Glaucus, king of Corinth, who, for having wished to scale Olympus mounted on Pegasus, was pursued by the wrath of the gods; for Nebuchadnezzar, see the book of Daniel,* iv, 33. ——*"Like Ishmael . . . Metabus . . . Timon of Athens": for Ishmael, see* Genesis, xvi, 12; *on Metabus, see the* Aeneid, xi, 540 f.; *Timon is pictured as a misanthrope by Lucian and Plutarch.* ——*"Aesop in his fable": the fable of "The Members and the Stomach."*

Continuation of Panurge's Speech in Praise of Debtors and Lenders

"ON THE other hand, picture another world, one in which everybody lends, everybody owes, and all are debtors, all are lenders. Oh, what a harmony will there be, in the

regular movements of the heavens! It seems to me that
I can hear that harmony, quite as well as Plato ever did.
What a sympathy among the elements! Oh, how Nature
will then delight in all her works and productions, with
Ceres laden down with corn, Bacchus with wine, Flora
with flowers, Pomona with fruits, while Juno, in an
atmosphere of serenity, remains always gentle and
health-giving! I lose myself in the picture.

"Among human beings, there will be peace, love,
affection, fidelity, repose, banquets, feastings, joy, and
merriment, as gold, silver, small change, rings, jewelry,
and other merchandise scurry from hand to hand. No
lawsuits, no wars, no arguments. No man will there be a
usurer, none a glutton, none a miser, and none will
refuse anything. My God! won't that be the age of gold,
the reign of Saturn, the incarnate idea of Olympus,
where all other virtues cease, and Charity alone reigns,
rules, dominates, and triumphs. All will be good, all will
be beautiful, all will be just. O happy world! O citizens
of that happy world! O thrice and four times blessed
ones! It seems to me that I'm there now. It's the God's
truth I swear to you, that if this world, this blessed
world, in which everybody lends and nobody refuses
anything—if this world had a pope, with plenty of
cardinals in his Sacred College, you would, within a
few years, see the saints a lot thicker and a lot more
miraculous, with more readings, more vows, more staffs
and candles than you will now find in all the nine bishoprics of Brittany, excepting only St. Ives.

"Consider, I beg you, how the noble Patelin, wishing
to deify and, by divine praises, to raise to the third
heaven Père Guillaume Jousseaume, can find nothing
better to say of the latter than

> . . . that this his fame:
> He lent his income to whomsoever came.

"Oh, what a fine tribute!

"After this pattern, picture that microcosm of ours, *id est,* that little world which is man, with all his members lending, borrowing, owing, that is to say, performing their natural functions. For Nature created man for no other purpose than to lend and borrow. No greater harmony will be found among the spheres than in the well-ordered functions of such an organism. The intention of the Founder of this microcosm is to support the soul (which He has placed in it as a guest) and life. Life consists in blood, and blood is the seat of the soul. There is only one task incumbent upon this world, and that is the constant manufacture of blood. In this process, all the members have their individual functions, and the hierarchy existing among them is such that each incessantly borrows from another, each lends to another, each is debtor to another. The material, the metal, suitable for transmutation into blood, is supplied by Nature: bread and wine. In these two are included all species of nourishment. And for this reason it is that they are called *companage* in the Gothic language.

"To find and prepare these, the hands labor, the feet travel and carry the mechanism about, the eyes direct the whole, the appetite, down in the orifice of the stomach, by means of a certain bitter and melancholy humor transmitted to it from the spleen, gives warning when it is necessary to supply food, the tongue tries the food out, the teeth chew it, and the stomach then receives it, digests it, and turns it into chyle. The mesentery veins, thereupon, suck from this what is good and suitable, casting aside the excrements, which, by an expulsive property, are emptied out through conduits expressly provided for the purpose; following which, the veins carry what is left to the liver, which transmutes it anew and makes blood out of it.

"What joy, then, do you think there must be among these various officers, when they look upon that golden stream that is their only Restorative? No greater is the joy of the alchemists, when, after long and arduous labors and great expense, they behold the metals that have been transmuted in their furnaces. In the same fashion, each member here bestirs himself afresh to purify and refine this marvelous treasure. The kidneys, through the emulgent veins, extract from it that bitterness we call the urine, and by means of ureters, conduct it down below. There the urine finds a suitable receptacle, the bladder, which at the proper time empties it out. The spleen draws from the blood-stream the earthly part and the dregs, which you call melancholy; the gall-bottle substracts from it the superfluous choler; and then, the blood is transported to another factory, to be still further refined. That factory is the heart, which by means of its movements, known as systole and diastole, subtilizes, purifies, and perfects the blood, in the right ventricle, and then sends it coursing through the veins to all the members. Each member takes a little to itself, and nourishes itself in turn: feet, hands, eyes, all. And thus it is that they are all made debtors who before were creditors.

"In the left ventricle, this substance is rendered so subtle that it is termed spiritual, and it is then sent to all the members, through the arteries, in order to warm and winnow the other blood. The lungs, with their lobes and breathing, refresh it unceasingly; and in recognition of this benefit, the heart sends to the lungs, through the arterial vein, the best part of the blood. Finally, all is so refined in the Marvelous Net as to be afterwards made into animal spirits, by means of which the individual is enabled to form concepts, to discourse. to make judg-

ments, to solve problems, to ratiocinate, and to remember.

"I swear to God! I'm over my head, I'm lost, I'm
drowning, as I sink into the profound abyss of this world
which is so ready to lend, so ready to owe. You may take
my word for it that it is a divine thing to lend, and that to
owe is a heroic virtue.

"But I'm not through yet. This world, lending, owing,
borrowing, is so generous a one that, when the work of
alimentation has been completed, it then thinks about
lending to those who are not yet born, with the idea of
multiplying itself in images like itself—that is, in children. To this end, each member sets aside and cuts off
something from the most precious part of its nourishment, and sends it down below. Nature there has prepared convenient vessels and receptacles, by means of
which this substance descends into the genitals, through
long ambages and flexuosities, there to assume an appropriate form and to find its proper place, in man or
woman, for the conservation and perpetuation of humankind. This is all done by means of lending and debts,
between one part and another, and it is from this that we
get our expression, 'the duty' (or debt) of marriage.

"Nature inflicts a severe penalty on the one who is
stubborn in his refusal, in the form of a bitter vexation
among his members and a fury of his senses; but to the
one who lends, she has assigned a fitting reward, in the
form of pleasure, voluptuousness, and lightness of heart."

*The sustained seriousness of this passage is to be
noted. For once, there is not a single note of levity. It is
true that this type of fine-spun reasoning is not out of
keeping with Panurge's character, that of a clever rogue,*

*as previously developed; but nevertheless, there would
seem to be no doubt that Rabelais is in earnest here. The
physician is very much in evidence, and Dr. Dorveaux,
the commentator, in his annotations has brought out the
general accuracy of the author's anatomical and physiological descriptions, in the light of the medicine of his
day. The basic concept is that of the physiological division of labor in society; but as indicated in the second
paragraph, the idea with Rabelais goes deeper than that.*

"Quite as well as Plato": the celebrated "music of the
spheres"; see Plato's Republic, x, 617. ——"The reign
of Saturn": the "saturnia regna" of Vergil, Eclogues, iv,
6. ——"O thrice and four times blessed ones": Vergil's
"O terque quaterque beatus," Aeneid, i, 94. ——"With
more readings": the more venerated the saint, the more
readings in his honor at matins, the more croziers, etc.
——"All the nine bishoprics of Brittany, excepting only
St. Ives": The Bretons were, and are, noted for their
firmness in the faith and their devotion to their saints,
special homage being rendered to St. Ives. ——"Patelin
. . . Père Guillaume Jousseaume": allusion to the farce
of Patelin, in which the master-rogue who is the hero,
by way of persuading the merchant, Père Jousseaume, to
trust him for some cloth, launches into praise of Jousseaume's dead father. ——"Called companage in the
Gothic language": companage is related to compagnon,
companion, comrade; in the langue d'oc, companatge is
everything that is put on the table in addition to the
bread and wine. ——"Which you call melancholy":
much of the mystical terminology of the old medicine
lingers in that of the sixteenth century; but note that
Rabelais says: "which you call." ——"The Marvelous
Net": this was supposed to be the network of blood-
vessels at the base of the cranium, on either side of the

sphenoid bone, the admirabilis plexus retiformis *of Galen; but modern anatomists have demonstrated its non-existence in man (Dorveaux).*

How Pantagruel Detested Debtors and Borrowers

"I UNDERSTAND," replied Pantagruel, "and you impress me as being a very good special-pleader. But you may preach and lecture from now to Pentecost, and when you are through, you will be surprised to find how far you are from having convinced me; and for all your fine talk, I have no intention of falling into debt. *Owe no man anything,* says the Holy Apostle, *but to love one another.*

"You have made use of pretty metaphors and figures of speech, and I like them well enough. But let me tell you that, if you can picture a brazen and importunate borrower coming into a city where his habits are known in advance, you will find the inhabitants of that city more dismayed and frightened by his coming than if the plague were entering their town in the same garb in which the Tyanian philosopher encountered it at Ephesus. The Persians were by no means wrong in their opinion, when they held that the vice of second magnitude was to *lie,* the first being to *owe,* since debts and lies commonly go together.

"I would not, however, have it inferred that one is never to contract a debt, never to lend. No man is so rich that he does not, sometimes, have to owe, and none is so poor but sometimes one may borrow from him. One should be governed by circumstance, as Plato sets forth in his Laws, where he lays it down as a rule that one should not permit one's neighbors to draw water from his well, unless they shall first have digged and scraped on their own premises until coming upon what is known as potter's clay, without finding any spring or faintest trickling of water. (For this earth of ours, by the nature of its substance, which is thick, firm, compact, and dense, tends to retain all humidity, and is not readily compelled to give up any exhalations.) But it is a great shame, always and anywhere, for any one to borrow, in place of working and earning. And so, in my opinion, one should only lend when the borrower, after having labored, has not been able to accomplish his ends by toil, or when he has suddenly fallen upon an unexpected streak of bad luck and has lost all his property.

"However, suppose we drop the subject; and from now on, see to it that you do not get tangled up with any creditors. As for your past obligations, I am going to take those off your hands."

"The least I can do, and the most, in this case," said Panurge, "is to thank you, and if thanks were proportionate to the affection displayed by benefactors, my own would be infinite and everlasting; for the affection you have shown me is beyond all estimation; it transcends all weights, all numbers, all measures, since it is infinite and eternal. The attempt to measure it by the nature of the material benefits conferred and the satisfaction of the recipient would be very unfair. You have given me much, indeed, and a great deal more than is my due— more, I must admit, than my merits call for—but you do not know the half of it! Debts—that is not what gives me a pain, that is not what cooks my goose and eats me up. What I am worrying about is this: what kind of face am I going to put on in the future, when I am out of debt? Don't you think I'll make rather a spectacle of my-self for the first few months, seeing I have not been brought up in, and am not accustomed to, such a mode of life? I'm very much afraid I shall.

"What's more, from now on, there won't be a fart let in Salmagundi that doesn't backfire under my nose. All the farters in the world will remark, as they fart: 'Take this for your receipt'. I'm not going to last long, I can see that. I leave it to you to compose my epitaph, for I'm going to die pickled in farts. And if, some day, the doctors happen to want to make some good woman with a bad case of colic fart, and find their ordinary medicines don't work, why, then, the mummy of my whoremastering and befarted body ought to prove a very good remedy for them. Let the patients take ever so little, and they'll fart more than they mean to. And that's the reason why I would beg you to leave me a few hundred debts— just as Louis XI, when he wanted to throw the lawsuits of Miles d'Illiers, Bishop of Chartres, out of court, was implored to leave the latter one or two, just to keep him in form. I'd rather give up the whole of my snailshellery, along with my cockchafery, deducting nothing thereby from the principal."

"Let us drop this conversation," said Pantagruel. "I have settled the matter once and for all."

By giving the last word to his hero, the kingly Pantagruel, the author tones down somewhat the effect of Panurge's socio-political heresy (for that is what it amounts to), while at the same time rounding out his own views on the subject; having pictured for us a world society based upon cooperation and a recognition of essential interdependence, he once more emphasizes, as has Friar John has done in Book First, the virtue of productive labor. It is not until the close of this passage that, after a tone of high seriousness has been preserved for a length of time that is unusual in these pages, Panurge breaks the spell with his buffooneries.

"From now to Pentecost": Molière here borrows from Rabelais; see L'Ecole des Femmes, i, 1. ——"Owe no man anything": Epistle to the Romans, xiii, 8. ——"The Tyanian philosopher . . . at Ephesus": Apollonius is supposed to have viewed a visible embodiment of the plague as it entered the city of Ephesus; see Philostratus, Life of Apollonius of Tyana, vi, 4-10. ——"The Persians were by no means wrong," etc.: the author is translating a phrase of Plutarch, On Avoiding Usury, v. ——"Plato in his Laws": Laws, 866 B; but Rabelais gets it from Plutarch, to whom he is indebted for this entire train of reasoning (Plattard); see On Avoiding Usury i, 827. ——"The lawsuits of Miles d'Illiers": Des Périers, in his thirty-sixth nouvelle, tells us of this prelate that "He had a million lawsuits against him, and it is said that one day the King wished to settle them all, but the Bishop would not hear of it, remarking that to take away his lawsuits would be to deprive him of his life at the same time."

How Panurge Had a Flea in His Ear and Left Off Wearing His Magnificent Codpiece

THE next day, Panurge had his right ear pierced in the Jewish fashion, and then fastened to it a small gold ring of damascene workmanship, in the setting of which he had a flea enchased. And the flea was a black one, in order that there might not be any doubt about it. (It's a fine thing always to be well informed on everything.) The upkeep of this ring, as it came through his office, did not amount to more than the marriage of a Hyrcanian tigress would have cost, some 600,000 maravedis, you

might say. Panurge was very much put out about having
spent so much on it, after he was through paying for it,
and from then on, in the fashion of tyrants and lawyers,
proceeded to take it out of the sweat and blood of his
subjects.

He then took four ells of coarse gray material, rigged
himself out in a long robe of simple cut, left off wearing
his breeches, and attached a pair of spectacles to his
bonnet. In this outfit, he made his appearance before
Pantagruel, who found this disguise a strange one,
especially when he missed seeing Panurge's handsome
and magnificent codpiece which had formerly been a
sacred anchor and last refuge against all the storms of
adversity. Not being able to understand the mystery,
the good Pantagruel proceeded to question him, inquiring what was the object of this latest prosopopoeia.

"I," replied Panurge, "have a flea in my ear: I want to
get married."

"I hope you do, and that soon," said Pantagruel. "It
does my heart good to hear you say it. But I wouldn't
hold a hot iron in my hand by way of swearing that you
will go through with it. This is not the getup for lovers;
they don't go around with their breeches hanging down
like that, in a long robe, gray in color, that is not the
shade employed in full-length robes by good and virtuous folks. If a few persons, heretics and sectarians, may
sometimes have got themselves up like that (even
though many have imputed it to quackery, humbuggery,
and a desire to tyrannize over the minds of the crowd), I
should not go so far as to blame them, or to pass an unfavorable judgment on them. Each has his own sense to
guide him, and this is particularly true in alien, external,
and indifferent matters which in themselves are neither
good nor bad, inasmuch as they do not spring from our
hearts and minds, which are the factory of all good and

all evil: of good, if our hearts themselves are good and rule the affections with a pure intent; of evil, if, through injustice and malignity, the affections have become depraved. The only thing that displeases me is the novelty of the thing and the contempt you display for common custom."

"As for the color," replied Panurge, "it is *âpre aux pots, à propos;* it is my *bureau,* and I propose to hold on to it, for I'm going to attend a little more closely to business after this. Now that I'm once out of debt, you never saw a more unpleasant fellow than I'm going to be, so help me God. Look at these spectacles. To see me coming, you would say, straight off, that it was Friar Jean Bourgeois. I shouldn't be surprised if, next year, I'd be preaching another crusade. God keep my balls from harm.

"Do you see this stuff I'm wearing? You may believe me when I tell you that it possesses some occult property that most people don't know anything about. I only put it on this morning, but already I'm crazy, I'm up in the air, I'm burning up to be married, and to work like the devil on my wife, without having to be afraid of a clubbing. Oh, what a fine head of a house I'll make! After my death, they'll burn me on an honorific pyre, so that they can have the ashes as a memento and keepsake of the perfect husband. By God, I swear by this *bureau* of mine, my cashier's not going to play any tricks on me by putting tails on his *s's;* for if he does, my fists will fly in his face. Look at my before and behind, will you? It's in the form of a toga, the garment worn by the ancient Romans in time of peace. I got the cut from Trajan's Column at Rome, and from the Triumphal Arch of Septimius Severus. I'm tired of war, tired of a soldier's bobtailed coat; my shoulders are all worn out from carrying battle-harness. Arms cease and togas reign, at least for a year to come, by the Mosaic law—if I get married, as you explained to me yesterday.

"With regard to the breeches, my great aunt Laurence used to tell me that they were made for the codpiece. I believe it, by the same process of induction which led good old Galen, *lib. ix, On the Use of Our Members,* to say that the head was made for the eyes; for Nature might have put our heads on our knees or on our ribs; but having invented the eyes for the purpose of seeing at a distance, she fixed them in the head, as on a pole, in the highest part of the body; just as we observe tall towers and lighthouses erected over harbors, so that the lantern may be seen from a long way off.

"And since I should like to take a little breathing-spell, of a year at least, from the art of war—I mean to say, since I should like to get married—I no longer wear the codpiece, or, as a consequence, my breeches; for the codpiece is the man of war's most important piece of harness. And I maintain, and I'll go through hell-fire to prove it, that the Turks are not properly armed, seeing that the wearing of codpieces is forbidden by their laws."

"Had his right ear pierced in the Jewish fashion": earrings were popular in the sixteenth century, but it was the custom to wear a ring in one ear only; the "Jewish fashion" is an allusion to Exodus, xxi, 6, *and* Deuteronomy, xv, 17, *with regard to the piercing of the ears of slaves.* ——*"This latest prosopopoeia": impersonation or disguise.* ——*"Âpre aux pots, à propos": a play on* à propos *and "hard on the jugs."* ——*"It is my bureau": a play on the word, which means a coarse cloth and also a writing-table, commonly covered with such a cloth.* ——*"Friar Jean Bourgeois": popular Franciscan preacher who died at Lyon in 1494, known as "the Gray*

Friar with the spectacles (Cordelier aux lunettes)."
——"*Putting tails on his s's*": that is, turning his ss, for
sous, into ff, for *francs*. ——"*Arms cease and togas
reign*": the famous line of Cicero, "Cedant arma togae,"
etc., De Officiis, i, xxii, 77. ——"*The Mosaic law . . .
as you explained to me yesterday*": alluding to a preceding conversation (passage omitted here) on "Why
Newly-Weds Are Exempt from Going to War"; for the
Bible reference see Deuteronomy, xx, 5-7. ——"*My
great aunt Laurence*": possibly an allusion to "la bonne
Laurence" of the farce of Patelin. ——"*Good old
Galen*": Rabelais has the reference wrong; it should be to
Galen's De Usu Partium, viii, 5.

*Following a brief disquisition by Panurge on "How It
Is That the Codpiece Is the Most Important Piece of
Harness Armor for Warriors," the subject of his pro-
posed marriage is resumed.*

Panurge Seeks Advice from Pantagruel as to Whether or Not He Ought to Marry

PANTAGRUEL making no reply, Panurge went on, remarking, with a deep sigh:

"My lord, you have heard my decision, which is to
get married, if it's not my luck to find all the holes shut,
nailed, and padlocked. I beg you, by the affection you
have so long shown me, to give me your opinion."

"My opinion," responded Pantagruel, "since you have
already cast the dice and firmly made up your mind, is
that there is no further use in talking about it; the only
thing to do is to carry out your decision."

"That's very well and good," said Panurge, "but I
didn't want to do anything without your able advice."

"My advice," replied Pantagruel, "is to go ahead."

"But," said Panurge, "if it were your opinion that it was to my best interest to remain the way I am, without taking on anything new, then it would be better for me not to marry, at all."

"Then, don't get married," said Pantagruel.

"Well," said Panurge, "but would you have me, then, remain single all my life, without any conjugal companion? You know that it is written: *Vae soli*, Woe to him that is alone. The single man never enjoys that natural consolation which you find among married folks."

"Then, marry then, for God's sake," said Pantagruel.

"But," said Panurge, "if my wife should make a cuckold of me—for you know, this is a great year for them— that would be enough to make me fly off the hinges of my patience. I like cuckolds well enough; they impress me as being good fellows, and I like their company; but for the life of me, I should not care to be one of them. That's a little too prickly a point."

"Then make it a point," said Pantagruel, "not to get married. For the maxim of Seneca is true, without any exception: *That which you have done to another, be assured that another will do to you.*"

"Do you mean to say," inquired Panurge, "that rule is true without any exception whatsoever?"

"Without any exception whatsoever, so he says," replied Pantagruel.

"Ho, ho!" said Panurge, "then, devil take me, if he mustn't mean either in this world or in the world to come. Which is it?

"But look here. Seeing I can no more worry along without woman than a blind man can without a cane— for my old gimlet must be kept going, or else I can't go on living—wouldn't it be better for me to take some decent and modest woman as a wife than to keep on changing from one to another, from day to day, always with the danger of a good clubbing or of the old pox at the worst? For find I never could a woman that was any good—to me—begging their husbands' pardons."

"Pardon me, then, but get married, for God's sake," replied Pantagruel.

"But," said Panurge, "if it should be God's will for me to marry some good woman who would beat me, why then I'd have to be more than a mate for Job not to go stark staring mad; for they tell me that a lot of these good women have a mean mug on them, and so they always have good vinegar in the house. I'd go her one better in that case, and so pound and thwack her giblets, that is, her arms, legs, head, lungs, liver, and spleen, and so tear her clothes to tatters that the old Dickens himself would stand at his door and wait for her soul. No, I think I can very well do without all that fracas, for this year, anyway, and be very well satisfied to be out of it."

"Then stay out," said Pantagruel, "and don't get married."

"Well," said Panurge, "but being in the condition I'm in, out of debt and not married—note that I said 'out of debt,' plague take it; for if I were very much in debt, my creditors would be only too careful to look after my paternity—but being out of debt and not married, I haven't a soul in the world to watch out for me and to show me that love they call conjugal affection; and if by any chance I should fall ill, I'd only be treated the wrong way. The wise man says: *Where there is no woman* (and by that is meant a mother of a family, by legitimate marriage) *the sick man is out of luck,* and I see only too obvious an example in the popes, legates, cardinals, bishops, abbots, priors, priests, and monks. No, you'll never have me there."

"Then, halve yourself off, in God's name," replied Pantagruel.

"But," said Panurge, "supposing that, if I should happen to fall sick and become incapable of the duties of marriage, my wife, impatient of my lassitude, should abandon herself to another, and not only fail to aid me in my necessity, but even make sport of my calamity and, what is worse, rob me, as I have so often seen happen: all this would be enough to make me go out and hang myself or run around the fields in my shirt-tail."

"Then curtail," said Pantagruel, "your intention to get married."

"Well, but then," said Panurge, "I'd never have, otherwise, any legitimate sons or daughters, by means of whom I might hope to perpetuate my name and arms, and to whom I might leave my legacies and the property I shall have acquired. For I'm going to acquire plenty, one of these fine mornings, you need have no doubt of that; and what's more, I'm going to be a great little mortgage-lifter, so that I'll have a little something to enjoy in my old age, instead of going around like an old curmudgeon. I see an example, every day, in the relations between your own mild and kind father and yourself, as well as in those of all good folk, in the privacy of their own homes. But being out of debt, not being married, and being, as it happens, put out about the matter, it seems that all I get is a laugh from you in place of condolences."

"Then," said Pantagruel, "for God's sake, condole yourself by getting married."

For his form in this passage, with Pantagruel in his replies echoing Panurge's last words in each instance,

Maître François is probably indebted to one of Erasmus'
Colloquies, *entitled* Echo. *Similar scenes are to be found
in Poggio's* Facetiae *and in J. B. Gelli's* Capprici del
Bottaio, *published in 1546. On the side of content he
has likely been influenced by Tiraqueau, Bouchard, and
other writers who participated in the* Querelle des
femmes. *He may also have drawn on Jean Raulin's sermon on widowhood and other theological and juridical
writings, where the tone in dealing with this subject is
frequently one of levity.*

"Woe to him that is alone": Ecclesiastes, iv, 10; *compare* Genesis, ii, 18. ——*"The maxim of Seneca":*
Seneca's *ninety-fourth* Epistle, "ab alio expectes alteri
quod feceris." ——*"They always have good vinegar in
the house": there is still a saying in Poitou that "when
the vinegar is strong, it's a sign that the housewife has
a good head."* ——*"The sick man is out of luck": reference to* Ecclesiasticus *(in the Vulgate),* xxxvi, 27, "Ubi
non est mulier, ingemescit egens." ——*"A great little
mortgage-lifter": refers to paying off the encumbrance
on an inheritance.*

*Pantagruel thereupon explains to Panurge how dif-
ficult it is to advise anyone on the subject of marriage
and proceeds to expound, with a great show of classical
erudition, the manner in which such questions were
answered through the Homeric and Vergilian lots, warning him, meanwhile, that it was illicit to practice divination by means of dice. They then have recourse to the
works of Vergil, and the answer, as always, is that
Panurge is destined to be a cuckold. After this, they
turn to dreams; and in one of his finest chapters Rabelais sets forth what is, it may be, his own basic life-view.*

Pantagruel Advises Panurge to Try to Forecast the Happiness or Unhappiness of His Marriage through Dreams

"WELL, since we cannot agree on the meaning of the Vergilian lots, suppose we take another method of divination."

"What's that?" inquired Panurge.

"A very good method," said Pantagruel, "an old one and vouched for. It is by means of dreams. For in dreaming, under the conditions specified by Hippocrates, *Lib. peri Enypnion,* as well as by Plato, Plotinus, Iamblichus, Synesius, Aristotle, Xenophon, Galen, Plutarch, Artemidorus Daldianus, Herophilus, Q. Calaber, Theocritus, Pliny, Athenaeus, and others, the soul is sometimes able to foresee things to come. I take it, there is no need of my going into detail in order to establish the point to your satisfaction.

"You have an everyday example of the same thing when little children, well cleaned, fed, and taken care of, have fallen into a deep sleep, and you then see their nurses who are at liberty stealing away, free to do what they please for the time being, since their further presence at the cradle would seem to be unnecessary. In the same fashion, our soul, when the body is asleep, when the physical processes have been thoroughly accomplished, and when there is nothing more for it to do until the body wakes, seeks its recreation by revisiting its fatherland, which is heaven. There it is intimately initiated into its divine origin, and in the contemplation of that intimate and intellectual sphere, the center of which is to be found in every spot in the universe and the circumference nowhere—the circumference being, according to Hermes Trismegistus, God—at that mystic center, where nothing happens, nothing passes, nothing falls away, and all time is as the present—there, the soul not only notes those things that have come to pass down below, but also things that are to come; and she then reports these back to the body; and when, through the sensory organs of the latter, she reveals these things to friends, she is then said to be a soothsayer and a prophet. It is true, she does not report them in the same purity with which she saw them, and this because of the imperfection and fragility of the physical senses—just as the moon, receiving her light from the sun, does not communicate that light to us in a form as lucid, as pure, as lively, or as ardent as that in which she received it.

"What these vaticinations of sleepers need is an interpreter, who must be nimble, wise, industrious, expert, rational, and an absolute oneirocrite and oneiropolist, as the Greeks call them. That is what Heraclitus means when he says that nothing is revealed to us by dreams and nothing concealed, but that we are given simply, a significant indication of future things, either for our own good or ill, or for the good or ill of another. The Sacred Scriptures afford examples of this, and profane historians support it, providing us with a thousand cases in which things have turned out in accordance with dreams, the dreams of the individual concerned or those of another.

"The Atlantides, those who dwell in the Island of Thasos, one of the Cyclades, are deprived of this faculty, and in their country no one ever dreams. This was true of Cleon of Daulia, of Thrasymedes, and, in our own time, of the learned Frenchman, Villanovanus, all of whom never knew what it was to dream.

"And so tomorrow about the time that rosy-fingered Aurora is engaged in driving away the nocturnal shadows, set yourself to dreaming profoundly. But you must be careful to rid yourself of all human passions: of love, of hate, of hope, and of fear. For, just as Proteus, the great soothsayer of olden times, who was in the habit of transforming himself into fire, water, a tiger, a dragon, and other strange disguises, yet never attempted to predict the future until, of necessity, he had been restored to his own proper and native shape, so man cannot receive divinity nor the art of vatication, unless that part in him that is most divine—that is, the *Nous*, the *Mens*—is quiet, tranquil, and peaceable, and not occupied or distracted by alien passions and affections."

"I am willing," said Panurge, "but must I eat a lot, or just a little, for supper tonight? I have good reason for asking, for if I don't have a very good and a very big supper, I don't sleep a wink that night, and do nothing but doze, with dreams as hollow as my belly is empty."

"It would be better," replied Pantagruel, "not to eat any supper at all, considering your ordinary eating habits and after a glance at that embonpoint of yours. Amphiaraus, the ancient soothsayer, directed that those who were desirous of receiving his oracles in dreams should eat nothing that day, and drink no wine for three days before. We shan't make use of any diet so extreme and rigorous as all that. Nevertheless, I believe that the man who is a glutton and filled with food will encounter great difficulty in establishing any sort of contact with spiritual things. On the other hand, I am by no means of the opinion of those who hold that after periods of long and obstinate fasting they are better able to enter into the contemplation of celestial things.

"You remember well enough how Gargantua, my honored father, often used to remark to us that the writings of those fasting hermits were as insipid, jejune, and bad-tasting as their bodies were unpleasant at the time they composed those same writings, and that it was a difficult thing for the mind to remain serene and in good condition when the body was suffering from inanition, since philosophers and physicians assert that the animal spirits are born, rise, and grow through the arterial blood that is purified and refined to perfection in the Admirable Net, which lies under the ventricles of the brain. And he used to cite us the example of a philosopher who, seeking solitude and a place somewhere out of the crowd, in order the better to shape his thoughts and compose his lectures and writings, found all around him dogs barking, wolves howling, lions roaring, horses neighing, elephants trumpeting, serpents hissing, asses braying, grasshoppers shrilling, and turtledoves lamenting—that is to say, found himself in the midst of a greater uproar than if he had been at the fair of Fontenay or Niort. For hunger was in his body; and seeking a remedy against this, his stomach barked and his sight blurred, while his veins sucked the substance that belonged to his fleshy members, all this tending to pull down that vagabond mind that had neglectfully treated its own natural and nourishing host, which is the body—just as the bird resting on the falconer's fist and wishing to take flight is pulled back by the leash.

"And speaking of this, we have the word of Homer, father of all philosophy, who tells us that the Greeks only put an end to their weeping and mourning for Patroclus, Achilles' great friend, when hunger spoke up and their bellies began to protest, declining to furnish them with any more substance for tears, since bodies exhausted by long fasting are no longer able to shed tears or to weep.

"Observance of the golden mean is praiseworthy in

all things, and see to it that you observe it here. And so at supper you will eat no beans, no hare or other meat, no fish or polyps, no cabbage, and no other dishes that may disturb and obfuscate your animal spirits. For just as the mirror cannot give back the objective images exposed to and projected upon it, if its polish has been marred by the human breath or by fog, in the same manner the mind is unable to receive divinatory dream-images, if the body has been upset and disturbed by the smoke and vapor of dishes previously eaten. This is due to the indissoluble sympathy that exists between body and mind.

"What you shall eat is good Crustumine and bergamot pears, an apple of the pippin variety, a few Tours plums, and a few cherries from my orchard. And there is no reason for you to fear that, on this account, your dreams may become doubtful, fallacious, or suspect, as certain Peripatetics have declared is the case in Autumn, when, as is well known, human beings eat more plentifully of fruits than they do in any other season. The ancient prophets and poets attempt, mystically, to teach us this, when they say that vain and fallacious dreams lie hidden under leaves that have fallen to the ground, since it is in Autumn that the leaves fall from the trees. This is not true, for the reason that the natural pungency that abounds in fresh fruit is readily evaporated, by reason of its ebullient quality, into the animal parts, as we perceive to be true in the case of must, and hence, is very soon dissolved and absorbed.

"And, in addition, you may drink good clear water from my fountain."

"Those conditions," said Panurge, "are a trifle hard on me. But I am willing. Cost what it may. But I promise you that tomorrow morning I'm going to have an early breakfast—just as soon as I'm through with my little job of dreaming. Furthermore, I commend myself to Homer's two gates, to Morpheus, to Icelus, to Phantasus, and to Phobetor. If they help me out in a pinch, I'll erect a jolly little altar to them, all made out of the finest sheep's down. If I were in Laconia, in the temple of Ino, between Oetylus and Thalamae, she would help me out by giving me a fine sleep and pleasant dreams."

Then, he inquired of Pantagruel:

"Would it be all right, if I were to put a few laurel twigs under my pillow?"

"There's no need of that," replied Pantagruel. "That is a superstition, and that which Serapion Ascalonites, Antiphon, Philochorus, Artemon, and Fulgentius Planciades have written on the subject is all wrong. I would say the same concerning the left shoulder of the crocodile and the chameleon, begging the pardon of old Democritus. And the same of the Bactrian stone called *Eumetris*, as well as of the horn of Ammon, which is the name given by the Egyptians to a precious gold-colored stone, in the form of a ram's horn, like the horn of the Ammonian Jupiter; for they assert that the dreams of those who carry this stone will always be true and infallible—in short, divine oracles.

"It may be that this is what Homer and Vergil had in mind, when they wrote about the two gates of sleep, to which you have commended yourself. One of these gates is of ivory, and it is by this gate that confused, fallacious, and uncertain dreams enter, as they might through ivory, even the thinnest that you can imagine; it is impossible to see anything through this substance, for its density and opaqueness impede the penetration of visual spirits and the reception of visible species. The other gate is of horn, through which enter certain, true, and infallible dreams, since through horn, on account of its resplendent and diaphanous quality, all species are visible, with certainty and distinctness."

"You mean to imply, I judge," spoke up Friar John, "that the dreams of horned cuckolds, such as Panurge will be, God and his wife aiding him, are always true and infallible."

"Lib. peri enypnion": *book on dreams.* ——*Of the less well-known writers mentioned in the third paragraph above: Iamblichus was a fourth-century philosopher; Synesius was a Greek writer of the fourth century; the second-century Artemidorus Daldianus flourished under the Emperor Antoninus Pius and was the author of a* Treatise on Dreams and Chiromancy *that was printed by Aldus Manucus, in 1518; Herophilus was a fourth-century Greek physician; Quintus Calaber, poet of Smyrna, also lived in the fourth century; Athenaeus was a third-century Greek antiquarian.* ——*"According to Hermes Trismegistus": Hermes Trismegistus (literally, "thrice great") was the false Hermes, the Egyptian god Thoth confused with the Greek divinity and looked upon as the founder of Egyptian science, art, religion, magic, etc.; forty-two "hermetic" books were attributed to him, the principal one of which had been translated into French, giving rise to passionate discussions among the humanists; his essential concept was that "God is a sphere"; M. Clouzot believes that Rabelais has here borrowed from some commentator, possibly Symphorien Champier.* ——*"Oneirocrite and oneiropolist": the former is an interpreter of dreams, the latter one who prophecies from them.* ——*"What Heraclitus means":* Plutarch's treatise On the Pythian Oracle, xxi (404 E); *Rabelais gets it through the* Lectiones Antiquae *of Cae-*

lius Rhodiginus. ——*"The Atlantides": the inhabitants of Atlantis; see Pliny's* Natural History, v, 8. ——*"In their country no one ever dreams": on Cleon of Daulia, see Herodotus, iv, 184; on Thrasymedes, see Plutarch,* On the Failure of the Oracles, 50 (417 E); *"the learned Frenchman, Villanovanus," is Simon de Neufville, who died at Padua, in 1530.* ——*"Amphiarius, the ancient soothsayer": see Philostratus,* Life of Apollonius of Tyana, ii, 37. ——*"The Admirable Net": this has been referred to ("the Marvelous Net") in a preceding passage.* ——*"When hunger spoke up":* Iliad, xiii, 20, *and* xix, 155 f. ——*"Good Crustamine pears": coming from Crustumenia in the land of the Sabines and celebrated by Vergil, Pliny, and other writers.* ——*"From my orchard": this, with "my fountain" below, is seen by the Lefranc editors as an allusion to Thélème.* ——*"Homer's two gates":* Odyssey, xix, 562, *and* Aeneid, vi, 894. ——*"To Morpheus, To Icelus," etc.: Morpheus is the god of sleep, Phantasus the god of apparitions, while Icelus and Phobetor are names designating the divinity of fright, according to Ovid,* Metamorphoses, xi, v, 640. ——*"If I were in Laconia": borrowed from Pausanias, iii, 26.* ——*"A few laurel twigs under my pillow": Galen recommends this,* "ad somnum conciliandum." ——*"Serapion Ascalanites, Antiphon," etc.: these are all writers who wrote or touched on the interpretation of dreams.* ——*"Begging the pardon of old Democritus":* Pliny, Natural History, xxvii, xxix, *and Aulus Gellius,* Attic Nights, x, 12. ——*"The Bactrian stone called Eumetris": Pliny,* xxxvii, x; *placed under the head, it was supposed to give an oracular character to nocturnal visions.* ——*"Like the Ammonian Jupiter": Pliny,* xxxvii, lx.

Panurge's Dream and Its Interpretation

ABOUT seven o'clock the following morning, Panurge appeared before Pantagruel. In the room at the time were Epistemon, Friar John Hackem, Ponocrates, Eudemon, Carpalim, and others. To these, at sight of Panurge, Pantagruel remarked: "Behold, this dreamer cometh."

"That remark," said Epistemon, "in days gone by, cost the sons of Jacob dearly."

Then, Panurge spoke up:

"I have been at Billy Dreamer's house," he said, "and I've dreamed a-plenty, and a little bit more; but deuce take me, if I have the faintest idea what it's all about. All I know is that in my dream I had a wife who was young, charming, and perfectly lovely to look at, and that she treated me like a spoiled baby. Never was a fellow better off, or gladder of it, than I was. She flattered me, tickled me, groped me, patted my curls, kissed me, hugged me, and then, just in fun, proceeded to plant a couple of little horns, right above my forehead. Just to keep up the joke, I told her that she ought to put them underneath my eyes, so that I might be able to see better what I was ramming with them. For I didn't want Momus to find anything wrong with them, or anything that had to be corrected, as he did with the position of bulls' horns. The silly girl, in spite of my scoldings, kept on pushing them in; but it didn't hurt the least bit, which is a very strange thing, indeed. A short while afterward, it seemed to me that I was transformed, I don't know how, into a tambourine and she into a screechowl. At that point, my sleep was broken, and I awoke with a start, all worried, perplexed, and out of sorts. So, there you are. There's a fine kettle of dreams for you; fall to and enjoy 'em, and tell me what you make of 'em. Come on, Carpalim, let's go in to breakfast."

"I," said Pantagruel, "if I am possessed of any ability whatsoever in divination by dreams, make out from that, not that your wife is going to put a real pair of horns on your forehead—horns on the outside, those that you can see, and such as the satyrs wear—but that she is not going to keep faith with you nor show you conjugal loyalty, that she will abandon herself to another and make a cuckold of you. Artemidorus explains this, very clearly, just as I have told you. And so, too, you will not really be metamorphosed into a tambourine, but you shall be beaten by her, like a drum at a wedding; and she will not be turned into a screechowl, but she will rob you, in accordance with the habits of the screechowl. Your dreams, you may see, agree with the Vergilian lots: you shall be a cuckold, you shall be beaten, you shall be robbed."

At this point, Friar John bawled out:

"He's speaking the truth, by God. You're going to be a cuckold, my dear fellow, I can assure you of that; you're going to have a pretty pair of horns. Ha, ha, ha! Our Parson *De Cornibus*, God save him! Just preach a little now, and I'll go ahead and take up a collection among the audience."

"It's just the other way around," said Panurge. "My dream means that in my marriage I'm going to have lots of good things from the horn of plenty. You talk about satyr's horns. *Amen, amen, fiat, fiatur, ad differentiam Papae.* Which is something the Pope doesn't say in his bulls. In that case, I'll always have the old gimlet in good working order, like the satyrs, and it won't lie down on the job, which is a blessing that everybody longs for and very few get from heaven. As a result, I'll never be a cuckold, since the lack of that thing I've been talking about is the one cause without which not, the one reason why husbands become cuckolds. What makes poor devils beg? It's because they haven't anything at home to stuff in their wallets. What makes the wolf leave the timber? Lack of meat. What makes women rips? You get me, I think. I'll leave it to our friends, the parsons, the judges, the lawyers, and legal advisers, the solicitors and other glossarists of that venerable rubric, *de Frigidis et Maleficiatis.*

"You'll pardon me, if I get a little bit hot under the collar, but it seems to me that you're obviously all wrong when you interpret horns as cuckoldom. Diana wore them on her head, in the form of a pretty crescent; and was she a lady-cuckold for that reason? How the devil could she have been a cuckoldess, when she was never married? You'd better be careful what you say, and watch out she doesn't make you a pair, like the kind she made for Actæon. Our friend Bacchus, likewise, wore horns, as did Pan, Jupiter Ammon, and so many others. Are they all cuckolds? Would you make Juno out to be a whore? For that would follow, in accordance with the figure of rhetoric known as *metalepsis*—just as when you call a child in the presence of his father and mother a foundling or an adulterous offspring, you are politely implying that the father is a cuckold and his wife a chippy. Let's get this straight. The horns that my wife made for me are horns of plenty and filled with all good things, I give you my word for that.

"What's more, I'm going to be as happy as a drum at a wedding, always making a noise, always snorting, always buzzing and farting around. Believe me, this is my lucky day. My wife's going to be as charming and pretty as a nice little screechowl. And whoever aoesn't believe it, let him go from hell to the gallows, Merry Christmas."

"I am just making a note," said Pantagruel, "of the last things you said, in describing your dream, and comparing them with the first. At first, you were very much delighted; then, you awoke with a start, worried, perplexed, and out of sorts."

"Yes," said Panurge, "but that was because I hadn't had anything to eat."

"Everything is going on the rocks for you, I can foresee that. For you may rest assured that whenever you awake with a start, when sleep leaves you worried or in a bad humor, it either points to some misfortune already existing or foretells one to come. Points, I say, to some misfortune—that is, to some cacoëthetic malady, malign, infectious, occult, and latent in the body which, during the process of sleep—for sleep, according to medical theory, always increases the intensity of physical reactions—has begun to make itself known and to move toward the surface. As a result of this unpleasant action, rest is broken and the sleeper is admonished to be prepared to suffer and to provide against some evil to come. Just as we speak, proverbially, of 'teasing the hornets, stirring up the Camarine Marshes, or waking a sleeping cat.'

"And when I say 'foretells some evil to come,' I am referring to cases where the soul, through divination in sleep, gives us to understand that some misfortune is destined or preparing for us that soon will materialize and become evident. You have an example in the dream and frightful awakening of Hecuba, and in the dream of Eurydice, Orpheus' wife, both of whom, Ennius tells us, awakened with frightful starts. And afterward, Hecuba saw her husband Priam and her children slain and her fatherland wiped out; while Eurydice, a short while later, perished miserably. You have a case in Aeneas, dreaming that he is speaking to the dead Hector, and suddenly awakening with a start; and it was that very night that Troy was sacked and burned. Again, he dreamed that he saw his household gods, his penates; and after awakening in terror, he suffered the following day terrible buffetings on the sea. There was Turnus who, being urged on by a fantastic vision from the infernal regions to declare war on Aeneas, awoke with a start and a shock, only to be, after long tribulations, slain by that same Aeneas. There are thousands of other instances.

"And while I am speaking of Aeneas, note what Fabius Pictor has to say, to the effect that Aeneas never did or undertook anything, and that nothing ever happened to him, that he had not first known and foreseen in a dream. And there is good reason, in all these cases, for assuming that sleep and rest are a gift and special blessing from the gods, as the philosophers maintain and the poet bears witness, when he says:

> It was the time when sleep, gift of the skies,
> Bent over human, tired and grateful eyes.

"Such a gift, accordingly, cannot come to an end in shock and annoyance, without some great infelicity being foreshadowed. Otherwise, rest would not be rest, the gift a gift—not a gift coming from friendly gods, but, rather, one from inimical devils, just as the common saying is: *echthron adora dora*, the gifts of enemies are not gifts. It is the same thing as though the father of a family, seated at table with a hearty appetite, were to be seen suddenly rising in alarm at the beginning of the meal. Anyone who did not know the reason would have a right to be astonished. But what is the reason? He has heard his servants crying fire, his maids crying robber, his children crying murder; and so, leaving his meal untouched, he has had to run to their aid in order to set things to rights.

"And at this point, I recall what the Cabalists and Masoretes, the interpreters of the Sacred Scriptures, have to say, in explaining how one may, with discernment, test the veracity of angelic apparitions; since it sometimes happens that the Angel of Satan is transformed into the Angel of Light. They state that the difference between the two visitations lies in the fact that when the benign and consoling Angel appears to man, he begins by frightening his host and ends by comforting him, leaving him content and satisfied; whereas, the malign and seducing Angel begins by gladdening man, but ends by leaving him perturbed, annoyed, and perplexed."

"*That remark . . . cost the sons of Jacob dearly*": Genesis, xxxvii, 19-20: "*Behold this dreamer cometh. Come now, therefore, and let us slay him.*" ——"*At Billy Dreamer's house*": chez Guillot le songeur, *a proverbial expression.* ——"*Momus . . . as he did with the bull's horns*": *he wanted the horns placed under the eyes; Aristotle* (De Partibus Animalium, III, ii, 7) *and Lucian* (Nigrinus, 32) *have the anecdote; see also Erasmus,* Adages, I, v, 74. ——"*Artemidorus explains this*": *in his* Treatise on Dreams and Chiromancy, *previously mentioned, Book* II, *chapter xii.* ——"*Our Parson De Cornibus*": De Cornibus *is the Latin form of De Corne; Pierre Cornu, or De Corne, was a Parisian doctor of theology, contemporary of Rabelais.* ——"Amen, amen, fiat, fiatur, ad differentiam Papae": "*Amen, amen, so be it, so mout it be, just to be different from the Pope*" (fiatur *being a barbarism for* fiat, *the term employed by*

the Roman chancelleries). ——"De Frigidis et Maleficiatis": *on the sexually cold and those beset by evil
spells;* Decretals, Book IV, Title 15. ——"Like the kind
she made for Actaeon": *Actaeon was changed into a stag
by Diana.* ——"Figure of rhetoric known as metalepsis":
metalepsis *is a transposition.* ——"From hell to the
gallows, Merry Christmas": *garbled tag of an old Christmas carol.* ——"Camarine Marshes": *these have been
mentioned before.* ——"Both of whom, Ennius tells
us . . .": *Cicero,* De Divinatione, I, xx *and* xxi, *and
Vergil,* Aeneid, VII, 408-9. ——"You have a case in
Aeneas": *for this passage and following, see the* Aeneid,
Books II, III, *and* VII. ——"What Fabius Pictor has to
say": *Fabius Pictor is the most ancient of the Latin an-
nalists; see Cicero,* De Divinatione, I, xxi, 43. ——
"Sleep, gift of the skies": *these verses are from the*
Aeneid, II, 268-9.

Panurge's Excuse, with an Explanation of the Monastic Cabala in the Matter of Salt-Beef

"GOD help," said Panurge, "the fellow who sees well
enough, but who can't hear a word. I see you very well,
but I can't hear you at all, and haven't the faintest idea
what it is you're talking about. For a hungry belly has
no ears. I'm belling like a deer, for the reason that I'm
crazy with hunger. I've just done a most extraordinary
little job of work, and it would take more than Master
Fly himself to make me do another stretch of dreaming
like that. Eat no supper, what the Devil! A chancre take
me! Come on, Brother John, let's go in to breakfast.
Whenever I've had a good breakfast and my stomach has
had a good supply of hay and oats, then I can, in a
pinch or a case of necessity, pass up my dinner. But no

supper? Another chancre! That's all wrong. That's a crime against nature. Nature made the day so that we could work and exercise in it and each one attend to his business; and that we may be able to do this more conveniently, she furnishes us with a candle, that is to say, with the clear and cheerful light of the sun. Towards evening, she begins to take it away from us, as much as to tell us: Children, you've been very good today; you've worked enough; the night's coming on, and so now you ought to stop your labor and refresh yourselves with a little good bread, good wine, and good victuals; after which, you should take a little recreation, and then go to bed and rest, so that tomorrow you will be as fresh and sprightly as ever for your tasks.

"That is the way falconers do. When they have fed their birds, they do not fly them on a full crop but leave them to digest their food on the perch. The good pope who first started the custom of fasting understood this very well. He directed that one should fast up to the hour of nones, but that the balance of the day was to be left free for feeding. In olden times, very few had any dinner—only, you might say, the monks and canons; and they may well eat, seeing they have no other occupation—all days are holidays to them, and they diligently observe a well-known cloistral proverb: *De Missa ad Mensam*, from Mass to the mess-hall: the only thing for which they put off sitting down at table is the coming of the abbot, and they wait for that gentleman as monks usually do, by falling to and guzzling, every man for himself, without stopping to worry about the other fellow.

"But while this was true of dinner, everybody had supper—everybody, that is to say, except a few mopers —and that is how it is that supper comes to be called *cena,* meaning *common* to all. You know all that very well, Friar John. Come on, my friend, hell's bells, let's go. My stomach's barking like a dog from hunger. Suppose we throw a plate of soup into its jaws to appease it, as the Sibyl did with Cerberus. You like monastery soup, but I prefer hound-soup, with a few slices of the laborer, salted down with nine readings."

"I know what you mean," replied Friar John. "Your metaphor is from the *Cloistral Frying-Pan.* The laborer is the bull, who labors or has labored, and the nine readings mean cooked to perfection. For the good monastery fathers, in accordance with a certain cabalistic science of the ancients, not written down, but passed down from hand to hand, were in the habit, in my day, when they rose for matins, of indulging in certain noteworthy preambles before entering the church. They would first dung in the dungeries, piss in the pisseries, spit in the spitteries, cough in the cougheries, most melodiously, and then mope a little in the moperies, in order that nothing unclean might be carried into divine service. When they had done all these things, they would devoutly betake themselves to the holy chapel—for that, in their lingo, was the name given to the cloistral kitchen —and there they would pray devoutly that the beef might be put on the fire at once, for the breakfast of the religious, brothers in Our Lord. And they themselves would frequently light the fire under the pan.

"Now, there being nine readings at matins, it follows that, when they for this reason got up earlier in the morning, their appetite and their thirst multiplied and increased to the barkings of the parchment a good deal more than it did on those occasions when they merely yodeled through two or three readings for morning service. And so, according to that cabala which I have

mentioned, the earlier they rose the sooner the beef was
on the fire; the longer it took the better it was basted;
and the longer it did cook, the tenderer it tasted—so that
they did not have to use their teeth so much, their
palates were more delighted, their stomachs less burdened, and the good brothers better nourished. Which is
the sole end and first intent of the founders, in view of
the fact that they do not, by any manner of means, eat to
live: they live to eat, and their lives are all they have in
this world. Come on, Panurge, let's go."

"I'm with you," said Panurge. "I heard you, old hairy
balls, old cloistral and cabalistic balls. I've a little business
of my own to attend to. I'll cancel the principal, usury,
and interest; I'll be satisfied with the costs, considering
that you have given us so learned a dissertation on this
particular chapter of the culinary and monastic cabala.
Come on, Carpalim. Friar John, old pal, let's be going.
Good day, my good lords. I've done enough dreaming to
earn a little drinking. Let's go."

The word was not out of Panurge's mouth, before
Epistemon exclaimed:

"It is a very common thing among human beings to be
able to glimpse, foresee, recognize, and predict the misfortunes of another; but Oh, what a rare thing it is for a
human being to be able to predict, recognize, foresee,
and glimpse his own misfortune! How wisely does Aesop
put it in his *Fables*, when he tells us that every man is
born into this world with a knapsack around his neck,
in the front satchel of which are the faults and mishaps
of others, always exposed to our view, always readily
recognizable, while in the rear satchel are our own mishaps and faults, which we never see nor hear of, unless
we chance to be one of the few who are favored of
heaven!"

"Master Fly": Maistre Mouche (in Italian, Maestro Muccio) was proverbial for the mountebank type. ——— *"The good Pope who first started the custom of fasting": see Polydorus Virgilius, De Inventoribus Rerum, vi, 3.* ———*"Up to the hour of nones": the canonical ninth hour; three o'clock in the afternoon, sometimes earlier.* ——— *"As monks usually do": "to wait as monks do for the abbot" was a proverb.* ———*"As the Sibyl did with Cerberus": Aeneid, vi, 417-23.* ———*"I prefer hound-soup": souppes de levrier, that is, a hare.* ———*"From the Cloistral Frying-Pan": an imaginary work.* ———*"To the barkings of the parchment": reference to the sound made by the turning of the leaves of the holy books.*

Following his experience with dreaming, Panurge is urged by Pantagruel to consult a certain sibyl, the Sibyl of Panzoult (Panzoult, incidentally, is in the Chinon country). The cryptic response in doggerel is the to-be-expected one: to the effect that Panurge will be a cuckold; and he, as always, stoutly disputes the interpretation. Pantagruel then advises him to seek counsel from a dumb man, and so, he visits Goatnose (Nazdecabre) and is answered by him in gestures. Panurge and his master then go to see "an old French poet named Raminagrobis," whom Professor Lefranc identifies as Jean Le Maire de Belges, an anti-clerical writer of the time who exercised a major influence on Rabelais' work and who was noted for the boldness of his religious and political ideas. After presenting Panurge with a number of symbolic gifts and a set of very obscure-sounding verses, Raminagrobis dismisses his guests with the following remarks:

"Go my children, may the great God in heaven keep you, but do not trouble me further with this or any other business. I have this very day, which is the last of May and the last of me, driven out of my house, with much effort and difficulty, a lot of unclean, villainous, and pestilential beasts, black, striped, tawny, white, ash-colored, and thrush-spotted. For they were unwilling to let me die in peace, but with fraudulent prickings, harpy-like clawings, and waspish and insatiable importunities, kept calling me out of those calm thoughts which I was enjoying so very much, as I viewed and contemplated, and even touched and tasted, the blessings and the felicity which the good God has prepared for his faithful and his elect in that other life, the state of immortality. Keep out of their way, and do not be like them; and do not bother me any more, but leave me in peace and quiet, I beg of you."

Rabelais takes this opportunity to give us another veiled and satiric attack on the Mendicant Friars, toward whom he cherishes a special animosity. The following passage, together with Panurge's preceding dissertation on the salt-beef cabala, may be taken as Maître François' ironic bow to the monks, in this his Third Book, where he is in general concerned with other things—above all, with that most absorbing of all contemporary topics: the Woman Question.

Panurge Pleads in Favor of the Order of Mendicant Friars and Urges That They Go Back to Raminagrobis

As THEY left Raminagrobis' place, Panurge, thoroughly frightened, remarked:

"By God, but I believe he's a heretic; devil take me, if I don't. He slandered the good mendicant fathers, the Franciscans and the Jacobins, who are the two hemispheres of Christianity, by whose gyrognomonic circumbilivaginations, as by two celivagous filopendules, the whole antonomastic matagrabolism of the Roman

Church, whenever it finds itself emburelucocked with any jabberings of error or of heresy, homocentrically bestirs itself. But what, in the name of all hell, have those poor devils of Capuchins and Minims ever done to him? Aren't they bad enough off the way it is, the poor devils? Aren't they sufficiently smoked out and stunk up with misery and calamity, the poor fish-eating wretches? Is he, I ask you, Friar John, in a state of grace? He'll get his, by God. He'll be damned like a snake, to thirty-thousand basketfuls of devils. Slandering those good and valiant pillars of the church! Is that what you call poetic fury? If so, I don't want any of it for mine. He's a hardened old sinner; that's what he is. He blasphemes against religion. I'm highly scandalized, I can tell you that."

"I," said Friar John, "don't give a hang. They slander everybody else; if everybody slanders them, that's no concern of mine. Let's have a look and see what's here."

Panurge read through, attentively, what the old man had written.

"He's raving," he said, "the old toper. But I'll overlook it. That's because he's about done-for. Come on, let's compose his epitaph. From the answer he gave me, I'm every bit as wise as I was before. But listen here, Epistemon, old dear. Doesn't it seem to you that he's a trifle too cocksure in his answers? He's a crafty, quibbling, and clever sophist, by God. I'll bet, he's a Moorish renegade. Holy smoke, but he's careful enough not to go wrong in what he says! He only answers in disjunctives. He can't help telling the truth, for only one part of what he says has to be true for it to be the truth. Oh, what a rascally clown he is! St. Iago of Bressuire, are there any more like him left?"

"That," said Epistemon, "is exactly what Tiresias, the great soothsayer, used to state at the beginning of all his divinations. He quite frankly informed those who came to seek his advice: 'What I am about to say will come to pass, or it will not come to pass.' And that is the style of all prudent prognosticators."

"Yes," said Panurge, "but Juno scratched out both his eyes."

"Oh, that," said Epistemon, "was out of spite, for the reason that he had given a better answer than she on a knotty point raised by Jupiter."

"But," said Panurge, "what devil possesses this Master Raminagrobis that he should thus, without rhyme or reason, and with no excuse, start in slandering those holy fathers, the Jacobins, the Minors, and the Minims? I am, I assure you, vastly scandalized, and I can't keep still about it. He has sinned, grievously. His soul is headed straight for thirty-thousand hamperfuls of devils."

"I do not get you at all," replied Epistemon, "and you yourself scandalize me greatly, when you interpret as unfavorable to the Mendicant Friars what our friend, the poet, had to say about black, fawn-colored, and other-colored beasts. In my opinion, he was not indulging in any sophistical or fantastic allegory. He was speaking, purely and simply, of the fleas, bugs, mites, flies, gnats, and other such animals, some of which are black, some fawn-colored, some ash-colored, some tanned and tawny, and all of them importunate, tyrannic, and pestiferous, not only to the sick, but to healthy and vigorous persons, as well. It may be that he has ascarids, or tape-worms in his innards. It may be, as is a very common occurrence in Egypt and on the borders of the Erythrean Sea, that he is suffering, in his arms or legs, from the sting of those little speckled dragon-worms which the Arabs call *Meden*. By interpreting his words in any other fashion, you wrong both the good poet, through misrepresentation, and those same friars, through the implication that they are in wretched circumstances. One must always look on the best side of everything in dealing with one's neighbor."

"So, you'd teach me to know flies in milk, would you!" cried Panurge. "I swear to God, he's a heretic. And what I mean is, a full-fledged heretic, a mangy heretic, a heretic every bit as burnable as a jolly little steeple-clock. His soul is going straight to thirty-thousand cart-loads of devils. Do you know where he's headed for? God damn me, old top, if it isn't straight for Proserpina's toilet-stool—straight for that infernal basin where she empties the fecal results of her enemas—you know where, to the left of the big kettle, about six yards from Lucifer's claws, on the way to the Demiurge's big black room. What, ho, the villain!"

"Let's go back," continued Panurge, "and talk to him about salvation. Let's go, in the name of God. That would be the charitable thing to do on our part. If he must lose his body and his life, don't let him damn his soul at the same time. We'll bring him to repentance for his sin, and make him beg the pardon of those same holy fathers, absent as well as present; and we'll take a deposition of the fact, so that, after his death, they will not be able to declare him a heretic and damned, as the goblins did with the provost's wife at Orléans. We'll make him give them satisfaction for the insult, by order-ing plenty of handouts, plenty of masses, and plenty of obituaries and anniversaries for all the good conventual fathers throughout this province. We'll make him see to it that, on the anniversary of his death, they shall always have a quintuple pittance, so that the big leather-boy, filled with the best, may trot the rounds of all the tables —those of the rough-serge lads, the lay brothers and the heavy-feeders, as well as those of the priests and parsons—those of the novices as well as those of the professed friars. In this way, it may be, he can prevail upon God to forgive him.

"But whoa, there! I'm all wrong. I don't know what I'm saying! The devil take me, if I'm going back there! Holy Christ! that room is full of devils. I can hear them already, tousling and beating hell out of one another, to see who'll be the first to suck up the raminagrobidic soul and carry it, jug-to-mouth-wise, to Master Lucifer. Better stay away from there. I'm not going. The devil take me, if I'm going! Who knows but they may employ a little *qui pro quo* and, in place of Raminagrobis, grab poor Panurge, now that he's just out of debt? They've failed many times when he was head over heels and bankrupt. Stay away from there. I'm not going, I tell you. I'm scared to death, by God. What, go among a lot of hungry devils! Among a lot of quarrelsome devils! Among a lot of business-like devils! Stay away. I'll bet you that there won't be a single Jacobin, Franciscan, Carmelite, Capuchin, Theatine, or Minim at his funeral. And they're wise! For he hasn't left them a solitary thing in his will. The devil take me if I'm going back there.

"If he's damned, let him be damned. Why did he want to go and slander the good convent fathers? Why did he chase them out of his room, at the very minute when he had most need of their assistance, of their devout prayers and holy admonitions? Why didn't he leave, in his will, at least a few handouts, a few pickings, a few belly-furnishings for those poor fellows who have nothing in this world but their lives? Let any one who wants to, go back there; the devil take me, if I'm going! And if I went, the devil *would* take me. Chancres! Stay away from there."

"Jacobins": the Dominicans, whose principal convent in Paris was in the Rue Saint-Jacques. ——"By whose gyrognomonic circumbilivaginations," etc.: one commentator (Moland) "translates" this passage as follows: "By the circular turning of which, as by two celestial counterweights, the whole allegoric mechanism of the Roman Church, when it finds itself unpleasantly tormented by error or heresy, rights itself around the same center."
——"He only answers in disjunctives": term from logic for such a proposition as: It is either day or night. —— "St. Iago of Bressuire": allusion to St. James; Bressuire is in the Vendée, and like many other towns, had an almonry that bore the name of this saint. ——"His soul is headed," etc.: here, as in two passages below where the soul is mentioned, the first edition in place of âme, soul, has asne, ass, a pun that might be freely rendered by "ars-oul"; this got the author into trouble, and in one of his letters he disclaims responsibility for the pleasantry. ——"Erythrean Sea": the Red Sea. —— "Those little speckled dragonworms": the allusion is to threadworms (pinworms), scientifically known as Filaria (Dracunculus) medinensis Velsch.; Rabelais' "Meden" is for the French Médine, Medina. ——"As burnable as a . . . steeple-clock": allusion to a death-sentence pronounced against one of the first Huguenots at La Rochelle, a clock-maker by trade, an admirable specimen of whose workmanship in the form of a large wooden clock was ordered burned by the executioner because it had been made by a heretic. ——"The Demiurge's big black room": with the Greeks, this was the spirit that inhabited the bowels of the earth, with Chaos and Eternity as companions. ——"As the goblins did with the provost's wife at Orléans": according to the story, Louise de Mareau, wife of François de Saint-Mesmin,

Provost of Orléans, upon her death was interred in the church of the Franciscans, whereupon the religious imitated goblins and pretended that the soul of the deceased was haunting their monastery; their trickery was discovered and they were severely punished. ——— "Qui pro quo": *substitution of one for another.*

Epistemon then undertakes to advise Panurge and gives the latter a learned lecture on oracles, but reaches the discouraging conclusion that, since the advent of Christ, all the oracles have become "as dumb as fishes," and even if there were any left, he is doubtful as to the propriety of consulting them. There follows a passage in which the author gives us, in a single chapter, a résumé of the magical practices and superstitions of an age—the late Middle Ages and the early Renaissance— as summed up in the art of Herr Trippa, who is, without a doubt, the real-life Cornelius Agrippa. Agrippa (1486-1535) was a German-born cabalistic philosopher and professor of magic, author of a well-known work entitled De Incertitudine et Vanitate Scientiarum (On the Uncertainty and Vanity of the Sciences). *He was also the most enthusiastic of all the panegyrists of the feminine sex; his treatise,* De Nobilitate et Praecellentia Feminei Sexus *has been previously mentioned.*

Panurge Goes to Herr Trippa for Advice

"But look here," continued Epistemon, "I'll tell you what we might do, before we go back to our King, if you want my advice. Near l'Ile-Bouchard, there lives one Herr Trippa. You know how, through the arts of astrology, geomancy, chiromancy, metopomancy, and others of the same grist, he predicts all things to come. Suppose we go consult with him regarding this business of yours."

"I know nothing about all that," said Panurge. "But I do know very well that one day, while he was engaged in conversation with the great King, concerning celestial and transcendental things, the court flunkies behind the stair-doors tumbled his wife to a fare-you-well, for she was not a bad-looking wench. And he, who was able to see all things, ethereal and terrestrial, without spectacles and to talk about all things past, present, and to come, was not able to see one thing, and that was his own wife ringing the joy-bells; and for that matter, he never did get the news. All right, let's go see him, since you're in favor of it. A fellow can never learn too much."

The next day, they arrived at Herr Trippa's house, and Panurge after making their host a present of a wolf's-skin robe, a big bastard-sword, well gilded and with a velvet scabbard, and fifty nice little "angels," at once entered upon an intimate discussion of his personal affairs.

Herr Trippa immediately looked him in the face and said: "You have the metoposcope and the physiognomy of a cuckold. And what I mean is a scandalous and disgraced cuckold."

Then, inspecting Panurge's right hand very thoroughly, he added: "This false line that I see here, just above the *mons Jovis,* was never in the hand of anybody but a cuckold."

Then, with a pen he hastily made a number of points, and joining them by geomancy, said:

"Truth itself is not more true than that you are going to be a cuckold, and that very soon after you are married."

He then asked Panurge for his horoscope. When Panurge had handed it to him, Trippa at once began manufacturing his heavenly house, in all its parts; following which, after having considered the positions and aspects in their triplicities, he gave a deep sigh and remarked:

"I have already told you, very plainly, that you are going to be a cuckold; you cannot fail to be. And here, I have plenty of fresh proof. I assure you, once more, that you are going to be a cuckold. What's more, you will be beaten by your wife, as well as robbed by her, for I find the seventh house in an aspect altogether malign, and under the unfavorable influence of all the horn-bearing signs such as Aries, Taurus, Capricorn, etc. In the fourth, I find a decadence of the *Jovis*, along with a tetragonal aspect of Saturn in conjunction with Mercury. You're going to be peppered properly, my good man."

"A plague on you," replied Panurge, "you old fool, you stupid, silly joker, you. When all the cuckolds hold a meeting, you'll be carrying the banner in the procession. But where do I get this ringworm here, between my two fingers?"

Saying this, he stuck his first two fingers straight out towards Herr Trippa; they were spread out in the form of a pair of horns, the other fingers being closed into his palm. As he did so, he said to Epistemon:

"You see before you the true Olus of Martial, who devoted all his time to studying, observing, and reflecting upon the woes of others, while his wife was keeping a bawdy house at home. And he, for his part, poorer than Irus but still a swaggerer, more overbearing and unendurable than seventeen devils—in a word, a *ptochalazon*, a pompous beggar, as the ancients very appropriately termed the whole tribe of scoundrels like him. Come on, let's leave this crazy fool; he ought to be in a madhouse. Let's leave him to rave his belly full with his own private devils. I imagine the devils would love waiting on a bastard like that. He doesn't know the first principle of philosophy, which is: KNOW THYSELF, and while he's strutting around, just because he's found a wisp in some one else's eye, he fails to see a good-sized log that's poking his own eyes out. He's exactly such a *polypragmon*, a busybody, as Plutarch describes. He's another Lamia, who, in strange houses, in public, and in the presence of the common people, has more penetrating eyesight than a lynx, but in her own house is blind as a mole. She couldn't have seen anything at home, for when she returned there she was in the habit of taking her removable eyes from her head, like a pair of spectacles, and hiding them in a shoe hung up behind the door of her dwelling."

At these words, Herr Trippa picked up a tamarind-bough:

"He's right," said Epistemon. "Nicander calls that bough the divining-branch."

"Should you like," inquired Herr Trippa, "to know the truth more fully, through pyromancy, through aeromancy, described by Aristophanes in his *Clouds,* through hydromancy, or through lecanomancy, a method so renowned among the Assyrians and approved by Hermolaus Barbarus? In a basin full of water, I'll show you your future wife, ringing the joy-bells with a couple of rustics."

"When you stick your nose up my arse," remarked Panurge, "don't forget to remove your spectacles."

"By catoptromancy," continued Herr Trippa, "by which method Didius Julianus, Emperor of Rome, foresaw all that was bound to happen to him? You won't need any glasses for that. You'll see her, in a mirror, throwing up her rump as plainly as if I were to show her to you in the fountain of the temple of Minerva near

Patrae. By coscinomancy, formerly so religiously practised by the Romans, as a part of their ritual? Let's have
a sieve and a pair of nippers, and you'll see devils. By
alphitomancy, mentioned by Theocritus, in his *Phar-
maceutria*? Or by aleuromancy, which consists in mixing
cheese with flour? By astragalomancy? I've got the implements all ready. By tyromancy? I have here a very
suitable Brehemont cheese. By gyromancy? I'll make
you turn a number of circles here, and I assure you, they
will all fall on the left side. By sternomancy? My word,
but you have a badly proportioned chest. By libano-
mancy? All you need is a little incense. By gastromancy?
It is a method which for a long time was employed in
Ferrara by the lady Jacoba Rhodigina, an engastrimyth.
By cephalonomancy, a method which the Germans were
in the habit of employing and which consists in
roasting an ass' head on glowing coals? By ceromancy?
As the wax melts in the water, you will see your wife and
her drummer-boys going to it. By capnomancy? On the
glowing coals, we will place the seed of the poppy and
the sesame. Oh, but that's a lovely method! By axinomancy? All you have to do is to provide yourself with an
ax and a Gages-stone, or piece of jet, which we will place
upon the embers. Oh, what a splendid use Homer made
of this method in the case of Penelope's suitors! By
onymancy? Let's take some oil and a little wax. By
tephramancy? You will see ashes in the air, showing you
your wife in a pretty pickle. By botanomancy? I have
some sage-leaves here, all ready. By sycomancy? Oh,
divine art! Here are the fig-leaves. By ichthyomancy?
This method was praised and practised by Tiresias and
Polydamas, just as it likewise formerly was in the ditch
of Dina, in the grove sacred to Apollo, in the land of
the Lycians. By chœromancy? Let's take plenty of pigs;
you shall have the bladder. By cleromancy? The same

way they find the bean in the cake on Epiphany Eve. By anthropomancy? Heliogabalus, Emperor of Rome, made use of this method. It is a trifle annoying, but you won't mind that, seeing you're a predestined cuckold. By sibylline stichomancy? By onomatomancy? By the way, what is your name?"

"Chewshit," replied Panurge.

"Or by alectryomancy? I will draw a neat little circle here, which I will divide, with you looking on, into twenty-four equal portions. On each, I will draw a letter of the alphabet. On each letter, I will place a grain of cheese. Then, I will let a handsome virgin rooster walk across the circle. You will see, he'll eat the grains on the letters

C. U. C. K. O. L. D.   T. O.   B. E.

as fatidically as in the case of the Emperor Valentinian. When the latter was anxious to know the name of his successor, the soothsaying and alectryomantic rooster ate the grains upon the letters T. H. E. O. D., which stood for Theodosius.

"Should you like some information through the art of haruspicy, through the extispicine art, through auguries based upon the flight or upon the song of birds, or upon the solistime dance of ducks?"

"I'll take the turdspicine art," replied Panurge.

"Or, perhaps, by necromancy? I will resurrect for you at once some one who has just died, as Apollonius of Tyana did with Achilles, as the pythoness did in the presence of Saul; and this person will tell us all, as when, upon the invocation of Erichtho, one thus revived predicted to Pompey the entire progress and outcome of the battle of Pharsalia. Or if you're afraid of the dead, as all cuckolds naturally are, I'll use only sciomancy."

"Go to the devil, you crazy fool," replied Panurge,

"and have yourself buggered by some Albanian, if you happen to fancy a pointed hat. Why the devil don't you just as well advise me to hold an emerald or a hyena-stone under my tongue? Or to provide myself with pee-wits' tongues or green-frogs' hearts? Or to eat the heart and liver of a dragon, so that, by the song of swans and other birds, I might be able to make out my destiny, as the Arabians used to do, in the land of Mesopotamia? Thirty devils take this cuckold, cornuto, infidel, and sorcerer; to the devil with this Anti-Christ of an enchanter!

"Let's go back to our King. I'm sure he's not going to like it very well, once he hears that we've come here, into the den of this petticoated devil. I repent having come, and would gladly give a hundred nobles and fourteen commoners, provided only the chap who used to whistle in the bottom of my breeches would at once illuminate this guy's mustaches with his spit. Good God! how he's stunk me up with his nasty fooleries and his devilments, with his sorceries and his spells! Let the devil take him! Say *Amen*, and let's go have a drink. I shan't be myself again for two—no, not for four whole days."

"Near *L'Ile-Bouchard*": in the Chinon region. ——— "Metopomancy": divination by means of the lines in the forehead. ———"A big bastard-sword": one with a long, rigid, keen-cutting blade, used by archers. ——— "Fifty nice little angels": the "angel" was a coin with the figure of St. Michael; the name was also applied to a coin worth about eight francs in gold, current during the reign of Charles VI and Charles VII. ———"Metopos-cope": a reading of the forehead. ———"Just above the mons Jovis": the mons Jovis is the small elevation or prominence at the base of the index-finger of the right hand. ——"*You'll be carrying the banner in the procession*": this is the tag of an old song about the gathering of the cuckolds. ——"*The true Olus of Martial*": Martial, Epigrams, vii, 10. ——"*Poorer than Irus*": a beggar mentioned in the Odyssey, xviii, 1-116. ——"*In a word, a ptochalazon*": the word occurs in Athenaeus, and Erasmus picks it up in his Adages. ——"KNOW THYSELF": the gnothi seauton (nosce te ipsum) of the ancients, the words that Socrates loved to repeat; they were engraved on the pediment of the temple at Delphi. —— "*Polypragmon, as Plutarch describes*": see Plutarch, Peri Polypragmasynes, ii, 516 A; the anecdote of Lamia will be found there. ——"*Nicander calls that bough the divining-branch*": the Greek physician Nicander was the author of two verse treatises in which a number of medicinal plants are mentioned; the work was first printed at Venice, in 1499. ——"*Through pyromancy*," etc.: pyromancy is divination by fire; aeromancy, by air; hydromancy, by water; lecanomancy, through the reflection of an image in a basin filled with water. ——"*By coscinomancy*": divination by means of a sieve (Greek koskinon). ——"*Alphitomancy*": divination by means of barley-flour. ——"*Astragalomancy*": divination through the casting of knuckle-bones, or dice. ——"*Tyromancy*": another form of divination with cheese. ——"*Sternomancy*": divination through observing the human chest. ——"*Jacoba Rhodigina, an engastrimyth*": an engastrimyth is a ventriloquist; the story of Jacoba Rhodigina is told in Book Fourth; Rabelais is again drawing on the Antiquae Lectiones of Caelius Rhodiginus ——"*Capnomancy*": divination by smoke. ——"*Axinomancy . . . a Gages-stone*": the Gages-stone (so called from the Gages River in Lycia) is jet, and axinomancy consists in placing the jet on a hot ax; if it is not consumed, the consulting party gets his wish. ——"*Onymancy*": divination by means of the fingernail (Greek onyx) smeared with wax or oil. ——"Ichthyomancy": divination with fish. ——"Cleromancy": divination by lots. ——"Anthropomancy": divination through inspection of the human intestines; this explains Herr Trippa's remark to Panurge. ——"Sibylline stichomancy": divination through sibylline verses. ——"Onomatomancy": divination by names. ——"Alectryomancy": divination with cocks. ——"The extipiscine art": divination through entrails. ——"The solistime dance of ducks": Rabelais' bal solistime is a jocular rendering of the tripudium solistimum of the Romans, as explained by Cicero, De Divinatione, ii, 34; the term was applied by the ancients to sacred birds that in eating let fall a few grains that struck the ground (solum), this being looked upon as a favorable augury. ——"As Apollonius of Tyana did with Achilles": the philosopher was supposed to have brought a young woman back to life; see Philostratus, Life of Apollonius of Tyana, iv, 16. ——"As the pythoness did in the presence of Saul": the story of Saul and the woman of Endor, First Samuel, xxviii, 7-14. ——"Upon the invocation of Erichtho": Erichtho was a magician of Thessaly. ——"By some Albanian, if you happen to fancy a pointed hat": the headgear of the Albanians, mercenaries in the service of France, was a conical bonnet. ——"In the land of Mesopotamia": this is from Philostratus, Life of Apollonius of Tyana, i, 20. ——"This petticoated devil": that is, in a doctor's gown. ——"A hundred nobles and fourteen commoners": a play on the coins known as nobles à la rose.

Panurge next turns to Friar John Hackem, and as might be expected, the advice he receives from the monk is of a hilarious and bawdy kind. In the course of their conversation each addresses the other with 166 different *epithets applied to the male organ of generation. Incidentally, it may be noted that in this passage Rabelais draws upon a well-known preacher of the time, Jean Raulin, and this cleric's famous "Sermon on Widowhood"* (Sermo de Viduitate), *included in the same author's* Heavenly Journey (Itinerarium Paradisi), *which was printed at Paris, in 1524. The friar ends by offering Panurge a bit of consolation on his predestined state.*

Friar John Consoles Panurge on the Question of Cuckoldom

"I UNDERSTAND what you mean," said Friar John, "but time lays all things low. There is no bit of marble or porphyry that does not have its old age and its period of decline. You may be all there now; but a few years from now I think I can hear you confiding to me that they're hanging a little too low, from want of a jockstrap. I can already see your hair getting grisly on top. Your beard, with its gray, white, tan, and black sectors looks to me like a map of the world. Look here! There's Asia. There are the Tigris and the Euphrates. There is Africa. There are the Mountains of the Moon. Can you see the swamp of the Nile? Over there, on the other side, is Europe. Do you see Thélème? That tuft there, all white —those are the Hyporborean Mountains. By my thirst, oldtimer, when the snows are on the mountain-tops— I mean, the head and the chin—there's not a whole lot of heat left down in Codpiece Valley."

"You've got chilblains," replied Panurge. "You don't know what you're talking about. When the snow is on the mountains, that means that thunder, lightning, cyclones, plagues, and all the devils in hell are in the valley down below. Do you want to prove it? Take a trip into Switzerland and look at Lake Wunderberlich, four leagues from Berne, in the direction of Sion. You throw my grisling hair up to me, and you don't stop to think that it is the nature of leeks to have a white head and a tail that's straight, green, and vigorous.

"It's true, I do recognize in myself certain signs that would seem to point to old age—I mean a green old age, of course. Don't say a word about it to any one. It's merely that I find the wine a little better and a little tastier than I used to, while I dread falling in with bad wine worse than I ever did. All this indicates, you may observe, that something or other is setting; it means that the heyday is past. But what of it? You've always been a good fellow, I like you as much or better than I ever did; and I tell you, that's not what I'm afraid of, hell's fire, no; that's not what worries me. I'm afraid that, during some prolonged absence of Pantagruel, our King—for I should have to go with him, if he went straight to hell— my wife will make a cuckold of me. And there, you have it. For everybody I've talked to about it has threatened me with that fate, and has told me that I was pre-destined to it by the will of heaven."

"It's not every one," replied Friar John, "who can be a cuckold. If you're a cuckold, *ergo,* your wife will be beautiful; *ergo,* she'll treat you nice; *ergo,* you'll have plenty of friends; *ergo,* you're safe. These are monkish Maxims. You'll be all the better off, my sinner-friend; you'll be better off than you ever were in your life before; you'll have less to worry about than you ever had; and you'll get along better and better, every day in every way. If that's your fate, would you go against it? Seeing that you are predestined to it, would you set the planets back in their courses, throw all the celestial spheres out of gear, cause the motivating Intelligences to go astray, and blunt the spindles, put a kink in the wheels, slander the bobbins, cast a reproach on the reels, condemn the skeins, and unravel the yarn of the Parcae? Why, plague take it, you little prick! You'd do worse than the Giants did. Come out of it, you big prick, you. Which would you rather be, jealous without cause or a cuckold without consciousness?"

"I shouldn't fancy," replied Panurge, "being either one or the other. But once give me warning, and I'll see that everything's all right, or else all clubs will fail in this world. My word, Friar John, the best thing for me to do would be not to get married. Listen to what the bells are saying this very minute: *Marry not, marry not, Not, not, not, not, If you marry, marry not, marry not, Not, not, not, not, You'll repent, pent, pent, A cuckold you will be.* By the wrath of God! I'm beginning to get angry. You cowled heads, you, haven't you any remedy to offer? Has Nature rendered human beings so destitute that a married man cannot go through this world without falling into the dangers and the pitfalls of cuckoldom?"

"I'd like," said Friar John, "to show you a way to keep your wife from ever being able to make a cuckold out of you without your knowledge and consent."

"Go ahead," said Panurge; "go ahead, old hairy prick; tell me what it is, old top."

"All you have to do," said Friar John, "is to put on Hans Carvel's ring. Now this Hans Carvel, grand lapidary to the King of Melinda, was a learned man, able, studious, worthy, gifted with good sense and judgment, mild, charitable and philanthropic, philosophic, and, moreover, a good companion and a jolly all-around fellow, if ever there was one; but a trifle big in the belly, a wee bit shaky in the head, and not altogether as fit as might be in the matter of physique. In his old days, he had married the daughter of the Bailiff Concordat. She was young, pretty, frisky, gay, up-and-coming, and a little overly gracious toward her neighbors and her servants.

"And so, it came about that, after a few weeks had elapsed, he became jealous as a tiger, and began to suspect that she was having her buttocks drummed somewhere else. To forestall any such contingency, he proceeded to fill her full of nice little stories about the desolations wrought by adultery, frequently reading her the *Legend of Virtuous Wives*, preaching modesty to her, and uttering enough praises of conjugal fidelity to fill a book. At the same time, he endeavored to instill into her a strong and unwavering hatred of the wicked conduct of married hussies; and to top it all, he made her a present of a lovely carcanet, all covered with oriental sapphires.

"Notwithstanding all this, he observed her deliberately carrying on in such a manner with the neighbors that his jealousy increased more and more. One night, having gone to bed with her in a passion, he dreamed that he was talking to the devil and retailing his grievances. The devil comforted him and placed a ring on his master finger, saying:

" 'I make you a present of this ring. So long as you keep it on your finger, your wife will not have carnal relations with another without your knowledge and consent.'

" 'Many thanks, Mr. Devil,' said Hans Carvel. 'May I deny Mohammed, if I ever take it off my finger.'

"The devil disappeared, and Hans Carvel, glad as could be, awoke, to find that he had his finger in the what-you-may-call-it of his wife.—I almost forgot to tell you how his wife, when she felt it, fell back on her rump, and said: 'Here, here, that's not the thing you want to put there.' And then, it seemed to Hans Carvel that someone was trying to rob him of his ring. Now, isn't

that an infallible remedy? If you want to take my advice, follow his example, and see that you constantly
wear your wife's ring on your finger."

With this, they reached the end of their talk and the
end of the road.

*The Hans Carvel story is far from being original with
Rabelais. It will be found as the eleventh tale in the* Cent
Nouvelles Nouvelles. *Its literary source would appear to
have been the* Facetiae *of the Italian writer, Poggio.
Ariosto makes use of it at the end of his fifth satire. The
tale forms part of a collection of* Plaisantes Nouvelles
*published at Lyon in 1555. Celio Malespini later em-
ployed it in his* Ducento Novelle, *Venice, 1609; and La
Fontaine, in 1665, put the story into verse. There is yet
another rendering in Anacreontic Latin, and Prior has
made use of it in English.*

*"Switzerland . . . Lake Wunderberlich": Rabelais
writes "Vunderberlich"; there is no Swiss lake by this
name. ——"You'll do worse than the Giants did": allusion to their fabled assault on Olympus. ——"The Bailiff
Concordat": possibly a jocular personification, or possibly someone in those legal circles that were frequented
by the author. ——"Legend of Virtuous Women": there
was a whole moral literature of this sort in the Middle
Ages.*

*Panurge being still "up in the air" as to whether or
not he should marry, Pantagruel decides to summon a
theologian, a physician, a philosopher, and a man of law
to help settle the question. Accordingly, they first consult the theologian Hippothadeus, who is identified by
Professor Lefranc as Lefèvre d'Etaples, one of the
French leaders of the Reformation. Hippothadeus' advice*

is such as might be expected from one of his calling and lays stress on the moral aspect of marriage, the necessity of care in the selection of a proper mate, and the example which a husband should set his wife. It is then Dr. Rondibilis' turn. He has commonly been thought to be Guillaume Rondellet, who had studied medicine with Maître François at Montpellier, but some are convinced that he is none other than Rabelais himself—Rabelais, the physician.

Rondibilis, the Physician, Advises Panurge

PANURGE, continuing his remarks, then said:

"The first word that the one who deballed the drab-backed monks at Saussignac had to say, after he had finished with deballing Friar Hotear, was: 'And now, for the rest.' And I, likewise, say: 'Now for the rest.' Come on, Dr. Rondibilis, Sir, and help me out. Should I marry or should I not?"

"By my ambling mule," replied Rondibilis, "I don't know just what answer I ought to give to that question. You say that you feel within you the poignant prickings of sensuality. Now, I find in our science of medicine—and we've taken it from the ancient Platonicians—that carnal concupiscence may be bridled by five different means. By wine—"

"I believe you," said Friar John. "When I'm drunk, all I want to do is sleep."

"I mean, of course," said Rondibilis, "wine taken intemperately, for by intemperance in wine there comes to the human body a certain cooling-off of the blood, a certain letting-down of the nerves, a certain scattering of the generative semen, a certain stuffiness of the senses, and a certain misfire in physical movements, all of which are unfavorable to the act of generation. As a case in point you see Bacchus, the god of drunkards, commonly painted without his beard and in the costume of a woman, as though he were utterly effeminate, like a deballed eunuch.

"But it is different, when wine is taken temperately. The ancient proverb teaches us as much when it tells us that Venus catches cold without the company of Ceres and of Bacchus. And it was the opinion of the ancients, according to Diodorus Siculus, and especially of the Lampsacians, as Pausanias informs us, that Master Priapus was the son of Bacchus and of Venus.

"In the second place, there are certain drugs and plants that render a man chilled, bewitched, and impotent for the act of generation. There are, for example, the *nymphaea heraclia,* or pond-lily, the Amerine willow, hempseed, the periclymenos or honeysuckle, the tamarind, the vitex or chaste-tree, the mandragora, the hemlock, the smaller orchid, hippopotamus-skin, and other drugs that, when taken into the human body, by virtue of their elementary and specific properties, freeze and mortify the prolific germ, dissipate those spirits the duty of which is to conduct that germ to the places destined for it by nature, or else they obstruct the passageways and conduits by which the germ is expelled. Just as, on the other hand, we have certain ones that heat, excite, and accoutre a man for the venereal act——"

"I have no need of those," said Panurge. "Thank God! But please don't be offended, Doctor; there's no harm meant to you."

"The third method," continued Rondibilis, "is by means of assiduous labor, for in the course of such labor there takes place so great a dissolution of the bodily substance that the blood, which in this manner is dispersed for alimentary purposes throughout all the members, has no time or leisure, and is not able to prepare that superfluous seminal resudation which is the third primary reaction. Nature keeps it for herself, as being more necessary for the preservation of the individual than for the propagation of the species and the multiplication of the human race.

"And so it is that Diana, who is constantly occupied in hunting, is called the chaste. And so, also, in days gone by, the *castra*, or military camps, that is, *chaste places*, were so called for the reason that, in these places, athletes and soldiers incessantly labored. And Hippocrates, *lib. De aere, aqua, et locis,* tells us of certain peoples in Scythia who in his day were more impotent than eunuchs when it came to the venereal sport, for the reason that they were constantly on horseback and at work. On the other hand, the philosophers are in the habit of observing that idleness is the mother of lust.

"When Ovid was asked why it was that Aegistus became an adulterer, he could give no other reason than that the fellow was a loafer. If idleness were suddenly to be taken out of the world, all the arts of Cupid would very soon perish, his bow, his quiver, and his arrows would be merely a useless burden to him, and he would never hit a soul; since he's not half good enough as an archer to be able to bring down cranes flying through the air or deer starting up from a thicket, as the Parthians did—by which I mean, human beings stirring about and working. He has to have his target quiet and leisurely, seated or lying down.

"Theophrastus, on a number of occasions, when asked how he zoologically classified love-affairs, replied that they were the passions of idle minds. Diogenes, similarly, was accustomed to remark that whoremastering was the occupation of folks who were not occupied in any other manner. And so it was that Canachus, the

Sicyonian sculptor, wishing to convey the idea that idleness, laziness, and listlessness are the handmaidens of debauchery, proceeded to make a statue of Venus sitting down, and not standing up, as all his predecessors had done.

"The fourth means is by ardent study, for in the course of such study, there takes place so incredible a dissolution of the animal spirits that there are none left to be sent pulsing down to those places destined for the reception of this generative resudation, and the cavernous nerve, the function of which is to project these spirits outward for the propagation of humankind, remains unfilled. However this may be, I shall merely ask you to look at a man whose attention is fixed upon some studious pursuit. You will note in him all the arteries of the head drawn as taut as the cord of a crossbow, in the effort properly to furnish a supply of spirits sufficient for filling the ventricles of common sense, imagination and apprehension, ratiocination and resolution, memory and the mnemonic faculty; and you will behold these spirits agilely running from one faculty to another, through those conduits which the science of anatomy plainly reveals to us, at the base of the Admirable Net, where the arteries that take their rise from the left cupboard of the heart terminate, and through which the vital spirits flow, in long detours, to be made into animal spirits.

"As a result, in a studious person of this sort you will find that all the ordinary faculties have been suspended and all the external senses blocked. In short, you would think that such a one was no longer living, that he had been ecstatically lifted out of himself; and you might say that Socrates was not juggling words when he remarked that philosophy was nothing more nor less than a meditation on death.

"This, probably, was the reason why Democritus blinded himself, thinking less of the loss of his sight than he did of the diminution of his contemplative powers, which he felt were being interrupted through the distraction of the eyes. And so it is that Pallas, goddess of wisdom and patroness of all students, is called a virgin, as are the Muses, and as are also the Graces who dwell in a state of perpetual chastity.

"I recall having read that Cupid, when repeatedly asked by his mother, Venus, why it was he never attacked the Muses, replied that he found them too beautiful, too clean, too decent, too modest, and too ceaselessly occupied: one in the contemplation of the stars; another in the computation of numbers; another with the dimensions of geometric bodies; another with rhetorical inventions; another with poetic composition; another with musical arrangements. And he added that, whenever he approached them, he at once laid down his bow, closed his quiver, and put out his torch, from shame and from a fear of annoying them. Then he would lift the bandage from his eyes, in order to have a clear look at their faces, as he listened to their pleasing songs and poetic odes. He enjoyed this more than anything else in the world—so much that he often felt utterly ravished by their grace and beauty, and would fall asleep to the sound of their melody, it being the farthest from his thoughts to wish to attack them or to disturb their tranquil studies.

"And here, I may say that I understand what Hippocrates, writing on the same subject, has to say, in speaking of the Scythians, in his book entitled *On Offspring*. He says that all human beings in whom the parotid arteries have once been cut are impotent for the act of generation. For these arteries are at the side of the ears, as has been explained above, in speaking of the resolution of the vital spirits and the blood-stream, of which they are the receptacles; and when they are cut, a major portion of the generative substance is prevented from leaving the brain and spinal column.

"Fifthly, there is the venereal act—"

"I was waiting for that," said Panurge. "I'll take *it* for mine. You take any of the others you like."

"That," said Friar John, "is what Fra Scyllino, Prior of Saint-Victor-les-Marseille, calls maceration of the flesh. And this was, also, the opinion of the Hermit of Sainte-Radegonde, above Chinon, who believed that the hermits of the Thebaid could not more fittingly have macerated their bodies in order to get the upper hand of that old whore, Sensuality, and so put down the rebellion of the flesh than by doing it twenty-five or thirty times a day."

"I perceive," went on Rondibilis, "that Panurge is well proportioned in all his members, very moderate in his bodily humors, of a good complexion in his animal spirits, and of a suitable and opportune age, as well as possessed of a firm resolution to get married. If he should happen to meet a lady of like temperament, they ought to beget children worthy of some transpontine monarchy. And the sooner he does it the better, if he wants to see his offspring provided for."

"I will, Doctor, very soon," said Panurge. "You need have no fear on that point. During your learned discourse, this flea in my ear has been tickling me worse than ever. I hereby invite you to the wedding. We'll have a time and a half, I promise you that. You can bring your wife, if you like—and the neighbor women, too, that's understood, and a good time will be had by all."

In view of Rabelais' reputation for "obscenity"—his hilarious, essentially healthy horse-play attitude toward sex—it is of especial interest to read the words on the subject that he puts into the mouth of an enlightened humanist physician of his time—if, indeed, Rondibilis is not Maître François himself. The views expressed above, it may be noted, have to do with what we today speak of as "the sublimation of the libido." Commentators have been particularly enthusiastic in their admiration of the passage beginning "And so it is that Pallas . . . is called a virgin." "A passage," observes one of the older school, "in which Rabelais has shown, perhaps more than anywhere else, how much grace and chastity there may yet be in a book that is in general so free— such a passage is like a pearl buried in manure, amid the coarse and obstetric remarks on Panurge's marriage." Another modern scholar speaks of "the great poetic charm" with which the author develops his theme here.

"Friar Hotear": "frai Cauldaureil," a play on frai(s), *cool, and* cauld (chaud), *hot; the French Variorum adds: "one can guess what ears are meant."* ——*"Venus catches cold": well-known line from Terence, Eunuchus, iv, 5, "Sine Cerere et Libero friget Venus."* ——*"According to Diodorus Siculus": Diodorus Siculus, IV, vi, 1.* ——*"Lampsacians . . . as Pausanias informs us": the Lampsacians were the inhabitants of Lampsacus, in Lycia; Pausanias, IX, xxxi, 2.* ——*"The Amerine willow": a species of willow deriving its name from Ameria, in Umbria, mentioned by Theophrastus, Pliny, and other writers.* ——*"Hippocrates, lib. De aere, aqua, et locis": Book on Air, Water, and Places.* ——*"When Ovid was asked": see the Remedia Amoris, 161-2 and 139-40.* —— *"Theophrastus . . . when asked": Theophrastus, Fragment 114.* ——*"Similarly Diogenes": related by Diog-*

enes Laërtius, vi, ii, 51. ——"Why Democritus blinded himself": Plutarch's treatise On Curiosity, 531, and Cicero, Tusculan Disputations, v, xxxix, 114. ——"I recall having read": in connection with this much-admired passage Rabelais is under a debt to Lucian's dialogue on "Aphrodite and Love." ——"What Fra Scyllino calls . . .": this has been seen as referring to one Roscelino, or Roscelin, Prior of St. Victor's in the middle of the thirteenth century; at the Marseille convent the religious are said to have taken a vow of chastity "in so far as human fragility may be able to endure it." ——"The Hermit of Sainte-Radegonde": "Upon the hill overlooking Chinon is the ancient chapel of Sainte-Radegonde, hollowed out of the rock and occupying the grotto of a hermit known as St. John of Chinon" (Lefranc edition). ——"Worthy of some transpontine monarchy": some overseas monarchy.

Rondibilis Declares Cuckoldom to Be One of the Natural Appanages of Marriage

"There remains," Panurge went on, "one little point to clear up. You have observed, before now, on the Roman standards the letters: S. P. Q. R. *Si Peu Que Rien.* Little or nothing. That applies to the question I'm about to ask. It's really nothing at all. What I want to know is, am I going to be a cuckold?"

"For heaven's sake!" exclaimed Rondibilis, "what is this you're asking me? Whether or not you are going to be a cuckold? Listen, my friend, I'm married, and you're going to be. Well, you may write this on your brain with an iron pen: that every married man is in danger of being a cuckold. For cuckoldom is naturally one of the appanages of marriage. The shadow does not more naturally follow the body than cuckoldom does married folks. And whenever you hear those three words said of any one: 'He is married,' if you add: 'He is, therefore, or has been, or will be, or may be a cuckold,' you shall not be termed an unskilful architect of natural consequences."

"Belly-aching devils!" cried Panurge, "what's this you're telling me?"

"My friend," replied Rondibilis, "you should remember Hippocrates, who, in going one day from Cos to Abdera to visit Democritus the philosopher, wrote a letter to Dionysius, his old friend, begging that in his absence the latter would take his, Hippocrates', wife to her father and mother, who were respectable people with a good reputation, since he did not care to leave her at home alone. In spite of this precaution, he desired his friend to watch over her carefully, and to make note of where she went with her mother and what persons came to see her at her parents' home. 'Not,' he wrote in his letter, 'that I doubt her virtue or her modesty, with which I have had opportunity in the past to become thoroughly well acquainted, but she is a woman.'

"And there you have the whole thing in a nutshell, my friend. The nature of women may be represented by the moon, both in other ways, and in the fact that, in the sight and presence of their husbands, they mope, restrain themselves, and act a part; but when their husbands are absent, they at once proceed to take advantage of it, and go out for a good time, gadding and trotting around, throwing off their hypocritical airs, and demonstrating the fact they *are* like the moon, which, in conjunction with the sun, is visible, in heaven or on earth, only when it is in opposition to the sun, and which shines in all its fullness and is seen to be whole only at those times when it is at the greatest distance from the sun, notably at night.

"When I speak of woman, I speak of a sex so fragile, so variable, so changeable, so inconstant, and so imperfect that Nature impresses me—and I say it with all honor and reverence—as having lost, when she was building woman, that good sense with which she has created and formed all other things. I've thought it all over a hundred and five times, and I am sure I do not know what conclusion to come to, unless it is that, in turning out woman, Nature had more in mind the social delectation of man and the perpetuation of the human species than she did the perfecting of individual womankind.

"Plato, you will recall, was at a loss as to where to class them, whether among the reasoning animals or the brute beasts. For Nature has placed in their bodies, in a secret and intestinal place, a certain animal or member which is not in man, in which are engendered, frequently, certain humors, brackish, nitrous, boracious, acrid, mordant, shooting, and bitterly tickling, by the painful prickling and wriggling of which—for this member is extremely nervous and sensitive—the entire feminine body is shaken, all the senses ravished, all the passions carried to a point of repletion, and all thought thrown into confusion. To such a degree that, if Nature had not rouged their foreheads with a tint of shame, you would see them running the streets like mad women, in a more frightful manner than the Proetides, the Mimallonides, or the Bacchic Thyades on the day of their Bacchanalia ever did; and this, for the reason that this terrible animal I am telling you about is so very intimately associated with all the principal parts of the body, as anatomy teaches us.

"I call it an 'animal,' in accordance with the doctrine

of the Academics, as well as of the Peripatetics. For if movement, as Aristotle says, is a sure sign of something animate, and if all that moves of itself is to be called an animal, then, Plato was right, when he called this thing an animal, having noted in it those movements commonly accompanying suffocation, precipitation, corrugation, and indignation, movements sometimes so violent that the woman is thereby deprived of all other senses and power of motion, as though she had suffered heart-failure, syncope, epilepsy, apoplexy, or something very like death. In addition, we observe in women an unusual sense of smell, and note that they flee the unpleasant and are attracted by the aromatic odors.

"I am, I may remark here, aware that Cl. Galen has attempted to prove that these movements are not, in themselves, significant, but, rather, accidental, and that other members of the same sex do their best to prove that there is nothing in the least unusual about their sense of smell, and that if they are able to distinguish a number of different odors, it is simply because there happen to be a number of different odors to be distinguished. But if you look carefully into their remarks and the reasons that they give, and if you weigh them in Critolaus' scales, you will find that in this case as in a number of others these gentlemen are speaking from a love of jesting and a passion for taking their predecessors down a peg, rather than from an earnest desire to discover the truth.

"I shall not go any further into this dispute. I merely would say to you that those virtuous women who have lived modestly and blamelessly, and who have had the courage to rein in that unbridled animal and to make it obedient to reason, are deserving of no small praise indeed. And I may, in conclusion, add that once this same animal is glutted, if glutted it can be, through that alimentation which Nature has prepared for it in man, then all these specialized motions come to an end, all appetite is satiated, and all fury appeased. But do not be astonished at the fact that we are in perpetual danger of being made cuckolds—those of us who do not happen to be possessed of enough, every day, to enable us to pay the beast off and satisfy it."

"Gods and little fishes!" cried Panurge, "haven't you any other remedy than that?"

"Yes, indeed, my friend," replied Rondibilis, "and a very good one it is—one that I myself make use of. You will find it in a famous author of eighteen hundred years ago. Listen to this—"

"By God!" exclaimed Panurge. "But you're a good fellow, and I love you, a whole blessed bellyfull. Here, try a little of this quince pie. It properly closes the orifice of the ventricle, on account of a certain jolly stypticity that is in it, and thereby starts your digestive apparatus to working. But what's the idea? Here I am, talking Latin in front of the parsons. Wait till I give you a little drink out of this Stentorian tumbler. Should you like another little swig of the white hippocras? You needn't be afraid of the quinsy, not in the least. There is no squinancy, or quinsy-wort, no ginger or seed of Paradise in it. It contains nothing but cinnamon, very choice and high-grade, and some first-class refined sugar, mixed with the good white wine of La Devinière growth, from the Sorbapple vineyard, above the Hard Walnut."

In these remarks of Dr. Rondibilis, modern medical commentators have pointed out, Rabelais is displaying an intimate knowledge of the symptoms of uterine hysteria. At the same time, the donna è mobile *theme—*

compare Vergil's "varium et mutabile semper" (**Aeneid,** IV, 569)—*was a popular one of the day; Tiraqueau and other writers had employed it, and Francis I was in the habit of observing that* "toujours femme varie."

"*Hippocrates . . . in a letter to Dionysius*": this *letter, found in the old editions of Hippocrates, is generally regarded as apocryphal.* ——"*More frightful than the Proetides*": *the Proetides were the daughters of Proetus, King of Tiryns; because of their pride, they were punished with madness by Juno and imagined themselves to be cows; the Mimallonides (so named from Mt. Mimas in Asia Minor), and the Thyades (from the Greek verb,* thyein, *to sacrifice) were bacchantes, or priestesses of the god Bacchus.* ——"*As Aristotle says*": in the Physics, viii, 1-6. ——"*Then Plato was right*": Phaedrus, 245 C. ——"*I am aware that Cl. Galen*": De Locis Affectis, vi, 5. ——"*In Critolaus' scales*": *Athenian peripatetic philosopher who weighed moral and physical properties and discovered that the former outweighed the latter; Macrobius,* Saturnalia, I, v, 16.

Dr. Rondibilis Gives a Remedy for Cuckoldom

"Back in the days," remarked Rondibilis, "when Jupiter was taking a census of his Olympian household and drawing up the calendar of all his gods and goddesses, having set aside a feast-day and a special season for each one, and having assigned the seats of their oracles and pilgrimages and prescribed the nature of their respective sacrifices—"

"Are you sure," spoke up Panurge, "that he didn't do what Dinteville, Bishop of Auxerre, did? That noble prelate loved good wine, as every good fellow does, and so, he took over, under his special care and guardianship, the vineyard, which is Bacchus' grand-daddy. Now, it happened that, for a number of years past, he had seen the vintage lost through icy blasts, drizzling rains, frosts, sleet, cold spells, hail, and other calamities, all of which had happened about the time of the feasts of Sts. George, Mark, Vitalis, Eutropius, and Philip, and around Holy Cross and Ascension Days or thereabouts, all of which feasts fall within a period when the sun is passing through the sign of Taurus. And so, the good father became convinced that the saints mentioned were great hailers, freezers, and vineyard-spoilers; and he wanted to transfer their feasts to the winter-time, somewhere between Christmas and Epiphany, licensing them, in all honor and reverence, to hail and freeze then, as much as they liked. For a little frost at that time would do no damage, but would, obviously, be good for the vineyards. And in their old places, he wanted to set up the days of St. Christopher, St. John the Beheaded, St. Magdelene, St. Anne, St. Dominic, and St. Lawrence—which is what you might call putting mid-August into May; since, so far from there being any dread of freezing-spells in such a season, he reflected that there were no trades in the world that were then more in demand than those practised by the cold-drink-shakers, the junket-makers, the arbor-builders, and the wine-coolers.

"But Jupiter," Rondibilis went on, "forgot the poor devil, Cuckoldom, who did not happen to be present at the moment. The latter was at Paris, in the Palace, looking after some bastard lawsuit or other at the time for one of his tenants and vassals. I can't tell you how many days it was afterward that Cuckoldom, hearing of the slight that had been done him, dropped his legal soliciting, out of solicitude at being foreclosed out of house and home, and appeared before the great Jupiter in person, alleging his precedent merits and the favors that had previously been shown him, and urgently insisting that he be not left without a feast-day, without sacrifices, and without honor. Jupiter excused himself by pointing out that all the benefices had been distributed and that the lists had been closed.

"But Sir Cuckoldom begged so hard to be included in the census and the catalogue, and to have the proper honors, sacrifices, and feasts assigned to him on earth that, as a result, and in view of the fact that there was not one vacant place in the whole calendar, he was given the same day as the goddess Jealousy. His jurisdiction was to be over married chaps, especially those that had good-looking wives; his sacrifices were to be suspicion, defiance, grouchiness, watchfulness, hunting-down, and espionage, on the part of married men towards their wives, strict orders being given that every married man was to revere and honor him, and to hold a double celebration and offer the prescribed sacrifices on the god's day, the penalty being that those who failed to do this should be deprived of Sir Cuckoldom's favor, aid and succour. He was never to take any account of such ones, never to enter their houses, never to keep their company, no matter how many invocations might be made to him; but he was to leave all such fellows to rot alone, forever, with their wives, without any rival whatsoever; he was to spurn them sempiternally, as heretics and sacrilegious wretches, as is the custom of the other gods towards those who do not duly honor them: of Bacchus toward the vineyard-growers; of Ceres toward laborers; of Pomona toward fruit-growers; of Neptune toward sailors; of Vulcan toward blacksmiths; and of the other gods toward their respective followers.

"With this, on the other hand, was coupled the infallible promise that those who, as directed, laid off work on his day, who stopped all their business and disdainfully dropped all their other affairs in order to spy on, lock up, and jealously mistreat their wives, as prescribed in the sacrificial code, should be loved by Cuckoldom and have the pleasure of his constant company, day and night, in their homes. Such followers were never to be deprived of his presence. Now, then! I've said my say."

"Ha, ha, ha!" laughed Carpalim, "there's a remedy for you more ingenuous than Hans Carvel's ring. Devil take me, if I don't believe in it! That's the nature of the beast. Just as lightning never strikes or burns any but hard, solid, and resistant substances, just as it never stops for soft, empty, and yielding things, burning the steel sword without damaging the velvet scabbard, and consuming the bones of the body without touching the flesh that covers them—in the same manner, the subtle, stubborn, and contradictory minds of women are never directed towards anything except what they know to be forbidden and prohibited."

"Some of our doctors," commentated Hippothadeus, "tell us that the first woman in the world, whom the Hebrews call Eve, would hardly have been tempted to eat the fruit of the tree of wisdom if it had not been forbidden her. However that may be, we do know that the cunning Tempter reminded her, with his very first words, of this prohibition, as much as to imply: 'It is forbidden, and so, you ought to eat it; else, you're not a woman.'"

We by now have a new and somewhat different light on Rabelais' attitude toward the Woman Question— especially, if we are to assume that Dr. Rondibilis is Ra-

*belais. He is here found to be satirizing not so much the
cuckolded as the over-jealous husband. Indeed, a case
might be made out for asserting that what he is attack-
ing is, rather, the masculine seclusion and mistreatment
of women, as well as the hypocrisy of the institution of
marriage as frequently practiced.*

*This passage is by way of being an adaptation of one
in the* Consolations *of Plutarch, Rabelais' "Cuckoldom"
being substituted for the "Grief" of the original text.*

*"What Dinteville . . . did": Rabelais has Tinteville;
the reference is to François de Dinteville, Bishop of
Auxerre and ambassador to Rome, who died in 1530; he
seems to have been confused here with an episcopal
predecessor, Michel de Crenney, who abolished a
number of feast-days in his diocese.*

How Women Commonly Seek Forbidden Things

"BACK in the days," remarked Carpalim, "when I was a
roystering student at Orléans, I found that I had no
rhetorical flourishes that stood me in better stead and
no argument that was more persuasive with the ladies, in
bringing them into the toils and attracting them to the
sport of love, than the habit of pointing out to them
plainly, vividly, and shamelessly, how jealous their husbands were of them. And I wasn't half wrong. You will
find examples and reasons a-plenty in literature, in law,
and in everyday experience. Once let them get this idea
into their noodles, and by God (and I don't mean to
swear, either), they will infallibly make cuckolds of their
husbands. They will do the same thing that Semiramis,
Pasiphaë, Segesta, the women of the Island of Mendes in

Egypt (made famous by Herodotus and Strabo), and other such bitches did."

"That reminds me," said Ponocrates, "of a story. Pope John XXII, happening one day to visit, in passing, the Abbey of Bumperhome, was requested by the Abbess and the circumspect mothers to grant them an indulgence, permitting them to confess their sins to one another. They pointed out that the good sisters have sometimes little secret imperfections which it is a shame for them to be compelled to reveal to a masculine confessor, and that they would confess these with much greater freedom and intimacy to one another, under the seal of the confessional.

" 'There is nothing,' replied the Pope, 'that I would not gladly do for you. I see only one drawback, and that is that confessions must be kept secret. You women would have a hard time doing that.'

" 'We would do it very well,' they insisted, 'even better than the men.'

"Accordingly when the time came the Holy Father gave them a box to keep, in which he had had a tiny linnet placed. He requested them kindly to keep this box in some safe and secret spot, giving them his word as pope that he would grant their request, provided they did keep the box secret, but absolutely forbidding them to open it in any manner whatsoever, under pain of ecclesiastic censure and eternal excommunication.

"The sisters no sooner heard this prohibition than they at once began to long ardently to see what was on the inside, and they barely waited until the Pope was out of the door to set about finding out. The Holy Father, having given them his benediction, retired to his own lodgings; and he was not three paces from the abbey when the good ladies came running up in a crowd to open the forbidden box and have a look inside.

"The day following, the Pope called upon them once more, for the purpose, as they supposed, of conferring the indulgence they had asked. Before coming to the point, however, he requested them to bring him the box. It was brought in, but the birdie was not there. And then, he proceeded to show them what a difficult thing it would be for them to conceal what had been told them in the confessional, seeing that, for so short a period of time, they had not been able to keep the little secret of the box that had been left in their care.

"My good sir, you are a very welcome guest, indeed. I have taken, praise God, a very great pleasure in listening to you. I don't recall having seen you since you were playing at Montpellier, along with our old friends, Anthony Saporta, Guy Bouguier, Balthazar Noyer, Tollet, Jean Quentin, François Robinet, Jean Perdrier, and François Rabelais, in the moral comedy of *The Man Who Married a Dumb Wife*."

"I was there," said Epistemon. "The good husband wanted her to talk. She talked, through the art of the physician and surgeon, who cut an ancyloglot which she had under her tongue. When she had recovered her speech, she talked so much that the husband returned to the physician for a remedy to make her keep silent. The physician replied that he knew many remedies to make women talk, but that he had none to make them keep still, the only one he knew of being to render the husband deaf, as a protection against the interminable babbling of his wife.

"And so, the bastard became deaf, by means of some charm or other; whereupon his wife, seeing that he was deaf and that she was talking in vain, since he couldn't hear her, went mad. Then the physician came to ask for his fee. The husband replied that he was deaf and could not hear what the physician was saying. The physician then threw some kind of powder or other on the husband's back, by virtue of which the latter became a fool. Following this, the fool of a husband and the crazy wife banded together and proceeded to beat the physician and surgeon, leaving him half dead. I never laughed so much in my life as I did over that fool clowning."

"Let's come back to our sheep," said Panurge. "Your words, translated from jargon into French, mean that I may go ahead boldly and get married, and that it makes no difference if I do become a cuckold. Damme, if you haven't turned clubs. Sir, I'm very much afraid that when my wedding day comes around, you'll be detained elsewhere by your practice and won't be able to put in an appearance. Oh, well, I'll excuse you:

> Stercus et urina medici sunt prandia prima;
> Ex aliis paleas, ex istis collige grana.
> Feces and urine are the doctor's dish;
> From these he gets his grain; all else is chaff.

"You have it wrong," said Rondibilis. "The second verse should be:

> Nobis sunt signa; vobis sunt prandia digna.
> For us but signs, for you they are fitting food.

Now if my wife should take sick," he continued, "I should want to have a look at her urine, feel her pulse, and inspect the condition of the lower abdominal region and the umbilical parts, as Hippocrates recommends, 2 Aph., 35, before proceeding any further—"

"No, no," said Panurge, "that has nothing to do with the case. It's a matter for us legal lights, with our statute De ventre inspiciendo, On the Inspection of the Belly. I'll be glad to lend her an injection of hot fat. But please don't leave your other and more urgent business. I'll send some of the leftovers around to your house, and we will remain good friends."

Then Panurge went up to the doctor and, without saying a word, placed four rose nobles in his hand. Rondibilis took them right enough at first, then appeared, suddenly, very much put out about the matter.

"Ah, I say! that is not at all necessary, sir. Many thanks, just the same. I never take from the unworthy, nor refuse anything from the deserving. I am always at your service."

"When I pay you," said Panurge.

"That," replied Rondibilis, "is understood."

"Same thing that Semiramis . . . did": Semiramis loved a horse (see Pliny, Natural History, viii, 42); Pasiphaë, daughter of the sun, and wife of Minos, sister of Circe and mother of Ariadne, fell in love with a white bull and from their union the Minotaur was born; Segesta, daughter of the Trojan prince Hippotes, abandoned herself to a river-god metamorphosed as a bear or dog and became the mother of Acestes, founder of the Sicilian city of Segesta; Mendes, a city of lower Egypt, on one of the mouths of the Nile, was noted for the worship that was there paid to the goat and to the god Pan; see Herodotus, ii, 46, and Strabo, xvii, 802. ——— "Since you were playing at Montpellier": Rabelais introduces a reminiscence of his days as a medical student; the names mentioned are those of fellow-students, only one of whom, Pierre Tollet, was later to attain distinction as a physician; Antoine Saporta was a professor of medicine and chancellor of the university. ———"Let us come back to our sheep": Retournons à nos moutons, a favorite expression of Rabelais, taken from the farce of Patelin. ———"Damme, if you haven't turned clubs": the sense appears to be to speak out of turn, mal à propos. ———"Stercus et urina": these verses, with varia-

tions, were widely prevalent. ——"Nobis sunt signa. . . .
For us but signs": an old legal brocard. ——"De ventre
inspiciendo": *on the necessity of examining the belly and
saving the child; reference to the* Pandects, xxv, 4. ——
"*An injection of hot fat": the meaning of the original,* "un
clystère *(literally a clyster, or enema)* barbarin," *is in
doubt—as to whether the sense is* "rhubarb," "barbarous," *or* "barbed"; *Urquhart has* "a plaster of warm
guts," *which agrees with Cotgrave; the expression,* "injection of hot fat," *is current in America and is close to
the meaning.* ——"When I pay you. . . . That is understood": *a doctor's little joke on the subject of doctor's
fees.*

*The next personage to be consulted by Panurge is the
philosopher Trouillogan, one for whom a satisfactory
real-life identification has not as yet been established,
although a number of modern scholars, persuaded by the
nominalist-like skepticism that Trouillogan reveals, are
inclined to see in him the figure of William of Occam,
the fourteenth-century English Franciscan. The name,
from the Poitevin dialect, means "reel-" or "skein-
winder."*

How Trouillogan, the Philosopher, Handled the Difficult Question of Marriage

WHEN this conversation was over, Pantagruel turned to
Trouillogan, the philosopher, and said:

"Now, our loyal friend, the torch is being passed along
to you. It is your turn to speak up. Should Panurge
marry, or should he not?"

"Both," replied Trouillogan.

"What's that you're telling me?" inquired Panurge.

"You heard me," replied Trouillogan.

"Ah, ha!" exclaimed Panurge, "so that's how we stand, is it? I hold no flush; I pass. And now, tell me: should I get married or not?"

"Neither one nor the other," said Trouillogan.

"Devil take me," said Panurge, "if I don't believe I'm losing my mind, and the devil *may* take me, if I understand a word of what you're saying. Here, hold on a minute until I fasten my specs to my left ear so that I can hear you a little better."

At that moment Pantagruel perceived, near the door of the dining-room, Gargantua's dog which was called Kyne, that being the name of Tobias' dog; and he remarked to the rest of the company: "Our King is coming; let us rise." He had no sooner said this than Gargantua entered the room, each one rising to do him reverence.

Having extended a pleasant greeting to all present, Gargantua said:

"My good friends, I trust you will show me the favor of not interrupting your talk. Bring a chair for me to this end of the table, and let me have some wine, that I may drink to everyone here. You are all very welcome, indeed. And now, tell me what it is you were discussing."

Pantagruel replied by informing him, as the second service was brought in, that Panurge had propounded a problematic question—namely, as to whether or not he should marry, that the good father Hippothadeus and Dr. Rondibilis had just finished giving their opinions and that Trouillogan had been about to give his when he, Gargantua, had entered. Pantagruel also told him that Trouillogan, in response to Panurge's question, "Should I get married or not?" had replied: "Both," and the second time: "Neither one nor the other," and that Panurge had been complaining of such conflicting and contradictory answers, asserting that he did not understand what it was all about.

"I think I understand," said Gargantua. "That answer is like the one which an old philosopher gave, when asked whether or not he had a certain woman for a wife."

"I have her," said he, "but she does not have me; I possess her, but am not possessed by her."

"A similar answer," remarked Pantagruel, "was given by a wench of Sparta. When asked if she had ever had an affair with a man, she replied that she never had, but that men had sometimes had affairs with her."

"That," said Rondibilis, "is what we call the *neuter* in medicine and the *mean* in philosophy, implying a participation of two extremes, through an abnegation of both extremes and a temporal partition between the two."

"The holy Apostle," said Hippothadeus, "appears to me to have stated the matter more clearly, when he says: *Let those that are married be as though they were not married, and they that have wives be as though they had none.*

"I," said Pantagruel, "interpret having and not having a wife, at one and the same time, in this manner: To have a wife is to have her for that purpose for which Nature has created her, which is for the aid, pleasure, and companionship of man; while not to have a wife means not to be constantly hanging on her skirts and not, on account of her, to impair that single and supreme affection that man owes to God—not to forsake the duties that he naturally owes to his country, to the State, and to his friends, and not to neglect his business and personal pursuits in order to be always pleasing his wife. If we take the having and not having a wife in this manner, I can see no contradiction in terms."

"Our loyal friend": the young prince speaking. ——*"I hold no flush; I pass": passe sans flus, equivalent to passons outre! let's get on to something else.* ——*"Dog called Kyne . . . Tobias' dog": "Kyne" is from the Greek kyon, kynos, a dog; see, in the Apocrypha, Tobit, xi, 9; but the name of Tobias' dog is not given there.* ——*"By a wench of Sparta": Plutarch's Conjugal Pre-cepts, 18.* ——*"Let those that are married": a paraphrase of* First Corinthians, vii, 27 f.

Following a cross-purposes dialogue between Panurge and Trouillogan that is in reality a take-off on skeptical (probably on nominalist) philosophers, Pantagruel advises his companion to "take a fool's advice" by con-sulting with Triboulet, the court-jester. After they have "blazoned" Triboulet, in heraldic fashion, by applying to him more than 200 epithets—another of those cata-logues of which Maître François is so fond—they set out for the mythical city of Myrelingues, Pantagruel observing that he will first have to be present at the trial of Judge Bridlegoose. This affords an excuse for Rabelais' most extended and biting and, at the same time, uproarious satire on the legal profession.

Pantagruel Attends the Trial of Bridlegoose Who Decided Cases by the Fall of Dice

THE day following, at the appointed hour, Pantagruel reached Myrelingues. The presiding judge, senators, and counsel begged that he would sit with them and hear the case and assist them in reaching a decision as to the causes and reasons set forth by Bridlegoose as to why he had pronounced a certain sentence against an official by the name of Toucheronde, a sentence that did not appear in the least equitable to the centumviral court.

Pantagruel readily agreed and, upon entering the courtroom, found Bridlegoose seated in the center of the room. The latter, upon being duly interrogated, would give no reasons or excuses and make no answer, except that he had grown old and had not, upon the occasion in question, been able to see quite so well as usual. He proceeded to cite the divers miseries and calamities that old age brings with it, the which are noted *per Archid., d. lxxxvi, c. Tanta;* and for this reason, he had not been able to recognize the points on the dice so distinctly as in the past. And so, just as Isaac, an old man with failing sight, had taken Jacob for Esau, it was possible that he had taken a *four* for a *five*, especially since, it was to be noted, he had made use of his small dice, and the law expressly provides that imperfections of nature are not to be imputed as a crime; as clearly *ff. De re milit., l. Qui cum uno; ff. De reg. jur., l. Fere; ff. De edil. ed (per totum); ff. De termo., l. Divus Adrianus, resolu. per Lud. Ro. in l.: Si vero, ff. Solv. matri.;* and that whoever did otherwise would be accusing not man but Nature, as is evident in *l.: Maximum vitium, c. De lib. praeter.*

"What dice, my friend, do you mean?" inquired Bluster, the presiding judge.

"The dice of judgment," responded Bridlegoose, "the *alea judiciorum,* the dice of judgment, those specified in *Decr., c. 26, q. ii, c. Sors; l. Nec emptio, ff. De contrah. empt.; ' Quod debetur, ff. De pecul., et ibi Barthol.,* and of which you gentlemen commonly make use in this your sovereign court, as do all other judges in the decision of cases, in accordance with the notation of D. Henr. Ferrandat, *et no. Gl. in c. fin. De sortil., et l. Sed cum ambo, ff. De judi., ubt Doct.* who observe that games of chance are decent, respectable, useful, and necessary in the voidance of suits and dissensions at law. *Bal., Bart.* and *Alex., c. Communia, de l. Si duo,* have spoken still more clearly on this subject."

"And just how," queried Bluster, "do you work it, my friend?"

"I will reply briefly," said Bridlegoose, "according to the prescriptions of *l. Ampliorem, ∫ in refutatoriis, c. De appela.,* and the statement of *Gl. l. i, ff. Quod met. caus. gaudent brevitate moderni.* I do the same as you gentlemen; I act in accordance with judicial custom, to which our laws advise us always to defer, *ut no. Extra., De consuet., c. ex. literis, et ibi, Innoc.*

"What I do is this. Having well viewed, reviewed, read, reread, rummaged, and leafed through all the complaints, summonses, appearances, warrants, interrogatories, preliminary hearings, exhibits, citations, bills, cross-bills, petitions, inquiries, answers, rejoinders, trijoinders, documents, exceptions, pleas, rebuttals, briefs, collations, hearings, libels, appeals, letters-royal, examinations, demurrers, injunctions, changes of venue, mittimuses, remands, decisions, nolle-prosses, stipulations, mandamuses, statements, processes, and other such tidbits on the one hand or the other, as a good judge ought to do, according to the notations *Spec., De ordinario, ∫ iii, et tit. De offi. om. ju., ∫ fi., et De rescriptis praesenta, ∫ i*—having done this, I place at one end of the table, in my chambers, all the defendant's bags, and then give him the first throw, just the same as you other gentlemen, *et est not., l. Favorabiliores, ff. De reg. jur., et in c. Cum sunt, eod. tit., lib. vi,* which says: *Cum sunt partium jura obscura reo favendum est potius actori.*

"Having done this, I place the plaintiff's bags, just as you other gentlemen do, at the other end of the table, *visum visu, car opposita, juxta se posita, magis elucescunt, ut not. in l. i, § Videamus, ff. De his qui sunt sui vel alieni jur., et in l. i, Munerum mixta, ff. De muner et honor.:* and then, I proceed to give him a due and equal chance."

"But, my friend," inquired Bluster, "how do you become familiar with the obscure points of law brought up by the two parties to the proceedings?"

"The same way you other gentlemen do," answered Bridlegoose, "that is, by the number of bags at one end and at the other. And then, I proceed to make use of my small dice, just the same as you other gentlemen, according to the law: *Semper in stipulationibus, ff. De reg. jur.,* and the versal law in verse, *p. edo. tit. Semper in obscuris quod minimum est sequimur, canonized in c. In obscuris, edo. tit., lib. vi.*

"I have other big dice, very pretty and melodious, of which I make use, just like you other gentlemen, when the matter is more fluid, that is to say, when there are fewer bags."

"And when you have done that," said Bluster, "how do you set about handing down a decision?"

"Just like you other gentlemen," replied Bridlegoose. "I give the decision to the one who wins the throw, in accordance with the judicial, tribunary, praetorian, first-come-first-served dice. For we are thus instructed in our laws *ff. Qui po. in pig. l. Potior, leg. Creditor., c. De consul., l. i., and De reg. jur., in vi.: Qui prior est tempore potior est jure."

Professor Lefranc believes that Bridlegoose (Bridoye) had his counterpart in real life and that this passage in Rabelais may be based upon an incident that actually happened; he even thinks the documents may some time be found among the archives of the Parliament of Paris. The French scholar is inclined to identify Bluster (Trinquamelle), presiding magistrate at Bridlegoose's trial, as André Tiraqueau. He rejects the etymology of the name that is usually given—fanfaron, fendeur de naseaux, a swaggerer or boaster, or "nose-splitter" (compare our "bruiser")—and sees, rather, an anagrammatic allusion to the author of the De Legibus Connubialibus.

"*This chapter and the following one are filled with citations from the* Corpus Juris Justiniani *and the* Decretals. *It would be pointless to reproduce them all in extenso and to undertake to explain them here. It will be sufficient to remark that, in general, they are correct but facetiously applied by way of showing the unreflecting use which Bridlegoose made of them*" (Marty-Laveaux).

"*By the name of Toucheronde*": Toucheronde (meaning round wood or copse) is not an invented name but that of a hamlet in Poitou, near Ligugé. ——"*The centumviral court*": a court composed of a hundred men; one of Rabelais' Latin neologisms. ——"*Just as Isaac had taken Jacob for Esau*": Genesis, xxvii. ——"*The dice of judgment*": play on the expression: "*the hazard of judgments.*" ——"*Et ibi Barthol.*": and there is your Bartolus for you; Bartolus was professor of law at Bologna and Pisa, in the fourteenth century. ——"*With the notation of D. Henri Ferrandat*": Ferrandat was a commentator of the Decretals. ——"*Gaudent brevitate moderni*": the moderns like brevity. ——"*Cum sunt partium jurum obscurum*": when the law in the case is obscure, one should lean to the defendant rather than to the plaintiff. ——"*Visum viso*": directly opposite, vis-à-vis. ——"Car opposita, juxta si posita": "*for opposed things, being juxtaposed, become more clear.*" ——"*The versal law in verse . . .* Semper in obscuris": *this law, as a matter of fact, forms a Latin pentameter; the some-what doubtful sense of the adjective* versale *would ap-pear to be that of* "*capital*" (majuscule), *but our* "*versal*" *is a fairly adequate rendering; the meaning of the law is: in case of doubt, we always take the course that entails the least consequences.* ——"Qui prior est tem-pore": *the first in date has the preference at law.*

Bridlegoose Sets Forth the Reasons Why He Employed Dice in the Cases That He Was Called Upon to Decide

"WELL, my friend," persisted Bluster, "but since you give your decisions by throwing dice, why do you not have the throwing done the very day and hour that the parties to the controversy appear before you, without any further postponement? Of what use to you are the documents and records contained in the bags?"

"The same use that they are to you other gentlemen," was Bridlegoose's answer. "They serve me for three ex-quisite, requisite, and authentic purposes.

"*First,* as a Formality, without which whatever is done is of no value, as is very well proved, *Spec., tit. De instr. edi., et tit. De rescrip. praesent.;* moreover, you know only too well that very often, in judicial procedure, the formalities destroy the materialities and substance, for *Forma mutata, mutata Substantia, ff. ad exhib., l. Iulianus; ff. ad leg. Falcid., l. Si is qui quadrigenta, et Extra., De Deci., c. Ad audientiam, et De celebra. Miss., c. In quadam.*

"*Secondly,* as with you other gentlemen, they serve me as a dignified and salutary form of exercise. The late M. Othoman Vadare, a great physician as you might say, *C. De comit. et archi., lib. xii,* has very often remarked to me that a lack of bodily exercitation is the sole cause of the unhealthiness and shortness of life of you other gentlemen and of all the officers of justice. Which had been very well observed before him by Bart. *in l. i. C. De senten.* 'quae' *pro* 'eo quod.' Gentlemen, to us, respectively, *quia accessorium naturam sequitur principalis, De reg. jur. lib. vi. et l.: Cum principalis, et l. Nihil dolo., ff. eod. titu.: ff. De fidejusso., l. Fidejussor, et Extra. De offi., deleg., c.i.,* are conceded certain forms of respectable and recreative diversion, *ff. De al. lus. et aleat., l. Solent, et Autent. Ut omnes obediant, in princ., coll. vii, et ff. De praescript. verb., l. Si gratuitam., et l. i, C.: De spect., lib. xi,* and such is the opinion *D. Thomae, in Secunda Secundae, quaest, clxviii,* very patly cited by D. Alber. de Ros., who was *magnus practicus* and a solemn doctor, as Barbatias attests, *in prin. Consil.* The reason is set forth *per Gl. in Praemio ff., § Ne autem tertii:*

Interpone tuis interdum gaudia curis.

"That is to say, mingle occasional joys with your cares. And the truth is, one day, in the year 1489, having a little fiscal business to look after before the Gentlemen of the Excise Court, and entering the said court by pecuniary permission of the bailiff, like you other gentlemen, for you know that *pecuniae obediunt omnia,* as has been observed by *Bald. in l. Singularia, ff. Si certum pet., et Salic., in l. Receptitia, C. De constit. pecun., et Card., in Cle. i, De baptis.,* I found them all playing fly, which is a most salubrious exercise, either before or after meals, it is all one to me, provided that *hic no.* that the said game of fly is respectable, salubrious, ancient and legal, *a Musco iventore, de quo C., De petit. haered., l. Si post motam, et Muscarii, i.,* those who play at housefly are excusable in law, *l. i, C., De excus. artif., lib. x.*

"For the moment, M. Tielman Picquet was the fly, as I remember, and he was laughing because all the gentlemen of the said court were ruining their bonnets from drubbing his shoulders so hard; but he added that, notwithstanding, they would not be excusable for this spoiling of their bonnets upon their return from the Palace to their wives, by *c. i, Extra. De praesump., et ibi Gl.*

"And now, *resolutorie loquendo* I should say, like you other gentlemen, that there is no other such exercise, and none more aromaticizing, in this palatial world, than voiding bags, leafing through papers, indexing portfolios, filling baskets, and examining pleas, *ex Bart. et Jo. de Pra., in l. Falsa de condit. et de mon. ff.*

"*Thirdly,* like you other gentlemen, I am mindful of the fact that time ripens all things, and in time all things come to light; time is the father of truth, *Gl. in l. i, C. De Servit. Autent., De restit. et ea quae pa., et Spec. cit., De requis. cons.* That is why, like you other gentlemen, I suspend, delay, and defer judgment until the case, having been well aired, sifted, and argued, comes in the course of time to its maturity; and the outcome which comes after will then be more gracefully borne by the condemned parties, as *no. Gl., ff. De excu. tut., l. Tria onera: Portatur leviter, quod portat quisque libenter.*

"In judging it roughly, greenly, and in the beginning there would be danger of that inconvenience that the physicians say is incurred when an abscess is opened before it is ripe or when the human body is purged of some noxious humor before the reaction is complete. For, as we read *in Autent., haec Constit. Inno. const., in prin., and this is repeated by Gl. in c. Caeterum, Extra.,*

*De jura. calum.: Quod medicamenta morbis exhibent,
hoc jura negotiis.* Nature, moreover, instructs us to pluck
and eat fruits when they are ripe, *Instit., de re di., ∫ Is
ad quem, et ff. De acti. empt., l. Julianus,* and to marry
off the girls when they are ripe, *ff. de donat, int, vir. et
uxo., l. Cum hic status, ∫ Si quia sponsa, et xxvii. Q., i.
c., sicut Gl.* says: *Jam matura thoris plenis adoleverat
annis Virginitas.*

"Do nothing except in all maturity, *xxiii. Q., c. ii, ∫
ult., clxxxiii. d., c. ult.*"

"Forma mutatur . . .": *"when the form is changed, the
substance is changed."* ——*"M. Othoman Vadare":* unidentified personage, possibly a German. ——"Quia
accessorium . . .": *"because the accessory follows the
nature of the principal."* ——*"D. Alber. de Ros.":* Al-
berico de Rosata, fourteenth-century canonist of Bergamo. ——*"Who was* magnus practicus": *"who was a
great practitioner."* ——"Pecuniae obediunt omnia":
"all things are obedient to money." ——*"All playing
fly":* a schoolboys' game in which one plays the part of
the fly (la mouche) *and all the others fall upon and
chase him; this was one of the infant Gargantua's pastimes.* ——"Hic no.": *"note here."* ——*"A Musco* in-
ventore": *this is a play on the Latin* musca, *Italian*
mosca, *a fly, and certain expressions that occur in the
legal texts.* ——*"M. Tielman Picquet":* the Picquet
family was a prominent one in Montpellier, furnishing a
number of professors of medicine for the university.
——"Resolutorio loquendo": *"speaking judicially."* ——
"In this palatial world": that of the Palace of Justice.
——"Quod portat quisque libenter": *"that which one
bears willingly is borne lightly."* ——"Quod medicamenta morbis exhibent": *"what medicines do for dis-*

eases, judgments do for business." ——*"Jam matura thoris . . .":* *"long ripe for the nuptial couch, virginity has been maturing for many years."*

Bridlegoose then narrates an anecdote having to do with a certain "fixer of cases" (apoincteur de procès) *and what befell him, and follows it up with an illuminating discourse on the origin of suits at law.*

How Lawsuits Start, and How They Are Brought to Perfection

"THAT is why," continued Bridlegoose, "like you other gentlemen, I temporize, and wait for the case to mature and to come to perfection in all its members—I am referring to the documents and lawyer's bags. *Arg. in l. Si major., C. Commu, divi. et De cons., d. i, C. Solennitates, et ibbi Gl.*

"A lawsuit, when it is first born, impresses me, as it does you other gentlemen, as being something imperfect and unformed. Just as a newborn bear has neither feet nor hands, neither skin, wool, nor head, and is but a piece of rude and formless flesh; it is the mother-bear who, by licking her cub, brings its members to perfection, *ut no. Doct., ff. ad leg. Aquil., l. ii. in fi.*

"And thus, I observe, just as you other gentlemen do, that lawsuits at their birth, in their beginnings, are formless and without members; they have then but a paltry brief or two to stand on, and are an ugly enough beast. But once they have been well heaped, piled, and bagged up, why, then, they are what you might call fleshy and well formed. For *Forma dat esse rei, l. Si is qui, ff. ad leg. Falci, in c. Cum dilecta, Extra.; De rescrip.,*

Barbatia, Consil. 12, lib. 2, and before him *Bald. in c. Ult. Extra. De consue., zi l. Julianus, ff. Ad exib., et l. Quaesitum, ff. De lega, iii.* The procedure is that set forth in Gl., p. q. j. c. Paulus: *Debile principium melior fortuna sequetur.* Just as you other gentlemen, and likewise the sergeants, bailiffs, sheriffs, shysters, solicitors, trustees, lawyers, investigators, reporters, notaries, clerks, and standing judges, *De quibus tit. est lib. iii. Cod.,* by strongly and constantly sucking on the purses of the parties to a suit, beget for their cases heads, feet, claws, a beak, teeth, hands, veins, arteries, nerves, muscles and humors—by which, I mean the bags; *Gl. De cons., d. iii., Accepisti. Qualis, vestis erit, talia corda gerit. Hic no.* that in this respect, the parties are better off than the ministers of justice, for *beatius est dare quam accipere, ff. Comm., l. iii. et Extra. De celebra. Miss., c. Cum Marthae, et 24 Q., j. c., c. Odi., Gl. Affectum dantis pensat censura tonantis.*

"In this manner, they render the case perfect, comely, and well formed, as is stated in *Gl. Can.: Accipe, sume, cape, sunt verba placentia Papae.*

"The same thing has been more clearly set forth by *Alber. de Ros., in verb. Roma:*

> *Roma manus rodit, quas rodere non valet, odit;*
> *Dantes custodit; non dantes spernit et odit.*

"The reason why? *Ad praesens ova cras pullis sunt meliora. ut est Glo., in l. Quum hi., ff. De transac.* The inconvenience of the contrary is set forth in *Gl. C. allu., l. fi.: Cum labor in damno est, crescit mortalis egestas.*

"The true etymology of lawsuit (*procès*) lies in this: that in the proceedings (*prochats*) there must be many bags (*prou sacs*). And we have some deific legal maxims on this subject: *Litigando jura crescunt; Litigando jus acquiritur; Item Gl. in c. Illud, Ext. De praesumpt., et*

C. De prob., l. Instrumenta, l. Non epistolis, l. Non nudis.

"Et, cum non prosunt singula, multa juvant."

"Well, my friend," inquired Bludter, "but how do you proceed in a criminal action, the guilty party being taken *flagrante crimine?*"

"Just as you other gentlemen do," responded Bridle-goose. "I permit and order the plaintiff to take a good nap before entering the courtroom, and then summon him to appear before me with a valid and legal affidavit to the effect that he *has* had a good nap, according to *Gl. 32, Q. vii. c.: Si quis cum, Quandoque bonus dormitat Homerus.* For this act engenders another, and from this other still another is born, just as link by link the hauberk is made. Until, finally, I find the case, through divers interrogatories, well formed and perfect in all its members. And then, I go back to my dice. And I have not adopted such a course without good reason, based upon a most notable stock of experience.

"I recall that, in camp at Stockholm, there was a certain Gascon by the name of Gratianauld, a native of Saint-Sever. Having lost all his money in gambling, and being greatly put out by it, since you know that *pecunia est alter sanguis, ut ait Anto. de Butrio in c. accedens, ii., Extra., Ut lit. non contest., et Bald. in l. Si tuis, C. De op. li. per no., et l. Advocati, C. De advo. div. jud.: Pecunia est vita hominis, et optimus fidejussor in necessitatibus,* at the door of the gambling-house he sang out to all his companions in a loud voice:

" 'By the bull's head, my lads, I hope the old keg bowls you over! And now, seeing I've lost my twenty-four calves I can punch, pound, and slug all the better. Is there any one of you wants to fight me? I'm giving you a good excuse.'

"When no one answered him, he went on over into the camp of the Hundredpounders and repeated the same words, inviting them to fight him. But all they had to say was:

"'That Gascon talks about fighting anybody and everybody, but he's more interested in what he can lay his hands on. You womenfolks had better keep an eye on the baggage.'

"Accordingly, nobody on their side offered to fight him. Whereupon, the Gascon went on over into the camp of the French freelances, repeating what he had said before and inviting them all, most handsomely, to do battle with him, accompanying his dare with a number of little Gascon monkeyshines. But no one took him up. Then, the Gascon went off and lay down, at the far end of the camp, near the tent of the big Christian Knight of Cressé, and there dropped off to sleep. In due time, a freelance, having similarly lost all his money, came out with drawn sword and a firm determination to fight the Gascon, seeing that they both were losers:

Ploratur lachrymis amissa pecunia veris.

That is to say, true tears are shed for money lost, as we find in *Glos. De poenitent., dist. 3, c. Sunt plures.* Having looked all through the camp, he finally found the sleeping Gascon and said to him:

"'Hey, there! sonny-boy, what the devil, get up! I've lost my money just like you. Come on, what do you say if we have a jolly good fight and rub our bacon down? This Verdun sword of mine is no longer than that spade of yours.'

"The Gascon replied, in a daze:

"'St. Arnaud's noddle! who are you, and what do you mean, waking me up like that? I hope the urine goes to your head. St. Sever, patron of Gascons! And here I was having such a good snooze, and this pest has to come around!'

"The freelance once more invited him to the fray, but the Gascon replied:

" 'You poor bastard, you, I'd break your back, now that I've had my rest; come on and take a little nap like me, and we'll fight it out afterwards.'

"For, having forgotten his loss, he had, at the same time, lost all desire to fight. The short of it was, in place of mauling and, perhaps, killing each other, they went off afterward, to have a little drink together, over their drawn swords. It was sleep that brought about this happy state of affairs, for it had quelled the downright madness of the two doughty champions.

"And here, we have the golden saying of Joan. And. *in c. ult. De sent. et re judic., libro sexto: Sedendo et quiescendo fit anima prudens.*"

"Forma dat esse rei": *"the form gives being to the thing."* ——"Debile principium . . .": *"a better fortune will follow a weak beginning."* ——"Standing judges": *judges of inferior jurisdiction, probably so called because they rendered their judgments standing.* ——"Qualis vestis . . . talia corda": *"like garment, like heart."* —— "Beatius est dare": *"it is more blessed to give than to receive";* Acts, xx, 35. ——"Affectum dantis pensat . . .": *"the censure of the thunderer is proportionate to the disposition of the giver"; in French the rhyme is* La censure de celui qui tonne Pèse la disposition de celui qui donne. ——"Accipe, sume . . .": *"Receive, take, get, are pleasing words to the Pope."* ——"Roma manus rodit . . .": *"Rome gnaws (feeds on) hands, hates those she cannot gnaw, watches over those that give, spurns and hates those that do not give."* ——"Ad praesens ova . . .": *"today's eggs are better than tomorrow's chickens."* ——"Cum labor in damno . . .": *"when labor is in jeopardy, mortal need arises."* ——"Litigando jura crescunt": *"rights grow by litigation."* ——"Et, cum non prosunt singula . . .": *"when isolated efforts are of no avail, multiplied ones are useful."* ——"Flagrante crimine": *we commonly say* "in flagrante delictu." —— "Quandoque bonus dormitat Homerus": *"when the good Homer nods"; Horace,* Ars Poetica, 359. ——"Pecunia est alter sanguis . . . pecunia est vita hominis": *"money is man's blood . . . money is the life of man and his best guaranty in case of necessity"; compare Erasmus,* Adages, II, viii, 35. ——*"By the bull's head": this speech is in the Gascon dialect.* ——*"Seeing I've lost my twenty-four calves": that is, pieces of money.* ——*"Into the camp of the Hundredpounders": Rabelais' word is* Hondrespondres; *this was a sobriquet of the lansquenets.* ——*"The Gascon talks . . .": this passage is in German.* ——*"The big Christian Knight of Cressé": the Cressé family was of Anjou, related to the Du Bellay family.* ——*"That spade of yours": "spade" is an Italianism for sword (Italian* spada). ——*"The saying of Joan. And.": Jean André, the jurisconsult.* ——"Sedendo et quiescendo . . .": *"by sitting quietly the soul is rendered prudent."*

When the evidence against Bridlegoose has been heard, Pantagruel, in one of our author's tongue-in-cheek passages, finds that the dice-throwing magistrate is, after all, deserving of pardon, by reason of his age, his simple-mindedness, and the fact that all his decisions in the past have been upheld by the judges who are trying him! Pantagruel and Panurge then consult with the court-jester, Triboulet, on the marriage question. Once again there is a Sibylline response as to the interpretation *of which Panurge and his master cannot agree. The fool having placed a bottle of wine in Panurge's hand, this is taken by the recipient as an omen: "Triboulet is sending me to the bottle." They accordingly resolve to visit the oracle of the Holy Bottle (Dive Bouteille), making the journey by way of the "Lanternese country." First, however, it is necessary to obtain Gargantua's permission.*

Into Gargantua's mouth the author puts a speech that introduces one of the burning topics of the day, the subject of clandestine marriages contracted without the knowledge and consent of the brides' parents. The ecclesiastic authorities had held that such consent was not required where the sanction of the Church was given; and as a result, according to the accounts of the time, numerous abuses were committed, with the monks— "those dreaded mole-burrowers," as Gargantua calls them—acting as go-betweens. French magistrates and jurists had launched a campaign to right this abuse, and Maître François is raising his voice in the chorus. The following chapter not only shows, once again, Rabelais' extreme sensitiveness to the life and thought-currents of his day; it also serves to round out his views on the Woman Question and constitutes at the same time yet another attack on the evils of monasticism.

Gargantua Explains Why It Is Unlawful for Children to Marry without the Knowledge and Consent of Their Fathers and Mothers

As PANTAGRUEL entered the great hall of the castle, he came upon the good Gargantua emerging from the Council Chamber, and proceeded to give the latter a full account of their adventures, explaining their plan, and

begging his father to give them his permission to put it
into execution. Gargantua, good man, had both hands
filled with two big bundles of notations, of business
attended to and to be attended to. These he handed to
Ulrich Gallet, his veteran Master of Requests; and drawing Pantagruel aside, he said to him, with a more than
usually happy expression on his face:

"I praise, my very dear son, the God who keeps you in
the path of virtuous intentions. I am quite willing that
you should make this journey; but I wish that you likewise would acquire a desire and the determination to
marry. It seems to me that you are now of suitable age.
Panurge has done his best to overcome the difficulties
that might stand in his way; so, speak for yourself."

"Mildest of fathers," replied Pantagruel, "I have not
even thought of it as yet. In all that I do I act in accordance with your good will and paternal commands. And I
pray God that, to avoid your displeasure, I may sooner
lie rigid in death at your feet than live and be married
without your consent. It has never been my understanding that, by any law whatsoever, either sacred, barbarous, or profane, it was permitted to children to marry
without the will and consent of their fathers, mothers,
and nearest relatives. All legislators agree in depriving
children of this liberty, reserving the decision for parents
alone."

"My dearest son," said Gargantua, "I believe you, and
I thank God that you have never displayed an interest in
any but good and praiseworthy things, and that, through
the windows of your senses, nothing has entered the
domicile of your mind except a liberal understanding.
For in my day, there was on this continent a certain
country in which were to be found certain indescribable
mole-burrowing image-toters, who, while full of sala-
ciousness and lasciviousness, were yet as opposed to mar-

riage as the Phrygian priests of Cybele, or as though they
had been capons instead of priestly roosters; and these
fellows set up to give the people laws in the matter of
marriage.

"I do not know which is the more to be abominated,
the tyrannic presumption of these dreaded mole-burrowers—who, instead of staying behind the lattices of
their own mysterious temples, had set themselves to
meddling with affairs absolutely foreign to their station
in life—or the superstition and the stupidity of the married, who have sanctioned and lent obedience to laws so
malicious and so barbarous, failing utterly to see that
which, none the less, is clearer than the morning star: how
such connubial sanctions as these are altogether to the advantage of the mystery-mongers, and not at all for the
profit or well-being of married folk; which consideration
should have been of itself sufficient to render such laws
suspect, as being iniquitous and fraudulent in character.

"The victims might, with equal justice, lay down laws
for those same mystery-mongers, concerning the latter's
ceremonies and sacrifices, seeing that they are in the
habit of decimating and gnawing away the fruit of the
people's labor, the result of the sweat of their hands, in
order to nourish and keep themselves in plenty. And such
laws, in my opinion, would not be so perverse or so impertinent as those others that the people receive from
them. For as you have very well said, there is no law in
the world that gives children the right to marry without
the knowledge and consent of their fathers.

"Thanks to those laws of which I have been speaking,
there is not a ruffian, criminal, scoundrel, gallows-bird,
stinkard, louse, moral leper, schemer, thief, or rascal in
their countries who may not violate and ravish any maid
he chooses to pick, no matter how noble, beautiful, rich,
modest, and respected she may be, taking her from her

own father's house, from the arms of her mother, in spite of all her relatives, provided the pimp has once associated with him some mystery-monger, who will one day share in the booty. I ask you, were the Goths, the Scythians, or the Massagetae ever guilty of a worse deed or one more cruel, even in an enemy's place which, after a long siege, they had taken by storm?

"And when the grieving fathers and mothers behold some unknown person, some stranger, a barbarous, stinking cur, chancrous, cadaverous, mean, and wretched— when they behold such a one abducting and taking from their own houses their daughters, so beautiful, so delicate, so well cared for, and so wholesome, whom they have so tenderly and virtuously reared in a decent and respectable way of life, with the hope, in time, of giving them in marriage to the sons of their neighbors and old friends, who are bound to them by ties of blood—all this, that their daughters may find happiness in marriage and have offspring that will inherit the manners as well as the goods and property of their fathers and mothers—when the parents behold all this, how do you think they must feel?

"You may believe that the desolation of the Roman people and their allies was no greater upon learning of the death of Germanicus Drusus. You may believe that the sorrow of the Lacedaemonians was no more piteous when they beheld the Grecian Helen furtively abducted from their land by the adulterous Trojan. And do not believe that the grief and lamentations of these parents are any less than were those of Ceres, when Proserpina, her daughter, was snatched away from her, or than those of Isis were at the loss of Osiris, of Venus at the death of Adonis, of Hercules at the straying of Hylas, or of Hecuba at the abduction of Polyxena.

"Yet these parents are so beset with superstition and

fear of the Devil that they do not dare raise their voices when the mole-burrower has been present as a party to the transaction; and so, they remain in their homes, deprived of their beloved daughters, the father cursing the day he was married, the mother regretting that she had not aborted instead of giving birth to a daughter. The result is, they end in tears and lamentations a life that had every reason to end in joy and kind treatment. Others have so gone out of their heads and have become so insane that, out of grief and regret, they have drowned, hanged or otherwise slain themselves, being unable to endure so undeserved a fate.

"Others still have displayed a more heroic spirit and, following the example of the sons of Jacob, when the latter revenged the rape of Dinah, their sister, have hunted down the pimp and, having found him in the company of his mole-burrower, engaged in treacherous and clandestine parleyings with their daughters, have hewed the both of them to pieces, on the instant and in cold blood, afterwards casting their bodies to the wolves and the ravens of the fields. At such manly and valiant action, the mole-burrowing mystery-mongers have miserably groaned and whined and then have formulated hair-raising complaints, imploring and insisting, relentlessly, that the state and the secular arm of the law see to it that such an offense be exemplarily punished.

"But neither in natural equity nor the code of peoples nor in any imperial law whatsoever is there to be found any rubric, paragraph, jot, or title in accordance with which pain or punishment is to be inflicted for such a cause, since reason resists and nature is opposed to any such course. For there is not a virtuous man in the world who, naturally and with good reason, would not be more moved and perturbed at hearing the news of the rape of his daughter than he would be at hearing of her death. It follows, then, that any one finding the murderer, iniquitously and stealthily engaged in the act of committing homicide upon the person of his daughter, may with reason, and ought by natural instinct, to slay the wretch, instantly and without being brought to justice for the deed.

"There is, accordingly, small room for wonder if, when he finds the pimp, at the instigation of the mole-burrower, engaged in betraying his daughter and stealing her out of her own home, even though it may be with her consent—there is little cause for wonder if he puts them both to death, ignominiously; he may and ought to put them to death, and to throw their bodies out to be torn to pieces by the beasts, as being unworthy of receiving the gentle, the desired, the last embrace of our great and cherishing mother, the Earth—that embrace we know as *Burial*.

"And so, my beloved son, after my death, see to it that such laws are never enacted in our realm. So long as I am alive and in the flesh, I myself will look after it very well, with God's help. Since, therefore, you refer the question of your marriage to me, I may tell you that I am in favor of it and will take the proper steps.

"Go, then, and make your preparations for the journey with Panurge. Take with you Epistemon, Friar John, and any others whom you may select. Take, also, whatever you may need from my treasury. Anything you may do, I am sure, cannot fail to meet with my approval.

"From my arsenal at Thalasse, take such equipment as you wish, and such pilots, sailors, and interpreters as you may think best; and when you get a favoring wind, set sail, in the name and under the protection of God, our Savior.

"During your absence I will both provide a wife for you and prepare a wedding feast, if ever there was one."

Etienne Pasquier, in one of his Letters *(Book III, Letter 1), deals with the subject treated here.* "I am well aware," *he writes,* "that for several hundred years certain monks, patchers of old glosses, have endeavored to propagate the barbarous and uncivilized opinion that, in canon law, the consent of fathers and mothers was not necessary to the marriage of their children, such consent being sought only out of respect and not from obligation." *The question involved came up for discussion in the Council of Trent, which began in 1545, that is to say, about the time that Book Third was published. Erasmus had raised his voice in the matter, and many other writers had done the same.* "It is remarkable," *observes M. Marty-Laveaux,* "to see the comic authors and the poets taking upon themselves with so much eloquence and authority the defense of those paternal rights of which the clergy, falling back upon the canon law, were inclined to take no account." *And the same commentator adds:*

"This fine chapter, filled with so elevated a morality, is a thorn in the side of those fantastic biographers of a merely smutty Rabelais; for which reason it is that it has always been left in the shade, as though there were an understanding that it was not to be quoted."

Rabelais is here expressing an attitude that has long been deeply rooted in France. Henry II finally published a decree annulling such marriages. But back of the Maître's violent defense of parental rights lies an even more violent animus toward the Church for usurping those rights and toward the monks for their self-interested scheming in such cases.

So far as the Woman Question is concerned, it may be noted that the author ends by having his princely hero decide in favor of marriage.

"Image-toters": *Rabelais' word is* pastophores; *these*

*were Egyptian priests, spoken of by Macrobius (Book
xi), who bore the images of the gods in procession.
——"As though they had been capons instead of priestly
roosters": the word in the original is* galls, *a play on the
Latin* gallus, *meaning at once a cock and a priest of
Cybele.* ——"Behind the lattices of their own mysterious
temples": *allusion to certain* loges grillées *at the Sorbonne.* ——"Upon learning of the death of Germanicus
Drusus": *see the passage in Tacitus on the death of
Drusus;* Annals, ii, lxxii, 82. ——"When the latter revenged the rape of their Dinah": *Genesis, xxxiv.* ——
"My arsenal at Thalasse": *from the Greek* thalassa, *the
sea.*

  As Pantagruel and his followers set out on their new
voyage, Book Third draws to a close with several enig-
matic chapters on "the plant called Pantagruelion," its
mode of preparation and the uses to which it is put, the
origin of its name, its "admirable virtues," and its ability
to resist fire. The Pantagruelion is identified as hemp,
the Cannabis sativa of Linnaeus, and this passage, so
filled with botanical lore, has been compared to Pliny's
dissertation on flax at the beginning of Book xix of his
Natural History; Rabelais, indeed, is indebted to the
Roman writer for the idea and the general outline of his
description. The digression may have been suggested by
the hempen sails of Pantagruel's ships; although others
see in it an allusion to the introduction and frequent use
of the rope as a punishment for criminals during Francis i's reign. In any event, it is an extremely learned little
essay and a mystic-sounding one. For one reason or another, it is not unusual for Maître François to begin or
close his books with an "enigma" of this sort. There may
have been a method in his madness—there usually was.
In the meanwhile, he has given us in the pages of his

Third Book his profoundest thinking and most mature view of life and the world, the best that his genius has to offer; and that is a best that was not bettered by any writer of his age.

END OF THE SECOND BOOK OF THE PANTAGRUEL, OR BOOK THIRD

The Fourth Book

THE FOURTH BOOK

Of the Heroic Deeds and Sayings

OF THE WORTHY

PANTAGRUEL

Composed by M. François Rabelais

Doctor of Medicine

NEITHER DEATH   **NOR POISON**

With Book Fourth Rabelais returns to the theme of Pantagruel's voyagings. As has been stated, in connection with the concluding portion of Book Second, these voyages have a very definite relation to the geographical explorations and discoveries of the age and the ever expanding world that was thus revealed; they are a reflection of the exotic impulse introduced into French literature by the discovery of America and the search for the northwest passage; the influence of Jacques Cartier, discoverer of Canada, is apparent, and it has even been thought that Rabelais may have known Cartier personally and that it was from the explorer that he picked up his seagoing terms. M. Plattard, however, thinks it more likely that Maître François acquired his nautical language in Italy.

This book is of interest not only from the geographic

519

*but from another point of view as well: that of Rabelais'
life and his relations with the French throne, as a propagandist for its policies. When Book Third appeared, with
its Royal Privilege, it had seemed as if his troubles might
be over. He had dared for the first time to sign his name
to a portion of his romance; he had dedicated the work
to Marguerite of Navarre and throughout its pages had
upheld the royal view on the issues of the day and, in
his treatment of the Woman Question, had catered to the
conversational interests of the King and his courtiers.
Gone were the usual overt or but slightly veiled attacks
on the Sorbonne; indeed, it seemed at times that he was
endeavoring to appease these censorious ogres. Yet for
all of that, Book Third met with the same fate as its
predecessors—it was suppressed. This came as a shock.
So tired was its author of being eternally hounded by
"cannibals, misanthropes, and agelasts" that, as he tells
us in the Epistle to the Cardinal of Châtillon which
serves as a dedication to Book Fourth, he was "more
than of a mind not to write another iota."*

*The suppression of his Third Book marked a turning
of the tide for Rabelais. He was under a cloud and
things now began to go against him, old friends to desert, among them Tiraqueau, patron of his youth. The
upshot of it all was that he deemed it safer to go into
voluntary exile at Metz, and it was here, doubtless, that
he worked on Book Fourth. He still had powerful
friends, it is true, and the court as always was inclined
to protect him; Henry II had renewed the Royal Privilege granted by Francis I, and the latter's Readers and
His Majesty himself had been able to find not "a single
suspect passage." There was, nevertheless, a limit to
the protection that even the throne could accord him
against the Sorbonne heresy-hunters; and the Sorbonnists, so it is said, did not like that pun on "soul" and*

"*ars-oul*"; much less did they relish the scene in which Raminagrobis (the heretical Jean Le Maire de Belges) drives the monks from his domicile. Those flaming fagots were always in the background.

But Rabelais keeps on writing, as a real writer almost invariably does, whatever the odds. He continues, at the same time, to support the royal policies. In this instance, it is a question of the relations of the Gallican Church to the See of Rome. At the very moment when Book Fourth was being brought out, Henry's edict against the abuses of Rome was being promulgated to the sound of trumpets in the streets of Paris, all of which has a light to throw on the "Popejiggers," the "Papimaniacs," and "Decretalists" satirized in the following pages. But once again the Maître was to find that luck was against him. A partial edition of Book Fourth, in eleven chapters and a prologue, had been brought out at Lyon, in 1548; it breaks off in the middle of a sentence, as if the author had been pressed for time. The complete version was first published by Michel Fezendat, at Paris, in 1552; and it was in April of that year that a reconciliation was effected between Henry II and the Holy See. This meant that Rabelais' satires were now decidedly out of place and no longer represented the views of the court. Even before this, on March 1, 1552, the sale of the book had been stopped by order of a magistrate—André Tiraqueau! Is it any wonder if the writer who gave us the Gargantua and Pantagruel became an embittered man? It is to be noted that this is the last book published during his lifetime, the last to bear his own indelible imprint all the way through.

Book Fourth is less literary than its immediate predecessor; there is in it less of classical erudition, with fewer Latinizings and Hellenizings and more of popu-

lar speech. In this book the author has borrowed to a greater extent than usual from the Italian Folengo. He has been both criticized and defended for his employment of nautical terms in the storm scene; but we may be assured that he was concerned with the artistic effect rather than with technical exactitude. Despite an anticlericalism which is his chief stock-in-trade, Voltaire did not like this portion of the Rabelaisian romance.

"His (Rabelais') book," he remarks, "was printed with a privilege; and the privilege for this satire was granted on account of the ordures it contains. . . . This book has never been forbidden in France (!) for the reason that everything in it is hidden under a mass of extravagances which never give one time to disentangle the true aim of the author."

The text of the Michel Fezendat edition has in general been followed here. The title page indicates that the work came "From the Printery of Michel Fezendat, at Mont-St.-Hilaire, at the Hotel d'Albret," at Paris, and bears the words "With the Privilege of the King" (allusion to the Royal Privileges granted for Book Third, applicable to "such other, new works as he may plan to publish"). The phrase "Neither Death Nor Poison" has reference to the proverb to be found in modern French: "Morte la bête, mort le venin," when the beast is dead, the poison's dead. There are two Prologues to this book, one written for the partial edition of 1548, a second and more timely one for the Fezendat edition of 1552. It is the second that is given here.

Monseigneur Odet,

Cardinal of Châtillon

You are duly aware, Illustrious Prince, by what great persons I have been, and still am daily requested, urged, and besought to continue my Pantagruelic mythologies, it being set forth that a number of the ill and languishing, or those who are otherwise grieved and troubled, have by the reading of those mythologies been enabled to outwit their cares, to pass the time cheerfully, and to find new mirth and fresh consolation. To which persons it is my custom to reply that, having composed those tales for my own amusement, I could lay claim to no praise or glory whatsoever; that all I had had in mind in putting them into writing had been what little solace I might be able to bring to the afflicted and to my absent patients, and that I am very happy to console in the same manner and in person, when opportunity offers, those who avail themselves of my art and my services.

Sometimes, I make a long speech to them, explaining what Hippocrates in a number of passages, but especially in the sixth book of his *Epidemics,* has to say concerning the profession of the physician, his remarks being addressed to his disciple; also what Soranus the Ephesian, Oribasius, Cl. Galen, Hali Abbas, and other later authors have had to say on the same subject, regarding the physician's gestures, bearing, glance, touch, countenance, manners, personal appearance, facial cleanliness, clothing, beard, hair, hands, mouth—even going so far as to specify the care he should take of his nails, just as though he were about to play some amorous rôle or other or the part of suitor in some distinguished comedy, or as though he were about to enter the martial lists to combat some powerful enemy. And to tell the truth, the practice of medicine has been very aptly compared by Hippocrates to a battle, or to a farce with three characters: the patient, the physician, and the disease.

In reading this, I have sometimes thought of what Julia had to say to Octavianus Augustus, her father. She had presented herself to him one day in costly, dissolute, and lascivious garments, and had greatly displeased him thereby, though he did not say a word. The next day, she changed her clothes and dressing herself modestly as was the custom then among respectable Roman ladies, she once more presented herself, thus clad, to her father. And he who the day before had refrained from indicating in words the displeasure he had felt at seeing his daughter clad in immodest garments, was unable to conceal the pleasure he found upon seeing her thus altered in attire. And so he exclaimed to her: "Oh, how much more fitting and praiseworthy are such garments as those in Augustus' daughter!" But she had an answer ready, and replied: "Today I have dressed myself for my father's eyes. Yesterday I was dressed for my husband's pleasure."

Similarly might our physician, thus disguised, as it were, in face and in clothing—even going so far as to provide himself with an expensive and charming robe with four sleeves, as was formerly the custom (this robe being known as the *philonium*, as Petrus Alexandrinus informs us, in *Epid.*)—even so might he reply to any who found such a prosopopoeia a trifle strange: "I have dressed myself like this, not to play the dandy and trig myself out, but for the pleasure of the patient whom I am going to visit, since he is the only one I am interested in pleasing, and since I do not wish to offend or to annoy him in any way."

But there is more to come. In a certain passage of Father Hippocrates, in the work above quoted, the thing that he is all in a sweat to have us know is not that a peevish, grouchy, crabby, Catonian, unpleasant, unhappy, gruff, and severe mien on the part of the physician tends to give the patient the blues, while a jovial, placid, gracious, open, and pleasing countenance cheers him up—no, that has all been established and is most assured; the point is, rather, that such low spirits on the patient's part and such cheering-up come from a certain susceptibility in the sick person, who tends to absorb the attitudes that he observes in his physician, guessing from the doctor's manner at the outcome of his malady and conjecturing that a cheerful manner means a cheerful and hoped-for outcome, while an unpleasant demeanor implies a displeasing and a dreaded one; or else it is that these states of mind come about through a certain transfusion of dark or placid, terrestrial or aerial, melancholy or jovial spirits from the physician to the person of the patient, which latter theory is in accordance with the opinion of the Platonicians and of Averroes.

Above all, the aforementioned authors have had special advice to give the physician concerning the words, remarks, discourse, and conversation that should take place between him and the patients by whom he is summoned, the object being that all should tend to one end, namely, the cheering of the patient (without any offense to God) and the avoidance of anything that may in the least serve to make him sad. And so it is, we

find Herophilus severely blaming the physician Callianax who, when asked by a sick man: "Am I going to
die?" impudently answered:

> "Patroclus died, there's nothing is more true;
> He was, by far, a better man than you."

While to another, who wanted to know how his disease
was getting along, and who said to the doctor, after
the manner of the noble Patelin:

> ". . . and my urine:
> Does it not tell you I am going to die?"

—to this one, he replied: "No, not if Latona, the mother
of those two fine youngsters, Phoebus and Diana, was
your mother also."

Likewise, we find Cl. Galen, *Lib. iv, Comment. in vi,
Epidemi.*, calling Quintus, his medical instructor, hard
names for the reason that the latter, when a certain
Roman patient, a most decent sort of chap, remarked to
him: "You've just dined, Doctor; your breath smells of
wine," arrogantly replied: "Yours smells of fever; which
is the better smelling of the two, fever or wine?"

But the slanders of certain cannibals, misanthropes,
and agelasts, directed against me have been so atrocious
and so beyond all reason as long ago to have vanquished my patience; and I was more than of a mind
not to write another iota, especially seeing that one of
the least of the slanders they employed against me was
the report that my books were crammed with heresies
of various sorts. And yet, they were not able to cite a
single instance, in any passage. There were jolly bits
of tomfoolery, without any offense either to God or the
King, that is true; such is, indeed, the one theme of my
books; but heresies there were none, unless one were,
perversely and against all reason, as well as against every

usage of language, to read in an interpretation which
I would a thousand times rather have died than permit
to creep in, or even so much as think of such a thing.
It is as though for *bread* one were to read *stone*, *serpent*
for *fish*, and *scorpion* for *egg*.

Complaining of all this in your presence, upon occasion, I have remarked to you, quite freely, that if I
did not consider myself a better Christian than they
show themselves to be, or if in all my life, writings,
words, or even thoughts I were able to recognize one
scintilla of heresy, why, then, I should, of my own accord, following the Phoenix' example, set about piling
up the dry wood and lighting the fire for my own funeral.

And then, you proceeded to tell me that the late King
Francis, of eternal memory, was well aware of these
slanders, and that he, being curious in the matter, had
had those books of mine read to him by the most learned
and capable readers of his realm, listening to such reading most attentively. (And note that I say *my* books, for
the reason that a number of false and infamous ones
have been maliciously attributed to me.) And you likewise informed me that His Majesty did not find a single
suspect passage, but that he had expressed a horror for
whatever serpent-eater it was who had endeavored to
find the basis of a mortal heresy in an N that had been
put in place of an M, through the fault and negligence
of the printers. As a result of it all, his son, the good and
virtuous Henry, blessed of heaven, may God long preserve him, granted you in my behalf a privilege and
special protection against the slanderers. These glad
tidings you in your great goodness of heart confirmed
for me at Paris; and you again and more fully confirmed them at the time when you were paying a visit to
Monseigneur the Cardinal du Bellay who, being then
convalescent from a long and serious illness, had retired

to Saint-Maur, a place, or, to speak more fittingly, a paradise, of good health, amenities, serenity, comfort, delight, and all the worthy pleasures that come from a rustic and agricultural way of life.

That is the reason, Monseigneur, why I now, without being in the least intimidated, proceed once more to put a quill in the wind, trusting you in your kind favor to be to me, against my slanderers, as a second Gallic Hercules in knowledge, wisdom, and eloquence, an *alexicacos* in virtue, power and authority, and one of whom I may say what was said of Moses, the great prophet and captain in Israel, by the wise King Solomon, *Ecclesiasticus, xlv, 45:*

"A man fearing and loving God, pleasing to all human beings and well beloved of God and men, one whose memory is blessed. God in His Glory hath made him like unto the valiant, He hath raised him up as a terror to his enemies, and in his behalf hath done mighty and dreadful things; in the presence of kings, He hath honored him; to the people, through him, He hath declared His will, and by him hath His light been shown; He hath consecrated him, in faith and in meekness, and hath elected him from among all flesh; through him He hath willed that His voice should be heard, and that to them that are in darkness he should be the living law of wisdom made manifest."

In conclusion, I promise that if I happen to fall in with any who would congratulate me on these merry writings of mine, I shall swear to all of them that the whole of the credit is yours, that you alone deserve their thanks, and that they should pray our Lord to preserve and to increase that mighty stature of yours, but that they should give me credit for nothing more than a humble subjection and a voluntary obedience to your own good commands. For it is you who, through your honorable exhortations, have given me both courage and inventiveness; without you, my heart would have failed me and the fountain of my animal spirits would have remained dried up at the source. May our Lord keep you in His holy grace. From Paris, this twenty-eighth of January, 1552.

Your most humble and very obedient servant,
FRANÇ. RABELAIS, physician.

The Cardinal of Châtillon was the elder brother of the Admiral de Coligny. Made a cardinal by Clement VII *at the age of eighteen, he held a number of important ecclesiastical posts, but later embraced the reformed religion, gave up his cardinal's hat, and was married—in a red cassock, so it is said. Pope Pius* IV *deprived him of his episcopal honors and excommunicated him. Châtillon then went to England, where he died.* "He was a man of intellect," *the French Variorum informs us,* "devoted to letters but still more devoted to his pleasures."

"Soranus the Ephesian": *physician of Ephesus who practiced at Alexandria and Rome about the year 125* A.D. ——"Oribasis": *physician and friend of the Emperor Julian.* ——"Hali Abbas": *Persian physician who flourished about the year 980.* ——"Known as the philonium": *one commentator (Le Duchat) says that this was a sleeveless robe, like a priest's cope.* ——"As Petrus Alexandrinus . . . in Epid.": *Rabelais means to refer to Joannes Alexandrinus, author of a commentary on Hippocrates; reference to Hippocrates' treatise on* Epidemics. ——"Catonian . . . mien": *like that of Cato the Censor.* ——"The opinion of Averroes": *Averroes (or Averrhoës) was a celebrated Arabian physician of the twelfth century.* ——"We find Herophilus . . . blaming": *Herophilus was a fourth-century physician of Alexandria. These answers are given in the sixth book of Hippocrates, except that it is another (Bacchius) and not Herophilus who blames Callianax; Herophilus was the leader of the school to which Callianax belonged.* ——*"Patroclus died":* Iliad, II, 21-2; *the lines are spoken by Achilles.* ——*"We find Galen":* Book IV *of his commentary on Hippocrates'* Epidemics. ——*"Certain . . . agelasts": those who never laugh; from the Greek.* ——*"If I did not consider myself a better Christian . . . ": this sentence, tangled and obscure, reads as follows in the original: " . . . that if I did not consider myself a better Christian than they show themselves to be, or if in all my life, writings, words, or even thoughts I were able to recognize one scintilla of heresy, (why, then) they would not fall, in so abominable a fashion, into the lakes of the Spirit of Slander, that is to say, the* Diabolos, *who through their ministry raises up such a crime against me. I should of my own accord . . . ," etc.* ——*"Whatever serpent-eater": allusion to a passage in Pliny's* Natural History, *Book V, Chapter viii, descriptive of the Troglodyte population in the interior of Africa.* ——*"An N in place of an M": this is the "ars-oul" pun,* âne *(ass) for* âme *(soul).* ——*"Had retired to Saint-Maur: Saint-Maur-les-Fossés, the Cardinal's celebrated château, a humanist resort.* ——*"An alexicacos": one who wards off evil (Greek).* ——*"King Solomon, Ecclesiasticus xlv, 45": from the book of Ecclesiasticus in the Apocrypha; Rabelais paraphrases the first five verses of the chapter.*

Prologue of the Author

M. FRANÇOIS RABELAIS

**FOR THE FOURTH BOOK OF THE HEROIC
DEEDS AND SAYINGS OF PANTAGRUEL**

TO HIS BENEVOLENT READERS

MY GOOD folks, may God save and keep you. Where are
you? I can't see you. Wait a minute till I straddle my
specs. Ah, ha! Fine and fair is Lent! You've had a good
vintage this year, from all that they tell me, and I'm
not the least bit sorry for it. You've found a never-failing
remedy against thirst: that's a fine piece of work. But
you yourselves, your wives and children, your families
and relatives, are you all in as good health as you could
wish? That's fine, that's good, that suits me. May God,
the good God, be eternally praised for it, and if it be
His holy will, may you long remain so. As for me, by
His holy grace, I'm all there; I can speak for myself. I
am, thanks to a little Pantagruelism—and that, you
understand, is a certain cheerfulness of disposition, preserved in spite of all fortuitous circumstances—very fine
and fit and ready to have a little drink, if that suits you.
Do you ask me why, good folks? An irrefutable answer:
Such is the will of the good and almighty God, in which
I acquiesce and which I obey, holding in reverence His
most holy word which we find in the Good News, that is

531

in the Gospel, where, in *Luke iv*, we hear the physician who is negligent of his own health being reproved with terrible sarcasm and annihilating bitterness: "Physician, heal thyself."

Cl. Galen was always careful to keep himself in health, and this not out of respect for the passage I have quoted, though he did possess some acquaintance with the Holy Scriptures and had known and kept company with the Christian saints of his day, as we clearly see, *lib. ii, De Usu Partium; lib. ii, De Differentiis Plusuum, cap. iii, et ibidem lib. iii, cap. ii et lib. De Rerum Affectibus,* if this last be Galen's work: no, he did it, rather, from fear of laying himself open to the popular and sarcastic jest:

> *Ietros allon, autos elkesi bryon . . .*
>
> He comes to others with his doctor's lore;
> Yet he himself is but one running sore.

And so it is, we hear him making the boast that he would not look upon himself as a physician if from the day he was eighteen to his old age he had not always lived in perfect health, with the exception of a few ephemeral fevers of slight duration; and this, though his constitution was not naturally one of the strongest, and though he had, it is obvious, a bad stomach.

"For," he remarks, *lib. v, De sanit. tuenda,* "it is hard to have any faith in a physician's ability to look after the health of others, when he is careless of his own health."

And the physician Asclepiades went even further in his boasts, asserting that he had struck a bargain with Fate to the effect that he was not to be considered a physician if he fell ill for a single day from the time he began practicing his art to his extreme old age. And as a matter of fact, he did live to a ripe and vigorous old age, and thus may be said to have outwitted Fate; until finally one day, without having been previously ill in the slightest degree, he died as a result of falling down a badly built and rotting staircase.

And now, if by any misfortune the health of your lordships happens to be anywhere at large—above, below, in front, behind, to the right, to the left, within, without, far away, or near at hand—wherever it may happen to be, may you, with the help of our blessed Savior, be enabled to meet up with it right soon again. And as soon as you encounter it, let it that very minute be claimed, seized, laid hold of, and appropriated by you. The laws permit it, the King wills it, and I advise it, neither more nor less than did the old legislators when they authorized the master to claim his fugitive slave, no matter where the latter might be found.

Why, good God and my good fellows, is it not prescribed (and practiced) in the ancient code of this realm of France, a land so noble, so venerable, so beautiful, so flourishing, and so rich—is it not prescribed that *the dead seise the quick?* See the exposition that was recently made of this point by the good, the learned, the wise, the human, the mild, and the just And. Tiraqueau, councilor to the great, victorious, and triumphant King Henry, the second of his name, in the latter's most august Parliamentary Court at Paris.

For health is our life, as Ariphon the Sicyonian has very well said. Without health, life is not life, life is no longer livable. ABIOS BIOS, BIOS ABIOTOS. Without health, life is but a languishing thing, life is but the image of death. And so, then, if you are deprived of health, that is to say, if you are dead, seize the quick; lay hold of life, which is health.

I have this trust in God, that He will hear our prayers,

in view of the firm faith with which we utter them, and that He will grant this our wish, seeing that it is a moderate one.

Moderation has been termed golden by the wise men of old, that is to say: precious, praised by all, everywhere a pleasing thing. Run through the Holy Scriptures and you will find that the prayers of those who have asked in moderation have never been among the slighted ones.

We have an example in little Zacchaeus, whose body and relics the monks of St. Garlic, near Orléans, boast that they possess. (They call him St. Sylvan.) He wanted nothing more than to see our blessed Savior in and about Jerusalem. That was a very moderate wish, and one that anybody might cherish. But he was too small and in all that mob of people couldn't see a thing. And so, after stamping and ranting around, pushing and shoving and getting nowhere, he went off to one side and climbed a sycamore tree. Now, the good God knew how sincere and how moderate was the desire of this man's heart, and so, was careful to see that the little fellow had a good glimpse of Him; and Zacchaeus not only saw the Lord, but what's more, the Lord heard him and came to his house and blessed his family.

As another case, a certain prophet's son in Israel was splitting wood near the river Jordan, when the end of his hatchet slipped away from him, as we read in IV *Reg. vi* and fell into the stream. He prayed God to give it back to him. Now, that was a little enough thing to ask for; and he with firm faith and confidence proceeded to hurl—not the hatchet after the handle, which is a scandalous error propagated by certain censorious and sing-song devils—but the handle after the hatchet, as you might very well say. And then suddenly a double miracle occurred: the iron rose from the bottom of the water and fitted itself to the handle. If he, on the other hand, had wanted to go up to heaven in a chariot of fire, like Helios; if he had asked for as numerous a posterity as Abraham's; if he had demanded to be as rich as Job, as strong as Samson, or as good-looking as Absalom, do you think he would have got his wish? It's a question.

And while we are speaking of moderate wishes in connection with hatchets—let me know when it's time to take another drink will you?—I will tell you a story that is to be found among the fables of that wise man, the French Aesop—excuse me, I mean the Phrygian and Trojan Aesop, as Max. Planudes assures us, from which people, according to our most veracious chroniclers, our French nobility is descended. Aelian makes the statement that Aesop was a Thracian, while Agathias, following Herodotus, maintains that he was a Samian. It's all one to me.

In Aesop's time there was a poor villager, a native of Gravot, by the name of Ballocks, he was a hewer and a splitter of wood, and in this humble calling contrived to eke out a miserable, so-so sort of existence. One day, he lost his hatchet; and maybe you think he wasn't cut up about it? That he was; since on his hatchet depended his income and his life. With his hatchet he might continue with some self-respect and reputation to hold up his head among all the rich wood-choppers of the neighborhood; but without his hatchet he was sure to die of hunger. Death, meeting him six days afterwards without his hatchet, would have been sure to mow him down and weed him out of this world.

In this state of mind, he began to cry out, to pray to, implore, and invoke Jupiter, with many eloquent prayers —for you are aware that Necessity is the mother of Eloquence—lifting his face toward heaven, planting his knees in the earth, spreading out his hands, and repeating ever so often, in the course of his loud and tireless invocations:

"My hatchet, O Jupiter, my hatchet, my hatchet! Nothing more, O Jupiter, nothing except my hatchet, or the pennies to buy another one. Alas! my poor hatchet!"

Jupiter at the time was engaged in a very important conference, and at that moment old lady Cybele was just giving her opinion on the business in hand—or, we'll say, it was that handsome young chap, Phoebus, if you must have it your way. But the exclamations coming from Ballocks were so loud that they created considerable consternation in the council-meeting of the gods.

"Who the devil," demanded Jupiter, "is that fellow down there who's making such a horrible racket? I'm a son of old Styx, haven't we enough on our hands here, with all these important matters to be settled? We've already taken care of that little matter of Prester John, King of the Persians, as well as that of Solyman, Emperor of Constantinople; we have patched up that little difficulty between the Tartars and the Muscovites; we have looked into the Sherif's petition; we've taken care of our friend, Golgots Rays; that Parma matter's off our hands; also the Magdeburg matter, the Mirandola matter, and the Africa matter (for that's the name mortals give to the region on the Mediterranean that we call Aphrodisium). Tripoli has changed masters, out of pure carelessness; but her time had come, anyway. And now, here are those Gascon renegades, demanding the return of their bells. Over in that corner are the Saxons, Osterlings, Ostrogoths, and Germans, the last named a people who were once invincible but who are now ABERKEIDS, having been subjugated by one little crippled runt of a chap. They are demanding of us vengeance, assistance, and the restitution of their former good sense and ancient liberties.

"But what are we going to do with this Ramus and this Galland here, who, flanked by their scullions, tools and trusties, are throwing the whole Academy of Paris into an uproar? I'm very much perplexed about the matter and don't know yet just what course I ought to take. Both of them impress me as being likely enough fellows and well-hung lads. One of them has plenty of sunny crowns—and when I say that, I mean, nice, big, heavy ones—while the other would like well enough to have some. One of them has learning while the other is by no means ignorant. One of them likes the right kind of people while the other is liked by the right kind of people. One of them is a fine, crafty little fox; the other is a slanderer in speech and in his writings and is always yelping like a dog against the old orators and philosophers. How does it look to you, you old ass-walloper of a Priapus? Come on and let's have it. I have often found your advice very fair and to the point. *Et habet tua mentula mentem.* That member of yours has a mind of its own.

"King Jupiter," replied Priapus, raising his flaming-red face and holding his head as stiff as a poker, "since you have compared one of these fellows to a snarling dog and the other to a cunning fox, it seems to me that, without working yourself up into any more of a thirst, you ought to do with them what, in the old days, was done with a certain dog and a certain fox."

"What was that?" inquired Jupiter, "and when was it? Who were they? Where did it all happen?"

"Oh, what a fine memory you have!" replied Priapus. "This venerable Father Bacchus of ours that you see over there with the crimson face, in order to get revenge on the Thebans, had a fairy fox made, of such a sort that, no matter what damage he might do, he could never be captured or harmed by any other beast in the world. At the same time our noble Vulcan had made a dog for himself, out of Monesian brass, and, by sufficient lung-work, had succeeded in animating the beast and bringing him to life. He gave him to you, and you gave him to Europa, your little sweetie. She gave him to Minos, and Minos gave him to Procris. Procris, finally, made a present of him to Cephalus.

"Now this hound, also, was a bewitched one and, like the lawyers of today, took every beast that came his way; nothing got away from him. One day the two met. And what do you think happened then? The dog, by Fate's decree, simply had to take that fox; the fox, by Fate's decree, simply could not be taken. The case was brought up to your council-board. You protested that you could not go against Fate. But the Fates were contradictory in this case. The outcome of the whole bally business was that the thing was declared to be a physical impossibility. You sweated a-plenty over that, I'm telling you. And from your sweat as it fell to earth sprang cabbage-plants. In the meanwhile this honorable consistorial body of ours, from failure to come upon a categoric solution, underwent a most miraculous thirst and in this very council-room there were consumed no less than seventy-eight barrels of nectar.

"And then, acting on my advice, you turned them into stone. Whereupon, the whole thing was as clear as day, and a truce to thirst was declared throughout the length and breadth of this great Olympus of ours. That was the year, if you remember, of the Flabby Balls, down near Teumessus, between Thebes and Chalcis.

"Following this precedent, I am of the opinion that the best thing you can do is to turn this present dog and fox of yours into stone. Both of them are named Pierre.

And since, according to the Limousin proverb, it takes three stones to make the mouth of an oven, you might add Master Pierre du Coignet, the candle-snuffer, whom you some while back petrified for similar reasons. And a pretty little equilateral triangle they will make in the big Temple of Paris, or out in the middle of the courtyard, these three dead stones being there set up to perform the function of extinguishing with their noses (as in the game of Squirrel) lighted candles, tapers, dips, links, and torches, seeing that they during their lifetime were in the habit of lighting, most testicularly, the fires of faction, hidden hate, testicular sectarianism and prejudice among the good-for-nothing students. This will serve as an enduring memento of the fact that these two little testiculariform and self-conceited asses have merited your contempt, rather than your condemnation. I've said my say."

"You're a little too easy on them," said Jupiter, "from all that I can see, Master Priapus, my friend. You're not quite so easy with others. For don't you see, since all they are after is to hand their names down to posterity, it will be a lot better for them, after their death, to be turned into hard and marble-like stones than to have to go back to dirt and rot.

"Just have a look down there behind you, over there by the Tyrrhenian Sea and the neighboring Apennine regions, and note what tragedies are being provoked by certain image-toters. That madness will last its time, like the Limousin ovens, and then will end, but not quite so soon as all that. We're going to have plenty of good sport. I can see just one drawback, and that is that we are rather short on thunderbolts, ever since that day when you, my fellow gods, by my express permission and for your own amusement, started hurling them down with no economy whatever on New Antioch. Just as,

later, following your example, the dandified champions
who had undertaken to guard the fortress of Apery
against all comers proceeded to squander their ammuni-
tion by firing at sparrows, and as a result, had none
when the pinch came and they were forced to defend
themselves; the upshot of it was, they evacuated the
place and surrendered to the enemy, who, as a matter of
fact, had been just about to lift the siege, being frantic
with despair and having but one thought, which was to
beat a hasty and a shameless retreat.

"Look lively, there, son Vulcan. Wake up your sleeping Cyclops, Asterlopes, Brontes, Arges, Polyphemus,
Steropes, and Pyracmon. Put them all to work, and give
them plenty to drink. Fiery folk should never be sparing
with the wine. And now, let's take care of that bawler
down there. Take a look, Mercury; see who he is, and find
out what it is he wants."

Mercury looked down through the trap-door of
heaven, that door through which the gods hear what is
said on the earth below. (This trap-door is like the hatch-
way of a ship; and Icaromenippus used to remark that it
was like the mouth of a well.) Mercury looked down and
saw that it was Ballocks, asking for his lost hatchet, and
he duly reported the matter back to the council.

"Well!" exclaimed Jupiter, "that's a fine howdydo for
you! I suppose we have no other business on hand now
than to return lost hatchets? Oh, well, let him have it.
It's in the books of Destiny—you hear that, don't you?
—just as much as if it were worth the whole Duchy
of Milan. To tell the truth, his hatchet is worth as much
to him as his realm is to a king. Tut, tut, give him his
hatchet, and let's hear no more about it. Let's get at that
business about the clergy and the Molehill of Landerousse. Where were we, anyway?"

Priapus, all this while, was leaning against the chimney-piece. After listening to Mercury's report, he very politely but with jocular frankness spoke up and said:

"King Jupiter, back in the days when by your special permission and command I was the guardian of gardens on the earth, I made a note to this effect: a *hatchet* is equivalent to a number of things. It signifies a certain instrument by means of which wood is split and cut. It signifies also—at least, it used to signify—a female who has been well and frequently diddledaddled. And you will observe that every rounder calls the daughter-of-joy who is his sweetie: my Hatchet. For with this tool" (and as he said this, he exhibited his dodrental shooting-stick) "they ram the old hatchet so boldly and so doughtily up to the hilt that their lasses are immune for ever after to a certain fear that is epidemic with the feminine sex: namely, the fear that this too will some day drop down from the lower belly to the heels, through want of a good set of hooks-and-eyes to hold it up.

"I remember, for I've a very fine member—I mean a very fine memory—and one quite large enough to fill a butter-jug—I remember, one day, at the feast of the Tubilustria—it was on Vulcan's holiday, in the month of May—I remember listening in a pretty garden-plot to Josquin des Près, Ockeghem, Hobrecht, Agricola, Brumel, Camelin, Vigoris, De la Fage, Bruyer, Prioris, Seguin, De la Rue, Midy, Moulu, Mouton, Gascogne, Louis Compère, Pinet, Fevin, Rouzée, Richafort, Rousseau, Constantio Festi, and Jacquet Berchem, as they warbled most melodiously:

> When Big Ted went to bed that night,
> With his new-wedded wife,
> He hid a mallet out of sight—
> It was to save his life!
> "Dearie"—her voice was like a knife—
> "Why the mallet, if I might

Be so bold to ask?"—"To drive her tight."
"What! a mallet? That's a farce.
When Big John comes, he treats me right:
He drives it with his arse."

"And nine Olympiads and one intercalary year after that—Oh, what a member—damn it, I mean a memory! (I'm always getting the meaning of those two words mixed up)—I listened to Adrien Willaert, Gombert, Jannequin, Arcadelt, Claudin, Certon, Manchicourt, Auxerre, Villiers, Sandrin, Sohier, Hesdin, Morales, Passereau, Maille, Maillart, Jacotin, Heurteur, Verdelot, Carpentras, Lhretier, Cadéac, Doublet, Vermont, Bouteiller, Lupi, Pagnier, Millet, du Mollin, Allaire, Marault, Morpain, Gendre, and other jovial musicians, in a private garden, under a pleasant arbor and surrounded by a rampart of flagons, hams, pasties, and various sorts of tufted quail, as they, in the most charming fashion, rendered the following:

Since a hatchet or a tool is of no use,
Unless it has a handle that will match it,
Let's put a handle in, and not too loose:
Let's play that I'm the handle, you're the hatchet.

"And you can judge from this what kind of hatchet it is that rowdy fellow, Ballocks, is yelping for."

At these words all the venerable gods and goddesses burst out laughing, like a microcosm of flies, while Vulcan with his peg-leg, to cut a figure in the eyes of his sweetie, did three or four nice little somersaults on the platform.

"Tut, tut," said Jupiter to Mercury. "Go down there right away and throw down three hatchets at Ballocks' feet: his own, one of gold, and a third one of silver, all of them heavy and of good caliber. Give him his choice, and if he takes his own and is satisfied with it, give him the other two. If he takes either of the others, chop his head off with his own hatchet. And do the same, here-- after, to all hatchet-losers."

When he had said this, Jupiter twisted his own head around, like a monkey swallowing pills, and made so frightful a face that all Olympus trembled.

Mercury with his peaked cap, his short cloak, his winged heels, and his caduceus let himself down through the trap-door of heaven, clove the atmospheric void, descended lightly on the earth, and cast the three hatchets at Ballocks' feet, saying to the latter:

"You've yelled enough to be wanting a drink by this time. Your prayers have been heard by Jupiter. Look these three hatchets over, see which is yours, and take it."

Ballocks, lifted the golden hatchet. He looked it over and found it quite heavy. Then, he turned to Mercury and said:

"'Pon my soul, that's not mine at all, at all; I don't want it."

He did the same with the silver hatchet, saying:

"It's not this one, either; you can have it."

Then, he took the wooden one in his hand, looked at the end of the handle, and discovered his own mark; and leaping with joy like a fox that has fallen in with some stray chickens, and grinning at the same time through the end of his nose, he said:

"By golly, if this one here's not mine! If you want to leave it with me. I'll make you a sacrifice of a nice big jug of milk, all covered with fresh strawberries, on the Ides—that's the fifteenth—of May."

"My good man," said Mercury, "I'll leave it with you, all right. Take it and welcome. And seeing that you have been so moderate in your wishes in the matter of the hatchet, I, by Jupiter's will, hereby make you a present of these others. That's enough to make you rich for life; run along now and be a good little man."

Ballocks thanked Mercury politely, payed his wor-
shipful respects to the great Jupiter, and fastened his old
hatchet to his leather belt, tucking it up under his arse
like a second Martin of Cambrai. The two others, which
were heavier, he strung around his neck. In this outfit
he went strutting through the country, making a fine
appearance among his neighbors and fellow parishioners,
as he inquired of them, in the words of Patelin: "Have
I got mine, or haven't I?"

The day following, clad in a white smock and with the
two precious hatchets about his neck, he betook himself
to Chinon, a most distinguished city, a right noble city, a
most ancient city—indeed, one might say, the first city
of the world, according to the opinion and the statements
of the most learned of the Masoretes. At Chinon, he
changed his silver hatchet into perfectly good Heads and
other white money, while his golden hatchet he changed
into Saluts, nice big woolly Sheep, pretty little Riders,
some charming Royals, and some fine big sunny crowns.
With the money, he bought a lot of farms, a lot of barns,
a lot of fields and country houses, tillable ground, pas-
tures, ponds, mills, gardens, willow-groves, oxen, cows,
sheep, lambs, nanny-goats, sows, hogs, asses, horses,
hens, roosters, capons, pullets, geese, ganders, ducks,
drakes, and other small-fry. And in less than no time, he
was the rightest man in the country—richer, even, than
Maulevrier the Lame.

The backwoods lads and the Jimmy Goodfellows of
the neighborhood, observing what luck Ballocks had
fallen into, were thoroughly astonished at it, and the
pity and commiseration they had always felt towards
the poor fellow in the past was changed into envy for
his wealth which was so great and so unlooked for. And
so, they began scurrying around, making inquiries, be-
wailing their own ill luck and trying to find out where

and by what means, on what day, at what time by the
clock, and just exactly why and how this big windfall
had come Ballocks' way. When they learned that it was
through the loss of a hatchet, they cried:

"Hee, haw! And is that all it takes, the loss of a
hatchet, for us to become rich? That's an easy way and it
costs very little. So then the heavens, constellations,
stars, and planets are in such a position that whoever
loses his hatchet will at once become rich? Hee, Haw!
Hee, Haw! By God, old hatchet, but you're going to be
lost, whether you like it or not."

And they all went straight out and lost their hatchets.
Devil a one there was, when they were through, that had
a hatchet to his name. I'm telling you there wasn't a
single mother's son that didn't mislay his hatchet. The
result was, there was no more wood felled, no more wood
split in the whole country, on account of the great
scarcity of hatchets.

And the Aesopic fable goes on to state that certain of
the avaricious small gentry who had sold their small
meadowland and mill-holdings to Ballocks so that they
might be able to dress up and step out—the fable says
that when these same ones learned that Ballocks' luck
had come to him in this fashion and by this means alone,
they at once hawked their swords in order to buy
hatchets, that they might lose them like the peasants and,
through this loss, obtain a heap of gold and silver. You
might, very properly, have said that these were little
Romeward-bound ones, selling their all and borrowing
from others in order to be able to buy a mass of favors
from some newly created pope. All they did was cry and
pray and lament and invoke Jupiter:

"My hatchet, my hatchet, Jupiter!" (My hatchet here,
my hatchet there.) "My hatchet, Oh, ho, ho! Jupiter, my
hatchet!"

The air all round about resounded with the cries and yelpings of these hatchet-losers.

And Mercury was right there when it came to bringing them fresh hatchets. He offered each one his own, the one he had lost, another of gold, and a third of silver. All of them picked the golden one and were about to rake it in, with many thanks to their benefactor, the great Jupiter; but that very second, while they were bending over to pick the hatchet up from the ground, Mercury busied himself and chopped off their heads, in accordance with Jupiter's command. And the number of chopped heads was equal and correspondent to the number of lost hatchets.

There you are. You can see what good fortune comes to those simple ones who wish and long for moderate things. Take warning from this, all of you, you back-country bumpkins, you who are always saying that for ten thousand francs in income you wouldn't give up the thing you've set your heads on. Take warning and, hereafter, don't go around talking quite so impudently, as I have heard you in the past when you were wishing:

"Would to God that I had right now a hundred-seventy-eight-millions in gold! Ho, ho! what a figure I'd cut!"

You've got chilblains, that's what's the matter with you. How could a king, an emperor, or a pope wish for any more than that, I'd like to know. You've had plenty of opportunity to find out, by experience, that all you get from your outrageous wishing is the old sheep's-rot, and not a penny in your pockets, any more than those two wishful beggars who did their wishing in the Paris fashion, one of whom wished that he had all the nice sunny crowns that had been spent there from the day the first foundation stones were laid down to the present time, the whole to be figured at the rate of sale and value of the dearest year there had been in all that lapse of time. There was nothing bashful about that lad, now, was there? Do you suppose he could have been eating bitter plums with the peel on? Do you suppose it had put his teeth on edge? Well, anyway, the other one wanted Notre-Dame, filled up with steel needles from the pavement to the highest vault, and he wanted to have as many sunny crowns as could be put in as many bags as could be sewn with each and every needle, until they were all broken or pointless. There's a wish for you! How does it strike you?

And what did they get for it all? By evening, each one of them had chilblains on his heels, a chancre on his chin, a bad cough in his lungs, catarrh in his windpipe, a big boil on his behind, and a devil of a crust of bread to pick his teeth.

Do your wishing, then, in moderation, and you will get all you wish for and more still, providing that you duly work and labor in the meanwhile.

"Well," you protest, "but God might just as well have given me seventy-eight thousand as the thirteenth part of a half, since He is all-powerful. A million in gold is no more than a penny to Him."

Tee, hee! And who, pray, taught you to speak like that of the power and predestinating will of God, you poor devils, you? Peace. Ps-s-t, humble yourselves before His holy face, and become conscious of your own imperfections.

And that, my gouty friends, is what I found my hope upon. I am firmly convinced that if the good God pleases, you shall obtain the gift of health, seeing that, for the present, that is all you ask. But hold on a minute; a half ounce of patience there. That's not the way the Genoans do, when, in the morning, having thought it all out in their rooms and decided from whom they will get their nickels that day, and who by their wits is going to be fleeced, trimmed, tricked, and out-sharpered—having done all this, they go out and greet each other by saying: "Good Health and Good Gain, Signor." They're not satisfied with health; they want gain (*guadagno*) too; as witness the crowns of Guadagne; and so, it quite frequently happens that they get neither one nor the other.

All right, then, assuming that you are in good health, take a good cough for yourselves; take, also, a good triple-sized drink; wiggle your ears for all get-out; and be ready to hear marvels told of our friend, the noble Pantagruel.

"Cl. Galen . . . De Usu Partium," *etc.: reference to works of Galen on various medical subjects.* ——"A *popular and sarcastic jest"*: Plutarch, *in his* Discourse against the Epicurean, Kolotes, *attributes this verse to an unnamed Greek tragic poet.* ——"De sanit. tuenda": *on the care of the health.* ——"The physician Asclepiades"*: Pliny, Natural History, vii, 37. ——"The dead seise the quick"*: play on the legal term* seise *and the verb* to seize. ——"The good . . . André Tiraqueau"*: who was soon to suppress this very book!* ——"Ariphon the Sicyonian"*: of Sicyon, a village in Achaea: the poet is referred to by Athenaeus in the last chapter of his fifteenth book.* ——"Little Zacchaeus"*: the story of Zacchaeus the publican, in* Luke, xix. ——"The monks of St. Garlic"*: Rabelais means the monks of Saint-Ay, but he puns by writing Saint-Ayl.* ——"They call him St. Sylvan"*: a play on Silvanus, god of the woods, and the fact that Zacchaeus climbed a tree; St. Sylvan (Saint-Sylvain) is confused with Zacchaeus in certain apocryphal legends.* ——"In IV Reg. vi"*: the fourth book of* Kings, *sixth chapter; in the King James version, Second Kings, vi; Rabelais*

cites the Vulgate in which the two books of Samuel are regarded as First and Second Kings. ——"Certain censorious and sing-song devils": allusion to the Sorbonnists. ——"Like Helios": the sun god. ——"As Max. Planudes assures us": Maximus Planudes, fourteenth-century Greek monk noted for his learning. ——"Aelian makes the statement": Aelian was a second-century Greek writer. —— "Agathias . . . maintains": Agathias was a Greek poet and historian of the sixth and seventh centuries. —— "A native of Gravot": near Chinon. ——"In Aesop's time . . .": the story is from Aesop's fable of Mercury and the Woodsman; compare the first fable of La Fontaine's fifth book; Poggio has a somewhat similar one. ——"The little difficulty between the Tartars and the Muscovites": this has been seen as referring to the victory of the Muscovites over the Tartars in 1550; these allusions show Rabelais' awareness of the events of his age, but a number of them can only be guessed at, and the element of fantasy enters in. ——"The Sherif's petition": a sherif is an Arabian chief or prince. ——"Our friend Golgots Rays": probably the Turkish admiral, Dragut Rays, who about this time was committing depredations in the Mediterranean. ——"The region . . . that we term Aphrodisium": this was the name of a maritime town in Latium, in the province of Lavinium, noted for its temple of Venus. ——"Those Gascon renegades, demanding the return of their bells": the inhabitants of Guienne in Gascony having revolted against the salt-tax, their bells had been taken from them. ——"Osterlings": the Hanseatic cities to the east of France, England, and the Low Countries; "Osterling" is equivalent to "Easterling." ——"Who are now ABERKEIDS": Swiss patois (abakeit) meaning "done for." ——"One little crippled runt of a chap": the Emperor Charles v. ——"This Ramus and this Galland": Rabelais writes Rameau *(branch or bough), but he means Ramus, or Pierre La Ramée, professor of philosophy and mathematics at the Collège Royal; Ramus was also a grammarian and philologist and had attacked Aristotle, Cicero, and Quintilian; Pierre Galland was principal of the Collège de Boncourt and rector of the University of Paris; he defended Aristotle against Ramus, and the controversy had divided university circles; Galland had attacked Rabelais. ——"Procris . . . made a present of him to Cephalus": Procris was the wife of Cephalus, who shot her in a wood, mistaking her for a wild beast. ——"Down near Teumessus": this fable will be found in Pausanias, Ovid, Suidas, Caelius Rhodiginus, and other writers; Pausanias states that the fox came from Teumessus. ——"Both of them are named Pierre": Pierre in French means rock or stone. ——"Master Pierre de Coignet . . . whom you . . . petrified": allusion to a statue of one Pierre de Cugnières, an advocate-general who under Philip of Valois had defended the royal authority against the clergy; a grotesque effigy, it was used for snuffing candles. ——"As in the game of Squirrel": in which the player has to put out a lighted torch with his nose; one of Gargantua's games. ——"The fortress of Apery": Rabelais' word is* Dindenaroys, *the sense of which is the land of those who foolishly ape the manners and gestures of others (Sainéan). ——"By firing on sparrows": possibly a play on* moineaux, *sparrows, and* moines, *monks. ——"Through the trap-door of heaven": described in Lucian's* Icaromenippus. ——"The Molehill of Landerousse":* taulpetière, *or molehill, with Rabelais means monastery; Landerousse has not been explained. ——"His dodentral shooting-stick": from the Latin* dodentralis, *half a cubit long, or nine Roman inches; compare the* "sesqipedalis mentula" *(foot-and-a-half-long penis) of Martial. ——"The feast of the Tublilustria": Roman*

festival in honor of Mars; the feast of trumpets. ——*"I remember listening to . . .": Rabelais of the encyclo-pedic mind here displays his musical erudition by listing the outstanding composers of his age and the century preceding; almost all have been identified.* ——*"Do the same to all hatchet-losers": a dig at cuckolds, those who cannot hold their wives.* ——*"Like a second Martin of Cambrai": Martin and Martine (masculine and fem-inine) were the names given to two clock figures, each provided with a hammer* (marteau) *to strike the hours, that were to be found on the steeple-clock of Cambrai.* ——*"Have I got mine, or haven't I?": Patelin's "En ay-je?"* ——*"Changed his silver . . .", etc.: the "Heads" were coins known as Testons; the "Salut" was an Anglo-French coin that had circulated during the reign of the English Kings, Henry* v *and Henry* vi, *at Paris; the "Riders"* (riddes) *were gold pieces with the figure of a knight; the other coins have been previously mentioned.* ——*"Maulevrier the Lame": this was probably Michel de Ballan, Seigneur de Maulevrier, near Lerné in the Chinon country; he is mentioned in the* Gargantua. ——*"Crowns of Guadagne": Thomas de Guadagne, a financier of the time, had lent money to Francis* i *when the latter was taken prisoner by Charles* v; *there is a play on Guadagne and the Italian* guadagno, gain.

How Pantagruel Put Out to Sea to Visit the Oracle of the Holy Bacbuc

IN THE month of June, on the day of the Feast of Vesta—the very day on which Brutus conquered Spain and sub-jugated the Spaniards, and the day, also, on which the miserly Crassus was defeated and vanquished by the Parthians—on that day Pantagruel took leave of the good Gargantua, his father. The latter, as was the praiseworthy custom among Christian saints of the primitive Church, prayed for a prosperous voyage for his son and all the latter's company, as Pantagruel put out to sea from the port of Thalasse, accompanied by Panurge, Friar John Hackem, Epistemon, Gymnastes, Eusthenes, Rhizotome, Carpalim, and other servants and domestics of long standing, together with Xenomanes, the great traveler and Hero of Perilous Crossings, who a few days before had duly arrived at Pantagruel's command.

The last mentioned for certain very good reasons had left with Gargantua, in the latter's big universal Hydrography, a complete chart of the route they were to follow in their visit to the oracle of the Holy Bottle Bacbuc.

The number of ships has already been stated, for your benefit, in the Third Book, and they were convoyed by an equal number of triremes, long rowing-boats, galleons, and Liburnian light-craft, all well equipped, well calked, and well furnished with an abundance of Pantagruelion. Before setting out, all the officers, interpreters, pilots, captains, seamen, cabin-boys, rowers, and sailors gathered on the *Thalamege*. That was the name given to Pantagruel's big flagship, which had on its poop, by way of ensign, a large, commodious bottle, half of smooth and polished silver and half of gold, enameled a carnation red; from which it may readily be deduced that white and red were the colors of these noble travelers, as an indication that they were on their way to consult the Bottle.

On the poop of the second ship was reared an antique lantern, fashioned with much fine workmanship of transparent phengites stone, by way of denoting that they were to pass through the Lantern country. The third for device had a fine deep porcelain goblet. The fourth, a little gold jug with two handles like an ancient urn.

The fifth, a distinguished-looking spit of sperm-emerald. The sixth, a monastic flagon made of four metals combined. The seventh, an ebony funnel all embroidered with gold and damascene workmanship. The eighth, an ivory goblet, very precious, inlaid with damascened gold. The ninth, a flask, made of refined gold. The tenth, a drinking-glass of fragrant agalloche, which is what you call wood of aloes, threaded with Cyprian gold and Persian-work. The eleventh, a mosaic vintage-basket. The twelfth, a *barraut*, or old-time measure, of tarnished gold, covered with vignettes of big Indian pearls and topiarian work.

As a result, no one, no matter how sad, downcast, crabbed, or melancholy he might have been—not even Heraclitus, himself, that old Weeper—could have refrained from feeling quite elated or from smiling right cheerfully as he looked upon this noble convoy of ships with their various devices. And there was no one who would not have sworn, at once, that these voyagers were all good drinkers and good fellows, and who would not have predicted without any hesitancy whatsoever that their voyage, both going and coming, would be a merry and a healthful one.

We left them, then, gathered on the *Thalamege*. There Pantagruel first made a brief and pious speech, all based upon sayings taken from the Holy Scriptures, on the general subject of navigation. When this was ended, he prayed to God in a loud, clear voice as all the shopkeepers and citizens of Thalasse, who had gathered on the quay to witness the embarkation, listened most attentively. Following the prayer they rendered, with very fine harmony, the Psalm of the Holy King David that begins: *When Israel went out of Egypt*. When the Psalm was finished, tables were spread upon the deck and food was promptly brought in. The Thalassians who had joined in the singing of the above Psalm caused many victuals and much wine to be sent from their homes, and all drank to them and they drank to all.

And this is the reason why it was that not a manjack of the crew was afterwards seasick or suffered any disturbance whatsoever in either his stomach or his head, something which they could by no means so readily have prevented by drinking salt water, either pure or mixed with wine, for some days before, or by employing quinces, lemon-rind, the juice of bitter-sweet pomegranates, by going on a prolonged fast, by covering their stomachs with paper, or any of the other fool things that the doctors prescribe for those who are about to take a sea voyage.

After their cups had been filled time and again, each one retired to his own ship; and at an early hour they set sail, to an east-by-southeast wind, in accordance with the route that had been charted by the chief pilot, one Jamet Brayer, who himself had set the needles on all the compasses.

For his opinion, and that of Xenomanes likewise, was to the effect that, seeing that the oracle of the Holy Bottle was in Cathay, in Upper India, it was best not to follow the route ordinarily taken by the Portuguese. The latter were in the habit of passing through the torrid zone and rounding the Cape of Good Hope at the southern end of Africa, beyond the Equinoctial, thus losing from sight the North Pole, which should have served them as a guide; and in this manner they made a tremendous voyage of it. The better thing to do was to keep as close as possible to the parallel of India and to swing around the North Pole to the west in such a manner that, coming in from the north, they would find themselves in the same latitude as the port of Olonne, but without going any farther north than that, from fear of being drawn into the Arctic Sea and marooned there.

By making, then, this canonical detour and by keeping to the same parallel, they would have to their right and toward the east what at their departure had been on their left, which was a very great advantage for them. And so, without shipwreck, danger, or the loss of any of their men, but very tranquilly, except for one day near the island of the Macraeons, they made the voyage to Upper India, accomplishing in less than four months what the Portuguese were barely able to do in three years, not to speak of a thousand sufferings and innumerable dangers which the latter were forced to meet and undergo.

And I am of the opinion—standing, of course, to be corrected—that this quite likely was the route followed by those Indians who sailed to Germany and who were so respectfully treated by the King of the Suevians, at the time when Q. Metellus Celer was proconsul in Gaul, as we read in Cor. Nep. Pomp. Mela, and in Pliny who follows these authors.

That Rabelais, in the navigations of Pantagruel, had in mind the search for the northwest passage, is here indubitably indicated.

"The Oracle of the Holy Bacbuc": "Bacbuc," from the Hebrew, is equivalent of "Bottle." ——"Xenomanes . . . Hero of Perilous Crossings": the name Xenomanes, from the Greek, means one who is passionately interested in things that come from abroad; this personage has been seen as the captain-pilot Jean Fonteneau, known as Alfonse de Saintongeois, who died in 1545; the identification is doubtful, however. ——"Big univer-

sal Hydrography": that is, marine chart. ——"Of transparent phengites stones": the phengites *is a stone mentioned by Pliny* (Natural History XXXVI, xxii, 46) *and by Suetonius* (Life of Domitian, xiv); *it was selenite or crystallized gypsum and was used for making windowpanes. ——"Of sperm-emerald": this was a bastard emerald, the* prasius lapis *of Pliny* (Natural History, XXXVII, viii, 34). ——"Of fragrant agalloche": from the Greek* agallochom, *the bitter aloe. ——"Barraut, an old-time measure": an old measure of twenty-seven pints employed in the langue d'oc country. ——"Of topiarian work"; ornamental work in imitation of vegetables; from the Latin* topiarius, *pertaining to landscape gardening. ——"Heraclitus himself": the "weeping philosopher." ——"When Israel went out of Egypt":* Psalm cxiv *in the King James version; Rabelais here quotes a translation by Clement Marot. ——"One Jamet Brayer": probably a famous pilot and navigator of the day. ——"Port of Olonne": mentioned in Book First; today Sables d'Olonne, in the Vendée. ——"The island of the Macraeons":* Macraeons *is from the Greek, meaning those who live a long time. ——"Those Indians . . . King of the Suevians": the reference is to East Indians; the Suevians, or Suevi, were a powerful Germanic people of northeastern Germany. ——"Cor. Nep., Pomp. Mela": Cornelius Nepos the Roman biographer and Pomponius Mela the geographer who lived in the first century* A.D.

In the course of their voyage Pantagruel and his followers put in at a number of exotic ports of call. But however he may attempt to disguise his satiric intent with the trappings of fantasy, Rabelais still stays close to life, the life of mid-sixteenth-century France. An example of this is his passage on the Shysteroos, where

*he launches yet another attack on the members of the
legal profession and the conniving monks who work
with them. This passage also introduces a direct reminiscence of one of the two or three writers to whom he
is most deeply indebted—François Villon.*

How Pantagruel Passed Pettifoggery and the Strange Mode of Life among the Shysteroos

CONTINUING on our way, on the day following we passed
Pettifoggery, which is a country all blotted and blurred.
That's all I can tell you about it. There, we saw some
Pettifoggers and some Shysteroos, or writ-servers, fellows capable of anything. They did not invite us to have
either a drink or a bite to eat. The only thing they did do,
with a lot of pretentious bowings and scrapings, was to
inform us that they were wholly at our service, providing
we paid them for the said services.

One of our interpreters gave Pantagruel an account
of how these people earn their living in a very strange
fashion, the direct opposite of that followed by the
Romicoles. At Rome, an endless number of fellows
earn their living by poisoning, mauling, and murdering.
The Shysteroos, on the other hand, earn theirs by taking
a good thrashing; and as a matter of fact, if they go for
too long a time without being trounced, they die of
hunger—they, their families, and their offspring.

"These fellows," said Panurge, "are like those that Cl.
Galen tells us of, who are unable to erect the cavernous
nerve above the equatorial circle, if they are not well
drubbed. St. Theobald! anybody who did that to me
would produce just the opposite effect and unsaddle me
completely, I swear it by all the devils in hell."

"The way it comes about," went on the interpreter,

"is this. When a monk, priest, money-lender, or lawyer happens to have it in for some gentleman in his neighborhood, he sends one of these Shysteroos to see the party. The Shysteroos will serve and summons the gentleman and impudently offend and insult him, according to instructions, until his victim, if the latter is not paralyzed or more stupid than a flabby frog, is forced to give him a good clubbing over the head with a sword or a few telling kicks in the shin, or, better yet, he tosses the intruder out of the loopholes or windows of the castle. Once this is done, behold, your Shysteroo is rich for four months to come just as though blows from a club were his regular diet. For he will be well paid by the monk, the money-lender, or the lawyer and in addition will recover damages from the gentleman—damages sometimes so heavy that his victim will lose all he has in paying them, until he is in danger of dying like a rat in jail. You would think it was the King himself he had struck."

"I know," said Panurge, "a very good remedy against that, and one which the Lord of Basché made use of."

"What is that?" asked Pantagruel.

"The Lord of Basché," replied Panurge, "was a courageous, virtuous, magnanimous, and chivalrous gentleman. Having returned from a long war in which the Duke of Ferrara with the aid of Francis i defended himself against the madness of Pope Julius ii, he found himself daily served, summonsed, and beshystered, and all to please a certain fat prior of Saint-Louand.

"One day, as he was lunching with his retainers—for he was very kind and human in his relationships—he sent for his baker, whose name was Loire, and for the latter's wife, together with the curate of the parish, whose name was Oudart and who acted as my lord's butler, as was then the custom in France. When they

were all there, he addressed them, in the presence of
his gentleman retainers and the others of his household:

"'My friends, you can see how every day I am
persecuted by these paid bandits of Shysteroos. It has
come to such a point that, unless you aid me, I have
made up my mind to flee the country and go fight for the
Sultan, or else, go straight to the lower regions, it does
not much matter which.

"'And so, from now on whenever they come around
here I want you, Loire, and your wife to be ready. I
want you to be in my great hall, in fine wedding attire,
and to make out that you have just been married. You
are to act just as you did when you were first married,
you understand. Look; here are a hundred gold crowns;
take them and buy what you need. And you, Father
Oudart, be sure not to fail to appear in your best stole
and surplice with a little holy water for the wedding.
And you too, Trudon' (for that was the name of his
drummer) 'you be there with your flute and drum.

"'And then, when the words that make them man and
wife have been pronounced, and when the bride has
been kissed and while the drum is beating, I want you
all to give each other little wedding souvenirs, that is,
blows with your fists—you'll enjoy the supper all the
more afterwards for it. But when it comes to the Shysteroo, flay him as you would green rye. Don't be easy
with him. Hit, swat, and pound him, I beg you. Wait a
minute—I'll give you right now these jousting gloves
covered with goat-hide. Give him more swats than you
can count, this way, that way, an t'other way. The one
that swats him the hardest I'll look upon as my best
friend. And don't be afraid of being arrested for it; I'll
stand backer for you all. Your licks, of course, are to be
given with a smile, as is the custom at all weddings.'

"'That is all very well,' said Oudart, 'but how are we

going to know the Shysteroo? For there are all sorts of persons in your house every day.'

" 'I've taken care of that,' replied Basché. 'Whenever there comes up to the gate some fellow on foot or badly mounted, with a huge, thick silver ring on his thumb, you'll know that's the Shysteroo. The gatekeeper, having courteously let him in, will ring the bell. That is the time for all of you to stand by and to come into the great hall to play the little tragicomedy which I have sketched for you.'

"And that very day, as God would have it, there came up a big, fat, red-faced Shysteroo. When he rang at the gate, the gatekeeper recognized him through the fellow's large heavy gaiters, his paltry mare, a bag filled with writs that hung at his girdle, and especially by the heavy silver ring which the Shysteroo wore on his left thumb. The gatekeeper treated him courteously enough, let him in without ceremony, and then merrily jangled the bell.

"When they heard it, Loire and his wife put on their wedding finery and with merry faces came down into the great hall. Oudart put on his stole and surplice and, as he emerged from his sacristy, bumped into the Shysteroo. He at once took the latter back in with him, to have a prolonged swig at the bottle; and while the others were bringing in gauntlets from all sides, Oudart remarked to the visitor:

" 'You could not have come at a more opportune moment. Our master's in a fine humor today. We're going to have a rousing time of it and no expense will be spared. For we're right in the middle of a wedding. Here's to you; drink up and be merry.'

"While the Shysteroo was having a drink, Basché, observing that all his followers were on hand and ready for the fray, sent for Oudart. Oudart came in, bringing the holy water, with Shysteroo trailing along behind him. The latter as he entered the room did not forget to make a number of bows and scrapes, and then turned and served a summons on Basché. Basché gave him the finest reception in the world, made the fellow a present of an "angel" and begged him to be so good as to be a witness to the wedding contract. Which was done.

"Towards the end, fisticuffs began to fly around. But when it came the Shysteroo's turn, they so belabored him with blows from the heavy gauntlets that, when they were through, the fellow was knocked dumb and half murdered, with one eye poached in black butter, eight ribs broken, his breast-bone caved in, and his shoulder-blades knocked helter skelter, while his lower jaw was in three slices; and it was all done with a laugh. God only knows what good work Oudart got in, covering with the sleeve of his surplice the big steeled gauntlet, lined with ermine, for he was a powerful rascal.

"And so, Shysteroo, looking like a striped tiger, went back to l'Ile-Bouchard, quite satisfied with the reception the Lord of Basché had given him. With the assistance of the good surgeons of the country, he lived as long as any one could wish, and nothing was said about the matter afterwards. All recollection of it died with the sound of the bells that did a carillon for his funeral."

Though his hero may be voyaging amid the Arctic wastes of a fabled northwest passage, Maître François in spirit is back in his own "cow country," with this anecdote of one of the local gentry of the Chinon region; for the fief of Basché was in Anjou, on the borders of Touraine and Poitou, not far from Rabelais' birthplace.

"The Shysteroos": Rabelais' word is Chicquanous, *related to the modern French* chicaneur, *a pettifogger.*

——*"The Romicoles": dwellers at Rome.* ——*"The cavernous nerve . . . if they are not first well drubbed":* playing upon the erotic sense of the Latin *caverna*, the author elsewhere refers to the "cavernous member"; allusion to flagellation and its effects upon erection in the male. ——*"The madness of Pope Julius II":* allusion to the quarrel of Julius II and Louis XII. ——*"A certain fat prior of Saint-Louand":* Louand was a village on the right bank of the Vienne, a little below Chinon; it possessed an ancient abbey; M. Clouzot writes: "For some unknown reason, Rabelais appears to have had little sympathy for the monks of Saint-Louand." ——*"With a huge . . . silver ring on his thumb":* the ring was used as a notary's seal. ——*"Made him a present of an angel":* reference to the coin with the image of St. Michael.

How, Following the Example of Master François Villon, the Lord of Basché Commended His Followers

"Shysteroo, having left the castle and remounted his *esque orbe*, which was what he called his one-eyed mare, Basché, seated under the arbor of his private garden, sent for his wife, her ladies-in-waiting, and all his followers. He then had them bring in wine and a number of pastries, hams, fruits, and cheeses; and after drinking to all present right merrily my lord proceeded to tell them a tale:

" 'Master François Villon in his declining years retired to Saint-Maixent in Poitou under the patronage of a good man, the abbot of that place. There to amuse the populace he undertook to put on a Passion play in the

Poitevin language and with appropriate gestures. When
the players had been selected, the parts assigned, and
the theatre prepared, he informed the mayor and aldermen that the Mystery play would be ready about the
end of the Niort fair, adding that it only remained to
provide suitable costumes for the actors. The mayor and
aldermen at once passed a resolution looking after that.

" 'Now, Master François, in order to furnish an old
peasant who was to play the part of God the Father with
a suitable costume, requested Friar Stephen Taptail,
sacristan of the Franciscans of the place, to lend him a
cope and a stole. Taptail declined, asserting that by
their provincial statutes the members of his order were
strictly forbidden to give or lend anything to players.
Villon replied that the statute only had to do with farces,
masquerades, and dissolute performances, for such was
the manner in which he had seen it applied at Brussels
and elsewhere. Notwithstanding this, Taptail's answer
was that Master François might look elsewhere if he
liked but that he need expect nothing from his, Taptail's,
sacristy, for he would not get anything, that was certain. Villon in great disgust reported this to the players,
with the prophecy that God would take vengeance on
Taptail and see that the latter was properly punished,
and that very soon.

" 'On the Saturday following Villon was advised that
Taptail, mounted on the convent filly (for that was the
name they gave to a mare that had not yet been covered), had gone to beg a handout at Saint-Ligaire, and
that he would be coming back about two o'clock that
afternoon. Accordingly Villon proceeded to stage a
parade of his Devil Show through the village and the
market-place. His devils were all caparisoned in wolf,
calf, and ram skins, trigged out with sheep's-heads, bull's-
horns, and big kitchen-crooks, with huge leather thongs

for belts, from which dangled great cow-bells and little mule-bells, and they all kept up a terrific jangle. In their hands, the actors carried black sticks loaded with rockets, while others carried long lighted firebrands upon which at every street-corner whole handfuls of pitch and rosin in powdered form were thrown, this producing a most terrific fire and smoke.

" 'Having thus paraded his troop to the great enjoyment of the populace and the great terror of little children, Villon finally led them for a banquet to a country house that was near the gate by which one left on the road to Saint-Ligaire. As they came up to the villa Master François caught sight of Taptail at a distance, returning from his little job of begging. Whereupon the poet addressed his followers in macaronic verse:

> *Hic est de patria, natus de gente rascali*
> *Qui solet antiquo scrappas portare in sacco.*

" ' "Christ almighty!" cried all the devils then, "that's the fellow who wouldn't lend God the Father a measly cope, is it? Let's throw the fear of God into him."

" ' "An excellent idea," replied Villon, "but let us hide and let him pass, and then up with your rockets and your firebrands."

" 'When Taptail came up to where they were, they all piled out into the road in front of him, in great confusion, hurling fire from all sides upon the monk and his mare, jingling their bells, and yelling like the devil: *"Hoo, hoo, hoo, hoo, brrrourrourrr, rrrourrr! hoo, hoo, hoo! hoo, hoo, hoo! Aren't we nice little devils, Brother Stephen?"*

" 'The filly scared to death began to trot and fart, and to leap and bound and gallop, kicking up her heels and wiggling her arse, pedaling and pifflicating in double-quick time, until she finally threw Taptail, although he was hanging on to the saddle with might and main. His stirrup-straps were of rope, and on the mounting side his windowed shoe got so thoroughly tangled up that he couldn't get it out. And so the filly dragged him along, flaying all the skin off his arse and kicking him with her heels time and again until at last, running wild with fright, she tore into the hedges and through the brush and over the ditches. As a result she knocked his head clean off, the brains falling out near the Hosanna Cross, after which she tore him limb from limb, first one arm and then the other, and the legs after them, ending by making a long bloody trail with his guts, and doing so thorough a job of it that by the time she arrived at the convent she carried only his right foot and the shoe that had caught fast.

"'Villon, observing that everything had turned out just as he had planned, turned to his devils and said:

"'"You're going to do some tall acting, gentlemen devils, you're going to do some tall acting, I can assure you of that. Oh, what tall acting you're going to do! I defy the Devil Show of Saumur, of Doué, of Montmorillon, of Landres, of Saint-Espain, of Angers, or even, by God, of Poitiers, with all their fine auditoriums, to put on a better show. I'm just telling you this, in case anybody tries to make comparisons. Oh, what tall acting you're going to do!"

"'And in the same way,' continued Basché, 'I can see that you're going to do some tall acting after this, in this little tragic farce of ours, in view of the fact that at the first performance—the rehearsal, you might say—Shysteroo has been so eloquently swatted, thumped, and tickled by you. I hereby double your wages on the spot. And you, my dear,' he added to his wife, 'go ahead and do the honors as you may see fit. All that I have is in your hands and keeping.

"'As for myself, I, first of all, drink to you all, my

good friends. Drink up; it's nice and cool. In the second place: You, Mr. Majordomo, take this silver basin. I make you a present of it. You squires, take these gilded-silver cups. As for you pages, you shall not be whipped for three months to come. Sweetheart, give them my pretty white feathers with the gold tassels. Father Oudart, I present you with this silver flagon. This other one I give to the cooks. To the bedroom flunkies, I give this silver basket, while this gilded-silver service goes to the grooms. To the porters, these two plates; to the mule-drivers, these ten soup-spoons. Trudon, take all these silver spoons and this spice-dish; and you lackeys, take this big salt-cellar.

"'Serve me faithfully, friends, and I will reward you; for I am sure of one thing, and that is that I would rather, in God's name, go to war and take a hundred mace-blows on the helmet in the service of our good King than be once summonsed by those hounds of Shy-steroos, and all to please a big fat prior like that.' "

There has been much discussion as to the authenticity of the Villon anecdote related here (compare the "Spectrum" dialogue of Erasmus); one commentator (Des Marets-Rathery) observes: "But no one had read or studied the works of Villon so thoroughly as had our author; it seems impossible that he should not have been familiar with the life of the poet, or that he should have fallen into error concerning incidents that were almost contemporary and which he relates with details so precise."

"His esgue orbe": a langue d'oc expression for blind mare. ——"About the end of the Niort fair": Niort is in the Deux-Sèvres region, and Saint-Maixent is in the same arrondissement (that of Niort); the fair was a

famous one of the time; Saint-Ligaire was in the same vicinity. ——"Hic est de patria": *as stated in the text, this is macaronic Latin, that is, a mixture of Latin and French or, in translation, of Latin and English, the sense being: Here comes a native of Beggarland who is used to going around carrying scraps in an old bag.* ——"His windowed shoe": *Franciscan foot-gear with leather thongs.* ——"The Hosanna Cross": *one of the landmarks of the neighborhood.* ——"The devil-show of Saumur," etc.: *the places mentioned were all noted for their mystery plays, passion plays, and "devil-shows," or farces.*

How Pantagruel Passed the Islands of Tohu and Bohu, and the Strange Death of Nose-splitter, the Windmill-Swallower

THAT same day Pantagruel passed the two islands of Tohu and Bohu in which we found nothing on the fire. For the great giant Nosesplitter had swallowed all the stoves, saucepans, kettles, earthen pots, drip-pans, and frying-pans in the country, from lack of windmills, which were his regular diet. As a result of this, shortly before daybreak at the time he was ordinarily engaged in digesting his food, he had fallen seriously ill, his illness being due to a certain rawness in the stomach provoked, as physicians stated, by the fact that the digestive faculties of that organ, adapted by nature to windmills swallowed whole, had not been equal to the task of assimilating perfectly the stoves and earthen pots. As for the kettles and frying-pans, they had been digested easily enough, as the doctors could tell from the sediment and precipitation of four wine-vats full of urine which the giant had twice passed that morning.

To give their patient relief, the physicians employed various remedies prescribed by their art. But the disease had proved stronger than the remedies, and the noble Nosesplitter had that morning passed out, in a fashion so strange that you need no longer be astonished at the death of Aeschylus. The latter, having been warned by the soothsayers that on a certain day he would be killed by something falling upon him, had on the fatal day gone as far away as he could from the city and from all houses, trees, rocks, and other things that might drop and kill him in their fall. All day long he stayed out in the middle of a big prairie, trusting in the good faith of a free and open sky, and feeling safe (as he thought) against any mischance other than the heavens themselves falling, which he deemed to be impossible. They say, by the way, that the larks are very much afraid that the heavens will fall, for if the heavens fall, they are sure to be caught.

The Celts on the banks of the Rhine—that is, the noble, valiant, chivalrous, warlike, and triumphant French—used to fear the same thing. They were once asked by Alexander the Great what thing in this world it was that they feared most. He hoped they would make a solitary exception of himself, in view of his great prowess, victories, conquests, and triumphs. But they replied that the only thing they feared was the falling of the heavens. For they really feared this, rather than the danger of refusing to form a friendly alliance with so valorous and magnanimous a king, if you believe Strabo, *lib. vii,* and Arrian, *lib. i.* Plutarch, also, in the book which he has written, *On the Face That Is Seen in the Moon,* cites the example of one Pharnaces, who greatly feared that the moon would fall upon the earth and who felt a vast pity and commiseration for what would happen to those peoples, such as the Ethiopians and the Taprobaneans, who dwelt under it, if so great a mass should chance to descend upon them. He would in the same manner have been afraid of the heavens falling upon the earth, if the heavens had not been duly sustained and supported upon Atlas' columns, according to the opinion held by the ancients, as we are told by Aristotle, *lib. vi, Metaphys.*

But to come back to Aeschylus, he, notwithstanding all his precautions, *was* killed—by a falling turtle-shell which, slipping from between the claws of an eagle high up in the air, came down upon his head and split his brain.

There is, moreover, the example of the poet Anacreon, who died by strangling on a grape-seed. There is also Fabius, the Roman praetor, who choked to death on a nanny-goat's hair while consuming a bowl of milk. There was, likewise, the bashful chap who, from holding in his wind and fearing to let even a tiny fart, died suddenly in the presence of the Roman Emperor Claudius. Then there is the gentleman at Rome, buried in the Via Flaminia, who in his epitaph complains of having been bitten by a cat in his little finger. There is Q. Lecanius Bassus, who died suddenly from a pin-prick in the thumb of his left hand, so minute that it was barely visible. And there is Quenault, the Norman physician, who died of a sudden at Montpellier from having, with a penknife, removed a ringworm sideways from his hand.

Nor should we forget Philomenes, whose lackey had brought him new figs for the first course of his dinner. While the lackey was gone to get the wine, a big-balled jackass entered the house and, with some compunction, began eating the figs. Philomenes watched with much

interest and amusement the manners of this asinine
sycophage, and remarked to the lackey, who by that
time had returned:

"It is only right, since you left the figs for this zealous
ass to eat, to go ahead and give him some of that good
wine you have just brought in." As he said this, he went
off into such a burst of merriment and laughter and kept
it up for so long that the exertion proved too much for
his spleen and he at once died.

Then there is Spurius Saufeius who died sucking a soft
egg as he came out of his bath. And there is the one of
whom Boccaccio tells us, who died instantly from picking
his teeth with a sprig of sage. There is

> Phillipot Flatbutt, aye,
> Who, being high and dry,
> Did suddenly die

while paying an old debt, without having been ill before
that. Finally, there is Zeuxis the painter, who died very
unexpectedly from laughing too much at a portrait of an
old woman which he had painted.

There are a thousand other cases of which you may
read in Verrius, Pliny, Valerius, Baptista Fulgosus, and
Bacabery the Elder.

As for the worthy Nosesplitter, alas! he died from
strangulation from eating a lump of fresh butter at the
mouth of a hot oven, on the advice of his physicians.

Here, too, it was that we learned how the King of
Culan in Bohu had defeated the satraps of King Mechloth and had sacked the strongholds of Belima.

Later, we passed the islands of Nargues and Zargues,
also the islands of Teneliabin and Geneliabin, which
were very pretty to look at and very fruitful so far as
enemas were concerned. Also the islands Enig and Evig,

from which there had formerly come the stroke of a penknife to the Landgrave of Hesse.

"The Islands of Tohu and Bohu": tohu *and* bohu *are
Hebrew words found at the beginning of Genesis: "And
the earth was without form* (tohu) *and void* (bohu)*"; in
modern French, the expression* tohu-bohu *means a confusion, uproar, hurlyburly. ——"Nosesplitter, the Wind-
mill-Swallower": Rabelais' "Bringuenarilles" in the past
has been rendered, by Cotgrave, Le Motteux, and others,
as "Widenostrils"; however, as M. Sainéan points out, the
name means "fendeur de naseaux." ——"We found
nothing on the fire": "ne trouvasmes que frire," literally,
"nothing to fry"; compare our slang phrase, "what's
cooking?" ——"If the heavens fall, they are sure to be
caught": "hope to catch larks, if the heavens fall" is a
proverbial expression. ——"Arrian. lib. i": Flavius Ar-
rianus, the Greek historian, second century* A.D. ——
*"The Taprobaneans": natives of Ceylon; Taprobane was
the Greek name for the present island of Ceylon. ——
"In the presence of Claudius": in Suetonius' Life of
Claudius, the victim does not die but merely comes
near dying. ——"Q. Lecanius Bassus": Pliny,* Natural
History, XXVI, i. ——*"Quenault, the Norman physician":
the partial edition of 1548 reads: "Guinemauld, a Norman physician, a great glutton for dried peas and a most
illustrious card-player, who died suddenly," etc.; "Guinemauld" ("one who squints") is a travesty of the real
name. ——"Philomenes": Philemon is the form found
in Valerius Maximus and Lucian, but the form Philomenes occurs in the folio edition of the former, published
at Paris, in 1517; see Valerius Maximus,* XI, xii, *and*
Lucian's Discourse on Those Who Have Lived for a

Long Time. ——"*Sycophage*": *fig-eater.* ——"*There is Spurius Saufeius*": *the name in Pliny* (Natural History, Book VII) *is Appius Saufeius.* ——"*Of whom Boccaccio tells us*": Decameron, Fifth Day, Seventh Tale. —— "*Phillipot Flatbutt*": *in the original, Phillipot Placut.* ——"*Being high and dry*": "*estant sain et dru,*" *literally, in good health and sturdy.* ——"*Baptista Fulgcsus*": *writer of Geneva, author of a treatise* De Inusitatis Mortis Generibus (On Unusual Ways of Dying). ——"*Bacabery the Elder*": *it is not known whether this is a real or fantastic person; to this list of writers the partial edition adds* "*Sausageater*" (Riflandouille). —— "*The King of Culan in Bohu*": *this is a locality in Berry.* ——"*King Mechloth*": *the meaning of the name is not certain; the Hebrew* makloth *is maladies (Sainéan).* ——"*The strongholds of Belima*": Belimah *is Hebrew for land of nothingness.* ——"*Nargues and Zargues*": *fanciful names.* ——"*Teneliabin and Geneliabin*": *these are Arabic pharmaceutical gums.* ——"*Enig and Evig*": *a play on the German words* einige *and* ewige, *which one commentator (Le Duchat) explains as follows:* "*One of the clauses of the treaty between the Emperor Charles* V *and the Landgrave must have been that the latter was to remain in the former's train* ohne einige Gefängnisse *(without any imprisonment)* . . . *so that the Landgrave was quite astonished when it was pointed out to him that, by the substitution of the word* ewige *(perpetual) in place of* einige *(that is, without perpetual imprisonment), he had become the Emperor's prisoner for as many years as that monarch might see fit; it is to this trickery that Rabelais applies the term 'stroke of a penknife'* (estaïilade)."

How Pantagruel Escaped from a Mighty Tempest at Sea and How Panurge and Friar John Behaved Themselves during the Storm

THE next day, on the right-hand side, we ran into nine transports full of monks, including Jacobins, Jesuits, Capuchins, Hermits, Augustinians, Bernardines, Celestines, Theatins, Egnatins, Amadeans, Franciscans, Carmelites, Minims, and other holy brothers, all of them on their way to the Council of Chesil to sift the articles of faith against the new heretics.

Seeing them, Panurge was excessively joyful, feeling assured that we would have good luck all that day and many others following. And after courteously greeting the holy fathers and commending his soul to their devout prayers and small favors, he had seventy-eight dozen hams, a quantity of caviar and dozens of Bologna sausages, and hundreds of slices of caviar, as well as two thousand pretty "angels" for the souls of the dead, cast into their boat.

As for Pantagruel, he remained thoughtful and melancholy. Friar John perceived this and was inquiring as to the source of this unaccustomed lowness of spirits when the pilot, observing the whipping of the ensign on the poop and foreseeing a coming tempest, suddenly ordered all hands on deck, including sailors, deck-hands, and cabin-boys, as well as us passengers. He at once had them lower the sails: the mizzen-sail, the counter-mizzen-sail, the lugsail, the mainsail, the tackle, and the spritsail. He had them haul in the small-sails, the maintopsail, and the fore-topsail and run down the main-mizzen-sail, commanding that of all the yard-arms they should leave only the shrouds and the ratlines.

And then, of a sudden, the sea began to puff and swell and rage from its lowest depths, and the great waves began to beat against the sides of our vessels; following which, there came the nor'wester, accompanied by an unbridled squall, huge banks of black clouds, terrible whirlwinds, and deadly hurricanes, whistling through our yard-arms. From the heavens came thunder, lightning, rain, and hail. The air lost its transparent quality and became darkly opaque and somber. The only illumination we had was from the lightning, and the rents it made in the flaming clouds. Storms, squalls, and tempests burst about us in sheets of flame, with, on all sides, thunder-claps, blinding flashes, zigzag streaks, and other ethereal ejaculations. We did not know which way to look and were too frightened to look anywhere. The terrific typhoon raised up and suspended mountainous waves from the deep. You may well believe that this seemed to us like the Chaos of old, with fire, air, sea, earth, and all the elements tossed together in one vast and refractory confusion.

Panurge, having fed the scatophagic fishes thoroughly and well with the contents of his stomach, was crouched on the deck, half dead from fright. He called upon all the saints, male and female, to aid him, promising that he would go to confession as soon as time and place offered. Then, he began to bawl out in mortal terror:

"Hey, Mr. Steward, my friend, my father, my uncle, bring out a little salt-meat, will you? We're going to have more than enough to drink, from all that I can see. Eat little and drink much is going to be my motto from now on. Oh, I would to God and to the blessed, worthy, and

sacred Virgin, that I were on *terra firma* right now, nice
and comfortable—and I mean this very minute!

"Oh, how happy—thrice and four times happy—are
they who plant cabbages! O Fates, why did you not spin
me out for a planter of cabbages! Oh, how few in number are those on whom Jupiter has conferred that favor,
of destining them to plant cabbages! For they always
have one foot on the ground and the other's not far
away. Talk about sovereign happiness all you want to,
but whoever plants cabbages is at this moment, by my
edict, declared to be blessed. And I have better reason
for saying this than Pyrrho had, when, being in the same
danger that we now are, and catching sight of a hog
munching barley-grains on the shore, he declared that
the hog was blessed for two reasons: first, because he
had plenty of barley to eat; and second, because he was
on dry land. Ha! for a godlike and lordly mansion, there's
nothing like a cowshed!

"That wave there is going to sweep us away—O God,
our Savior! O my friends! A little vinegar! I'm sweating like Jazus! the yard-arm gears are broken, the ropes
are in shreds, the rings are bursting, the lookout-mast
is dipping into the sea, our keel's as high as the sun, our
cables are nearly all gone. Jazus! Jazus! where are our
small-sails? All is frelore, bigoth! Jazus! Who's going to
claim this wreck? Here, friends, let me get behind one
of those piles. My lads, your tow-line's down. Alas!
don't give up the helm, nor the tackle, either. I can
hear the pintle trembling. Is it broken? For God's sake,
save the cannon-rope; don't bother about the oarlocks.
Baa, baa, boo, hoo, hoo!

"Watch the needle of your compass, please, Master
Astrophilus. Who started this storm, anyway? My word!
but I'm scared. Boo, hoo, hoo, boo, hoo! It's all up with

me, I can see that; I'm shitting from fright. Boo, hoo, boo, hoo! Otto, to, to, to, to, ti! Otto, to, to, to, to, ti! Boo, hoo, hoo, oo, oo, oo, boo, hoo, boo, hoo! I'm drowning, I'm drowning, I'm dying! Mates, I'm drowning!"

Pantagruel, having first implored the aid of the great God, our Savior, and having made a public, fervent, and devout prayer, proceeded on the advice of the pilot to take the ship's mast and hold it, strongly and firmly. As for Friar John, he had stripped to his doublet, in order to lend the seamen a hand; and Epistemon, Ponocrates, and the others had done the same. Panurge alone remained sitting on his rump on the deck, weeping and wailing. Friar John caught sight of him from the quarter-deck and exclaimed:

"By God, if there isn't Panurge, the booby-calf! It would be a lot better if you'd give us a hand here, instead of sitting there on your balls like a baboon and bawling like a heifer."

"Baa, baa, boo, hoo, hoo!" replied Panurge. "Friar John, my friend, my good father, I'm drowning, I'm drowning, my friend, I'm drowning! It's all up with me, my spiritual father, my friend, it's all up! Your broadsword can't save me. Jazus, Jazus! we're way up above high C; we're clear out of the scale. Baa, baa, boo, hoo, hoo! Jazus! Right now, we're way down below low G! I'm drowning! Ho! my father, my uncle, my everything! The water's running into my shoes through my collar. Boo, hoo, hoo, pish, hoo, hoo, hoo, ho, ho, ho, ho, ho, I'm drowning! Baa, baa, boo, boo, boo, boo, boo, ho, ho, ho, ho, ho! Jazus, Jazus! Right now, I'm like a forked tree with my feet in the air and my head down below. I would to God that I was in that transport with the good and holy council-going fathers that we met this morning. Oh, how devout they were, how fat, how jolly, and what nice ladylike manners they had! Help, help, help! Jazus, Jazus! that devilish wave—*Mea culpa, Deus*—I mean, that godly wave is going to sink our ship. Jazus! Friar John, my father, my friend, confess me! Look, here I am on my knees. *Confiteor*. Give me your holy benediction."

"Come here, you damned gallows-bird," said Friar John, "come here and lend us a hand. Thirty legions of devils, come on! Is he coming or not?"

"Don't swear," said Panurge, "my father, my friend, don't swear at this time. Tomorrow you can swear as much as you like. Help, help! Jazus! Our ship's taking water, I'm drowning! Jazus, Jazus! Baa, baa, baa, boo, hoo, boo, hoo! We're at the bottom this very minute. Jazus, Jazus! I'd give eighteen-hundred-thousand crowns in income to any one who would set me down on land, all shitty and loose in the bowels as I am, if there ever was such a chap in all my shitty country. *Confiteor*. Jazus! One little word for my will—or a codicil, at the very least!"

"I hope," exclaimed Friar John, "that a thousand devils jump all over that cuckold's body! Why, damn his soul! Talking about a will at a time like this, when we're in such danger and every man-jack of us ought to be getting a move on, if he ever expects to again. Are you coming or not, what the devil?—That's the way, Matey, my lad. That's a good little first mate for you! Over this way, Gymnastes, this way, over the poop. By God, but I think we're done for this time. There goes our lantern! She's gone straight to hell."

"Jazus, Jazus!" cried Panurge, "Jazus! Boo, hoo, boo, hoo! Jazus, Jazus! Was it here that we were predestined to perish? Help! mates, I'm drowning. I'm dying! *Consummatum est*. It's all up with me."

"*Magna, gna, gna*," grumbled Friar John. "Rats! what an ugly bastard he is, that beshitted booby over there!

Here, boy, what the hell, watch this pump. What's the matter? Did you hurt yourself? Damn it all!— Here, fasten her to one of these blocks. Over this way with her, what the devil, there you are! That's it, sonny!"

"O Friar John," cried Panurge, "my spiritual father, my friend, let's not swear. You're sinning. Jazus, Jazus! Baa, baa, boo, hoo, boo! I'm drowning, mates, I'm dying! I forgive everybody. Goodby. *In manus.* Boo, hoo, boo, hoo, hoo! St. Michael of Aure, St. Nicholas, help me just this once and never again! I make you a nice little vow, and one to Our Lord, that if you help me out this one time—I mean, if you set me down on land and out of danger—I'll build you a big little chapel, or maybe two of them, between Candé and Montsoreau, where no cow or calf to feed shall go. Jazus, Jazus! More than eighteen buckets or two of water have swilled into my mouth. Boo, hoo, boo, hoo! How bitter and salty it is!"

"I swear," said Friar John, "by the blood, body, belly, and head of Christ, that if I hear you whimpering just one time more, you damned cuckold, you, I'll flay you like a seawolf! Holy Christ! why don't we toss him to the bottom of the sea, anyway? Here, sailor, what, ho, my lad; that's right, old man! Keep her up there. That's sure some thunder and lightning! I think all the devils in hell must be let loose today, or else Proserpina's having a young one. For all the devils are dancing around with bells on 'em, that's one sure thing!"

In connection with this tempest scene, Rabelais is under a debt to the twelfth book of Folengo's Opus Macaronicum. *The scene has been put into verse in a work, now rare, by the Marquis de Culant, printed in Holland, in octavo format, in 1783. The controversy over Rabelais' use of nautical terms has been mentioned.*

Another point that may be noted is the degeneration of Panurge's character by this time: he is now an arrant braggart and a coward. By contrast, the character of Friar John is deepened and developed; and the stress, in his case, on useful communal activity attains a climax in the crisis of the storm.

"The Council of Chesil": the name, according to Sainéan, corresponds to the Hebrew kessil, fool, and so is equivalent to "Lanternese." ——"Scatophagic fishes": ordure-eating fishes. ——"Jazus!": the 1552 edition has Zalas, which is Saintonge patois for Hélas, or Alas; but the partial edition of 1548 has Jarus, which according to Sainéan is "simply the Parisian pronunciation of the name of Jesus." ——"All is frelore, bigoth!": Swiss patois for "All is lost, by God!" ——"Master Astrophilus": the name means "friend of the stars." ——"Mea culpa, Deus": "my fault, O God." ——"Confiteor": "I confess." ——"In all my shitty country": "en ma patrie de bren," a play on ma patrie de bien, my good country. ——"Consummatum est": "It is finished"; the words of Christ on the cross. ——"In manus": "Into thy hands (I commend my spirit)"; this is another instance of Rabelais' sacrilegious audacity. ——"Between Candé and Montsoreau": Panurge is here quoting a proverb.

The storm keeps up and Panurge, more frightened than ever, continues to insist on making his will. For this he is reproved by Epistemon; whereupon there follows, put into Panurge's mouth, a dissertation on wills made at sea. Finally the storm subsides and land is sighted.

How, When the Storm Was Over, Panurge Played the Good Fellow; but Friar John Insisted That He Had Been Unreasonably Frightened

"Ah, ha!" cried Panurge, "everything is fine! The storm's over. I beg you, permit me to be the first to disembark. I have some very important business to attend to. Can I lend you a hand there? Toss me that cable, and let me twist it for you. I've plenty of courage; anybody can see that. No, no—not a pennyworth of fear. It's true, that decuman wave that just swept over the deck from prow to poop, speeded my pulse a little, but that's all."

"Lower the sails!"

"That's talking. Look here, Friar John, how does it come you're not doing anything? Is this any time to be having a drink? How do we know but St. Martin's flunkey may be brewing another storm for us? Can't I come over there and lend you a hand? Holy Christ, I'm sorry (but it's too late now) that I didn't remember the teachings of the good philosophers who tell us that to stroll near the sea and to sail near the land is a very safe and delightful proceeding, just as it is to walk on foot, leading one's steed by the bridle. Ha, ha, ha! By God, but everything's lovely! Are you sure I can't lend you a hand there? Fork it over; I can turn that little trick, or else the devil himself is in that cable."

Epistemon had one hand with the flesh all torn off and bleeding as a result of his having held on too hard to one of the cables. Hearing Panurge's remarks, he said:

"You may believe, my lord, that I was afraid, and not any the less afraid than Panurge. But what of it! I didn't spare myself when it came to helping out the rest. I reflected that, if death is, of a truth (as, indeed, it is) a fatal and inevitable necessity, then it must, accordingly, be God's holy will that we should die at such or such a time, in such or such a fashion. We should, of course, incessantly implore, invoke, pray to, entreat, and supplicate Him. But that should not be the limit of our exertions. It behooves us, at the same time, to bestir ourselves and, as the holy Apostle says, to be workers together with Him.

"You know what the consul Caius Flaminius said, when, through Hannibal's astuteness he had been cooped up near that Perugian lake that bears the name of Trasimenus:

" 'Lads,' he said to his soldiers, 'you need not hope to get out of here, either through vows to or through help from the gods. But by strength and courage we *must* get out and, with the edge of the sword, hew a path through the midst of our enemies.'

"Similarly, in the pages of Sallust, we hear M. Portius Cato informing us that the aid of the gods is not to be obtained through idle vows or womanly lamentations. But by watching, working, and bestirring ourselves all things come about in the end as we would wish them to, and all turns out for the best. If in necessity and danger a man is negligent, idle, and unmanned, it is vain for him to implore the assistance of the gods. The latter, in such a case, are merely irritated and indignant."

"Well," said Friar John, "may I go straight to hell—"

"I'm half way there already," interrupted Panurge.

"—may I go straight to hell if the Close of Seuilly wouldn't have been wholly devastated and destroyed, if I had done nothing but sing: *Contra hostium insidias* (it's a matter of the breviary) as those other damned monks did, without running out to save the vineyard with my crozier from those pillagers of Lerné."

"Let the good ship go free!" cried Panurge. "Everything is lovely, and the goose hangs high. Look at Friar John over there, doing nothing. His name is Friar John Donothing. And just look at me, sweating away here and working to help out this Good Man Sailor, first of the name. Hey, there, Skipper, what, ho! Just a word or two with you, begging your pardon. Exactly how thick are the planks of this ship?"

"They are," replied the pilot, "a good two inches thick; you need have no fear on that score."

"Damme," said Panurge, "if we're not, then, constantly within a couple of inches of death. Is that what you call one of the nine joys of marriage?"

"Ha, sailor, you're right, if you measure danger by the yardstick of fear—"

"There's no fear so far as I'm concerned. Fearless William, that's my name. I've courage and to spare. And I don't mean a sheep's courage, either. What I mean is the courage of a wolf, the nerve of a murderer. I don't fear anything except danger—"

"Good day, gentlemen," continued Panurge, "good day, a very good day to you all. I trust I see you all quite well today. *Dieu mercy*, and you? You are very welcome, indeed. You've come at just the right minute. Let us disembark. Sailors, ho! let down the gangplank. Draw up alongside that ship. Can I lend you a hand there? I'm as hungry as a wolf from all the work I've been doing. I've been drudging like a double yoke of oxen. My word, but this is a pretty place—and such nice folks, too! Are you quite sure, my lads, that there's nothing I can do to help you?

"For the love of God, don't be sparing with the sweat of my body. Adam—that is, Man—was born to work and labor as the bird was to fly. It is our Lord's will, as you are very well aware, that we should all eat our bread in the sweat of our bodies, and not by loafing around like that tattered monk you see over there—Friar John, who does nothing but guzzle and die from fear.

"What nice weather we're having. As I think of it now, the answer which Anarcharsis, that noble philosopher, gave is true and founded in reason. He, as you will recall, when asked what ship seemed to him the safest, replied: 'The one that is in port.'"

"Better than that," said Pantagruel. "He, when asked whether there were more persons dead or living, put the further question:

"'In which group do you include those that sail the seas?'

"Subtly implying that those who sail the seas are constantly so very near to death that they live dying and die while they live.

"And so, too, Portius Cato used to remark that there were only three things that, if he had ever done them, he looked upon as cause for repentance: if he had ever revealed a secret to a woman; if he had ever passed a day in idleness; and if he had ever traveled by sea to any place that he might have reached by land."

"By the worthy frock that I wear," said Friar John to Panurge, "but you, my big-balled friend, were certainly most unreasonably afraid during the storm. Unreasonably, because your fate and your destiny is not to die by water. You're certainly going to swing high in the air, or else be burned merrily, like a father. My lord, should you like a nice raincoat? Let me have those wolf-skin and badger-skin coats of yours, and then take Panurge and skin him alive and use his hide to cover

you. But don't go near the fire and never walk in front
of a blacksmith's forge, for God's sake; for if you do
you'll be burnt to a cinder in a minute. But expose yourself as much as you like to rain, snow, and hail, and
even, by God, take a dive to the bottom of the ocean,
and you won't so much as get damp. Make your winter
boots out of it, and they will never take water. Make
bladders out of it to teach the youngsters how to swim,
and they'll learn without the least danger."

"His hide, then," said Pantagruel, "must be like that
plant that is called Venus' hair, which is never known to
be wet or damp, but which always would remain dry,
even if you were to cast it to the bottom of the sea. For
this reason, it is named *Adiantum.*"

"Panurge, old top," said Friar John, "never be afraid
of the water, I beg you. For your life is going to be
brought to an end by a contrary element."

"That's all right," replied Panurge, "but those damned
cooks sometimes lose their heads and make mistakes.
They often put on to boil what was meant to be roasted,
so that in the kitchens of the master-chefs we frequently
see them larding the partridges, ringdoves, and pigeons
with the very likely intention of roasting them, yet it
turns out that they put the partridges on to boil with
the cabbage, the ringdoves with the leeks, and the
pigeons with the turnips.

"But listen, my good friends. I hereby announce, in
the presence of this noble company, that as for the
chapel that I vowed to Monsieur St. Nicholas, between
Candé and Montsoreau, I intend that it shall be a
chapelle (alembic) of water-of-rose, where to feed no
cow or calf goes—for I'm going to dump it to the bottom
of the sea."

"And there you are!" said Epistemon. "There's a fine

fellow for you. There's a fine, fine fellow and a half! But after all, he's only verifying the old Lombard proverb:

Passato il pericolo, gabbato il santo.
Once the danger's past, the saint is mocked."

"*St. Martin's flunkey*": the Devil, who was always at the saint's heels. ——"*It must be God's holy will*": the partial edition of 1548 has: "partly God's will, partly a matter of our own free will." ——"*To be workers together with Him*": Second Corinthians, vi, 1; the edition of 1548, after "bestir ourselves," reads: "and lend our help by finding a remedy and a way out; if I do not speak according to the edicts of the mateologians, they will have to pardon me, for I speak by book and on authority"; Marty-Laveaux observes that "He (Rabelais) regarded it as safer, in his second edition, to cite his authority." ——"*What the consul Caius Flaminius said*": Livy, xxII, 5. ——"*That . . . lake that bears the name of Trasimenus*": the modern Lago di Perugia. ——"*In the pages of Sallust*": in his Catiline. ——"*One of the nine joys of marriage*": allusion to the work known as the Quinze Joies de Mariage, or the Fifteen Joys of Marriage. ——"*I don't fear anything except danger*": see Villon's Monologue du Franc-archer. ——"*Eat our bread in the sweat of our bodies*": Genesis, iii, 19: "in the sweat of thy face." ——"*Portius Cato used to remark*": Plutarch's Cato, xviii. ——"*Be burned merrily, like a father*": commentators have disagreed as to what Rabelais means by "guaillard comme un père." ——"*The plant that is called Venus' hair . . . named Adiantum*": a delicate fern, the Adiantum capillus veneris, common all over the world; adiantum, from the Greek, means unwetted.

Following a stop at the Macraeon Islands, or land of the aged folk, and a rather lengthy discourse on the death of heroes in which Rabelais eulogizes his late friend and protector, Guillaume du Bellay, the Seigneur de Langey, the Pantagruelians reach the Island of Sneaks and we are given a description, or better, an anatomical inventory, of its monarch, Lentkeeper, that ought to interest the modern devotees of Surrealism.

How Pantagruel Passed the Island of Sneaks, Where Lentkeeper Reigned

THE ships of the joyous convoy having been repaired, made over and revictualed and the Macraeons being more than satisfied with the amount of money Pantagruel spent with them for this purpose, our men, even jollier than was their wont, took advantage of the serene and delightful *Aguyon* and set sail with great good cheer.

About midday, Xenomanes pointed out to us, from some distance off, the Island of Sneaks, where Lentkeeper reigned, of whom Pantagruel had heard something before, and whom he would have liked very much to meet in person, if Xenomanes had not discouraged the idea, as much on account of the considerable detour they would have to make as because of the slim pickings which he stated were to be found in the way of sport, either at the court of that lord or in the island as a whole.

"All you will find there," he asserted, "is a big swallower of dried peas, a big lummox of a keg-smasher, a big overgrown mole-catcher, a big hay-bundler and half-giant with downy wool and a double tonsure, of

Lanternese descent, a gonfalonier of the Ichthyophages, dictator of Mustardland, and a flogger of little children, a calcinator of ashes, the father and chief support of physicians, rich in pardons, indulgences, and stations of the cross, a good man, a good Catholic, and extremely devout: he weeps three times a day. And you will never, never find him at a wedding.

"It is true, he is the most industrious manufacturer of larding-pins and skewers to be found in forty kingdoms. It must be about six years ago now that, putting in at Sneaks Island, I brought back a gross of them and presented them to the butchers of Candé. They thought very highly of them, and they had good reason to do so. I will show you when we return a pair of them hung up in the church doorway. The food which Lentkeeper consumes consists of salted small-hauberks, helmets, salted morions, and salted sallets, a diet that sometimes causes him to suffer with a very oppressive hotpiss. His clothes are quite jolly, both in cut and in color, for he wears: Gray and cold; nothing in the foreground and nothing in the backfield; sleeves of the same."

"You would give me a great deal of pleasure," said Pantagruel, "if, having described for us his clothing, his food, and his amusements, you would also tell us about his bodily form and shape, in all its details."

"Yes, please do, my little Ballocks," said Friar John, "for I've found it all in my breviary. It comes right after the movable feasts."

"I shall be very glad to do so," replied Xenomanes, "and we may hear more about him, when we pass the Wild Island, which is ruled by the plump Chitterlings, his mortal enemies, against whom he wages a sempiternal warfare. And if it had not been for the aid of the noble Carnival, their protector and good neighbor, that great lantern-bearer of a Lentkeeper would long ago have driven them out of house and home."

"Might those Chitterlings," inquired Friar John, "be male or female, angels fair or mortals frail, wedded wives or virgin-tail?"

"They are," Xenomanes replied, "females in sex, mortals in condition, and some of them are virgins and some are not."

"Why, damn me!" exclaimed Friar John, "if I'm not for 'em. What kind of unnatural carryings-on is it, anyway, to be making war on women? Let's go back and chop that big villain to pieces."

"Make war on Lentkeeper!" cried Panurge, "what the devil! I'm not so dumb and foolhardy at the same time. Quid juris, if we happen to find ourselves bagged up between Lentkeeper and the Chitterlings? Between the sledge-hammer and the anvil? Chancres! Stay away from there. Let's head in some other direction. Goodby, old Lentkeeper. Take good care of the Chitterlings; and don't forget the Black Puddings as well."

"Where Lentkeeper reigned": in rendering Rabelais' Quaresmeprenant as Lentkeeper, the present translator is following Marty-Laveaux's interpretation of the word. ——"The serene and delightful Aguyon": a term for zephyr in nautical patois. ——"A gonfalonier of the Ichthyophages": standard-bearer of the fish-eaters. —— "It comes right after the movable feasts": that is, where the readings for Lent occur in the breviary. ——"Quid juris": "what law (can save us)?"

Xenomanes Describes and Anatomizes Lentkeeper

"LENTKEEPER," said Xenomanes, "so far as his internal organs are concerned, has—or, at least, had in my time— a head precisely resembling in size, color, substance, and vigor, the left nut of a male ringworm;

"Ventricles of the same like a gimlet;

"A vermiform excrescence like a croquet mallet;

"Membranes like a monk's hood;

"A funnel like a bricklayer's bird;

"A mug like a gomphosis;

"A pineal gland like a bagpipe;

"A *Rete mirabile* like a chanfrin;

"Mammillary projections like old leather;

"Tympanums like a little mill;

"A petrified bone like a goose or turkey wing;

"A neck like a lantern on a stick;

"Nerves like a water-plug;

"An uvula like a pea-shooter;

"A palate like a big woolen mitten;

"Saliva like a shuttle;

"Tonsils like a pair of eye-glasses;

"An isthmus like a vintager's hod;

"A gullet like a grape-basket;

"A stomach like a girdle;

"A pylorus like a pitchfork;

"A tracheal artery like a hedgebill;

"A throat like a lump of tow;

"Lungs like an amice;

"A heart like a chasuble;

"A mediastinum like a drinking-horn;

"A pleura like a crow's beak;

"Arteries like a Béarn-cloak;

"A diaphragm like a bonnet fastened under the chin;

"A liver like a two-bladed ax;

"Veins like a window-sash;

"A spleen like a quail-whistle;

"Bowels like a dragnet;

"A gall-bladder like a chip-ax;

"Entrails like a gauntlet;

"A mesentery like an abbatial miter;

"A hungry gut like a forceps;

"A blind-gut like a breast-plate;

"A colon like a vase with handles;

"A rump-gut like a monastic flagon;

"Kidneys like a trowel;

"Loins like a padlock;

"Urinal pores like a pothook;

"Emulgent veins like toy squirt-guns;

"Spermatic vesicles like a beaten cake;

"Prostates like a feather-pot;

"A bladder like a crossbow;

"A bladder-neck like a clock-hammer;

"A *mirach* like an Albanian's hat;

"A *siphach* like an arm-brace;

"Muscles like bellows;

"Tendons like a bird-glove;

"Ligaments like a money-bag;

"Bones like cheesecakes;

"Marrow like a mallet;

"Cartilages like a brushwood-turtle;

"Adenoids like a bill-hook;

"Animal spirits like great blows with the fist;

"Vital spirits like prolonged knuckle-raps;

"A boiling blood-stream like repeated punches in the nose;

"Urine like a Popefigger;

"Genitals like a hundred lath-nails; and his nurse told me that, when he had married Midlent, the two of them begot a number of local adverbs and certain double-fasts;

"A memory like a scarf;

"A supply of common sense like a drone of bees;

"An imagination like a peal of bells;

"Thoughts like a flight of starlings;

"A conscience like an unnesting of herons;

"A gift of deliberation like a sack of organs;

"A faculty of repentance like a cannon-carriage;

"A faculty of enterprise like the list of a galleon;

"An understanding like a torn breviary;

"Intellective powers like slugs, crawling out of a strawberry-patch;

"A will like three nuts in a shell;

"Desires like a bale of holy hay;

"A judgment like a shoehorn;

"A sense of discretion like a block-and-tackle;

"A reason like a foot-stool."

The External Anatomy of Lentkeeper

"LENTKEEPER," continued Xenomanes, "so far as his external organs were concerned, was a little better proportioned, except for his seven ribs, which were preternatural in shape.

"He had great-toes like a tuned piano;

"Feet like a guitar;

"Heels like a club;

"Soles like a crucible;

"Legs like a trap;

"Knees like a stool;

"Buttocks like a helmet;

"Haunches like a centerbit;

"A pointed-toed belly, buttoned up in the old-fashioned way and girdled over his chest;

"A navel like a hurdy-gurdy;

"Hairy parts like a tart;

"A member like a slipper;

"Balls like a big bottle;

"Genitals like a carpenter's plane;

"Testicle-muscles like a tennis-racquet;

"A perineum like a flageolet;

"An arse-hole like a crystal mirror;

"Thighs like a harrow;

"Loins like a butter-jug;

"An *Alkatin* like a billiard-table;

"A back like a huge crossbow;

"Vertebrae like a bagpipe;

"Ribs like a spinning-wheel;

"A breast-bone like a baldachin;

"Shoulder-blades like a mortar-board;

"A breast like a hand-organ;

"Teats like a cowherd's horn;

"Armpits like a chessboard;

"Shoulders like a wheelbarrow;

"Arms like a masquerade-hood;

"Fingers like fire-dogs at a fair;

"Carpal bones like a pair of stilts;

"Forearms (*fauciles*) like sickles (*faucilles*);

"Elbows like rat-traps;

"Hands like a currycomb;

"A neck like a drinking-glass;

"A throat like a hippocras-filter;

"An Adam's-apple like a barrel, from which dangled two bronze goiters, very pretty and melodious, in the shape of a sand-dial;

"A beard like a lantern;

"A chin like a pumpkin;

"Ears like a pair of mittens;

"A nose like a half-boot, turned up in front into an escutcheon;

"Nose-holes like a baby's bonnet;

"Eyebrows like a dripping-pan—and over the left brow, he had a sign of the shape and size of a urinal;

"Eyelashes like a rebeck;

"Eyes like a comb-case;

"Optic nerves like a briquet;

"A forehead like a catch-all cup;

"Temples like a sprinkling-can;

"Cheeks like a pair of wooden shoes;

"Jaws like a goblet;

"Teeth like a javelin—and of such milk-teeth as his, you will find one at Colonges-les-Royaux in Poitou, and two at Brosse in Saintonge over the door of the cellar;

"A tongue like a harp;

"A mouth like a saddle-cloth;

"A face cut up like a mule's pack-saddle;

"A head twisted like an alembic;

"A cranium like a game-pouch;

"Sutures like a fisherman's ring;

"Hide like a gabardine;

"An epidermis like a sieve;

"Hair like a shoe-scraper;

"Wool as above stated."

More about Lentkeeper and His Reactions

"Lentkeeper," Xenomanes went on, "was a marvelous person to see and know:

"If he spit, it was baskets of artichokes;

"If he blew his nose, it was salted eels;

"If he wept, it was ducks and onions;

"If he trembled, it was big hare-pies;

"If he sweat, it was codfish in butter;

"If he belched, it was oysters on the half-shell;

"If he sneezed, it was barrels of mustard;

"If he coughed, it was boxes of marmalade;

"If he sobbed, it was penny-packages of water-cress;

"If he yawned, it was jugfuls of mashed peas;

"If he sighed, it was smoked beef-tongues;

"If he sucked in his breath, it was basketfuls of green monkeys;

"If he snored, it was wicker-vases full of shelled beans;

"If he frowned, it was pigs' feet in the sty;

"If he spoke, it was heavy sackcloth from Auvergne, so far was it from being that bright-colored silk, of which Parysatis wished to have woven the words of those who spoke to her son, Cyrus, King of the Persians;

"If he whistled, it was indulgence-boxes;

"If he blinked his eyes, it was waffles and wafers;

"If he scolded, it was March cats;

"If he shook his head, it was wagon-spokes;

"If he made a mouth, it was broken sticks;

"If he muttered, it was light sport at Bench and Bar;

"If he stamped, it was five years' respite;

"If he fell back a step, it was cockcranes;

"If he slobbered, it was baking-ovens;

"If he was hoarse, it was the entrance of Moorish dancers;

"If he farted, it was brown cowhide leggings;

"If he pooped, it was Cordovan boots;

"If he scratched himself, it was new statutes;

"If he sang, it was peas in the shell;

"If he dunged, it was pumpkins and mushrooms;

"If he sucked in his breath, it was cabbages in oil;

"If he discoursed, it was the snows of yesteryear;

"If he worried, it was the shaved and shorn;

"If he gave nothing, the cheat had the same;

"If he reflected, it was flying pricks, crouching against a wall;

"If he moped, it was new leases;

"And another strange thing is: he worked at doing nothing and did nothing when he worked; he corybanted sleeping and slept while he corybanted, with his eyes open, as rabbits do in Champagne, fearing some surprise assault on the part of the Chitterlings, his ancient enemies; he bit when he laughed and laughed when he bit; he ate nothing fasting and fasted eating nothing; he nibbled by suspicion and drank by imagination, bathed himself on top high steeples and dried himself in ponds and rivers, fished in the air and caught decuman crabs, hunted at the bottom of the sea and found ibexes, mountain-goats, and chamois; he ordinarily poked out the eyes of all the crows he caught on the sly, feared nothing but his own shadow and the yelpings of fattened kids, pounded the pavement on certain days, played holy cords and made a mallet of his fist, and wrote on rough parchment, with his big inkstand, prognostications and almanachs."

"There's a fine fellow for you," said Friar John. "He's a man after my own heart. He's the lad I'm looking for. I'm going to send him a challenge."

"You have there," remarked Pantagruel, "a strange and monstrous limb of a man. You remind me, as I listen to you, of what is said of the appearance of Amodunt and Discord."

"What appearance," inquired Friar John, "did they present? I've never heard tell of 'em, God forgive me for it."

"I will tell you," Pantagruel replied, "what I have read in the old fables.

"Physis, that is, Nature, at her first pregnancy gave birth to Beauty and Harmony without carnal copulation, being of herself very fecund and fertile. Antiphysis, who is always the opposite of Nature, at once began to envy the latter so beautiful and respectable a progeny; and she, on the other hand, gave birth to Amodunt and Discord, as a result of copulation with Tellumon. These children had heads that were entirely spherical and round, like a balloon, and not gently flattened at the two sides, as is the normal human head; their ears were reared aloft like asses' ears; their eyes protruded from their heads, being fastened on heel-like bones, without eyebrows, and hard as those of crabs; their feet were round like little balls; their hands were turned backwards and upwards, toward their shoulders; and they traveled upon their heads, constantly turning wheels, arse over head and feet foremost.

"Now you know that monkey-bitches think their little monkeys are the loveliest things in the world. And so in the same manner Antiphysis praised her offspring and endeavored to prove that their form was more beautiful and impressive than that of Physis' young ones. She insisted that traveling wheel-fashion like that was a very perfect mode of locomotion and one that had in it something of the divine, since it was in such a manner that the heavens and all things eternal revolve. To have one's feet in the air and one's head to the ground was, therefore, an imitation of the Creator of the universe. For she pointed out that the hair in man is like roots and the legs like the branches of a tree, adding that trees are more properly fastened in the earth by their roots than they would be resting upon their branches.

"Arguing along this line, she asserted that her chil-

dren were much better and more natural, being like an
upright tree, than those of Physis, which were like a
tree upside down. As for the arms and hands, she argued
that it was more sensible for them to be turned back
towards the shoulders, for the reason that that part of
the body should not be left without protection, drawing attention to the fact that the front part was ably
protected by the teeth, which the individual could use,
not only for biting, without the assistance of his hands,
but also for defending himself against anything that
threatened.

"Thus, through the testimony and suffrages of the
brute beasts, she won over to her view all the fools and
senseless ones and found herself vastly admired by all
the brainless and those deprived of all good judgment
and common sense. And afterwards she begot the Old
Apes, Moral Lepers and Hypocrites, the maniacal *Pistolets,* the demoniacal Calvins, those impostors of Geneva, the rabid Putherbs, the Begging Brothers, Humbugs, Whining Tomcats, Cannibals, and other deformed
and unnaturally misformed monsters."

"A mirach *like an Albanian's hat*": mirach *is Arabic
for the abdomen.* ——"A siphac *like an arm-brace*": the
siphac *(Arabic) is the peritoneum.* ——"An alkatin *like
a billiard-table*": the alkatin *is the lumbar vertebrae.*
——"Parysatis *wished to have woven*": Rabelais takes
this from Plutarch's Apothegms of Kings and Emperors.
——"What I have read in the old fables": the commentator La Monnoye traces this fable to Caelius Calcagninus, whose works were printed at Basel, in 1544; he
points out that Rabelais merely translates Calcagninus
down to the sentence beginning "She begot the Old
Apes"; and another commentator, M. des Marets, notes

that Calcagninus was neither an ancient nor a well-known author; it may be of interest to compare this passage with the opening lines of Horace's Ars Poetica, having to do with the artistic creation of monsters. ——
"The maniacal Pistolets*": the* pistolet *was originally a firearm brought in from Italy; it had come to be applied to a false coin, and finally came to signify little or insignificant men.* ——*"The demoniacal Calvins, those impostors of Geneva": this passage, with the "predestinators" and "impostors" allusion in the Prologue to Book Second, may be taken as the definitive statement in print of Rabelais' break with the Calvinists.* ——*"The rabid Putherbs": this is a reference to Rabelais' bitter and relentless enemy, Gabriel de Puy-Herbault (Putherbus), monk of Fontevrault and author of a treatise entitled* Theotimus, Sive de Tollendis et Expurgandis Malis Libris (On the Suppression and Expurgating of Evil Books), *published at Paris, in 1549; in this book Puy-Herbault attacks Maître François as an enemy of the faith; this was one of the things that turned the tide against the author of the* Gargantua *and* Pantagruel.

After sighting a "monstrous physeter," or whale, which is slain by Pantagruel, the voyagers come to Wild Island, "the Chitterlings' old homestead." Here they learn more of the ancient quarrel between the Chitterlings and Lentkeeper, and here the former lay an ambuscade for Pantagruel, whereupon he calls a council of war. In the meantime, the author holds forth in defense of Chitterlings.

Showing That Chitterlings Are Not to Be Looked Down Upon by Human Beings

You may laugh here, you drinkers, believing that it was not all just as I am telling you. I am sure I don't know what to do with you. Believe it, if you like; if you don't like, then go and see for yourselves; but I know well enough what *I* beheld with my own eyes.

All this happened in the Wild Island, I would have you understand. And I would remind you of the strength of those ancient giants who endeavored to pile Mt. Pelion on Ossa and with the latter to cover cloud-wrapped Olympus; for they were fighting the gods and attempting to unnest those deities from the skies. Theirs, you must admit, was no ordinary or vulgar degree of strength; and yet, they, so far as half of their bodies was concerned, were nothing but Chitterlings—or serpents, if I am not to tell a lie.

The serpent that tempted Eve was Chitterlingish; yet notwithstanding, we read that it was a fine and crafty specimen, more so than all the other animals. The same is true of the Chitterlings. And it is still maintained in certain academies that this tempter was none other than the Chitterling named Ithyphallus, into which our friend, Mr. Priapus, was formerly transformed—he, the great tempter of ladies in *paradise,* as we say in Greek —in *gardens,* as we say in French.

Take the Swiss (*Suisses*), today a bold and warlike race—who knows but that they may formerly have been sausages (*saucisses*)? I, for one, wouldn't put a finger in the fire by saying. The Himantopodes, a very notable people of Ethiopia, are, according to Pliny's description, Chitterlings and nothing else. If this reasoning fails to satisfy your lordships' incredulity, I may tell you that I expect, right away, directly after drinking, to have you visit Lusignan, Parthenay, Vovant, Mervent, and Pouzauges in Poitou. There, you will find hoary witnesses of good mettle and reputation, who will swear to you upon St. Rigome's arm that Melusine, their original founder, had a feminine body down to the satchel, but that the rest of it, down below, was a serpentine Chitterling— or, if you will, a Chitterlingish serpent. And yet, she had a very charming gait, of the sort that you today will see imitated by the Breton dancers doing their trilling *trioris*.

What was the reason that led Erichthonius to invent coaches, litters, and chariots? It was that Vulcan had begot him with Chitterling legs, and to hide these he preferred going in a litter to riding horse-back; for in his day Chitterlings were not yet in repute.

The Scythian nymph, Ora, likewise had a body that was half woman and half Chitterling. And yet, she struck Jupiter as being so beautiful that he slept with her and had by her a fine son named Colaxaïs.

And so, you may as well stop shaking your sides, and believe that there is nothing so true as the Gospel.

"Upon St. Rigome's arm": St. Rigome was a saint of Maine whose arm was a much venerated relic in Rabelais' time. ——"Doing their trilling trioris*": the* triori *was a quick-measured Breton dance. ——"Erichthonius to invent coaches": the legendary Erichthonius, son of Vulcan and king of Athens, is mentioned by a number of classical writers as being the first to yoke horses to a chariot. ——"The Scythian nymph, Ora": Ora was Hersilea, wife of Romulus, as a goddess; see Ovid's* Meta-morphoses, *xiv, 851;* Valerius Flaccus, *Argonautica, vi, 48.*

Chitterlings, or sausages, are properly combatted by cooks; and Friar John, accordingly, draws up the latter for this "straw battle." In imitation of the Trojan Horse, he has the engineers construct a huge sow and the cooks enter it. The Chitterlings attack; and we are then given a passage in which at least one scholar, Professor Lefranc, sees an uncanny premonition of modern aerial warfare.

How Pantagruel Brought the Chitterlings to Their Knees

THE Chitterlings came on, and came so close that Pantagruel was able to see how they were using their arms. They were already beginning to lower wood.

At this point, he dispatched Gymnastes to hear what they had to say, and to find out why it was that, without any provocation, they thus wished to make war on their old friends, who had never done or said anything to harm them. Gymnastes, having come up to the front ranks, made a profound bow and cried out as loudly as he could:

"Yours, yours, yours, we are all very much yours, and at your service. We are all of us for Carnival, your old confederate."

Some folks told me afterwards that he said *Gradimars* in place of *Mardigras*. However this may be, no sooner had he heard the word, than a big, fat wild-Bologna, darting out in front of their battalion, tried to grab our friend by the throat.

"By God," said Gymnastes, "you'll never get in there, except in slices; for you're too big to go in whole."

Saying this, he with both hands whips out his trusty sword, *Kiss-me-arse* (for that was what he called it) and whacks the Bologna into two pieces. Good God! but he sure was fat! He reminded me of the big Bull of Berne, the one that was killed at Marignano at the defeat of the Swiss. You may believe me, there were no less than four inches of bacon on his belly.

When this Bologna had been beheaded all the Chitterlings came pouncing upon Gymnastes and were about to down him in most dastardly fashion, when Pantagruel and his men came running up, top speed, to the rescue.

And then, the martial combat began, pell-mell. Colonel Sausageater ate sausage and Colonel Puddingcarver carved puddings as Pantagruel brought the Chitterlings to their knees. As for Friar John, he from his sow was watching everything, when all of a sudden the Meat Pies who were lying in ambush leaped out and fell with a great hullabaloo upon Pantagruel.

At this point Friar John, seeing the confusion and tumult, opened the doors of his sow and leaped out with his trusty followers, some of them bearing iron spits, and others andirons, fire-dogs, stoves, shovels, pipkins, grills, grates, tongs, drip-pans, brooms, sauce-pans, mortars, and pestles, etc., all in the best military order, yelling and bawling most frightfully, all at the same time, like a lot of house-burners:

"*Nebuzaradan! Nebuzaradan! Nebuzaradan!*"

With cries like this and a great uproar of all sorts, they charged the Meat Pies and tore through the Sausages. The Chitterlings quickly became aware of the reinforcements and took to their heels, galloping away furiously, as though they were bound straight for hell.

Friar John with a big iron bar mowed them down like flies; and his men did not by any means lay off. It was a piteous sight. The field was soon strewn with Chitterlings, dead or wounded; and the tale goes on to say that, if it had not been for God's hand in the matter, the Chitterlingish race would have been wholly exterminated by these culinary troops. But just then a marvelous thing happened. You may believe as much of it as you see fit.

From the north, a big, fat, gray pig came flying up, with wings as long and wide as those of a windmill. Its feathers were a brilliant red like those of a phenicopter, which in the languegoth langue d'oc is called a flamingo. Its eyes were as red and flaming as those of a carbuncle, its ears as green as a green emerald, its teeth as yellow as a topaz, its tail as long and black as Lucullian marble, and its feet as white, diaphanous, and transparent as a diamond, being widespread, like those of geese, or like those which *la Reine Pedauque* formerly had, at Toulouse.

And the pig wore around its neck a gold collaret, inscribed with certain Ionic letters of which I was able to make out only the two words: HYS ATHENAN, the *Hog Teaching Minerva*. And though the weather up to then had been fine and clear, at the coming of this monster it began thundering so strenuously, from the left-hand side, that we were all quite astonished.

The Chitterlings as soon as they perceived the apparition threw their arms and clubs to the ground and all fell upon their knees, raising their clasped hands high in the air without saying a word, as though they were worshiping it. Friar John and his men kept on laying about them and bespitting Chitterlings; but at Pantagruel's command, a retreat was now sounded and all arms ceased.

The monster, having flown back and forth a number of times between the two armies, now cast down more than twenty-seven kegs of mustard upon the earth, then flew away through the air and disappeared, crying incessantly:

"*Carnival! Carnival! Carnival!*"

"*Began to lower wood*": *the wood of their lances.* ——"*Gradimars in place of Mardigras*": *the former is the southern dialectical form.* ——"*La Reine Pedauque*": "*Tradition has preserved in the region of Toulouse, the memory of a more or less fantastic queen, Regina Pedauca, the queen with the feet of a goose; la Reine Pedauque has statues in many cities of the south, monuments still bear her name, and her tomb is even pointed out in the cemetery of the church of Notre Dame de la Daurade*" *(Du Mège).*

The latter part of Rabelais' Book Fourth contains an extended and bitterly satirical attack on the Papacy and the Decretals of the Church. The following passage will serve to convey the flavor of this portion of the book. After Wild Island and the Chitterling episode, the Pantagruelians first put in at "the desolate island of the Popefiggers," that is, those who mock the Pope; after which they proceed to "the blessed island of the Papimaniacs."

How Pantagruel Disembarked at the Island of the Papimaniacs

LEAVING the desolated island of the Popefiggers, we sailed very peacefully and pleasantly for a day and then the blessed Island of the Papimaniacs hove in sight.

As soon as we had cast anchor in the harbor and

before we were done fastening our cables we saw coming towards us in a skiff four individuals variously clad. One wore the garments of a frocked monk, dirty and booted. Another was dressed as a falconer, with a lure and bird-glove. Another as a trial-lawyer, with a big bag full of briefs, citations, shysterooings, and summonses in his hand. The fourth as a wine-grower of Orléans, with handsome linen gaiters, a large basket, and a bill-hook at his belt. No sooner had they come up to our ship than they cried out in a loud voice, all in unison:

"Have you seen him, good travelers? Have you seen him?"

"Whom?" asked Pantagruel.

"Him," they replied.

"Who is he?" demanded Friar John. "By the old bull, but I'll beat him to death."

For he thought they must be inquiring after some robber, murderer, or sacrilegious wretch.

"What!" exclaimed they. "Strangers, don't you know the One and Only?"

"Good sirs," said Epistemon, "we don't understand such expressions as that. But explain to us, if you will, just what you mean, and we will tell you the truth, without any beating around the bush."

"He is," said they, "the One Who Is. Have you ever seen Him?"

"The One Who Is," replied Pantagruel, "according to our doctrine and our theology, is God, for that was His word to Moses. Most assuredly, we never saw Him, for He is not visible to bodily eyes."

"We are not speaking," said they, "of that great God, who rules in the heavens; we are speaking of the God on Earth. Have you ever seen him?"

"They mean the Pope," said Carpalim, "upon my word, they do."

"Yes, yes," spoke up Panurge, "yes, indeedy, gentle-men, I've seen three of 'em, but I can't say that the sight of them did me a whole lot of good."

"What!" they cried, "why, our sacred *Decretals* tell us that there has never been but one living."

"I mean, of course," said Panurge, "successively, one after another. I've never seen more than one at a time."

"O men," said they, "thrice and four-times blessed, you are very welcome, indeed; you are more than wel-come!"

They at once fell upon their knees in front of us and wanted to kiss our feet, a thing that we would not per-mit them to do, pointing out to them that they could not do any more than that to the Pope himself, if he should happen to visit them in person.

"We'll do that, right enough," they said, "we've made up our minds to it. We'll kiss his behind without any leaves, and his balls likewise, for he has balls, the good holy Father: we read that in our beautiful *Decretals;* for otherwise, he would not be pope. In the subtle Decretaline philosophy, that is a necessary consequence: He is pope; therefore, he has balls. And when balls fail in this world, the world will have no more pope."

Pantagruel, meanwhile, had inquired of a cabin-boy aboard their skiff who these individuals were. The lad replied that they were the four Estates of the island; and he added that we were sure to be well received and well treated, in view of the fact that we had seen the Pope. Pantagruel communicated this to Panurge, who re-marked in an aside:

"That's the stuff, I vow to God. Everything comes to him who waits. I never got any good before from the sight of a pope; but now, by all the devils in hell, we're going to profit by it, from all that I can see."

And then, we disembarked; and all the people of the

country, men, women, and little children, passed in front of us as if on parade. Our four Estates kept crying out to them, in a loud voice:

"They've seen Him! They've seen Him!"

At this proclamation, all the people fell to their knees in front of us, raising their clasped hands in the air and crying:

"O blessed ones! Oh, more than blessed ones!"

And these acclamations kept up for more than a quarter of an hour.

Then, a schoolmaster came running up, with all his pedagogues, little urchins, and upper-grade pupils; and he began flogging the scholars most masterfully, the way they used to flog little children in our country when some criminal was being hanged, so that they would be sure to remember it. Pantagruel was vexed at this, and said to them:

"Gentlemen, if you do not stop flogging those children, I shall go back."

The people were greatly astonished at his stentorian voice, and I overheard one little long-fingered hunchback inquiring of the schoolmaster:

"I'm a son of the Extravagants! but do those who have seen the Pope grow as big as that fellow who just threatened us? Oh, I just can't wait to see the Holy Father, so that I can grow some and become big like that!"

So loud were their exclamations that Dumbell, for that was what they called their bishop—now came cantering up on an unbridled mule, caparisoned in green. He was accompanied by his vassals, or, as they put it, by his tools, all bearing crosses, banners, gonfalons, baldachins, torches, and holy-water-fonts. And he like the others was bent upon kissing our feet, as the good Christian Valfinières did Pope Clement's; for he told us that one of their hypophetes, a grease-scraper and glossarist of their holy *Decretals,* had made the statement in writing that just as the Messiah, so long awaited by the Jews, had come to the latter at last, so, similarly, in this island the Pope would one day come. As they waited for that blessed day, if any one who had seen him, at Rome or elsewhere, arrived upon the scene, it was their duty to fête the visitor and to treat him with all reverence.

"A son of the Extravagants": the Extravagants were extraordinary decrees not contained in the regular collection of Decretals. ——*"The good Christian Valfinières": Le Duchat thinks the allusion is to some Piedmont lord and Pope Clement* vii. ——*"One of their hypophetes": hypophetes is a Greek word meaning an interpreter or expounder.*

Anyone who is inclined to doubt that François Rabelais possessed a keen and profound awareness of the economic forces at work in human society, an awareness of society's economic base, has but to read the following passage, describing the visit of Pantagruel and his followers to the home of Sir Gaster (in other words, Sir Belly). Not only does the author see hunger as the motive force in social relationships; he further perceives its relation to man's development of the arts, including the art of human slaughter. What he has to say about the introduction of artillery will have a familiar ring in this dawning atomic age of ours. In the light of such passages as this and a number of others that have been given—the discourse on borrowers and lenders, the Prologue to Book Third, the Abbey of Thélème, etc.—it is hard to see how Rabelais could ever have been regarded as a

*mere jester, an erudite buffoon whose only answer to life
is a deep belly-laugh.*

In the following passage Chapters LVII *and* LXI *of
Book Fourth have been combined.*

How Pantagruel Disembarked at the House of Sir Gaster, Foremost Master of Arts in the World, and How Gaster Invented the Means of Getting and Preserving Grain

THAT same day, Pantagruel disembarked at a most wonderful island—wonderful on account both of its situation
and of its governor. On all sides, to begin with, it was
rough, rocky, mountainous, and infertile, being very unpleasant to view, very hard walking, and only a trifle
less inaccessible than the mountain of Dauphiny that
gets its name from the fact that it is shaped like a
pumpkin, and which, within the memory of man was
never climbed by anyone except Doyac, commander of
Charles VIII's artillery, who by the aid of certain miraculous mechanical contrivances succeeded in scaling it—
and all he found on the top was an old ram. It was a
hard job guessing how it had got there, though some
folks said that, having been carried there when it was a
little lamb by some eagle or screech-owl, it had saved
itself by running off through the bushes.

Having with great exertion and not without a deal of
sweat climbed the first difficult ascent, we found the top
of the mountain so pleasant and fertile, so healthful and
altogether delightful that I thought this must be the true
garden and earthly paradise concerning the location of

which our friends, the theologians, do so much talking and expend so much labor. But Pantagruel informed us that this was the house of Arete, that is, Virtue, described by Hesiod—saving, always, a better opinion.

The governor of this place was Sir Gaster, foremost master of arts in the world. If you believe Fire to be the great master of arts, as Cicero states, you are all wrong, for Cicero never believed it himself. If you believe, as did our ancient Druids, that Mercury was the first discoverer of the arts, you are likewise way off the track. For the satirist is right when he says that Sir Gaster is the master of all arts.

With the latter there dwelt in peace the good lady Penia, otherwise known as Poverty, mother of the nine muses, from whom, in days of old, in union with Porus, the Lord of Abundance, there was born Love, that noble child who is a mediator between Heaven and the Earth, as Plato says *in Symposio*.

To this knightly king, it is our duty to do reverence, swear obedience, and show honor; for he is imperious, rigorous, round, hard, difficult to please, inflexible. He cannot be made to believe anything, he cannot be shown anything or persuaded of anything, for the very good reason that he does not hear a thing. And just as the Egyptians used to say that Harpocrates, god of silence, called *Sigalion* in Greek, was *astome*, that is to say, without a mouth, so Gaster was created without ears, being, in this respect, like the image of Jupiter in Candia.

He speaks only by signs, but these signs are obeyed by all the world, more quickly than are the edicts of praetors and the command of kings; he permits no delay, no tarrying whatsoever in connection with the serving of his summonses. You may remind me of how when the lion roars all the beasts tremble for far around—as far, that is, as his voice can be heard. That, I know, is a matter of record. It is true. I know by experience. But I wish to certify to you that at Sir Gaster's command all the heavens tremble and the earth shakes. And his command is: *Do what you must do, without delay, or die.*

The pilot told us a story of how one day following the example of the bodily members who, in Aesop's fable, conspired against the belly, the whole kingdom of the Somates conspired against Gaster and took an oath not to obey him any more; but they very soon came to their senses, repented, and returned to Gaster's service in all humility; otherwise, they would have perished of famine.

Into whatever company he may go, there can be no discussion there of first rank or preference; for he always goes before all others, even though they be kings, emperors, or the Pope himself. And at the Council of Basel, he went first of all, even though they may tell you that the council in question was a seditious assembly, on account of the conflicting ambitions of those present and the contentions over first place. To serve him, all the world is busy, all the world labors; and as a recompense, he does this for the world: he invents for it all arts, all machines, all trades, all implements, and all refinements. He even teaches the brute beasts arts that have been denied them by Nature. Crows, jays, popinjays, starlings —he makes poets of them all; and of the magpies, he makes poetesses, teaching them to speak and sing in the tongue of human beings. *And all for the guts.*

Eagles, gerfalcons, falcons, sakers, lanners, goshawks, sparrowhawks, merlins, wild birds, migratory birds, flying birds, birds of prey, savage birds—he domesticates and tames them all, in such a manner that, turning them loose in the heavens when he sees fit and leaving them free to fly as high as he wishes, holding them there suspended in their wandering and hovering flight while they flirt with him and pay him court from above the clouds, he is still able suddenly to bring them down to earth. *And all for the guts.*

Elephants, lions, rhinoceroses, bears, horses, dogs—he makes them all hop and skip and dance, fight, swim, hide themselves, and fetch and carry for him, taking what he would have them take. *And all for the guts.*

Fishes—both sea-fish and fresh-water ones—whales and marine monsters,—he causes them all to leap up from the lowest depths; he hurls the wolves out of the forests, the bears from off their rocks, foxes out of their holes, and serpents out of the earth. *And all for the guts.*

The short of it is: he is so enormous that, in his fury, he eats everything, beasts and men, a sight that was witnessed among the Vascons, at the time when Q. Metellus was besieging them in the Sertorian wars; among the Saguntinians, when the latter were being besieged by Hannibal; among the Jews when they were besieged by the Romans; while six hundred other examples of the same sort might be cited. *And all for the guts.*

When Penia, his queen-regent, takes the war-path, wherever she may go all parliaments are closed, all decrees are mute, and all statutes vain. For she is subject to no law, but is exempt from all. Everybody, everywhere, flees her approach, preferring to run the risk of shipwrecks at sea or to pass through fire, over mountains, or through the depths of abysses to being apprehended by her.

Pantagruel now devoted his attention to studying Gaster, the noble master of arts.

You are aware that by a decree of nature bread with all its appanages has been apportioned to him as a provision for his sustenance, a benediction from Heaven being added to the effect that in his efforts to get and guard his bread nothing should be withheld him. To begin with, he invented agriculture and the blacksmith's art, to enable him to cultivate the earth so that it might produce grain for him. He invented the art of war and of arms in order to defend his grain, and invented medicine and the requisite mathematical sciences to preserve his grain in safety for a number of centuries and to put it beyond the reach of atmospheric disasters, the depredations of brute beasts, and the thievings of brigands.

He invented water-mills, windmills, hand-mills, and a myriad other contrivances, to grind his grain and reduce it to flour, invented leaven to ferment the dough and salt to give it flavor—for he knew very well that nothing in the world renders human beings more subject to ailments than the employment of unfermented, unsalted bread. He also invented fire to bake with and clocks and dials to mark the time that his bread, which is the creature of grain, took in baking.

But it sometimes happened that there was a shortage of grain in some country, and so he invented the art and means of bringing it from one country to another.

Displaying further a vast degree of inventiveness, he proceeded to mix two species of animals, asses and mares, in order to produce a third species, which we call mules, beasts that are more powerful, less delicate, and capable of enduring more labor than the rest. He also invented carts and chariots to haul his grain more conveniently.

If sea or rivers stood in the way of its transportation, he invented boats, galleys, and ships—a thing at which the elements are quite astonished—in order to be able to travel beyond the sea, beyond streams and rivers, and to bring grain from barbarous, unknown, and widely separated lands.

It has sometimes happened, for a certain number of years back, that, as he cultivated the soil, he did not have the proper amount of rain, or did not have it at the right time; and from want of moisture his grain would remain in the earth and rot. Certain other years, the hail spoiled it, the winds husked it, and the tempest beat it down. But he, already, before we arrived upon the scene, had invented the art and means of evoking rain from the skies, merely by cutting down a certain plant which is very common on the prairies but known to very few folks; and this plant he showed to us.

He expressed the opinion that this was the plant by casting one single branch of which the Jovian pontiff had cast into the Agrian fountain on Mt. Lycaeus in Arcady, in time of drought, and so had stirred up vapors which had formed huge clouds; and when these clouds dissolved in the form of rain, the whole region was nicely irrigated. Gaster had, in addition, invented the art and means of staying and suspending rain in the air, and of causing it to fall into the sea. He it was who invented the ways and means of destroying hail, laying winds and turning aside the tempest in the manner practiced by the Methonesians of Troezene.

Other misfortunes also came. Plundering brigands would steal the grain and bread in the fields; and so he invented the art of building cities, strongholds, and castles, where he might store it and keep it in safety.

It sometimes happened that, not being able to find any bread in the fields, he would learn that there was grain stored away in these places, being more carefully watched and guarded by the inhabitants than the golden apples of the Hesperides were by the dragons. Accordingly, he invented ways and means of battering down and demolishing such strongholds by means of machines and *tormenta bellica,* rams, ballistae, and catapults, the designs for which he showed us—but our own architectural engineers and disciples of Vitruvius appear to find some difficulty in understanding them, as Master Philibert de l'Orme, King Megistus' great architect, admitted to us.

When these had proved to be of no further use on account of the malign subtlety and subtle malignity of those engaged in the art of fortification, he had more recently invented cannons, serpentines, culverins, big-gauge guns, and basilisks, hurling iron, lead, and bronze bullets weighing more than great anvils, this being accomplished by a horrific concoction of powder in the presence of which Nature herself is lost in astonishment and confesses herself vanquished by art. All this he did with a contempt for the practices of the Oxydracians, who by means of thunder, lightning, rain, and tempest were in the habit of vanquishing their enemies and putting the latter to a speedy death. For one single basilisk shot is more horrible, more frightful, more diabolic, and murders, mangles, and wipes out more people, and, in general, more greatly perturbs the human senses, as well as demolishing more walls, than do a hundred thunderbolts.

"The mountain of Dauphiny": *"Mont Aiguille (Needle Mountain), a very high rock two leagues and a half from Dic, which, under the name of the Inaccessible Mountain, was formerly counted among the seven wonders of Dauphiny"* (Des Marets-Rathery). ——*"By anyone except Doyac"*: *Jean Doyac, architect and engineer under Charles* VIII *and Louis* XII; *he was commissioned to provide a passage across the Alps for Charles* VIII*'s artillery.* ——*"As Cicero states"*: De Natura Deorum, iii. ——*"The satirist is right"*: Persius (Prologue, 10):

"Magister artis ingentique largitor Venter." ——"As Plato says": Symposium, xxiii. ——"Gaster . . . without ears": compare the proverb, "a hungry belly has no ears." ——"The whole kingdom of the Somates": the bodily members (Greek somata; soma, the body). —— "Among the Vascons": old name for Basques. ——"The Sertorian wars": the campaigns waged by Sertorius, the general of Marius, against the partisans of Sylla in Spain. ——"Among the Saguntinians": the inhabitants of Saguntum, a town in Spain besieged and destroyed by Hannibal; now Murviedro. ——"The Agrian fountain": In Pausanias this fountain is called Agno; Rabelais takes the form Agrie from a work by Nicolas Léonic, the Histoires Diverses. ——"The Methonesians of Troezene": inhabitants of Methone, a city of Argolis, between Epidaurus and Troezene. ——"Tormenta bellica": machines for hurling stones or other projectiles. ——"Master Philibert de l'Orme": architect to Henry II, Francis II, and Charles IX; Rabelais possibly had made De l'Orme's acquaintance in Rome. ——"The practices of the Oxydracians": a people of India mentioned by Philostratus and Quintus Curtius.

This volume, perhaps, could not be brought to a close more fittingly than with Maître François' account of the "thawed words" that Pantagruel came upon in the course of his voyagings. This excerpt constitutes Chapters LV and LVI of the Fourth Book.

How Pantagruel, on the High Seas, Heard Various Thawed Words and among Them Came Upon Some Good Throaty Ones

ON THE high sea once more, as we were feeding, nibbling, chattering, and engaging in merry banter, Pantagruel arose and gazed around him to see what he could see. Then, he turned to us and said:

"Friends, don't you hear anything? It seems to me that I can hear people talking on the air; yet I cannot see any one. Listen."

At his command we were all attentive and proceeded to suck in the air through our ears like nice little oysters in the shell, to see if we could hear any sounds or voices scattered around. And not to lose anything, some of us followed the example of the Emperor Antoninus and cupped our hands behind our ears. Still we insisted that we could not make out any voices whatsoever.

But Pantagruel kept at it, maintaining that he could hear various ones on the air, some of them masculine and some feminine, until we came to believe either that we also heard them or that our ears must be tingling. And so we persisted, listening harder than ever; and then we began to distinguish the voices, even to the point of catching whole words. This greatly frightened us, as well it might, since while we saw no one, we still could hear the various sounds made by men, women, children, and horses, until Panurge exclaimed: "Cock's belly! Is some one playing a joke on us? We're lost! Run! There's an ambush around here. Friar John, old friend, are you there? Stay close to me, please! Do you have your broadsword? Be sure to keep it out of its scabbard. You don't half take the rust off it. We're lost! Listen! By God, but those are cannon-shots! Run! Run! and I don't mean with feet and ·hands, as Brutus said at the Battle of Pharsalia; I mean with sails and oars. Run! Run! I have no courage at all at sea; but in a cellar and elsewhere, I've enough and to spare. Run! Fly! And I don't say that from fear, for *I fear nothing except dangers.*

"That's what I always say, and that's what the Franc-Archer of Bagnolet used to say. Let's not take any chances, so that we'll be sure not to get any raps in the nose. Run! Right about face! Turn that helm around there, you son of a whore! I would to God I were in Quinquenais this very minute, even if I never get married! Run! We don't want to have anything to do with them. They're ten to one, I can assure you of that. What's more they're on their own manure-heap, and we don't know the country. They'll murder us. Run! That won't be any disgrace on our part. Demosthenes says that *He who fights and runs away, will live to fight another day.* At least, let's retreat a little. Larboard! starboard! look to the mizzen-mast! look to the small-sails! We're goners! Run! In the name of all the devils in hell, Run!"

Pantagruel, hearing the rumpus that Panurge was making, said:

"Who is that coward down there? Let us find out who they are first. It may be that they are our own men. I do not perceive anyone as yet, and I can see for a hundred miles around; but wait.

"I have read that a philosopher named Petronius held the opinion that there were a number of worlds touching each other, in the form of an equilateral triangle, in the heart and center of which was the House of Truth, and there it was that Words dwelt, Ideas, Exemplars, and the Portraits of all things, past and future, while around these lay the secular universe; and every so

many years, at long intervals, a portion of these words
would fall upon human beings like catarrhs and as the
dew fell on Gideon's fleece, the other portion being
reserved for time to come and for the consummation of
all worldly things. I also recall the saying of Aristotle, to
the effect that the words of Homer are fluttering, flying,
moving and, as a consequence, animate.

"There was also Antiphanes, who observed that the
doctrine of Plato was like certain words which, when
they are uttered in some country in time of winter, are
frozen over with the coldness of the atmosphere and are
not heard. He added that what Plato taught to young
children, the latter would scarcely be capable of understanding when they had become old men.

"And so, it is our business now to do a little philosophizing, and to make a search to see if this may not be
the place where such words are frozen. We should be
highly astonished, if we were to come upon Orpheus'
head and lyre. For after the Thracian women had hacked
Orpheus to pieces, they cast his head and lyre into the
river Hebrus, and the head and lyre descended that river
into the Pontic sea, going as far as the Island of Lesbos,
floating all the time side by side. And from the head
there issued incessantly a lugubrious wail—a lamenta-
tion, as it were, for the death of Orpheus—while the
lyre, as the wind played over its chords, chimed in har-
moniously. Let us see if we can discover anything of
them around here."

The pilot answered:

"My lord, don't let anything frighten you. We are on
the borders, here, of the Glacial Sea, on which, at the
beginning of last winter, the great and awful battle between the Arimaspians and the Nephelibates was fought.
At that time the cries of men and women froze upon the

air, along with the clashing of armor, the shock of battle-harness and of barbs, the neighing of horses, and all the other uproar of the fight. But now that the rigor of winter is past and serene and temperate weather has come once more, those sounds melt and are capable of being heard."

"By God," said Panurge, "I believe it. But couldn't we see one of them? I remember having read that, on the edge of the mountain where Moses received the law of the Jews, the people actually saw voices."

"Hold on," said Pantagruel, "take these. Have a look at them. Those are a few that are not thawed out yet."

And with this, he cast down upon the deck whole handfuls of frozen words, and they were like striped candy of various colors. We saw there throaty words, quartz-green words, azure words, sable-colored words, golden words, which, when they had been heated a little between our hands, melted away like snow; and we could really hear them, but we could not understand them, for they were in a barbarous tongue.

Except for one big little word which, after Friar John had warmed it up between his hands, made a sound such as chestnuts do when, having been thrown on the fire without being cut open, they suddenly burst. The popping of this word made us all jump from fright.

"That," said Friar John, "was a falcon-shot in its day."

Panurge requested Pantagruel to give him some more. Pantagruel replied that to exchange words was lovers' business.

"Sell me some, then," said Panurge.

"That's lawyers' business," said Pantagruel, "selling words. I prefer to sell you silence, and at a higher price, the way Demosthenes sometimes sold it, by means of his quinsy of the purse."

Notwithstanding, he threw down three or four hand-fuls upon the deck.

And I saw there some very sharp words, and some bloody ones. The pilot told us that these sometimes returned to the place from which they came, but that place was a slit crop. I saw other terrible words, and none too pleasant ones to look at; and as they melted, we heard:

"*Hin, hin, hin, his, ticque, torche, lorgne, brededin, brededac, frr, frrr, frrr, bou, bou, bou, bou, bou, bou, bou, bou, traccc, trac, trr, trr, trr, trrr, trrrrr! On, on, on, on, ouououououon! goth magoth.*"

I cannot tell you what other barbarous words I heard. And the pilot said that these were the clash and neighings of horses in a battle-charge. And then we heard other big ones that gave out a sound as they thawed—some of them a sound like that of fifes and drums, and others a sound like that of trumpets and clarions. You may believe that we had plenty of sport.

I wanted to pickle a few of the throaty words in oil, just as one does snow and ice, between straw; but Pantagruel would not hear of it. He said that it was foolish to preserve something that one never had a lack of, but always kept on hand—such as is the case with good throaty words among all good and joyous Pantagruelists.

If the flying hog of the Chitterlings is, as Professor Lefranc would have it, a premonition of the modern bombing-plane, what shall we say of the foregoing episode—that Rabelais is here dreaming of our radio? In reality, this is simple Platonism, which was then very much in vogue, having been introduced into France largely through the influence of Marguerite of Navarre; and Pantagruel's "thawed words" represent Plato's heaven of ideals.

As for the fable itself, which is based upon a passage

in Plutarch's Moral Works, *it had been made use of before Rabelais by Castiglione in his* Il Cortegiano, *an edition of which was published by Aldus in 1528, followed by a French translation in 1537 (see Castiglione's second book). There are also two fables of Caelius Calcagninus, published at Ferrara, in 1544, bearing the titles:* Voces Frigoris Vi Congelatae *and* Voces Frigore Concretae.

The "throaty" (or throat-colored) words, motz de gueule *in the French, is a play on* gueule, *meaning throat (mouth or jaws), and the heraldic* gueules, *or* gules, *the color of which is red. It is an allusion once more to the role of Pantagruel as the little devil of thirst.*

"As Brutus said": Brutus, *as a matter of fact, said just the opposite (see Plutarch's* Brutus, *63):* "We must flee, that's plain . . . but it is with the hands and not with the feet"; *that is to say,* "We must save ourselves by fighting." ——"In Quinquenais": *the vineyard near Chinon.* ——"He who fights and runs away": *the Greek is* "Aner ho pheugon kai palin machesetai"; *the saying is quoted by Aulus Gellius, xvii, 21.* ——"A philosopher named Petronius": *In Plutarch's treatise* On the Oracles Which Have Ceased, *this system is developed as that of Petronius, a Sicilian philosopher, who had composed a work on the subject.* ——"On Gideon's fleece": *Judges, vi, 37-40.* ——"The words of Homer": *compare Homer's* "winged words *(epea pteroenta)".* ——"Between the Arimaspians and the Nephelibates": *the Arismaspians were a people of Scythia (Pliny, vii, 2, and vii, 19, and Herodotus, iv, 27);* "Nephelibates" *("Cloud-walkers") is undoubtedly a Rabelaisian coinage.* ——"The people saw voices": *Exodus, xx, 18:* "And all the people saw the thunderings and the lightnings and the sound of the trumpet," *etc.* ——"A falcon-shot": *that is, from the cannon known as a "falcon."* ——"To exchange words

. . . *lovers' business": Ovid's* "Verba dat omnis amans."
——*"Quinsy of the purse": according to the story, when
Demosthenes declined to plead a certain case on the
ground that he had a sore throat, the people cried out
that it was not the quinsy that he had, but rather "quinsy
of the purse."*

THE END